Eileen Townsend was born in Scotland, but spent most of her childhood in Cumbria. A graduate of Dundee University, she and her family still live in Tayside, in the former fishing village of Broughty Ferry. This is her first saga.

EILEEN TOWNSEND

Of Woman Born

This edition published by Grafton Books, 1999

Grafton Books is an Imprint of HarperCollins*Publishers*
77–85 Fulham Palace Road,
Hammersmith, London W6 8JB

Published in paperback by
Grafton Books 1989

First published in Great Britain by
Grafton Books 1988

ISBN 0-261-67180-4

Printed and bound in Great Britain by
Mackays of Chatham PLC, Chatham, Kent

The extract from 'Instructions to the Orphic Adept',
taken from *Collected Poems 1975*, by Robert Graves, is
reproduced by permission of A. P. Watt Ltd on behalf of
The Executors of the Estate of Robert Greaves.

For Sasha

Man that is born of a woman is of few days,
And full of trouble.
He cometh forth like a flower,
And is cut down.

Job 14:1–2

BOOK ONE
Blood upon
the rose

I see his blood upon the rose
And in the stars the glory of his eyes,
His body gleams amid eternal snows,
His tears fall from the skies.

I see his face in every flower;
The thunder and the singing of the birds
Are but his voice – and carven by his power
Rocks are his written words.

Joseph M. Plunkett, 1887–1916
Executed, Easter 1916

Chapter 1

Dublin, Easter Monday, 1916

'Dear Mother of God, let it stop!'

The ensuing scream escaped the confines of the small room and reverberated in the narrow, brick-walled close outside, as the young woman thrashed wildly on the dishevelled bed. Her swollen body, beneath the pink flannel nightgown, was bathed in perspiration, her knuckles standing out white under the pale skin of her hands as she gripped the iron bedrails behind her head.

'No–o–o . . . pl–e–e–ease . . . !' Nobody had warned her it would be like this. Nobody. Certainly not her mother, for happenings below the belt did not exist in the refined world around St Stephen's Green.

Another long groan escaped her lips, to be immediately censured by the old woman at the foot of the bed. 'Whisht there, Maeve, he's coming – and he's a head o' hair like his father. I can see it now!'

Although untutored in the craft of midwifery, Mrs Mahoney had seen it all before, for Maeve Donovan's was getting on for the hundredth infant she had brought into this world, in the warren of narrow, sunless streets that cowered behind the elegant Georgian façade of fashionable Dublin. And she had no doubt that Danny Donovan's first child would be a son. Hadn't his mother carried him so high up that you could have played a game of shove ha'penny on her stomach?

'One more push should do it. Come on then, girl – shove!' The old woman's swollen-knuckled hands fastened themselves around the bloodied head of the child, gently working it loose from its raw pink prison.

'A–a–ah . . . !' Using what strength she had left in her arms, the young woman gripped tightly to the cold metal of the bedhead and hauled her distorted body into a more upright

11

position, as the painful ripping of unyielding flesh between her legs was followed by a wet, emptying feeling, unlike anything she had ever experienced.

The child slithered its bloody way into the world and landed with a satisfying plop into the waiting hands of the midwife. Its tiny fists flailed the still, fetid air of the room as it filled its dormant lungs with the first breath of life to announce its arrival into the world.

The squawk that was emitted from its tiny mouth brought a wide smile to the old woman in whose arms he lay. 'You'll be a bonnie fighter an' no mistake, so you will! Just listen to that, Maeve, ma vourneen! Won't his daddy be right proud of him this day?'

She wrapped the bawling infant into a waiting towel, carefully wiping its puce-coloured face with the edge of the well-washed cotton, before handing it to the young woman on the bed.

Maeve Donovan looked down at her son and felt a great emptiness well within her. An emptiness not born out of the expulsion of the human cargo her slight frame had carried so unwillingly for the past nine months, but an emptiness born of something much deeper; it was an emptiness of the human soul itself. Was it possible to feel something akin to mother love towards this small scrap of human flesh? Human flesh that was also part of *his* flesh. She doubted it, and a bitter bile rose in her throat. This was not how it was supposed to be.

'Well, what do you think of him?' Ellen Mahoney rinsed her hands in the chipped enamel basin on the washstand by the bed and looked round at the younger woman. 'You'll be calling him Danny, after his father, no doubt?'

The young woman shook her head. That was the last thing she would be doing. 'No, I'll call him Kieran. He'll take after nobody, in name or character, if I have my way. He'll be his own man . . .'

The midwife dried her hands on the corner of her apron and gave a perfunctory but puzzled nod. She'd heard tell it was a queer one Danny Donovan was married to. A little bit of a girl from one of them Protestant families from the big houses overlooking the Green, who called themselves Irish, but were as English as King Billy himself . . . But, wait a minute, King Billy was a Dutchman, wasn't he? . . . It was all getting quite beyond her.

'Would you be liking a cup o' tea, then?' Her red, arthritic fingers fiddled with the hat-pin that held the soft, brown felt hat firmly fixed to the greying topknot, as she got down to really important matters. 'We can get you cleaned up after that. I think we can both do with a pot, after the battle that one has had in making his entrance into the world, don't you?'

Maeve nodded, as her fingers stroked the damp wisps of hair back from the wrinkled brow of the child. 'A cup of tea would be lovely.'

Mrs Mahoney hobbled her way painfully to the door of the bedroom. Long, difficult births like this had been were getting beyond her – what with her phlebitis and all. She could never have refused to help bring another Donovan into the world, though, for wasn't this child's grandfather one of the finest and bravest men ever to walk God's earth? In the eighties, hadn't Seamus Donovan, along with her own husband and Michael Davitt himself, waged that glorious campaign against the crucifying land rents being forced on the poor – her own family amongst them? Folk didn't forget the debt owed to men like him in a hurry.

His eldest child, Dermot, had been born on the very day of Charles Stewart Parnell's funeral – surely an omen in itself, folk had said, as she delivered him with her own hands. Those that had joined the thousands who had congregated to mourn the passing of Ireland's great Home Rule leader still spoke with awe of how, at the very moment the coffin was lowered into the ground, a falling star had lit the heavens overhead.

Ellen Mahoney believed profoundly in signs – and there was one that day, as sure as God. And what was more, the events that were now taking place at the very moment of this child's birth, in this very city, only a few streets away, would surely go down with just as much glory in the annals of their country's history. Her sons Jackie and Ned, and all seven of her grandsons, were out there now, their uniforms newly pressed, their boots shined as they never were for church, as they congregated with their comrades, ready to do their duty. 'There'll be history made in this city today, Mammy,' they had told her, and she believed it. Oh yes, this infant's entrance into the world would be on just as momentous a day for the Irish people, even though his mother hardly merited the honour of the name Irish.

'Can we see her, Mrs Mahoney? Can we see Maeve and the baby?'

Ellen Mahoney's pale eyes alighted on the tiny figure of the girl waiting behind the bedroom door. 'Sure and you can that, Katie. It's a nephew you've got, and as bonnie a one as you'll see in a long time.'

'Can Willie-John come too?' The nine-year-old girl glanced towards the stooped figure of her elder brother standing by the black range, on which a kettle hissed persistently. 'He's looking forward to seeing the baby as much as I am, Mrs Mahoney. Honest to God he is!'

The midwife's eyes took in the gormless, bent figure of Seamus and Bridie Donovan's second son, who looked at her imploringly from across the tiny kitchen. Poor devil, it wasn't his fault he was half daft. Plenty of other families had a similar heartache to him to contend with and there was no harm in him, the big soft lump . . . 'Away in ye go, the pair o' ye! But only for a minute, mind. I haven't even got either o' them cleaned up yet.'

A deep sigh escaped the toothless lips of the old woman as the two Donovans made for the bedroom, and the new life that lay beyond, and, wrapping a cloth round the handle of the kettle, she lifted it off the hob and poured the scalding water into the teapot that was sitting at the ready on the kitchen table. Four blue and white earthenware cups were then lifted from the middle shelf of the dresser and a splash of milk poured into the bottom of each one.

'Is there enough in the pot for an extra one?'

The old woman's eyes turned to the outside door behind her, where a tall, spare-framed young man, in the long black cassock of a Roman Catholic priest, stood uncertainly on the doorstep. 'Why, Father Dermot, come away in with ye! My, but it's good to see you, although I'd have thought you'd have been elsewhere in the city today, seeing what's afoot.'

'Priorities, Mrs Mahoney, priorities . . .' The dark eyes in the pale, fine-boned face glanced towards the closed door of the bedroom. 'Has Maeve been delivered yet?'

'She has that. You're an uncle, Father. It's the finest wee fella you're likely to see in many a long day. Kathleen and Willie-John are in there with her now, but I said they'd to be only a minute, and not tire her out. Maybe you'd like to take Maeve's cup o' tea in to her and chase the pair of them out?'

Father Dermot Donovan smiled his agreement, as he picked up one of the steaming cups from the table. 'I'll do that, with pleasure . . .'

'Dermot!'

'Hello, Maeve . . .' He walked forward towards the side of the bed, gesturing to his brother and sister to take their leave, as, setting the cup down on the bedside table, he sat down on the rush-seated chair and took his sister-in-law's damp hand. 'He looks a fine wee fella.'

Maeve looked down at the bundle in her arms and nodded without speaking. He knew. Dermot knew all right what emotions – or lack of them – were churning within her, but he was too much the gentleman to ever let on.

The brown eyes in the pale, sculptured face smiled down at her as, with his free hand, he tentatively touched one of the small, curled-up fists of the child. The tiny, pink fingers spread outwards, then clasped themselves tightly around his index finger. 'Danny will be right well pleased. Doesn't every man want a son first time round?'

Again the young woman on the bed nodded, but found herself unable to look down at the child. Dermot was right; there was nothing Danny wanted more than a son to carry on the fight when he was dead and gone, as he had done for his own father before him, and backwards through the generations to time immemorial.

But maybe that would be no longer necessary after today. Maybe it would be all over before this very day ended. She shook her head in mystification at the thought. Centuries of English domination all over in a few hours – a few minutes maybe. 'Has it begun yet? Has the Rebellion taken place?' Her voice was little above a whisper as she looked up into the eyes of her brother-in-law.

The young priest extracted his finger from the infant's grasp and looked down at the white, slim fingers of its mother that clasped his own hand, on top of the faded pink bedspread. 'Twelve noon, I've heard tell, Maeve . . . It'll be any minute now. But Danny will be all right, have no fear. God will protect those whose cause is just.'

A wry smile flickered across the flushed face of the young woman on the bed. 'You mean, for today He is exclusively an Irish God? He will be studiously ignoring all those caught up in the fighting not of Republican persuasion?' Her blue eyes looked steadily into the dark brown ones of the young man in the black cassock and, seeing the embarrassment on his face, she sighed deeply. 'I'm sorry, truly I am. But there's been so much fighting – so much killing of late . . . What with this wretched German war and Charlie across in France and all . . .' Her voice trailed off with a sigh, as she thought of her elder brother wallowing in the mud of some bloodied Flanders field, in the 'War to end all Wars', as the newspapers constantly referred to it.

Dermot remained silent. He, perhaps above all others, knew what her brother meant to her. Of all the family she had been forced to reject when she chose to defy convention and marry his brother Danny, Charlie Ballantine was the wrench that was hardest to come to terms with, especially since news of his transfer to the trenches of the Western Front came to her ears barely a week ago.

'He shouldn't be out there, you know. He's far too young. They said it would all be over by the Christmas before last, and if that had been the case, he'd still be here in Dublin.' Hot tears spiked her eyes and she lowered them in embarrassment, to fall on the sleeping bundle in her arms. So much had happened since she had last seen him. Her parents' ultimatum to her of either rejecting Danny's proposal of marriage, or leaving the family home forever, had come as a real shock. This was the twentieth century, wasn't it? Surely you could marry a Catholic in this day and age without being cast out into the cold like some poor Victorian wretch?

When she had left home last year to marry Danny, Charlie had seemed little more than a child. But then, she herself had been a mere child – barely seventeen – and now here she was, a grown wife and mother, and Charlie, dear, dear Charlie, hundreds of miles away, a fully-fledged soldier of the King . . . But not the Irish King – Danny was always the first to make that much plain, and thereby hung the tale that ripped her very soul apart. But then she often doubted if she had much of a soul left in her body these days, for souls were nurtured on dreams and dreams quickly died. When you had a husband that drank, that was.

She bit her lip as painful memories etched their mark across the clear skin of her brow and the silence of the small room crowded in on her. She made a brave attempt at a smile in response to Dermot's comforting squeeze of her hand. 'Did – did you speak with him – with Danny – before he left this morning?'

He nodded. 'Just long enough to offer up a short prayer. They'll be needing it about now, if everything's gone according to plan.'

Everything was indeed going according to plan for, as he spoke, his brother Danny, along with his comrades of the rebel army, whose sworn intention it was to overturn British rule in Ireland, were marching along Middle Abbey Street, and wheeling a sharp right turn into Upper O'Connell Street. They were heading for the main seat of foreign power in the land – Dublin Castle itself and the General Post Office.

'Bloody Sinn Feiners! Away wi' ye and join the real army! It's the Hun you should be attackin' not playing soldiers on a fine day like this!'

Danny Donovan's eyes swivelled to the left, to fall on the irate face of an elderly man in plus-fours, shaking his fist at the marching men. A recruiting poster for the British army fluttered from the shop wall behind him. Little did the old boy know, he thought. Little did very few of those milling holiday crowds know there would be no playing at soldiers this day. No more would they be stopped in the street to be offered the white feather, or have to face the jibes of those who felt they

17

should be dying in the Flanders mud with the rest of the British army. No — after today, it would be a very different story indeed!

As his booted feet marched in time with his comrades, his eyes continued to scan the well-dressed holidaymakers that crowded the pavements of Dublin's fashionable shopping centre and a surge of pride swelled in his breast, despite the ironic smiles on the faces of so many of the onlookers. They could smile — bloody ignorant, the lot o' them — but the marchers would have the last laugh! Although even he had to admit they must be making a pretty odd-looking spectacle as their motley band marched towards its destination. This was no ordinary army on the attack. For a start, there was little semblance of unity in the uniforms. Many sported the dark-green tunics of the Citizen Army, whilst others were clad in the heather-green uniform of the Irish Volunteers. But after today, it had been decreed by their leaders, no distinction was to be made. After today, the Citizen Army and the Volunteers would be one united band of men. Today the Irish Republican Army was born.

Danny's chest swelled with pride as his eyes scanned the marching ranks. The fact that the majority, himself amongst them, had no military costumes whatsoever was of little consequence. The bandoleer straps criss-crossing their worka-day clothes and the yellow armbands on their left sleeves were uniform enough. The important thing was what was in their hearts this day, not on their backs.

Most carried a weapon of some sort — either a Lee Enfield rifle, such as the one on his own shoulder, or whatever they could lay their hands on, be it a battered Winchester, an old American Springfield, or even the odd single-shot German Mauser, already considered obsolete during the Boer War. His pal Con O'Malley, several rows behind, carried just such a weapon.

But as they had congregated with the others at the start of the march, neither he nor Con could resist a smile, at the sight of the mystifying array of pickaxes, crowbars, spades, and even a number of antique spears and pikes carried by some of the others. And there had been some ribald comments, into the bargain, when their military transport rolled into view, for bringing up the rear of their unlikely army, jolting precariously over the cobbles, were a hansom cab and a jaunting car, both piled high with ammunition boxes held in place with an odd assortment of old suitcase straps and ropes.

Con had been assigned to walk alongside one of the ammunition wagons, along with a few others, to make sure none of the valuable cargo was lost before they arrived at their destination, but Danny was never one for taking a back seat in any form of action. He preferred to march as near to the head of the assault as possible. And here he was now, striding out just three rows behind the leaders.

His eyes squinted, in the strong spring sunshine, at the backs of the heads of two very different men: James Connolly, a man after his own heart, the rugged, down-to-earth leader of the Irish Transport and General Workers Union, and founder of the Citizen Army, and Patrick Pearse, the tall, gentrified, dreamy-eyed ex-headmaster and poet of the revolution.

Danny's dark brows furrowed, as his hazel eyes fixed on the back of the head of the dark-haired Pearse. While he had every sympathy for Connolly, whose Marxist beliefs in direct action by the workers against their masters he could understand and applaud, the genteel, bourgeois Pearse was another kettle of fish altogether.

'Bloody pansy,' his pal Con insisted. 'Another bloody Oscar Wilde, if you ask me!'

But Danny usually avoided asking him and tried not to be quite so uncharitable. If somebody wanted to dedicate their life to the preservation and propagation of the Irish language and culture, then that was up to them. But it was really the way the man looked at you through those smouldering, dark eyes that sent a shiver through Con's brawny body and made his own skin crawl. It was whispered that the intellectual headmaster preferred young boys to women and the very idea caused his fists to clench in revulsion.

But now was not the time for such suspicions. Pearse had a way with words that never failed to rouse the troops and that was what counted; his sexual preferences were his own affair.

'There are worse things than shedding blood,' Pearse had

19

declared to them all as they assembled for action this morning. 'And one of them is slavery . . .' And every man and boy of the seven hundred had cheered himself hoarse, before setting off in their respective divisions to carry out the plan of attack so carefully mapped out by Connolly at last Wednesday's conference.

Danny braced himself, and put even more vigour in his step. To hell with Con's dirty mind, it was an honour to be marching only a few rows behind such men as Connolly and Pearse, not forgetting the other poet, and son of a papal count, Joe Mary Plunkett, who flanked Connolly's left shoulder. For no other men, and no other cause, could he have torn himself from his wife's side this morning – on the very day his first son was about to be born. And it would be a son, he had no doubt about that. Anyways, he wouldn't really have been welcome in the house at a time like this. Giving birth was women's work, and women around McIntyre Street were not known for making a fuss about such things. Now was the time for Maeve to show her mettle; she was too given to harking back to the feather-bedded ways of her relations and their like who lived the life of Reilly around St Stephen's Green.

Aye, Maeve could get on with doing her bit in providing him with the son he so badly wanted; his part would come later. Danny Donovan's son would be no namby-pamby boyo like that gentrified sop of a brother of hers – he would see to that. He'd be the bonniest fighter ever to come out of McIntyre Street – and that was saying something!

They were almost there! Only a few more yards to go! Despite his excitement, nerves churned in his stomach in anticipation of what lay ahead, as the column ground to a halt in front of Nelson's Pillar, opposite the elegant Palladian-columned edifice that was the General Post Office. He wished Maeve could see him now. Maybe then she wouldn't assume that cool disdain in those blue eyes that never failed to rouse him to anger whenever the subject of the planned Rising was raised.

A bead of sweat broke on his forehead – this was the moment they had been preparing for for weeks . . . No, for centuries! The pain in his gut grew stronger and he cursed the extra whiskey he had downed before leaving the small kitchen in McIntyre Street.

His hazel eyes narrowed, in the warm April sunshine, as they watched the booted figure of James Connolly step forward, sword in hand, to declare at the top of his voice, 'Soldiers of Ireland, left turn – the GPO!'

Rows of booted feet swivelled on the dusty road, as all eyes moved from their leader to the object of their march, and then back again. Connolly seemed to physically grow in stature as he pulled himself up to his full height and, at the top of his voice, yelled, 'Soldiers of Ireland – CHARGE!'

Danny felt a surge of pride run through him, that erupted in a wild cheer akin to a war-cry that was echoed by the other rebels in the closed ranks behind him as, to a salvo of pistol shots, they broke ranks and hurled themselves at the portico of the Post Office.

'You men over there rush the main hall and make for the upper storeys, to stop the bastards from shooting us from above!'

Finding himself behind Patrick Pearse, Danny obeyed the poet's shouted command, as they launched themselves up the wide steps of the building and into the main hall.

In the rush that followed, he found himself being pushed up the wide sweep of the staircase behind Mick Staines, a man he knew only slightly, as the assault on the upper storey began. He could see little for the pushing and shoving that was going on, as he struggled to keep his footing on the polished stairs. Then an English voice from above penetrated his hearing, making him stop immediately in his tracks.

'Halt! Stand still – or we shoot!'

They gaped upwards, their mad dash halted, as a posse of soldiers appeared on the landing above them, covering them with their rifles.

'J–e–esus!' The name exploded from his lips as, before anyone could draw breath, Mick Staines, his face aglow with the fervour of the moment, fired his revolver at the sergeant in charge.

With a strangled gasp, the man fell wounded over the steps in front of them, blood spurting from his brow.

'Bloody hell!'

'Let's have 'em, boys!'

As if buoyed up by the sight of enemy blood, the rebels sprang forwards with renewed vigour at the remaining soldiers. Danny glanced back at the wounded man on the top step, who was moaning pitifully. The bastard was still alive.

White-faced, the other soldiers, aghast at the fate of their sergeant, threw down their guns and surrendered immediately. 'Don't shoot, for Chrissake . . . It's only bloody blanks we've got in here!'

They stared at their instant prisoners in incredulity, as an inspection of their weapons proved it to be true.

'Jesus – this is too easy!'

Elated by the ease of this victory, Danny and a few others gathered up the surrendered guns and ran back downstairs into the main body of the Post Office, where stupefied, half-hysterical customers and postal clerks were panicking wildly, as Connolly exhorted them to leave the building as quickly as possible. They needed little encouragement, and an immediate stampede for the door began.

'Let's get these into the ammo wagons!' Danny yelled to the others, as they pushed their way through the terrified crowd surging towards the main door.

In the middle of the mêlée, a lieutenant of the 14th Royal Fusiliers was attempting to enter the Post Office. Taking it upon himself to reassert law and order, he exchanged sharp words with Joe Plunkett and Mick Collins, on the steps outside, as Danny and the others emerged with the captured rifles.

'Get him, boys!' Connolly snapped impatiently, and they needed no second telling.

The guns were thrown to the ground and the Englishman was seized immediately, Danny grabbing his feet as the other two bound and gagged him, before carrying him down the steps and dumping him on the floor of a telephone box at the foot of Nelson's Pillar.

From his cramped, makeshift prison, the hapless lieutenant glared out through the dusty glass panels of the box at his jailers, as their eyes of one accord turned skywards.

'Will ye take a look at that!'

Two uniformed figures were making their way precariously along the ornamental ledge above the main door of the Post Office, to the spot where the Royal coat of arms hung. Bracing themselves against the fresh breeze, the men produced two small bundles from inside their tunics, which they proceeded to attach to the halyards of the twin Post Office flagstaffs. Under the bemused gaze of the onlookers below, the two little parcels unfurled themselves into the ancient green flag of Ireland, with the harp in the centre and the words Irish Republic embroidered in Celtic lettering, and the orange, green and white tricolour.

As the flags fluttered against the blue, almost cloudless sky, a ragged cheer, accompanied by a few catcalls, went up from the onlookers on the crowded pavements below.

'At last! Will ye take a look at that!' If only his father had lived to see the day. Tears sprang to the eyes of Danny Donovan as his own voice joined in the rejoicing, before a volley of shots rang out to announce the appearance before them of Patrick Pearse, clutching a roll of parchment in his right hand.

The rebel leader stood white-faced in the centre of the main doorway, looking around at the assembled crowd.

'Shut your bloody gobs, damn you!' A faceless rebel soldier in the crowd exhorted his fellow onlookers to silence, and, as if by magic, a deathly hush fell on the gathered crowd, as they looked in curiosity towards the man on the Post Office steps.

Danny's hazel eyes glowed amber in the sunlight, almost matching the colour of his flame-red hair, as his leader cleared his throat and proceeded to declaim, in a peculiarly flat voice, in the name of the Provisional Government:

'Irishmen and Irishwomen: In the name of God and of the dead generations from which she receives her old tradition of nationhood, Ireland, through us, summons her children to her flag and strikes for her freedom . . .'

A half-embarrassed, half-amused murmur rose from the gathered crowd, causing Pearse to pause for a second before continuing in a slightly louder voice, 'We declare the right of the people of Ireland to the ownership of Ireland and to the unfettered control of Irish destinies, to be sovereign and inde-feasible . . . Standing on that fundamental right and again

23

asserting it in arms in the face of the world, we hereby proclaim the Irish Republic as a Sovereign and Independent State, and we pledge our lives and the lives of our comrades in arms to the cause of its freedom, of its welfare and of its exaltation among the nations . . .'

Danny stared at the tall, dark-haired figure on the steps, as Pearse concluded the proclamation. Emotion almost suffocated him, but then reality broke in.

A bowler-hatted citizen to his right, outside the closed public lavatory, urinated gleefully against the wall of the Post Office, declaring, 'Now we have a Republic we can do what we bloody well like!'

He averted his face from the spectacle, as a few – very few – perfunctory cheers rose from the assembled crowd, to be followed by as many jeers and catcalls. White-faced, Pearse looked towards Connolly to save the situation. This, after all, was the greatest moment in Irish history in their lifetime.

'Thanks be to God, Pearse, that we have lived to see this day!' The union leader strode across to clasp his comrade by the hand, and Danny Donovan, watching less than ten yards away, breathed a sigh of relief. Dignity had been maintained. Just wait till he told them at home. Just wait till he told Maeve!

'Maeve!' His wife's name escaped his lips. She could have given birth by now! He could be the father of a son! And what a legacy his generation had just bequeathed to the next . . .

Chapter 2

'Maeve, why is it you and Mary-Agnes don't get on?'

Maeve moved her son of two days to the other breast and looked across at the sparrow-like figure of the nine-year-old girl by the kitchen door. 'Why, Katie Donovan, whatever makes you say a thing like that?'

Her tiny sister-in-law moved from one foot to the other, and toyed with a long corkscrew curl of red hair, which she began to chew thoughtfully, as she watched the baby suck greedily at the nipple. 'Lots of things,' she said at last. 'She hasn't even been in to see the baby, for a start, and he's two days old now!'

'Mary-Agnes is a busy woman, Katie. I don't have to tell you that. Your big sister has a lot on her plate, what with you and Willie-John to look after, as well as her own husband and family. *And* she's cooked all my meals while I've been abed.'

'Aye, but she's not brought them over herself. She's let me do that.'

Maeve looked across at the scrap of a girl. For so tiny a child, she missed very little. She could be a cut-down version of her big brother Danny, with her flame-red hair and freckled-faced, almost pugnacious features; even the way she so often stood, with her two feet planted firmly apart on the stone-flagged floor, reminded her of her absent husband. But there the resemblance ended, for Kathleen Bernadette Donovan had no temper; in fact, she was the sweetest-natured of all God's creatures.

'Is it because Mary-Agnes wanted Danny to marry somebody else? Was she angry because he didn't marry Cissie O'Rourke – what with her having his baby, an' all?'

Maeve's already pale cheeks drained of what little colour they had left. Dear God, did they all know? It was the first time the O'Rourke girl had been mentioned in her presence by anyone in Danny's family, although it had been cast up plenty by her own family, in Jubilee Avenue, when the battle was in

25

progress over her proposed marriage to him. The child – a girl – must be almost walking by now, but she had never set eyes on the poor wee thing, and doubted if he had either.

'Who told you about that, Katie?' The words choked in her throat as she looked across at the child.

Katie shrugged her narrow shoulders. 'They're always speaking about it, so they are. Mary-Agnes says that Cissie's a real hard worker. She's behind the counter in her Daddy's shebeen all God's hours, an' the baby's there an' all. Mary-Agnes knows her right well. She buys her invalid port there.'

Maeve drew in her breath sharply. So this Cissie O'Rourke and her little bastard were almost part of the family, were they? Nothing surprised her any more. 'Do you happen to know the name of this – this shebeen where she works, Katie?' It was hard to keep her voice steady.

'Oh aye, it's on Kildare Street – next to Mr Shaughnessy's wee post office on the corner. Mary-Agnes often sends me for the port, if she's real busy and runs out of it on washing-day or something like that . . . Will Danny be home today, Maeve?'

A deep sigh shuddered through Maeve's body, as she heaved the satiated child from her breast and placed him up on her shoulder. 'I wish I knew, Katie astore . . . They're still fighting it out in the city centre, so I believe, and God only knows what's happening up there. I'm hoping your brother Dermot will call by and bring some news with him.'

The child's amber eyes lit up. 'But Dermot's with us now, so he is! He was having some of Mary-Agnes's broth for his tea when she sent me across with yours. Shall I tell him, Maeve? Shall I tell him you want to see him?'

Maeve's slim fingers did up the buttons of her blouse as her other hand rubbed absent-mindedly on the child's back. A loud belch filled the tiny kitchen and she lifted her son down to her lap once again, to wipe the creamy froth of undigested milk from his lips. 'It's time you were back in your crib, young man.'

'Will I tell him then, Maeve? Will I tell him you want to see him?'

Maeve looked up from the wooden cradle, as she tucked the gurgling infant tightly into the woollen shawl. 'Aye, you could say that, Katie. It seems that you and he are my only link with the outside world at the moment – and God only knows what's been happening while I've been in that bed through there!'

She listened as the child's tackety-booted feet ran back down the rough stone cobbled street beyond the kitchen door, towards the home she shared with Mary-Agnes and her family. It was a shock to hear her come out with that about the O'Rourke girl, but it didn't surprise her that it was a subject much talked about in the Kellys' two-up-two-down across the street.

There was no love lost between herself and Mary-Agnes Kelly, *née* Donovan. There never had been since the day Danny first brought her home to meet his remaining family. A shudder ran through her to this day when she remembered the way Mary-Agnes had taken her best chinchilla fur-collared coat, to hang it up on the back of their kitchen door, as she gestured to Maeve to take one of the only two easy chairs in the room. 'I'm afraid we don't run to maids to do this kind of thing over here, on this side of town, Miss Ballantine,' she had said, with a smile that had chilled Maeve to the bone, as her rough, red hands had stroked the soft, smooth fur. 'Our kind of folk are the ones that have to do the fetchin' and carryin' for the likes o' yerself!'

Things had started badly that day and had never improved. It was not the way she would have wished it, especially when she no longer had her own family to turn to. And when, almost immediately after the wedding, she found herself expecting her first child, she bitterly regretted the fact her husband's elder sister seemed to have taken such an instant dislike to her.

Danny had lived with Mary-Agnes and her family before their marriage, their parents having died a good few years before. But when his Uncle Hughie joined his Maker almost two years ago and left his little two-roomed cottage across the street empty, at just about the time that his nephew was thinking seriously about taking a wife, it seemed only natural that the young husband-to-be should move in.

Maeve looked around the cramped kitchen with a sigh. It wasn't exactly the palace she had dreamt of as a child, in her pink and white satin-frilled room in Jubilee Avenue, across the other side of St Stephen's Green. That all seemed another world away now. And, in fact, might as well be, for she had never ventured anywhere near her old home, nor those of any of her old friends, since the day she walked out of number nine Jubilee Avenue for ever.

She had placed herself beyond the Pale of the Anglo-Irish Protestant society into which she had been born by marrying Danny Donovan, just as surely as if she had announced she was to marry the Pope himself. Not only was he Catholic, and proud of it, but he was a staunch Republican, and, perhaps most damning of all, the Donovans were poor. Marrying into a family like that — well, that her parents could neither understand nor forgive, and never would.

But all that seemed a lifetime ago now. Reality was here and now, in this little kitchen with her new son. She flexed her shoulders and rubbed the small of her back, giving a small moan as she did so. Feeding the baby herself took a lot out of her and she wondered if her body would ever feel the same again. It was almost as if her spirit were locked into a prison of alien painful flesh that bore no resemblance to the healthy, firm body that had been Maeve Margaret Donovan only nine short months ago.

The clock on the mantelpiece above the range struck six brittle, musical chimes that matched the delicacy of the dainty Dresden china figures that clustered around its ormolu base. It was a present from her Aunt Maud, in Wicklow — one of the few of her relatives to brave the wrath of her parents by sending her a wedding present; and it looked incongruously out of place in the tiny kitchen.

She walked over to where it sat and stared listlessly into the oblong, bevelled mirror in the centre of the overmantel behind it. Not only her circumstances had changed. She had too. The face that stared back at her had faint, bluish-black shadows beneath the blue eyes, the once smooth pink skin had grown sallow, through lack of sunlight and proper nourishment, and the skin seemed to be stretched far too tightly over the high cheekbones. Even her hair, once her pride and joy, seemed to be drained of all vitality, like herself. Instead of being done up in the fashionable roll around her head, as she had worn it in her past life, it seemed to spend its time bound into a loose, blue-black braid that hung, thick and heavy, half-way down her back.

She was still staring into the mirror a few minutes later, when, in the reflection of the glass, she saw the door open.

'Dermot!' She whirled round to greet the tall young man in the long black cassock, who entered the room wearing a broad smile. His shock of thick, dark auburn hair was dishevelled from the gusting wind that always seemed to funnel down the narrow street outside the kitchen door. He looked so young, much too young, to have already taken Holy Orders; hardly more than her own age really, but he had already seen twenty-four Easters before this one.

'Did you think I'd forgotten you, then?' He walked across to his sister-in-law and kissed her fondly on both cheeks.

'No – no, of course not! You're a busy man – and don't I know that as well as anybody? You have your flock to see to!' Automatically her hands smoothed back the stray wisps of dark hair from her face and made sure her blouse was neatly tucked into the waistband of her skirt.

He watched her, with a look of wry amusement on his face, and gave a short laugh as he seated himself on a hard-backed chair by the range. 'My flock? Sure and there are not many of *them* left around here at the moment – more like a lot of straying sheep, if you ask me. Only they're not exactly little lost lambs, for I know where they're all to be found – and the majority, like your own good man, are on the roof of the General Post Office!'

Maeve stared at him. 'They're still holding out up there, then? The Tommies haven't gone in to clear them all out of there?' She could hardly believe it. What on earth were the British playing at? Could it be that this piece of foolhardy nonsense was actually turning into a real Rebellion that Danny and his pals might possibly win? Her eyes gazed at her brother-in-law in amazement.

He scratched his chin thoughtfully, as, with the toe of his right shoe, he gently rocked the wooden cradle containing the child. 'Well, I'll not say they haven't tried. They sent in a company of Lancers yesterday afternoon, presumably to scare the pants off our lads and send them running back home, but that proved to be a bit of a fiasco, so I believe, although three or four of the English were killed before they managed to retreat. I heard tell they turned tail and scarpered with a good deal more energy than they showed on their arrival in O'Connell Street!'

'People are really getting killed out there?' It seemed a daft thing to say, but somehow the thought had never really occurred to her.

'Oh, aye, they're getting killed all right! I was down along the Quaysides this morning and didn't stay around there long, I can tell ye! The Volunteers were volleying from all sides around the Four Courts and Church Street area, right along as far as Ringsend and Cabra. And it's not only the Shinners that are firing off their ammo at all and sundry – one of my colleagues, Father Desmond from St Stephen's, was due at Trinity College this morning to see some Protestant students and he couldn't get near the place. British machine-gunners were swarming like ants all over the roof and aiming at everything on two legs.' He gave a rueful laugh. 'But, I dare say, even our four-legged friends aren't exempt – going by the number of dead horses there are littering the city centre!'

'Holy Mother of God!' She didn't usually take Our Lady's name in vain in front of Dermot, but what he was saying shocked her to the core. People – even animals – were dying out there. 'But what about Danny, for God's sake? Is *he* all right?'

Dermot got up from the chair and walked over to where she was standing. Placing his two hands on her shoulders, he bent his head to hers and said softly, 'Do you want me to find out, Maeve? Is that it?'

She shook her head in despair. 'No, no – I don't want you, of all people, mixed up in that carry-on!' Their eyes met and a shiver ran through her. His were very brown. Very soft and brown. Nothing like Danny's, whose eyes often seemed not hazel at all, but could blaze as red as his hair when he was aroused, which was all too often these days. 'I don't know, Dermot, really I don't . . .'

Her voice trailed off and she trembled again, more visibly this time, so that he drew her to him, resting her head on the dark cloth of his cassock, as he stroked her hair. 'Maeve, Maeve, it's not easy for you, is it, girl? And don't think I don't know. You could have done without this – especially at this time – with the baby, an' all. This past year, since you've been married to him, has been a baptism of fire, and no mistake. But we all make our own bed in this world . . .'

'And we've got to lie on it, with a brave smile on our face, for the rest of our lives, is that it, *Father*?' The bitterness in her voice surprised them both, as she cut in sharply, and wrenched herself free of his arms. She stood glaring at him across the rag rug in front of the fire. Two bright pink spots of colour had risen in her cheeks and she found it hard to control the tears that were choking her throat. The last thing she wanted right now was a lecture on marriage – especially from him!

'Nobody forced you, you know. Nobody held a gun to your head and said that you had to marry him – that you had to become Mrs Daniel Donovan. It was your own free choice. It's not as if there was another life on the way.'

His voice was soft – maddeningly soft, as if he were talking to some half-wit child, instead of a grown woman who had already had more experience of marriage than he would ever have. Anger flared in her eyes once more. 'No, there wasn't that, was there, Dermot? Somebody else had already beaten me to it in that particular race! There was another little Donovan brat of his already running around in this city before I even fell pregnant by your precious brother!' She gestured wildly to the sleeping infant in the cradle at their feet.

'That's wild talk, Maeve! It ill becomes you.'

'Is it? Is it really wild talk, Dermot? Don't tell me you've never heard tell of Cissie O'Rourke – or her daughter! Why, it wouldn't surprise me if you were the one that baptised the child! She is your niece, after all!'

Now it was the turn of his colour to heighten, so much so that she stared at him in incredulity. 'Dear sweet Jesus, is it true? Are you telling me it's true?'

'Children enter this world free of sin, Maeve. They do not ask to be born. They are merely the innocent by-products of sins of the flesh committed by their parents.'

'Sins of the flesh? Is that what it is? Is that what you call it?'

Her voice rose to a high-pitched treble and her mouth twisted into a derisive laugh. 'And what would you know about that, pray? You, a career-virgin, an' all!'

Pain flashed in the dark brown of his eyes as his right hand grabbed her wrist, twisting it back, until her face was just below his. There was a look in his eyes that she had never seen before – a mixture of hurt, anger and frustration that combined to distort the familiar, gentle features into those of a stranger. A curious excitement welled within her. It was as if the very devil himself had taken possession of her soul.

'Well, Dermot, deny it – deny it if you can! Tell me there's a man – a real, flesh and blood man – beneath that cassock! You can't – you bloody well can't – for you murdered your manhood when you entered the priesthood. You might as well be a bloody eunuch!'

The slap that caught her squarely across the right cheek sent her staggering backwards towards the hot range and her ensuing scream sent him dashing forwards to break her fall. He caught her beneath the arms and pulled her roughly towards him, holding her trembling body tightly against his, as she sobbed all the pain that was in her into the black cloth of his cassock.

'I'm sorry, Maeve, I'm sorry, ma vourneen . . . Forgive me . . .' His words were muffled in the soft, dark depths of her hair as he pleaded for her forgiveness. What, in heaven's name, had come over him? He had never struck a woman in his life before.

She clung to him, moving her head slightly, and, suddenly, his lips were against the smooth skin of her brow, and he was kissing the twin dark arches of her eyebrows. She caught her breath and a small moan broke in her throat as she felt them reach the delicate skin of her closed eyelids, kissing the salt tears that spilled over her flushed cheeks. His body moved against hers. It felt different from Danny's – softer, more pliable somehow. The heat of the fire in the range less than two feet away seemed to envelop them and a faint sweat broke from every pore in her body, bathing her in a glistening glow. Her hands that had been pressing defensively against his shoulders relaxed momentarily, then stiffened again as his lips found

hers, his tongue forcing her lips apart, until her mouth opened
beneath his and she gasped for breath as his kiss grew deeper.

> 'He is handsome, she is pretty,
> He is the boy from the Golden City,
> Katie Donovan says she'll die
> For the lad from the . . .'

The childish voices from the street beyond the small lace-
curtained window jerked them apart, as if wrenched to opposite ends of the kitchen range by unseen arms. They stared at
one another in a silence that echoed like the loudest thunder
in her brain. His eyes were glowing — scorching her very soul —
as she drew a hand across her glistening brow.

'Mary-Agnes has sent me for the bowl!'
Both pairs of eyes turned towards the small child in the open
doorway.

Katie looked from one to the other in turn. Why were they
staring at her like that — all pink-faced and funny-like? Grown-
ups were right queer sometimes. 'Did you enjoy your broth,
Maeve?'

Maeve stared in embarrassment at the full bowl of now cold
broth on the kitchen table. 'I — I wasn't too hungry, Katie ma
chree. But I'll not keep Mary-Agnes waiting.'

She turned and walked to the enamel basin on the marble
slab beneath the window and, after emptying the broth into an
empty jug, rinsed out the bowl and handed it back to the
waiting child. 'You're playing with Pegeen tonight, then?'

Katie turned to the mouse-haired child at her shoulder. 'I'm
doing my lessons at her house after I've done all the messages
for Mary-Agnes. I might even get to sleep there on Friday
night, if I'm right good this week. I like it at Pegeen's. She's got
a room all to herself.' The child paused a moment to muse on
this wondrous phenomenon, then turned to her brother. 'Are
you going back to your own house now, Dermot?'

He glanced at Maeve, then shook his head. 'No, not yet . . . I
think I'll be taking a walk down to the Post Office to see if I
can get some word of Danny first.'

'No! There – there's no need for that!' Abashed at her own outburst, Maeve's cheeks flamed. 'I – I mean, there's really no need. I'm sure he's fine. I – I wouldn't want you to put yourself in any danger on my account.'

'Oh, it won't be just on your account, Maeve. He *is* my brother too, don't forget. And I reckon it's high time he was told he's a father, don't you?'

Maeve looked at the sleeping child in the cot and back at the young man in the priest's robes in front of her. An image of Cissie O'Rourke and her daughter, two human beings she had never even seen, rose in her mind, blotting out everything else. 'I think that's something he's known for a long time, don't you, Dermot?'

Chapter 3

The bullet whistled past the shock of dark hair, missing the scalp beneath by less than two inches. If he had been wearing his biretta, Dermot thought, it would have been shot clean through the crown. A film of sweat broke on his brow and beneath his armpits. Dear God, this was turning out to be a foolhardy exercise! The Rising was ceasing to be the bit of a lark most people had put it down to, for the British were hitting back at the Shinners with a vengeance.

He had already had to make a longer detour than he intended, for the government had brought a gunboat up the Liffey which was now pounding the hell out of Liberty Hall, the Labour headquarters. And, not content with that, from positions in Tara Street, two eighteen-pounders were attempting to make mincemeat out of the building. The daft thing was, from what he'd heard on his house calls around the parish this morning, the hall had been evacuated by the rebels yesterday afternoon, leaving only Peter Ennis, the caretaker, in charge. The poor man must be wetting himself by now!

In the side streets, across the quays along the River Liffey, hardly a pane of glass remained intact in any of the windows, due to the constant barrage of the guns. Hadn't anyone the gumption to tell the Tommies that there were no rebel positions nearer than Hopkins and Hopkins' corner on O'Connell Street? If even he, a mere parish priest, knew that much, it didn't say much for British intelligence that they still hadn't tumbled to that fact!

But at least all this warfare was helping to take his mind off what had just occurred in the house in McIntyre Street that he had just left. His own brother's house – with his own brother's wife. The sweat oozed more profusely from his pores at the thought and trickled down his pale skin beneath the thick white cotton shirt he wore under his cassock. Dear God, what had come over him? Whatever had possessed him? What devil had got into him that had allowed such a thing to happen? He would have to confess it, of course. But who to? The very idea of relating the episode to Father O'Reilly brought a cold, sick feeling to the pit of his stomach that made him almost oblivious of the danger all around him, as he made his way carefully through the streets towards the city centre.

It took the best part of an hour to reach the General Post Office building, and, with every step, the frequency of the bullets increased. But at least half of them now were rebel ammunition. The knowledge gave him a curious satisfaction.

'Eejits – the lot o' yez!' As he approached the tall, pillared edifice that was Dublin's main Post Office, an old woman in a black woollen shawl shook her fist and yelled upwards towards the rebels on the rooftop above them. 'Come on down from yer perches up there an' we'll tan the arse from yer bloody Sinn Fein britches!'

Seeing the priest approach, the shawlie remained unabashed. 'Have ye ever seen such a bunch o' traitorous eejits, father? The divil the one o' them is worth a roasted fart to Ireland! Bloody traitors, the lot 'o them, firing on good folk like ourselves an' good Irish lads in the service o' King and country. I spit on the lot o' them when I think o' the thousands o' men like my Donal dyin' in France for the likes o' that lot. Connolly that ignorant little yahoo o' a red flag socialist an' his gang – I spit on every last one o' them!'

Dermot lowered his head, and hurried on past, ashamed of his own cowardice in ignoring the old woman's invective. If he had stopped and attempted to justify his brother's and the others' actions, he would only have been invested with the title of 'a bloody Commie sympathiser', or some even more colourful label. Feelings were running high in this city just now and the strange thing was, most people were targeting their abuse towards the rebels, and not the British.

Rumours were abounding – German ships and transports were filling Dublin Bay – a full-scale British attack was on its way that would lay waste to the entire city centre in minutes. But, looking around him as he had zig-zagged between the tall buildings on his way down here, it had seemed like there wouldn't be a great deal left to destroy, if things went on at this rate.

'Evening, Father!'

The soft, lisping voice broke into his musing and he turned to find himself looking straight into the eyes of Willie Pearse. The Good Lord must be smiling on him tonight, for here, in the shape of Patrick Pearse's younger brother, was his passport into the Post Office itself. A few words, and several seconds later he was accompanying the thin, delicate-looking young man with the receding chin in through a back entrance of the building.

The sight that met his eyes was only slightly worse than the smell that made him gag and reach for his handkerchief. The main hall looked like an outpatients' branch of the nearby Jervis Street Hospital, with casualties lying around the floor in various states of injury. And, by the look of them, some were little more than young boys.

His first instinct was to go over amongst them and offer what little comfort he could, but he decided his ministering could wait a few moments while the family business was attended to. But before he could climb the staircase to make his way upstairs, where he was reliably informed he would find Danny, he was called upon to administer the last rites to a young boy, who could have been no more than fourteen years old. He recognised him as a lad from one of the houses that backed on to his sister Mary-Agnes's home, but the boy himself was too far gone to know anybody. The experience left him feeling numbed and dismayed – a feeling that persisted when, eventually, he came face to face with his brother.

'Jesus, Dermot, what in God's name are you doing here?' The hazel eyes stared out of a smoke-blackened face, as Danny got up from his perch by an open window. Even the familiar freckles were barely visible beneath the soot and grime, and the clothes that clad his stocky figure were spattered with dried blood. He laid down his rifle, propping it up against the window-sill, as he took out a handkerchief and wiped the perspiration and some of the grime from his face. 'Is it Maeve? Has something gone wrong?'

Dermot shook his head. 'No, there's nothing wrong. You're a lucky man, boyo. You've got a fine son!'

He was rewarded by a great bear-hug that sent him staggering backwards, as a whoop of pleasure filled the air, momentarily blotting out the sound of gunfire all around them. Danny's eyes shone out of the blackened face. 'A son – a son for Ireland! How are they? How is the little bugger?'

'Why don't you go and see for yourself? Sure and the revolution is not going to be over by the time you get round to McIntyre Street and back!'

The two men looked at one another, and Dermot could see his brother's brain considering the proposal. 'Jeez an' I'd love to, Dermot – you know that, but . . .'

'But nothin'! What's more important, for pity's sake, fighting the Tommies or seeing your son for the first time?'

Danny's eyes hardened. 'This is, of course. Surely even you can see that? What we're doing here is for the likes of him, and all the others of his generation. That's why it's so important we win this fight. Can't you see that?' He stared long and hard at his brother, then gave a despairing shrug. 'Well, maybe you can't, but one thing's for sure, if you don't, then you're no different from any of those other buggers out there!' He nodded derisively towards the city beyond the broken glass of the window. 'There's hardly more than a couple of hundred of those bastards joined us since the Rising began. Can you credit it, Dermot? Can you really believe it? We're doing it for them, damn it all!'

His brother's silence brought a bitter smile to his lips. 'Aye, you can. I can see that. It's too much bloody bother, isn't it? They'd rather be at the races, or picnicking in Phoenix Park, on a Bank Holiday than fighting for the freedom of their country.' He spat in disgust at their feet.

'Well, are you going to see your son or not?'

The two brothers' eyes locked, then Danny turned to pick up his gun. 'Give Maeve my regards, boyo. Tell her . . .'

'Give her your what?' Dermot's dark eyes widened, then narrowed in derision. 'Regards! Is that all she's entitled to after what she's been through? Take a hold of yourself, man! She's all but on her own down there, with Mary-Agnes still determined never to darken her door, even at a time like this, and her own family not giving a tuppenny curse.'

'Holy Jesus!'

The scream came from Jim Connolly, as a young man who had been standing between them and the Citizens' leader suddenly jack-knifed and collapsed on the floor beside them, blood spurting from beneath the green tunic covering his chest. A middle-aged man wearing a Red Cross armband sprinted across, bent almost double to avoid the fire from the windows across the street, to attempt to stem the fountain of blood.

'Get out of here, Dermot,' Danny ordered, between gritted teeth. 'You can do more good amongst the living down below. But do me a favour, will you? Go back to Maeve and give her this.' He felt deep into the right hand pocket of his trousers and extracted a black string of wooden rosary beads. 'Tell her it's to go to the wee lad if anything happens to me.'

The two brothers looked at one another, then Dermot shrugged and attempted a smile, as he pocketed the beads. 'I'll do that, Danny. I'll do that.'

It was almost three hours later before he could keep his promise. He stood in the chill twilight outside the green painted door of number seven McIntyre Street and fingered the wooden beads of the rosary nervously. For the first time in his life he was not looking forward to coming face to face with the young woman within. What on earth was he to do? Should he apologise for what had occurred between them, or simply pretend it had never happened? 'Hail Mary, full of grace, have mercy on us miserable sinners . . .'

He knocked three times with the knuckles of his right hand on the rough wood panels, as he clasped the rosary with the other.

Inside the small kitchen, Maeve looked up at the clock on the mantelpiece with a puzzled frown. It was almost eleven o'clock. Who on earth was that knocking at this time of night? Was it the police? Had something happened to Danny?

White-faced, she leapt up from the chair, where she had been dozing by the fire, and tightened the belt of the woollen dressing-gown around her waist.

'Who is it?' She opened the door only a fraction, just enough to make her voice heard.

'It's only me, Maeve. It's Dermot. I've come from Danny.'

She pulled open the door and stared into the face of the young priest on the doorstep. He had never knocked in his life before. 'You'd better come in.'

He followed her into the room and, for a moment, both stood awkwardly on either side of the scrubbed pine table. Neither could meet the other's eyes and did not attempt to.

'Would you be wanting a cup of tea?' It was a rhetorical question, for she did not even glance at him, to see his grateful nod, before she walked to the pail of cold water by the sink and quarter-filled the kettle, scooping out the water from the bucket with an enamel mug.

He watched as she set it on to the glowing fire in the range, but still could not bring himself to sit down.

'For God's sake, take a chair – you're making me feel right uncomfortable standing about like that!'

They sat down opposite one another on either side of the range and Dermot felt in his pocket. 'He asked me to give you this. You're to give it to the baby if anything should happen . . . if for any reason . . .'

Maeve rose and took the beads, staring down at them, before turning back to the young man beside her. 'It was too much to expect him to come himself, then?' There was a scathing quality to her voice that did not go unnoticed.

'They need every able-bodied man up there, Maeve. There are only a few hundred of them, and God knows how many government troops.'

'Need? *They* need? Who are *they* to need anything? Who are they to risk the life of my husband at a time like this? Whose need is greater, Dermot, tell me that? That child's down there, not to mention my own, or some airy-fairy notion of "the good of Ireland"?'

He watched in silence as she walked to the dresser and tossed the beads into a drawer, before turning to face him with real anger in her eyes.

'Is being prepared to die for your country so bad a thing, Maeve? Is it really so great a sin?' His voice was soft, placatory, but only served to raise her ire even more.

A mocking laugh rang out. 'Tell me, Dermot, why do so-called patriots always talk of *dying* for their country and never of *killing* for their country – for doesn't it amount to the same thing? Can you, as a man of God, really condone the fact that there are young men out there right now who are quite prepared to kill other women's husbands, other children's fathers, other mothers' sons – in the name of this patriotism that is always spoken of in such reverent tones?'

He had never seen her like this and his face flushed at her words. He had never thought of it in quite that way before. 'They are only doing their duty, as they see it, Maeve.'

'Duty! Is that what it is – duty? Well, what about their duty to their own families, or doesn't that come into it? Is it all right that that child in the crib should grow up without a father, and me without a husband, because your brother saw it his duty to serve some mystical notion called Ireland, and not to look to our welfare?'

'Patriotism is a noble emotion, Maeve. Self-sacrifice can never be any other.'

She stared down at him, with a look that verged on contempt on her face, as she took two cups from the dresser and placed them on the table, with an impatient shrug. 'I'm sorry, Dermot, but to me it can never be a noble thing that my brother is risking his young life in the trenches in France for some quarrel that has nothing to do with him – with any of us. And it can never be a noble thing that my own husband would rather stay out there shooting at other young men than come home and see how his own wife and child are doing. Good God, I could have died yesterday when he was out there playing at soldiers! If you ask me, we'll never have a peaceful world until we knock patriotism out of the human race . . . But, then, nobody ever does ask the women, the wives and mothers, especially in this country, do they, Father?'

She only called him 'Father' when she was being ironical, or pulling his leg about something, but there was no humour in her eyes as they looked across and found his. He shrugged uneasily. 'Women have one role in this life, Maeve, men have another . . .'

'Men are born to cause the suffering, while women are born to suffer. Is that it?'

He shook his head. They were getting into deep water now and he had no wish to get too far out of his depth. Danny's wife was a clever one and no mistake. For years he had been the brains in the Donovan family, but in this young woman he could not help feeling he had met his match.

The silence that followed was broken by the hissing of the kettle on the fire and he watched as she bent down to remove it, and pour the scalding water into a brown earthenware teapot. In the firelight, her face seemed to take on an almost translucent glow, and the thick lashes that fringed the blue eyes cast long, curling shadows on to her cheeks. Even her hair, released as it was from its braided prison, seemed to add an almost ethereal dimension to her presence, as it tumbled down around her shoulders almost as far as her waist at the back. There were paintings of young women like her in the Cathedral, and in the Bishop's palace – Madonnas painted by the old Italian masters. Botticelli, Giotto, Raphael, Titian . . . none could have possessed so exquisite a sitter. He sat transfixed on the rush seat of the chair, unable to drag his eyes away, as she went through the motions of brewing the tea. The palms of his hands grew damp and he wiped them on the black cloth of the cassock covering his knees. Feelings were stirring within him that had no right to occur. Sins of the flesh that he, above all others, should know about and beware of. To allow them to occur was to allow the triumph of the devil over our Lord. It was unthinkable.

'Your tea, Dermot!'

'Th–thank you, Maeve.'

She had a curious smile on her face as she sat down opposite him. It was almost as if she knew what agonies were going through his mind – what stirrings were taking place beneath the tense exterior of his body, as he sat bolt upright on the chair. It was almost as if she was enjoying his discomfort. 'Tell me, Dermot, why did you never marry? Was there never a girl that interested you? Or have you never been attracted to a woman?'

Her voice was soft, intimately soft, and the sweat broke out on his body once more, causing him to push the chair back slightly from the fire. But it was not the heat from the coals that was making his cheeks flame in the firelight – and, drat it all, he was not the only one who realised that. He took a gulp of the tea. Far too big a gulp, for it scalded the tender flesh of his mouth and throat as it burned its way down to his stomach. 'Those are very personal questions, Maeve.'

'Do you mind me asking them?'

'Is there a purpose behind them?' It was difficult to keep his voice under control – to play the cool cleric he would have her believe him to be.

'Sisterly interest. We are family now, after all.'

Her eyes were blue, very blue, and seemed to dance in the firelight as they searched his. 'It – it's not a dislike of women that makes a man give himself to God, Maeve. It's love. The love of God transcends all earthly loves and is beyond the comprehension of all but those who have experienced it.'

'Like you.'

'Pardon?'

'You. You have experienced this unearthly love?'

There was the very faintest hint of a smile on her lips that he chose to ignore. 'Yes. Yes, I have.'

She nodded slowly. 'But the other type of love, Dermot. The plain, old-fashioned earthly kind that ordinary mortals like me understand – the love between a man and a woman – have you ever experienced that?'

He stared at her over the top of the teacup, as he downed the remainder of the steaming drink in one go. The ormolu clock above their heads struck eleven. Its brittle, tinkling chimes seemed to ring in his head. 'I – I really think it's time I was going, Maeve. It was good of you to bother with the tea.'

He stood up and made to place the cup on the table beside them, but she was too quick for him. 'I'll take that.' She stood beside him, less than a foot away. Only the blue-rimmed piece of crockery stood between them, as the fingers of her right hand reached up to touch his glistening brow. 'Dear me, you're sweating. It was stupid of me to have had such a fire in on as warm a night as this . . . Although, to be honest, I really wasn't aware of it being all that hot in here before you came.'

Such an innocent conversation, but why were fireworks exploding beneath the thick dark cloth of his cassock? 'Aye, well, maybe it's a touch of 'flu I'll be having. Sure and there's plenty of it about in this town at the moment.'

He made for the door, squeezing himself between the slight, dressing-gowned figure of his sister-in-law and the table. 'Well, I'll be going now. See and take care of yourself now . . .'

'Dermot!'

He turned to see the softest, most appealing of smiles on her face. 'You usually give me a goodbye peck afore you go? I haven't said anything to offend you, have I, that's made you forget?'

The colour flamed in his pale cheeks. 'Of course not! There's a daft thing to say, and no mistake!'

He walked over to where she was standing, his heart beating crazily beneath the black cloth of his cassock, as he bent down to place the most chaste of kisses on her brow.

You can do better than that – I know you can, for you've already proved it! The words formed in her brain, but got no further. Now was neither the time, nor the place . . .

'Goodnight, Dermot, sweet dreams . . .'

'Goodnight, Maeve.'

She stood quite still, in the firelight, in the quietness of the small room, as she watched the silhouette of his tall, slightly stooped figure pass the window outside. He was hurrying – as if he couldn't wait to put distance between himself and what had just occurred in his brother's house. She felt ashamed. Ashamed as she had never felt about anything in her entire life. But with the shame came an exhilaration creeping through her body that made her already long for his return.

She had loved his brother once. She had loved Danny with a passion that had glowed white-hot within her young body for a whole summer, then had cooled as quickly come winter, when his ring weighed as heavily on her heart as on her finger.

Drink could change a man. She knew that now. But it could also change a woman. And it had changed her. She was no longer the naïve young girl she had been only a few short months ago and he, her fine rebel husband, might not realise it – but his brother did. Yes, Dermot knew. And the knowledge sent a shiver through her as she turned her back to the window and gazed down at the sleeping form of her young son.

'I loved him once – your father,' she whispered into the silence of the room. 'I loved Danny Donovan once . . .'

She closed her eyes and threw back her head as a low groan was emitted from the very depths of her being. Hot tears spiked her eyes beneath the closed lids. Her fists clenched, her fingernails digging into the soft flesh of her palms. She would not cry. She *must* not cry. Too many tears had already been spilt in the few short months since her wedding last summer.

She opened her eyes and stared blindly out through the dusty glass of the window. What had gone wrong? What had become of him – of her? What had happened to her Danny-of-the-laughing-eyes who would pick her up and whirl her off her feet and tell her she was an angel sent from heaven itself especially for him? 'Heaven . . .' She repeated the word beneath her breath, almost spitting it out. Never mind heaven! These last few weeks leading up to the birth had been all she needed to know of hell. And it wasn't just the drinking. She could just about put up with that. It was the other times – the long evenings and nights she was left alone, here in this small shoebox of a house, knowing he was out there enjoying himself. But not with her.

Tears blinded her once more as the name of Cissie O'Rourke echoed in her head. What a stupid, naïve little fool she'd been to believe all those tales. How could she possibly have believed he had had a political meeting six nights out of seven? But believe it she had. For the first six months of their marriage at least. After all, wasn't one of the first things that had attracted her to him the fact that he was so political – the very first young man she had ever met who actually cared about something – had an ideal, a dream of how the world should be, and had set out to do something about it?

Her mind went back to the others of her own social circle – she hated the word class – the namby-pamby bunch that had hung around her brother Charlie, and accompanied them to the weekend house parties that had taken up so much of their time before the war. After meeting Danny, they had seemed like children, the lot of them; spoilt children who thought of nothing outside their own little world of cards, horses and shooting, and who had gone off to war against the Germans as if to some extra-special outing. It was all a game – life was all one huge game to them. What did they know of the *real* world that lay beyond the elegant Georgian squares around St Stephen's Green? Had they even *heard* of Tone, Parnell, or even of Marx himself?

No, Danny Donovan might not have had their money or fancy clothes, but he had had something else – a zest for life that had swept her off her feet from almost that first moment those hazel eyes had held hers in their golden glow. If she had waited to know him better, she could have found out before it was too late that those laughing eyes had smiled into more than her own before now, and would continue to do so. It had been a big step – the biggest she would probably make in her entire life – giving up her own family and friends to marry him, but she had truly believed it would be worth it. With all her heart and soul she had believed that a love such as theirs the poets had written about, and other men had died for, yet never known. What a fool . . . What a silly little fool . . .

The child in the cradle stirred and she bent down to pick him up, pressing her lips to the soft down of red hair that clung damply to his scalp. If she was entirely honest with herself, the doubts about his father had begun to creep in even before Danny had slipped this gold band on to her finger. They had begun during the long evenings she had sat in this very room taking instruction in the Catholic religion from his brother Dermot.

She stared past the baby's head into the grey street beyond the window. She could talk to Dermot – really talk – and he would listen. Oh sure, it was his job and all that, but there was a gentleness about him that she had never found in Danny, a willingness to listen, and, with no one from her old life left to confide in, that had been important. So very important. She had even begun to wonder before the wedding what it might have been like if she had met Dermot first. But that was almost blasphemy, wasn't it? Dermot was no ordinary man, after all. He was a Catholic priest. She clasped the baby even tighter to her breast. 'Please God, let me remember that,' she whispered. 'Please God, let us both remember that . . .'

Chapter 4

Danny stifled a yawn, his pale-lashed eyes squinting out through the darkness over the surrounding rooftops. In the distance fires blazed, where British shells had found their targets throughout the past twenty-four hours: the Dublin Bread Company, the Imperial Hotel, and even the Post Office itself – little had escaped the battering of the government guns.

Most worrying of all, the flames were creeping ever nearer, with most of the buildings on Lower Abbey Street and O'Connell Street now ablaze. It was only a matter of time before the Post Office itself would have to be evacuated, then where would they be?

He sighed and eased the weight of the rifle on his shoulder. These night vigils were the worst and few of the men within these walls had had more than a couple of hours sleep since they took over the building on Monday. Three bloody days ago and what had they to show for it? Precious little.

But wait. Something – or somebody – was moving out there, on the rooftop of that building in . . . he peered round further to the west . . . Yes, Henry Street it must be. It was the Tommies, it had to be, the bastards were everywhere now. They must have them surrounded. It was time Jim Connolly was told.

He crept back to where his leader was lying. Jim Connolly's stocky body was almost unrecognisable beneath the greatcoat that served as a makeshift blanket. It was the first sleep he had had in twenty-four hours and a faint whistling sound was coming from his open mouth. Danny stared down at him. It was a shame to waken him, but it had to be done. To hell with Pearse and the others – this was the man in whom he put his trust. The only man he could trust to get them out of this mess alive. He shook him gently by the shoulder and delivered his message in an urgent whisper. When there was no immediate response, he repeated the information, louder this time.

'. . . Do you hear me, Jim? They're there, I tell ye – dozens of them!'

The sleep-heavy pale blue eyes stared up at him in the darkness. 'They are not!' The response was quite emphatic and, with that, he turned over and went back to sleep.

Danny looked helplessly at Winifred Carney, Connolly's secretary, who lay a few yards to his right, and she shook her head. 'Let him be, Danny. Can you not see the man's dead beat?'

Danny gave a shrug and crept back to his post. He was probably getting too jittery stuck up here at the window. What if it *was* the Tommies on that roof out there? A fat lot they could do about it now with their meagre numbers. Where were all those true Irishmen they had believed would rally to their country's call? Sleeping in their bloody feather beds, the lot of them! He spat on to the floor in disgust. No one could accuse him of not being prepared to give his all at a time like this. Why, his firstborn son was nearly three days old and he hadn't even set eyes on him yet!

His eyes clouded at the thought. It wasn't Maeve he missed. Sure, if he was honest with himself, it was a blessed relief to get away from her for a few days, but he did regret not having seen his son. He had told her it would be a son, but she hadn't listened. But then she listened to very little he said these days. It had been different before they were married – then she couldn't see or hear enough of him.

His mouth twisted into a cynical smile. Oh aye, he remembered how she would whisper to him that he was nothing like that lot of pansies her folks had picked out for her to walk out with. And neither he was.

He still recalled how she had smiled with pleasure that day on St Stephen's Green when he had caught her bonnet as it sailed over the flowerbeds on the frisky April breeze, and returned it freshly adorned with a bright yellow daffodil plucked from a carefully-tended bed before her astonished eyes.

He had walked with her as far as the gates of her house that day and she had glanced nervously up at the great bay windows in case either her mother or father should be watching. They made an unlikely couple, if it was dress you were judging them by; her in her flower-sprigged, white muslin Sunday best, and him in his dirty corduroy trousers and checked wool shirt.

'You'll be nervous at being seen with the likes of me, then?'

She had blushed to the roots of her blue-black hair. 'Of – of course not! What a perfectly stupid thing to say! My parents are no snobs, they are true democrats, Mr . . . ?'

'Donovan – Danny Donovan. And you are?'

The blush had deepened. 'Maeve – Maeve Ballantine.'

'Well, Maeve Ballantine, what do you say to putting that "true democracy" to the test and walking out with me tomorrow?'

Shock, apprehension, then another more indefinable emotion had appeared in the bright blue eyes. She was intrigued. He stood before her – five feet nine inches of flame-red hair, solid muscle, and colossal cheek – and she was hooked. There was no other word for it. A spark had been lit that day that was to blaze into life and consume every doubt or inhibition that threatened to whisper a warning of parental disapproval into her besotted mind.

And so it had remained throughout the coming summer, for he had shown her a world she had never even guessed existed. A world of vibrant, real people, who poured more emotion into their everyday lives and loves than she had ever dreamt of in her sheltered seventeen-year-old world of governesses and house parties.

She had listened entranced when he had told her of his dreams for an Ireland free of British domination, and she had even attended some of the meetings, where romantic figures like Paddy Pearse, the intellectual, poetic headmaster, and the glamorous Countess Con Markiewicz and others had declaimed their idealistic visions of the future before them. Oh yes, she had assured him this was a new world all right, and one that she could not wait to grasp with both hands. He was opening her mind to all sorts of things that she had never come across before. Things they would not dream of discussing in the elegant parlour of her family home on Jubilee Avenue. And it excited her. Oh, how it excited her!

But the fascination for Maeve hadn't all been in the mind.

Not at all. He knew that better than anyone. For he was the one who had transformed her from a girl into a woman. A smile twisted the corners of his mouth at the memory. She couldn't get enough of him then, and even his prodigious energy was in danger of flagging by the time they finally said good-night, on those hot summer nights, and she crept quietly back into her house on the Green by the servants' entrance.

Oh, he had had women before, of course -- and plenty of them. Wasn't he bedding Cissie O'Rourke at every opportunity all the time he was leading on his little, innocent Miss Ballantine? No, even the fact that that silly bitch Cissie was in the family way with his own child had not cooled his ardour for and determination to both bed and wed his little St Stephen's Green Miss. Such a marriage was something no one -- no, not a single one -- from his own little world around McIntyre Street had ever accomplished. But then, wasn't Danny Donovan as good as any of that Protestant bunch who lived in those grand houses around the Green and had the brass neck to call themselves Irish? Too bloody true he was. Of that he had no doubt. And, when Maeve's relations tried to make out otherwise, he left her, and them, in no doubt about it.

He frowned, adjusting the smooth wooden butt of the gun against the rough stubble of his right cheek. If he thought about it, maybe that was half the trouble why they weren't seeing eye to eye now. If he'd swallowed his pride and kowtowed a bit more to old Charlie Ballantine and his missus, then maybe Maeve wouldn't have turned so queer lately. Yes, if she'd still been able to visit them, say, before the baby was born, then maybe she might have been a bit more accommodating towards him.

It wasn't as if he'd ended up returning to Cissie's bed by choice lately. For hadn't Maeve forced him into it by complaining of feeling unwell so much of the bloody time during the past nine months? To hear her, you'd think she was the first female ever to get herself in the family way. No, it certainly wasn't his fault . . . After all, a man had to get relief somewhere, didn't he?

* * *

'Je—e—e—esus God!' A sniper's bullet whistled past his head, missing him by inches, and ricocheted off the wall opposite, causing quite a commotion among the men propped up against the damp stonework trying to catch a few minutes' much-needed sleep. It didn't pay you to daydream for too long on this job! He leapt up from the window as another shot hit the stonework outside, then a whole volley of shots reached their target, sending showers of masonry fragments on to the pavement beneath. There was no way Jim Connolly or anybody could sleep through this!

He was right, for, within minutes, everyone was up off the floor and at their posts ready for another day of bombardment. The British guns were getting nearer and nearer, battering down rebel positions around the O'Connell monument.

By mid-morning they were having to shout to one another to make their voices heard above the gunfire. Willie Pearse, who had been standing next to Danny staring out over the rooftops as if mesmerised by the noise and confusion, started to sing, in his strange lisping voice, the words of 'The Soldier's Song':

'Soldiers are we, whose lives are pledged to Ireland . . .
'Mid cannon's roar and rifle's peal
We'll chant a soldier's song . . .'

A few others joined in, their voices strident and defiant in the midst of the smoke and din.

The singing continued on and off throughout the remainder of the morning, and, as nerves began to fray, it became more discordant, almost painful to ears already smarting from the continual shooting. Willie Pearse disappeared, along with his brother, around midday to survey the O'Connell Street positions and the others awaited their return with trepidation. The news was not going to be good.

'Hey, Danny, they're back!' A voice from somewhere in the confusion behind him made him turn round. 'The Pearses — they're back. Paddy's giving a speech down on the ground floor now. You'll better come down if you don't want to miss it.'

He followed a trickle of others who were making their way back downstairs, just in time to catch the main points of the address. Patrick Pearse was standing, pale-faced and gaunt, in the middle of a crowd of battle-weary men, reading from some sheets of paper, clasped tightly in his right hand:

'. . . For four days you have fought and toiled, almost without cessation, almost without sleep, and in the intervals of fighting have sung songs of the freedom of Ireland. No man has complained, no man has asked, "Why?" Each individual has spent himself, happy to pour out his strength for Ireland and for freedom.'

He paused. His eyes seemed to glow like hot coals from out of the deeply-shadowed sockets as he looked around him. For a fleeting second he caught Danny's gaze and the latter automatically straightened his shoulders. Although he had never regarded the man with as much reverence as Connolly, there was something about him that commanded respect.

As if reading his silent thoughts, Pearse looked him straight in the eye once more as he continued, 'If we do not win this fight, we will at least deserve to win it, although we may only win it in death. Already we have done a great thing. We have redeemed Dublin from many shames, and made her name splendid among the names of cities . . .'

A thin cheer went up when he had finished; there was little energy left for more boisterous shows of enthusiasm. A voice from behind him on the stairs, that Danny took to belong to Sean MacLoughlin, said quietly, 'The boss is looking for men to accompany him on a reconnoitring exercise. Any of you men game?'

He needed no encouragement. He hadn't seen the outside of this place since Monday, and Pearse's words had given a transfusion of new, vital blood to his veins.

Within minutes a detail of around thirty men had been gathered and cautiously followed the stocky figure of their leader out of the fortified bulk of the Post Office and across Prince's Street, where Connolly ordered several of the men to take up positions in the Metropole Hotel to bolster the protection of the south side of the Post Office. To the remaining others went the task of constructing barricades on Prince's

Street itself. While they worked, requisitioning what material they could gather for the fortifications, including Michael O'Rahilly's beloved Ford car, their leader strode fearlessly from position to position, encouraging his weary troops to greater effort.

From his stance in the Lucas lamp and bicycle shop directly opposite Middle Abbey Street, Danny marvelled at the bravery of the man. 'Just take a look at him,' he urged the freckle-faced youngster at his side. 'Any other poor bugger would have been felled by one of the Tommy snipers long ago! The man's indestructible, I tell ye. There's not a Tommy born who can stop the likes of him!'

Within seconds he wished the tongue could have been torn from his loud mouth, as a government bullet whistled down the street to hit the pavement beside Jim Connolly's gesticulating figure and ricochet off the pavement to shatter their leader's left ankle. He fell immediately and, as a further volley of fire opened up, he attempted to drag himself out of the street into a side alley.

Danny watched in mute horror for a second or two, then his young companion felt a tug on his arm, 'Come on, kid, we're needed out there!' Oblivious to the gunfire around them, Danny, pulling the boy behind him, shot out of the shop doorway to run crouching across the street to where their injured leader lay.

With the help of two others who had witnessed the incident, they carried him back up the road into the Post Office building. None could bear to look down at the agony of the man they so revered. In severe pain, small beads of sweat ran down Connolly's face and clung to the thick dark bristles of his moustache, but he made no sound.

'Hey, you two, over here – quick!' Danny yelled out to a couple of medical students who were manning the makeshift hospital on the ground floor.

They laid their leader down on top of a table as the two young men hurried across to meet them. The horror on their faces was obvious when they recognised the patient. And, to the astonishment of the men who had just brought him in, the medics informed them it was the second wound suffered by their leader that day. The first he had kept secret, lest it lower the morale of his already exhausted troops. But a cursory examination of this wound told them it was far more serious than the first and certainly well beyond their medical capabilities. George Mahoney, a captured British army doctor, was immediately summoned and only then did Danny and the others take their leave, as the call went out for morphine.

'They'll not find enough, you know. They've been eking it out with distilled water since last night. Old Jim's in for a bloody awful time, if he pulls through this, with nothing to ease the pain.'

Danny stared at the speaker, Sean McLoughlin, but could not bring himself to speak. No bloody morphine now. No bloody anything, he thought in despair. Never since the Rising began had spirits been so low. It was as if the bullet that had shattered Jim Connolly's ankle had also knocked the feet from the rebellion itself. The man had given them pride in their cause and the strength to carry on, even when all the odds seemed stacked against them. But now . . . He shook his head as he made his way back upstairs. The incessant din seemed to be pounding into his very brain. What wouldn't he give for it to be all over and to be out of this hell hole for good?

For the first time in hours his thoughts flew back to the small house in McIntyre Street and his young wife and son. God, how she would smile to see him returning home with his tail between his legs! Or maybe it would please her better if he didn't return home at all? The bitch had probably never even given him a second thought since Monday morning.

He was wrong, for Maeve had thought about very little else since she had given birth to their son. Just how could a man walk out on his wife at the moment of the birth of their first child? Even now, the thought still filled her with a barely suppressed anger as she shed her blue woollen dressing-gown and donned a freshly-laundered blouse and skirt.

The blouse smelt of lavender from the heart-shaped sachet she had filled just after her wedding and laid in the middle of the top drawer of the dressing-chest in their bedroom. Her slim fingers fussed with the high frilled collar in front of the mirror of the overmantel in the kitchen, then moved to the wide leather belt that encircled her waist. She had taken special care of her looks today, even moulding her long hair into the fashionable roll of her pre-marriage days.

She glanced at the clock on the mantelpiece. It was gone six o'clock and Dermot still hadn't appeared. Was he really such a coward that he was staying away on purpose? Her lips pursed as she teased out the carefully curled fringe with her fingers. She couldn't really believe that. He was a Donovan after all, and what Donovan was ever afraid of a mere woman?

She was to ask herself that same question many more times over the next four hours, until a tap on her door made her jump up from the chair by the fire and glance at the clock. It was almost ten o'clock. Surely that couldn't be him at this time of night?

It wasn't. And the look on her face when she opened the door could not disguise her astonishment, and disappointment, as she stared incredulously into the face of her sister-in-law, Mary-Agnes Kelly.

Chapter 5

'Mary-Agnes!' Maeve stared into the light brown eyes of the young woman on the doorstep. What on earth did she want? The eyes that stared back into hers were unblinking, hostile even, but she must at least give her the benefit of the doubt. 'You – you'd better come in . . .'

She stepped aside to allow the other woman to enter and closed the door behind her. They stared uncomfortably at one another from across the small kitchen. Not a word had passed between them during the ten months she had been Danny's wife and, by the look on his elder sister's face, she had not exactly come here tonight for a pleasant chat. 'Can – can I offer you something? A cup of tea, perhaps?'

Mary-Agnes moved her small daughter on to her other hip and looked round the sparsely furnished room, missing nothing. ''Tis not idle gossip I've come here for, so I'll spare you the bother of that.'

Maeve's eyes narrowed as she looked at her sister-in-law, a wave of relief sweeping over her that she had actually tidied up before sitting down for the evening. Why did she always feel so intimidated by her presence? There was no need for it, but the feeling was there all the same. Maybe it was something to do with the way she looked her up and down with those cold, sparsely-lashed, muddy brown eyes of hers. And Mary-Agnes was a good head taller, of course – that didn't help. She must be all of five feet ten, and built in proportion, with a positive shelf of a bosom and wide, ample hips that seemed to grow in width with each succeeding child. 'You've not come of your own accord, I take it?'

'I'll not lie to you – Dermot asked me to come. He thinks that you're maybe not quite right since the baby's birth.'

'Not quite right!' Maeve exploded. 'And just what is that supposed to mean?'

Mary-Agnes pushed a stray lock of lank brown hair back

56

behind her ear, with an impatient shrug. The movement sent a hairpin rattling to the floor, from the plaited bun at the nape of her neck, but Maeve made no move to pick it up. Let the bitch do it for herself.

'He knows that women sometimes take queer-like after having a baby and felt you could do with some company.'

Maeve gave a hollow laugh. 'And you're the company, are you, that's supposed to put me right? Just how many Hail Marys did he have to threaten you with to agree to this little act of mercy?'

'Mind your tongue, Maeve Ballantine! Nobody had to threaten me with anything, let alone Dermot. As Danny's sister it was the least I could do – what with him away there risking his life for his country an' all!'

'So that's it, is it? It was the thought that I could well be a widow by now, and how would you hold your head up in company again if I made it clear you weren't welcome at the funeral? I feel real sorry for the likes of you, Mary-Agnes. I really do!'

She walked to the window and stared out into the night sky. A deep pink glow lit the horizon. There were buildings ablaze out there. Whole streets of them. And Danny was in the thick of it all. 'It was a sad day for you when he married me, wasn't it?'

'Sure and that had nothin' to do with me!'

'No, but you've made it your business ever since to show your disapproval by totally ignoring me! What a pity for you he didn't marry that little tart Cissie O'Rourke, then you could have had one of your own kind as a sister-in-law!'

'Bitch!' Mary-Agnes's normally florid complexion went even redder. 'Cissie's no tart! She's more of a woman than you could ever be – otherwise why should Danny still be feeling the need to bed her, with you living under his own roof?'

Maeve whirled round. The words hit her like a sledgehammer. The knowledge shouldn't hurt – but it did. Oh God, how it did! 'You're lying! You're saying that to rile me, but you'll not succeed!'

A look of pity mingled with contempt crossed Mary-Agnes's face, as she shook her head slowly. 'I'm not lying, Maeve.

There's no need to lie. If you don't believe me, ask anyone – it's no secret around here. But don't go expecting any sympathy, mind, it's not you that folks feel sorry for – it's Danny. You've always felt you're a cut above the rest of us, haven't you? Well, folk take exception to that. Those who go around with their heads in the air get tripped up before long!'

The small child on her hip started to grizzle and pull at her mother's hair with outstretched sticky fingers and Mary-Agnes slapped them away impatiently, as her eyes met those of the white-faced young woman by the window. 'Well it's time I was going. I've done my duty. I've done what Dermot asked and come round. The good Lord knows, it's hardly my fault if I've not been made welcome!'

Maeve opened her mouth, but no words came out. She hadn't come here out of kindness at all. She had come here to demean her – and succeeded. The bitch. The big, fat, bloody bitch!

Mary-Agnes made for the door, an unctuous smile contorting her pursed lips, stopped for a moment, as if about to say something else, then changed her mind and went out, with a shrug of her shoulders. The door slammed shut behind her, making the crockery on the dresser shudder and waking Kieran, who lay dozing in his cradle beneath it. He started to whimper and Maeve went over and picked him up.

'There, there . . .' She stared at the closed door, as she rubbed her hand up and down the woollen matinee jacket that clothed the infant's tiny frame. What sort of world had she brought him into?

A wave of revulsion filled her. Revulsion for the woman who had just left – and everything she stood for. She was actually condoning what her brother was doing behind his own wife's back – they all were. God, how they must hate her round here! She wasn't one of them and they would never let her forget it. But neither did she want to be any more. Maybe Dermot was right. Maybe she was turning queer!

But that wasn't what he meant, was it? A perverse smile quirked the corners of her lips as she sat down on the chair by the fire and dandled the baby on her lap. That was simply how he was coping with what had passed between them the other night. He was putting it down to an aberration brought about by childbirth that had made her take momentary leave of her senses! And maybe so it was. She gave a bitter smile that faded almost as soon as it reached her lips. Perhaps it was better that he did believe that, for she was not proud of what had passed between them. She thought too much of him for that. But it had happened and there it was. It was something they would both have to live with. And if she could live with it, then so could he, surely? And, if that was the case, why had he been too scared to call by today? Why had he seen fit to send Mary-Agnes instead? It was the first day he had missed in months – and surely that spoke for itself? He was probably kneeling by his bed right now, begging absolution for what had, and hadn't, passed between them. A wave of guilt ran through her. But it was a guilt tinged with something else. A feeling that she couldn't quite put her finger on; a feeling that brought the pale skin of her arms out in gooseflesh and ran an icy finger down her spine as she leaned over and placed the baby back in its cradle.

With a sigh, she began to pull the pins from her hair and place them on to the polished top of the mantelpiece. As the long, dark locks tumbled around her shoulders, a deep frown etched itself across the clear skin of her brow. The last thing she wanted to do was to upset or embarrass Dermot – to change anything between them. He was the only one who understood – or at least tried to understand how things had changed between her and Danny over the past year. Mechanically her fingers began to undo the tiny pearl buttons of her blouse. Perhaps they'd all be better off in bed this night. It had not been a good day.

Dermot, in fact, was nowhere near his bed. He was less than five hundred yards away, standing by the fire in Mary-Agnes's kitchen listening, grave-faced, to his sister. 'For pity's sake, Mary-Agnes, the idea wasn't that you fell out even more with the girl – it was that you made it up!'

His sister's mouth was set. 'Then tell her that – the stuck-up little madam! I'm sorry, Dermot, I know you're well intentioned, but Maeve Ballantine's not one of us and never will be.

59

I knew that from the very first time I set eyes on her. Her with her fancy clothes and fancy ways!'

'But I like Maeve's clothes, Mary-Agnes! She lets me try them on sometimes.'

The mud-coloured eyes turned in irritation to the small girl on the edge of the fender. 'Shut up, Katie! You don't know what you're talking about. She tolerates you, that's all.'

'T–o–lerates . . .' The child moved the word around on her tongue. It sounded good. 'Then she tolerates Willie-John too, Mary-Agnes, for she's good to him as well.'

Her elder sister flung her an 'if looks could kill' glance and lifted the kettle off the hob, with a sigh. 'Willie-John – that gormless lump! I'd wager it was him that put Madam wise to poor Cissie's existence, for nobody else would be that daft!'

Katie stared up at her, her small mouth suddenly dry. 'Did Maeve not know about Cissie, then, Mary-Agnes? Did she not know about Uncle Dermot's other babby?'

'She did not! Not to my knowledge, at least! And whoever it was that put her wise to it will surely burn in hell for their sins in divulging such a thing!' She shook her head as she poured the hot water into the enamel teapot and replaced the kettle on the range. 'Unless the Good Lord takes pity on the likes of Willie-John, of course, and realises the poor creature doesn't know what he's saying half the time!'

Katie's stomach turned over as she gazed up at the bulky figure of her sister, then across at Dermot. It wasn't Willie-John – it was her – Katie – that told Maeve! She was the one that would be burning in hell. Hot tears sprang to her eyes and she blinked them back as she looked up at the young man in the priest's robe. 'Can I speak to you, Dermot? Can I speak to you in private for a minute?'

'Take no notice of her, Dermot. It's time she was off to bed. That one's too keen by half of listening in to adult conversations that don't concern her!'

But Dermot already had his small sister by the hand. 'Come on then, Kathleen astore . . . Let's be hearing what you've got to say for yourself!' With one mighty swing he had swept her up on to his back, as they made for the door that led to the upstairs bedrooms.

Her confession, blurted out in between stifled sobs, from the edge of the double bed she shared with Willie-John, was listened to in silence by the young priest. 'Tell her I'm sorry, won't you, Dermot? Tell Maeve I didn't mean to be sinful and tell her about Cissie and the babby. I thought she knew. Honest to God, I thought she knew.'

'I know you did, Katie. And there's no sin on your part.'

The brimming eyes widened. 'I'll not burn in hell, then? Mary-Agnes was wrong? I'll not be punished for telling about Danny and Cissie O'Rourke?'

Dermot took the small, damp hands in his. 'No, child, you'll not be the one that's punished. The sin is not yours . . . if there is to be punishment in the hereafter in that regard, you'll not be the one that suffers the torments.'

'But you'll tell her all the same. You'll tell Maeve I didn't mean it. I thought she knew. Promise me, Dermot. Promise me!'

He nodded slowly. It was not a promise he relished keeping.

The night went slowly for those on the roof of the Post Office and in the other rebel positions around the city. The British forces were now outnumbering the rebels by about twenty to one and had driven a wedge across the city, roughly in line with the River Liffey. In the Post Office itself morale was at an all-time low since the shooting of James Connolly. There had been other shootings – many others killed – but somehow the wounding of the man regarded by all as their most capable leader was a hard cross to bear.

By mid-morning many of the surrounding fires had burned themselves out, but it was little comfort to those still inside the barricaded building, where the exhausted men were fighting a never-ending battle to keep the flames at bay. They were now completely surrounded by British artillery; the shelling was intensifying by the hour, and incendiaries were flying towards them like homing pigeons. Word came from above that the whole of the roof was ablaze. 'Evacuation' had become the key word on everyone's lips.

Pearse and Connolly decided that the female nurses of the Cumann na mBan should be the first to leave, along with the worst of the wounded, who would be taken to the nearby Jervis Street Hospital. A deep melancholy pervaded those left inside as, despite several very vocal protests, the women prepared to leave.

Danny watched them go from the same window as Winifred Carney, Connolly's secretary. He had strangely mixed feelings, as the small procession of about twenty girls walked out of the Henry Street door under the protection of a Red Cross apron tied as a makeshift flag to a pole. Relief for those on their way out to normality, and apprehension for the rest of them still inside, showed clearly in the deeply furrowed brow above the bloodshot hazel eyes.

Before they reached the end of the street the nurses, and their patients, were immediately taken into custody by British soldiers. It was no more than they had expected.

Winifred Carney, who had refused to obey her boss's order to leave, glanced across at Danny and shook her head. There were tears in her eyes. There was no need for words.

Throughout the afternoon the bombardment increased, with incendiary bombs exploding everywhere. Like everyone else, Danny was dog-tired and soaked through, as every available man ran with water hoses to attempt to dampen the flames of the fires that were breaking out all around them. By around six o'clock, however, they knew it was a losing battle and the two upper storeys were abandoned to flames. Blazing beams were crashing down from the roof to land at their feet, scattering their burning fragments on the exhausted men as they struggled in vain to save the ground floor with sandbags and water.

Jim Connolly himself was attempting to give orders from a bed in the middle of the chaos and, hearing from Winifred Carney that he was about to make an important announcement, Danny made for the iron bedstead that housed his leader.

Pearse, MacDermott, Clarke, Plunkett and O'Rahilly were already there, gathered round their wounded comrade, as Connolly propounded his plan. There was nothing for it, the building would have to be evacuated as soon as possible, and, since the sewers were proving impenetrable as a means of escape, they would have to fight their way through to a new headquarters above ground, taking their chances against the waiting British artillery as best they could. The Williams and Woods soap and sweet factory was the building decided upon as the one most suitable.

'But that's on Parnell Street,' Joe Plunkett interrupted. 'It's quite a way north from here. That'll mean taking on the British guns that are positioned all the way up Moore Street.'

He looked from one to the other, his face deathly pale, the earrings that dangled from beneath the officer's hat glinting gold through the thick dust of pulverised mortar that hung like talcum powder in the air around them. The white bandage round his throat – the constant reminder of the glandular tuberculosis that was slowly killing him – was now a dirty dark grey, and his eyes seemed to burn from hollow sockets in his head.

Tom Clarke, the old Fenian in whose tobacconist's shop in Parnell Street they had all met so often to plan and to dream, took off his pince-nez and cleaned it with a grubby handkerchief. Like almost everyone in the beleaguered building, his seamed face was haggard and bleeding from the jagged splinters of stone and brick that pierced the air with each enemy strike.

A silence fell and Danny found himself staring at the old man. Funny how he had never noticed how scrawny his neck was before. Like a thrawn chicken's it was, with an adam's apple as big as a golf ball jiggling about above the dog-eared collar.

'I'll be willing to lead a party up there when the time comes. You just have to say the word, Jim.' It was Michael O'Rahilly who spoke, and all eyes turned to look at him, but there was no reply to his offer. It would be a suicide mission and every man there knew it. But what was the alternative?

Danny turned away, walking over to where Winifred Carney was sitting slumped in a corner. He was followed by Joe Plunkett, the silver spurs jangling from the heels of his hand-tooled riding boots as he sat down beside her, and looked up at Danny with a strange, haunted look in his eyes. His long white fingers caressed the automatic Mauser pistol that dangled from his belt, as he said softly, 'You're married to a Protestant, aren't

63

you, Dan? Isn't it old Charlie Ballantine the accountant's daughter you've made an honest woman of?'

Danny nodded, the surprise showing in his face. He was not aware it was such a well-known fact among the leadership. And certainly he never suspected Count Plunkett's poet son took an interest in his personal affairs. 'Sure, I'm married to Maeve Ballantine and she was a Protestant – still is, if she's anything . . .' He gave a short laugh. Religion had never had too high a profile in their relationship.

Joe Plunkett nodded. 'There's a strange comfort to be gained knowing someone else has been in the same boat as yourself. My fiancée Grace – Grace Gifford – is a Protestant too. She's been estranged from her family for some time now because of our engagement. She's converted to the faith for my sake and her family just can't come to terms with it.'

There was real grief in his voice as he spoke and Danny and Winifred Carney looked at him curiously, wondering what was coming next. They glanced at one another in apprehension as he proceeded to pull an exquisite filigree bangle from his left wrist, followed by one of his huge antique rings. Extracting an empty envelope from his inside pocket, he dropped the jewellery into it and handed it across to Winifred. 'I'd like you to give these to Grace when you get out of here, Win. I – I'd like her to have something to remember me by.'

With that, he got up and disappeared into the mayhem around them. Danny and Winifred looked at one another. It was the first time anyone had admitted out loud that they believed they would not come out of here alive.

An almighty crash from somewhere deep in the building was followed by a series of explosions that shook the very fabric of the stonework around them. The flames had swept down the liftshafts and were now taking hold in the cellars where the explosives and most of the ammunition were stored.

'Holy Mary and Joseph!' Danny was flung from his feet to land on his back on the soaking floor. He lay there, eyes closed, for some minutes, as if paralysed. Every bone in his body ached and all the hammers of hell were pounding in his head. What, in God's name, was he doing here when there was a soft, comfortable bed waiting for him less than a mile away? For the first time real doubts crowded his mind and he cursed himself inwardly. He was turning into a bloody girl. Who was he to wish he was out of it all when the likes of Winnie Carney were still willing to stick it out?

The day dragged to a close, amid choking dust, water and more explosions as the flames claimed the remaining boxes of ammunition. By eight o'clock there was no disguising the fact by gallant words any longer; they would have to fight their way out. What was left of the building around them was like a scene from hell itself, as the remains of the upper floors crashed about them in flames. Through the belching smoke they could look out to the street beyond, where the ruins of the Imperial Hotel seemed to mock the dreams they had once held so fervently – and still held – for their beautiful city.

'The O'Rahilly is organising his party to make the break for the factory in Parnell Street. Are you game, Danny?'

He turned to find himself looking into the eyes of Con O'Malley. 'Con, you old sod! Sure an' it's been more than a day since I've set eyes on you!'

His friend grinned, his teeth gleaming white through his smoke-blackened face. 'You'll come, then? You'll not let the old boy down?'

He did not need a second invitation and the two made their way across to where Pearse and Plunkett were setting about rounding up the remainder of their beleaguered troops to march them from the raging inferno that had been their home for four days into the courtyard by the side gate.

As the men lined up to make their way towards the Henry Street exits, The O'Rahilly, his bloodshot eyes gleaming out of a smoke-blackened face, gathered his volunteers into a separate advance group and Danny and Con slipped in towards the rear. They looked a sorry sight compared to the high-stepping soldiers who had marched so proudly into the building just four short days ago, but a lot had happened since then, Danny reminded himself, as Patrick Pearse strode across to wish them luck on the task ahead.

His last words, 'Go out and face the machine-guns as though you were on parade,' rang in their ears as they marched towards the yard gates. Michael O'Rahilly, cocking his hat at a jaunty angle, broke into the words of 'The Soldier's Song' and, for the first time in years, Danny felt the hot sting of tears in his eyes, as he forced one painful foot after the other behind the closed ranks of his comrades.

They had got less than three hundred yards, and were on the point of turning into Moore Street, when a terrific volley of gunfire opened up on them from all sides. The man directly in front of him was hit in the groin and collapsed groaning to the ground. Danny stumbled over him, but raised himself in time to see a burst of machine-gun fire mow down The O'Rahilly and Pat Shortis, the man next to him. They were dead before they reached the ground.

'Let's get the hell out of here!' Liam Daly yelled from the row directly in front of him, and automatically he followed the small group that broke ranks and made for the left-hand side of the street, to escape down one of the small alleyways that led to some stables beyond. The bullets whistled past their ears and one hit Daly in the left arm. He stumbled and Danny stopped in his tracks, but was urged on by Con, who pulled him by the arm. 'Come on, Danny boy, we're going home! The Rising's over for us!'

They were the last words he was to hear his friend speak, for a bullet caught Con cleanly through the back of the head and came out through his forehead, leaving a hole the size of his fist above the wide-open blue eyes. He made no sound as he fell, but lay spread-eagled on the cobbles staring up at the narrow patch of blue sky above the rooftops that bordered the alley. There was a look of astonishment on his boyish features, as if he could not quite comprehend it had happened to him – not now, after having survived the past four days of hell.

Danny stared down at him for a moment then ran on blindly down the narrow close. Tears were streaming unashamedly down his cheeks, making dirty grey rivulets through the smoke and grime.

He was going home all right, but not with Con. There was no need for Con to flee the British guns like a hunted animal. The bastards had got him. The Rising was over for him all right.

Chapter 6

The insistent banging on the door made Maeve sit up with a
jolt, clutching the bedclothes to her. Her heart pounded
beneath the light flannel of her nightgown. Who on earth was
that at this time of night? The banging continued, joined now
by the impatient rattling of the door-handle, as she threw back
the bedclothes and slipped down on to the rag rug by the side
of the bed.

The noise woke the baby who had been sleeping in his cradle
at the side of the bedside cabinet and his high-pitched wail
almost drowned out the racket from beyond the bedroom door.

'Maeve! Maeve! For God's sake open up!'

It was him! It was Danny! There was no mistaking the voice,
even through the thick pine panels of the door. Not waiting to
bother with slippers, she ran barefoot to the closed door. Her
fingers were all thumbs as she struggled with the heavy cast-
iron key in the lock, then pulled back the rusty bolt.

'You took your time!' He almost fell into the room, staggering
over to the chair by the range, as she closed the door behind
him. 'Lock it!'

She obeyed his barked command, then turned to face him,
her back pressed against the pile of coats that hung from a
hook at the back of the door. 'You look awful!'

'So would you if you'd spent four days in that bloody place!'

She continued to stare at him. It was like looking at a
stranger, as he leaned thankfully against the bentwood back of
the chair and let out a long, groaning sigh. He didn't even
bother to look at her as he opened his jacket and extracted a
pistol from his belt and laid it on the table beside him. So this
was it – this was the romantic reunion after the birth of their
firstborn. 'I'll make you a cup of tea.'

'To hell with tea – get me a whiskey. And make it a big one!'

She was aware of his eyes on her as she went to the dresser
and uncorked a half-full bottle of Jameson's that was kept for

special occasions. The irony was not lost on her as the golden liquid sloshed into a glass and she carried it across to him. 'I take it it's all over, then?'

He nodded, swigging half the whiskey down in one. It burned its way down to his stomach, filling his insides with a mellow glow that belied his jagged nerves, as he said tersely, 'They got Con. The bastards got Con!'

Her mouth went dry. Not Con! 'You mean he's been shot?'

'Dead . . .' His voice cracked as he spoke. 'In front of my own eyes.' He finished the whiskey and thrust the glass back at her. She refilled it automatically and he took another gulp, pushing a hand through the thatch of unruly red hair. It was all of two hours ago now, but the sight was still a livid scar on his mind, and his head still rang with the sound of gunfire. At one point he thought he would never make it back to his own home, for the British seemed to be everywhere, and two hours of creeping around back alleys and hiding in cold, damp wash-houses had just about done for him.

A wail from the bedroom beyond made him look round as the image of his friend's blue sightless eyes faded from his mind and the reality of the present broke in. The faintest hint of a smile flickered at the corners of his lips. 'I've got a son.' There was little enthusiasm in his voice.

She nodded. It was typical of him to put it that way. 'I'll get him.'

The child was bright red and fretful as she plucked him from his cradle and brought him through, to place him in his father's arms for the first time.

'He's going to have red hair.' Danny's fingers plucked at the small tufts of reddish down that covered the child's scalp. 'I'll call him Seamus after my old man. How'd you like to be called after your grandfather, eh kid?'

'His name's Kieran.'

Danny's head jerked up, as he looked at her in amazement. 'What'd you say?'

'I said his name's Kieran.' She was determined to stand her ground.

'And who the hell is Kieran, may I ask?'

'He is! He's his own man, Danny — or will be some day. I

68

don't want him called after anybody else. I don't want him to have to live up to anybody else – dead or alive – or to have to prove anything to anyone.'

He took a long breath, letting it out noisily through gritted teeth. He wasn't in the door five minutes and they were at it again, but this time he was too exhausted to argue. All he wanted was a wash and change of clothes then he'd be out of here, to a safer place. The Tommies would be battering that door down before the night was through and he wasn't going to end up with a bullet through his head like Con. No, sir, they wouldn't catch up with him in a hurry.

He handed the child back to her without a word and got up and walked to the basin on the washstand by the window.

She watched in silence as he stripped off his filthy clothes and washed the grime and smoke from his face and body. In the lamplight his clean skin was pale, almost translucent, and covered with a fine down of golden hair that transformed itself into a thick, deeper red curling mat on his chest. For a smallish man, he was powerfully built, but his body no longer held the power to thrill her as it once had. She found she could look at it quite objectively now, and the knowledge brought no feeling of relief, merely a cold emptiness that came over her in a wave and caused her to shiver physically and clasp her arms around her as he pulled a clean checked wool shirt over his head.

'Do I get to know where you're going?'

They stood facing one another at the door, a few minutes later, and he shook his head. 'It's better you don't. That way there's nothing the Tommies can do that can harm you – or me. But I'll be okay – I'll be well looked after, you need have no fear about that.'

She looked straight into his eyes, and shook her head as a vision of Cissie O'Rourke and her child obscured her vision. 'I have no doubt about that, Danny. No doubt at all.'

He leaned forward and kissed her, a perfunctory, dry kiss in the middle of her forehead. Then he was gone.

She turned to the table where his gun still lay and walked over and picked it up. The metal felt cold and heavy in her hand. Then she caught sight of herself in the mirror above the mantelpiece – a gun in one hand, a newly-born child in the other. The sight sent a shiver through her that chilled her blood. 'You'll never hold one of these in your hands if I have anything to do with it, Kieran Donovan,' she whispered into the uncomprehending ears of the infant. 'If you do it'll be over my dead body – or his . . .'

The bed felt cold and empty when she finally returned to it, to lie staring up at the cracked ceiling of the small bedroom. What was happening to her? What would happen to Danny, now a fugitive out there in the city? Even Cissie O'Rourke could not protect him from the wrath of the British for ever.

She was still musing on the question, too emotionally exhausted to sleep, when, at just after three o'clock, an almighty explosion seemed to rock the building to its very foundations.

White-faced and shaking, she clambered out of the bed and ran to the window. There was no moon, so she could see nothing but the pink glow that lit the sky in the direction of the Post Office. The explosion seemed to come from there . . . Please God, don't let there be any men left in there . . . God help them if there are . . .

She repeated her silent prayer as she made her way through to the kitchen and lit the lamp from the dying embers of the fire. The bottle of Jameson's was still sitting on the dresser and she poured herself a generous drink, before sitting down in the chair by the fire. Thank God the noise hadn't wakened the baby. All she wanted was a few minutes' peace and quiet to collect her chaotic thoughts. A few more coals soon brought the fire flickering back to life and the whiskey, for the first time in her life, tasted good on her tongue.

She had almost finished it and was contemplating pouring another when a noise outside the door made her whirl round in her seat. Was it him? Had he come back? Her heart pounded crazily against her ribs as she gripped the edges of the chair. It couldn't be Danny. He would have made himself known by now.

A faint tapping brought a film of nervous perspiration to the palms of her hands and she wiped them on the blue flannel of her nightgown as she stood up and stared nervously at the locked door. The handle turned, rattling slightly in its socket, and the tapping became more insistent. It couldn't be the British looking for Danny, for surely they would have kicked it in by now.

'Who – who's there?'

'It's only me, Maeve. It's Dermot.'

A wave of relief swept through her. But what on earth was he doing here at this time of night? Puzzled, she unlocked the door and pulled it open to find herself face to face with her brother-in-law.

'Is he here?' His voice was low and urgent as he peered into the lamplit interior behind her.

She shook her head as she stepped back to allow him to enter. 'He's gone ... I don't need to tell you where.' It was impossible to disguise the bitterness in her voice.

Dermot looked puzzled for a moment, then comprehension dawned and he nodded mutely, avoiding her eyes as he strode over to the heat of the fire. He stood with his back to it, his hands clasped behind him, as she locked the door and made for the bottle of whiskey. It didn't seem a night to be offering tea, somehow.

She poured them both a drink and walked over to the fireside and handed him his. He took it with a murmur of thanks and their eyes met for a flickering second, before both looked away much too quickly.

He cleared his throat noisily before speaking. 'He's been here, then? Was he all right?'

She took a sip of the whiskey and nodded. 'Con's dead, though – and God knows who else. Danny said very little, and I didn't like to ask, I could see the state he was in. What's happening out there, Dermot? Have they all gone mad?'

'It's madness all right. I've just seen with my own eyes what's left of the Rising and it's a pitiful sight.'

'Have they surrendered? Has the leadership given up? Are they in British hands by now?'

Dermot gave a mirthless laugh. 'No, they're in Cogan's grocery store on Moore Street! At least Connolly, Plunkett, Clarke and MacDermott and some of the others are – Pearse seems to come and go as he thinks fit. Maybe he imagines he's

71

still holding some kind of control on the situation, but it's useless, Maeve, it's useless. There's some wild talk of knocking holes through all the adjoining houses and making some kind of escape that way. Have you ever heard of anything so daft?'

He shook his head and took another swig of the drink, letting out a satisfied sigh as the pungent liquid made its way down his throat. 'If you ask me, they'll get as far as Hanlon's fish shop and that'll be an end to it. Jim Connolly's foot will see to that. Any fool can see already that gangrene has set in and the man's in mortal pain.'

'You've seen him? You've been there?'

He nodded. 'I was called for to assist Father O'Reilly give the last rites to some of the wounded. They've got a couple of Cumann na mBan girls there, Julia Grenan and Elizabeth O'Farrell, and of course Winifred Carney, Connolly's secretary, to nurse them, but most of the poor devils have got precious little hope of surviving the night. And, if Jim Connolly doesn't get help for that ankle soon, neither has he.'

A silence fell between them, as both pondered on their own thoughts, then Dermot reached out and picked up Danny's pistol from the table-top. 'I see he's left this.'

'It's probably safer. If he was found by the British with a weapon on him, I wouldn't give out much hope for his chances.'

'You're right there.' He replaced the gun on the oilcloth and turned to face her. 'I'm sorry it's come to this, Maeve. I really am. It's not been the best start to married life and starting a family that you could have wished for. How old are you now – eighteen?'

She nodded. He was only twenty-four, but he made eighteen sound no more than a child. 'Don't patronise me, Dermot Donovan, sometimes I feel old enough to be your own mother!'

He laughed and reached out and touched her cheek. It felt soft and warm beneath his fingertips. 'You don't look it. You'll never look that, Maeve.'

Their eyes met and, for the first time, she noticed how the dark brown of his seemed to glow gold at the centre in the firelight. They were softer than Danny's, much softer and much more gentle, as was his touch on her skin.

72

She made a slight movement with her head and a lock of hair fell forward across her cheek. He brushed it away, aware of how silkily soft it felt – so soft he wanted to touch it again; stroke it and feel the smoothness of it through his fingers.

She was different from Mary-Agnes, and almost all the other young women from round here. Her beauty had not yet been tarnished by the hard grind of poverty. There was a softness, a glow, about it – a purity that did not belong in this wretched kitchen, waiting for a man who they both knew was already in someone else's bed. When he looked at her, he was reminded there was another world beyond the confines of McIntyre Street and its surrounding alleyways; there was a world of beauty, of art and literature – all the things he had never been able to discuss with his own family. Before she became part of it, that was . . .

'Why did you come here like this, at this time of night?' Her voice was huskily low as she spoke.

Embarrassment crept in a pink glow up his neck. 'I – I came straight from the Cogan place, in Moore Street. The British are searching all known rebel houses – I wanted to warn Danny, if he was here, that he'd have to get away fast.'

'Oh.' She turned from him, tossing her hair over her shoulders, as she stared into the flames of the fire. What he said was true, she knew that, but it was only half the truth . . . But not a man – or woman – on this earth would get him to admit the other half. 'Well, I don't think I have to spell it out where you'll find him, do I? He'll be at the O'Rourkes', so 'tis to there you'd better be taking yourself.'

'I don't think I'll be knocking on her door at this time of night.' The hair that cascaded in coils down the back of her nightgown shone like polished jet in the lamplight and his fists clenched as he gazed at it. He mustn't reach out and touch it. On no account must he reach out . . .

'Well, in that case, 'tis home you'll better be heading for, don't you think?'

His right hand jerked back to his side as she turned to confront him. There was the scent of lavender about her that was even stronger in the warmth of the fire. It almost overpowered his senses. Just standing here letting her presence flood through him was almost sin enough to bring him to his knees and beg absolution. He nodded, without speaking, and turned and walked to the door.

She followed him, standing by him as his hand reached for the handle. Her face was upturned, as it always was, waiting for the expected brotherly peck on the cheek. He leaned forwards and gripped her by the shoulders, but, as his mouth skimmed the light pink skin of her right cheek, she moved her head slightly, so that for an instant their lips touched. He jerked back, as if stung, and drew in his breath sharply. Her cheeks flamed in the firelight as she met his eyes. May the Good Lord forgive her. The devil had entered her soul this night. Her voice was almost inaudible. 'Goodnight, Dermot. Thank you for coming.'

He stood for a long time leaning against the outside of the door as she closed it behind him. He listened as she turned the key in the lock and slid the bolt back into position. A few seconds later the lamp went out, plunging the small house into darkness. The night was chill, but there was a thin film of perspiration covering his body beneath the black cassock. Every nerve end of his being was on edge. There was no way he could go home right now and endure the tortures of the turmoil that was in his mind. He would return to Moore Street and see if he could be of some help. Even the British wouldn't shoot a priest down in cold blood.

Cogan's grocery store was on the corner of Henry Lane and Moore Street and next to it, adjoining the yard, was a small cottage occupied by a family with ten children. A short time before his first visit a few hours previously, one of the daughters, a young girl of sixteen, and her father had been shot and mortally wounded by one of the rebels. Dermot crossed himself and said a silent prayer for their souls as he walked quickly past. So many in the city were suffering this night and this could be just the beginning of it now the round-up of the rebels had begun in earnest.

The sight that met his eyes in Cogan's shop made him wish he had gone straight home. The ground floor was littered with wounded men, very few of whom were able to sleep, for what little they had in the way of painkillers had run out long ago.

The morphine had been diluted with distilled water until there was no relief to be gained from it, bar the psychological, and a low moaning sound filled the air.

Jim Connolly had been put to bed in the back room. He lay in perhaps the greatest pain of all. Mrs Cogan was endeavouring to tend them all as best she could, but the task was beyond the strength of one human being. The two Pearse brothers, he was informed, were upstairs asleep, stretched out side by side on top of a table.

Dermot took up a position in the small back kitchen, near the stove, and attempted to doze. Somehow he felt his presence there was important, although there was very little he could give in the way of help, except in spiritual support.

Almost all were relieved when morning came and the discussions on future plans began again in earnest. An air of unreality pervaded everything, made more so by the bright sunlight that began to filter through the dusty net of the curtains on the narrow windows. Could such a thing really be happening here in civilised Dublin, during Easter week? Dermot could only shake his head in disbelief, and settle down quietly at the rear of the proceedings to listen to the arguments that ensued.

None of the acknowledged leaders could agree on a plan, so finally Jim Connolly turned to young Sean MacLoughlin. His bravery the previous night had won him a field commission and his opinion was as valid as any of theirs. He was only too willing to say his piece, he had spent most of the night thinking about it and knew exactly what should be done. He would lead a diversionary assault on the Tommies lying in wait for them outside. By doing so he would give their remaining comrades a chance to make a dash for the Four Courts, the law courts on Inns Quay, where Ned Daly and his men were still holding out. That would be the ideal place to set up headquarters for a last stand. With a bit of luck, it could succeed – it had to.

'How many lives will it cost?' It was Patrick Pearse who asked the question. For the time being, the poet had given way to the realist.

'Around thirty. Certainly no more, with a bit of luck.'

They agreed it was worth a try. At this stage they had little

75

left to lose. So the tunnelling began again in earnest, from one house in the row to the next, up the east side of Moore Street, to the point where the diversionary charge would have most hope of succeeding. Dermot's prediction to Maeve proved uncannily accurate, for by the time they got as far as Hanlon's fish shop, at number sixteen, it was decided to go no further to save Jim Connolly any further agony. To get him through the knocked-out holes in the brickwork, his carriers were having to transfer him from his mattress to a blanket sling, which afforded his shattered limb no protection.

Dermot followed directly behind his makeshift stretcher and his admiration for the man grew by the minute, as he watched him grit his teeth, and stare with glazed eyes out of a face that had become a mask of pain. His skin was ashen and bathed in sweat, but he was determined not to add to the difficulties of his bearers by moaning out loud.

The smell of fish only added to the incongruousness of the situation as they gathered in the back room of the shop and laid their leader and the other wounded on the floor. Joe Plunkett, his face now whiter than the grubby bandages that swathed his ailing neck, stood by the door, his right hand resting on the antique sabre that hung from a scabbard at his waist. Dermot looked at him in wonder. He looked like an escapee from a comic opera, but there was no denying the courage of the man. Not for a minute had he allowed his tubercular condition to inhibit his contribution to the cause. 'You're Danny Donovan's brother, aren't you, Father?'

Dermot nodded in embarrassment. He must have been aware he was staring at him. 'I have that distinction.' He meant it humorously, but Joe's eyes were serious as he looked across at him.

'He was one of the bunch that set off in the advance guard with The O'Rahilly. I hope to God some of them made it. His family should be proud of him, Father. One day their names will be written in gold in the annals of this country.'

'I don't know about that,' Dermot said, with a wry smile. 'What is it the good book says: "A prophet is not without honour, save in his own country, and in his own house" . . . I reckon the same could be said for freedom fighters too.'

The Pearse brothers exchanged looks. The priest's words had the uncomfortable ring of truth. Just how would history – and, more important, their own people – judge them all? Could they ever understand the emotions, the dreams, that lay behind the happenings of the past four days? Would generations of children, as yet unborn, bless them, or curse them – or, even worse, laugh at what they had done this Easter week, in the name of Ireland?

Pat's eyes rested on the pale, haggard face of his brother Willie. Dear, dear Willie . . . Was there ever a brother who could have meant more?

> In direst peril true to me . . .
> Of all the men that I have known on earth,
> You only have been my familiar friend,
> Nor needed I another . . .

The words of his own poem rang in his head, and he felt a surge of love for the thin, stooped, young man by his side. But he must not allow himself to get maudlin . . . He averted his eyes from his brother's weary face and, as three shots rang out, shattering the quiet of the room, he walked quickly to the front window and peered down the empty street.

A house belonging to a local publican was burning on the opposite side of the road, a few doors down, and lying sprawled on the pavement were the bodies of the man and his wife and daughter: each had a white handkerchief clutched in their right hand. They had obviously been picked off by government snipers as they ran to escape the flames that were consuming their home.

'What is it, Paddy? Who's doing the shooting?' Winifred Carney pushed past him to stare out through the dusty glass. Sick at heart, she turned away. Both were speechless as they returned to the group. Dermot knew they had seen something out there in the street and felt, in his position as a priest, he should say something, offer some comfort perhaps, but the look on their faces told him silence was infinitely preferable. There came a time when words were of little consolation.

A silence descended that was broken only by a rough

scuffling sound from the mouth of the tunnel that was being dug through the walls. Within seconds the two Seans, Mac-Loughlin and MacDermott, appeared, their already dirty uniforms almost indistinguishable beneath the thick covering of brick dust that covered the green. They had obviously finished the tunnelling, but there was no pleasure, or look of accomplishment, on their faces.

'Well, did you get through?' It was Jim Connolly himself who spoke.

The two men nodded, then MacDermott said quietly, 'We saw The O'Rahilly. His body's still out there in the street, riddled with holes.'

'Sure and we'll all be shot to pieces as soon as we poke our noses outside! Bloody sieves they'll make of the lot o' us!' Mick Feeney, who had been sitting quietly cleaning his rifle with an old handkerchief voiced the thoughts of quite a few of the others.

All eyes turned to Patrick Pearse. After what he had just witnessed, he had never heard truer words. It would be criminal to allow a suicidal assault on the street. They would be mowed down before they got to the end of the road. Those poor blighters lying out there on the pavement, in their own blood, were evidence of that. But it wasn't his place to impose his will on anyone. They must all have a say in their own fate. He glanced again at his brother Willie, then stepped forwards, clearing his throat. 'We'll have a free vote on it. Do we come out fighting to the last, or go in for a conditional surrender?'

Willie Pearse's pale face went paler still, then he turned and disappeared through a door on the far wall to give the news of the vote to his friend Desmond Ryan and the others crowded in the adjoining room. Seeing him go, Dermot rose quietly to his feet and slipped out of the back door. This was their decision. They had been in it together from the beginning. He had no right to witness their agonies at the end.

It took only a few minutes to end the torment. When he re-entered the room a strange calmness hung in the air. Old Tom Clarke stood by the window, his face ashen, and Winifred Carney sat on the floor behind him sobbing quietly. Dermot went over and stood beside her, resting a hand on her shaking shoulder as Sean MacDermott went over to ask Elizabeth O'Farrell, one of the nurses, if she could find a white flag of surrender.

She produced a white handkerchief which was hung on a stick outside the window and Tom Clarke, who until then had remained silent, burst into tears. Seeing the old man's grief, MacDermott wept too.

Another handkerchief was found and this she clutched in her right hand. There was complete silence, save the muffled sobbing from inside the room, as she made for the front door of the shop. Her friend Julia Grenan started to weep noisily and had to be restrained by Patrick Pearse from going after her.

'God go with you, Elizabeth,' Dermot said quietly, voicing the thoughts of them all.

She paused on the doorstep and turned to him, a determinedly brave smile on her lips. 'Pray for me, Father. Pray for all of us.'

He kissed her on both cheeks and, taking a long, shuddering breath, she stepped out into Moore Street, waving the flag in front of her.

Somewhere over the rooftops a church clock struck noon. The Rising was over. It had lasted exactly four days.

Chapter 7

'Hell, Cissie, I feel like a rat that's deserted the sinking ship!' Danny's red-rimmed eyes gazed in anguish out through the net-covered window to the street beyond. 'I should go back. I shouldn't be cowering here like a bloody woman!'

'And what might you mean by that? Sure and weren't you the one to say there were still some women there to the last?' Cissie O'Rourke turned from the table, where she was piling a meal of freshly-boiled potatoes on to a plate, to cast a glance at the young man at the window.

He gave a sheepish shrug and nodded briefly, letting the curtain drop back against the dusty window-pane. He was in no mood for a battle of the sexes, he got enough of that at home with Maeve. If only he had word of what exactly was happening out there. This was the worst bit, the not knowing.

He sat down at the table and cut a wedge of butter off the dish with his fork and dropped it into the middle of the potatoes, passing one across to the small girl seated on the chair next to him. She took it with a gap-toothed smile and stuffed it into her mouth.

'What do you say, Caitlin?'

The child looked at her mother and beamed a mashed-potato smile in her direction. She was barely eighteen months old, but she already knew that her mother did not scold her when the red-headed man was visiting them.

Danny looked from one to the other. He still found it hard to think of this little bundle of pink cheeks and golden curls as his daughter. Not that he'd recognised her officially as such. It was purely her mother's name on the birth certificate and the child would be Caitlin O'Rourke as long as she was on this earth – unless a man changed it for her by marriage, of course. But Cissie had never made a thing of her lack of a wedding ring, she was the uncomplaining sort. She was never likely to cast up the hurt she felt when he took Maeve Ballantine to the altar and not her.

'Are the potatoes to your liking, Danny?'

'A drop of your Pa's best Irish would make them taste even better!'

She had smelt the whiskey on his breath when he arrived, but had, as usual, made no comment. Anyway, it was only him she kept the good stuff in the house for, and well he knew it. She went through to the kitchen and reached for the bottle of Paddy from the shelf above the sink. She was on the point of pouring a glass when she heard voices in the room beyond. Two men's voices. Danny was speaking to someone. Please God, don't let it be the Tommies! The Sherwood Foresters had been up and down the street all day and she had been on tenterhooks for hours, feeling sure they would come barging in at any minute.

The sight of the dark-haired young man in the priest's robes brought an immediate sigh of relief. 'You'll join Danny in a wee drop o' Paddy, Dermot?'

He shook his head. 'Thank you, no, Cissie. I fear I'm light-headed enough this night without making myself more so, with any more of the hard stuff.'

'Dermot's been with Pearse and Connolly and the others, Cissie,' Danny interrupted. 'For Chrissake, man, come and sit down and tell us what's been going on out there.'

His brother pulled out a chair from the table and sat down heavily on it. He looked across at Danny's expectant face and sighed deeply. 'It's not good news, boy.'

'I never expected it to be.' Danny gripped the knife and fork in his hands even tighter, his knuckles showing white through the pale, slightly freckled skin. 'It's surrender, isn't it?'

Dermot nodded. 'Unconditional. The British demanded it. Nothing less would do.'

'And Pearse, Connolly and the rest – where are they now?' His pale-lashed hazel eyes stood out in the drawn face as he waited for the inevitable.

'Taken into custody, the lot of them. I believe Pearse was taken to the British HQ at Parkgate, but word has him being transferred to the Arbour Hill Detention Barracks, then him and the rest of "the main ringleaders", as the Tommies are referring to them, are to be taken to Kilmainham Jail.'

'Je–e–e–z . . .' Danny hissed the word out through gritted teeth. 'Who's been telling you all this?' It was crazy, but there was still the faint hope it might be simply a rumour.

'I was there myself – like I said. It's the truth, boyo, believe me.' He fell silent, his mind flying back to the small back room of Hanlon's fish shop, in the final minutes before surrender.

After Elizabeth O'Farrell had come back with a thirty-minute time limit for complete surrender from Brigadier-General Lowe, the officer commanding the government forces in the city, he had got down on his knees with the rest of the remaining men to say the rosary, before they gave themselves up. The memory of that moment was etched on his heart for ever. They had knelt in a circle, each man clutching the rifle he was so soon to surrender to the waiting British. 'Hail Mary, full of grace, blessed art Thou . . .' The responses had been muffled, as tears choked the familiar words in their throats. The dream was over, for the time being at least – maybe for ever for some of them.

Led by Willie Pearse, who held the white flag of surrender aloft in his right hand, and young Sean MacLoughlin, they had filed out into Moore Street and marched in perfect time towards the Parnell Monument. There he had watched from the pavement as they were disarmed and taken to the forecourt of the Rotunda Hospital.

The night had been cold, bitterly cold for April, but they were left to spend it in the open air, until, come daybreak, they were taken to the detainment compound at Richmond Barracks. He had offered to go with them, but had been prohibited. Captured rebels in the detested green uniform were one thing, but sympathetic priests in clerical robes were quite another.

'I should be there with them.' Danny's anguished voice interrupted his thoughts. 'Wherever they are now, I should be there too.'

'Don't talk daft, Danny!' It was Cissie who cut in. Her blue eyes clouded with worry. 'Sure an' that would do a lot of good, wouldn't it?'

Danny pushed the empty plate from him and sat back in his

chair, his fists clenched on the checked tablecloth. 'But we were in it together from the beginning . . . I should be there with them at the end, no matter how it turns out.'

'Even if it means swinging on the end of a British rope?' Cissie's voice expressed her anguish, as she picked up their daughter and held Caitlin to her aproned breast.

'If it comes to that.'

'Then that's just crazy talk!' She turned to Dermot for confirmation. 'Tell him, Dermot, tell him he's being just plain stupid! Can't you see, Danny, if Pearse and Connolly and the rest of your leaders are to be executed by the British, and the others locked up for God knows how long, then that's all the more reason for the likes of yourself to remain free. There has to be someone left to keep the free flag flying, hasn't there?'

Dermot nodded. 'She's right, Danny. You'll do the cause a lot more good outside Kilmainham prison walls than inside. But that's not to say they'll not come looking for you. I have it on good authority they're already trying to round up all known insurgents. Come what may, you'll have to lie low for quite a while yet.'

'He can stay here.' Cissie cut in. 'They'll maybe knock his own door in, in McIntyre Street, but they'll not come looking for him here. As far as the English authorities are concerned there's no man on the premises here, I'm just a fallen woman with a bastard daughter. They'll have no need to come storming in here in the middle of the night.'

The two men flinched at her bluntness, then Danny nodded slowly, acknowledging the accuracy of her words. It would be no penance to lie low under Cissie's roof for the time being. It might even make Maeve appreciate him more the few times he did manage to drop by. He wouldn't tell her where he was staying, of course. That would be asking for trouble. But, yes, a few weeks of lying low here might not be that bad an idea. It would probably be some weeks before the British decided what to do with the likes of Connolly and Pearse and the others . . .

He was never to be more wrong. The following Wednesday, the third of May, Patrick Pearse was executed by firing squad, along with Tom Clarke and the university lecturer Tom Mac-Donagh, in the yard of Kilmainham Jail.

The following day, his brother Willie joined him in death, along with the poet Joseph Plunkett, Ned Daly and the writer Michael O'Hanrahan.

On Friday, Major John MacBride was executed. He had joined the Rising almost by accident. On Easter Monday afternoon, he had come across a detachment digging themselves in on St Stephen's Green and, being an old soldier, he couldn't resist the temptation to join them. He faced death with a smile, smoking a cheroot.

On Monday, the eighth of May, Michael Mallin, Con Colbert, Sean Heuston and Eamonn Ceannt were put to death. The following day, Thomas Kent.

On the twelfth, it was the turn of Sean MacDermott and James Connolly. The latter's wounds had not healed, and he was still in great pain. After kissing and embracing his family, he was carried in a chair to face the firing squad.

'The bastards, Maeve, they've actually shot and killed an already wounded man! Is nothing beyond them?' Danny's clenched fist crashed down on the kitchen table of number seven McIntyre Street as he glared his anger across at his wife. 'And Willie Pearse — what harm had that poor sod ever done anyone? He was no fighter. He was only there because he was Paddy's brother — and that's why they've killed him!'

He shook his head in incomprehension. 'And poor bloody Plunkett . . .' His voice trailed off as he remembered the bejewelled poet taking off his bracelet and one of his rings and giving them to Winnie Carney to give to his fiancée. He had married his beloved Grace in the death cell. They had executed him only four hours after putting the ring on his bride's finger.

It was sick. The whole thing was sick. He knew those men — they were no desperadoes, but idealistic dreamers who had made a valiant gesture in the face of the enemy.

'Say something, damn you! Don't you think it's beyond human belief? Or can it be that you privately think your English cronies have done the right thing?'

She looked at him — a cool, blue-eyed gaze that gave nothing away. He had been cursing and swearing like this ever since he arrived out of the blue about half an hour ago. Never a word of affection, or concern about how she or the baby were faring, with him living God knows where for the past few days. 'I don't know what you're acting so surprised about, to be sure. You were all grown men – surely you knew it wasn't a game you were taking part in? You can't expect to go around starting rebellions and just shake hands at the end of it and go on home as if nothing has taken place.'

She placed the baby back in the cradle and smoothed the stray wisps of dark hair back from her brow, as she straightened up, to turn and face him. 'And, anyway, it's not just Englishmen you were fighting. You had little or no support among the local population, you know that fine. Most of them in this town think the Shinners are a load of lunatics – and this little shenanigan has done little to disprove that!'

He glared at her. The truth always hurt. Especially when it was delivered with such a supercilious look in those ice-cold eyes. He slumped back in his chair and stared moodily into the fireplace. 'Have you seen anything of Dermot these last few days?'

'No.' She spoke the truth. 'Have you?'

He shrugged. 'Not since Sunday. And he was looking pretty done in then. He was talking about getting a transfer to Cork before he left.'

'Cork!' Maeve's mouth dropped open. 'He said nothing about that to me. What's brought this about?'

He shrugged. 'Your guess is as good as mine.'

She walked to the window and looked out along the grey length of the close beyond. Could she guess? Could it have anything to do with . . . No, surely not . . . 'Maybe the fighting's just sickened him of life in the capital, for the time being.'

'Well, if that's the case, he'll have to stay away for years to come, for this is not over, Maeve, mark my words! Not by a long chalk. They may think they've put an end to it by killing our leaders – by knocking off the head – but the heart is still intact, and beating as strongly as ever.'

He got up from the chair and walked to where she was standing by the window. 'You'll have to put up with it, you know. Life's not going to be easy for any of us from now on. But there are more important things than a quiet life.'

'Really? And what may they be?' Their eyes met and held. There was a challenge in hers that made him bridle immediately.

'You know damned well. You'll have to get used to the fact, Maeve, that Kathleen ni Houlihan's the most important woman in my life. I'd lay down my life for her, if need be. You may be my wife, but she's my mistress — and always will be.'

A red flush crept up Maeve's pale cheeks, as he spoke the old literary name for Ireland, and a bitter smile twisted her lips. 'So it's Kathleen ni Houlihan — it's old Ireland — that's your mistress, is it, Danny? Well, she makes a change from Cissie O'Rourke, I suppose.'

His breath caught in his throat, and he stepped back as if physically struck. 'What do you know of her?' The words were barked out.

'Enough.' There was a look of almost triumph on her face.

'Tell me, damn you, tell me!' His hands gripped her shoulders, shaking her like a rag doll, as his eyes blazed down into hers.

'What? What should I tell you, Danny? That I know all about her — and your little bastard daughter? Is that what you want to hear? Then I do . . . God help me, I do!' Despite her resolve to stay calm and retain the upper hand, hot tears sprang to her eyes as she gazed up into the freckled blur of his face.

He let go her, almost pushing her from him, a look of anger mingled with disgust on his face. 'Well, if it's sorry you're expecting me to say, then you'll be disappointed, that's for sure!'

'I'm not expecting that, Danny. I'm not expecting anything from you any more. I stopped having expectations about you, or our marriage, months ago.'

'And what might that mean?' His right hand shot out and grabbed her left wrist, jerking her towards him. His breath stank of whiskey and she averted her face as he spat his fury at her. 'You're still my wife, damn you, and you'll treat me with the proper respect. You've food on the table, haven't you? And clothes on your back. That's a darn sight more than many folks have in this town right now.'

'And precious little more of that I'll have with you on the run. Just how do you expect to get work around here and earn a living wage now you're a wanted man with a price on his head?'

He let go her wrist with a dismissive shrug. 'There are other ways of earning money than slaving away for a pittance. You'll not starve.'

'What do you suggest I do, then, go on the streets? Is that what you're after? You want to make a whore out of me?'

'Don't be so bloody stupid. You'll not have to lift a finger, let alone your skirts. I've got my own methods of making money in mind that need be no concern of yours.'

The contempt in her face gave way to fear. 'You're not getting into anything illegal? I'll not have my son brought up with a common criminal for a father!'

'*Your* son, is it now?' His hazel eyes blazed a flaming red that matched the thick head of curling hair as he glared at her. 'It's not Ballantine he's called, my girl, he's a Donovan! And he'll be a fighter, the same as his father, and grandfather, and great-grandfather before that. Donovans have fought for Irish freedom for generations and there's nothing you can do that will ever change that fact!'

'Don't bet on that, Danny. Just don't bet on that.' Her voice was low and expressed a positiveness that she did not feel as she backed towards the fire. But in so small a room it was impossible to put any distance between them.

The cold anger in her eyes seemed to arouse him to an even greater fury and he advanced towards her, like some predatory creature stalking its prey, causing her to move backwards, in the only direction possible, towards the bedroom door.

His eyes moved from her face, down her long slim neck, and over the white, frilled lawn blouse that tucked neatly into the handspan waist. It was months since he had seen her figure as anything but a pregnant hulk that inspired no emotion in him other than a peculiar disgust that sent him round to Cissie's almost every day. But now – now the swollen, heavy flesh had returned to the slim, tantalising shape that had aroused him almost to madness last summer ... Now that latent passion that had lain dormant for so long was rising again. He could feel it within him . . . 'Come here, girl . . .'

She continued to back away, until she could go no further, and her back came in contact with the closed door of the bedroom. There was no mistaking the look in those glittering eyes, but the thought disgusted her. There was no love there any longer, merely a blatant lust that he did not even bother to disguise as he pulled her towards him.

His mouth aimed for hers, filling her nostrils with the stench of whiskey, as she jerked her head to one side. Her resistance seemed to act as an even greater spur. His hands pinned her arms to her side as his lips found the soft white flesh of her neck. His teeth dug into the skin, bringing an immediate moan of pain to her lips. 'That's it, girl, enjoy it! Enjoy it!'

'Let – let go . . .' The words came out with difficulty as he pressed against her. 'Please, Danny . . . Please . . .'

His breath came faster as the blood pulsated within him. It was normal for her to feign resistance. It was all part of the game, wasn't it? She had been waiting for this for weeks, just as he had been. His right hand moved up, his fingers seeking the tiny pearl buttons that ran down the left shoulder of her blouse, but she squirmed even more beneath his grasp.

'Don't, please don't!' Her voice was louder now as panic overcame her. What on earth was he doing? Didn't he know she was still red raw from Kieran's birth? Didn't he care?

The delicate material ripped beneath his fingers, sending two of the pearl buttons bouncing down to the floor beneath their feet. Then the lace-trimmed strap of her chemise was pulled down over her shoulder and his hand moved roughly down over her swollen breast. The pain of the pressure of his rough palm made her wince and cry out in pain, but, instead of pulling back, his fingers dug deeper into the blue-veined, tender flesh, as his right knee forced her legs apart.

He was going to have his way. The heartless bastard didn't give a damn about her feelings! With all the strength she could muster, her own right knee came up and caught him in the groin. Then again, and again, until he staggered backwards clutching at the agony that brought tears to his eyes and made him yell out loud.

'You bitch! You little bitch! I'll kill you for this!'

Chapter 8

'What in the name's going on in here?' Dermot stood in the open doorway, his dark eyes widening in horror at the sight before him.

Maeve was lying on the floor by the kitchen table, her blouse half-ripped from her body, and her hair pulled from its carefully arranged roll, to hang in long tangled coils, totally obscuring the tear-stained face, as she fought to cover herself. Her skirt had been ripped from her with the same frenzy. It lay at the other end of the room, by the range, where it had been tossed, and the white cotton chemise that barely covered her knees was blood-stained.

'Get the hell out of it, Dermot. It's got nothing to do with you!' Danny's voice came from the back of the room, where he sat slumped in a chair, an almost empty bottle of whiskey in his hand. 'Just piss off, will ye? My wife and I have had a little difference of opinion about marriage rights, that's all.' His voice was slurred and he waved a dismissive hand at his brother, but the other was not to be moved.

'Are you all right, Maeve?' Dermot knelt beside the trembling figure of his sister-in-law and tenderly swept the hair back from her face. Her mouth was bleeding and a deep-blue swelling was rising just below her left cheekbone.

She nodded mutely as she struggled to raise herself to her knees, one arm crossed protectively across her bared breast. She winced as his fingers touched the area above her left shoulder-blade. There was a perfect set of teeth-marks in the pale skin from which blood oozed.

'You bastard! You sadistic little bastard!' Incensed, Dermot strode across the room and hauled his brother from the chair, sending the bottle of whiskey flying out of his hand, to land with a crash of broken glass beneath the washstand. A blow from his right fist sent Danny flying backwards, to sprawl in a heap on the floor.

He stared up at his brother, disbelief in his red-rimmed eyes. 'What was that for?' The voice was petulant, child-like almost.

'You know damned well what that was for! What in tarnation's got into you, man? You've no right to treat a helpless woman like that!'

'She's not a helpless woman! The bitch is a divil – a ragin' divil!' He pulled himself up, with the help of the chair, and staggered towards his brother, who knocked him away in disgust.

'You shame me, Daniel Donovan! You shame all of us – but most of all you shame yourself!'

Danny made a lurch towards him once more, his fists clenched. 'You shut your bloody gob, Dermot! You've no right to say that to me – nobody has!'

Dermot's right hand moved upwards, his own fist clenching once more, as Maeve scrambled up from the floor and ran towards him, grabbing him by the arm. 'No, Dermot, no! Leave him be! Can't you see he's drunk? He doesn't know what he's doing!'

He looked down at her, his eyes taking in the tear-swollen, bruised face. 'He knows what he's doing, all right. Have no fear about that! And so do I. And right now I'm putting him out of here.'

'You can't, for heaven's sake! He'll be picked up as sure as God. The British will have him before he gets the length of the street!'

'In that case, I'll take him as far as Mary-Agnes's. She can sober the little bastard up!' He yanked his brother by the arm and pulled him roughly towards the door. 'Come on, you're coming with me!'

Danny made a feeble attempt at a struggle, then gave up. The half bottle of Jameson's he had consumed had got the better of him, even more than Dermot's superior strength. Under any other circumstances he could make mincemeat of his Holy Willie of a brother, but not tonight . . . No, not tonight. 'I'll be back soon, don't you worry, Maeve me darlin'!'

She watched stony-faced as he disappeared out the door, stumbling behind Dermot's tall, black-robed figure. A shiver ran through her and she crossed her hands once more over her half-naked breasts. Neither the Church nor the law recognised the fact that a woman could be raped by her own husband, but she did. And so did Danny. If he got any pleasure at all from the coupling that had just taken place on the floor of this room, then, if there was an ounce of scruples in his body, he would blush into his pillow this night, once he had sobered up.

A wail from the cradle in the room next door reminded her that it was time the baby was fed. With a sigh, she walked painfully through to the bedroom and picked him up. 'Now, now, enough of that noise . . .'

His face was bright red from the exertion of crying and he squirmed in her arms, as if not willing to be pacified by soothing words. She held him at arm's length and a knife twisted in her heart. She saw only his father in the look in the eyes that blinked back into her own. They were still the dark, indeterminable colour of infancy, but one day they would be hazel, she had absolutely no doubt about that.

As she sat down in the chair by the fire, something made her look up at the window. Her heart gave a jolt as a pair of eyes stared back at hers. 'Kathleen Donovan – what are you doing out there?'

The child gave a nervous smile and disappeared from view. A couple of seconds later, the door opened. 'Can I come in, Maeve?'

'Sure an' it looks like you're already in!' She kept her voice light. There was something about the way Katie's eyes darted nervously from her own towards the door, then back again, that told her she had borne witness to the scene that had just occurred. It didn't surprise her. Any chance she got she was to be found hanging around her brother Dermot's cassock tails.

'Would you be fancying a cup of tea? The water in the kettle should be hot enough, if you care to brew us both a cup.'

The child nodded gratefully. At home at Mary-Agnes's she was not allowed to have extra cups of tea when she felt like it.

Maeve watched as she executed the task with solemn concentration etched on the freckled features of her young face. She looked so much like Danny, it was almost like watching him in miniature, for her tiny sister-in-law had not yet reached the age of puberty, and her face and figure still had the sexless contours of extreme youth. But there the resemblance seemed to end, for it was to Dermot and not Danny that the child gravitated, when given the chance.

'Thank you, Katie.' Maeve sipped the hot brown liquid and smiled at the child, as she prepared herself for the baby's feed, carefully balancing the cup and saucer within easy reach on the edge of the table. 'Is Willie-John not with you tonight?' The pair of them usually made an appearance some time in the early evening, when Liam, Mary-Agnes's stonemason husband, got back from work. He liked peace and quiet to have his wash and evening meal.

'Sure 'tis home he's gone to, Maeve. He's a real scaredy-cat an' no mistake!'

Maeve's brow furrowed. 'What's that supposed to mean?'

The child pouted, swinging her grasshopper legs backwards and forwards on the wooden chair. 'He's scared, that's what he is. He's the same at home when Liam has a go at Mary-Agnes. Runs and hides under the bed upstairs, so he does. I'm not like that.'

Maeve avoided the child's eyes and stared down at the infant at her breast. She knew there was violence in almost every home round here, but the thought of Katie and poor Willie-John having to suffer it sent a shudder through her. 'They don't touch you, do they Katie? Liam – he doesn't harm you?'

The red head shook emphatically. 'Oh no, not Liam. Mary-Agnes does though. But not often. I'm lucky, it's usually Willie-John that gets the hammering from her. He's just a gormless eejit, she says – but he's not, Maeve, he's not. He understands things. I know he does!'

Maeve looked up at the intense little face. She was his only champion. She would defend Willie-John to the death.

'But it'll not always be like this. I'm going to take him with me, Maeve. When I get married, Willie-John's going to come and live with me. He knows he is, for I've told him so and he likes the idea right well.'

'I'm sure he does, Katie.' She changed the baby to the other breast and took another sip of the tea. She had no doubt Katie would keep her word. This country was full of strong women, who had once been children exactly like her. Children for whom family violence was as commonplace as death, yet who knew instinctively that did not make it right. The child had principles, although she didn't yet even know the meaning of the word.

'I wish it was Dermot you'd married, Maeve.'

Maeve caught her breath. 'But Dermot's a priest, Katie. Priests are not allowed to marry.'

The child pouted, a deep furrow crossing the clear skin of her brow. 'Who says so?'

'Well, the Pope I expect.' She was floundering now, knowing very little about the Catholic religion.

'And does the Pope say only men can be priests, too?'

'Well, yes, I think he does.'

'And why is that?'

'Well, because Christ wasn't married, I expect.'

'But Ruth Goldberg, at school, says Jesus was a Jew, so if priests aren't allowed to get married because He wasn't married, that means only Jews should be allowed to be priests, because He was a Jew!'

'Really, Katie!' It was all getting quite beyond her. 'What things you do think about – and talk about! But I'm afraid I'm not the person to be asking when it comes to questions about the Church. Dermot's the one, not me.'

Katie nodded. 'Mary-Agnes says you're the next thing to godless, being a Pres-ba . . . whatever it is, an' all.'

'Presbyterian.' Maeve said, tight-lipped. 'And Mary-Agnes should keep her big mouth shut on matters that don't concern her.'

'Sure an' Dermot's always telling her that. But it doesn't make much difference, she says what she thinks anyway. I'm not going to be like her when I grow up, Maeve. I'm going to be like you.'

Maeve gave a hollow laugh. 'Sure there are better things to aspire to than that, Katie aroon!'

She was still smiling wistfully at the thought half an hour later when the child had disappeared into the gathering dusk of the street and she settled the baby back into the cradle for the coming night. It was funny how a particular grown-up could appear all things wise and wonderful to a child. She had felt the same about her Aunt Maud.

Maud Ballantine lived in a big house just outside the village of Ballinalea, at the foot of the Wicklow Mountains. Much too big it was for an old woman living alone, but that never troubled the old lady. She was Maeve's father's eldest sister and had always been something of a rebel.

Her niece's blue eyes turned wistful as she walked slowly back to the kitchen and sat down by the fire. She could picture her now, striding across the soft green parkland that surrounded the house, her two collies, Jet and Jade, at her heels. She had never married, which was surprising for one so full of life. But rumour had it that she had fallen in love with a Catholic boy from Wicklow and the family hadn't approved. Rumour also had it that that same boy had then taken Holy Orders and Maud, much too worldly to ever contemplate entering a convent, had remained an old maid.

A deep sigh was emitted from her lips as she leaned back in the chair and closed her eyes. The Church, and the bigoted attitudes it fostered on both sides, had a lot to answer for in this country. A wry smile flickered at the corners of her mouth. Katie's little friend Ruth was right – Christ was a Jew. And the world would be a far less complicated place if his followers had been contented to remain such themselves. But she couldn't change history any more than she could change what had happened in this very room between herself and Danny tonight. The best you could do was to try to come to terms with it.

Sleep came with difficulty that night and she was just on the point of dropping off at last when a pounding at the door brought her back to consciousness with a gasp. 'Dear God, don't let it be him back! Don't let it be Danny!'

For a few seconds she sat quite still, the bedclothes clutched to her thumping heart, but then the shouting began. It wasn't one man's voice – it sounded like there was a whole streetful of them out there. 'The Tommies!' She gasped the word aloud as she scrambled from the bed. They had come for Danny!

Grabbing her dressing-gown from the foot of the bed, she

pulled it on as she raced for the door. Delay meant it would be smashed in, she knew that much, for she had seen the results of these night-time raids with her own eyes at the homes of others further up the street.

'I'm coming! I'm coming! Hold your horses, can't you?'

Her fingers pulled frantically at the bolts and catches as the hammering continued, and shouts of, 'Open up, there!' sounded through the wooden panels.

'You're bloody lucky there, missus. A few seconds later and we'd have been through.'

She stared in a mixture of horror and apprehension at the small posse of soldiers on the step. All had guns cocked and ready and pointed directly past her into the kitchen.

'Where is he, then? Where's the bleedin' Shinner?' The accent was English – from somewhere around the Midlands, she guessed.

'There – there's nobody here, only me and the baby.' She had intended to keep her voice steady, but failed miserably.

'You're Mrs Donovan – Danny Donovan's missus?' It was put as an accusation and barked at her, as the sergeant in charge pushed past her and they entered the room.

'There's nobody here, I tell you. Nobody!' She attempted to run on ahead of them and regain the attention of the leader, as drawers and cupboards were pulled open, spilling their contents on to the floor.

'Where is he, then? You'd better tell the truth. You'll only make it worse for yourself – and him – if you don't!'

She shook her head in desperation. What could she say to convince them. 'I don't know. I swear to God I don't know. I only wish I did!'

The sergeant, a small stocky man, sporting a thick handlebar moustache, looked closely at her, his brown button eyes taking in the livid swellings on her face. 'Never seen 'im, eh? Seen neither 'ide nor 'air of 'im, you say? Well, do you mind telling us 'ow you came by those shiners? Walk into the door, did you?'

Her fingers flew to the bruising around her cheek and mouth. 'I – I fell and hit myself on the edge of the range,' she said quietly. 'I – I must have fainted. I've only just had a baby, you see.'

'She's right, sarge. There's a nipper in here all right!' A voice from the bedroom backed up her excuse, as the sound of bedding being ripped from the mattress and clothes being pulled from the wardrobe filled her ears.

The sergeant grunted. He'd had enough experience of these Shinner wives already to know that they'd lie through their teeth to save their men.

She watched, her heart in her mouth, as he strode through to join his men in the bedroom. By now the noise had awoken Kieran who was bawling his head off in the midst of it all. A shrieking infant was all the soldiers were needing. It had already been one of those nights and each and every one of them was itching to get back to barracks.

As his men congregated at the outside door once more, the sergeant turned to Maeve. 'You tell 'im, lady. Just you tell that bleedin' rebel bastard of a husband of yours that we know all about him. We know all about all the sons of bitches that took part in that little pantomime over Easter. He's a marked man, missus – a marked man. Just you make sure he knows that, for if he as much as shows his nose in this city again, we'll get 'im, I swear to God we will!'

She could only stare at him and shake her head as he shouted an order to his men, before disappearing out of the door behind them. It rattled on its hinges as he banged it shut and she stared at it for a long time, before sinking slowly to her knees and burying her face in her hands.

Going back to bed was unthinkable. Her face and body still ached from Danny's physical assault and now her nerves were shattered. Painfully she picked herself up off the floor and replaced the kettle on the dying embers of the fire. There was no whiskey left in the house, the fight between Danny and Dermot had seen to that, so a cup of tea it would have to be.

She fell asleep after it, in the chair by the fire, and was awakened by Kieran yelling for his morning feed. She took twice as long in tending to him, relieved just to be sitting at peace with her child in the quietness of the early morning.

After the events of the night, it was something to be appreciated.

When finally she had settled him back into his cot, she grimaced at the swollen mass of flesh that was her face, as she confronted herself in the glass over the mantelpiece.

'Good God, I'll never be able to go out like this!' Her fingers tenderly touched the blue-black skin of her cheek, then moved down to the side of her lip which was swollen to twice its normal size. Shame filled her. She had now joined the ranks of young women that she had looked upon with pity, and, to be honest, very often contempt, as she stood next to them in the butcher's or grocer's, when out doing her daily shopping. How could they bear to show themselves to the world like that, she used to think, as her eyes studiously avoided the brilliantly coloured bruises and missing teeth that so often bore silent testimony to the wrath of a drunken husband. And now she was one of them.

Sick at heart, she lifted her blue wool coat from the back of the door and slipped it on. She still stubbornly refused to adopt the plaid shawl of the other women of this area, no matter how conspicuously she stood out in the local shops. And this morning it was important that she looked her best. She had a mission to accomplish. This morning she would see Mary-Agnes and demand she tell her where Danny was living. It would mean swallowing her pride, but it had to be done. They had to have this thing out between them. There was no way she could carry on there alone with the baby, not knowing when, if ever, he would come home.

Her heart thudded in her breast as she stood, with the baby in her arms, outside the green-painted front door of the Kellys' house. There was no response and she knocked again, louder this time. She was on the point of turning away to retrace her steps when the door was flung open. Mary-Agnes stood there, her grey stuff dress covered in an ankle-length rough calico apron. Her sleeves were rolled up past the elbow and her muscular arms were still damp and steaming from the washtub. Her red, rough-skinned hands were clenched in a pugilistic pose on her ample hips.

'Well? What can I do for you?'

Despite her firm intention to remain cool and in command of the situation, Maeve felt her confidence ebb away by the second. 'If you've a minute to spare, Mary-Agnes, I'd be grateful.'

'Have your say, then!'

Maeve glanced around her in embarrassment. 'I — I'd rather we spoke inside, if you don't mind.'

Her sister-in-law grunted and moved slightly to the side, indicating with a brief nod of the head for her to enter. A damp steamy atmosphere from the small wash-house off the kitchen pervaded the whole house. It was only the second time she had been over Mary-Agnes's doorstep and the dark L-shaped living-room was even more cramped than she remembered it. The room had the stale, fetid smell of too many human beings living at too close quarters, and her stomach turned over as she looked around her.

The three Kelly children, all under school age, lay in the box-bed, in the deepest part of the L, and Willie-John sat in his vest and combinations by the fire. He made a welcoming grunting sound at the sight of Maeve and the baby and she went over and stroked his cheek. It was rough with stubble. He might have the mind of a child, but he must be all of twenty-three years old.

'Ye'll excuse the state of Willie-John. I trust it'll not offend your fine sensibilities. His clothes are in the wash. The poor bugger can't always control himself and by the end of the week the stink is something awful, so it is.'

Willie-John giggled nervously and received a cuff in the ear from his sister for his pains. 'You'd not find it so bloody funny if it was you that had to do the washing, you great eejit!'

Maeve stood awkwardly in the middle of the mat by the still open door wishing fervently she had stayed at home.

'Well, what's bothering you enough to bring you here this fine day?' There was no invitation to sit down, no offer of a cup of tea — nothing.

Maeve bridled. If that was the way she wanted to play it . . . 'I want you to tell me where Danny is.'

'And if I say I don't know?'

'Then I'll call you a liar.'

The two young women faced one another across the few feet of floorspace. Mary-Agnes's strong jaw was set, her fair, reddish-brown brows furrowed above the slightly protruding eyes. 'He's on the run, ye know that fine!'

'He wouldn't have run all the way to Cissie O'Rourke's, by any chance?' Maeve drew in her breath immediately she had uttered the words, as the anger rose in the face of the woman opposite, and a nervous, high-pitched laugh came from the fireside. Willie-John could sense in an inkling when his sister was getting riled and it could mean only one thing – someone was in for it, usually him. A strange, slightly hissing sound of running water broke the silence of the small room.

Both looked round to see a steaming puddle of golden liquid trickle towards them from under Willie-John's chair. Cowering, he got up and backed towards the wash-house door, fear contorting the vacant features of his face.

'Ye filthy brute! That's the third time this week!' A pewter candlestick was plucked from the table in the middle of the room and aimed at the retreating figure. 'I'll tan the gormless hide from ye when I get hold o' ye!'

Anger rose in a wave within Maeve. 'You'll do nothing of the kind! He can't help himself. You'll not touch him!'

'And just what can you do to stop me, pray?' Mary-Agnes's look was scathing. 'It's not you, my fine lady, that's got the bother of coping with the likes o' him. Or are you offering to take your share? He's Danny's brother too, after all. Are you offering to take Willie-John into your own home and dirty those lily-white hands of yours cleaning up his messes, is that it?'

Maeve stared at her, her embarrassment all too obvious in the deep pink that crept up her neck and infused her face. Her shame burned brightly in the swollen skin of her cheeks. She should say yes. She should show her mettle and offer to take Willie-John off Mary-Agnes's hands and into the sanctuary of her own home. But no matter how she tried, the words would not come.

Mary-Agnes's scathing laugh rang in her ears as she turned and fled from the steam and shame of the small room, and tears blinded her as, clutching the baby to her breast, she ran back down the cobbled street towards her own home.

Chapter 9

The air inside the confessional was stale, and even through the dividing grille it still smelt strongly of the old woman who had just left. It was a sickly, fetid smell – the stale sweaty stench of a body that had known little cleansing, combined with the pungent smell of mothballs from the black Sunday-best coat that was faithfully unearthed from the back of the wardrobe for the daily Mass and weekly confession. Poor old biddy, Dermot thought wearily, she had more than her fair share of troubles. He should be praying for her, not sitting here complaining inwardly about the stench.

His silver fob watch lay on the small shelf beneath the grille. It was five to four: with a bit of luck that should be the last of them today. He had had just about half the population of the parish in here today confessing their sins, and the weight of all that guilt was enough to sink a much better man than he was.

A frown clouded his face in the dim light of the box. Almost every other man who had the privilege to wear the robes and cross of Christ, as one of his priests, must be a better man than him. It should be his own sins he was putting his hands together for, never mind other people's. Not that he hadn't spent time in prayer for himself over the past few weeks ... few weeks, that was a joke! Over the past year would be nearer the mark. For it was just over a year since Danny had first introduced him to his young bride-to-be.

He could still remember the moment as if it were yesterday. Maeve wore a satin blouse of peacock blue, beneath a matching darker blue jacket and skirt, and a hat with a dazzlingly brilliant peacock's feather that curled right round behind her ear. He had never seen anything like it – nor anyone quite like her – before. That pale complexion, contrasting so dramatically with the shining blue-black hair, and those wide, baby-blue eyes, with lashes that seemed to curl right up to the beautifully marked eyebrows that rose delicately in interest as he took her hand.

The second their fingers touched something had happened. He knew it instantly and he was sure that she did too. What it was exactly he would probably never know; but something had ignited within his soul that day – a spark that had, despite all his prayers, continued to grow and grow, until it was now becoming a raging inferno within him that was threatening to engulf them all.

He could hear her now: 'A priest, how interesting! If I become a Catholic shall I have to come and confess all my sinful thoughts to you, Father?'

He had blushed to the roots of his hair. There was something about the way she looked at him when she said it that had brought a hot flush to his entire body. 'I – I'm sure there will be very little to confess, Miss Ballantine,' he had answered lamely, and she had laughed.

'I wouldn't be too sure of that, if I were you!'

And Danny had joined in, as they exchanged meaningful looks; looks that sent a stab of jealousy towards his younger brother into his guts; and that pain had remained to this very day.

It was not only sinful, it was downright perverse that the only woman he had ever felt this way about should belong to his own brother. He had known her for six weeks before the wedding. Six weeks that had proved the most tortuous of his life. Six weeks in which for the first and only time in his life he had actually considered renouncing the priesthood.

The week before the wedding his agony had been at its height, for Maeve had moved into his Uncle Hughie's old house and was living there alone till Danny moved across the road from Mary-Agnes's after the wedding. They had asked him to give her some extra instruction on the tenets of Catholicism and he had spent several evenings alone with her there, while Danny attended his Citizen Army parades, or other political meetings related to the cause at Tom Clarke's house or the like, which were taking up so much of his time last summer.

He had thought hard before agreeing to it, making up Bible study groups to avoid a situation that he longed for, yet dreaded. But Danny would have none of it. 'If you can't find time to do your own brother's "intended" a favour, what can you find time for?' he had said, clasping his arm around his shoulder. 'Do it for me, Dermot boy . . . Apart from anything else, I don't want Maeve to feel lonely during her week across the road there. I can't understand what's got into Mary-Agnes these days, she's acting like a real bitch. Whenever I suggest she spends some time getting to know Maeve better she always has some bloody stupid excuse at the ready.' He had paused, his eyes imploring him to help. 'Don't you let me down too.'

He had agreed of course. What option had he? But it was with a crazily beating heart that he walked the dusty pavements between the presbytery and his Uncle Hughie's old house in McIntyre Street, where Maeve now waited.

The evenings always followed the same routine: she would make him a cup of tea, he would sit down on one of the chairs by the range and she would come and sit at his feet. He could picture her now – those wide saucer-eyes looking up at him, hanging on every word he uttered. She had a disconcerting habit of chewing her bottom lip as she listened and he would find his eyes transfixed on that small but beautifully-formed mouth, and those small even teeth, as he talked. But all too often those lips, with the darting pink tongue, would win the battle for his concentration and he would lose the thread of what he was saying. Was she aware of it – of her power over him? To this day he could still not be sure. Sometimes, during those quiet hours, he thought he could sense a feeling – a bond growing between them that made it harder and harder to say good-night. But then he had always been a bit of a dreamer. And perhaps that's all it ever was . . . his dreams.

Their last meeting had been the worst. Their very last meeting together before she tied the knot with his brother that Saturday. He had to let her know – give some inkling just – of the way he felt about her, so that he could know if the feelings were reciprocated. She had looked particularly beautiful that day, dressed in a rust-coloured plaid tea-gown, with her long hair loose behind her head, caught in a matching satin ribbon.

'This will be our last meeting, Dermot. I'll no longer be yours

– be your student – I'll be Danny's wife the day after tomorrow.' Her voice was low as her hand took his and she closed the outside door against the balmy July evening, and led him into the room.

He had kept hold of her fingers, astonishing himself as he raised them to his lips. 'It's what you want, Maeve, isn't it? It's what you really want?' The urgency in his voice had embarrassed him, but seemed to come as no surprise to her.

She withdrew her hand slowly and placed her right index finger on his lips. 'Your job is to make me a fit person to marry a member of the Church of Rome – your brother – not to interrogate me on my motives in doing so.' There was a quiet smile on her lips as she spoke, but her eyes were not smiling. Was it his imagination, or were they telling him things that she could not say aloud?

The look on his face brought a pucker to the clear skin of her brow, beneath the frizzed fringe. She looked at him intently for a long time, then hugged him to her. The movement brought a sharp intake of breath to his lips as her hands clung to his shoulders, and her head rested against his chest. 'I'm sorry, Dermot. Forgive me, I didn't mean to be rude. You must ask me anything you wish – anything!'

His hands slid up her back, over the fine cashmere of her gown, and she moved slightly beneath his touch. The fire that had been smouldering within him, since that spark had been struck at their first meeting, burst into life. The ache in his loins was matched only by the white heat that engulfed him, bathing his whole body in a sea of perspiration. He could say it now – he could beg her to forget Danny and marry him. He could tell her he would renounce the Church – turn his back on Christ – for her. What more could a man do? His heart pounded against his ribcage, as her breasts pressed even closer to the wall of his chest. She must feel his heart beating there – she must feel it! He lowered his head slightly and his lips touched her hair; the scent of her filled his nostrils. Dear God . . . Dear God . . .

'After all, there must be no secrets in the same family, must there?'

Her voice was incredibly, heartbreakingly light as she disentangled herself from his arms and walked over to the kitchen table. 'And we will be part of the same family very soon, won't we, Dermot?' Her hands had reached up behind her neck to adjust the bow of the satin ribbon that imprisoned the waist-length dark hair as she threw him a dazzling smile across the few yards separating them. The gesture emphasised the tight fit of her bodice and the small firm breasts imprisoned in the smooth, plaid-patterned cashmere and made his breath catch in his throat once more.

It was as if he had never held her, as if she knew nothing of the havoc she was playing with his body – with his very soul. Either that or she was taunting him, playing with his emotions as a child would with a favourite toy, before it was cast aside in boredom. He tried to speak, but his throat had closed up. He coughed and pushed a hand through the thick fall of dark auburn hair that shadowed his brow. His palm was sweaty, as was his entire skin.

'I thought we might have a wee sip of whiskey tonight, instead of tea . . . By way of celebration . . .'

He watched as she poured two glasses of the golden liquid and handed him one. He took it, nodding his thanks.

'What shall we drink to, Dermot? To love – and marriage?' She whispered the question, her words caressing his ears as her eyes found his.

He looked down at the whiskey in the glass, then back at her. 'How about simply to love, Maeve?'

He could taste it still, that warming, pungent spirit, as it filled his mouth and throat. He got up and pushed open the door of the confessional. He needed air. He was suffocating in there. A thin film of perspiration bathed his face in a pale pink glow and a bead of sweat formed on his brow and trickled slowly down the narrow channel between his brows. The ache in his groin was almost overpowering, but nothing compared with the pain in his soul. He was contaminating this place – this House of God – with thoughts of her. He was spitting in the face of the Lord. A low groan found its way from the very depths of his being to his lips . . .

'Are ye all right, Father? I'm not too late, am I? Sure an' I missed my usual tram, but I've run all the way, so I have.'

He turned dully to look down into the face of the old woman at his elbow. 'No, Mrs Finnegan, it's not too late . . . For some of us, maybe . . . But not for you.'

The poignancy of the remark was totally lost on its recipient, as her priest took her by the elbow and made his way back into the confessional.

'May the Lord be in your heart and on your lips, to worthily confess your sins . . .'

'Forgive me, Father, for I have sinned . . .'

Father O'Reilly's faded blue eyes widened as they peered over the top of the half-moon spectacles. He recognised that face coming up the drive. It would come back to him – just wait a minute. His brow furrowed as he got up from the desk to crane his neck round the corner of the bay window as the young man in question made for the door. It was Danny Donovan. As sure as God, it was Father Dermot's young brother! What in the name of goodness was he doing here – him wanted by the Peelers and all?

''Tis a real chance you're taking and no mistake, aren't you, Danny? Coming here in broad daylight is tweaking the Tommies' tail a bit much, isn't it?' He held out his hand to be shaken by the younger man as he stepped back to allow him entrance to the oak-panelled hall. 'I take it it's your brother you're here to see?'

Danny nodded. 'If he's in, Father. I heard he wanted to see me and I was in the district, anyway.'

'He should be in all right.' The elderly priest led the way into the small library to the right of his own study. 'If you'd like to wait here, I'll take a look upstairs and see.'

Danny entered the room indicated. It smelt of old books and beeswax, but had a comfortable feel to it. Books stood in well-thumbed piles on almost every surface and in uniform rows in the glass-fronted bookcases that lined three walls. A large print of Holman Hunt's *Light of the World* hung above the carved mantelpiece and he averted his eyes. Somehow since killing his first man last Easter, during the Rising, he had been unable to look any picture of Christ straight in the eye.

His fingers caressed a coloured statue of the Virgin Mary on an Indian table by the window. There was a chip out of her nose; the white plaster of Paris gleamed through the pink blush of the painted skin. It looked incongruous – indecent somehow, and he grimaced as he replaced it on the lace tablemat.

'Mrs Shea's fault, I'm afraid. It's the rheumatics in her hands.'

Dermot's voice made him look round almost guiltily as his brother came in through the open door. The two men shook hands. It was the first time they had met since Dermot had deposited his young sibling unceremoniously at Mary-Agnes's after the fight in Danny and Maeve's kitchen.

'Cissie said you wanted to see me.'

Dermot poured two glasses of home-made cider from a flagon on a cabinet by the side of the fireplace and handed his brother one. The two men eyed each other warily over the top of the glasses as they took their first gulp, then Danny spoke. ''Tis a dressing-down I expect you've got in mind. I can tell by that look in your eyes.' Ever since childhood his elder brother had employed that same reproving dark-eyed stare whenever Danny had done something to be ashamed of – in Dermot's eyes that was. His own interpretation of the deed was usually very different.

'Far be it for me to tell anyone how to live their life, especially you.'

'But . . . ?'

'But I think it's time someone put you straight on a few things, Danny boy. I didn't feel it was my place to say anything in front of Mary-Agnes and Liam the other night.'

Danny gave an impatient grunt and walked to the window, staring out sullenly over the well-manicured lawn and flower-beds. 'If you're going to get on your high horse about the other night, then I was drunk. It's as simple as that.'

'It's not quite that simple, boyo. You're not playing fair by either of them – Maeve or Cissie.' He paused, as if choosing his words carefully. 'I don't know what your relationship is like with Cissie, not really, but I do know I can't stand idly by and watch what you're doing to Maeve.'

'It's none of your bloody business.'

'Yes, it is. I like Maeve . . .'

'Like Maeve!' Danny mimicked, turning round with real anger in his eyes. 'Love Maeve more like! That's nearer the truth, isn't it Dermot?' He hadn't grown up in his elder brother's shadow for all these years, slept in his bed until they were grown men, without sensing what went on behind those dark, inscrutable eyes. 'I'm sorry for you, man, I really am. But it was me she married and there's nothing you can do now to change that fact. What goes on between a man and his wife is nothing to do with anyone else.'

Dermot's fingers tightened round the glass as his ire rose, but he had to keep calm; losing his temper would solve nothing. 'I won't stand by and see her abused.' He did not bother to deny the accusation. He could not discuss his feelings for Maeve with anyone else, let alone her husband.

Their eyes met and it was Danny who looked away first, shrugging his shoulders helplessly as he sighed. 'She's a cold bitch, Dermot, an ice-cold bitch. Can you imagine what it's like to go to bed with the Snow-Queen herself?'

Imagine it — could he imagine what it was like to go to bed with Maeve? Suddenly his collar felt much too tight; his pulse raced, as he fought to control his voice. 'No, Danny, I can't imagine . . .'

Ignorant to the irony in the reply, Danny thought he could sense an ally to his cause of the wronged husband. 'Well, it's not easy, I'll tell you that! I've got to fight for my rights almost every bloody time . . .' But seeing the look that came into Dermot's eyes, he added hastily, 'But not always like that time! Honest, Derm, she pushed me too far that night, that's all. It won't happen again. To be honest I'm getting fed up with it — what with Cissie always so accommodating and all that . . . Why the hell should I bother with Miss High-and-Bloody-Mighty Ballantine?'

Miss High-and-Bloody-Mighty Ballantine . . . It was Dermot's turn to walk to the window and stare out into the garden beyond. What if she really was Miss Ballantine still? Would he still be cherishing this yearning for her? Or was half the attraction that of the forbidden fruit — the fact that she was now, for better or worse, his brother's wife? So many questions, so few answers . . .

Chapter 10

Maeve breathed deeply, gazing up at the cloudless blue of the heavens. For the first time in months she actually felt happy, although her mission today was a far from happy one. No, it was simply being in the fresh verdant sanctuary of St Stephen's Green again that had this effect on her. The park, with its cool blue lake and sparkling waterfalls and fountains, was part of the Dublin she knew and loved, the Dublin she felt she had lost since her marriage to Danny. Her Dublin was not the slum heart of the city to the north of here, where she was now destined to spend her days, but down here where the air was fresh, the scenery was green, and the houses were elegant examples of the very best in Georgian architecture. This was her home.

But even as she reminded herself of that fact, she felt guilty. She was no longer the carefree young woman, with no responsibilities, who had lived only yards from where she now walked with so light a step. She was a wife and mother, even if her son had been left for the afternoon with Mrs Maloney, the old lady two houses but one down the street, and her husband was someone who came and went at will.

A frown creased her brow. It was almost three months now since that fateful Easter week, but she had seen very little of Danny in the intervening period. Even the British seemed to have given up on him, for she had had to suffer the indignity of two more raids in rapid succession after the first one, but since then she had been left in peace. Perhaps they believed her that he had left the country. At any rate they seemed to be making no more attempts at finding him, and many's the time she wished her lies on his behalf were the truth. Over the past few months he had called perhaps half a dozen times in all, usually the worse for drink and almost invariably to claim his marital rights after a laughable attempt at showing concern for her welfare.

The last time he had appeared, almost a week ago now, he had left twenty pounds in five-pound notes in an envelope on the table. She hadn't opened it until he had gone. To do otherwise always made her feel like a whore, somehow. In he would come, his breath smelling of old man O'Rourke's poteen, to make polite noises about how Kieran was growing, then take her straight into the bedroom. A shudder ran through her. It was a wonder he hadn't taken to leaving the money under the pillow, for that was what they did with that type of woman, wasn't it? And it was exactly what it made her feel like.

But what on earth was she doing, spoiling her first chance of a breath of freedom with such depressing thoughts, especially on a lovely day like this? She had never dreamt when she got up this morning she would be heading for Harcourt Street and a meeting with her old schoolfriend Amy Grafton this afternoon. It had come as quite a shock when she had opened the newspaper this morning to read of her fiancé Will Lovett's death in France. Knowing her brother Charlie was somewhere in the trenches over there, she never failed to scan the newsprint, first thing in the morning, her heart in her mouth, as the columns of the killed, wounded and missing grew longer with each passing day. But it had still been a shock this morning to see Willie Lovett's face staring back at her from out of the assembled ranks of those who had given their all for king and country, and could give no more. He had joined up the same time as Charlie, in the same regiment, the 36th Irish Division, and that made it all the worse. There was just no way she could let today pass without coming round to the Graftons to offer her condolences.

Her feet slowed as they left the freshness of the Green to traverse the sweeping majestic curve of Harcourt Street. She had not seen Amy for over a year – not since she left her family home to marry Danny, and the prospect of re-entering the world she had given up so dramatically last summer made the nerves churn sickeningly in her stomach.

She ignored the brass lion's head in the middle of the Graftons' front door for the small bell-pull at the side. It clanged somewhere in the depths of the house and within a minute the door was opened by a young housemaid in a frilled white apron and cap. Miss Amy, she was informed, was not really intending to receive visitors today, due to her recent sad bereavement, but since it was a personal friend calling, she would see what she could do, if Maeve would care to step this way and wait in the library.

Maeve followed the tiny, bird-like figure into the main hall and through a panelled door on the right. The sun streamed through the tall sash windows in golden shafts that caught the gilt bindings of the leather-bound books that lined the walls in just as much profusion as in her father's library in Jubilee Avenue. In a cut-glass bowl in the middle of the table was an enormous arrangement of purest white and blood-red roses, the latter matching the heavy velvet curtains that skirted the Indian carpet on either side of the window. Everything in the room seemed golden, and was made even more so by the entrance, a few minutes later, of Amy herself.

Her long corn-gold hair was done up on top of her head in a very full top-knot, and the frizzed fringe that covered her brow did little to disguise the red, bloodshot condition of the eyes beneath. She was dressed totally in black, in a gown of heavy antique moiré silk that emphasised the paleness of her complexion. The two young women looked at each other from across the room, then Maeve rushed up and hugged her friend to her.

'Amy – I'm sorry, so very sorry about Will!'

They sat on the button-backed sofa by the window, lapsing into silence as they waited for the parlour-maid to finish serving the tea and petit-fours that Amy had ordered. Then, once they were alone again, it all came spilling out.

'Oh, Maeve, I still can't believe it. Will was too young – far too young to die! And the worst part is, I encouraged him to go!' The blue eyes widened at the horror of the revelation. 'We were to be married as soon as it was all over. Nobody thought it would last this long, did they? You know that, too! We never imagined it would come to this.'

It was true. 'Over by Christmas' was the cry throughout that fateful August, two summers ago, but the carnage was never-ending.

'I trust your brother Charlie's all right? There seems to be this big offensive going on at the moment . . .'

'Somewhere called the Somme, I think they call it.' Maeve's voice was little above a whisper. 'I don't know, Amy. I don't know if he's there or not. I don't know anything about Charlie. I heard the 36th arrived in France in October of last year, but I don't know if he's on the Somme or not. I was hoping you might have heard something yourself.'

Her friend shook her head. 'Will was never one for writing very long letters and it's almost a month since I heard anything until . . . until this awful news. They usually score out place names and things, you know, for security and all that. He must have been wounded somewhere – lying in some God-forsaken French field – and I never knew.'

She got up and walked to the window, gazing out into the cloudless blue of the sky. 'A beautiful summer's day like this makes a mockery of their suffering, doesn't it? People shouldn't be dying out there, not on a day like this . . .' Her voice tailed off and she turned to Maeve, anger suddenly flaring in the bright blue of her eyes. 'It makes me so mad, Maeve, it really does, when I see all those cowards walking about out there, as if there's no war going on. If I had a basket of white feathers, I swear I'd go out this very minute and pin one on every last one of them! It's mainly Shinners, you know. You'd never get decent Unionists turning their backs on their king and country in time of trouble. And what did you make of that tomfoolery last Easter? A bunch of hooligans playing soldiers, if you ask me – doing their best to divert attention from the fact so many of our boys were over there in France doing the real fighting for them!'

Maeve avoided her eyes, looking down at the clasped hands in her lap. A year ago those words could have come out of her own mouth. She took a sip of the tea, to cover the embarrassment of her silence.

Amy was looking at her, with delicately-winged brows furrowed above the bright blue eyes. 'I'm sorry – you married a Catholic. I forgot. That was tactless of me. Is he a Shinner too?'

'He took part in the Rising, if that's what you mean.'

A flush rose to Amy's cheeks. 'Is he in prison?'

Maeve shook her head. 'He's on the run. I'm a fugitive's wife, Amy. Whatever would Miss Devine say?'

The faintest hint of a smile crossed Amy's rosebud lips. Miss Devine was their headmistress at Baldwin's Ladies College, and the old lady was anything but typical of her name. 'I really can't imagine. I don't believe she's ever met a criminal in her entire life. Come to think of it, neither have I – but there you are married to one!'

This time it was Maeve's turn to flush. However she now regarded Danny, it was not as a common criminal. A man of principle who had taken the wrong path, perhaps, but a criminal – never.

'I heard you had a son a few months back. These things get around, you know, even if you don't announce them in the *Irish Times*. Will you be bringing him up as a Catholic?'

She did not wait for the answer, as she rushed over and sat down beside her friend on the sofa. 'Oh, Maeve, you can't, you just can't. The Shinners are out to ruin this country – to take all power and influence away from London and give it to Rome. Is that what you want? Do you really want an old bachelor thousands of miles away in Italy telling us all how to run our lives?' She shuddered visibly as she leaned over and took a sip of the tea.

Maeve replaced her own cup in the gilt-bordered saucer on the small table in front of them. No, it was not what she wanted, but to her own amazement she found herself bound by a peculiar loyalty to her absent husband. 'I'm sure the Pope has the interests of Ireland at heart, Amy, just as the King does. To be honest, I've begun to feel of late it doesn't really matter who's in power, the lot of the poor never really changes. And I should know, for I'm one of them now!'

Amy regarded her sceptically, her blue eyes fixed firmly on Maeve's face, as if searching for the tongue she was sure was wedged firmly in the other's cheek. 'Well, be that as it may, no one can deny these are awful times we live in, when brave young men like Will are being mown down in their thousands.' Her eyes took on a faraway look as she thought of her fiancé and the future they had planned together.

'If you do hear anything of Charlie, you will let me know, won't you, Amy? I'd never get over it if anything happened to him and I didn't know about it.'

'You don't trust your parents to inform you?'

Maeve shook her head, as she felt in the pocket of her coat for a piece of paper to write on. A few screwed-up tram tickets were all she could come up with, so she was forced to ask Amy to search the writing-desk against the opposite wall for a pen and paper.

The back of an old envelope was produced and a half-chewed indelible pencil. 'Here we are. Will these do?'

Maeve smiled her thanks as Amy sat down beside her once again, then, wetting the lead of the pencil with the tip of her tongue, she balanced the sheet on her knee and wrote: Maeve Donovan, 7 McIntyre Street, Dublin, in her attractive flowing hand, then handed it back to Amy. 'There, that's my address now. You will inform me, if there's any news? Please.'

A glance at the ormolu clock in the glass dome on the mantelpiece told her it was after four o'clock. Kieran would be about due for another feed. She got up from the sofa and looked down at her friend. In a funny way Amy seemed suddenly older. It was as if coming into contact with the hand of death had somehow left its mark. She searched her mind for the right thing to say. Somehow, it seemed quite improper to say she would get over it, or babble some inanity about time being a great healer, as people felt compelled to do at a time like this. People didn't want to get over it — not yet, anyway. 'If you need me, you know where to find me.'

This time they shook hands. It was as if two young school-friends had entered the room ten minutes ago, but two grown women were about to leave it.

'Come back soon, Maeve. Don't let us turn into strangers.'

Maeve shook her head and gave a small smile. 'Of course not. I'll be back soon, don't you worry.'

But, as she walked slowly down the front steps a few minutes later, she already knew that was not true. To try to re-enter the world she had left behind would be as impossible as attempting to live her previous Jubilee Avenue life-style as Danny's wife in McIntyre Street. You couldn't do it. You just couldn't do it. The two worlds could never meet; they could only collide, and she knew that better than anyone. She belonged nowhere in this city any more. And the knowledge brought a cold, sick feeling to her heart.

The baby was glad to see her. At almost three months, Kieran was recognising people by now and a smile creased the chubby pink skin of his face as she collected him from Mrs Maloney's arms.

'Been good as gold, so he has,' the old woman informed her, taking care not to notice the two-shilling piece that Maeve slipped on to the brown oilcloth of the table. 'You've got roses in your cheeks, Mrs Donovan. Sure and it'll do you good to do this more often!'

'I just might, Mrs Maloney.'

As they walked to the door, an arthritic hand was rested on Maeve's arm. 'I'd never bother wi' that divil, Mary-Agnes, if I were you. He's far better off here. The shoutin' and carryin' on that goes on in that house is nobody's business – how Liam Kelly puts up with it I'll never know. I 'clare t'God the poor man hasn't the life o' a dog with that one!'

Maeve nodded. 'You've been a great help, Mrs Maloney. I appreciate it.' She had lived in this area long enough to know to keep her counsel when other people were being torn to pieces, especially relatives. But even the depressing thought of Mary-Agnes was unable to dominate her thoughts for long as she walked briskly along the cobbled street back to her own home.

This afternoon had unsettled her. Just being back in the area around St Stephen's Green had affected her more that she had ever dreamed it could. It was astonishing how her whole world seemed to have shrunk to these few streets over the past few months, and to travel out of them was almost like entering a foreign country. She had taken so much for granted before; the clean streets; the elegant houses and well-kept gardens; the glittering balls in the winter; the picnics in the summer; and rides to the hounds in the autumn and spring at their second home of Mountclare, just outside the little village of Tullyallen, near Drogheda . . . But all that was in the past now and it was stupid to dwell on what couldn't be changed.

As she closed her own front door behind her, she held Kieran aloft in her arms. 'This is our home now, isn't it, son? And all the wishing in the world can't change that fact.'

He kicked his chubby legs in the air and, opening his mouth to laugh, sent a long dribble of saliva down her chin. She wiped it away with the back of her hand and he laughed again, an infectious giggle that made her own mouth curl at the edges. He was a good-natured little devil and no mistake, even if he did have Daniel Donovan for a father.

After feeding and changing the child and settling him back down in his cradle, she cut herself a wedge of cheese and buttered a piece of bread. This was almost her staple diet these days, but there was a certain comfort to be drawn from the pungent taste of the cheese and the cup of strong, hot tea that she sipped standing in front of the window. It was almost nine o'clock, but it was still broad daylight and the sky had taken on that translucent look that preceded the coming dusk.

The tinny sound of distant laughter rang from one of the neighbouring houses, followed by the barking of a dog. Across the street, old Seamus Healey wove his way along the pavement towards Mullen's shebeen on the corner. He spent his life staggering those fifty yards, but seemed happy enough with his lot, so who was she to cast judgement?

She was on the point of turning away when a tall, dark shape in the distance caught her eye. A priest had rounded the corner, lifting his biretta to the old man. Her heart skipped a beat.

'Dermot!' The name escaped her lips in a gasp. It was almost two weeks since she had last seen him. Was he headed here, or to see Mary-Agnes?

She rushed to the glass above the mantelpiece. Her face was not as pale as it had been of late. Maybe that walk over to Harcourt Street had done her good this afternoon. Nervously she smoothed the stray tendrils of dark hair into the roll that framed her face. She was glad she still had on the deeply ruffled pale blue taffeta blouse and darker blue skirt that she had worn to Amy's this afternoon. He didn't often see her in such attractive attire.

Too nervous to go back to the window, she stood by the range and listened for the sound of footsteps crossing the road towards the front door. It was ridiculous – sinful even – but she had not felt this excited at the prospect of seeing anyone since the first heady days of her romance with Danny.

The thought of her husband brought a fleeting frown to her brow. For heaven's sake, what had got into her? It wasn't Danny out there, it was Dermot. And Dermot was not only her brother-in-law, he was a Roman Catholic priest! She must be calm, collected and, most of all, act her age. She was not a silly impressionable young girl any more. She was a responsible wife and mother.

A sound at the door made her look round as two light taps were followed by a turning of the handle.

'Hello, Maeve.'

He stood in the doorway, his tall dark figure filling the narrow entrance. His face looked thinner and there was a strange intensity in his eyes as they smiled across the room at her.

'Dermot!' In five short steps she flew across the room and into his arms.

Chapter 11

Dermot's heart thudded against his ribs as Maeve clung even closer, her full breasts pressing against the black, fine wool of his cassock. Her hair tickled his mouth and the sweet scent of lavender filled his nostrils – the same perfume that had filled his dreams so often recently; dreams that still made him blush to the roots of his dark auburn hair in the confessional every day.

He had seen very little of her lately – a deliberate decision, more than justified by what was now taking place. His hands hovered above her back, unable to move that last vital inch that might seem to encourage and condone their embrace.

'I'm sorry, forgive me – I'm just so glad to see you, that's all!' As if reading his thoughts, of her own accord she pulled herself away and led him over to a chair by the fireplace.

Her face was flushed, with two bright pink spots above her cheekbones, and there was a sparkle in her blue eyes that he had not seen for months. She had never looked more beautiful as she flung a delighted smile in his direction.

He was being stupid – there was no shameful motive behind her embrace – it was only youthful impulsiveness. He was reading too much into perfectly innocent behaviour. He must not burden her with his own guilty thoughts. She was not to know what went on in a man's mind in the wee small hours of the night, for no matter what his dog collar and cassock might indicate, he was still a man – and a very normal man in every sense of the word. And he trusted his own body even less than hers.

'It's good to see you too, Maeve.' His voice was huskier than normal and his attempt at a casual smile did not quite come off.

She sat down on the chair opposite, her eyes shining as she looked at him. 'I thought you'd deserted me.'

'I wouldn't do that. You know that.'

117

She gave a light laugh. 'I should hope not! But I expect you've been busy, working all hours for your flock and all that.'

'I do get some time to myself.'

The smile faded from her lips and she looked at him with an intensity that made him look away. 'What do you do in your spare time, Dermot Donovan?'

He sat back in the chair, stretching out his long legs in front of him, as he raked the fingers of his right hand through the shock of reddish-brown hair. 'It's confession time, is it? Well now, my dear young lady, what do I do? Let me think . . . I sleep a lot . . .'

'No – honestly – tell me honestly. I want to know.' It was true, suddenly she wanted to know everything there was to know about this dark, intense young man who was Danny's brother . . . He had listened to her often enough in the past.

The black-clothed shoulders shrugged. 'The truth is quite boring, really . . . I write.'

'Write!' she exclaimed. 'But that's wonderful! What do you write? Not just sermons, surely!'

He grinned and shook his head. 'No, Maeve, not just sermons.'

'What then, poems? Stories?' She leaned forwards, her slim white hands clasped round her knees; her eyes gleaming.

'Uh-huh.' He nodded again, the same quiet smile on his face. 'Both.'

'Then I want to read them . . . Or, better still, I want you to read them to me! Say you will, Dermot! Say you will!'

Her genuine enthusiasm surprised him. No one, absolutely no one, had taken the slightest interest in his scribblings, ever. He scratched the faintly blue stubble of his cheek and gave a sheepish grin. 'Well now, I don't carry them around in my head, you know.'

'Then get them. Please, Dermot, it's not that far to go – go and get them for me, please! It'll not take you an hour to get there and back. I'll put on a bite of supper. You'll not say no to that, surely?' She got up from the chair and looked down at him, then grabbed his right hand. Her mind was made up and there was no way she was going to take no for an answer. 'Come on – or I'll give you no peace!'

'Woman, you're a hard taskmaster!' Still looking slightly bemused, he allowed himself to be hauled to his feet and bundled out of the front door.

'Not more than an hour, mind! The toast will be burned to a cinder, otherwise!'

When he had gone, she leaned back against the pile of coats on the back of the door and hugged herself in delight. What a perfect end to the day! Although she could have wished her visit to Amy to have been under happier circumstances, it had whetted her appetite for further conversation. And, if the truth be known, there was no one she would rather talk to than Dermot. She would cut the bread right now and have everything ready for him when he got back.

A new loaf was unwrapped from the white enamel bread bin by the sink and placed on a wooden board in the middle of the table. Although cold, it still smelt delicious and she broke off a piece of the golden crust and popped it into her mouth, before attacking the whole with the knife.

She had just finished cutting the fourth slice, and was putting two cups on a tray by the plate of bread when a noise from the street outside made her look up. It surely wasn't him come back to say he'd changed his mind?

She opened her mouth to call his name when the front door burst open and, to her astonishment, Danny staggered in. She stared at him in horror. His hair and clothes were dishevelled, his face dirt-streaked and the sleeve of his jacket was holed and blood-streaked.

'What in God's name . . . ?'

There was a wild, hunted look in his eyes as he pushed the door shut behind him. 'Don't ask questions. Just get me something to eat and then tend to this!' He gave a cursory nod towards the bloodied arm, before staring down at the two cups and pile of freshly-cut bread on the table. 'Expecting company?'

Her eyes moved uncomfortably towards the half-prepared supper. If she admitted Dermot was due back, she'd never get rid of him, for he would insist on waiting to see his brother.

Resentment welled within her at this unexpected intrusion into her life on tonight of all nights. 'No, no – of course not.'

'Don't lie to me, woman! The baby's hardly at the cup of tea stage yet – so don't give me that!' He grabbed her right arm, his fingers digging into the soft flesh, as the hazel of his eyes glittered gold at the centre. 'Who is he? Who is the bastard? Tell me who your fancy man is an' I'll murder him! As sure as God I will!'

The fingers dug even deeper into her upper arm until she cried out in pain and attempted to jerk herself free. But a sharp slap across the face put a stop to that.

'There's no one, Danny, no one!' She almost screamed the words, for she knew that look in his eyes so well. Fear clasped its clammy hand around her heart. Please God, don't let him hit me again, please God . . .

It wasn't pity, but the pain inflicted on his injured arm by the violent movement of the slap that made him release his grip on her. She staggered backwards, rubbing the painful flesh with her fingers, as he tore off his jacket and threw it on the table.

'Good God, it's a bullet wound!' She felt sick to the stomach as she stared down at it. There could be no mistaking it. 'Wh – what's happened? Tell me, for God's sake!'

He grimaced as she rolled the sleeve of his blood-stained shirt as far up as it would go over his bicep, then tenderly touched the open wound with her fingertips. 'Don't ask questions and the answers won't upset you. Just get some hot water and disinfectant, will you? And be quick about it.'

She obeyed immediately, a thousand conflicting thoughts whirling round her head. He whistled softly through gritted teeth as she set to, to bathe the wound with a pad of cotton wool dipped in hot water and carbolic soap. Once the area had been wiped clean, it was not as deep as she first imagined and there was no sign of the bullet. But it had been a close thing. Whoever had fired that gun had not meant to miss. But who on earth was it? The question burned on her tongue, but she dared not voice it. The look in his eyes brooked no interrogation.

She bound the wounded arm with a length of linen that she

cut from the end of a sheet and fetched a clean shirt from the dresser drawer in the bedroom. He put it on, carefully easing the painful arm into the sleeve. 'If there's enough hot water left in that kettle, I'll have a cup of tea before I go.'

She nodded and poured what was left of the boiling water over two spoonfuls of tea leaves in the brown eathenware pot. It barely half-filled it. 'Can you manage a bite to eat?'

He shook his head, as he waited impatiently for the mixture to brew. Maeve watched in silence as he drank a full cup, then another, until only the dregs were left, and she carried the teapot to the sink to rinse it out. As the dark brown blob of coagulated leaves plopped into the sink, she glanced casually out of the window. Her mouth fell open and her heart missed a beat.

Dermot was rounding the corner into McIntyre Street. What was he doing back so soon? He must have run there and back. Panic welled within her. They must not meet. Wounded though he was, Danny wasn't going to do her out of the evening she had expected. Her heart thudding erratically, she turned to face him. 'Quick, Danny, it's the Peelers! They're heading this way. Get into the bedroom and out the window, quick!'

She dashed across the room and grabbed him by the uninjured arm, pulling him towards the bedroom door. 'I'll keep them out as long as I can and swear I've never seen you!'

He didn't need a second telling, but how on earth did they recognise it was him? Surely the balaclava he had been wearing made recognition impossible . . . ? But now was no time to puzzle on that!

She grabbed his jacket off the kitchen table and threw it after him as he vaulted the bed to get to the window. It was pushed up in a flash and he jumped down into the back alley below.

'Watch how you go!' She leaned out the sill and called after him in a loud whisper.

He half-turned as he clambered up the adjoining wall on to the roof of the wash-house opposite. 'No fancy man bastard tonight, mind! Or it'll not only be a bloody Peeler that has copped it from me tonight!'

She stared after him. What in God's name did he mean by

that? Surely he hadn't killed a man tonight? He'd been in some kind of shoot-out, that much was clear ... But to actually kill a man, a policeman only doing his job. A man with probably a wife and family at home like he had. A bitter bile rose in her throat as a voice from the bedroom door made her whirl round.

"Tis not even the full hour I've been. I took a jarvey cab to make sure of getting back in record time. Does that warrant an extra slice of that toast you promised me?'

'Dermot ...' She hardly had the strength to speak his name, and her legs seemed to turn to jelly as she looked at him.

The smile on his face faded as he rushed towards her. She had turned pure white. He helped her through to the kitchen. 'What is it, Maeve? Has something happened? It's not the baby, is it?'

She shook her head. 'No, it's not the baby. It's Danny, Dermot, he's just left. He was wounded. He came here to have the wound dressed ... He's killed a man tonight. I'm certain he's killed a man!' The words came flooding out as she sank down to her knees on the rug by the fire.

He knelt down beside her and put an arm round her trembling shoulders. 'Whisht now, don't excite yourself ... Just take it easy and tell me what's happened.'

The words came spilling from her lips as she sat with her head resting on his shoulder in the warm glow of the fire. What had just occurred seemed like a bad dream – a nightmarish interlude in an otherwise normal day. But then all Danny's visits had been much like that recently. Dermot listened in silence until she had finished, his hand resting protectively round her shoulders, then a long sigh broke from deep inside him.

'What am I to do, Dermot? How can I go on like this? Every time he comes home it seems to be worse than the last time. I keep waiting for it. First the drink, then the row, then the fight.'

She closed her eyes as the memories came flooding back, causing her to tremble involuntarily. She shook her head as if to dispel the pictures by doing so. 'It's as if he actually loves the fight because after it ...' Her voice broke, it was impossible to admit what happened next. But then he had seen it for himself once.

'I know, Maeve, I know. Don't distress yourself by talking about it. He's gone now. There's just the two of us. He'll not be back – not tonight . . . Make that supper you promised me and we'll just enjoy what's left of the evening together.' His voice was gentle, coaxing, caressing her tattered nerves, until she blinked back the tears that hovered behind the blue of her eyes, and got up and went to the table.

He watched, toasting the slices of bread in front of the fire on a long brass fork, as she brewed the tea. She spread them with butter and handed two across on a plate to him. He ate them slowly, the butter dripping in golden rivulets through his fingers as his eyes remained fixed on her face. His gaze disconcerted her. It was not usually so overt.

When he had finished, she gathered the dirty plates together and placed them back on the table, before settling down at his feet once more.

'Speak to me, Dermot, just speak to me.' She whispered the words, as if to speak out loud would be to break the magical spell that was being woven around them. Danny had receded into the background like the bad dream that he deserved to be, and there was just the two of them. Just them and the night.

'What would you have me speak about? What Father O'Reilly said at breakfast this morning? Or Mrs Burke's lumbago? I got a vivid account of that on the way back here tonight!' The feelings that were stirring deep within him made him attempt to make light of the situation – a situation that was fraying his resolve of self-control by the minute.

She playfully punched his knee, then rested her head against it. 'Read me some of your writing. I know you've got it there – I can see it beneath your cassock.'

She remained with her head resting against his knees, as he extracted the pages from an inside pocket, then sat quietly for a moment. He had never showed his writing to a living soul, let alone read any of it. What he had brought with him was a piece of whimsical nonsense, really. Something he had written on a day's outing to the Velvet Strand at Portmarnock last year. But, perhaps, if anyone was to understand – to appreciate it, then she might. And surely reading aloud was an innocent enough occupation for anyone — even a Catholic priest?

At last, he began to speak, in a low hushed voice, so that at first she had to strain to hear:

'It is the story of a dream I tell. But there are dreams and dreams: dreams of what has been and dreams of what is yet to be, as well as the idle fantasies of sleep. And this, perhaps, is one of those dreams whose gossamer is spun out of the invisible threads of sorrow; or may be, it is woven out of the tragic shadows of unfulfilled dreams . . . It is of little moment.

'I write in a quiet sea haven. Tall cliffs half enclose it in two white curves, like the wings of the solander when she hollows them as she breasts the wild north wind.

'These sun-bathed cliffs, with their soft hair of green grass, against whose white walls last year the swallows swooped and soared, and where tufts of sea-lavender hung like breaths of stilled smoke, now seem to be merely tall cliffs. Then — when we were together — they were precipices which fell into seas of dream and in the wind was born a most ancient, strange and haunting music.

'I do not sleep — but listen to the wind and sea. My dreams and thoughts are children of the wind . . .'

His voice seemed to fill her whole world. It had shrunk to this one small room and the two of them seated here by the smouldering embers of the fire. As he spoke, his right hand slowly stroked her hair, and her whole being was filled with the sense of him — his voice, his touch, his smell . . .

The rapture was broken by the sound of crying from the next room. It intruded on her world like a cruel douse of cold water, extinguishing the warmth that enveloped her. 'It's the wee one. It's Kieran. I'd better go.'

He did not speak, but watched her intently as she left the room. She moved with a lithe, almost animal grace that he had seen in no other woman. He could watch her all day and the knowledge of it shamed him.

Why had he come back here tonight? Why had he agreed to it? Was it mere vanity, to have an audience for his writing? He shook his head. No, there was more to it than that. But just how much more he still could not admit, even to himself, although the fire continued to burn deep in his loins, making him shift uncomfortably on the wooden chair as he waited for her return.

She was gone only a few minutes. Her face still flushed from the heat of the fire, her eyes gleaming a dark navy-blue against the blush of her skin. Her voice was breathless, whether with excitement or relief at settling the infant he could not tell. 'He'll be all right now. It was a touch of wind, that's all.'

He held out his hand. 'Come back to the fire.'

She did not take it – she could not take it – but came and sat beside him, clasping her arms around her knees as she looked up at him. Her eyes were troubled, mirroring the confusion within. 'Why does it have to be like this, Dermot? Why? Is this it? Is this life?'

He looked at her for a moment, without speaking. He knew exactly what she meant, but had no easy answers to offer. When at last he did speak, his voice was resigned. 'Yes, this is it, Maeve. We have to make the best of it.'

She continued to look at him intently. 'What about you, Dermot? What do you want from life?'

'Many things, I'm ashamed to say. But not material wealth, I can live without that.'

'But what most of all? Tell me. There must be something you want more than anything else out of life.'

He nodded thoughtfully. 'There is perhaps one thing above all others.'

'And that is?'

'Love.'

Her heart missed a beat. 'Is that all?'

'Is that not everything?'

They looked at one another for a long time. His gaze disconcerted her, sending icy fingers down her spine, as did the ambiguity of his answer. Did he mean the love of God . . . of humanity . . . Or . . . ? It was foolish, immoral even, to speculate. 'Recite me a poem, Dermot! A beautiful poem!'

He sat quite still in the chair, looking at her with a troubled expression in his dark eyes. Then, just when she thought he had not understood, he said softly, 'I know very few by heart, but there is one . . . You don't have the Gaelic, do you?'

She shook her head, for once almost ashamed of her Anglo-Irishness. 'No, I don't, I'm sorry . . . Maybe you can translate it into English for me?'

He stared into the fire for a moment, a frown creasing the skin between the dark brows. Then he nodded slowly. 'It's a theme as old as the hills, but as new as tomorrow.' Then he turned to face her, and, with his eyes holding hers, he began to recite:

> 'Girl, do not toy with my heart,
> Let our spirits become as one,
> Be thou my love and love me,
> Until forever is done.
>
> Place your lips on mine,
> You with skin as soft as foam,
> And as white, embrace me now,
> Forbid the morrow to come.
>
> My gentle, graceful love, come
> Lie with me this night,
> The pain of life will fade from view
> As we soar from height to height.
>
> I offer you freely from my heart
> All the love I have to give,
> Return to me, with body and soul,
> That love without which I cannot live.'

'It – it's very beautiful.' The colour blazed in her cheeks and the words choked in her throat as she got up from the rug and stood with her back to him, her fingers clutching the edge of the table. Why was he doing this to her? Why?

Then, suddenly, he was behind her, his hands on her shoulders. The ormolu clock on the mantelpiece behind them struck ten. Its tiny, brittle chimes rang in her head.

'Is it time I was going, Maeve?'

She nodded, too confused to think properly, her heart too full to speak.

Chapter 12

'This morning a police officer was shot and killed during a raid on a sub-post office in the Sandymount area of Dublin, by two or more armed men. The officer, Constable Kevin O'Dade, had seven years' service in the force and was a married man with three children. Police are pursuing their enquiries into the killing, which, it is believed was carried out by Republican sympathisers . . .'

Cissie O'Rourke's pink face drained of all colour as she closed the evening paper and turned to stare at the young man slumped at the table.

Danny took another swig from the whiskey bottle in front of him and waited for her reaction. It was not long in coming.

'It was you, wasn't it? It was you who killed that Peeler.' Her pale, fair-lashed eyes stood out of her head like a startled rabbit. She had guessed something like this had happened, of course, but actually seeing it in black and white was quite another thing. 'Could ye not have got the money without gunning down the poor man?'

'He bloody asked for it – coming at me like that! What was I supposed to do – let him arrest me? How were we to know he'd be in the back shop drinking tea? If he'd been out on his beat doing what he was paid to do it would never have happened.'

Her heart sank. 'It *was* you that killed him, then, and not one of the other two?'

'They've no evidence. They'll never prove it.'

The certainty in his voice was so typical. Other people got arrested and killed – not Danny. He seemed blessed with the luck of the devil, and the worst part of it was, he knew it. She sighed deeply and lifted up their daughter who was tugging at her skirts. The child's chubby fingers poked playfully in her mother's eyes and Cissie pushed them away impatiently, before smoothing the long strands of curly golden hair that had escaped the pink bow on top of her head. 'Who was it fired at you?'

Another mouthful of whiskey was gulped down. 'Some bastard in the constabulary. They were passing in an armoured car just as we were making our escape and one of them fired at us. We'll get even, though, don't you worry. We'll get our own back on the sods. John-Joe O'Malley has a good idea where they're billeted.'

'Why, Danny? In heaven's name, why? Is that type of thing really necessary? Why do you do it?'

'You know why. The cause needs the money.'

'But you can get the money without killing for it, surely?' There was real despair in her voice, and it wasn't just sympathy for the man who had died. She feared for him. What if it was his turn next? How would she survive without him? Even imagining the unimaginable for a fleeting second brought the hot sting of tears to her eyes.

'Don't talk to me about killing! Those bastards had no scruples about murdering our leaders a couple of months back! Legalised murder it was – nobody can deny that!' He spat the words out. The injustice of the deaths had eaten away at him the whole summer.

She nodded miserably. She had been as shocked as he was at the execution of Pearse and Connolly and the rest. 'You're sure they don't know it was you, then? There'll be nobody bursting the door down tonight?' The anxiety in her voice was reflected in her eyes as she gazed across at him.

He got up from the table and came over to where she was standing. His right hand cupped her chin as he gazed down into the fear-filled eyes. 'I'll be long gone before they get round here, don't you fear. John-Joe's uncle's got a place out in the country somewhere down around Kildare. We're going to lie low there for a while until this thing blows over.'

'The country! God's truth, and what will you be doing with yourselves stuck in the country?' The Danny she knew and loved was a city boy, born and bred. Why, even a half hour spent in Phoenix Park made him homesick for the narrow grey streets he had left behind!

He grinned, for the first time since he staggered back into her life less than half an hour ago. 'Making fireworks, Cissie, that's what. Fireworks to entertain those gallant gentlemen of the constabulary!'

Her brows furrowed for a moment, then comprehension dawned. 'Bombs! You're to be making bombs! Holy Mother of God, you've taken leave of your senses an' no mistake! It's blowin' yourselves up you'll be doin' and it's ten stones of mince they'll be burying in your coffin, by the time they've picked up all the bits!'

He gave a mirthless laugh. 'Well, if that's the case, I'll tell the old boy O'Malley not to bother with a funeral. He can feed my remains to his pigs. John-Joe tells me it's a pig farm we'll be living in, so what could be handier?'

Their eyes met and she tried very hard to smile, but it was getting harder and harder these days.

It was next morning before, half a mile away in the small house in McIntryre Street, Maeve read of the raid at Sandymount, on the second page of the *Irish Times*. When Danny was at home she was not allowed to have such a Unionist rag, as he termed it, in the house; but, with him absent so much of the time now, she could indulge herself in its familiar pages. Anyway, close scrutiny of the casualty lists from the Western Front was essential, with Charlie over there in the thick of it.

She gasped aloud, sitting down clumsily on the chair at the table as she re-read the newsprint a second time. So it was a married man with three children he had done for, was it? Sick at heart, she closed the paper and stared with unseeing eyes at the closed door facing her. So she was married to a murderer now.

She got up from the seat and walked to the window, staring out into the pale sunshine of the midsummer morning. It was funny really – he must have killed other men during the week of the Easter Rising, but somehow she could live with that. They weren't men with wives and families, they were nameless creatures whom she would never know. But the man in the paper existed. In fact, he had a face – a round, boyish face, with a thick, dark moustache and good-natured dark eyes that gazed back out of the page at her. And he had a wife, probably not much older than herself, with three small children, who would grow up never really knowing their father. Knowing only that he was killed by 'a bad man' – for that was what their mother would tell them, wasn't it?

Her eyes travelled over to her own son, sitting propped up in a wooden barred crib to the left of the range. What, in the name of God, had she wished upon him? Had she ever imagined this time last year, when her whole world revolved around Danny and their love for each other, that she would be wishing a murderer on her son for a father? . . . No, not even in her wildest dreams.

A glance at the clock on the mantelpiece told her it was just after nine o'clock. Dermot would still be in the presbytery. He never usually started his morning rounds till after ten. She wondered if he had seen it yet, and what his reaction would be. As the thought of him filled her mind, she could feel her heart beating faster beneath the thin cotton of her blouse, as it had done almost all night. For that was how long she had relived those moments with him since he left the house so abruptly yesterday evening.

Sleep had finally come, as the first grey fingers of dawn had touched the rooftops, beyond the small window by her bed, where Danny had made his escape only a few short hours before. But even in sleep it was his brother's face that had risen before her. It was Dermot who haunted her dreams.

No matter how often she attempted to rationalise it – to try to explain to herself what was happening between them – the more confused she became. To begin with she could pretend that it was all her imagination. In years, she was still a young girl, after all, and young girls were known for their romantic fantasies, weren't they? And what could be a more romantic fantasy than to have a Catholic priest fall in love with you – or even fall in love with one yourself? Didn't that have to be the very ultimate in forbidden fruit?

Yes, from the beginning she had been aware, painfully aware, that Dermot was not only a priest, but an undeniably attractive man. But he could never belong to her – he was married to the Church. And she could never belong to him – she was his brother's wife. Somehow the unshakeability of

130

those two facts should have made things easier, but it didn't. It made no difference at all. The fact that they had both, one fine day, said certain words that religious people called vows, did not make the slightest difference to the fact that he was a man and she was a woman, and when they were together something happened between them that she could not explain. No, she could not explain it; she could only feel it – and knew that he could feel it too. All the certainties in life – her love for Danny, her marriage – were toppling around her and the only thing she was really sure of any more was that she longed to see his brother again. She longed to see Dermot so much that it was becoming a physical ache within her.

But what went on in her mind was her own private affair. Surely he wouldn't – he couldn't – take it amiss if she called round this morning, to show him the article in the *Times*? She simply had to share her fears with someone. And didn't Mrs Maloney say she didn't mind her leaving Kieran with her any time she fancied an hour or so's break?

Dermot was at his desk in the morning-room of the presbytery, immersed in a pile of correspondence, when she was shown in by Mrs Shea, the housekeeper.

'Maeve, this is a surprise!' His face mirrored his astonishment as he came forward and took her by the hand to lead her to a high-backed, two-seater settee in front of the empty fireplace.

He had just been thinking of her and to see her suddenly here in front of him, in the flesh, was like seeing a ghost come to life. He fought to control his voice as his eyes darted across and met hers. Even exchanging a glance was akin to sharing a peculiarly intimate experience. 'Is anything wrong?'

It was the first time she had ever set foot in here and that didn't help matters. It almost made it worse, for having her here in the presbytery brought his guilt home to him, right to his own doorstep – and across it.

The newspaper was clasped in her right hand. She passed it over to him without a word, opening it at the appropriate page and pointing to the article in question, so there could be no mistake.

He read it in silence and when he had finished, he leaned

back and closed his eyes. His lips were moving soundlessly and she knew he was praying.

'What do I do, Dermot? Tell me, please.' Her plea came from the heart.

He shook his head. 'Only you can decide that, Maeve.'

'But I'm asking for your opinion. You must at least have an opinion, for God's sake!'

'You've already got your answer, Maeve . . . For God's sake, is the key to the whole question. But not only for our Lord's sake, for your child's sake as well, for Kieran's sake, you must simply remember what you promised before God when you married his father. You must remember the vows you made. For better, for worse, meant exactly that. You can't desert him now. Now is the time he needs you – needs all of us – the most, to help him find his way again.' He said the words mechanically, as if reading them from a book.

'You're telling me to go home and forget this ever happened? To come to terms with the fact that the man I married is a cold-blooded murderer?' She gestured towards the newspaper, a look of utter despair in her eyes.

'I'm not telling you anything. You asked my opinion, I gave it, that's all.' His voice was patient, infuriatingly patient.

She rose to her feet and looked down at him, contempt in her eyes. She should have known better than come here. She should have known what his reaction would be. A parrot, that's all he was. A pathetic parrot, mouthing the words of those higher up the clerical scale. 'You don't care, do you, Dermot? You really don't care. As long as I'm obeying the rules and not rocking your precious religious boat, I can go through hell without anyone giving a damn!'

She swung round on her heel and made for the door, but he caught up with her before she got to it. His fingers dug painfully into her upper arm, through the soft woollen cloth of her jacket. 'You know better than that!'

'Do I, Dermot? Do I?'

Their eyes met and held. His face was set and a tiny nerve flickered beneath the shadowed skin at the edge of his jaw. When he spoke, the intensity in his voice sent a tremor through her. 'Yes, Maeve, you know. You know and I know. But I prayed to God all last night that no one else but He and us will ever know just how much of a damn I give, as you so delicately put it.'

She opened her mouth to speak, but no words came. Her throat had closed up and a thin film of perspiration broke on her brow. 'You – you won't desert me, though? You won't stop coming?' She forced the words out with difficulty.

He let go her arm and shook his head. 'I don't know, Maeve, I really don't. It could be asking for trouble – real trouble. You know that.'

'Trouble for whom?' Anger flared in her eyes. 'We're responsible adults, for heaven's sake. No one's going to force you to do anything you don't want to do, least of all me!'

There was a look of pity in his eyes at her naïvety as he gazed down at her. 'But that's the whole trouble, can't you see? It wouldn't be something I didn't want to do!'

Danny's fair, freckled face was bright red with the effort, and perspiration stood out like glistening raindrops on the skin of his brow. Why did John-Joe's uncle have to live right at the top of a bloody hill? Pedalling down to the village for provisions every morning, and back up again with a heavy saddle bag full of groceries was almost killing him. He'd never even learned to ride a bike before they arrived here at Ballymeath two weeks ago and his thigh muscles still protested painfully with every mile.

Old Willie O'Malley's cottage stood fully three miles outside the village, if you could call four houses and a pub a village. But at least the pub, owned by Paddy Garoghan, a local small farmer, sold just about everything they needed to keep body and soul together, stuck out here in the wilds.

Why he had been landed with the job of fetching and carrying the groceries, Danny still wasn't quite sure. Maybe it was because John-Joe pretended to some kind of superior knowledge of the way bombs were manufactured, so could be of more help to his uncle. This was probably an exaggeration, with downright laziness being nearer the truth, Danny reckoned, but up to now it hadn't seemed worth making an issue over. With a bit of luck, they'd be out of here and on their way back to Dublin by the end of the week.

Just how they were going to transport the produce of their creative energies, he was not quite sure, but they certainly had quite a pile in the wash-house in old man O'Malley's back yard to show for it.

Since arriving here he'd learnt to make black gunpowder and had also turned his hand to producing hand-grenades by filling tin cans with blasting-powder. They had spent hours collecting every available sporting cartridge and refilling them with buckshot. Each and every one would be essential in the coming fight. For the longer he had been out here, the more determined he was to fling himself wholeheartedly into direct action once he was back in the capital. And John-Joe agreed completely. Con's death, as well as all the others, must be avenged at all costs.

He was within five hundred yards of the small cottage, and looking forward more than anything to a generous glass of the old boy's poteen, when the sudden noise and sight that met his eyes sent him sprawling off his bike on to the grass verge.

'Bloody hell!'

The whole roof of the wash-house went sailing into the air with an explosion that must have come from the boiling bowels of the earth itself. As orange and yellow flames leapt into the heavens, a succession of loud bangs rent the still morning air. Hand-grenades, dozens of them, were exploding left, right and centre. The bloody fools had sent the place up!

Leaving the bike and groceries in a heap by the roadside, he started running towards the inferno. The flames hadn't yet reached the main part of the house, but it could just be a matter of time — and worse, John-Joe and the old man could be in there. If they weren't already blown to smithereens, that was!

As he ran panting up the path towards the front door, Willie O'Malley came staggering out of the house. The old man's face was pure white and his already bandy legs were buckled at the knees with shock. 'B'Jasus, Danny, John-Joe's still round the back, so he is! If he's not in kingdom come by now!'

'Stay there, and keep that damned dog quiet. I'll see what's happened!'

Willie's collie, Ben, was barking crazily at Danny's heels as he ran round the corner of the cottage towards the yard, but, thankfully, a shouted command from his master made him retreat unwillingly to the old man's side.

The smoke was suffocating as he neared the destroyed wash-house and shrapnel from the exploding grenades still flew through the air like lethal confetti. John-Joe was lying sprawled on his back about twelve feet from the blown-out door of the building. His eyes were closed and his face was pitch-black, as were his clothes, but from what Danny could tell, there was a chance he was still breathing.

'Hold on, boyo. Hold on, there. I've got you!' The comforting words were more for his own benefit than his unconscious friend's, as he squatted down behind him and raised him under the armpits, hauling him over the debris-strewn yard towards the water pump that stood in the corner by the back door.

Carefully he laid his friend's head under the spouted mouth of the pump and gave the iron handle three hefty jerks. The cold water burst forth in a hissing deluge, covering John-Joe's smoke-blackened face and the upper half of his body.

The commotion that ensued brought the old man and dog running round to see what in heaven's name was going on.

'Lay off, you bloody eejit! You're drowning me!' John-Joe's yell almost drowned the explosions behind them as he scrambled up, out of the line of fire of the pump.

'Yer not dead, then?' His uncle looked at him closely out of his one good eye, as his nephew rose to his feet, dripping, in front of them.

'If he is, he's a bloody noisy ghost!' Danny put in, with a grin, stepping deftly aside, to avoid the clout that was aimed in his direction.

Then all three turned to gaze in sombre awe at what was left of their bomb factory.

Chapter 13

Maeve read and re-read the letter. She held it tenderly between her fingers, as if scared it might fall to pieces at any moment, as her eyes took in the familiar spiky handwriting. It was written on the twelfth of July, from a place called Beaumont Hamel on the Somme. That was almost a month ago now – at least he was alive then! Charlie was alive! 'When did it come?'

'Yesterday. I would have come straight away but Mama had arranged a dinner party and wasn't keen on me taking off in the middle of all the preparations.' Amy Grafton sat on the edge of her seat, her dainty hands clasped tightly in her lap as Maeve gazed down at the piece of paper she had just handed her. 'It was really thoughtful of Charlie to write and offer his sympathy on Will's death, don't you think?'

Maeve nodded. Charlie was always one to think of others, often to the detriment of his own welfare.

'I know he doesn't say much about his own circumstances – I don't expect they're allowed to, really. But I felt you'd like to see it anyway.'

'Yes, oh yes, I'm so grateful, Amy, I can't tell you!' Thank God, she had had the gumption to leave her address when she called round to the Grafton house last month.

'I'll write back, of course – straight away. It – it's comforting somehow, writing to someone in Will's old regiment. I haven't been able to talk to anybody – not really – about Will being killed, but I feel Charlie will understand. He's been through it too, hasn't he?'

'And is still going through it.'

Amy nodded gravely. 'I – I thought I'd send him your address. Would that be all right, Maeve? You wouldn't mind that?'

'Mind?' Maeve shook her head, a bemused look in her blue eyes as she reluctantly handed back the letter. 'Oh, Amy, it's the best thing that happened in so long, I can't tell you!' To be in touch with Charlie again after all this time was more than she could have hoped for.

'The mail seems to be taking a long time to come, but at least it's getting here,' Amy said, slipping the letter back into its envelope. 'It must be really awful for them over there, although the papers keep on about all the victories we're supposed to be winning. All I can say is, if all those obituaries in the columns of the *Irish Times* are anything to go by, then it's an awful cost our boys are paying.'

'You're right there.'

The two young women looked at one another. Both were still in their teens, but they had had a baptism of fire into the world of womanhood this past year. Maeve's eyes rested on Amy's face, with its pretty, china-doll features. There was a set look to the pink rosebud mouth now and it was not just the black mourning-dress that had drained the colour from her normally pink complexion. As for herself, she could not even begin to explain to her old friend what she was now going through.

She had seen nothing of Danny since he had leapt from the bedroom window over a month ago, although she had heard he was back in Dublin. He had even been to visit Mary-Agnes on one or two occasions, if Katie was to be believed.

'Is there nothing else I can do for you, Maeve? I'd be only too glad, you know that.' Amy's eyes moved around the cramped little kitchen, with its cheap furniture. It had required courage for her to venture into the area of McIntyre Street to see Maeve today. The cave-dwellers, the middle classes around the Green called the inhabitants of the tenements on Dublin's seamier side, and it had always been forbidden territory throughout her young life in the city – and Maeve's, come to that. Certainly Maeve didn't actually live in a tenement, but even they couldn't be much worse than this . . .

'It's pretty awful isn't it?' As if reading her thoughts, Maeve shrugged helplessly as she looked around what was now her private world. There was hardly a stick of furniture in the place that was worth more than a couple of pounds. Almost everything had been inherited, along with the house, from Danny's uncle, and its antiquity showed in every dent and stain. 'Do you know, Amy, I no longer possess a single book of my own? It's funny the things you miss when you're suddenly cut adrift from your old life.'

'It – it must have taken courage to leave like that . . .' Amy began uncertainly.

'Courage?' Maeve's laugh was bitter. 'Romantic stupidity would be nearer the mark!'

'You really regret it, then? You're sorry you eloped?' Amy's blue eyes opened wider as she attempted to comprehend what on earth had got into her friend last summer to act as she did. 'You know they said you only did it because you imagined yourself as some kind of a second Countess Markiewicz!'

'A second Countess Markiewicz!' Maeve hooted. 'Sure and if that's how I saw myself, would I have gone and married a penniless Irish rebel? Another Polish Count like she got hold of would have been a much better proposition!'

She shook her head in a mixture of amusement and despair. It was true that Constance Markiewicz had been influential in winning her over to the Republican cause. As the daughter of a well-to-do Anglo-Irish Protestant family, the Gore-Booths, Constance Markiewicz's espousal of the rebel cause had caused an even greater shock in influential Unionist circles than Maeve's marriage to Danny. The defection of both young women to the other camp had caused much tut-tutting and shaking of heads in Dublin society, but, while the beautiful Con was already a living legend in Ireland for her part in the Rising last Easter, there was little glamour about her own situation – nor was there ever likely to be.

'There'll be a few dos coming off in the autumn – you know, whist drives and sales of work, and that type of thing, to collect funds for the war effort . . . I don't suppose you'd like to be involved?' Amy studied her nails as she waited for the reply. The last thing she wanted to do was to embarrass her friend by suggesting something that for one reason or another would be out of the question.

Excitement leapt for a split second in Maeve's heart, then doubt set in. What on earth would Danny say? How could she ever justify it to him? To him, what was happening in France was criminal – an Imperialist war, he called it. A war between the two great capitalist nations, Britain and Germany, to settle who would become masters of the world in the twentieth century. 'Those poor buggers at the Front are merely cannon fodder!' She could hear his voice now. 'The capitalist bosses are getting their poor bloody wage slaves to do their dirty work for them, while they sit at home on their fat arses rubbin' their hands!'

She shook her head reluctantly. 'I'm sorry, Amy, I'd like to, you know that, but . . .'

'But what, for heaven's sake?'

'But I might run into my mother, or one of her friends . . . It, it would be just too embarrassing.' There was no way she could give the real reason. And, anyway, that one was genuine enough.

Amy gave an exasperated shrug. 'Have it your own way. But I think you're being just plain silly. I'm sure if you did run into your mother, she'd be only too happy to make things up. It's been a whole year, Maeve. How long do you intend this exile to go on for?'

Maeve stared silently into the empty grate. 'I don't really know. For ever if need be. I know one thing, Amy, after what was said by both Mama and Papa, I'm not the one who's going to go crawling back there in a hurry. If I never set eyes of either of them again, it'll be too soon!'

'But what if anything happens to Charlie? It could happen, you know, Maeve – look at poor Will.' Memories clouded the bright blue eyes and her lower lip quivered slightly. She dug her teeth into it. 'Sure and it's a terrible time for us all.'

'I'll make a cup of tea!' Maeve walked quickly to lift the kettle from the cold hearth. It would mean lighting the fire, but it would be worth it. A cup of tea was the answer to everything, wasn't it? . . . Almost everything, that was . . .

She was to think often on Amy's offer as the summer dragged into autumn and the leaves around St Stephen's Green and her old home on Jubilee Avenue turned from green to gold. And, although Danny was hardly at home enough to warrant paying heed to his views, somehow she could not bring herself to take up Amy's invitation and re-enter the world she had left behind, no matter how good the cause.

He said little on the visits he *did* make to her and the baby, stopping long enough only to secure his conjugal rights and leave a small pile of notes under the clock on the mantelpiece. She knew where the money was coming from, for its frequency tallied too closely with break-ins and raids reported in the local newspapers to be pure coincidence. She should say something, she knew that, but his temper made such a thing unthinkable.

The only person she had divulged her fears to was Dermot, but all he could do was shake his head, and promise to offer up prayers for the soul of his brother. A frown crossed her brow as the pale face, with the dark intense eyes, filled her mind. She tried so hard to keep him out of her thoughts these days. They were both holding each other at arm's length and had been for weeks now. Nothing had been said – nothing overtly, that was. But then it didn't have to be. They both know that. Things happened between them that didn't have to be explained in words. They only had to be in the same room, talking about the most mundane of things, and they each knew exactly what the other was feeling.

The opening of the door brought her out of her reverie and she turned to see Katie slip inside, closing it quietly behind her. It was three days since her last visit and Maeve's eyes lit up at the sight of the pert, freckled face. Only tonight there was no bright smile to greet her.

'What is it, Katie? You look like you've lost a sixpence and found a ha'penny!' She folded the last of the baby's nappies off the rack in front of the fire and placed them in a neat pile on the table, as the child came and pulled herself up into a sitting position on the brown oilcloth.

'Danny's at our house, Maeve. I think he's coming in to see you.'

Maeve's heart turned over, but she attempted a bright smile. 'Oh, really, that's nice.'

Katie shook her head emphatically. 'It's not, Maeve, it's really not. He's had a least half a bottle since I got home from school. I know he has 'cause Liam called him a stinking drunk. Danny was going to hit him, but Mary-Agnes stopped him, so he called Liam a lily-livered rude word instead. He said if he'd an ounce of guts he'd be out working for the cause in an evening instead of sitting stuffing his fat face by the fire.'

A shudder ran through Maeve's body. She could just imagine it. 'Well then, Katie, if things are so bad across the road, maybe it's just as well he's coming on here. It can't be very nice for you and Willie-John and the wee ones with grown-ups arguing like that.'

Katie nodded. ''Tis not the wee ones that it worries,' she said, 'but Willie-John gets all worked up, so he does. If he pees himself again this week, Maeve, Mary-Agnes will kill him, so she will!'

The memory of her last encounter with that particular problem flashed painfully into Maeve's mind. She had felt guilty ever since, each time she thought of poor Willie-John. She glanced round at a pot of stew she had simmering on the fire. The biggest favour she could do both Katie and her poor half-wit brother was to get Danny out of there fast. 'Go and tell Danny I'm taking supper up, Katie, there's a good girl. Tell him it's his favourite – stew and dumplings – that should make him come round at the double.'

As soon as the tiny figure had disappeared out of the door to deliver her message, Maeve regretted her words. But it was too late now. Two plates were lifted down from the dresser and set at opposite ends of the table, then a knife and fork placed carefully on either side. She would brew a good strong pot of tea, that should help combat the whiskey.

She had got as far as pouring the hot water into the teapot when the door opened and Danny walked in. As first, she thought that Katie had been exaggerating, for she had seen him much more the worse for drink than this. But he wasn't staggering drunk, merely argumentative – and that, she knew to her cost, was far worse.

'If you think it's more money I've come to dole out, you'll better think again, me darlin'!'

'Sure and what makes you say that?' She forced a laugh. 'It's plenty of money I've got at the moment!'

She had meant it as a joke, but he was in no mood to see it

that way. 'And where would you be getting that, may I ask? Whoring round the Quays, if I'm not mistaken!'

'Danny, really!'

A loud wail from the bedroom beyond prevented her from carrying her protest further as she rushed through to lift Kieran from his cot. He was wet and she breathed a sigh of relief that she had got his nappies dried in time.

Carrying him through under one arm, to avoid the wetness seeping through even more, she took a nappy off the top of the pile and, with one hand, spread it out on the table-top, before proceeding to undress the infant's lower half.

'What the hell do you think you're doing?'

She looked up in surprise at the vehemence with which the question was delivered. 'I'm changing your son, that's what I'm doing.'

'Not in here you're not! You're not stinkin' this place out just before I have my supper. Get it out of here!'

'It? It?' She repeated the words, almost screaming them at him. 'You're not referring to your son as It by any chance?'

'Less lip and get the little brat out o' here! Find somewhere else to wipe his arse – not in front of my face with supper on the table!'

Red-faced with fury, Maeve chose to ignore the command completely and continued to undress Kieran, laying him down alongside the nappy.

'I'm warning you, woman!'

Still she ignored him.

'I'm warning you!' White-faced with anger, Danny got up and came round the table. 'I'm warning you!'

Her mouth set in a lipless line, she worked even faster, unpinning the fouled nappy and throwing it on to the floor down by the hearth.

'Bitch! Bloody bitch!' With one mighty swipe of his arm, he pushed her aside, sending her staggering back against the clothes rack, which toppled with a sharp crack on to the floor. Then, to her horror, the baby was yanked by the left leg off the table, as his father marched towards the bedroom.

'Danny – no!' Her scream filled the room and she scrambled to her feet to dash after them. As she watched in horror the child was swung by the leg, like a rubber doll, and thrown on to the bed. He bounced in the middle of the patchwork quilt and, for a second, lay quite still and totally soundless.

'Dear God ... Kieran!' She stared down aghast at the tiny figure, then turned and attacked his father with all the strength she could muster as a piercing yell came from the child on the quilt.

'You bastard! You inhuman bastard!' Her fists flailed at the grinning, triumphant figure beside her, as Kieran shrieked in the background. 'You could have killed him! You could have killed your own child!'

Amazingly, he stood and took it, with that awful infuriating grin on his face, which enraged her even more.

Breathless, she stood back and looked at him, contempt twisting the delicate features of her face. 'But that would be nothing new for you, would it, Danny? Murder would be nothing new to you. It's just part of your everyday life these days!'

'Shut up, woman, you don't know what you're saying.' He pushed past her and made for the kitchen once more.

'Don't I? Don't I? I've got enough on you to hang you a dozen times over, you little bastard!'

'Shut yer gob, woman, and take up that supper ... I'm warning you!'

'You're warning me nothing!' Nothing was going to deter her now from speaking her mind – not after the way he had just treated his son. 'I despise you, Danny Donovan, and all you stand for! Oh, aye, I was taken in by it in the beginning, but not any more. All those fine words were just a cover for murder – just an excuse to get your own way, and impose your own ideas through cold-blooded murder!'

'So it's a murderer I am, am I? Well, my lady, what does that make your precious British government? What does that make Asquith and Lloyd George and all the rest of those bastards who sentenced fine men like Jim Connolly and Pat Pearse and the rest to death? Carried Connolly to his death in a chair, they did! What is that if it's not murder? And even worse, it's murder perpetrated by one state on the citizens of another. How far back do we go, Maeve, in looking for murderers? Do we go back to Cromwell and beyond? Do we count all those bastards in the English parliament who refused to subsidise grain in the 1840s, so that my great-grandparents' generation died in their millions? Are they all murderers too, Maeve, or do you reserve that title only for me? Only for those of us with the guts to do something about it?'

He cast a glance towards the open bedroom door where Kieran was still screaming inconsolably. 'It's the likes of him we're fighting for, so his generation won't grow up under the British yoke. We're not murderers, damn you, we're liberators! It's the life of this country we're fighting for!'

They stared at one another through the falling dusk in the small room. Her parents had warned her that mixed marriages couldn't work. Why, in heaven's name, hadn't she listened to them?

Chapter 14

'Oh whisht, can't you! Stop that incessant whining!' Maeve looked across in exasperation at the grizzling child in the cot. The constant fretting had been going on for weeks now, ever since the last time Danny showed up, to be exact. It seemed to be worse when it came to changing his nappy. Whenever she held him by the ankles to wipe his bottom he would scream the place down. Had something happened that day his father had grabbed him by the leg and thrown him down on the bed like that? She really should do something about it; take him to the doctor, maybe. But he would only tell her it was something quite normal – teething problems or pain from the nappy-rash most probably, and that she was being a silly, over-anxious mother. Anyway, she had no money for the doctor, or anything else these days. She had lied when she had told Danny she had plenty of money left; she had had three pounds to live on for the past seven weeks and there was exactly three shillings and sixpence in her purse in the dresser drawer.

She got up from her knees, where she had been blackleading the kitchen range, and replaced the lid on the tin of Zebo. Her back ached, as did her head, and she looked down in despair at her polish-covered hands. Quite apart from the grimy stains of the blacking ingrained in the skin, her nails, once her pride and joy, were cracked and broken. Hot tears stung her eyes and she blinked them back angrily as she crossed to the wash-bowl to attempt to clean up.

Kieran's constant fretting had meant that she had put off leaving him with Mrs Maloney for the odd afternoon as she had anticipated and, day by day, the walls seemed to be closing in on her.

She gazed listlessly out of the window. A pale beam of late autumn sunshine accentuated the grime on the glass. She should get out there and clean it, just as she should spend ten minutes each morning scrubbing the front step like the other housewives did around here. The fact that she didn't and the grime was being left to accumulate had not escaped the notice of the clacking tongues of her neighbours, but she no longer cared. In fact, she no longer cared about anything very much these days.

A glance at the clock told her it was just after midday; time she made herself a bite to eat. A bit of cheese would suffice, but she had even run out of that. There was nothing for it but to take Kieran and run up the road to Sullivan's grocery store on Candlemaker Row. It was a bit further to go than Heaney's, on the corner of McIntyre Street itself, but it was worth it, for she got almost as good a selection of foodstuffs there as in the better-class haunts of her childhood shopping expeditions on the other side of town.

Slipping her dark blue wool jacket over her blouse and fixing a wide-brimmed felt boater on top of her head with two long hatpins, she picked up Kieran from his cot and wrapped him up tightly in his shawl. Luckily it didn't look too cold outside and the fifteen-minute walk should do them both good.

She deliberately only took a shilling from the purse in the drawer. What she didn't have with her, she couldn't spend. It was as simple as that.

Despite the sunshine, there was a fresh breeze blowing as she rounded the corner of McIntyre Street, into the street that ran between there and Candlemaker Row, and she was forced to hang on to her hat, despite the anchoring pins, as she gripped the baby tightly with the other arm.

What on earth was happening ahead? Her eyes narrowed against the sun and swirling dust. A crowd had gathered outside Campbell's, the pawnbrokers, and smoke was billowing out through the barred windows of the shop. Automatically she began hurrying in the direction of the commotion.

A woman in a shawl and heavily-stained skirt, whom she knew by sight, was hurrying towards her, a look of shock distorting the gaunt features of her face. 'I'd keep well clear o' there if I were you, girl. 'Tis a bomb that's gone off, so they say, killing the old man and a customer! I 'clare to God, I don't know what the world's coming to these days. An' me with my old man's Sunday best still in there. The Good Father knows how I'll get it out in time for Mass now, with that poor bugger Campbell lying as dead as a doornail behind what's left of his counter!'

A bomb! Fear clutched at Maeve's heart, her thoughts immediately turning to Danny. But that was stupid – and unjust. He couldn't be responsible for every explosion in the city.

The heels of her booted feet clicked even faster along the pavement and she got there just in time to see the body of what was left of a young man being carried from the shop and laid down on the pavement. A coat was spread over his head as Maeve pushed through the milling crowd.

'They'll not be able to do that to old Campbell,' a middle-aged woman carrying a parcel said knowingly, nodding towards the smoking interior of the shop. 'They'll have to collect the bits off the ceiling first!'

Sick at heart, Maeve looked down at the dead body on the pavement. The young man was lying on his back, with just his lower half visible; his corduroy trousers were patched and there was a big hole in the sole of his right boot. 'Poor blighter,' she breathed, with a sigh that came from the heart. 'Does he come from round here?'

The woman with the parcel nodded and gestured with her head back towards McIntyre Street. 'Oh aye, it's that daftie from down yonder. Donovan I think his name is.'

Maeve's heart turned a somersault as she looked from the woman back down to the body on the pavement. 'No – no, it can't be!' It couldn't be Willie-John! Please God, don't let it be Willie-John!

Clutching the baby to her breast, she pushed an old man who was blocking her sight out of the way and knelt down beside the half-covered corpse. Hardly daring to breathe, she peeled back the jacket from his face, then let out a scream. There was nothing left of it but a red, livid hole. Half the side of his head had been blasted away. But it was him all right. It was Willie-John. She recognised him by the Anderson tartan tie she had given him for Christmas. It had never been off his neck since.

'Do you know him, then, missus? Was he a friend of yours?'

The old man behind her leaned over and stared in morbid fascination at what was left of her brother-in-law.

Maeve nodded mutely. 'I know him all right. And he was a friend of mine . . . He was a very good friend of mine.'

Tears blinded her as she retraced her steps back towards Mary-Agnes's house. She had spoken the truth. Willie-John was a friend of everybody. Was there no justice in this rotten world? Why was it always the innocent who seemed to come off worst?

Willie-John's funeral took place that Friday afternoon, but she did not attend. It was not that she had been refused permission, she simply preferred to stay at home with Kieran and Katie and honour his memory in her own way.

'He'll be there by now, won't he, Maeve? Willie-John will already be in heaven. Jesus won't ask him to spend all that time in purgatory like the rest of us. Willie-John was so good.' The child's eyes brimmed with tears as she looked across at her sister-in-law.

Maeve laid the knitting needles with the half-finished child's bootee down on her lap and nodded reassuringly. 'Of course, Katie. Don't you worry, Willie-John has gone straight to heaven. He'll be smiling down on you right now. He's in a happier place than he ever was in this life – have no fear of that.'

The child nodded. She always believed what Maeve said.

Danny wasn't at the funeral. They couldn't trace him in time. Not even Cissie O'Rourke knew where he was. On some business down around Kilkenny was all he had said when she saw him last week. He was liable to be away a few days. That was all she knew. Dermot imparted the information with an embarrassed look as he called in after his brother Willie-John had been laid to rest. 'It'll not be a day too soon, will it?' He had guessed long ago of her financial plight, but had little of his own to offer.

She gave a bitter smile as she shut the door behind Katie, who had disappeared back to Mary-Agnes's for the end of the wake. 'If it wasn't for the baby I could earn my own money.' If – if – the world was full of ifs . . .

'Is he still as fretful?' Dermot cast a glance at the sleeping child in the cot.

'Every bit. And the awful thing is, he seems to cry even harder when I pick him up. It seems there's no end to it.'

He looked at her closely, his eyes taking in the dark shadows that wreathed the blue eyes, and the dispirited droop to the shoulders inside the grey flannelette blouse. 'I wish I could help. I really do.'

She opened her mouth to assure him that he did. He helped just by being here. But the door bursting open caused the words to freeze on her lips.

'Danny!' Maeve and Dermot chorused the name together.

'Surprised to see me?' He closed the door behind him and went over and shook his brother by the hand. 'I understand it was a fine service. I thank you for that. Willie-John deserved the best.'

Dermot coughed his embarrassment. 'He was my brother too, you know.'

'There's hot tea in the pot, if you fancy a cup.' Maeve's voice broke the momentary silence that had fallen.

'I will. Thanks.' Danny sat down in his usual chair as if he had never been away and looked at them both. There was an almost challenging light in his amber eyes. 'Well, this is a fine kettle o' fish, an' no mistake! Poor bugger, he deserved a better end than that.'

'Any idea who planted the bomb?' Dermot voiced the question that had haunted Maeve since that day.

'It wasn't one of ours, if that's what you're getting at. More like a Mickey Mullen affair, or one of those other half-wit maverick groups that think they're aiding the cause by letting off explosions left, right and centre. There's been a lot of bad feeling about old Campbell in some circles. He was a Proddy, you know.'

Maeve's hackles rose. 'What if he was a Protestant? Did that qualify the poor man to be blown sky high?'

'Don't be bloody stupid, woman. There's always more to it than meets the eye. Intelligence has it he was supplying money

149

for gun-running in the North.' He leaned back in the chair, his thumbs hooked into the armholes of his waistcoat, as he let the effects of his words sink in. 'Aye, he had connections with the Ulster Volunteers, there's little doubt about that. Folk who play with fire run the risk of getting burnt.'

'Or blown up.'

Dermot's laconic interjection brought a scowl from his brother. 'Don't you go getting all self-righteous, boyo. You know as well as I do you can't make an omelette without breaking eggs. It's Ireland's life we're fighting for – we're not kids playing cops and robbers. Some people get killed – that's life. If you'll pardon the expression.'

Maeve gave an impatient sigh as she poured the tea. She had heard all the old clichés too often. They no longer had the power of persuasion that they once did. Willie-John's death seemed such a cruel, pointless thing to have happened that no amount of rationalising could ever justify it. 'Are you back for long?' She handed the cup of tea across the table as she asked the question.

Danny threw a glance at the clock on the mantelpiece as he took the cup. 'About ten minutes. I brought you this.' He placed the cup on the table beside him and felt inside the back pocket of his trousers. He pulled out a bundle of notes which he threw down on to the table in front of her. 'That should keep you going for another week or so.'

She glanced down at them in embarrassment, then scooped them up and stuffed them into the pocket of her apron. Why did it always upset her so much to accept his money? Maybe if she knew where it came from – that it was legitimately earned – it would be easier.

But Danny was unaware of her discomfort, he had already turned to his brother to regale him with a story about a mutual friend. Their ensuing laughter seemed incongruous, with Willie-John hardly cold in the ground.

She walked to the window and stared out at the rain that was falling steadily in the street beyond. It ran in grimy streams down the window-pane and seemed to sum up her feelings exactly. She wished Danny would just leave – get out of her life for ever and leave her to get on with it. She would manage.

She could get a job — in a shop or something — and pay Mrs Maloney to keep Kieran. Once he was better, that was. She wouldn't wish him on anyone right now, howling his head off all day like this.

'Did you hear that, girl?'

Danny's shouted question made her look round. 'Sorry, no — I was day-dreaming.'

He got up from the chair and pushed it back under the table, before feeling into his back pocket once more. Another five-pound note was extracted and thrown on to the brown oilcloth. 'I've just been having a word with Dermot here, and he tells me you and the kid haven't been keeping too well lately.'

Maeve stared down at the note and gave a slight shrug, wondering what was coming next.

'We're agreed a breath of fresh air would do you both a power of good.' He nodded towards the note. 'That's to take you down to Kingstown for a couple of days. The sea air should be just what you need.'

'Kingstown!' A few days in Dublin's seaside suburb was the last thing she expected. 'But how . . .'

He came over and placed his hands on her shoulders, the amber eyes looking straight into hers. 'There's to be no argument. Dermot here has promised to take you down — and bring you back. So there'll be no excuses about not managing a case and a baby on your own.'

She glanced across at Dermot, who, amazingly, was nodding in agreement.

'Say you'll do it, Maeve.' Danny pleaded. 'Say you'll go. It'll do you good — and Kieran. I'm not a monster, you know, although you like to think so sometimes. I don't like to see you wasting away like this.'

She gave a helpless shrug and managed a strained smile. 'If — if that's what you both want.'

'It is,' they chorused.

'Right then, I'll go.'

'Great stuff!' Danny leaned forward and gave her fleeting kiss on the mouth. 'I've got to go now, but you can discuss the details of the trip with Dermot and let me know all about it next time I see you.'

151

With that, he was gone. They could hear his booted feet hurrying back down the pavement in the direction of Mary-Agnes's. Maeve glanced across at Dermot who was standing silently by the table. He gave her a quiet smile in return.

'It looks like you can't refuse, doesn't it? He'll be back in a week or so and will want a detailed report. When do you fancy going? Will Monday suit? I could probably get away then and bring you back on Wednesday.'

'Fine, that sounds just fine.' It was all happening too fast, but she was too tired to argue.

'Right, I'll be off now and fix it up with Father O'Reilly. He won't mind covering for me for a wee while. I've done it often enough for him when his mother was ill last year. You're sure you'll be all right, Maeve?' She had gone quite pale and it worried him.

He came over and lifted her chin with his right index finger. His eyes were gentle, very gentle, mirroring his concern, as they gazed down into hers. 'I'll be there, you know. There'll be nothing to worry about.'

A dark lock of hair had fallen over his brow, giving him a dishevelled, little-boy appearance. Nothing to worry about, because he would be there? The silly, silly fool. Couldn't he see that was exactly what was worrying her? And, if he had any sense, it was what should be worrying him too.

Chapter 15

'This'll do you fine, I reckon!' Dermot's eyes smiled across the table, in the well-appointed dining-room of Mrs Devlin's guest house overlooking Scotsman's Bay.

Maeve bit into the buttered scone and nodded happily. It was just what she wanted – a small, but well-run place, with good food and not too many other guests to disturb the peace and quiet. 'You don't have to rush back straight after tea, do you?'

Dermot looked down at the remaining crumbs on his plate and moved them around with the index finger of his right hand. 'Afraid so. There's a bible study class at half-past eight and I couldn't get anybody to fill in for me.' It was only half the truth: he could have cancelled it, and the temptation to do so had proved almost impossible to resist.

Her face fell. 'You'll be back tomorrow, then.'

He shook his head. 'No, you'll have to enjoy the pleasures of the seaside on your own tomorrow. But I'll come down early on Wednesday, I promise.'

'But I'm supposed to be travelling back on Wednesday night!'

'We'll have the whole day, Maeve. We can't be too greedy.'

'I can!' Her lower lip pouted as she pushed her plate from her. 'I'll be bored to death on my own.'

'No you won't. Anyway, you'll have Kieran. You'll have your hands full with him.'

'Mrs Devlin says she's got a young daughter who's mad on babies. I can leave him with her.'

'You'll have to provide her with a pair of ear-plugs first.'

Maeve managed a wry smile. 'The landlady said she used to use either Dr Jameson or Dr Paddy when any of hers played up when they were young.'

'Dr Jameson or Dr Paddy?' Dermot's dark brows furrowed. 'Sure and you've a good enough doctor of your own, haven't you?'

Maeve's laugh rang out in the almost empty dining-room. 'Oh, Dermot, you're a case and no mistake! Whiskey, you daft eejit. She used whiskey in their bottle to keep them quiet!'

A look of horror crossed his face. 'You'll not be trying that?'

She shook her head wearily. 'No, I'll not be trying that. One alcoholic in the family is quite enough. He is Danny's son, remember!'

Their eyes met across the white damask cloth and both gave a brave attempt at a smile.

'What will you do with yourself tonight when I've gone?'

'Think about you. Regret you're not here.'

His face hardened. It was the wrong thing to say. But, as she watched his tall figure stride back towards Marine Parade half an hour later, she knew she had spoken only the truth.

All was not lost, however. There were shelves full of good books in the guests' drawing-room and the whole evening ahead in which to enjoy them.

Mrs Devlin seemed to go in for bound volumes of magazines, for the bottom two shelves of the glass-fronted bookcases were filled with red morocco-covered copies of all her favourites. The *Strand Magazine* was there, with as many stories as she could read in a lifetime of holidays, plus *Blackwood's*, but her fingers reached for a past collection of the *Girl's Own Annual 1897–8* – the year she was the proverbial twinkle in her father's eye. She flicked through its pages, her eyes falling on a serial, *The White Rose of the Mountain*, and a love story, *Handsome Jack*. Yes, that would do nicely.

She slipped the book under her arm and made her way upstairs to her room. Kieran would be waking soon and she had better ask Mrs Devlin if she could warm the milk for his bottle.

She awoke next morning to a room washed with autumn sunshine and a feeling of perfect relaxation. Her eyes travelled around the floral-papered walls, with their Dutch prints, past the cot in the corner, where her son still slept. Everything was so light and clean, not dark and dingy like the bedroom back home in McIntyre Street. It reminded her of her old room in Jubilee Avenue.

Even the floor felt clean underfoot as she slipped out of bed and padded across to the window, throwing back the chintz curtains to gaze in sheer pleasure at the sparkling blue waters of the bay.

Her eyes travelled upwards to the sky. Dark clouds were gathering away out at sea, but they wouldn't come to much; they couldn't, not today. She would go for a walk this afternoon, that's what she would do. She would spend the morning here in the guest house with Kieran, then, when he had settled down for his afternoon nap, she would take a stroll along as far as Sandycove Harbour, and maybe, if she felt up to it, climb Killiney Hill.

The room was gloriously warm, for the maid had lit the fire in the grate a good half an hour earlier, and she washed thoroughly, standing on the small Persian rug in front of the washstand and sponging herself from top to toe, before donning her matching lace-trimmed chemise, drawers and petticoats.

She had brought one of her favourite day-dresses with her, a pale blue cashmere piped in navy that set off the colour of her eyes to perfection. Her hair, however, was in one of its rebellious moods and she abandoned the idea of an elaborate roll, settling instead for a simple top-knot, and teasing out the carefully crimped fringe with a pair of curling tongs, heated on the bars of the grate.

There were only two other guests in the dining-room when she appeared at a little after nine o'clock, an elderly lady, with an ear-trumpet that she rested by the side of her plate, and a youngish man with a fair handlebar moustache that had turned yellow in the centre through too much smoking. She studiously avoided his eyes as she sat down at a table for two by the window, and arranged Kieran comfortably in his high chair. At a little over six months, he could now use one, provided he was securely propped up with cushions, and the superior view from so high a position seemed to please him.

She had a traditional English breakfast of bacon and eggs, washed down with a pot of strong tea, then toast and marmalade to follow. When she had finished, and the other two had left the room, Mrs Devlin came to clear the dishes and Maeve stayed behind to chat to her. The relief of talking to someone who knew nothing of her present poverty-stricken existence was enormous. Poverty was nothing to be ashamed of, she knew that. But it was darned inconvenient. What was it Dr Johnson or someone said? 'Resolve not to be poor . . . Poverty is a great enemy to human happiness; it destroys liberty, makes some virtues impracticable and others extremely difficult.' She agreed with that wholeheartedly.

'So it's Jubilee Avenue you come from, Mrs Donovan? My, but that's a real nice area. Your husband will be across in France, no doubt?' The sympathy showed in the landlady's faded blue eyes as she piled the last of the used crockery on to the tray.

'Yes. Yes, he is.' She answered quickly, much too quickly. Why, oh why, was she lying? Her face coloured and she leaned across to wipe an imaginary dribble from Kieran's chin to cover her embarrassment.

'It's a sad business, so it is. Of course, Mr Devlin's passed on these twelve years since, and I've no sons of my own, but I've a couple of nephews across there. The Somme, isn't it? Poor lads, they'd little idea what was coming to them. 'Tis just a wee break you'll be having down here, I take it?'

Maeve nodded. The landlady spoke very rapidly, running her words together into one long sentence, and had a disconcerting habit of peering at her closely every time she asked a question. 'Yes . . . I – I've been a bit run down lately. The family thought the sea air would do me good.'

Mrs Devlin beamed her approval. 'And so it will, and no mistake! Take yourself along the shore this afternoon and leave the wee one to me. We'll get along just fine.' She smiled fondly down at Kieran. ''Twas four girls I had, God help me, and Mr Devlin would have happily swapped every last one of them for a son.' She sighed deeply at the memory as she lifted the heavy tray from the top of the table. 'Still, it doesn't do to always get what we want most from this life, does it, Mrs Donovan?'

Maeve swallowed hard. 'No, no, it surely doesn't.'

After lunch it took her all of an hour to leave the bustle of Kingstown behind and follow the path up the hill behind the town to reach the spot she wanted. She had come here on days' outings as a child. Nanny and Charlie would carry the wicker picnic hamper between them and they would spread the checked cloth on the dry, springy grass and unpack the mouth-watering goodies that cook had packed specially. It was funny the things you remembered. It was always a checked cloth, somehow, never a white or self-coloured one. And she could taste those home-made pies and cakes even now – and the lemonade and ginger-beer that came in those thick green bottles that you seldom saw nowadays.

Her eyes gazed back towards the houses huddled around the shore. The rain that had fallen earlier in the day had passed and a heavy curtain of dark grey mist hung above the horizon far out over the bay. There was an absolute stillness and peace about the whole scene that brought a feeling of serenity to her mind that she had not known in a long time.

The grass beneath her feet was moist and green after the rain and behind her great banks of white mist lay on the crest of the hill, moulding itself to the contours of the summit like a veil of virgin snow. Despite the dampness, there was a crispness in the air, a freshness that sent a tingle coursing through her veins and made her clasp her arms around her as she let her eyes roam slowly over her new world.

But wait . . . She was not alone. A figure was walking slowly up the steep path towards her. A tall dark figure. Her eyes strained against the light. It couldn't be . . .

But it was. Dermot was striding up the path towards her, his right arm raised in silent salute.

She picked up her skirts and ran back down the way she had just come, her dainty, button-booted feet skipping lightly over the stones and potholes in the rutted path.

'You said you couldn't come! You said it would be tomorrow before you could make it!' She panted for breath, her face flushed, as she reached him.

'I changed my mind. Do you mind?' There was a quiet smile on his face that made her heart turn over.

'No, no! How could I?' Her heart sang as she took his arm and they started to reclimb the path towards the summit of the hill.

157

They did not talk on the journey to the top. She was content to feel the strength of his arm beneath hers as they walked slowly, side by side, up into the heavens. For that was what it seemed like.

When they reached the top they turned as one, and gazed in silent awe on the scene beneath. The mist that from below had seemed like a portent of the snow of the coming winter, now swirled around them in ephemeral wraiths. Maeve felt Dermot's arm encircle her shoulders and she moved imperceptibly nearer, as his voice spoke softly in her ear.

'Do you know what this reminds me of?'

She shook her head. Her heart was thudding in her breast, making her breathing difficult.

'Do you know the story of Cuchulain?'

Again she shook her head. To her shame, her knowledge of Ireland's great mythical hero was minimal.

'They say he came from the Isle of Mist,' he said softly. 'He was the son of the chief of the Isle of Skye, before he went across the sea to take part in the Irish wars, leaving his beloved wife Bragela behind him. Long, long she mourned him, and gazed out across the waves for the first glimpse of his ship homeward bound through the mists, but he never returned.'

His voice sent tremors through her, as it continued in her ear. He was no longer here, in the second decade of the twentieth century, but had flown back into the mists of time. He was there on that Island of Mist, all those years ago, and he had taken her with him. He was Cuchulain . . .

Ossian the ancient bard's words mingled with his own, as his eyes darkened and gazed past her out over the endless waters of the bay. '"Dost thou raise thy fair face from the rock to find the sails of Cuchulain? The sea is rolling far distant, and its white foam shall deceive thee for my sails. Retire, for it is night, my love, and the dark wind sighs in thy hair. Retire to the halls of my feasts, and think of the times that are past, for I will return not till the storm of war is past."'

His fingers increased their grip on her shoulders. 'Imagine it, Maeve . . . Spread your white sails with me for the Isle of Mist and see Bragela waiting on her rock. Feel the salt tears in her eyes as she listens to the night winds, to hear the song of the rowers, but hears only the song of the sea, and the plaintive sound of Ireland's distant harp. Listen with her in vain, for the brave Cuchulain will never return . . . You call in vain for your departed lover, as the night comes rolling in from the sea and the face of the ocean fails you. You shall rise with the morning light, but your tears will return with the sun, and your sighs with the returning night.'

A silence fell when he had finished, such as she had never experienced before. A silence broken only by the whispering of the wind in the long grasses and the distant murmuring of the restless sea.

She wanted to say something, but her heart was too full. Only the right words would do and they would not come.

'Come, the dark clouds are gathering again. By the time we get back, they will be preparing tea.'

He was right. Dark clouds were scudding across the sky and the wind that had been merely whispering through the trees and bracken a few moments ago was now whistling ominously in their ears. She clasped hold of his hand as they began the long descent to the village. His fingers were longer than Danny's, longer and more gentle, as they enclosed hers. But, as they got nearer the houses, something made her withdraw her hand. He was still a priest, after all.

By the time they got to Sandycove Road the heavens had opened. Careless of the curious looks of passers-by, he grabbed hold of her hand once more as they broke into a run, head down against the horizontal spikes of rain that stung their cheeks and made them screw up their eyes as they ran blindly in the direction of the guest house.

Mrs Devlin was watching from the window as they came in sight and she had the door open waiting for them. 'Mercy me, you're soaked to the skin!' It was Maeve she looked at, her sympathy going out to this pale-faced young woman whom she had come to the conclusion was definitely a consumptive. 'You'll have to get out of those wet clothes before you catch your death!'

They stood panting on the rubber mat in the tiled foyer staring down at the small puddles that were forming at their feet, as the landlady shook her head. 'You get on up to your room and get out of those wet things, m'dear. There's a good fire in the grate and tea's about ready. I'll get the Father here to bring it up on a tray for you. The pair of you can have it upstairs if you prefer. Seeing the state of you, there's no sense in eating in a draughty dining-room if you can help it.'

Maeve and Dermot glanced at one another, then back at Mrs Devlin. 'That's very good of you,' Dermot said. 'We'd like that just fine, wouldn't we, Maeve?'

Chapter 16

'Here we are. Don't I make the bonniest maid you ever did see?' Dermot's brown eyes danced with amusement as Maeve held the bedroom door open and stood aside for him to enter.

He laid the heavily-laden tray on the dressing-table by the window and turned to smile at her. 'Herrings in oatmeal and the finest pile of mealy potatoes you'll see in many a long day!'

He glanced across at her with as broad a smile of satisfaction as if he'd made it himself. She had been kneeling in front of the fire when he had knocked, drying her hair. It hung long and loose over the shoulders of the pale blue dressing-gown she had slipped on. Her wet dress and jacket hung damply on hangers on the back of the door. Her cheeks were flushed and rosy from the heat of the fire and he thought she had never looked more beautiful.

'I'll pour the tea.' She came across and lifted the white porcelain teapot from the tray and filled the two cups, as he made himself comfortable on the edge of the bed. She lifted his plate across to him and placed the cup and saucer on the edge of the bedside cabinet within easy reach.

Never had a meal tasted better. She sat cross-legged on the floor by the fire, balancing her plate on her lap, and her cup on the gleaming brass fender. There was an intimacy born of a shared, almost mystical, experience this afternoon, and accentuated by the warmth of the fire and the soft light from pink-shaded lamps on either side of the bed.

She was aware of him watching her as she ate and sipped the tea and a warm glow permeated her whole being. When she had finished she got up and replaced the used dishes on the tray. Dermot got up immediately. 'I'll take them back down . . . Would you prefer it if I left now and gave you a while to rest before the landlady brings Kieran back up?'

She shook her head. 'No, I wouldn't prefer it. I wouldn't prefer it at all.'

They exchanged quiet smiles as he picked up the tray and she opened the door for him to return it to the kitchen.

He was gone less than five minutes and there was still a smile on his face as he closed the door behind him as he re-entered the bedroom. 'Mrs Devlin says to let you know her daughter Sinead's got back from Dublin and will be only too happy to mind the wee one for another hour or so, if you're agreeable. I said I was sure you wouldn't mind. Was I right?'

He needed no reply, for the look of relief on her face said it all. She was seated on the rug by the fire once more and patted the floor next to her in silent invitation for him to join her.

'It's years since I sat on the floor.' He smiled sheepishly as he settled down beside her, leaning back against a buttoned velvet easy-chair, as she threw another log into the flames. 'Yes, I was really young when I last did anything like this.'

'I'd like to have known you when you were young,' she said softly.

He laughed. At twenty-four, he had never regarded himself as exactly ancient. 'Oh, you wouldn't have liked me, Maeve. You wouldn't have liked me at all. I was a right little tearaway and no mistake!'

'I don't believe it.' She shook her head emphatically. 'You must have been a goody-goody from the beginning.'

The laughter faded from his eyes. 'Is that really what you think of me – as a goody-goody?' The hurt in his voice was obvious.

She flushed. 'No, not exactly.'

'Not exactly – but almost.' His mouth twisted bitterly and the brown eyes hardened as they stared past her into the flames of the fire.

She shifted uncomfortably on the rug. 'Don't take it amiss, please. I – I mean, it's only natural, isn't it? You would have to be a better person than the rest of us to join the priesthood in the first place.'

'If only that were true.'

The words were spoken so softly, she almost missed them, and she turned to him questioningly. 'But it must be true, mustn't it? You have to be different to give everything up like that.'

He gave a soft, mirthless laugh and shook his head. 'I'm no different from you, Maeve, or anyone else. What you feel, I feel – anger, humiliation, elation, jealousy, hate – love . . .'

The slight pause before the last word sent a shiver through her. It echoed in her head. Hadn't he once told her that was what he wanted most out of life? Her voice was huskily soft as she repeated it. 'Love, Dermot? You mean the love of God or the love between a man and a woman?'

'Either – and both. Do you really think the wearing of this cassock makes one bit of difference to what goes on in my heart – or anywhere else for that matter?'

He shook his head in mystification at the very thought. 'If that's what you think, Maeve, you don't know how wrong you are. The only difference between you and me is that you publicly acknowledged your love by marrying the person of your choice. I can never have that luxury.'

'Luxury?' Her laugh was bitter. 'I can think of another word for it. Maybe if I'd had the gumption to join a nunnery I could have saved myself a whole lot of heartache . . . Only they don't have nuns in the Presbyterian Church!'

He looked at her silently for a moment or two. He knew only too well what was going on in her mind. He had seen with his own eyes what life had deteriorated to with Danny. But she had her dignity. He must let her explain it in her own way, if she wanted to. 'Is it that bad, Maeve?'

She nodded, her fingers twisting in her lap, as she avoided his eyes and stared into the fire. 'It's worse.'

'Do you want to talk about it?'

His voice was soft and persuasively gentle, but what could she tell him? Could she tell him the truth – that she no longer loved his brother, but was now convinced she had fallen deeply, heartbreakingly, in love with him? Could she tell him that? Could she tell him that he filled a need in her that Danny could never fill? She had looked into his very soul today out there on the hilltop and it had touched a chord in her own psyche that would remain with her for ever. He had opened up a whole new world to her – a world of poetry and literature, with words that wove spells around her heart . . . A world of beauty and gentleness that Danny, with his guns and violence, could never enter . . .

'Do you want to talk about it, Maeve?' He repeated the words softly, hesitantly.

She shook her head. 'No, I can't – and please don't ask me . . .' Bitter tears filled her eyes and she brushed them away impatiently, determined not to spoil the evening by breaking down in front of him. But it was too late. His hand reached out towards her.

'Don't Maeve, don't cry. Please . . .' He knelt down beside her, brushing the teardrops from her cheeks with the tips of his fingers. His breath was warm on her face as he said softly, 'I know why not . . . God help me, I know.'

She turned from him, wrenching herself free from his grasp. A film of sweat had broken out on her skin, under the fine woollen cloth of the dressing-gown and the lace-trimmed lawn of the underwear beneath. He was too close to her, much too close. Surely he could realise that too?

She shook her head. 'I'm sorry . . . I'm being silly.' But still she could not look at him. There was no way she could turn and face the look in those dark unfathomable eyes.

'You don't have to apologise. Not to me.' His hand reached out and touched the nape of her neck, sending a shiver through her body that was impossible to disguise.

She half-turned towards him. 'Dermot . . .' She whispered his name. Then, suddenly, she was in his arms, and he was kissing the salt tears from her face, his lips burning a trail across her damp skin, as his hands cupped her cheeks.

'Maeve, my love, my love . . .' His mouth found hers and the depth and urgency of his kiss made her gasp helplessly and fight for breath. Her hands clutched at his hair, then pushed against the broad mass of his shoulders. Was she fighting against him, or simply responding in kind to the almost animal passion that had him in its thrall? She was sure of nothing any more. Nothing other than the undeniable fact that she wanted him. She wanted him more, much more than she had ever wanted his brother. She wanted him more than she had ever wanted any man.

She was not aware of them shedding their clothes, she was

164

aware only of his voice repeating her name over and over, and the exquisite agony of the touch of skin on skin as his body, smooth and white in the firelight, met hers.

He took her slowly, gently, with infinite tenderness, their bodies moving in perfect, silent unison on the soft wool of the rug. The love that had been denied for so long was transformed into an act of infinite beauty that bore no resemblance to what had ever taken place between her and Danny.

Tears spilled in streams from beneath her closed lids as he carried her higher and higher to the ultimate plateau. Then she cried aloud, her nails digging into the soft white flesh of his shoulders, as the dam of thwarted passion that had been threatening to explode for so long, burst forth and engulfed them both.

It was only when he lay back exhausted on the rug and threw an arm across his face that she realised that he had cried too.

She pulled herself up on the mat and gazed down at the motionless figure beside her. Her eyes moved in a slow caress over the white, almost translucent skin. It was covered from head to foot with a soft, dark down that thickened to a curling mass on the broad wall of his chest. She had never thought of a man as beautiful before, but he was truly beautiful.

Tears filled her eyes once more and she turned away, unable to bear to look any longer on what could never be hers. No matter how she might wish it otherwise, Dermot could never be her husband. She was married to his brother and he was married to the Church.

'Dear God, what a mess!'

Her hopeless cry made him sit up and place a comforting arm around her shoulders. He could say nothing to comfort her. What had just occurred between them was what he had longed for, yet dreaded, from the first moment he had ever set eyes on her. Oh yes, he had committed the ultimate sin many, many times in the privacy of his own thoughts.

They dressed with their backs turned to each other, as if a sudden shame had descended to blight the happiness of a few short moments ago.

He seemed like a stranger — a tall, dark stranger dressed in the robes of a Church that was not her own, and whose ways she could not begin to comprehend. But a Church that had claimed this man that she loved with both body and soul.

'It's not fair! It's just not fair!' She was not even sure she believed in this God that he had renounced the world for. She shook her head wildly, as she turned from him, ashamed of the tears that coursed once again down her cheeks.

She felt his hands on her shoulders. He knew exactly what she meant, but had no words of comfort to give. Tonight he had his own cross to bear. He had betrayed his Lord for the sins of the flesh, and the knowledge twisted a knife deep within him.

'I'm going now, Maeve. I'm sorry . . .'

She made no sound or indication that she had heard as he left the room, quietly closing the door behind him. What was he sorry for? For the fact that he was leaving – or the fact that he had just made love to her? She had no way of knowing. Both most probably.

She walked to the window and watched his tall figure disappear into the darkness of Marine Parade. If he was lucky he would be just in time for the last train back to Dublin. Back to the world of McIntyre Street and all the miseries that entailed.

With a sigh, she sat down on the edge of the bed and stared with unseeing eyes at the wall. The warm afterglow of their love still permeated her body, but her mind was a cold, dark, empty place.

She felt sorry for them both in a way – for both Dermot and Danny. As brothers, on the surface they were as different in character as could be, but beneath it all they were so alike – both dreamers, both sons of old Mother Ireland who would be condemned to pay the penalty exacted by those very dreams by which they lived. Danny, who attempted to fulfil his dreams of a free Ireland by action only to see that very dream reduced to blood and ashes amid the carnage of the Easter Rising, and Dermot, whose dreams would always be of the mind, but whose poetry and fine words could never make up for the frustrations of the flesh. He could spellbind her with his words, but words could never take the place of actions. His real mistress was the Church of Rome, and it demanded total fidelity. A bitter smile twisted Maeve's lips. What Rome really demanded was a clergy of eunuchs to administer its dogma. It did not require full-blooded men with normal, healthy desires. If they joined its ranks, it tore them apart. It subjugated them into total subservience. Unless they had the guts to say, *No, I can serve my God without denying my masculinity.* She closed her eyes and sighed deeply. Had Dermot the strength to make that decision? Had she the strength to ask him? And what of Danny? Between them for ever stood the pugnacious, red-headed presence of her husband – his brother. Where, in heaven's name, did she – did any of them – go from here?

All she had wanted out of life was a man to love her – love her above all else. She had thought that Danny would provide her with that perfect love, only to find that in Mother Ireland he had an even more demanding mistress than that slut Cissie O'Rourke. No, she would never come near to being the only love in her husband's life. And neither would she in his brother's. Had she remained in love with Danny, perhaps she could have come to terms with sharing him with another woman . . . But that was over now. That part of her life was as dead as the men who had fallen in the name of liberty in the General Post Office that awful day last Easter. She had moved on since then. She had grown up. She had finally admitted to herself that she was in love with another man. She was in love with Dermot. And just how did one come to terms with playing second fiddle to God himself?

A knock at the bedroom door made her look round with a start. It couldn't be? Or could it? Please, let it be . . . Let him have come back . . . Her heart in her mouth, she raced across the room and threw open the door.

'I've brought Kieran back, Mrs Donovan. He's been as good as gold. Have you have a nice rest?'

She stared uncomprehendingly into the eyes of the strange young woman in front of her. 'Oh – you must be Sinead . . . Yes, yes thank you. I had a very nice rest . . .'

Chapter 17

'Stay you here, John-Joe, boy, and I'll nip round to her old man's place for another bottle.' Danny got up from the chair in front of Cissie's kitchen fire and reached for his jacket. To run out of a drop of the hard stuff when they were on the point of setting out on a job was unthinkable.

'Are ye sure I can't go?' John-Joe O'Malley made to rise from his own chair, but a dismissive gesture of the arm from Danny made him sit down again.

'Naw, the old bugger won't part with it to the likes o' you. He will for me, though. I'm his blue-eyed boy, isn't that right, Cis?'

Cissie O'Rourke threw a strained smile in his direction. 'Aye, you could be right there.' He wasn't, though. She was certain of that. Her father was sick to death with the easy-come, easy-go way in which Danny seemed to be treating his youngest daughter. And the fact that he had gone and married yon snooty Protestant Maeve Ballantine instead of her had been enough to give the old man an apopleptic fit. 'You'll not be long, I take it?' She was all too used to his nipping out for a drink or cigarettes and not coming back for days.

'D'ye hear that, John-Joe? Always bloody keeping track of me, so she is. There's no apron string long enough to keep a woman happy!'

He turned to Cissie. 'No, I'll not be long. Ten minutes at the most. Have I not just spent ten minutes already telling you we're off to do the business for the cause tonight? Anyway, if I leave you any longer on your own wi' the likes o' him around, it'll not be just one squalling brat you'll be left to deal with!' He jabbed a thumb in his friend's direction, before winking broadly and tucking the ends of his scarf into his jacket as he headed for the street.

Cissie's pink cheeks turned puce as the door slammed behind him and, too embarrassed to look at John-Joe, she hurried through to the next room where an irate Caitlin was screaming to get out of her cot.

John-Joe watched her cross the room, his eyes taking in the well-rounded hips in the floral print, crossover apron. Even in her workaday clothes she was a fine figure of a woman. But then he had always thought so, ever since they had attended infant school together. He could not remember a time when his conception of idealised womanhood did not centre on Cissie O'Rourke.

In a way it had been a blessing in disguise when his brother Con had been killed last Easter, for it seemed only natural that he should step into the breach as Danny's right-hand man. Of course he had been sorry about Con, shattered even, for he was the one of his five brothers that he had been closest to, but being around Danny much more than in the past meant that he had a ready-made excuse to see more of Cissie. And that was the most important thing in his life. Yes, more important than the cause even. He had never been as politically minded as Con — never. He didn't mind using a gun now and then; it was quite exciting at times, but the other stuff — the spouting of endless quotes from Tone and Marx and the rest of them, and the hours of endless, pointless discussion . . . Well, that left him completely cold.

'She hears her Daddy's voice and wants to be in on things.' Cissie's voice sounded from the doorway, as she brought her daughter through and set her down on the rug in front of the fire. The small face, bright red from screaming, was now smiling broadly.

John-Joe looked down at her, then up at her mother. 'She's a fine-looking kid, so she is. D'ye not get fed up, Cissie, bringing her up on your own like this?'

Cissie looked surprised. 'Sure an' I'm not on my own — there's Danny!'

John-Joe shook his head. 'That's hardly the same as a proper husband now, is it? I mean, there must be times you'd like to have somebody permanent around the place.'

Cissie studied her nails, and she leant against the brass rail above the mantelpiece. 'Aye, I suppose you're right there. But life never turns out quite as we hope it will, does it? You should know that, John-Joe O'Malley, what with Con being gunned down just before his wedding an' all.'

John-Joe nodded, acknowledging the truth of her statement. Not that it had taken Con's fiancée long to get over it. 'I wouldn't worry about Maureen, if I were you. She's already walking out with a fella from the accounts department of Jacob's biscuit factory. Has been these past few weeks.'

He paused, as if searching for the right words, so as not to cause undue offence. 'But what about you, Cissie? What if anything was to happen to Danny? You'd surely not intend going around in widow's weeds for the rest of your life?'

A bitter smile twitched the corners of Cissie's lips. 'That would hardly be appropriate, would it now? Seeing as I'd not be his widow!'

He flushed and inwardly cursed his stupidity. 'You know what I mean.'

'Aye, I know what you mean all right,' she sighed. 'And you're right there. I'd never think of looking at another man while Danny's alive, but if anything was to happen to him . . .' She paused, then gave a rueful laugh. 'I'd marry the first stupid devil who was daft enough to ask me!'

John-Joe pondered on those words as the van rattled its way down the rutted road between Roscrea and Tipperary. It was only Tuesday afternoon, but they seemed to have been on the road for days. They were headed for a place in the Galtee Mountains; some cave or other, near a place he'd never heard of called Kilbeheny. According to Danny, they were to meet somebody there called McMahon who would take delivery of the explosives they had piled into the back of the van, under the sheaves of hay. He could think of better ways of spending his time, as he glanced across at his companion.

Danny, however, had his mind on other things. Maeve should have been in Kingstown for over twenty-four hours by now, ensconced in some nice little guest house, with Dermot to make sure the journey was as trouble-free as possible. A satisfied smile creased his face. It made him feel good to be able to dish out enough money for that type of thing. His pride had taken quite a knocking over the past year, knowing he could never provide her with the things she had been used to – but things were different now. His work for the cause had opened up a whole new world. One single raid could net as much as a hundred pounds or more and whatever cut he took in expenses was his own affair.

He felt in his back pocket with his left hand. The thick wad of notes that had been making a comfortable bulge for the past week was sadly depleted, thanks to Maeve. In fact, all he'd been able to leave Cissie when they left Dublin yesterday was three quid.

He pulled out the notes that were left and grimaced. 'One pound, ten bloody bob!' He glanced across at John-Joe. 'Got much on you, boyo?'

John-Joe felt inside the left-hand pocket of his trousers. Coins jingled as he extracted a small handful. A half-crown, three pennies and a bent silver sixpence lay alongside a screwed-up ten-shilling note. 'Thirteen and threepence,' he said, lifting his backside off the seat as he replaced them.

'That won't get you far.'

'What d'ye suggest, then? We print our own? There's no fund-raising raid planned for at least a week, is there?'

Danny nodded. 'You're right there.'

'So?'

'So we do something about it. Don't we?'

John-Joe's pulse raced faster as he stared out through the murky windscreen. 'Got anything special in mind?'

Danny nodded, a secretive, superior smile playing around the corners of his mouth. 'Wait and see.'

It took less than an hour for the secret to be revealed. 'There it is,' Danny said softly, as the van drew up slowly at the side of the road leading into a tiny hamlet. 'It doesn't look much, but, believe me, there's some amount of money goes over that counter on a Friday and Saturday night.'

John-Joe gazed in bemusement at the sign hanging above the door of the whitewashed, single-storey building. 'The Roaring Bull,' he said in a hushed voice. 'You're going to do it over?'

'Right first time. Got your handpiece?'

171

John-Joe's hand reached automatically for the Mauser pistol tucked into the waistband of his trousers, then he drew back. 'There's no need for that, is there?'

Danny put the van into gear once more and it began to creep slowly towards the target. 'Don't be dumb, boyo. It's the only protection we've got if anybody turns funny. And if they don't – well, it sure scares the hell out o' them, that's for sure.'

John-Joe nodded unsurely. He hadn't bargained for this type of excitement so early in the week. But the more he thought about it . . . 'I'm right behind you, Danny boy!'

Danny threw a grin across the tiny confines of the cab. 'Not literally, if you don't mind. I get kind o' nervous when somebody is following me with a loaded gun pointed at my back – friend or foe!'

A laugh came from the next seat. What a thing to say! Or was it? John-Joe frowned slightly, pursing his lips as his mind raced on ahead. Rumour had it quite a few personal feuds had been settled under the guise of the cause. He glanced back across at his companion. When you thought about it, if you wanted to get rid of someone, it would certainly be the easiest way to do it . . .

A faint screech of brakes brought the van to a halt in front of the pub and Danny turned to him, his hushed voice breaking into the train of thought. 'I'll go in first and you come right behind. Keep me well covered. You never know who's going to appear from the street door in a place like this. And I don't mean any old biddy – there are some real hard nuts among the Young Turks around here.'

They got out of the van together and John-Joe stood behind Danny as he pushed open the brown-painted door. It creaked heavily on its hinges, but the noise seemed to have no effect in raising any sign of the landlord.

They had entered a long room with a black varnished bar running most of its length. There were no other customers; it was too early in the day, probably, and for that they were grateful. A highly-coloured picture of the Virgin Mary, covered in a garland of flowers, looked down at them from the wall opposite and John-Joe studiously avoided her eyes.

'Get the shooter out and keep me covered!' Danny hissed, as

he vaulted the bar and landed with a clatter of studded boots on the other side.

John-Joe watched in silence as Danny searched for the usual cash-drawer beneath the counter. The latter cursed beneath his breath as his fingers touched only planed wood. Why hadn't he paid more attention when he was last here with Con?

'It's behind you!' John-Joe's voice ended the search abruptly as he spotted the unusual sight of a large, ornamental brass till in amongst the bottles on the shelf behind.

Danny turned and gave a delighted gasp at the sight of it. As he pulled open the drawer and stared down at the contents, John-Joe felt his pulse begin to race and a cold sweat broke out on the surface of his skin. His blue eyes stared as if fixated at Danny's back. His companion was muttering gleefully to himself as he stuffed his pockets with the contents of the till drawer, but all John-Joe could hear was Cissie's voice: . . . *If anything was to happen to him, I'd marry the first stupid devil who was daft enough to ask me.*

A bead of sweat formed on the stubble above his upper lip as his right index finger twitched on the trigger of the gun. She could be his. In the split second it took to pull the trigger, Cissie could be his. No one would ever know. They would assume he had been killed on the job. Cissie could be his! His pulse raced even faster at the sight, sound and smell of her filled his senses . . .

Crack! The sound of the bullet was followed by a much lower strangled, hissing sound that reminded him, for a fleeting second, of the air being let out of a tyre under water. Then Danny crumpled, as if in slow motion, to a heap on the floor.

He felt sick, physically sick, as he leapt over the counter to gaze in morbid horror at what he had done. Danny was slumped in an ungainly heap on the stone slabs, his head lolling at a ludicrous angle on his shoulders. The bullet had passed through the base of his neck, and a trickle of blood was forming at the corner of his mouth. He was dead all right; there could be no doubt about that.

John-Joe was so intent on gazing at his handiwork that he was totally unaware of the horror-stricken face staring at him from a side door to the left of the bar.

The shot that rang out was louder than the one that had killed Danny, but it had the same effect. John-Joe O'Malley never even glimpsed his killer as he slumped backwards on to the dead body of his friend. The pistol that had ended Danny Donovan's life, still smoking faintly from the barrel, clattered noisily to the stone floor and lay just out of reach of the outstretched lifeless hand.

'Holy Mary and Joseph!' The old man in the doorway gripped his rifle tightly in his knotted hands as he crossed the floor to gaze in a mixture of horror and relief at the body of the man he had just killed. 'There are two of the buggers!'

It was over twenty-four hours before Maeve heard of her husband's death. Identification had been difficult, but the police had eventually traced their identity through the owner of the van – a distant uncle of John-Joe's.

To add to her misery, it was Dermot who was called upon to break the news. It was like a vengeance wrought by God for what had happened in Mrs Devlin's upstairs bedroom in Kingstown. And Dermot felt the same, she was sure of that. He could not even look her straight in the eyes.

She shook her head for the umpteenth time. 'But what made that old man shoot them? They were only robbing a till, for heaven's sake!' Only robbing a till . . . At one time even that would have horrified her.

Dermot shrugged his shoulders helplessly. 'They say one of them was standing there pointing a gun at him, so he had no choice.'

'And is it true?'

'Two Mausers were found on them, and one had been fired.'

'The poor man must have had no choice then. It was self-defence.'

'It looks like it.'

It was no consolation. In fact, it made things even worse.

She walked to the window and closed the curtains on the coming night. Dermot would be taking the funeral. There would be no way he could get out of it and the knowledge made her feel physically sick. And God only knew how he felt about it. She could not bear to look at him as she said softly, 'The funeral's tomorrow, you say?'

He shifted uncomfortably on his feet. 'That's up to you, Maeve. You're his next of kin. You're his wife.'

She looked at him listlessly from across the dimly-lit room and shook her head. 'Wrong, Dermot. I'm his widow.'

Chapter 18

Maeve finished tying the string round the brown paper parcel and stood back in satisfaction. It was a bit bulky, maybe, but she should be able to manage it. If need be, she could wheel it round to Amy's in Kieran's pram.

It had taken the best part of six weeks to bring herself to sort out Danny's things. It was as if part of him still lingered there in the dark blue Sunday suit and the other oddments of everyday clothes that made up his half of the wardrobe. To throw them out was to acknowledge he had gone for good – that he really was dead and she was alone in the world. It was a big step to take.

It had been a good idea, though, to take them round to Amy's. To throw them out, or worse sell them, would be unthinkable, and to give them to a neighbour would be every bit as bad. She couldn't have borne it to see any old Tom, Dick or Harry walking down the street wearing Danny's clothes. No, taking them to Amy's meant that she would never see them again, but would have the satisfaction of knowing they would be put to good use. One of her war charities would see to that.

She lifted the parcel from the middle of the kitchen table and placed it on the floor by the door. Even that brief exertion found her sighing heavily afterwards. She had been so tired recently – really tired. And to make matters worse her period was late. It had been due almost a month ago and still hadn't arrived. It was probably the shock of Danny's death; emotional upheavals could play havoc with your monthly cycle, so she had heard.

Yes, it would be good to see Amy again, she decided. Even if she hadn't had a ready-made excuse like the clothes, she would have found some reason to see her old friend again. She no longer had to keep such visits to her old part of the city a secret; she was behoven to no one now that Danny was dead. She was free.

A wave of guilt washed over her. She would never have wished Danny dead, no matter how much she had come to hate her life with him, that was certainly true. In fact, the sense of liberation she had expected to feel had never really happened. Instead, she felt only a sense of bewilderment and, yes, loneliness; but over all other emotions, she felt a profound sense of guilt.

The fact that he had met his death on the very day she had made love with Dermot was a bitter pill to swallow. Divine retribution almost. She knew that was how Dermot felt about it and knowing that fact twisted a knife in her heart.

That Tuesday in Kingstown, both on Killiney Hill and afterwards in the bedroom of Mrs Devlin's guest house, had been the most enchanted few hours she had ever known. But Danny's death had tarnished them beyond redemption. Nothing could ever change that; no tears or wishing could ever change that fact.

It was snowing slightly when she left the house and at first she thought of leaving Kieran with Mrs Maloney, but changed her mind. The walk would probably do him good; he hadn't been out of the house very much recently. It would do them both good. She smiled at him over the top of the parcel of his father's clothes as they made their way along the frozen pavements. He had most of his front teeth now and it was Danny's face that chortled back at her from behind the rainflap of the pram cover.

She wished she could love him more – love him the way her own mother loved her brother Charlie. With a bit of luck, Amy might have word of Charlie. She crossed her fingers inside the angora mittens as she manoeuvred the pram carefully around a group of children pulling a sledge.

She deliberately avoided looking into shop windows with their colourful Christmas displays. To be poor at this time of year was surely the most cruel of all fates for a parent. She thought of the toy-filled nursery of her old home in Jubilee Avenue and of the meagre supply she had been able to buy Kieran: a threadbare golliwog bought at a local Salvation Army jumble sale, and two balls she had knitted with left-over remnants of wool. God only knew what he would get for

Christmas. She had exactly two pounds twelve shillings left of the money Danny had given her before he was killed, and what was going to happen when that ran out she shuddered to think.

As she rounded the corner into Amy's street the gaily decorated Christmas trees seemed to mock at her from the windows of the elegant drawing-rooms, where log fires blazed merrily in the shining grates. Just across the Green from here one such tree would be twinkling in the front window of number nine Jubilee Avenue; the only difference being, this year there would be only her mother and father left at home to trim it.

A rosy-cheeked maid whom Maeve had never seen before let her and the baby and pram into the front hall of the Grafton house. 'I believe Miss Amy's in the conservatory, ma'm, attending to the Christmas flowers. If you'll be good enough to wait, I'll let her know you're here. Who shall I say has called?'

'Maeve – Maeve Ballantine,' Maeve replied automatically, then stared in embarrassment after the disappearing figure of the maid. What on earth made her say that? It wasn't as if she was ashamed of the name Donovan, far from it. Maybe it was simply being back in this her old world once again. She shook her head, feeling vaguely uncomfortable as she waited for her friend.

As she expected, Amy was delighted to see her, and the baby, and more than touched that she should feel able to part with Danny's clothes. 'I'd no idea you'd been widowed, Maeve,' she said, aghast. 'You poor thing. And that poor wee mite – he'll never know his father. How did it happen?'

Maeve looked away, breaking Amy's concerned gaze, as the hot flush of embarrassment flooded her cheeks. 'It – it was an accident. He was working in Tipperary. I – I'm afraid I don't have too many of the details.'

'Of course, I understand.' Amy took her arm in a consoling gesture. 'We'll not dwell on it. It must be very painful for you still. Let's go into the drawing-room where it's warm and I'll tell Bridget to fetch us some tea.'

Relieved to have got the subject of Danny's death out of the way so quickly, Maeve obediently picked Kieran out of the pram and allowed herself to be led into the room with the Christmas tree. It smelt of pine needles and the crackle of burning birch logs greeted them as Amy led the way to a deep, buttoned-leather chesterfield settee in front of the fire. They sat down side by side, with Kieran propped up in the middle between two cushions, as Amy clasped her slim hands excitedly in her lap.

'I'm so glad you called, Maeve. I really am. I would have called on you anyway within the next few days. I had another letter from your brother Charlie last week.'

'From Charlie!' Maeve almost shouted the words. 'But that's wonderful! Is he all right? Oh, do tell me what he said, Amy, please. I've been so worried with all that fighting along the Somme. Is he there? Is he in the thick of it?'

Amy got up and walked to a rosewood writing-desk by one of the windows. 'They're not allowed to say very much – you know with censorship and all that – but I believe, when he wrote it, he was near a place called Beaucourt-sur-Ancre. It was only a few lines scribbled in reply to my own letter before his battalion went over the top again, but he did say he was so pleased to get your address. He was to write to you at the first possible opportunity. You should be hearing any day.'

She fished about in the pigeon-holes inside the desk for a moment. 'Here it is!'

Maeve took the stained envelope with a grateful smile and carefully unfolded the single page on her lap. It was dated just over three weeks previously:

13th November, 1916.

Dear Amy,

I can't tell you how good it was to hear from you again, and to have Maeve's address at last. I will write to her at the first possible opportunity, which will probably be in a day or two. From tomorrow my men and I will be kept pretty busy, but, with luck, once we have Fritz on the run again, there will be a few precious moments to put pen to paper. It tickles me to know I am an uncle. If you should see Maeve and her little son before she gets my letter, give her all my love and tell her I think of them both often. Our thoughts are with you all at home as Christmas draws near once more. Take special care of yourself and do write again. Your letters are a breath of fresh air in a polluted world.

> Till later,
> Believe me to be,
> Yours very truly,
> Charles W. Ballantine.

Maeve re-read the words before handing the letter back to Amy. She had the almost uncontrollable urge to cry. It was stupid, but there it was.

'It's hard to tell of course, but he sounds in quite good heart.' Amy moved over on the settee slightly to make room for the small Indian table the maid brought across and set down between them to put the tea tray on.

'Charlie always managed to put a good face on things. Not like me, I'm afraid. I've had the misfortune to wear my heart on my sleeve all my life, which is far from the best policy.'

Amy nodded sympathetically as they tucked into the cake and tea. 'It's easier for men, I always think. They're taught from childhood to keep a stiff upper lip. When my brother Harry's "intended" died of consumption last year he didn't seem to bat an eyelid, but I cried buckets over Will's death. They do say a woman feels things deeper, though, but a man's love lasts longer. Do you think that's really true, Maeve?'

Maeve placed a butterless pancake in Kieran's chubby fist and thought about the question. Had she been the more besotted of the pair between her and Danny? Certainly her love for him had appeared to wane much the quicker if lack of interest in the physical side of their marriage was anything to go by. 'I really don't know, Amy, and that's the truth. I haven't really had all that much experience of men as such.'

Amy's blue eyes widened. 'But, Maeve, you're quite the woman of the world now. I mean, being a wife, a mother, and a widow all before you're even twenty. Why, how many other girls do you know who can say that?'

She took another sip of her tea and replaced the cup in the saucer. The fine porcelain tinkled musically as she placed it back on the table-top. 'I – I know it's rather soon to ask, but do you think you'll ever remarry? I mean, if you do will it be

180

another . . .' she paused, her brow furrowing as she searched for the right word, '. . . another rebel?'

Maeve stifled a smile. She had spoken the word in a hushed, almost shocked tone. 'I hadn't even considered such a thing,' she said at last, 'any more than I suspect you've considered getting engaged again.'

Amy's delicate brows quirked above the blue eyes and she nodded mutely. The awful thing was, she *had* considered getting engaged once again. She had adored being engaged more than anything in her life and Will's death seemed to have plunged her into a limbo, to her mind, even worse than widowhood. At least Maeve had her baby for consolation. What did she have, but more endless years of boredom cooped up in this house with her mother and father?

The narrow shoulders in the black silk taffeta shrugged helplessly. 'Even if either of us had considered such a thing, it would be a fruitless desire, with every half-decent young man bogged down in the Flanders mud, don't you agree?'

Maeve thought a lot about her conversation with Amy over the next week, but most of all she looked for the postman. The fact that he never came brought all sorts of fears to her mind. Was Charlie dead? Had he been captured by the Germans? Or was he simply lying wounded somewhere? Every scenario her imagination painted was more lurid and depressing than the last. Her total absorption with getting a letter from her brother put even her thoughts of Dermot into second place.

Two very different men, two very different uniforms. One a soldier, the other a priest, but both meant more to her than any other living person, except perhaps Kieran. But although they seemed to absorb almost all of her inner life these days, she knew she was simply a figure on the periphery of theirs. They were out there in the real world, while she was stuck in here playing nursemaid to a young baby. In fact, it was even worse than that, for nursemaids got paid, while her own financial situation was becoming increasingly desperate. Not that she had ever mentioned it to anyone. She still had her pride, although she had little else left in the world.

It seemed a lifetime since she had last seen Dermot; in fact, it was only a little over a fortnight. But although she was seeing less and less of him these days, he was visiting Mary-Agnes just as regularly, she had learned that much from Katie, and the knowledge upset her. It shouldn't really, for she knew the reason for his absence, but that was no consolation. Every time the clock on the mantelpiece struck seven, something inside her would quiver in anticipation. That was usually the time he left his sister's and, in earlier times, would be heading for her own door. But not now.

'Dermot must be much busier these days, Maeve. Do you mind him not calling so much in the evenings?' Katie looked up at her curiously, sucking the end of a strand of curling red hair, as she rolled one of Kieran's woollen balls across the pram cover to him. The infant chortled in delight as his small fingers pushed it back. It was a game he never tired of.

'Sure and it's not up to me to monopolise his time. Your brother's a busy man, Kathleen Donovan. Parish priests always are. There are hundreds of other people out there hoping for a visit from him. People with real problems they want to discuss. He's got more to do than spend his time sitting around drinking cups of tea in here!'

Katie looked unconvinced. 'He always asks me how you're getting on, though, when he comes to see us.'

Maeve's eyebrows rose. 'Oh really? And what do you say to that, may I ask?'

'I tell him to go and see for himself!'

Maeve tried in vain to stifle the smile that came to her lips as she opened her mouth to reply, but a tentative knock at the door made her look round in surprise.

'D'you think that's him, Maeve? D'you think that's him?' Katie's excited question duplicated the one uppermost in her own mind.

'There's only one way of finding out, isn't there?'

She lifted her hands out of the sink and dried them on a hand towel hanging on a hook on the wall. He had never waited to be let in before. Surely it hadn't come down to this?

Casting a slightly anxious glance at her small sister-in-law, she walked quickly across the floor and, pausing only momentarily before the closed door, she opened it with a flourish. The smile that she had so carefully forced to her lips died instantly as she gazed in a mixture of horror and astonishment at the figure on the doorstep.

'Hello, Maeve.'

'Mother!'

Chapter 19

'Well, aren't you going to ask me in? You don't expect me to say my piece out here on the step, do you?' Emily Ballantine's bespectacled eyes peered first at her daughter, then past her into the lamplit interior of the room beyond.

Maeve's face had gone quite white. She had half-expected, half-hoped, to see the tall, slightly stooped figure of Dermot standing there on the ice-encrusted step. Her mother was the very last person she had imagined to find. 'Of – of course.'

She stepped aside, to allow the older woman to enter, the smell of gardenia-scented cologne assailing her nostrils as the heavily furred figure brushed past her and entered the tiny kitchen.

Emily Ballantine was an imposing figure, especially in so small a room. She was a good half-head taller than her daughter; all of five feet nine inches, and was made to look even bigger by the high-heeled brown leather boots at one end of her ample figure and the ostrich-feathered toque that adorned the other, beneath which a fine head of pure white hair curled. Her brown wool coat had an enormous shawl collar in the finest musquash fur, and the sleeves and hemline were also fur-trimmed.

Her grey-blue eyes, behind the half-moon glass of the spectacles, moved slowly round the room, coming to rest at last on the pram containing her grandson, and the young girl gripping tightly to the handle. Deliberately ignoring the infant, she decided to address the elder child. 'And who may you be, young lady?'

Katie gazed transfixed at the figure before her. Never in her life had she been addressed by such a grand lady before. Not knowing quite how to react, but desperate not to displease, she let go the pram handle and attempted a curtsy. 'Kathleen Donovan, if you please, ma'm.'

'Katie's Danny's younger sister,' Maeve said, finding her voice at last.

'And the child?' Her mother's eyes flicked back to the woollen ball-chewing figure of Kieran in the pram.

'He's my son.' Maeve coloured deeply as she spoke the words.

'He must look like his father. There's never been red hair in my family, or your father's. It's very Irish.'

Maeve bristled. By the way the last sentence was spoken, it might as well have been, 'It's very common.' 'No, it's a pity. We all seem to be very ordinary browns and blacks, don't we? Would you care for a cup of tea, Mother?'

'It's not a social visit, Maeve. I might as well make that clear at the outset. I'm here because Charlie has begged me to come.'

'Charlie? You've heard from Charlie?' It was impossible to contain the excitement in her voice.

Her mother nodded, the narrow lips pursing, as she said slowly, 'Charlie's home, Maeve. There was a consignment of wounded arrived back in Dublin from France last week and he was in it.'

'He's been home for a whole week and this is the first I've heard of it?' Maeve almost screamed the words. 'How badly wounded is he? It's not that serious, is it? He will live, won't he?' The words came tumbling out.

The head beneath the feathered toque nodded impatiently. 'If there had been any real doubt of that, you would have been informed before this. Anyway, there's no reason for you getting on your high horse. How were we supposed to inform you when you've never had the civility to give us your address?'

Maeve bridled, digging her nails into the palms of her hands to control herself. They had never asked for it, not once, nor made the slightest effort to find it out, as far as she knew. 'How did you get hold of it, then?'

'From Charlie – who do you think? It seems he got it sent by that Grafton girl on the other side of the Green. For all your father and I know, the whole of Dublin's been privy to it but us.' She flicked a leather glove impatiently at the melting snowflakes still clinging to her coat collar. 'Anyway, that's neither here nor there. Charlie has been asking for you. In fact, he's given us no peace whatsoever since he got back. He wants to see you, Maeve, and that's why I'm here. I tried to get your father to come, but he's still . . .' she paused, a pained expression on her face, 'he's still very upset about what you did to us. However, I hear your husband's been killed recently, so maybe it's the time to let bygones be bygones.'

Maeve stared at her, a cold anger rising within. She might just be acceptable now, might she, now that Danny was dead? With no Catholic rebel husband in tow, they might just deign to let her over the doorstep.

'Well, what do you say? Do you want to come and see Charlie, or not? As I said, your father and I are quite willing to let the past remain in the past now you're on your own in the world.'

'Not quite, mother. Not quite. You've forgotten Danny's child, haven't you? You've forgotten Kieran.' She almost added 'with his red Irish hair', but stopped herself in time.

Mrs Ballantine cast a glance across at the baby, causing Katie to move a defensive step nearer to him. 'Your father has never been one to shirk his responsibilities. He'll recognise the child, of course.'

'Recognise him?' Maeve shook her head in wonderment. What was this, some crude Victorian melodrama? 'What do you mean – he'll recognise him, for heaven's sake? What in God's name's the alternative? Would you have him wait outside the door in his pram in the snow while you allowed me inside for my audience with Charlie?'

It was now the other's turn to bristle. 'There's no need for that kind of language, Maeve, no need at all. I can see what living in a place like this for a year has done to you, and it's not a pretty sight. Of course the child can come in. Why, even the servants' offspring are remembered by a little something round the tree every Christmas, you know that.'

They stared at one another across the room, the minds of both women flying back to so many similar confrontations last summer, before Maeve finally walked out of the family home for good.

With a set face, Maeve squeezed past her mother to lift the kettle off the range to fill it from the enamel pail that stood on the table by the sink. But she had only got as far as lifting the lid when the sound of the door opening made her glance round, expecting to see her mother on her way out. Instead, a faint gasp of surprise left her lips.

'Dermot!'

He stood on the open doorway, a look of surprise and momentary embarrassment on his face at the sight of the roomful of people. 'I'm sorry, Maeve, I'll not disturb you. I didn't realise you had guests.'

Maeve stared across at him. His dark priest's clothing and hat were covered in fresh snowflakes, giving him a curious speckled appearance. But his face – his face still made her heart turn somersaults in her breast. 'You'll stay where you are! Anyway, it's not a guest, it's my mother.'

She turned to address the bulky figure in the middle of the floor. 'Mother, I'd like you to meet Father Dermot Donovan – my brother-in-law.'

Emily Ballantine's brows rose a good fraction of an inch in surprise. 'Why, Maeve, you never told me you had a man of God in the family!' She came forward and extended a beringed hand towards Dermot, who took it with a slightly bemused expression on his face.

''Tis a real pleasure to make your acquaintance at last, Mrs Ballantine.'

'And yours too, young man. You're Maeve's late husband's brother, I take it.'

Dermot nodded. 'Aye, I'm Danny's brother.'

'I'm afraid I didn't get the chance to know your brother well, Father, but may I extend my family's deepest sympathies over his death.'

'Why, thank you, Mrs Ballantine. I appreciate that.' He cast a quick glance at Maeve, who was still standing with the kettle in her hand.

Two angry red spots had risen on the pale skin of her cheeks. How dare she! How dare her mother say such a thing! The sanctimonious old bitch! Not once had she as much as expressed any kind of regret to her over Danny's death – and she was his widow!

An uncomfortable silence fell. Dermot coughed and backed

towards the door once more. 'Well, I only called in to make sure you were all right, Maeve. If you'll excuse me I'll better be getting back. It – it's been a pleasure to meet you at last, Mrs Ballantine.'

'Now just a minute, young man. You'll catch your death out in that snow without a decent coat on you. I'm just leaving anyway, and I've got a cab waiting just down the street. I'll tell the jarvey to let you off wherever you wish to go. I can't have my late son-in-law's brother catching his death as well now, can I?'

She turned and extended a smile in Maeve's direction. 'Maeve, dear, don't bother with the tea. I think it's much more important that this young man gets home warm and safe on a terrible night like this, don't you?'

Maeve looked from one to the other, the anger still boiling within her. 'Of course.'

Emily Ballantine beamed. 'Right then, that settles it. Now when can I tell Charlie to expect you? It had better be within the next few days or I swear he'll not believe I've even been here tonight!'

Maeve paused in her action of filling the kettle, aware of Dermot's, as well as her mother's eyes on her. 'Tell him I'll call round tomorrow afternoon, mother. And tell him I'll bring Kieran with me.'

Mrs Ballantine beamed. 'And why not indeed! He is one of the family, after all, isn't he? As is the good Father here.' She turned her gaze back to Dermot. 'Now why don't you come along too, young man? I'm sure partaking of afternoon tea in a Protestant household cannot be regarded wholly as one of your mortal sins!'

'Mother!' Maeve glanced across at Dermot, who looked distinctly uncomfortable.

'That's most kind of you, Mrs Ballantine, but . . .'

'No buts! I won't have them! I'll expect you both at three. In fact, I'll pay the jarvey tonight and instruct him to be outside this very door at half-past two, so there can be no excuses. Now, if you'll forgive me – the poor man is probably already frozen half to death waiting in that cab!'

Without further ado, she linked her arm into Dermot's and

walked him towards the door. He managed a hurried backward glance at Maeve before they both disappeared out into the night. The door rattled shut behind them as Maeve stared at it open-mouthed.

'Is that really your mammy, Maeve?'

She turned half-dazed to the questioning face of Katie. She had almost forgotten the child was in the room. She nodded slowly. 'Yes, Katie aroon, that's my mammy.'

Dermot settled himself in the padded seat of the cab, alongside the scented bulk of Emily Ballantine. He glanced across at her, finding it nearly impossible to believe this matriarchal mountain of a woman was actually Maeve's mother. Certainly there was no physical resemblance that he could discern, but when he thought about it, both seemed to like getting their own way in life.

'Now where is it you stay, Father?' Her voice broke into his musings.

'Oh, I'll not be going straight back to the presbytery, if you don't mind, Mrs Ballantine. There are one or two house calls I'd like to make first.'

'Have it your own way. Just give the jarvey plenty of warning, would you? In fact, you can give him a prod with this, for I swear he's as deaf as a doorpost!' She lifted up her umbrella and laid it across Dermot's black-robed knees in anticipation.

He managed a bleak smile. He could already envisage the type of man Maeve's poor father must be.

The jarvey, after the necessary prod, let him off in front of a familiar door. The curtains of the window alongside were not properly drawn and Dermot peered inside. Cissie O'Rourke was undressing her daughter Caitlin in front of the fire and the dark shadow at the window made her look up with a start.

'Dermot!' Her delighted exclamation filled the room as she sat the child on the rag rug and ran to open the door.

He hugged her to him before she closed the door against the swirling snow. 'It's good to see you, Cissie. You're beginning to look your old self again.'

She flushed prettily and drew a hand over her hair, tucking a stray curl back into the bun at the nape of her neck. 'It's good to see you too. You'll stay for a cup of tea. There's one in the pot.'

'In that case, thank you, I will.' He sat himself down in one of the two chairs on either side of the fire and lifted the beaming figure of Caitlin on to his lap. She was dressed only in a woollen vest and he lifted the long white nightgown from where it was warming over the brass fender and pulled it carefully over her reddish-blonde curls, then worked each plump pink arm through the frilled sleeves.

'That's some night out there!' Cissie commented, as she checked the tea in the pot on the table was still warm enough, then poured a cup and handed it across to him.

His dark eyes smiled up his thanks into hers as he took the cup. He ignored the remark on the weather; he was much more concerned to find out how she was. 'You're looking better today, Cissie. Did you go and see the doctor like I said?'

She flushed once again as she sat down on the chair opposite. 'That I did.'

'And what did he say? Did he give you something?' Dermot's eyes mirrored the concern he had felt at how she had been feeling recently. He had never seen her looking so ill. Danny's death must have really taken it out of her.

Cissie looked down, clasping and unclasping her hands in her lap. She had told no one, not even her sister Maggie, or her Da. 'No, he never gave me anything – not really.'

'He did examine you, though? He did check there was nothing wrong?'

'Aye, he did examine me.'

'He didn't find anything, did he? There's nothing seriously wrong, Cissie, is there?'

She looked up, giving a wan smile. 'He found something all right. But I can't really say there's something wrong . . . Wrong wouldn't be quite the right way to put it.'

She paused, glancing down at the beaming smile of Caitlin on Dermot's lap. 'A wee souvenir would really be a better way of terming it. Danny has left me another wee souvenir to remember him by.'

Their eyes met and Dermot let out a long, low breath as understanding dawned. 'You – you're not . . .'

'Aye, aye I am,' she sighed. 'I'm expecting another child – Danny's child, Dermot. How do you give birth to and bring up the child of a dead man?'

Chapter 20

The old jarvey was already waiting outside Maeve's door, sheltering from the cold beneath the hood of his cab, as Dermot turned the corner of McIntyre Street at a little after two-thirty in the afternoon. He nodded to the old man as he gave two light taps on the front door before pushing it open.

Maeve was standing, already dressed in her hat and coat, by the kitchen table, a half-finished glass of whiskey in her hand. She glanced at the clock on the mantelpiece. 'You're late.'

'I came as quick as I could. I was lucky to get away at all. December's a busy month for us, you know that.' His voice had an awkward edge to it as he closed the door behind him.

She nodded and finished the remainder of the whiskey in one gulp, grimacing as the pungent liquid found its way down her throat. 'I wasn't complaining. To tell the truth, I didn't really expect you to turn up at all today.'

He looked surprised. 'Don't you want me to come?'

She shrugged. 'It's not that. To be honest, I don't really want to go myself – I wouldn't go if it wasn't for Charlie.'

'He means a lot to you, your brother, doesn't he?'

'Everything. He's the only one who has never let me down.'

She looked straight at him as she spoke. She was including him in that, he knew that. He had let her down, just like everyone else. He had let her down by making love to her, then deserting her. For that was how she saw it, he was certain of that. And, God help him, so did he. He avoided her eyes, glancing back at the door. 'The jarvey's waiting. We'd better go.'

She nodded briefly and went through to the bedroom to fetch the baby from his cot. Dressed in a neat blue woollen suit, Kieran squirmed with excitement in her arms as they headed for the door. Already at eight months he knew that outdoor clothes meant a walk in the fresh air, but an even greater treat was in store today; it would be the first time he had ever ridden in a cab.

They spoke little on the journey across the city to Jubilee Avenue, but each was acutely conscious of the close proximity of the other. If they reached across a mere few inches they could touch one another, but each sat at the furthest edge of the seat, as if the other were contaminated by some dire plague. Luckily there was plenty to look at, for the pavements were thronged with Christmas shoppers, and, despite the shortages imposed by the war, the shops seemed to lack few of the essentials so necessary for the festive season.

Dermot's hands clenched and unclenched in his lap. He should at least make an effort; he must try to lighten the atmosphere between them. Whatever he was going through, she was going through too, in equal measure. He was sure of that. 'Will you be spending Christmas at home in Jubilee Avenue with your family, then?'

His question made her look round in surprise. 'Of course not,' she said indignantly. 'What an idea! My home's in McIntyre Street now, I thought you knew that. I'll be spending it in exactly the same way as last year, except this year Danny won't be here and Kieran will. Will you come and join us?'

The invitation took him completely by surprise. He looked uncomfortable. 'Well, I – I . . .'

'Oh, you don't have to if you don't want to – it's not obligatory!' Her head jerked back to stare studiously out at the shoppers once more. There was no way on earth she would beg him to come.

Dermot stared disconsolately at the back of her head. He should apologise – say, of course he would love to spend Christmas with her. But he couldn't. He had sworn, not only to himself but to Father O'Reilly in the confessional, that he would avoid, as far as he could, ever being alone with her for any length of time again. There was no way he could renege on that promise. It was made before God.

As the cab rattled up to the wrought-iron gates of the Ballantine home almost half-an-hour later, he could sense her tense inwardly. It would be the first time she had crossed the doorstep since she left home to marry Danny. His hand reached across to give hers a comforting squeeze. 'Are you all right, Maeve?'

She nodded, attempting to smile. It was not only the thought of entering her father's house again that had drained the colour from her cheeks. She shouldn't have had that whiskey before they left. Far from giving her the Dutch courage she had hoped for, she now felt physically sick. But then she had been sick on and off for the past couple of weeks – and it had little to do with the glass of Jameson's or the juddering of the cab over the cobbles on the way here.

Her mother was watching for their arrival from the drawing-room window, a handkerchief tightly screwed up between her fingers, and she glanced across at her husband as the cab drew up at the door. 'They're here, Charles. Remember now – no unpleasantness, please, for Charlie's sake.'

Charles Ballantine got up from depths of his favourite Queen Anne chair, stuffing his copy of the *Irish Times* down the side of the leather cushion. 'Grant me some gumption, woman!'

They stood side by side behind the flounced net of the bay window as the two figures got out of the cab. The sight of their daughter, clutching the child of that Republican tearaway to her breast and being helped up the stone steps by his brother in the dress of a Catholic priest, seemed to underline the humiliation they believed had been heaped upon their heads since Maeve had announced her intention to marry Danny.

A small pulse throbbed in one of the protruding veins on Charles Ballantine's left temple as he stood alongside his wife when his daughter and her escort were shown into the room by the maid.

'Maeve, dear – Father Donovan – how nice to see you!' Emily Ballantine rushed forward ushering Dermot towards her husband. 'Charles, dear, may I introduce Maeve's brother-in-law, Father Dermot Donovan.'

The two men shook hands. Dermot had seen Charles Ballantine from afar over the years, long before he knew Maeve, in fact. There were very few people in Dublin who did not know the affluent accountant, at least by sight. He had held almost every prominent Council post, bar that of Mayor, and had been a leading light in the business life of the city for the best part of a generation. 'I'm pleased to make your acquaintance, sir.'

The older man nodded and murmured an appropriate rejoinder. For a Catholic priest, at least he had a firm enough handshake, and could look you straight in the eye. That was something, at least. Deciding to reserve his judgement on the young man before him, he then turned and addressed himself to his daughter.

'Hello, Father.' Maeve's eyes looked directly into his, and she deliberately lifted her head that tiny bit higher than usual, although her heart was pounding unbearably in her breast.

'I hear you've called him Kieran.' The blue, slightly bulbous eyes rested on the child in his daughter's arms.

She nodded in surprise. It had taken her mother much longer even to acknowledge his presence in the room last night. 'Yes. There was no special reason. I simply liked the name.' She glanced down at the woollen-suited child in her arms. But Kieran was not looking at her. He was fascinated by the tall, red-faced man in front of him. His mouth broke into a beaming smile and his two chubby arms reached out towards him.

To her amazement, her father beamed back and reached out and plucked the baby from her arms. The red Irish hair peeping from beneath the blue woollen bonnet appeared to make no difference, this infant might bear the name Donovan, but he had the firm facial features of a Ballantine, the elderly man decided. 'You're a fine young man and no mistake!'

Maeve and Dermot exchanged a quick glance and his eyes remained on her face as she looked back at her tiny son in her father's arms. Already, in this elegant drawing-room with its rich brocade and velvet furnishings, they seemed a million miles away from that drab kitchen in McIntyre Street and he could feel the family ties extending once more to ensnare her. He was losing her, but she was not his to lose. The feeling brought a cold emptiness to the pit of his stomach.

He stayed on in the drawing-room drinking tea and eating petit-fours with her parents while Maeve went upstairs for her reunion with her brother. She left Kieran downstairs and her father squeezed him in beside him in the corner of the Queen

Anne chair. The old man, despite his cold exterior, was obviously entranced with the child, but Dermot's thoughts were on their way up the sweeping staircase with his mother.

Maeve did not even pause to collect her thoughts as she reached Charlie's room, but threw the door open and stood gazing across at the gaunt-faced figure propped up on the white pillows, in the middle of the four-poster bed.

'Maeve!'

'Hello, Charlie.' She breathed the words rather than spoke them, before breaking into a run and flinging herself into his arms.

'Hey, steady on there! I'm a dying man, remember!'

She pulled back immediately, only to see a smile on his face. But consternation still filled her eyes as she took his hand in hers. 'What *is* wrong, Charlie? Is it something very bad? They haven't told me yet.'

The smile on his face faded, emphasising the gauntness once more. There were deep black circles round his eyes, and they seemed to glow with an intensity that told her they had borne witness to things no man should ever see. 'You could say I've had a belly-full of the war.' Seeing her puzzled expression, he smiled gently and pulled down the bedcovers just enough for her to glimpse the thick wad of bandages that covered his lower stomach. 'Shrapnel,' he said simply. 'It could have been worse.'

She sat down on the edge of the bed, fighting back an almost uncontrollable urge to cry. Instead, she reached across and picked up a black clothboard-covered notebook that lay face down on the floral satin quilt. Her brows furrowed at the unfamiliar German words on the page:

> Was wirst du tun, Gott, wenn ich sterbe?
> Ich bin dein Krug (wenn ich zerscherbe?)
> Ich bin dein Trank (wenn ich verderbe?)
> Bin dein Gewand und dein Gewerbe,
> mit mir verliest du deinen Sinn . . .

'It's Rilke,' Charlie said quietly. 'It's a cry to the heavens, Maeve, in the midst of that hell they call Flanders.'

Maeve looked puzzled; unlike him she had never done any German. 'What does it mean?' she asked quietly.

'It's a young man coming face to face with death and his God. Roughly translated, he's saying, "Can't you see, God? In killing me, you kill yourself." I found a copy of it in the pocket of a young German lieutenant I shot.' Seeing the look of horror on her face, he continued, 'Yes, I'm a killer, Maeve. They made us all killers over there. His name was Martin Schnelldorfer and he came from a small village near Hamburg. I wrote to his parents last week, but I doubt if they'll ever get the letter.'

She shook her head, trying desperately to find the right words of comfort, as he continued. 'It doesn't hurt quite so much when you don't actually see the result of your pulling the trigger, or throwing the grenade. But I saw that poor bastard. I fired right into his trench. It was the least I could do – find out his address, I mean. His parents have a right to know . . . he was only eighteen.'

Tears sparkled in the grey-blue of his eyes and, unable to bear witness to his grief, Maeve got up from the edge of the bed and walked to the window, to look out over the snow-covered trees of St Stephen's Green. There had been so much death, so many needless, needless deaths, since she had last seen him. 'I suppose you heard that Danny was killed.'

She turned to look at him and he raised his hands in a helpless gesture. 'I'm so sorry, Maeve, so very sorry. What does one say . . . ?'

'If you're our mother, you say, if that's the case then I'm allowed to enter their precious home once more.' It was impossible to keep the bitterness from her voice.

Charlie shook his head. 'They've behaved abominably. I wouldn't have blamed you – not really – if you'd decided not to come today.'

She came back to the bedside and took his hand. 'Some things in life are worth more than standing on your pride, Charlie. Like you, for instance.'

They did not return home by cab, for her father insisted on driving them home personally in his car. Maeve sat in the high padded leather seat behind the driver with Dermot, while

Kieran, tired out by the excitement and attention of the afternoon, slept soundly in her arms.

'Can I drop you off first, Father?' Charles Ballantine glanced round at Dermot, as he manoeuvred the vehicle along Earlsfort Terrace, between the horse-drawn carriages and late afternoon shoppers who seemed to feel they had a God-given right to walk where they wished on the busy road.

Dermot glanced across at Maeve, half-expecting her to protest, to ask him to stop off at her place instead. But Maeve remained silent, gazing out over the snow-covered scene as if she had never even heard the question.

'That'll be real kind of you, sir.'

As the slate roof of the presbytery came into sight, behind the high elms that hid the rest of the house from the road, Dermot shifted uneasily in his seat. Despite his resolve to keep well clear of situations when he might find himself alone with Maeve, he had no wish to go home yet. He had to talk to her – they had to talk together – before that gulf that he could feel growing between them became too wide to bridge.

But still she said nothing. As he climbed down from his seat and stood, with one foot on the running-board, facing her, she gave a polite smile. 'It was kind of you to come today, Dermot. I did appreciate it.'

His eyes searched hers for some sign – some light – that would belie the distance he was sure he could detect in her voice. But none was visible. 'Yes, well, there's nothing to thank me for – not really. It was a most enjoyable afternoon.'

He turned to her father and extended a hand. 'Please convey my thanks to your wife once more, sir, for her kind invitation.'

'Not at all, young man. The pleasure was ours.'

As the car took off down the road once more, Dermot stood on the edge of the pavement and watched it until it was out of sight. He wished he hadn't accepted her mother's invitation; he wished he had never gone there today and seen with his own eyes how the other half in this city lived. How she had lived. It made his own world, and the world Maeve now inhabited around McIntyre Street, seem even more shabby than he already knew it to be.

He thought of those few days in Kingstown, in pleasant

surroundings, and how she had come to life again, and he could see the young carefree girl she had once been. The young girl with whom his brother Danny had fallen in love and who, despite everything, had captured his own heart that very first moment their eyes met.

Since that day he had told himself that to admit those feelings, even to himself, was to make them a reality, and realities had to be dealt with. It had been far easier not to allow himself to even think about it. But he would have to be dead not to think about it. Waking or sleeping, she was foremost in his thoughts, permeating his being until at times he thought he would surely go mad. He had learnt long ago that there was a limit as to how far the head could rule the heart. The battle for his soul was still raging within him and, whatever happened, he knew he would be the loser.

The yearning to run after the car – to run all the way to McIntyre Street if need be – the yearning to simply see her again, to talk to her, to be with her, became an almost unbearable physical ache. He groaned out loud – a soft, plaintive sound, like a wounded animal in great pain, as he turned and stumbled towards the tall wrought-iron gates of the presbytery.

He was greeted on the other side of the black painted metal by the small, rotund figure of Mrs Shea, the housekeeper, running down the drive towards him. Even from a distance, he could see her face was flushed and there was a wild-eyed look to her eyes.

She clasped a hand to her heaving, black-crepe-draped bosom as she fought to regain her breath when she finally reached him. 'Oh, Father, I saw you arrive from the upstairs window. I'm so glad you're back. It's Father O'Reilly, Father! Oh, do come – he's lying on the floor in the library. He's dead, Father. He's dead!'

Chapter 21

'Doesn't he look a treat, Miss Maeve? You need have no worries about Master Kieran — he'll be right as rain up here with me. You just go downstairs and enjoy yourself now!' Mrs Brennan, the housekeeper, gazed fondly down at the sleeping infant in the cot, then transferred the smile to his mother.

Maeve stood before the rosewood mirror by the side of the bed and fiddled nervously with the blood-red velvet sash at her waist. She could hardly believe she was actually here in her old room, with Kieran sleeping peacefully in the cot that Mrs Brennan had resurrected, on her mother's instructions, from the nursery store-cupboard. Her parents' Christmas parties were legendary in the neighbourhood, but a few short weeks ago she could never have imagined that she would actually be present at one again. And what was more, she appeared to be the guest of honour, if the number of people her mother had lined up for her to meet was anything to go by. 'The prodigal daughter has returned,' she murmured, giving a final twirl before the glass.

'Beggin' your pardon, Miss Maeve?'

'Nothing, Brennie, nothing!' She picked up the black silk shawl from where it was lying on the satin quilt of the bed and draped it around her shoulders. Her fingers lovingly caressed the long fringes. It was wonderful to have the opportunity to wear such sensuous materials again. She had not even bothered to pack her evening clothes when she had left home, expecting there would be little call for them in McIntyre Street, and she had been right. But now, to open her old wardrobe and find them all again, just as she had left them — well, it was like greeting long-lost old friends. 'Do you think it's time I was getting downstairs?'

The housekeeper glanced at the clock on the bedside table as she draped a fresh Turkish towel over the rack by the wash-stand. 'I surely do. It's gone eight already and your mother has umpteen folk she'll want you to get round before the meal is served at nine. Both her and your father are thrilled to bits you're back home, you know.'

Maeve raised an eyebrow as she knotted the fringed ends of the shawl over her breast. 'Only till tomorrow, Brennie. I've got a home of my own now, and I'll be heading back there in the morning.'

The housekeeper gave a knowing smile, but had no opportunity for argument as Emily Ballantine herself appeared at the bedroom door. 'Aren't you ready yet, Maeve? Even Charlie's down before you!'

She entered the room and pursed her lips as her eyes travelled over her daughter's velvet and satin-clad figure. Maeve might be unforgivably headstrong and a never-ending source of disappointment to both her and her husband, but there was no denying there would be few prettier young ladies on the Dublin social scene this season. If she could be persuaded to re-enter it, that was. 'Mmm, it'll do. I must admit that I always tended to favour your blue watered silk, though.'

Maeve gave a quiet smile as she stole a last glance in the mirror. No matter what she had chosen to wear tonight, her mother would have preferred something else.

'Are you coming, or are you going to stand there in front of that thing all night?'

'Coming, coming . . .' Throwing a farewell smile at Mrs Brennan, Maeve followed her mother from the room and out on to the landing that overlooked the gaily decorated hall below.

A buzz of animated conversation and laughter wafted up the stairs towards them and her thoughts immediately flew back over the years to when, as small children, she and Charlie would creep out of bed in their nightclothes to peep over the banisters on just such a scene every Christmas. Sixteen had been the age of admission to the grown-up festivities and she could still remember the thrill of her first official party. Charlie had, of course, preceded her entry into this magical world by two years and her envy had known no bounds as he paraded proudly in his first black satin-collared evening suit before her.

Charlie was, in fact the only reason she had been persuaded

to attend tonight and to stay overnight into the bargain. The doctor had said he could be allowed downstairs for a short period in a bath chair and the devil had sworn he wouldn't leave his bed unless she agreed to come.

'Are there more people than usual this year?' She paused at the top of the sweeping staircase, her stomach churning nervously as she gazed down at the colourful scene below. It was all just as she remembered it: holly wreaths on all the doors and an eighteen-foot Christmas tree aglow with lights, its beribboned bells tinkling in the draught from the open door. It stood at the far end of the hall, to the left of the fireplace, totally dominating the assembled company, while white-coated waiters served them drinks of hot Christmas punch and the best cream sherry on silver trays. 'There must be at least a hundred people down there.'

'Hardly, my dear. Just over eighty accepted, if I remember rightly, and only three of the guest rooms are occupied just now.' Her mother lifted the lorgnette to her eyes and peered down into the elegantly-attired crowd. Vanity prevented her from wearing her spectacles with evening dress. 'But there are one or two in particular that your father and I would like you to meet.'

Maeve tried to disguise a grimace as they descended the staircase side by side. People her parents approved of usually turned out to be the most awful bores. But her spirits lifted almost immediately at the sight of Charlie, resplendent in evening dress with a tartan rug covering his knees, seated in a bath chair at the foot of the stairs. A pretty fair-haired young woman, in slate-grey satin, was standing with her back to them talking to him, and she turned to glance up as Maeve and her mother neared the foot of the steps.

'Amy!' Maeve's delight at the sight of her old friend was instantaneous.

Mrs Ballantine's hand fixed firmly on her daughter's arm. 'Now, Maeve, you'll have plenty of time for gossip later. Charlie is perfectly capable of keeping Miss Grafton company till then. Right now there are other guests waiting!'

Maeve looked back at Amy and Charlie and gave a helpless shrug as she allowed herself to be shepherded into the main throng. It was quite obviously going to be one of those nights. She wished she felt better. She hadn't been physically sick today, thank goodness. That seemed to be wearing off by now, but a faint feeling of nausea remained, especially in a hot, stuffy atmosphere like this.

A succession of introductions followed, mainly to young men in British army officer's uniform – Jeremy Curzon, Hector Lambert-Hughes, Brendan Carmichael-Scott – they fused into a khaki-coloured blur as she made the appropriate noises, then moved on, until her mother was spirited away by the dour-looking man from Ballsbridge employed as butler for the evening. There had been a minor emergency in the kitchen and only the mistress of the house would do.

'You look about as lost as I feel.'

The deep American drawl made her look round in surprise, straight into the eyes of a tall, fair man, wearing a bespoke tailored evening suit that looked a distinct cut above any other in the room. 'Allow me to introduce myself – Fullerton's the name – Frank Fullerton.' He had pale blue eyes that had an amused glint to them that she found herself responding to with a smile.

'Maeve – Maeve Donovan.' She extended a black-gloved hand to be shaken and he held on to it for a second or two longer than would normally be considered quite proper.

'Hello, Maeve Donovan. You don't come from round here, I take it. At least I don't think we've run into each other over the past week.'

He didn't know who she was! He really hadn't a clue. Maeve perked up immediately. 'No, you're quite right. I live in McIntyre Street. I'm only here until tomorrow morning.'

'You don't say! Now how's that for a coincidence! You mean you're staying with the Ballantines too?' He looked genuinely intrigued as he took her by the elbow and edged her towards a quiet spot by the fireplace. 'Have you known Chuck and his wife long?'

Maeve hid her amusement with difficulty. It was the first time she had ever heard her father referred to like that – Charlie maybe, but Chuck . . . ! 'Oh, more years than I care to remember, really. You say you're staying here in the house?'

Frank Fullerton nodded as they accepted a glass of sherry from a waiter bearing a silver tray. 'I've been over here from New York for the past week working in Ballantines' main office. Our two firms are merging next year, haven't you heard?'

Maeve shook her head. 'I'm afraid I don't keep up with the intrigues of the world of high finance. I take it this – this merger will be to your mutual benefit?'

'You bet your sweet life it will! I wouldn't be here right now otherwise. Fullerton-Ballantine will be one of the biggest and best accountancy and finance houses on Wall Street before the decade is out – or before this war is over, whichever should prove the quicker.'

'Fullerton-Ballantine . . .' Maeve tried the name for size on her tongue. 'And how does "Chuck" feel about taking second billing on the company notepaper?'

The tall American grinned. 'He doesn't know yet – enlightenment in that department will come later. Certainly not tonight. Tonight is for other things – introductions to beautiful young ladies, for example!'

'Did I hear someone say "introductions"?' Emily Ballantine appeared at her daughter's elbow, beaming a smile at the tall young man before her. 'I see you've already met my daughter, Frank. You young people certainly don't waste any time!'

Maeve suppressed a smile at the astonishment on the face opposite. 'We've been getting along just fine, mother. Wouldn't you agree, Mr Fullerton?'

Frank Fullerton nodded. For the first time in his thirty-three years he was speechless. He had heard that the Ballantines' daughter was a wild tearaway who had disgraced the family by marrying a Catholic rebel. It was impossible to connect that knowledge with this fragile-looking, beautiful young woman who stood before him. He was instantly intrigued, but given little time to muse on the matter.

'I see supper's ready,' Emily Ballantine announced, waving an acknowledgement to the gesturing butler at the door to the dining-room. 'What could be more convenient, Maeve, it seems you already have the most charming young man in the room to escort you!'

* * *

Frank Fullerton not only escorted her to the supper table, but remained by her side throughout the whole evening. He had a wryly cynical view of the world of high finance and life in general that she found refreshingly different and which coincided surprisingly often with her own. He also had an uncannily accurate perception of the Irish situation for one who had only recently arrived in the country. He had listened with interest as she attempted to explain the differences between her father's conception of Ireland and her late husband's.

'What happened during and after the Rising at Easter shocked me, Frank, really shocked me. It wasn't just the British versus the Irish; it was also the Irish versus the Irish. The guns and bombs were aimed by Irishmen at other Irishmen; the blood on the streets was Irish blood . . .' Her voice faltered as she remembered the fate of poor Con O'Malley and the others. It contrasted so strongly with the feelings of euphoria and patriotism that had characterised the early hours of that fateful Bank Holiday Monday, as Danny and his comrades prepared for their march on the seats of power in the city. 'What is it about this country and our people that makes this type of thing possible?'

The broad shoulders in the black evening jacket had shrugged and his eyes looked quizzically into hers as he took a thoughtful sip of the sherry. 'You're one helluva race and no mistake – if you'll pardon the expression. I guess I haven't really been here long enough, though, to pass judgement.'

'But you must have your opinion,' she insisted. She already knew him well enough to know that much. 'What is it, Frank? As an American, what do you really make of us?'

His lips twisted into a wryly cynical smile as he looked at her over the top of his sherry glass. 'Well, honey, if you ask me, it seems like the Irish people can't really make up their minds what they want – but they're sure as hell prepared to fight to the death to get it.'

'At least they have the courage of their convictions. You have to give them that.' Even in death, she felt obliged to stand up for Danny and his fallen comrades.

He gave a mirthless laugh. 'Ah, Maeve, Maeve – convictions! Convictions, my dear, can be a far more dangerous enemy of the truth than lies. You only have to look at the history books to find that nearly all our disasters are caused by enough fools having "the courage of their convictions", as the saying goes.'

He finished the sherry in the glass and signalled to a waiter hovering nearby to bring another. 'If you ask me, we'll never have a quiet world until we knock patriotism out of the human race, and the Irish seem to have more than their fair share of it. I reckon it's a trait that doesn't really bode well for a untroubled future as a people.'

She had nodded in silent agreement, as a frown etched itself across her brow. It brought an immediate reaction from the man at her elbow. 'Hey, why the long face! Life ain't that bad – not really. Fortunately for us, most folk are cowards and wouldn't dare act on what they believe, so there's hope for us all yet!'

Her eyes were on Charlie at the other end of the room, in his bath chair, as Frank spoke. It was easy to talk glibly about such things as patriotism when you weren't personally involved in a war. What she had seen of the casualty lists from the Front recently had sickened her of the very word. There was her own brother perhaps maimed for life, and barely twenty-one, and Amy's fiancé and God knows how many others already dead. Many would be cowards if they had courage enough, she was certain of that. 'I hate killing,' she found herself saying bitterly. 'I hate risings, rebellions, wars – whatever they like to call it. It's still murder, isn't it, Frank? It's still killing! Surely this can't be the natural state of things. Surely it can't be something endemic in the human condition that makes men behave like this?'

Her eyes turned to his and he shook his head. 'I don't believe so, honey. I really don't believe so. If you ask me, man has only two primal passions – to get and to beget; everything else is manufactured. Sex is really the driving force in all our lives.'

Maeve took a sip of the sherry, feeling her cheeks colour. They said Americans were frank talkers – but really . . . 'What about love? Doesn't that come into the reckoning?'

He grinned down at her. 'Ah, love . . .' His eyes gazed into the middle distance. 'I guess love is a bit like seeing a ghost; we all talk about it, but few of us have ever seen one.'

'You talk as if you don't believe in it.'

'Do I?' His lips twisted into a bitter smile.

She was skating on thin ice, she could sense it, but felt compelled to go on. 'How would you define love then? Don't tell me you've never experienced it!'

The expression in the blue eyes was as serious as she had ever seen it as he shook his head slowly. 'No, I won't tell you that. Just how *would* I define love? Jeez, that's a tall order . . . I guess the nearest I could get to it is to say, it's a bit like a fistful of quicksilver. Leave your palm open and it stays; clutch at it and it slips right through your fingers.'

His words had a bitter edge to them that told her she had unwittingly sprinkled salt in some well-hidden, but still open wound. Frank Fullerton might be a typical product of Ivy League America, but there was a heart beating there behind that bland all-American exterior. There was no doubt about that.

In fact, the longer the evening progressed, the more intrigued she found herself becoming with this handsome but shrewd New Yorker. But, perhaps, the greatest surprise of all was reserved for the early hours of the morning when they danced beneath the flickering candles of the chandelier to the strains of all her favourite Viennese waltzes. The four-piece band in the corner opposite the Christmas tree had just struck up again after a ten-minute break and they were halfway round the floor when he murmured in her ear, 'Did your husband dance?'

The question took her by surprise and she thought for a moment, then nodded. 'Yes, but you're better.' It was the truth. Danny would have to be half-drunk before he could be persuaded to take the floor – and for a very good reason; his dancing left everything to be desired.

The answer seemed to please him, for he smiled broadly and held her that bit closer than before. 'May I return the compliment? You're much better than my wife.'

'Your wife!' She had almost shouted the words back at him and came to a complete halt in the middle of the floor. 'You didn't tell me you were married.'

'"Were" being the operative word. I'm not any more – not since June 1913.'

'You – you mean . . .'

'I mean I'm divorced.'

'Divorced!' She had never met anyone who had actually been divorced before. Divorce in Ireland, after the Charles Stewart Parnell and Kitty O'Shea affair, still meant only one thing – scandal and disgrace for all those involved. 'I – I'm so sorry.'

'I'm not!' He grinned as his arms swept her away in time with the music once more. 'In fact, it's the best thing that ever happened to me. I highly recommend it to all my friends!' His teeth were white and even as he smiled down at her. It was difficult to tell whether he was joking or not. If he was, then he was a superb actor. But she suspected there was more than a grain of truth in his remark, despite his enigmatic comments earlier in the evening.

The revelation, however, had thrown her completely off balance and she found herself longing to know more about Mr Frank Fullerton's early love life. What was she like, this quicksilver female who had once captured his heart? Just what kind of woman attracted a man of the world like this? She did not have too long to wait for the answer. He told her part of the story ten minutes later, standing at the drawing-room window looking out at the canopy of stars that hung low over St Stephen's Green.

Estelle Walters had been the belle of New York society when they had married on Thanksgiving Day 1912 but, as Frank picturesquely put it, the only thanks he got for making an honest woman of her was to have her run off with 'a sweet-talkin' Yid' from California about four months after their wedding.

'Art Finkelstein his name was, but I hear he's changed it to Finlay. Can't say as I blame the guy – about getting rid of a handle like that, I mean. But I sure as hell blamed him at the time for charmin' Estelle away! Seems like he gave her some fancy ideas about taking part in some motion-picture-making nonsense that he's involved in out there. She used to spend so much time staring into a mirror anyway, I guess she thought it might be kinda nice to go the whole hog and see herself up on the screen!'

No matter what his feelings at the time, though, to Maeve's surprise, he seemed to have no regrets about it now, and appeared to view the whole affair with a certain amused detachment, as if he were relating the plot of a novel he had just read. Somehow it didn't quite tally with the bitterness she had detected in his voice earlier.

'It hasn't soured you of marriage, then?'

'Hell no! Does finding one rotten one in a barrel put you off eating apples for the rest of your life?' He had grinned down at her, shaking his head as if the question amused him. 'Mind you, I have been known to say it's put me off blondes for quite a while – but you have no need to worry on that score, do you?'

She had blushed as his hand reached up to stroke the smooth coiffure of blue-black hair specially arranged for the evening. She wished he wouldn't look at her like that – with that faintly mocking glint in those pale blue eyes. He made her feel like a child again; a nervous, naïve little child. Maybe it was the wine that she had indulged in at suppertime that was going to her head. Maybe it was simply the lateness of the hour. Whatever it was, she was enjoying this young man's company far too much. It was time she excused herself and retired for the night.

Next morning at breakfast, as she reiterated her intention of returning home to McIntyre Street with the baby, the look of genuine disappointment in the American's eyes was obvious for all to see. She felt as if she had meted out a personal slight to him and was unable to object too strongly as he begged her to stay, for a few more hours at least. They finally settled on her remaining at Jubilee Avenue for lunch.

In the afternoon, however, when she was absolutely determined to return home, her father offered his American guest the use of the car to drive his daughter and grandson back across the city.

She felt like Cinderella returning from the ball, as she settled into the squeaky leather seat beside him. Surely her father's gleaming automobile would turn back into the dreaded pumpkin at any moment? And what on earth would he think of McIntyre Street when they got there?

She spoke very little on the journey across the city as he chatted animatedly about his own home across the Atlantic. It seemed to her mind a million miles away from Dublin – especially the Dublin she was now heading back to in McIntyre Street. His servants were probably far better housed than the population of her street – and better fed and paid into the bargain. A peculiar defensiveness welled within her for these mean streets they were now driving through, but, if he noticed the change in environment from the area around Jubilee Avenue, and the increasing poverty of their surroundings, he gave no indication. And that alone sent his stock soaring in her eyes.

As he pulled the car up outside the green-painted front door of her home, Maeve felt her heart lurch crazily in her breast. All thoughts of Frank and his opinions vanished from her head. He no longer existed ... Dermot was coming out of Mary-Agnes's house at the end of the street and was heading their way.

She sat transfixed in the passenger seat as his black-cassocked figure strode towards them along the impacted snow of the pavement. Then, as he got to within twenty yards of the car, he stopped and stared straight at her. For what seemed a lifetime they looked at one another. Then he turned on his heel and walked off quickly in the opposite direction.

'Maeve, are you all right, honey?'

Frank's voice broke into her consciousness and she nodded bleakly. Her eyes were still glued to the now empty pavement and the corner round which Dermot had just disappeared. She clutched Kieran to her breast, acutely aware of the new life growing within her, as she felt a hand on her arm.

'Aren't you going to ask me in? I reckon as a rookie chauffeur I didn't do too badly, did I? Anyway, I could sure do with a cup of your good old British tea to warm me up!'

She turned her head to meet his blue-eyed gaze. 'Of course, Frank. Forgive me, I was dreaming. It must have been that extra glass of wine at lunch!'

He followed her into the small kitchen, his eyes widening at the bleakness of the surroundings. She had warned him last night that her life as Danny Donovan's wife, and now his widow, was nothing like that she had left back home in Jubilee Avenue, but this was like nothing he had ever experienced. It existed in New York, of course: even he was well aware of the conditions the immigrants lived in on the East Side, but to find a girl like Maeve actually enduring something similar . . .

Hanging his hat on the back of the door, he removed his astrakhan-collared coat and leather gloves and, despite her protests, got down on his knees to light the fire.

Maeve shivered in the cold dampness that seemed to permeate the whole house. It would take at least half an hour for the room to warm up, but she refilled the kettle all the same and placed it on the feeble flames. 'It'll take a while,' she said, by way of apology. 'Wouldn't you rather have a whiskey to warm you up?'

'If you'll join me.'

She shook her head reluctantly. 'I'm sorry, Frank. I really shouldn't. I've already had three glasses of wine today.'

He laughed. 'That's hardly enough to do you much harm!'

'No, but it can harm the baby.'

The smile on his lips faded. He cast a puzzled glance at Kieran, now placed safely in his pram at the other side of the range. But she shook her head. 'You – you don't mean . . . ?'

Her eyes dropped to the rag rug at her feet. 'Yes, yes, Frank, I do. I'm having another baby.' Tears burned in her eyes. She hadn't meant to tell him. In fact, she couldn't think what possessed her. It was bad enough that she should be a widow with an eight-month-old infant, at her age, but to be pregnant into the bargain . . . She turned from him, unable to look up and witness the expression on his face. She must have shocked him to the core. She couldn't blame him if he cleared out of her life right now.

But, far from being shocked, his expression held only compassion as he walked slowly forwards and placed his hands on her shoulders. 'There's no need to cry, Maeve,' he said softly. 'There's no need to cry, honey. You're not alone any more. You're not alone, Maeve. You've got me now.'

He turned her gently towards him, then lifted her chin with the index finger of his right hand. Her eyes brimmed over as she looked up at him. To be this close to a man again brought

visions of that enchanted afternoon in Kingstown rushing back
to her mind. But the eyes that looked down into hers weren't
dark brown, they were pale blue. And the voice that whispered
her name, as his lips moved nearer to hers, wasn't Irish, but
American.

'Maeve . . . Maeve . . .'

But, as their lips met, it was only Dermot's name she called
silently in return.

Chapter 22

'You can't mean it. New York's the other end of the earth!' Dermot gripped the small gaily-wrapped Christmas parcel between his fingers so hard that the paper burst, showing the edge of the cardboard box beneath.

'Sure and it's hardly that! It's only the other side of the Atlantic Ocean. There are ships leaving Dublin every week for the States.' Maeve attempted a light laugh, but Dermot wasn't having it.

He reached forward and grabbed her arm, his eyes blazing down into hers with an intensity that brought a fleeting look of fear to her own. 'How can you marry someone you don't even know?'

His voice was harsh, almost unrecognisable, and she winced with pain as she wrenched herself free from his grasp. 'I do know him! We've seen each other every day for . . .'

'For less than a week!' his voice interrupted harshly. 'For less than a week, Maeve, for pity's sake! It's only Boxing Day now. You only met the fella a few days ago!'

'It's long enough.'

'Long enough for what, may I ask?'

'Long enough to know he'll make a good husband to me – and a good father to Kieran and the baby.'

There was a long silence as he stared at her. 'A good father to Kieran *and* the baby?'

She held her breath, unable to speak as she avoided his eyes. Her fingers twisted the slim gold band on the third finger of her left hand. Finally she nodded dumbly.

'You – you're having another baby?' His voice was barely audible.

Again she nodded.

'Danny's baby.'

It was impossible to know if the words were uttered as a statement or as a question. She remained silent.

213

'Danny's baby, Maeve! I said – Danny's baby! Answer me, damn you!'

'That's my affair.'

'Oh, no, you're wrong there! It's far from being only your affair!'

She looked at him – a long, hard look that turned his blood to ice-water. 'I'm marrying Frank next week, Dermot, and I'm going to New York with him. And I will have my child in America and bring it up with him as the father.'

'Does he know? Does he know about this baby?' His voice was husky, with a harsh edge to it, and a nerve twitched at the side of his jaw as his eyes cut into hers.

'Of course.'

He let out a long whistling breath between his teeth and opened his mouth to speak, but she was too quick for him.

'You've no right to question me, Dermot Donovan! You are married to the Church. That's a choice you made a long time ago and, no matter what my own feelings about it, I would never dream of questioning that choice. Nor would you appear to dream of questioning it either – not even for me.'

He stared at her. The words were painful to his ears as they came spilling from her lips. If only she knew ... If only she knew of all the nights he had spent on his knees praying – tearing himself apart over that very question she was now dismissing so glibly. 'What exactly are you saying, Maeve?'

'I'm saying that you are married to the Church and I am getting married to a human being – to Frank Fullerton. And Frank Fullerton has never dreamed of questioning the paternity of the child I am expecting. No one has the right to question that, Dermot, not even you.'

'But *you* know. *You* have no doubt in your mind about who the father is.'

'Yes, I know. I have no doubt in my mind whatsoever.' The statement was delivered in a flat, unemotional voice that merely added to its impact on him.

Their eyes locked in a look that said everything and nothing. She wouldn't tell him, he knew that. There was no way on earth she would tell him if it was his child she was carrying.

This was her punishment to him. This was the penalty he must pay for choosing the Church and not her.

'If that's the way you want it, Maeve.'

'That's the way I want it, Dermot.'

She was the one who broke eye contact first, as she turned abruptly to stare into the fire. Her hands gripped the brass rail above the range as she fought to remain calm. To look into those eyes any longer – those dark fathomless eyes – would surely crack her resolve. And she must not crack; she had to remain strong, for all their sakes.

'I'll be busy next week,' he said quietly. 'There's double the work since Father O'Reilly died. They haven't given me a full-time replacement yet.' He paused, as if unsure whether to continue . . . 'You'll forgive me if I don't come to the docks to see you off.'

'I'll forgive you, Dermot.' She whispered the words, her back still to him.

'We'll say goodbye now, then?'

She turned to face him and extended her hand. He took it, and each thought how cold the other's skin felt.

'Goodbye, Maeve. May God go with you all.'

'Goodbye, Dermot.'

On the way out, he remembered the small present still clasped in his left hand, and he laid it on the edge of the table, whispering 'Merry Christmas,' as he closed the door behind him.

Numbly, she walked over and picked it up. The festive wrapping was already torn where his fingers had punctured the paper a few moments ago. She ripped off the remainder and threw it down on the table.

Inside was a small box bearing the name of McNaughton's, the jewellers on Northumberland Road. Her fingers trembled as she opened it and lifted out the tiny silver crucifix. The links of the chain shimmered through her fingers and she clasped it to her, biting her teeth into her knuckles as tears stung her eyes. He had no need to buy her anything, no need at all. She already had the only reminder of him she would ever need in this life.

* * *

The wedding was a quiet one, held privately in her parents' local church. She wore a gown of pale-cream lace, with a low sash belt in matching satin, and a loose-fitting satin jacket that diplomatically hid the slight thickening at her waist. On her left shoulder she wore a single white rose that had arrived on her bedside cabinet that morning from Frank. The corsage of orchids that had been ordered specially was left lying on her dressing-table. The single rose meant much more.

Her groom had turned to smile his adoration as she entered on the arm of her father and she had smiled back in return. He looked every inch the eligible young man of her parents' dreams – tall, fair, Protestant, and well-heeled.

Everything was just as she had known it would be – perfectly organised and executed. Charlie, sitting in his bath chair, resplendent in army full dress uniform, was best man and she had asked Amy Grafton to be her bridesmaid. There were no other guests, barring her father and mother, and there would be no honeymoon; they were sailing for New York the next day.

The thought of the Atlantic crossing filled her with trepidation. The sinking of the *Lusitania* by German submarines off Kinsale Head in May the previous year, with the loss of a thousand lives, was still a livid sore in everyone's mind. Seeing her anxiety, Frank had thoughtfully suggested that they could postpone the crossing and he would arrange with his firm to stay on in Dublin for a few more weeks. There would be no problem, he assured her: having been made senior partner on the death of his father last year, he was virtually his own boss. And, with the coming of spring, the crossing to New York would be much smoother and there was even the possibility of the war being over soon, which would rid the Atlantic of the dreaded menace of enemy submarines. Maeve had listened to all the good reasons for postponing their departure, then had shaken her head reluctantly and thanked him with a squeeze of his arm. They had been walking down O'Connell Street at the time.

'I mean it, honey, I really do.'

'I know – and I mean it when I say that all I want to do in

216

the world is to get to America and start building our life together.'

He had kissed her – right there in the middle of the pavement outside the blasted frontage of the General Post Office. There seemed a cruel irony in the situation and she wondered if Danny was up there beyond those snow-filled heavens looking down at her with a bitter smile on his lips.

An old soldier wielding an accordion had been standing at the foot of Nelson's Pillar watching them as he serenaded the Christmas shoppers. As she pledged her determination to Frank to travel to America with him, the strains of 'Silent Night' suddenly gave way to those of 'Danny Boy'. No one seemed to notice it, not even Frank, but she did, and a cold hand clutched at her heart. Her arm had clung even closer to his as they hurried on past the old busker to continue their search for her trousseau.

They had arrived home by cab, laden with parcels from all the best stores in town. One single morning-gown had cost more than she had had to live on for the past six months, but strangely she felt no elation at the knowledge, only a deep sense of guilt. And that guilt was to become even greater when the time came to return to her old home in McIntyre Street to pack up her belongings that still remained there. But the greatest guilt of all came when the time came to say goodbye to Katie.

The child sat on the edge of the table, sucking a lock of curling red hair, as Maeve set about filling a cabin trunk with her things. She had hardly said a word since her arrival ten minutes ago and the silence was as bad an accusation as Maeve could bear.

When the last item was in its place and the lid slammed firmly down, she stood up and looked down at the child. 'Don't take on so, Katie aroon. It's not the end of the world. I'll be back some day.'

The red head shook in disbelief. 'No, you'll not. I know you'll not. Me mammy lied to me just like that before she left. She told me we'd meet again too, when they came to take her away to hospital. In a far better place than this, she said. "We'll meet again in a far better place than this, Katie" . . . But we

217

never did. They never brought her home again . . .' Tears choked her throat and she averted her head, too proud to let them show.

Maeve looked at her – this scrap of a child who reminded her so much of the Danny she had known and once loved. She could just imagine her mother telling her that all those years ago. Bridie Donovan had known only too well she would never be home again when they came to take her away to St Thomas's. But, being a devout Catholic, she would have truly believed what she said, and known that one day her tiny daughter would believe it too.

'Your mammy didn't lie to you, Katie,' she said softly. 'She promised you you'll meet again in heaven. And you will. Heaven is a far better place than this. God called her to his home, she had no choice but go.'

'But you have a choice! You have a choice, Maeve!' There was desperation in the voice and in the eyes that turned back to plead with hers.

'Yes, child, I have a choice.'

'And you're choosing to leave me – to leave Ireland.'

Maeve could feel the sharp smarting of tears in her own eyes as they met those of the child before her. 'Does any one ever *choose* to leave Ireland, Katie? I don't believe so. I swear to God I don't believe so. This country has lost millions over the years and I don't believe there is a single one of them that hasn't gone with a heavy heart. Some went because of the great hunger, some because of their political beliefs, some to find fame and fortune . . .'

'And why are you going, Maeve? Why are you leaving?'

Maeve hugged the child to her, pressing her lips to the crown of her head, as the hot tears spilled down on to the thatch of curling red hair. She wished with all her heart she could say, *Because of love, Katie. Because of love.* But the words would not come. Now, at a time like this, if she owed her anything at all, she owed her the truth.

She would be leaving Ireland for a new life in a new land, carrying two children; one in her arms and one, as yet unborn, beneath her heart. Neither would know their fathers, but, if they remained true to their race, they would remember their

Mother Ireland. The words of an ancient Gaelic sage rang in her head:

> I am Ireland
> Older than the Hag of Beara
>
> Great my pride
> I gave birth to brave Cuchulain.
>
> Great my shame
> My own children killed their mother.
>
> I am Ireland
> Lonelier than the Hag of Beara . . .

BOOK TWO
Avoid
this spring

So soon as ever your mazed spirit descends
From daylight into darkness, Man remember
What you have suffered here in Samothrace
What you have suffered . . .
To the left hand there bubbles a black spring
Overshadowed with a great white cypress.
Avoid this spring, which is Forgetfulness;
Though all the common rout rush down to drink,
Avoid this spring!

Robert Graves

Chapter 23

New York, D-Day, 1944

At sunset, on the night of Tuesday 6 June 1944, the blazing torch of the Statue of Liberty, extinguished since the bombing of Pearl Harbor, shone forth once more, a beacon of hope directed towards a world at war. As its rays illuminated the darkening sky, Franklin D. Roosevelt, the President of the United States, led his country in prayer:

'Almighty God – our sons, pride of our nation, have this day set forth on a mighty endeavour, a struggle to preserve our Republic, our religion, and our civilisation, and to set free a suffering humanity ... Lead them straight and true, give strength to their arms, stoutness to their hearts, steadfastness in their faith. They will need Thy blessing ... Give us faith in Thee; faith in our sons; faith in each other ...'

The middle-aged woman, listening alone in the elegant drawing-room of her Park Avenue apartment, switched off the radio with an impatient click and downed the remains of the gin and tonic in her glass. 'Faith in each other.' The words were repeated bitterly, as she stood up and stared out through the open window over the glittering skyline of Manhattan. 'Faith in each other – did you hear what the President said, Frank? Did you hear what he said, you bastard?' She yelled the words into the silence around her, knowing Frank would not hear, for Frank was not with her tonight. Frank had not been with her for so many nights. There was only one place Frank would be tonight or any night ...

She threw the glass against the marble fireplace, a bitter smile contorting her features as it shattered into a hundred crystal fragments. Then, without a backward glance, she walked unsteadily towards the door.

She was not aware of getting into her car and driving through the lamplit streets. She was aware only of the great emptiness that filled her soul. She had given up everything for this man. She had given up the only man she had ever loved, only to find that that had not been enough. An emptiness filled her soul; an emptiness that had been growing with each passing day, until finally she could bear it no longer.

She parked her car at the foot of East 14th Street, and stared out over the East River. The moon hung like a poised silver scimitar above central Manhattan, a curved sword of Damocles ready to fall at any second and wreak vengeance on the sleeping multitudes of sinners beneath.

Maeve Fullerton shivered, although the night was warm. A grey mist hung in wraiths over the water and Williamsburg Bridge loomed ominously out of the night, its presence vaguely threatening, as she walked slowly and deliberately towards it. Somewhere out on the river foghorns moaned their mournful cries into the night and street lights blinked haloed yellow eyes through the mist. It was just as well she wasn't a true Catholic – to them suicide was a mortal sin against God. But they would all condemn her, nevertheless. Dermot most of all.

Her high heels tapped out their unsteady staccato rhythm on the asphalt as she neared the water's edge. How long would it take? Five minutes, maybe ten? She had had no experience of drowning, although she had read once that an English writer, Virginia Woolf, if she remembered rightly, had taken her own life like this a few years ago. Walked into a river, so the papers had said, with her pockets full of pebbles to weigh her down. Maybe she should have brought something heavy with her. Maybe she would simply float around on the surface to be spotted and picked up by some stevedore on the night shift. A wave of panic overtook her. She had to do this properly. There could be no question of her muffing it and being plucked like a half-drowned rat from the water.

She hated this city and everything it stood for; every concrete and glass skyscraper full of sinners. For that's what the majority were, she was convinced of it; you couldn't live here for over twenty years and not believe it. She screwed up her eyes as she peered through the mist-shrouded night at the twinkling lights of Manhattan. How many of them were at it now? How many of them were deceiving their partners as Frank had deceived her?

She took a deep, shuddering breath and let it out slowly as she closed her eyes and let the pain wash over her once more. It had happened before of course, many times over the years, but never, never had it felt like this. For your husband to be unfaithful with some cheap little secretary was one thing; even the occasional high-priced tart she could tolerate; but with his ex-wife – well, that was another ball game altogether.

'Estelle . . . Estelle . . . Estelle . . .' Her voice whispered the name like some demonic incantation, as she ploughed her hands deep into the pockets of her linen jacket and walked as deliberately as the half-bottle of gin she had consumed would allow towards the bridge. Estelle Finlay, ex-socialite, ex-wife of Frank Fullerton of Fullerton Finance International, and the brightest jewel in the crown of Phoenix Films, was back in town. And back in Frank's arms. It shouldn't hurt, but it did. God, how it did.

She stared with unseeing eyes into the darkness. To think that for all these years she had thought that she had never really loved him, that she could never love anyone after Dermot. Maybe it was true, maybe she had never loved Frank in that heart-stopping way she had loved Danny's brother, but you couldn't live more than half your life with a man and not feel something at a time like this. She had coped with the other women over the years; in a way it had often been a relief to know that some other female was being called upon to satisfy his voracious sexual appetite, but this – this was different. He had once been married to this woman. He had placed a gold band on her finger years before his ring had ever graced her own hand. He had loved Estelle probably as much as she had loved Dermot – and that was what really hurt. For half a lifetime she had unknowingly played second fiddle in her husband's heart. Estelle was back and was calling the tune that was becoming louder and louder in her ears – so loud that she knew she could bear it no longer.

She shivered and dug her hands deeper into the pockets of the jacket. Maybe other women, much stronger than she was, could cope with this – could grin and bear it as their whole life fell apart, but she couldn't. Life wasn't so big a deal that she could simply hang around and wait for it to happen. For he would ask for the divorce this weekend, there was no doubt about that. He had practically promised Estelle that much last night. She still felt sick, even now, as she recalled the cold, empty feeling in her heart as she replaced the phone extension by the bed, then moved over to the very edge of the mattress as Frank came upstairs from his den to climb in beside her, totally unaware that she had overheard every word.

He would be with her now, she had no doubt about that. They would be together, somewhere out there in this dirty, sprawling city, planning a future together that did not include her. At forty-six she was already obsolete – surplus to requirements – as far as he was concerned.

The water lay below her, an inky darkness that reached down as far as hell itself. It would require no courage – simply a few seconds' exertion to clamber over the parapet and that would be it. The gin numbed the fear beautifully.

Her eyes scanned the immediate vicinity. Now was as good a time as any; if she lingered any longer someone would be bound to stop and ask what she was doing here . . .

Then suddenly she was falling; an involuntary scream echoing in the blackness as she toppled downwards towards oblivion.

'Mrs Fullerton . . . Mrs Fullerton . . . ? If you can hear me squeeze my hand.'

The voice came from the end of a great echoing tunnel . . . a woman's voice, insistent, yet concerned. It had been drifting in and out of her hearing for so long now, but the effort of obeying the request was simply too great. Why couldn't it just leave her in peace?

'Mrs Fullerton, your daughter's here to see you.'

Warm fingers took hold of her hand. 'It's me, Momma, Kitty . . .'

A deep tremor ran through the body of the woman in the hospital bed.

'She's trying, Miss Donovan. I'm sure she can hear us.' The nurse turned to the auburn-haired young woman on the chair

226

by the bed and patted her shoulder reassuringly. 'Just talk to her – keep talking and I'm sure you'll get a response before too long.'

The voices were nearer now, filling Maeve's head as she floated in and out of consciousness. Kitty was here – Kitty, her favourite child. She must try – she must try to respond.

'You're safe now, Momma. You're safe. There was a terrible accident, but you're going to be just fine.' Kitty Donovan held on to her mother's hand and gazed in concern at the drawn face on the pillow. It was no accident, none of them would be fool enough to believe that; in fact, if that truck driver hadn't spotted her throw herself off the bridge and raised the alarm immediately – well, she shuddered to think. But, thank God, at least she had been at home when the police called. What the others would make of it when they found out, heaven only knew. Of all women in this city, surely her mother had more to live for than most? Of course, they did say that women often did crazy things around the menopause, but this crazy . . . ? She could only muse at the unreality of it as she continued to stroke the limp hand in hers.

'Kitty . . .' Her mother mouthed the name; her lungs were far too painful to allow a deep enough breath to say it aloud.

Kitty's brown eyes lit up as she leaned forwards and smoothed a stray lock of damp hair back from the pale brow. 'Don't try to talk, Momma. Everything's going to be all right.'

'The others . . .' The words came out with difficulty.

'They don't know yet, Momma. There was only me at home.'

Maeve closed her eyes once more. Of course there was. That was why she had chosen tonight. There would be less of the family around to notice her absence. Kieran was out with some of his literary friends from Greenwich Village, and Maudie was staying the night with a friend on Lexington; while Charles, dear, dear Chuck, was over there on some Normandy beach, defending his country. But his father – well, she knew only too well where Frank would be.

'Poppa called earlier to say he'd be home late tonight. Something's come up – some problem to do with Lend-Lease. He's to see some guys from the Chase Manhattan and it'll probably be a pretty late night session.'

Kitty's excuse for her stepfather came almost on cue and Maeve managed a faint nod in response. His excuses were always so plausible – infinitely plausible. Why did they have to rescue her? Why couldn't they just have left her to drown?

Footsteps neared the bed and Kitty glanced round to find the buxom figure of the nurse at the foot of the bed. 'She's conscious,' she said, with a relieved smile.

It was almost a week before they let her home. She was to be discharged in the morning, after the doctors' round at ten, but Frank persuaded them to allow her to stay until he could pick her up personally at six o'clock. He stood in the doorway of her room, a tall, much broader figure than when Maeve first knew him, in a slate-grey business suit, with a bunch of red roses in his hand. His fair hair was now silver-grey, and his clean-cut features had long since taken on a craggier look that ideally suited the successful financier in his sixties that he now was.

They talked little on the journey home, but that was nothing new. After twenty-seven years of marriage the conversation had run out long ago. He had not even asked why she had done it when he first came to visit her in the hospital. The omission merely hardened her conviction that he already knew the reason.

'The girls wanted to arrange something a bit special for your homecoming, but I figured you'd rather just take things easy for a bit.' He smiled across the elevator at her as it carried them up to the seventh-floor apartment that had been their Park Avenue home for the past ten years.

Maeve attempted a wan smile. They had only allowed visitors in one at a time in the hospital, but now to have to face the whole family, minus Chuck of course, in one fell swoop was something she could well do without.

They were all congregated in the main lounge, Kitty and Maudie seated at either end of the large white leather sofa and Kieran standing behind them, a glass of bourbon in his hand. The girls were sipping Indian tonic water. Maudie was the first to rise, uncurling her slim dancer's limbs with a feline grace, before rushing across the Persian carpet towards her as soon as they entered the room.

As they hugged, Kieran and Kitty came across to join them, and Maeve embraced each one in turn, before turning to Frank. 'I think I could manage a drink.'

'Gin and tonic suit?'

'Yes, fine.'

There was an awkward silence after he handed it over and made one for himself. Maeve stared down into the clear liquid in her glass. They were waiting for her to say something – anything – to ease the tension that they could all feel. Should she say it was an accident? And, if she did, would they even believe her? The glass-domed clock on the piano struck seven; its melodic chimes echoed in the silence. Finally Kitty spoke. 'It's wonderful to have you back again, Momma. Sarah is preparing your favourite lobster salad for tea – you know, just like she makes it at the Cape.'

'Speaking of Cape Cod,' Frank cut in, 'I guess we could all do with a bit of a break after this. What do you say to us all taking a couple of days off at the weekend and heading over there?' He looked from one to the other expectantly.

Kieran was the first to speak. 'I'll have to have a word with them at the office. I guess I could always take a couple of books up with me to work on.' His position as an editor at Hayes and Hamilton, the publishers on 49th and Madison, meant that occasionally he could decant some of his required reading to his own home.

'I'm off at the weekend anyway,' Kitty said. 'I'll have to be back for a preview of our new exhibition on Monday evening, but if we're leaving Friday it would be just about worth it.'

'How about you, Maudie?' Frank Fullerton looked across at his nineteen-year-old daughter. Maud Amy Fullerton was always a law unto herself, but hopefully this time she would agree to put her mother's welfare first.

Maudie tossed a drape of blonde hair back from her left eye and looked thoughtful. They usually frowned upon you skipping classes at the Academy of Drama and Dance she attended on West 42nd Street, but maybe the odd day wouldn't matter too much. 'Sure, why not?'

'That settles it then. We'll head up to Nauset Friday morning.' Frank beamed as he finished the gin and tonic in one gulp and placed the glass on the coffee table in front of him. 'I'll have a word with Sarah myself to make sure there are no hitches.' He paused to pat Maeve on the shoulder on the way out. 'You take it easy now, honey. Bed would be the best place, if you ask me. I'll see you when I get back.' There was not even the dry peck on the cheek any more.

Maeve stood motionless as he left the room. He hadn't even asked if she felt like driving all the way up to the Cape for the weekend. And if he had she would have said no. The last thing she needed right now was to be cooped up in that great barn of a place with the family – all of whom would be wishing they were back in New York getting on with their own lives.

'Can I get you anything, Mom?' It was Kitty who spoke.

Her mother shook her head. 'No, thanks, honey. I think I'll just be heading on up to bed now. It looks like your father's too busy to stay for Sarah's lobster special, so I guess I'll just get on up to bed now like he suggested and have mine sent up. Please don't feel you've all got to stay around here tonight on my account.'

She looked from one to the other, but all avoided her eyes. 'I won't do anything silly like throwing myself from the bedroom window, I promise.'

The strained smiles that ensued were anything but genuine.

It was the first time they had been up to their summer house at Cape Cod that year and Maeve had even made a silent promise to herself that she wouldn't consider driving up there until Chuck was home from Europe. Somehow it seemed an obscenity to be here in this beautiful place while he was fighting a deadly war thousands of miles away on a foreign shore. She closed her eyes as she leaned back on the padded headrest of her lounger on the wooden balcony of the sprawling white clapboard house that overlooked the golden expanse of Nauset Beach. She could see him now, her beautiful, blond son. For he was beautiful; it would be ridiculous to call him anything else, with his tanned six-foot frame, pale blond hair and clean-cut, even features. Named after her beloved brother

Charlie, and born in New York three years after Kathleen, and followed five years later by his sister Maudie, her two children by Frank couldn't be more different in appearance to her Irish two.

Her Irish two – her lips creased into a rueful smile, for that was always how she referred to them; Kieran, red-haired, stocky and hazel-eyed just like his father, but as different from Danny as chalk from cheese. A pronounced limp in his left leg, the only legacy left by his rebel father to his son, had kept him out of the war, but he would have evaded the draft anyway, she was certain of that, for Kieran was a pacifist and as anti-violence as Danny had been for it, as a political tool. He was much more interested in his books and music. The fact of his Irish birth meant absolutely nothing to him. 'Nationalism's the curse of the twentieth century, Mom,' he had said to her more than once. 'How can a mere accident of birth influence anything? How can that possibly be an excuse to kill your fellow human beings?'

She could just picture the look in his sister Kathleen's eyes whenever he came out with a remark like that. It was the greatest regret in Kitty's life that, although she had been fortunate enough to be conceived in Ireland, she was actually born in New York. All the Irish patriotism that was lacking in Kieran was to be found tenfold in her. All the fire and passion that Ireland had once inspired in Danny were present in her slim young body. Her dark brown eyes burned with an eternal flame for the country she had never visited, but loved with all her heart. Yes, it was Danny's daughter she should have been, not Dermot's. But then, the biological truths of her conception were of no consequence. No one on this earth knew the real truth – knew that Dermot was her father – and no one ever would. The secret would go to the grave with her and Maeve had absolutely no qualms about it. The truth could only cause untold unhappiness, to Kitty most of all. Her greatest pride was in the fact that her father had taken part in the Easter Rising of 1916, and had actually died for the cause.

Maeve opened her eyes and gazed out over the endless blue of the sea. Perhaps that was the reason why she had never returned to Ireland since she had left on that blustery January day in 1917. To have gone back would have meant taking the children, and Dermot would only have to set eyes on Kitty to know the truth. It was all there – the dark auburn hair; the pale complexion; the dark brown eyes and tallish, slim figure, with a slight stoop to the shoulders that Kitty, in her innocence, believed came from too much book work during her adolescence. As a young girl she had begged her mother to take her back to Dublin, of course. And when her pleas fell on deaf ears she had resolved to go herself when she had left art college, but the war had intervened. Hitler and Hirohito had made sure that her beloved Ireland would remain only in her dreams as long as the U-boats placed the Atlantic out of bounds.

Out of bounds for unnecessary trips, that was, but not for summer fun, for the laughter that reached Maeve's ears from the sea shore made her open her eyes and sit up on the chair. Kitty and Maudie were splashing in the surf at the water's edge and calling on Kieran to join them, but he was having none of it, as he lay sprawled in the sun-bleached grass about twenty yards away. They could plead all they wanted, but he would not budge. He was as stubborn as the rest of the family when it came to getting what he wanted out of life.

'Well, that's me ready, honey. You take it easy now, like I said, and I'll see you back home on Tuesday.'

Frank's voice made her turn round, pushing her sunglasses up into her greying hair. He was standing in the doorway of the porch, case in hand, looking every inch the reluctant returnee. But she knew differently. He bent down to kiss the top of her head, his lips barely skimming the hairs.

'Mind how you go.' She kept her voice deliberately light.

'I will, don't you worry. I'll give a ring tonight when I get back to the apartment. Be good!'

Be good . . . Be good . . . The words rang in her head as he waved his goodbyes to the rest of the family on the beach.

When he had gone, she leaned back on the lounger once more and pulled out the magazine she had stuffed beneath the cushion behind her head. Deliberately she flicked through the glossy pages, stopping only when she came to a double-page spread featuring a beautiful blonde woman standing outside the Alhambra Theater on Broadway, her arms flung wide above her head. 'Estelle takes New York by storm' proclaimed the two-inch-high headline. 'New York's favourite blonde star Estelle Finlay has returned home to star in a new musical based on the life of Flaubert's celebrated adultress Madame Bovary. The love affair will not be confined to the stage, for all New York is set to fall in love again with glamorous blonde star . . .'

'All New York,' Maeve whispered, as she pulled down her sunglasses to hide the tears that had already sprung to her eyes. She didn't give a damn about all New York, one man's love affair with this woman had been quite enough to turn her secure, comfortable little world upside down. 'Why, Frank, why?'

But her words were lost in the eddying breeze that swept in from the great ocean that lay beyond the bay.

Chapter 24

Kitty glanced out over the balcony of her mother's room. Maeve was asleep on the lounger below on the veranda, the magazine still open at the offending page.

Kitty's eyes fixed once more on the open-armed figure of Estelle in the glossy black-and-white centre spread, then she grimaced as she walked back quickly into the bedroom. It all made sense now – her mother's moods over the past couple of weeks, the unexpected bursts of temper and the red, swollen eyes over the breakfast table, which finally resulted in the trauma of Saturday night. She pulled open the top drawer of the dressing table and rifled through the jumble of silk under-wear within. It was usually here, she knew that much from her earlier nosy-parkering as an inquisitive child.

'Got it!' Her fingers closed around the white, leather-bound diary and extracted it from beneath a pile of sable-coloured nylons.

Estelle . . . Estelle . . . Estelle . . . The one name written in Maeve's familiar scrawl leapt from every page over the past few days' entries. Kitty closed the book with a shudder, and replaced it in the drawer, unable to stoop to actually reading the contents. 'Damn Estelle Finlay! Damn the woman! Damn the woman to hell!'

She made her way to her own room and threw herself down on the bed, staring up at the pink fringed lampshade in the centre of the ceiling. Something would have to be done – that woman would have to be told what she was doing. She sat up on the bed, tucking her bare feet beneath her as she pondered on the problem. The theatre would have Estelle's address; she would get it and go round there in person; put it to her straight; tell her what she was doing – not just to her mother, but to their whole family. If she was any kind of a woman, surely she would lay off and find some other guy to amuse her?

* * *

Eight o'clock that evening found her standing outside a penthouse apartment overlooking Central Park staring at the name *Finlay*, etched in brass on a plate in the centre of the door. Kitty took a deep breath; she had always prided herself in fearing nothing and no one but . . . 'Easy, girl, easy . . .' She closed her eyes and took a deep breath before reaching out to press the bell, then took an automatic step backwards to await the result.

It was exactly three minutes in coming. But it was not what she expected. 'Is – is Mrs Finlay at home?' Her eyes blinked in surprise at the sight of the tall, thin figure on the doorstep.

'Nope.' The young man had soft dark hair that flopped in a rebellious quiff over a pair of dark brown eyes that stared back at her curiously from behind a pair of horn-rimmed spectacles. 'You a friend of Ma's?'

'Estelle Finlay's your mother?' Her astonishment was impossible to disguise.

'The good lady has that misfortune.'

Kitty took a deep breath. This wasn't at all what she had expected. He must be at least twenty-five and looked far too serious and intelligent to be the son of a sex symbol like Estelle. The only claim the, until now, falling star had to being a highbrow was the number of times she'd had her face lifted. According to the film mags she had a bust measurement of 40 and from what Kitty had read she reckoned the buxom blonde had an IQ to match.

'You a friend of hers?'

'Not exactly.' She moved uncomfortably from one leg to the other. 'More of a distant relative, I guess.'

'Really?' The brown eyes widened behind their glass frames. This was becoming interesting. 'Care to come in and introduce yourself?' He stepped back and made a slight bow and gesture of welcome with his right hand.

More than a little flustered, Kitty entered the apartment and gazed about her with interest. The furnishing was pure Hollywood – mainly white and gilt rococo furniture, with dashes of art deco in the form of alabaster and bronze young women in athletic poses holding up various designs of Tiffany lampshades. Above the mock-Adam mantelpiece was a life-size portrait in oils of Estelle herself at the height of her beauty and success. She walked over and gazed up at it thoughtfully.

'It was done for one of her films,' the young man commented as he closed the door behind him. 'They let her keep it. But then they let her keep most everything she fancies.'

'Even other people's husbands?' The words were out before she could stop them.

The young man let out a whistling breath. 'You've come here to complain that Ma's having an affair with your husband?'

'No, Mr Finlay, with my father, actually.'

'Jeez! And just who might your father be?'

'Frank Fullerton.'

'Ma's first husband?' He stared at her in astonishment.

'The same.'

'This calls for a drink!' He made for a drinks cabinet to the right of the mantelpiece. 'What'll you have, Miss – Fullerton, I take it?'

'Donovan, actually,' Kitty replied. 'Frank's my stepfather. A gin and lemon will be fine, if you have it.'

'One gin and lemon coming up.' He made two and handed her one with a wry smile. 'And what comes before the Donovan – another fine Irish name?'

To her annoyance she felt herself blush. 'Kathleen, but my friends call me Kitty.'

He nodded in approval. 'Kitty Donovan – I like it. It's got a good ring to it. Mine's Finkelstein – Leon Finkelstein. Despite Pa's anglicisation to Finlay, I reckoned if it was good enough for my grandfather it's good enough for me. But you can call me Lee.'

Their glasses touched and each took a sip of the tart liquid within. 'Would you care to sit down?' He gestured towards a gilt carved settee by the huge plate-glass window and she walked across to it and perched on the edge of the flowered satin cushion as he opened an onyx cigarette box on the drinks cabinet. He extracted two, placing both in his mouth and lighting them with a single flick of a matching table lighter.

He walked slowly towards her, removed one of the cigarettes from between his lips and handed it over. The gesture struck her as curiously intimate and momentarily disconcerted her as she took it with a murmur of thanks. He hadn't even asked if she smoked.

He sat down beside her and looked at her curiously as he let the smoke out slowly from his nostrils. They were narrow and slightly flared; his whole face had a finely-hewn sensitivity that she felt must owe more to his Jewish father than the bland Anglo-Saxon looks of his famous mother. 'I have no influence, you know. Over Ma's affairs, I mean. She goes her own way – always has done. I'm sorry this time it's had to be Frank though.'

Kitty looked down at the clear liquid in her glass. The anger she had felt on the doorstep a few moments ago had vanished. She genuinely believed that he was sorry. 'I – I don't make a habit of this type of thing – acting as my mother's protector. There have been other affairs before, I'm pretty sure of it, and Mom has coped with them, but this one was different . . . She attempted suicide at the weekend. I felt Estelle should know.'

'Holy Moses!' He got up from the settee and stubbed the cigarette out roughly in an ashtray. 'Is she all right? She's not going to die or anything?'

Kitty shook her head. 'She's fine, thank God. She's recovering in our house at the Cape right now. She – she doesn't know that I know, or that I'm here. I made an excuse to come back early. I guess I was scared that if she discovers it's still going on when she gets back to New York she'll try again.'

He stared down at her as the words sank in. Then he finished the drink in one gulp. 'What do you say to talking about this over a pizza? I know a little Italian place only a couple of blocks from here that does a marvellous tuna and shrimp special.'

The meal was every bit as delicious as he had promised and as they finished the bottle of wine and relaxed in the candlelit glow of Mario's wood-panelled interior, Kitty could not remember having felt so comfortable in anyone's presence. She found herself telling him of her life as assistant curator of the Bellini Fine Art Gallery on 54th Street, and listening with genuine interest as he told her of his life as a research scientist at the Massachusetts Institute of Technology. It seemed he was now affiliated to the government's Office of Scientific Research and Development, but was deliberately cagey about what exactly they were experimenting in. His chronic myopia had kept him out of the draft and she wondered if it bothered him at all.

'At times,' he replied with a shrug. 'Those Nazi bastards are doing God-awful things to my race over in Europe. Sure there are times I regret I can't be over there with the rest of the boys, but I know that the work I'm doing here will be just as relevant – more so even – in winning this war.'

'And when it's all over, Lee, what then?'

His eyes took on a dreamy look as he leaned forward on his elbows and said softly, 'Then, my dear Kitty, then I'll get my chance. I'll go to Palestine and help build a new world from the ruins of the old.'

'Go to Palestine! You mean you're a Zionist?'

'You make it sound like a dirty word.' He took another sip of the wine and leaned back in his seat. 'You've just told me you believe in a free Irish state, haven't you? Then why shouldn't I believe just as passionately in a free Jewish state? Surely you can understand how I feel?'

She looked across at him; his brown eyes burned with the same fervour as her own when she spoke of Ireland – that beloved land across the sea that was her spiritual home. 'I can understand that, Lee,' she said softly. And she could.

He walked her to the door of her parents' apartment, but refused her invitation to come in for coffee. 'I guess it might take some explanations if ol' Frank's at home, don't you, honey?'

She smiled up at him. He was standing very close and smelt faintly of tobacco and the peppermints they had been sucking in the cab on the way here. 'It's an odd feeling that your mother and my stepfather are – are having an affair.'

His lips quirked into a smile as a hand reached out and touched her cheek. 'It would seem much more appropriate somehow if it was us and not our parents, wouldn't it, Kitty?'

Her cheeks flamed and she stepped backwards, searching inside her purse for the door key. 'Thanks for the meal, Lee. I enjoyed it, I really did.'

'Enough to see me again?'

She shook her head, her mother's distraught face on the hospital pillow filling her mind. 'I don't think so, somehow.'

He stared down at her, as if not quite sure he had heard properly, then, without another word, he reached out and touched her hair. His slim fingers lifted a smooth dark auburn lock from the side of her cheek and for a few seconds he caressed it between his thumb and index finger as his eyes searched her face. He was waiting for her to speak, to change her mind; she was sure of it, but loyalty to her mother prevented her uttering a word. She could feel her heart beating rapidly beneath the cool white cotton of her blouse; he had incredibly long lashes for a man, and the glass of his spectacles seemed to make his eyes even bigger as they gazed down into hers. She wanted so much to dislike him, to punish him for what his mother was doing to hers, but it was as futile as whistling for the moon. She could only shake her head in despair as his fingers gently moved from her hair to place an invisible kiss on her lips before he turned and headed for the elevator.

The few days at the Cape seemed to do Maeve some good and Kitty found herself scrutinising her mother's face after the rest of the family's return to New York. But while it was true that the tell-tale swelling of her eyelids had gone down, the eyes themselves had a curiously vacant expression. The only person she seemed to pay any attention to was Frank and he was seldom there. It was useless trying to bring up the subject when they were alone, for Maeve would merely give a dry laugh and tell her not to be so theatrical and worry so much over what had been simply a silly accident. It was as if they were living on the edge of a volcano and any minute her mother would let slip her tenuous hold on the edge and tumble back down into the inferno within. By the end of the first week Kitty knew she had to confide in someone. To tell Maudie seemed unthinkable – Frank was her natural father, after all. But Kieran, that was quite another matter.

Kitty glanced across at her brother as he sat sprawled on an easy chair by the window of the lounge, a pile of typewritten sheets of a novel on his lap. She had never found it easy to discuss their mother with him. The fact that she was Maeve's favourite had been obvious to them both from as far back as she could remember, but what made it worse, much worse, was that of all her four children Kieran was the one who cared most for the woman who had borne him. He cared with an unspoken passion unknown to all but perhaps his sister, and Kitty could not believe that he did not already have some ideas of his own on the subject she was about to raise.

He listened in silence as she began hesitantly at first to relate her discovery, his normally placid features hardening as the words poured out of her as she neared the end. A hand was pushed through the short shock of flame-red hair as he took a deep breath. 'How long has the bastard been at it?'

Kitty shrugged helplessly. 'God knows. It's thirty years since he divorced Estelle – she must have been back in the city countless times since then.'

Kieran gave a wry grimace. 'Estelle Finlay, the original good time that was had by all – including ex-husbands! She's been through two more of them since she divorced that Jewish guy she ditched Frank for originally, and, if I remember rightly, the latest one only hit the dust in Reno last Christmas.'

Kitty frowned. Trust Kieran to keep up with all the scandal mags. 'That's probably just before she agreed to come back to Broadway with this show.'

'Right!' Kieran bunched the typescript pages together loosely and laid them on the floor as he got up and began to pace the area in front of the window. 'How could we be so stupid, Kitty, for God's sake? How could we be so bloody stupid?'

'Us?'

'Yeah us! We should've known something was going on before this. I noticed Mom had been out of sorts lately, but put it down to the change of life. I knew she'd been seeing the doctor quite a bit recently, but all that guy seems to do is to ply her with sleeping pills.' He paused, his hands plunged deep into the pockets of his brown cord pants, then he turned to stare wild-eyed at his sister. 'Jeez, Kitty, she must have enough of those things to commit suicide a dozen times over!'

He was right and she could only nod bleakly.

'Something positive's got to be done. It's no good you pissing about pleading with that guy Finkelstein, I doubt if he'll even mention it. He probably lives off the damned woman and daren't say a word in case dear Momma cuts off his allowance.'

'He does not! He's a scientist – he told me so. And he doesn't live with her permanently, he was simply down here spending a few days.'

'Easy, easy! What's with you and that guy anyway?'

'Nothing, nothing at all.' She brushed her hair back behind her ears with an impatient gesture, vaguely annoyed that she should find herself having to defend any relation of Estelle Finlay's, but equally irritated at hearing Lee so abused. 'And just what is this positive action you reckon is necessary anyhow? What do you intend doing – taking out a court order to stop them seeing each other?'

He glared across at her. 'Don't worry, I'll think of something.'

She watched him as he gathered up the manuscript from the floor and strode from the room. Maybe it wasn't such a good idea after all to share her discovery with Kieran.

Chapter 25

A bead of perspiration formed at the nape of Maève's neck and trickled down her back beneath the white linen dress. New York in late June was not a comfortable place to be, but be here she must, despite all Frank's entreaties to go up to the Cape for the summer. How could she? How could she leave New York and leave him to the clutches of that woman?

She passed a hand across her brow as she turned the corner of 6th Avenue on to the hot grey asphalt of Broadway itself. She had come here every weekday for the past fortnight, ever since she discovered that Estelle attended rehearsals at two every afternoon. There was always a small knot of fans outside the side entrance that she used and it was quite easy to make herself inconspicuous. Somehow there was a curious comfort to be gained from seeing her enter the building and knowing she would be there until five. For those precious three hours she could not be with Frank.

At two minutes past two exactly the familiar black Cadillac drew up and discharged its valuable cargo. Estelle looked stunning as usual; her silver-blonde hair worn loose on her shoulders, with a lock falling seductively over one eye. Her figure, for a woman well advanced into middle age, was exquisite, and made Maeve all the more aware of the thickening around her own waist and the generous sprinkling of grey in her once glossy dark hair. If Estelle recognised the figure in the dark glasses and white sleeveless shift dress from previous afternoons, she gave no indication as she swept into the entrance, with her usual beaming smile and regal wave of the hand for the waiting fans.

When she had disappeared and the door had shut firmly behind her, Maeve stood staring at it for several minutes. The urge to rush across those few yards and turn the bronze handle to enter that other world was almost irresistible. It took the greatest resolve to tear herself away and cross the street, where she turned once more to gaze back at the closed door. A cab was drawing up outside it, momentarily obscuring the view and a flicker of irritation crossed her face. Then her mouth fell open in horror. A man was getting out. A tall, well-built man, with silver-grey hair. A man carrying a large bunch of red roses wrapped in pink tissue paper. It was years since he had given her such roses. 'Frank . . .'

The name was lost in the ceaseless roar of the traffic as she watched in hopeless dejection. Perhaps this was what she had really been coming here every afternoon to see. Perhaps it wasn't Estelle at all she waited for, in the searing heat each day . . . She turned and stumbled on into the crowd of summer shoppers and sightseers who thronged the sidewalk of New York's most famous street.

It took almost half an hour to get home to Park Avenue, to be greeted in the front hall by Sarah. 'No, I don't want anything, Sarah, before you ask.' It was impossible to hide the irritation in her voice and she hated herself for it.

The air inside the apartment felt blissfully cool, and the drowsy hum of the air conditioning was curiously comforting as she made her way to the drinks cabinet in the drawing-room. A full half-bottle of Gordon's gin was extracted and tucked inside her clutchbag, which she replaced under her arm, before proceeding through to her own room. If the oblivion of death had been denied her, then drink was a convenient substitute.

There was a small bottle of tonic water by her bedside and she used that to dilute the spirit as she lay down on the bed. Her system must be getting too used to it now, she decided, for it took almost twice as many gulps before that delicious couldn't-care-less feeling submerged her usual depressed state of mind. The wonder of it was why she felt like this at all. She hadn't really given a damn over Frank's other affairs. In fact, there was something comforting in the knowledge that she had never loved him deeply enough to care. The only real love in her life, her love for Dermot, was something hidden deep within her, something to be taken out occasionally, when she was quite alone, and mulled over, its memory cherished and polished with infinite tenderness and care.

Her fingers found the tiny silver crucifix around her neck; his last present to her. It was almost thirty years now since they had said goodbye that day in her small kitchen in Dublin's McIntyre Street. It all seemed a million miles away, and a million years ago. Was there any resemblance still remaining to that dark-haired young girl? Was there any resemblance still remaining in him to that idealistic, intense young priest? She had deliberately not written personally to him after she left Ireland, preferring to get news from Katie. Dear, dear Katie . . .

Two large teardrops squeezed from beneath her closed eyelids and trickled down the pale cheeks as she shook her head on the pillows and remembered the tiny, flame-haired child she had had to leave behind. Katie was nearly forty now – a grown woman living in Belfast with a family of her own; two girls and a boy. The eldest child, Deirdre, had been given the second name of Maeve after her and was now a beautiful, auburn-haired young woman of nineteen, on the threshold of womanhood herself.

She had seen photographs, many of them over the years, but none of Dermot. Whether this was a deliberate decision on his part, she had no way of knowing, for he was certainly present at many of the family gatherings that had been recorded on film by Katie's husband Eamon's little box Brownie. He was still in Dublin, in the same parish in fact, she knew that much. According to the family, he had had the chance of becoming a Monsignor but had turned it down, preferring to stay close to his flock. She could believe that; their good was always more important to him than his own. Even she could not compete with his calling; she knew that to her cost, and that bitter fact had remained an open sore within her heart for over quarter of a century.

A deep sob rose within her, shuddering up through her body to explode from her lips in a low moan, as she rose on the pillow and reached for her glass once more. Another splash of clear spirit filled the bottom of the glass and this time she did not bother with the tonic as she downed it in one.

Was it really Frank's unfaithfulness that was making her crack up now, after all these years? Or was it something deeper – much deeper? Could it be that the knowledge that he too might have nurtured a secret yearning for his first wife – kept it hidden deep within his soul throughout all the years of their marriage, just as she had done – could that be what was really impossible to take? She had chosen his love in preference to the qualified love offered by Dermot all those years ago, only to find half a lifetime later that her husband's feelings too were qualified – given with only half a heart. The other half belonged to another woman – to Estelle – just as the other half of Dermot's heart belonged to the Church. Even Danny's affection had been shared with another woman, with Cissie O'Rourke. Never had she merited the complete love of one man. She knew now she had given up the only real love of her life for a man who had over all these years nurtured a secret yearning for his first wife, and that was an enormous cross to bear.

Faces and places swam in a haze behind her closed eyelids, but one face loomed largest in her mind's eye. It was his face – Dermot's face; the dark eyes burning with the same flame that had consumed her soul all those decades ago . . . The pain was real within her; the keen-bladed knife of memory twisting deep inside, so that she cried aloud as she reached across for the remains of the gin in the bottle. This time she did not bother with the glass. The neck found its unsteady way to her lips, the burning spirit trickling down the sides of her mouth as she gulped down the remainder of the pungent painkiller before throwing the empty bottle into the bedside cupboard and closing the door.

More than anything else she wanted to be out of here – out of this life with Frank – and out of this apartment, in this soulless city of concrete and glass. She wanted to be back in Ireland – back in Dublin. She wanted to be back in the arms of the only man she had ever loved. She wanted Dermot. Oh God, how she wanted Dermot . . .

Kieran was the first home that evening, to be greeted by a distraught Sarah. 'Ah jist can't rouse her, Mista Kieran, Ah swear to God Ah can't!'

Cursing his lame left leg which wasted precious seconds, he ran through to his mother's room, closely followed by the puffing buxom figure of the housekeeper. Maeve was lying diagonally across the satin quilt of the bed, one arm thrown up behind her head. Kieran grabbed her wrist in one hand and placed his other hand on his mother's brow. It felt cold and clammy, but at least she appeared to be breathing.

He snatched open the drawer of the bedside cabinet, emitting a sigh of relief at the sight of the still half-full bottle of sleeping pills. Then the door beneath was pulled open and the empty bottle of Gordon's fell out on to the carpet.

'Is that bastard home yet? Is her husband home?' For the first time in Sarah's hearing he did not refer to Frank as 'my father'.

The housekeeper stared at him in confusion, her round dark eyes bulging in the sweating brown face as she glanced nervously towards the open door behind them. 'Mista Frank's not here yet.'

'And ain't likely to be, no doubt – the bastard!' He threw the empty gin bottle into a wastebin at the side of the dressing-table and turned to Sarah once more. 'Ring for the doctor, will you – right away. I'm going over there.'

'Over where, Mista Kieran?'

'To Fullerton Finance, where else? That bastard's going to be taught a lesson he won't forget in a hurry!'

Frank Fullerton's shaggy silver brows rose in astonishment as his stepson burst into his office. Placing his glasses on the blotter in front of him, he got up from behind the polished walnut desk. 'Kieran – is something wrong?'

'You know the answer to that, you bastard!'

A frown creased the skin above the pale blue eyes as Frank came round the edge of the desk and made for the drinks cabinet built into the bookshelves that lined the wall to the right of the desk.

'Don't bother for me.'

The older man gave no indication of having heard, but, nevertheless, he poured only one glass of bourbon, splashing two ice cubes from a silver ice-bucket into the golden spirit. 'And to what may I attribute this unexpected visit?' He took a swig of the drink and turned to face his stepson.

'Don't come the innocent with me, for Chrissake. You know darned well why I'm here.'

The two men faced one another across the expanse of grey wool carpet, then finally Frank spoke. 'It wouldn't be about your mother, would it?'

'Darned right it would.'

'Has something happened?'

'She's out cold right now, with an empty gin bottle by her side, but that's only to be expected, ain't it, *Daddy*?' He spat the last word out, resolving never again to acknowledge this man as any type of relative. 'It would have been more convenient for you if she stayed that way – or, better still, if they'd never pulled her from the East River, wouldn't it?'

'You little bastard!' Almost throwing the whiskey glass from him, Frank bounded across the floor and grabbed his stepson by the throat. 'What the hell do you mean by that?'

Kieran brought his two arms up and wrenched the older man's wrists downwards. 'You know exactly what I mean. You're killing my mother, you bastard, with your whoring around with that old slag Estelle Finlay!'

Frank's face turned puce and a film of sweat broke on his brow. His fists clenched, then he took a swing in Kieran's direction. The blow missed its mark, causing the intended recipient to grin triumphantly.

'Come on then, hit me! It's the only answer you've got, ain't it, old man?'

'Don't you "old man" me, you young faggot! At least I'm still capable of "whoring around" as you put it. At least it's women who still turn me on, not tight-assed little fairies from Greenwich Village!'

Kieran's face went quite white behind the rust-coloured freckles. Holy Mother of God, what did he mean by that? Did he suspect? Did they all suspect? His mouth went dry and his throat closed up as he tried to speak, to refute the unspeakable that had just been uttered by the red-faced man in front of him.

A superior grin distorted the craggy features of Frank's face. 'You've got no answer to that, have you, sonny boy? Thought you could hide it from *decent* people like your own family.

247

Well, we weren't born yesterday. We all know you and that fruitcake pal Carelli ain't discussing the merits of modern literature when you spend all those evenings at his place over on Bedford Street.'

'You shit – you . . .' Kieran made a rush at the tall, grey-suited figure in front of him, but a hefty shove from the older man sent him staggering backwards.

'Don't mess with me, son. Just keep your lily-white fairy hands off of me. There ain't a queer born who can tangle with me and come out with his features intact.' As if to emphasise the truth of his statement, he walked back to his desk and sat down on the leather swivel chair and picked up his glasses from the pad in front of him. 'And don't try coming here again and playing the hard man. You're not up to it, Kieran boy. You're in the world of real men here on Wall Street, it'd serve you well to remember it.'

Trying to salvage what little pride he could from the encounter, Kieran straightened his shoulders and looked directly into the pale, ice-cold eyes. 'I take it, beneath all that foul-mouthed slander, you're telling me you've no intention of giving up that actress bitch?'

'Whether Estelle and I see each other or not is our own affair, and nobody else's.'

'Not even my mother's?'

His patience at an end, Frank laid his glasses on the desk once more and glared across at the young man standing so awkwardly in front of him. For a fleeting moment he felt something akin to sympathy for this pale-faced young cripple. Maeve had never loved him, he was well aware of that, and, despite a real effort in his early years as a stepfather, neither had he. 'Just get the hell outa here, Kieran, will you? And if you can't get out of my life, just get the hell out of my sight!'

Chapter 26

'They know, Louie. God help me, they know!'

'Aw shit, Kieran, you've no evidence of that. From what you say only your old man knows — or at least suspects.'

'Don't call him my old man, for Chrissake! He ain't my old man and never will be. My old man died twenty-eight years ago in Ireland. He was no fat slug getting rich on the backs of poor bastards fighting this dirty war. He might have been misguided in thinking he could change things with the gun, but at least he didn't two-time my mother like that bastard is doing.' Kieran sat up on the edge of the dishevelled bed and pulled a crumpled pack of Lucky Strikes from his jeans pocket. He lit one and leaned back against the bed end, before tossing the packet across to his friend and lover.

Luigi Carelli, better known as Louie, struck a match on the sole of his shoe and dragged a lungful of smoke through his well-drawn lips. His dark, thickly-lashed Italian eyes looked across at his friend in concern. It didn't bother him, it never had, if people recognised his sexual preference for his own sex, but then, with his parents both dead, he had no relatives over here in the States to bother about. Maybe he would feel differently if he were still back in their home town of Palermo, and his mother was still alive. 'I figure he ain't gonna tell your ma anyhow. What good would it do to cause more trouble? Most likely he reckons he just needs to scare the shit outa you to get you off of his back.'

Kieran's eyes narrowed as he took a long drag on the cigarette and let the smoke out slowly through his nostrils. 'Yeah, you're probably right. It sure don't help matters, though. He ain't gonna stop seeing that old bag, that's for sure, and Mom's cracking up over it.'

He got up from the edge of the bed and walked to the window. Twilight was falling over the grey street down below and a young couple, a boy and girl barely out of their teens, were necking in a shop doorway across the way. His mouth tightened. He had never experienced that – the desire to lay a hand on the opposite sex. He had never felt any powerful emotion for any woman but his mother. And though that love had never been reciprocated it made no difference to the agony he was now going through watching her suffer like this.

'What do you reckon on doing then? You can always move in here permanently. There ain't much room, but you're welcome to what little space there is.'

Kieran turned and threw a grateful smile at his friend. 'Yeah, I know that, Louie. And thanks, but no. Right now I figure it's more important to stick it out over there on Park Avenue. That way I can see what's going on. But as soon as I see her getting over this, I'll sure as hell get outa there. If I never set eyes on Frank Fullerton again it'll be too soon.'

'And if she gets worse? If your mom don't get over it, what then?'

'Then I'll kill the bastard with my own hands!'

Louie fell silent, staring across at his friend. A nerve was twitching beneath the freckled skin at the base of Kieran's jaw and the knuckles of his right hand showed white through the pale skin as he gripped the cigarette. There was hate in his eyes, real hate, such as he had never seen before. Gone was the gentle, dreamy-eyed young man who had first smiled at him so shyly, then grew slowly bolder, his glances more intimate, making his own heart beat faster beneath his new blue silk shirt, when he first joined the firm of Hayes and Hamilton, on 49th and Madison, as Kieran's office dogsbody.

Aware of the other's eyes on him, Kieran glanced across at his friend and attempted a smile as he held out his hand. Louie took it, clasping it to him, then raising it to his lips, as he moved closer and pressed the red head to his chest. The evening was hot and sticky; the air conditioning in the small bed-sitting-room inadequate for the ninety-degree temperature within. The young Italian-American was dressed only in a pair of faded denim jeans and Kieran's cheek lay motionless against the damp, curling hair of his bare chest. There was nothing he could say or do to relieve the pain he knew his friend was now going through, but it did not prevent him trying. 'Let's go to bed, *bellissimo* . . .'

Kitty pushed the sunglasses up into her hair and glanced down at her watch. Trust her to be late this morning of all mornings, but there was no way she could have left for work without waiting to see how her mother was. The doctor had prescribed yet another new batch of tranquillisers to be taken when Maeve finally awoke from her drunken stupor and Kitty felt it incumbent on her to wait and see how she was after breakfast. Heaven only knew had happened to Kieran last night. He had phoned just as she was preparing for bed to check on how things were, but had obviously spent the night elsewhere, for his bed had not been slept in. And both her stepfather and Maudie might as well have been living somewhere else too, for it was the early hours of the morning before either of them got in. She knew for she had checked with Sarah before she left. The housekeeper had the small room next to the elevator and was a light sleeper; there were very few nocturnal comings and goings that she missed.

The tiny hands of her watch indicated ten-twenty. It gave her exactly one hour and forty minutes to get the information she needed for the brochure she was writing for their next exhibition. It was due at the printer's by lunchtime, but she should make it if things went smoothly from now on.

Fifth Avenue mid-morning in high summer was not the most pleasant place on earth to be and it would be a relief to get inside into the cool spacious precincts of the Public Library.

As her high heels clicked up the wide marble steps, her eyes glanced upwards to the inscription above the main door: 'But Above All Things Truth Beareth Away The Victory'. The words had an ironic ring this morning. Was that always the case? Certainly there were no winners in their family now the truth was out.

Attempting to put all thoughts of family affairs behind her, she crossed the great hall with its display of Renaissance maps and miscellaneous literary relics. Then, too impatient to join the small knot of people waiting for the elevator, she hurried on past and ran up the gleaming marble steps leading to reading room 315. Passing the enormous oil painting of 'Blind Milton Dictating Paradise Lost To His Daughters' with scarcely a glance, she raced through the echoing third-floor halls to arrive finally at the catalogue room with its wall-to-wall drawers of well-thumbed card indexes.

Her books finally located, she slung her white leather bag further back on her shoulder and, clasping her hefty bundle to her breast, headed for one of the great golden-varnished tables so peculiar to room 315. For midsummer the room was surprisingly full, but she was lucky enough to locate a spare seat to the right of the door. She sat down with a sigh and opened the first volume.

Soon her pen was scribbling across the page of her notebook, transferring all the desired information to the clean page. Someone across the table coughed; a rather forced cough that merited only a faint flicker of a frown across her brow as the pen moved steadily onwards. Then the cough was repeated, and repeated once more, until finally she looked up in irritation.

The eyes that smiled into hers were walnut brown and instantly familiar. 'Lee!'

He placed a reproving finger to his lips and cast a glance around the other silent occupants of the room. He had obviously finished his business for the morning for his books were already placed back in a neat pile, but as she smiled awkwardly across the wide expanse of table, he took out his notebook and, extracting a page, he scribbled something on it, then sent it skimming across the table at her.

She reached out and caught it with an embarrassed glance at the two elderly men seated on either side of her. 'Mario's, eight o'clock. Be there – please.'

A quiet smile crossed her lips, as she re-read the spiky, slanted handwriting, then carefully refolded the paper. But when she looked up to find its author he had already gone. She leaned back in her seat and took a deep breath as the smile returned to her lips. To have waited for a reply would surely have been to invite another refusal. Mr Leon Finkelstein was no fool. But then she knew that all along.

* * *

'You're pretty sure of yourself. How did you know I'd turn up?' Kitty slipped into the empty high-backed chair at the table for two in the window alcove of the restaurant and picked up the single pink rose that lay on the napkin between her knife and fork.

Lee Finkelstein's face broke into a slow, knowing smile. 'Just intuition, I guess. But I'm glad you came.'

The delicate perfume of the bloom filled her senses as she stroked its velvet petals against her cheek. She had never been given a rose by a man before and the gesture touched her. 'Are you usually so romantic with your dates?'

'Are you usually so inquisitive with yours?'

'Touché.'

They grinned at one another across the checked gingham cloth as the waiter appeared at Lee's elbow. He ordered for both of them; lasagne napoli, followed by fresh fruit salad and coffee. The house wine was a full-blooded claret that brought an immediate glow and calmed the few qualms remaining in her mind about her decision to come tonight.

Conversation came easily. For a scientist, Lee Finkelstein had an enviable way with words and a dryly ironic sense of humour and Kitty found herself laughing more than she had done in a very long time. Unlike her, he was an only child, Estelle having preferred abortions to more offspring, and admitting the fact was the only time she was aware of a bitterness creeping into his voice. As a child of Hollywood he had been imbued with a decidedly jaded view of family life. Listening to him relate some of his early experiences, Kitty could not help feeling that her reaction to her mother's predicament might have seemed a trifle theatrical. However, unwilling to spoil what was turning out to be an uncommonly enjoyable evening, she deliberately avoided mentioning the reason behind her first meeting with him.

As they reached the coffee stage, a small three-piece band appeared at the far end of the floor, playing a seductive selection of Neapolitan love songs, and Lee looked across at her and raised an expectant eyebrow. 'I warn you I have two left feet, but I'm game if you are.'

Giving her no time to consider, he stood up and proffered his right hand, slipping it behind her waist as she rose from her seat. She slid comfortably into his arms. His cheek, although clean shaven, felt slightly rough against her brow as he hummed along with the music into her ear. After a few minutes, his left hand let go hers and slid around her back. Her hands moved up around his neck as they moved slowly around the cramped dance floor. By now at least half a dozen other couples had joined them, making movement almost impossible, but it no longer mattered. All that mattered was the fact that they were in each other's arms and enjoying every minute of it. It was almost two months since she had been out with a man. Somehow dates had ceased to be a high priority in her life over the past year or so, as she worked to build up a reputation for the gallery. But she was glad she had come tonight. Very glad.

When the music stopped, they remained together in the middle of the floor, each as unwilling as the other to let go, to break the spell that had been woven around them. And when the music started up again their bodies moulded even closer, moving slowly, seductively to the evocative strains of 'O Sole Mio'. She could feel his lips, warm on her brow, start to move down her cheek. A tremor ran through her body as his tongue traced the outline of her inner ear and his hands moved in a slow caress across the bare skin of her back.

It was over half an hour before they made their way back to their table, to be faced with cold coffee in the pot and an almost empty wine bottle. Kitty's body, beneath the apple-green cotton sun-dress, was bathed in a film of perspiration and was emitting signals to her that she had never experienced with any other man. She sensed he knew it too and was probably experiencing something similar, for his eyes were burning with a deep golden glow as they smiled down into hers. 'Fancy going on elsewhere?' His voice was huskily low as he leaned across and whispered into her ear.

Her mind flew back to her parents' apartment and she cursed the fact that she was still living at home. All she wanted right now was to be alone with him, to learn more about this dark, intense young man both mentally and physically. 'It — it's difficult . . .' she began.

'I've got a place — a pretty scruffy dive over on Brooklyn Heights, but it's private. Fancy taking a chance?'

He knew the answer before she nodded her head.

His apartment was exactly as he described it: a pretty scruffy dive that had decidedly seen better days, half-way up an apartment block on Brooklyn Heights. He offered coffee, but she declined. Instead she accepted a beer, cold and refreshing from the icebox.

'It feels as if we're in for another scorcher of a night,' Lee commented, as he divested himself of his jacket and tie and yanked open the top buttons of his shirt.

Kitty's eyes fixed on the mat of curling dark hair that adorned the tanned chest beneath. He was no beefcake specimen it was true, but there was something undeniably attractive about him. He possessed a sinewy, almost animal-like grace, and the dark hair and deeply-tanned olive skin made an intriguing change from the red and blond heads and fair skins of the males in her own family circle.

Suddenly aware of her eyes on him, he smiled across as he sprawled casually across the low-slung corduroy sofa opposite and took a swig of the beer. 'Feel free to do the same,' he grinned, indicating his discarded clothing.

'You'd get a shock if I did.'

She meant it in fun, but he shook his head, his eyes suddenly serious. 'No, I wouldn't.'

'You're quite used to girls taking their clothes off round here then?' It was difficult to keep her tone as light as she intended.

'It happens.'

'Often?' Incredibly, a pang of jealousy shot through her.

'Does it matter?'

They stared at one another across the few feet of living-room. Suddenly the air was electric. This was no time for lying and both knew it.

'Yes, dammit, it does!'

Chapter 27

Kitty awoke first and turned her head slowly in the crook of the masculine arm that lay sprawled across the pillow. A ray of bright sunshine had penetrated a broken slat in the blind on the window at the foot of the bed and it lay like a spotlight on the face beside her. The tanned skin was shining, a testimony to the heat of the night that had just gone. For a man in his late twenties his face was curiously unlined. Only the faint laughter lines that fanned upwards from the corners of the closed eyes and two narrow troughs in the skin between the dark straight brows gave any indication that this was no inexperienced adolescent lying here beside her. Perhaps the nose was a mite too large and the cheekbones too pronounced for it to be called a handsome face, but its minor imperfections did nothing to lessen its attraction. Every now and then a small nerve in his right eyelid flickered and she waited expectantly for the brown eyes to open on the new day. When, after a minute or so, they didn't, she leaned across and said softly, 'Lee, are you awake?'

Her whispered query brought no response as the man beside her moaned softly in his sleep, the ghost of a smile hovering across the finely-drawn lips. He must be dreaming, she thought. She had dreamed herself last night, in between the long periods she had lain awake in the sultry darkness, content just to be lying there next to him, naked and unashamed.

She had never slept with another man before, never, not once in her twenty-seven years. She had had love affairs before – at least two of which had almost ended in marriage. She had even been officially engaged once, to Guy, one of her stepfather's financial whizz-kids over on Wall Street. But, as with the other, she had got cold feet before she got anywhere near taking that fateful walk down the aisle.

She closed her eyes and smiled wryly at the memory. It had been a never-ending bone of contention between her and Guy that she would not agree to 'proving her love for him', as he insisted on putting it, by sleeping with him before the wedding. She had even felt guilty about it, wondering if there was something wrong with her that she did not feel as he did on the subject. Her eyes opened and fell once more on the sleeping man by her side. Now she understood why. There had been nothing wrong with her; she had simply never been in love before.

'I'd ask you to move in if it wasn't such a God-awful place.'

She looked across at him in astonishment. His eyes were closed and she had thought he was still fast sleep. He opened them and a slow, satisfied smile crept over his face as they moved from her dishevelled head of dark auburn hair down over her brow to the startled eyes. 'Did any one ever tell you you look beautiful first thing in the morning?'

'No,' she answered truthfully, sitting up beneath the single cotton sheet and cupping her knees with her arms. 'I've never spent the night with anyone before, so how could they?'

He continued to regard her thoughtfully for a moment, as if evaluating her confession, then he reached over and plucked two cigarettes from a pack on the bedside table. He lit them both and handed her one. 'No regrets?'

She shook her head. 'None.'

'You realise you're now a woman with a past?' he grinned. 'But most guys prefer that – they figure there's always a chance of history repeating itself!'

She looked across at him as his laughter rang in her ears. So that's what she was now, was it? She stared stony-faced at a spot in the peeling plaster just above the window-frame, before drawing deeply on the cigarette.

Unaware that his amusement was not reciprocated, he stuck the cigarette in the corner of his mouth as he adjusted the pillow behind his head. 'How does it feel to be a "fallen woman", Miss Donovan?' His eyes smiled at her through the series of smoke rings that left his lips to drift lazily towards the ceiling.

'If I'm a "fallen woman" now then I guess that must make you a "fallen man" several times over!' She rolled away from him as the anger welled within her.

'Easy, easy, honey!' He sat up on one elbow on the pillow. The bite in her voice took him totally unawares. 'I was only joking.' His hand reached out and touched her bare back. His touch sent an involuntary tremor through her body.

She gave no reply and he repeated himself. 'I was only kidding, Kitty, honey.'

She rolled back on to her back, but could not look at him. 'I know,' she said softly. 'It's just that it's true, isn't it? In the eyes of the world, I mean. A man can sleep with as many women as he has a mind to, but a woman only has to do it once and she's automatically placed beyond the Pale. In the marriage stakes her rating is zero.'

'Not in mine it ain't!'

She turned to look at him as he sat up on the mattress beside her. His eyes were serious as they looked into hers. 'Your rating will never be zero in any stakes where I'm concerned. I'd even consider that formidable institution marriage, if you absolutely insisted.'

She looked at him in astonishment. 'I do believe you would.'

'You'd better believe it, honey. And I swear to you, it's something I've never said to any other female.'

'Wow!' She passed a hand through her hair and took a deep drag of the cigarette, filling her lungs with the white smoke and closing her eyes as she let it out slowly through narrowed lips. He was serious. He was perfectly serious. 'You're crazy, do you know that?'

'About you I am.'

She smiled up at him, shaking her head. 'It wouldn't work, you know.'

'Give me one good reason.'

She grinned. 'I don't fancy being Mrs Finkelstein, for a start!'

'That's no reason – you could keep your own name. Lots of women in Europe do. You'd better come up with something better than that.'

'I don't believe in marriage.' The words came out of their own volition. But as soon as she uttered them, she knew it to be the truth. 'I'll sleep with you, Lee, for as long as you like. I'll even bear your child. But I'll never marry you.'

He looked at her for a long time without speaking, a strange mixture of hurt and confusion in his eyes. Then a grin transformed his face. This conversation had taken him totally by surprise. Marriage was a subject that had barely entered his head until now. But as he looked down at her he could think of many worse things. And he couldn't really take what she had to say about it too seriously ... What was it they said about ladies having the prerogative to change their minds? And this was certainly some lady he had shared his bed with last night ...

Maeve stood up once Sarah had served the Sunday lunch and fingered her napkin nervously as she looked around the dining-table. 'Kieran – girls – your father and I have some rather special news this morning. We heard about it late last night but thought it would be nice to wait till the family was all together ...' She extracted a buff-coloured envelope from a pocket in the skirt of her dress and laid it on the table. 'You're probably wondering why it's champagne we've got on the table today instead of the usual middle-of-the-road vintage ...'

Kieran and his sisters glanced simultaneously across at the bottle in the ice bucket in the centre of the table. Only Kitty had even noticed its presence and she had thought it had simply been a gesture of goodwill by their father. It was the first Sunday he had joined them for lunch in three weeks.

'What is it, Mom? For heaven's sake, get on with it, I'm starving. And apart from that I've got a date in just under an hour.' Maudie fidgeted irritably in her seat. They were all far too old for these childish guessing games.

Maeve took a deep breath and looked across at her husband. For once there was real warmth in the smile he returned. 'Chuck's coming home. He should be with us any day now.'

'What!' Maudie got up from the table and hugged her mother in delight. 'How do you know? How can he? You can't just walk out on a war when you feel like it!'

Maeve sat down as Frank set to to open the champagne and clutched the telegram to her, as if mislaying it might make the whole thing fall through. 'It's not all good news,' she said haltingly. 'He's been injured. Quite badly, in the leg we believe, so they're furloughing him back to the States. Pop reckons it'll

259

probably mean a desk job when he recovers, don't you honey? But it's wonderful news – he's done his bit for his country and that's something we can all be proud of. He'll most likely be decorated too . . .' There was undisguised pride in her voice as she looked round her other offspring before accepting the first glass of champagne from her husband.

'Let's all stand and drink a toast on this momentous occasion,' Frank said, raising his glass. 'To Chuck – a son to be proud of!' He looked directly at Kieran as he spoke the words.

'To Chuck!'

The talk was all of Chuck throughout the meal. None of the others had seen Maeve so animated for weeks. Her face positively shone as she made plans for her younger son's homecoming. 'We'll give a party, of course, won't we, Frank? It's not every family that has the return of a hero to celebrate!'

Kieran's heart sank. He could just imagine it now – Chuck standing there in all his military glory, while the whole of New York society paid homage. Or, at least, anyone that mattered. But then it had been like that throughout their lives: Charles Ballantine Fullerton had lived up to and beyond every expectation of his parents and had been suitably rewarded, while he himself had not only proved a disappointment, but had failed spectacularly in the process.

While Chuck was voted 'The One Most Likely to Succeed' throughout his high-school career, and had been both Junior and Senior Sports Champion, Kieran had left under a cloud. Not exactly expelled; it had been tactfully suggested to his parents that he should leave the week before his eighteenth birthday, his crime being the most heinous of all: anti-Americanism. He had had the temerity, as editor of the school magazine, to publish an article declaring that the United States had only entered the First World War for selfish imperialistic reasons and, as the coming generation, they should make sure such a thing never occurred again. The principal, an ex-West Point man, was appalled and insisted he print a retraction and full apology immediately. Despite his parents' entreaties, he had refused and was forced to graduate from another private college upstate.

* * *

'I just can't take any more of that hero crap, Louie. I've had it up to here!' Kieran made a gesture at throat level and threw down his pen on the paper-strewn desk as he swung round in his chair to gaze disconsolately out of the office window. 'They reckon he'll be here by the weekend and I don't aim to be on the welcoming committee waiting at the door to greet him.'

'What do you figure on doing then? You're welcome to move in with me, you know that.'

Kieran shook his head. 'Nope, I won't give that bastard Frank the satisfaction. I'll look for a place of my own over the next couple of days. I've already got a couple of addresses to look into.'

'You'll come over tonight, though. It's been almost a week.' Louie's voice was seductively soft as he adjusted the mail satchel on his shoulder and reached for the door handle. 'A guy gets kinda lonely . . . Why don't ya come up and see me, my little chick-a-dee!'

Kieran grinned. Louie did one of the best Mae West take-offs he'd heard. He stubbed the cigarette out in the overflowing ashtray in front of him and let his eyes roam possessively over the stocky body in the white T-shirt and blue jeans. Louie worked out in the gym on the corner of Green Street and Grand for a least an hour most nights – and it showed. Even under the white cotton, the muscles of his upper torso stood out like roped steel beneath the thin fabric. He was even thinking of entering for some local body-building competitions, and the fact that it would require shaving off most of his body hair was proving a bone of contention between the two men. Right now, however, differences of opinion were the last thing on Kieran's mind as the thought of a night in his friend's arms filled his mind. He felt a rush of blood from the neck to his face as his imagination traversed the hours between. 'I'll be there, buddy. Count on it.'

His eyes kissed those of the younger man across the few feet of office space and Louie beamed his approval as he took his leave.

Kieran took a deep breath and leaned back in his chair, shoving a freckled hand through the short crop of red hair. It was hot in here – too hot. He loosened his tie even further, then impatiently tore it from his neck and flung it down on the desk, as the telephone at his elbow let out a sharp buzz.

'Yeah, Donovan here.' Balancing the receiver between his left shoulder and chin, he took a cigarette from the pack of Lucky Strikes in front of him and stuck it in the corner of his mouth, lighting it with a flick of his lighter.

'Kieran, it's Maudie!'

The breathless female voice on the other end of the line made him sit up in the chair. It wasn't like her to phone him at the office. 'Hi, kid! Nothing wrong is there?'

'No, quite the contrary! I've been trying to phone Mom, but there's no answer from the apartment. Seems like even Sarah's out and I've simply got to share my good news with someone! I've landed a part in a show – a good one!'

'Yeah? You don't say! That's great, honey – really great! Have I heard of the show?'

'You bet your sweet life you have! Or at least you will have shortly – it's going to be the smash hit of next season!'

It could have been the Irish blood in him that made him too susceptible to premonitions. But most likely it was simply the uppermost thing in his mind at the moment. His lips clenched more firmly round the cigarette as he shifted uncomfortably in his seat. Jesus Christ – don't let it be that one . . .

'It's that new Estelle Finlay show – *Madame Bovary*!' Maudie's excited voice continued, confirming his worst fears. 'I'm to play one of the younger tarts!'

'Typecasting, huh?' Why, in God's name, hadn't they told her? Why had neither he nor Kitty the guts to reveal their discovery? The poor devil was quite oblivious to the fact that her father was that bitch Finlay's fancy-man.

A groan came from the other end of the line. 'I've already heard that line at least a dozen times!'

'Yeah, well, I never was the most creative thinker. If I were I'd be writing these damned manuscripts on some Californian beach right now, and not slaving here in this seventh-floor oven correcting the darned things!' Then, realising he hadn't even offered his congratulations, his voice softened. 'But that's great news, honey, it really is . . .'

'Thanks, Kier . . . I knew you'd be pleased. You've always

encouraged me to follow my dream. And I reckon Pop should be just as happy. At least he won't have to shell out on tuition fees next term – I'll be earning some money for a change.' A babble of other voices sounded down the line and Maudie's voice rose. 'Look, I'll have to go now – some of the guys have just appeared with some bubbly. See you later!'

He held on to the receiver for a good half minute after it had been replaced at the other end. The dialling tone droned monotonously in his ear, then, very slowly he replaced the handpiece in its cradle. 'Jeez . . .'

What happened now? There was no way Maudie could take that role – it would kill their mother. Yet there was no way he could tell her why she shouldn't take it. She idolised her father and if someone was to be the iconoclast in that particular relationship, it certainly wasn't going to be him. No, there must be another way out of it . . .

He rose from the desk and walked to the window, prising open the slats of the blind with his fingers as he gazed down into the street below. He could always call Kitty – leave her to deal with it, but that would be the coward's way out. No, he had to do something himself. But what? He took a deep drag of the cigarette and let the smoke out of his lungs in a slow, hissing stream. He had to talk to Estelle. There was nothing else for it. She was the only one who could get Maudie off the show without spilling the beans. A glance at his watch told him it was almost lunchtime. He'd grab a hamburger and a quick coffee at the delicatessen on the corner of the block and head on to Broadway and the Alhambra straight afterwards.

Chapter 28

Estelle Finlay's glossy pink lips pouted thoughtfully as she toyed with the wine glass. She was much younger-looking and much prettier than Kieran had anticipated. Her voluptuous figure was encased in a shell-pink sweater that matched her lips and nails, and a pair of hip-hugging burgundy slacks that left little to the imagination. 'I get your point – Kieran, isn't it? But I really don't see what possible advantage is in it for me, denying your sister this chance. On the contrary, it should be real nice getting to know Frankie's daughter . . .'

'Real nice for whom, dammit?' Kieran's eyes narrowed as he looked accusingly at the woman in front of him. 'Certainly not for my mother! Your tatty little affair has already nearly killed her once. If Maudie takes that part then God knows what'll happen.'

'But isn't that for Maudie herself to decide? She is old enough, after all.'

Kieran shook his head in frustration. Why couldn't she see what he was getting at? It didn't take a huge IQ to figure out that if Maudie joined her show it would completely crack their mother up. But maybe that was the general idea. Maybe that's what she wanted all along . . . 'You wouldn't have had anything to do with the offering of auditions to those Academy students, would you?'

Estelle's blue eyes widened and she shrugged lightly as she took a sip of the drink. 'I believe in encouraging new talent. Is that a crime?' She looked directly at him, her eyes defiant.

She hadn't denied it. It had been her idea all right. 'You bitch! You selfish bitch! You really want to cause trouble in our family, don't you? Nothing would please you better than for my mother to do herself in. You'd have Frank all to yourself then, wouldn't you?'

Estelle tossed a lock of blonde hair back from her face and gave a light laugh. 'Listen, sonny, nobody – not even me – can

264

break up a marriage that's worth anything. Only those that are not worth the paper they're written on are at risk. If Frankie and Maeve's ain't worth a dime any more, it sure as hell's got nothing to do with me. Do you really believe Frank's been a good little boy for the past twenty-five years or so?' She threw back her head and laughed at the incredibility of the idea. 'Honey, when it comes to your stepfather finally collecting his wages of sin, they'll have to pay him double time for all the overtime he's put in!'

Kieran's face set. It was obvious he was getting nowhere. It was simply no use appealing to her better side — she simply didn't have one. 'I take it you've got no intention either of giving up your sleazy little affair, or of getting Maudie out of the show, then?'

Estelle sighed. 'You make it sound so drastic. I really don't see that it's got anything to do with me at all. And as for not seeing Frank again . . . do I look like an ogre with some terrible hold over him? Do you really think I have to beg him to see me?' A pink tongue slicked across the even pinker lips and her long lashes lowered seductively as she smoothed an imaginary wrinkle from her left thigh. Turning on the charm was as second nature to her as breathing.

Kieran felt himself colour. Could it be that Frank hadn't mentioned the fact that his stepson had no physical interest in women? Or maybe Estelle merely figured that, as a homosexual, he was an even greater challenge.

'Well, you haven't answered me.'

He sighed. 'No, Estelle, you're no ogre. In fact, you're a mighty bright lady. You've probably gotten just about every darn thing you've wanted in this life. I wish to God I could say I hope you get Frank Fullerton, if he's what you really want right now, 'cause I think you both deserve each other. But I can't because of Mom and the others.'

'How noble. How very noble.' Estelle sat down on the chair in front of her dressing-table mirror and crossed her legs, dangling a high-heeled mule from the tip of her right toe, as she sipped her drink. 'But what about you, Kieran? What about you? Do the others appreciate all this worrying about their welfare? Do they care just as passionately about you as you seem to care about them? Does dearest Momma give a damn about all this energy you seem to be expending on her welfare? Or could it be that neither she, nor any of the others in that precious family of yours, gives a tinker's cuss about you and your problems?'

'You know nothing of my problems!' She had him on the defensive now and the knowledge infuriated him.

'Want to bet?' She looked at him with a secret, superior smile, before continuing, 'But, unlike you, I prefer not to sit in judgement on my fellow beings. It doesn't shock me, you know – about you being a . . . well, "one of those", shall we say . . . You can't be in this business as long as I have and stay shocked about anything for very long.' She gave a knowing laugh. 'Anyway, half the he-men in Hollywood are fairies! Honey, I could tell you stories that would make that red hair of yours curl so much you'd never get a comb through it again! It ain't just the gals that get the best parts by frequenting the casting couches, you know.'

'What goes on in that whorehouse of a place has got nothing to do with me.'

'But what goes on right here in New York has, huh?' Her eyes were cold now and looked right through him.

He shifted uncomfortably. This conversation was going nowhere – at least not in the direction he intended. He made a move towards the door. Estelle got up quickly from her chair and reached out a restraining hand on his arm. 'Look, Kieran honey. I'm really not the bitch you think I am. And I do understand about your problems. Why, we've got some real nice guys right here in the show who I'm sure you'd get on with real well. What do you say I introduce you to one right now?'

'One good turn deserves another – is that it, Estelle? You furnish me with some bedtime companions and I leave you the field free to pursue your little peccadillos with that two-timing bastard Frank.' The contempt in his voice was matched by that in his face as he shrugged his arm free. 'Forget it, glamour girl! This is one guy your charm doesn't work on!'

He strode out and slammed the dressing-room door behind him. The sound of one of her high-heeled mules bouncing off the lacquered wood brought a grim smile to his face. He hadn't won, but neither had he been totally defeated. With a woman like Estelle maybe it was as much as he could hope for.

The thought of going back to the office did not appeal in the slightest; he had too much on his mind to concentrate on work. House-hunting might be a more productive way of spending the next couple of hours.

He picked up a newspaper from a nearby kiosk. There might just be something in there that would do, if the addresses he already had didn't come up to much. There was a picture of General MacArthur on the front page, and the leading article referred to his ongoing offensive in New Guinea. It was funny how, even after all this time, he still felt an underlying sense of guilt at the thought of all those other guys out there. Even if he hadn't failed the medical, he would have refused the draft, he was certain of that, but still the guilt remained . . .

Louie had remarked recently that heroes exterminated each other for the benefit of other people who were not heroes. Was that how he saw *him* – as a non-hero? Could you – could anyone – love a person who went out of their way to be a 'non-hero'? He shoved the paper in his jacket pocket and made for the subway. The middle of Broadway on a hot summer's day was no place to be delving into the human psyche . . . Besides, he had some places to look at.

His first address was a two-roomed apartment, four floors up in an old red-brick block across the East River in Queens. And an hour later found him standing in the middle of the main room, the jacket of his suit slung casually over one shoulder as he looked around him. It was further from Louie's place than he would have liked, but the rent was reasonable and at least it was clean. A pin-up calendar, featuring Betty Grable, hung at an askew angle above the dresser. That would be one of the first things to go . . .

'I'll take it,' he said, to the surprise of the landlord, a small, wizened Pole named Zelinski. He had been in the L-shaped living room less than two minutes.

'It's twenty down – returnable when you leave, and a month's notice in advance. You sick or somethin'? Why ain't ya in the war?'

267

Kieran coloured slightly beneath the freckles. 'Yeah, I'm sick. What's it to you anyway?'

'It's just my country that Fascist pig Hitler has overrun, that's all. I still got relatives in and around Lvov, God help 'em.' He crossed himself, before sticking out a hand in Kieran's direction. 'Twenty dollars I said, if ya want it. But no noisy parties or carrying on. I live right underneath.'

Kieran reached into his back pocket and took out a billfold from which he extracted a twenty-dollar note. 'When can I move in?'

The old man shrugged. 'Suit yourself. It's free now.'

'Right. It'll be some time over the weekend, most likely. But I'll take the key now, if that's okay by you.'

The old man handed it over, after carefully folding the twenty-dollar bill and placing it in his shirt pocket. 'Give me a knock next time you're here and we'll get the paperwork sorted out. I'd do it now, but my old lady she ain't too well today.'

Kieran watched him as he shuffled back out of the door. He must be pushing seventy at least. What on earth was a guy like that doing here in this dingy block in downtown New York? He looked like he'd be a hundred times happier back in his native village, Hitler or no Hitler. But maybe not. What did he know about conditions over there in Europe? Precious little. But no doubt he'd be well informed in a few days' time when Chuck got back. He grimaced as he shoved the key in his trouser pocket. With a bit of luck he'd already have moved into here by then, so he should be spared the worst of the hero's war memories.

He glanced at his watch, once back out on the sidewalk. It was almost four o'clock – hardly worth making his way back to the office; the rest of them would be getting ready to pack up for the day shortly. But Kitty should be still at work; the gallery didn't close till seven o'clock. It mightn't be a bad idea to have a word with her before heading back to Park Avenue.

She was surprised to see him, her brown eyes widening in astonishment as he walked in through the glass swing doors. 'Well, big brother, what brings you here? Not artistic reasons, I trust?' She finished adjusting a rectangular watercolour on the wall in front of her and stepped back to examine it before turning to look at him curiously. 'There's nothing wrong, is there?'

He began to shake his head, then halted. 'Well, not exactly. I had a call from Maudie this morning. She's landed a part in Estelle's show.'

'You're kidding!'

'It's true. I've just been to see the lady in question to ask her to get Maudie off the cast, but she won't hear of it. If you ask me she's engineered the whole darned thing.'

Kitty stared at him. 'You mean you've actually been and spoken to Estelle Finlay?'

'The same.'

'What on earth was she like?' The knowledge that her brother had actually spoken to Lee's mother amazed her.

'Blonde, bosomy – bright. To tell the truth I didn't expect the latter.'

Kitty nodded. After knowing Lee, it came as no surprise to her. 'What do you want me to do?'

'God knows. Any ideas yourself?'

She tapped her lower teeth thoughtfully with the end of a pencil, which she stuck behind one ear, as her mind returned to Lee Finkelstein, the man whose bed she now shared. 'I might, brother dear. I just might . . .'

She did not mention Lee to Kieran, preferring only to say that she would make a phone call or two after he had gone, and asking him to keep his fingers crossed. They shared a glass of iced coffee in the back room before Kieran left and she couldn't help noticing how pale and drawn he was looking. She wished they could be closer. It was years since they had exchanged anything vaguely resembling a confidence and she knew little of his life outside the family home. His friends were as much a mystery to her as they were to all the family. If he had ever had a girlfriend she was not aware of it, but despite the occasional suspicious comments from her own friends over the years, she couldn't really believe there was anything untoward about her brother's sexual predilections. Many men of his age hadn't yet settled down with the right girl; it didn't automatically mean there was anything wrong with them.

269

But, as she pulled the shutters down on the gallery windows at just after seven, doubts began to creep in to her mind. Lee was in Massachusetts at the moment and wouldn't be back in New York until the weekend. She'd better ring him now, before returning home. In her parents' apartment there was no telling who might be listening on an extension.

An excited tremor ran through her body as she dialled his number and waited anxiously for the phone to ring at the other end. 'Please let him be in . . .' she murmured, as her fingers drummed nervously on the polished top of the desk.

'Yes!'

His abrupt response made her catch her breath momentarily. Just hearing his voice again affected her more than she anticipated. 'Lee, it's Kitty.'

'Sweetheart – how are you?'

'Fine,' she assured him, relaxing now at the obvious enthusiasm in his voice. 'I have a favour to ask you.'

'Anything. Name it and it's yours!'

She smiled, imagining the look in those walnut-brown eyes at the other end of the line. 'It – it's not that easy,' she began. 'It's to do with Estelle . . .' He groaned audibly as she continued, 'Maudie, my kid sister, has landed a part in her show . . .'

'And you want me to get her out of it?' he interrupted. 'Is that fair? It's a chance in a lifetime for someone like her.'

'I know, Lee. Believe me, I know. I just happen to believe the consequences of her carrying on with it may be more drastic than if she gave it up.'

'Isn't that up to her?'

'Yes. But that would mean telling her the reason. She has no idea about Frank and Estelle.'

'Kitty, honey, how old is she? Nineteen – twenty? Either way she's no child any more. You're asking me a helluva lot – to sabotage a young actress's career to protect a woman who, let's face it, should be quite capable of taking care of her own family problems.'

Kitty stared down into the black handpiece of the phone. The bastard – he was actually refusing to help!

'Are you still there?'

'I'm still here.'

270

'But you're pretty sore at me now, huh?'

'You could say that.'

There was a momentary silence at the other end, then he sighed and said, 'Look, Kitty, what do you say to us talking this over properly Saturday night? I should be back in New York sometime in the afternoon. What do you say I give you a ring around teatime?'

Kitty's lips tightened. 'To that I say, forget it, Lee. Just forget it. In fact, forget I even called.'

'Forget we ever met?' His voice was cynical.

'Got it in one.' She replaced the receiver with a resolute click in its cradle and stared down at it. But it wasn't the man on the other end of the phone she felt a cold, unreasonable anger for. 'Damn you, Maudie! Damn you, Mom! Damn you all!' Here she was, in her late twenties, and her family were still messing up her personal life.

Chapter 29

The furrow between Frank Fullerton's shaggy silver brows deepened as he leaned his head back against the grey hide upholstery of the limousine and closed his eyes. 'Jesus, what a day . . .'

Mike, his chauffeur, continued to whistle softly beneath his breath in the driver's seat in front of him. Frank opened his eyes and stared at the back of the bullet-shaped head. He had often wished he had as little on his mind as the fifty-five-year-old from Park Slope who had driven him to and from the office for the past seven years, but never more so than tonight. Estelle's phone call before he left the office had made him mad – darned mad. Just who the hell did Kieran think he was barging in on her like that? The last thing he needed was for the whole damned family to get involved in what was going on right now between him and his ex-wife . . . But just what *was* going on?

His pale blue eyes moved from the back of the head in front of him to stare out of the side window of the Cadillac. Could it be – could it really be that after thirty years he was actually in love again? . . .

Love, he repeated the word in his head. Maeve had asked him about that word once, long ago. The conversation had remained with him to this day, a dim and distant memory in the back of his mind. It was the first and last time he had ever attempted to define this feeling – this madness that took hold of you, body and soul, and tore you apart. He had told her then it was something you must never grasp at, for then it would run like quicksilver from between your fingers. And he should know, shouldn't he? Wasn't that exactly what he had done all those years ago, after making Estelle his wife?

Estelle . . . A deep sigh escaped his lips as he closed his eyes once more. He had loved her, then . . . Oh God, how he had loved her; so much that after she ran out on him for that rat

Finkelstein he had vowed he would never allow that emotion into his life again. And he had kept that vow.

Poor Maeve, poor, poor Maeve . . . She wasn't to know. How could she know? And he had done his best; he had really tried to be a good husband to her – during the first few years of their marriage, at least. But no matter how he had tried, it had never been a success; their whole marriage, both physically and mentally, had been a charade; a charade carried out by two basically nice people who just weren't meant for each other. Maybe if they could have talked to each other more. But what was there to talk about – his affairs? A bitter smile quirked the corners of his lips. God knows, there had been enough of them over the years. But what the hell was a guy supposed to do when, after the initial gloss of the honeymoon had worn off, every time you went to touch your wife she lay back like a marble statue and thought of England – or goddamn Ireland – or wherever?

Oh, he could make excuses all right . . . Even the Wall Street crash had played its part. It had occurred at just about the time the rose-tinted spectacles had fallen from their eyes; when they both realised that, after a dozen years of marriage, maybe theirs wasn't made in heaven, after all. With his business – his whole career on the line at work, and his wife coming on like the proverbial ice maiden at home, was it any wonder he had turned now and again to someone else for comfort? At first it had just been the occasional one-night stand, but, as time went on, it became simply a way of life. You'd meet a good-looking dame, ask her to join you for a drink, maybe even dinner and . . . Well, it had been so easy, hadn't it? So goddamned easy.

He had no idea when Maeve first realised what was going on, but realise she certainly did, he was sure of that. And, in a perverse way, that was what had made it all so easy. She didn't seem to care. Maybe she was even glad that someone else was relieving her of having to 'do her duty' at least a couple of times a week.

His fingers gripped the soft leather of the attaché case on his knees as his mind probed into the painful recesses of his psyche once more. They had stopped talking not because there was nothing to talk about – but because there was too much to talk about. Some idiot had once said that to know all was to forgive all, but any fool knew that was a load of crap. To know all – to confess all – in their marriage would have simply meant that one helluva lot of heartache would have been needlessly paraded – and to what end? ... Would she have loved him more if he had confessed he had never really loved her – had never loved any other woman but Estelle? Would it have helped their marriage if he had confessed that, rather than impose himself on her so much, he had relieved his sexual frustrations with other women – dozens of other women – over the years? You bet your sweet life it wouldn't. So they had remained silent. And their marriage had survived because of that silence ... Until now. Now Estelle was back in his life. And that made it different. Estelle was not just any floozie he might choose to spend a few hours with at the Waldorf – Estelle was the woman he had married before her – and that Maeve could not handle.

Frank's jaw clenched, as the Cadillac drew to a halt before his apartment block. Why the hell did that interfering little bastard Kieran have to go and stick his nose into things today? Who was he trying to kid? All that crap about Maudie's part in the show was just an excuse. He was warning Estelle off – and nobody, let alone a little creep like his stepson, did that to her! His mind still seethed with fury at the knowledge. Estelle might have passed it off as a joke, but there was no way he was going to do that. It was high time someone taught that busybodying little sonofabitch a lesson! He glanced at his watch. It was just after seven. He should be home by now. Just wait, buster ... Just you wait ...

He could hear Maeve's voice in the kitchen talking to Sarah as he closed the front door and threw his attaché case on to the telephone table in the hall. The door to Kieran's room was shut and he could feel the ire rise within him as he stared at it.

He was barely aware of crossing the floor towards it before he flung it open and gazed down at the body sprawled on the bed in front of him. A flush of perspiration seemed to break from every pore in his body as he fought to keep his voice steady. 'Just what the hell do you think you're playing at?' The pale blue eyes glared in fury at the recumbent figure. 'What

274

gave you the right to go barging in on Estelle like that? Maudie got that part off her own bat and you've no damned business trying to take it off her! And you've even less business barging in uninvited on Estelle!'

Kieran sat up on his bed, blinking the sleep from his eyes at the sight of the older man in the doorway. 'Shout a bit louder, why don't you? Then Mom might hear.'

'To be honest, I don't give a shit who hears. I'm mad, Kieran, bloody mad. Estelle called me just before I left the office and told me about your sneaky little visit. Thank God, the lady's got spunk and sent you packing, from what I gather. You'd no right to go there in the first place. It's none of your darned business meddling into who gets a part in Estelle's show. You've no right at all trying to sabotage your sister's career. Maudie's thrilled – I know 'cause I've just spoken to Estelle about it, and if getting a part in *Madame Bovary* is what makes her happy, then that's fine by me.'

'You're kidding! You mean you're quite happy for her to take it – to work with Estelle Finlay?'

'Too right I am.'

'Mom's feelings don't come into it?'

Frank gave an exasperated shrug. 'Maeve's got to learn to grow up sometime. She can't expect Maudie to give up a chance like this just because she doesn't happen to like the company her daughter will be keeping.'

'In other words, you're quite happy to rub her nose in your shitty affair, by encouraging Maudie to take the part.'

'I don't have to encourage her. She accepted it of her own accord.'

'Will you tell her about you and Estelle?'

'I would've thought you would prefer to delight in that privilege.'

'You're a bastard, you know that, Frank – a real bastard!'

'A bastard that's kept you in a way you certainly don't deserve for almost the past thirty years!'

'You won't have to for much longer,' Kieran said, through gritted teeth. 'I'll be out of here by the weekend.'

'Don't tell me you've got an apartment at last.'

Kieran nodded. 'In Queens.'

Frank let out a great guffaw. 'How appropriate! How very appropriate!'

Kieran leapt from his bed and grabbed Frank by the necktie. 'Say that again, you bastard!'

'Goddam fairy queen, that's what you are!' The older man's face turned puce as the silk tightened around his neck. 'Goddam fairy queen!' he spluttered. But the more he struggled to free it, the tighter the knot became as Kieran clung on. Then, with a mighty swipe, Frank succeeded in breaking free of the younger man's grasp and loosening the silken ligature. His fingers tugging at the neck of his shirt to aid his breathing even further, he backed towards the door, his flushed face sweating profusely as he glared across at the younger man.

'What's wrong, Frankie boy – can't take it? Can't take on a fairy queen?'

His pale eyes bulging, Frank took a lunge towards his stepson. There was no way he was going to be taunted by a young queer like him. His right fist clenched as he aimed a swing in the direction of the freckled face, but Kieran was too quick for him. His own fist caught him clean in the middle of the gut, causing him to double over and sink to his knees. A long exhalation of breath was emitted from his lips like the sound of the air being expelled from a balloon. Then suddenly he was lying on his back, fighting for breath.

For a moment Kieran stared down at him in triumph, then concern clouded his hazel eyes. 'For Chrissake, man, get up!' He knelt down and heaved the grey-suited bulk up by the shoulders, as Frank's eyes rolled backwards into his skull. A peculiar rasping sound was coming from his throat as his chest heaved in vain for oxygen. Something was wrong – far wrong. 'For God's sake, breathe!'

But it was no longer certain that Frank could even hear him. His florid face was turning blue, as were his lips as he fought for breath. A red-hot vice was clamped around his chest and pain such as he had never known was making it impossible to draw breath into his lungs.

Panic filled Kieran's face and his voice was little short of a croak as he urged the man in his arms to breathe. 'Harder – try harder, damn you!'

But the colour was already draining from the face lying in the crook of his arm. A shudder ran through the stout frame in the immaculately-cut business suit, accompanied by a curious jerking movement of the upper torso, then he was quite still.

'No, for Chrissake, no!' Kieran shook the lifeless form, gently at first, then with more force as reality dawned. Uninvited tears sprang to his eyes, then rolled unashamedly down his cheeks. He had killed him. There was no doubt about it – he had killed him, this man who had been the only father he had ever known; the man loved so intensely by his mother that the thought of losing him had made her attempt to take her own life. A long groan escaped his lips, to hang in the air in the silent room. She had lost him now all right. She had lost him for ever. They all had. He was dead. Frank was dead. And he had killed him.

White-faced, he got unsteadily to his feet and stared down at the lifeless form. He couldn't leave him there, lying in that ungainly heap on the carpet. He would have to get him on to the bed. It was the least he could do. Heaving him up by the shoulders, he hauled Frank's body across the floor to the side of the bed. His weight astonished him and it took an enormous effort to get him on to the bed, finally collapsing on top of the corpse as he succeeded in rolling it into the middle of the silk counterpane. All the time the tears refused to cease, running in hot streams down his pale cheeks as he struggled to adjust the body and give it some semblance of dignity.

His fingers pulled at the white silk of Frank's collar. There was a slight redness where the tie had dug into the creased skin, but nothing too noticeable, thank God. But that doctor his mother insisted on using was a nosy son of a bitch. Feverishly he did up the button and straightened the tie as best he could. Awkward questions he could do without.

'Kieran, have you seen your father anywhere?' His mother's voice, from the passage beyond, made him jerk round in panic. She mustn't come in – not yet. But it was too late, the door burst open and Maeve looked across in curiosity at the figures of her husband and son on the single bed. 'What on earth . . . ?'

Kieran slid off the edge of the mattress, casting a concerned glance back at the corpse of his stepfather, before turning to the astonished face of his mother. 'Take it easy, Mom, please . . .'

'What is it? Is something wrong? Frank – what are you doing there? He's not drunk, is he?' She hurried across the floor to the bedside, pushing aside Kieran's restraining arm. 'What's wrong with him? He's not ill, is he?'

Speechless, Kieran could only look on helplessly as she shook the lifeless form again and again. 'Frank! Frank! Answer me!' The shaking got wilder, as did her cries as her entreaties evoked no response. 'Help me, Kieran! Help me!'

He could only shake his head. 'It's no good, Mom, he's gone.'

'No!' Wild-eyed, she turned on him, her fists flailing. 'Don't say that! Don't lie to me! Help me, darn you!'

Grabbing her wrists, he pinned them to her sides and shook his head as he stared fixedly at her. 'I'm not lying, Mom. And I can't help – no one can. He's dead. Frank's dead.'

'No, he can't be dead. He can't be . . .' Her voice dropped to an inaudible whisper as she shook her head in confusion. She turned back to the lifeless form of her husband on the dishevelled counterpane. His arms were lying awkwardly by his side and she picked them up gently and laid them across his chest, his hands clasped as if in prayer. Then she bent and kissed him on the lips.

Kieran expected her to break down, have hysterics even, but she remained quite calm as she stood looking down at the body. She asked no questions. But strangely this merely increased his sense of guilt. He was an active participant in Frank's death – his killer some might argue – and he felt a compulsive need to unburden himself. But what good would it do? It would simply alienate his mother even more. In her eyes, he had always been the disappointment – what on earth would she say if she knew he had played an active part in her husband's death?

'We'd better call Dr Carroll.' Maeve's voice was low but quite controlled as she turned from the bed and took her son's arm.

He led her gently from the room and through to the lounge, sitting her down in the corner of the settee, as he made for the drinks cabinet. Neither Kitty nor Maudie were yet home, so he fixed only two drinks: two stiff gin and tonics. He handed her one and she took it automatically, downing the tart liquid in two large gulps. He watched her in silence. Strangely, her eyes were still quite dry as they turned to him. 'She can't have him now, Kieran. Estelle can never have him. He's mine now, in death as he was in life.' A strange smile lit her face as she leaned back against the ruched satin cushions and closed her eyes. For the first time in weeks, he thought, she actually looked happy.

Of his two sisters, predictably Kitty took the news best, refusing to go and view the body after the doctor had departed, content to sit in silent companionship with her mother in the lounge. Maudie, however, refused to leave her father's side and had to have her fingers physically prised from his hand when the black-suited funeral attendants came to remove the body. Her long-lashed eyes were red and swollen with tears as, at a little after ten o'clock, she stood in the open door and watched them manoeuvre the walnut and brass coffin into the elevator. 'I didn't even get a chance to tell him about my part,' she whispered, to no one in particular. 'Poppa would've been so proud . . .'

At Maeve's request, the funeral was a private family affair, with Chuck as principal mourner. He arrived home the day before it was due to take place; an older-looking, more gaunt figure than when he had left two years previously, but, strangely, to Kieran much less intimidating. Probably due to the fact that he was in a wheelchair, so he no longer towered a good head above him, for the first time in at least five years.

To everyone's astonishment, the widow shed no tears, either before the ceremony or during it. 'It's probably delayed shock,' Kitty confided to Kieran as they returned home in the rear of the black funeral car after the service, but he was not so sure. His mother's words, spoken with such utter conviction, just after her husband's death, still rang in his ears. . . . *Estelle can never have him. He's mine now, in death as he was in life.* He stared out of the car window at the passing traffic. That was all she really wanted, wasn't it? Frank could never be unfaithful again.

* * *

'It's ironic, ain't it?' Chuck said, half to himself, as they sat in the lounge later that evening. 'I go half across the world to take part in this God-awful war, yet it's Pop who ends up six feet under before it's finished.'

'He worked too hard,' Maudie said bitterly. 'And none of us really appreciated it. We were all content just to remain here living off him, without giving a second thought to where the money came from.'

Kitty caught Kieran's eyes and both looked away immediately. There was too much truth in what Maudie had just said. Kieran cleared his throat and shifted uneasily in his seat. 'Yeah, it's ironic really – I was just telling him I was on the point of moving out when he had his heart attack.'

'Moving out?' Maeve cut in sharply. 'And where to, may I ask?'

'I've got an apartment over in Queens. It's not much – two rooms and a shared john, but I figured it was time I made a move.'

'There's something wrong with your home, then. Is that it?'

'No, dammit, that's not it. I'm twenty-eight years old, Mom. I'm not a kid any more. It's time I stopped living off you and . . .' His protest tailed to a stop. It was no good including Frank. He had gone.

'Well, you'll have no need to live off anyone in future. I made sure your father made a sensible will some years ago. There's no good me inheriting everything. I couldn't possibly use a fraction of all he's got stashed away in bonds and one thing and another. You'll all be getting your fair share just as soon as they can tie up the estate.'

Kieran's face paled. How could he? How could he possibly touch a cent of any of it? 'You'd better include me out.'

Maeve's brow furrowed. 'What's that supposed to mean?'

'It's his goddam Commie philosophy rearing its ugly head, that's what it is. Ain't it, Kieran? Who was it – Marx, or Lenin, or some other Commie bastard, that said that property was theft? The same goes for inherited wealth, I presume?'

'It was Proudhon, actually. Get it right, soldier boy. And, if you must know, then, yeah, you're right – I do believe that. I reckon I'm as capable as the next man of earning my daily crust.'

A scoffing laugh came from the direction of the wheelchair. 'And that's exactly what it'll be, if you stay on in that two-bit publishing house. Good God, man, with some real money you've got a chance to do something to be proud of with your life.'

Kieran's lips tightened. 'You'd know all about that, of course. The conquering hero returns, and all that bullshit.'

'Enough, Kieran!' Maeve said sharply. 'I won't have anyone, least of all you, running down Chuck's war record. It's second to none.'

'Naturally! But every single thing he's ever done in his blessed life has been second to none, hasn't it?' Kieran got up from his seat and looked from his mother to his brother seated in the wheelchair next to the window. There was a quiet, superior smile playing on Chuck's lips that infuriated him even further. 'He's God Almighty on earth, as far as you're concerned, isn't he? If you were a real Catholic, and not just a bloody sham, you'd even have him running for Pope, if he hadn't already disqualified himself by laying all those high-class tarts before he was even out of high school!'

'Well, at least I was capable, Kieran boy! At least one of us is worthy of the word "male" on our birth certificate.'

'Meaning I'm not.'

'You said it, buster.'

Kieran's mouth went dry as a gasp came from Kitty sitting behind him. He looked at his mother, his eyes searching hers for a sign that she disagreed with Chuck's words. But Maeve would not meet his gaze. Instead she sat quite still, staring into space, her face totally expressionless. Whatever she did, she would not disagree with her younger son. He had articulated the unspoken fear in her own heart over all these years. Her elder son was a queer. As sure as his father, Danny, had been a cold-blooded murderer. Which was worse? Her lips tightened even further. She had no answer.

She got up and poured herself another drink. She should have no favourites, she knew that. That was the unwritten creed by which every mother lived, wasn't it? They were watching her. They were all watching her. Why couldn't she say something – anything – to make it all right again, like she used to do when they argued amongst themselves as children? But they weren't children any longer. They were adults, just as she was, and responsible for their own actions, for their own failings. If she had favoured Chuck at Kieran's expense over the years, it was because he had given her cause to do so.

Maybe if she had talked to Kieran more – tried to understand what made him the way he was – things might have been different. But talking, really talking, was something she seemed to have lost the knack of as she grew older. Confessions of any type made her nervous. No one had a right to know what was hidden deep within another's heart. There was pain enough to be found by looking into your own. She often wondered if she even had a heart left to look into. There was an emptiness within her that nothing, not even the contents of this glass in her hand could fill. It was as if she had left part of her behind in Ireland, all those years ago. The most important part. Her very soul . . .

Chapter 30

Kitty stood in the dingy living-room of Kieran's apartment, a hot flush creeping up her neck as she nodded a perfunctory greeting to the young man lying sprawled on the chintz-covered settee. She had expected to find her brother alone, and the sight of this bronzed, well-muscled stranger, bereft of all clothes but a pair of striped boxer shorts and looking as though he owned the place, brought a spasm of nerves to her throat as she attempted to speak. 'I – I'm sorry, Kieran. I didn't mean to interrupt. I didn't know you'd have company.'

Her brother looked uncomfortably at Louie. Why the hell hadn't he disappeared into the bedroom and got properly dressed when the doorbell went? 'Kitty, this is Louie Carelli, an old buddy of mine.'

'Not so old, if you don't mind!' Louie protested, getting off the settee at last, to extend a hand to the young woman by the door. 'I can give you quite a few years, old man! Nice to meet you, Kieran's sister. May I call you Kitty too?'

'Sure.' Kitty gave a strained smile; Chuck's revealing jibe, the night Kieran had moved out of their family home for good, repeated in her mind. Could it really be true? Could this smiling piece of bronzed beefcake possibly be her brother's lover? She felt sick at the thought. This visit was proving impossible. How could she possibly talk over private family matters in front of this prize body-building specimen?

'How's Mom and Maudie?'

'They're fine,' she began, then corrected herself. 'Actually that's not quite true and that's why I'm here. Mom's been really low, what with Pop's death and then you moving out last month. I – I wondered if you could find your way to calling in now and then.'

'Not while that bastard is still in residence!'

Kitty's lips pursed. 'Chuck's not so bad, Kieran. Everyone

283

says things they regret now and then. I'm sure he regrets what's happened as much as you do.'

'And what makes you think I regret anything? To be honest, it's one almighty relief to be out of there. For the first time I feel actually in control of my own life. I'm behoven to no one – least of all my mother!'

'You make her sound like a tyrant. She's been through a lot recently and has just been widowed, for heaven's sake! She's to be pitied, Kieran, not despised.'

Kieran's face hardened as he met his sister's admonishing look. 'But isn't that the worst kind of tyranny, Kitty – that of the weak over the strong?'

'And you're the strong, I suppose?'

'I am now – yes. But I wasn't while I was living under that roof. Anyway, she doesn't need me to cheer her up. There are others far better fitted to do that – darling Chuckie, for instance!'

'Chuck's aiming to go back to Europe within a week or so. They've offered him an office job in Washington, but he'll have none of it. He wants to be back with his unit.'

Kieran bit back a bitter retort. No matter what he thought about him, the guy seemed to have guts. 'So what's the answer, then? I certainly don't aim to rush over there to take his place. Who shall we conjure up to cheer up the grieving widow?'

'I suggested she sends for Aunt Katie. She seems to be the one of Mom's relatives she was most upset at leaving in Dublin, apart from her brother. And Uncle Charlie's out of the question – he's too tied up in the war effort.'

Kieran's eyebrows shot up. 'Aunt Katie – which one's she again?'

'Our real father's younger sister,' Kitty said impatiently. 'You know well enough. I was named after her. She lives in Belfast now and all her own family are well able to look after themselves for a few weeks.' She found it impossible to disguise her enthusiasm for the idea. 'Just to be able to talk in person to her will be truly fantastic. Mom never would talk about our real father, you know that – but she will, I'm sure of it. He was a hero, Kieran – a real hero. We have a right to know about him.'

Kieran shrugged. He had heard this eulogy so many times. Hearing the exploits of a man long dead who happened to be his biological parent, and who lived and died by the gun, held no fascination. Violence in all forms was abhorrent to him, political violence most of all. 'Yeah, well I hope you have a real good time when she finally gets here.'

'You'll come and meet her. You'll at least agree to that.'

He nodded and made a half-hearted attempt at a reassuring smile. 'Yeah, I'll meet her, Kit. If it makes you happy.' He avoided saying it would be in Park Avenue. He had still to make his mind up about that. 'Fancy a coffee, or a beer? We've got a few bottles in the icebox.'

She shook her head. 'I'll not stay, thanks. It was only a flying visit, to keep you up with the news.' She threw a quick glance in Louie's direction. He was once more sprawled on the settee and regarding her thoughtfully through a haze of cigarette smoke. 'It was nice to meet you, Mr Carelli.'

'Louie, honey, Louie.'

Maeve bit her lip. At all costs, she must resist the urge to intervene. She watched Chuck's jaw clench as he forced his wounded leg to the floor. He had been pacing back and forth in front of the window for the best part of half an hour, doggedly determined to get back to full fitness as soon as possible. Nobody could claim he was walking normally again, but the difference in the past couple of weeks had been enormous. In a perverse way, she almost wished he hadn't recovered so quickly. The thought of him returning to the fray in Europe horrified her. It was funny how things could change so dramatically almost overnight. Just over a month ago she and Frank had been looking forward to having him home again – were even planning a marvellous party to celebrate his return, but now Frank was dead and the party had never materialised. How could you possibly hold such a thing with your husband not even cold in the ground?

'I'd call it a day for now, honey. You know what Dr Carroll said – a little exercise and often. It's more like a lot and all the time, where you're concerned!'

Chuck threw a grin in her direction and nodded. 'It gets

easier all the time, too. I never would've believed it a few weeks ago. To tell the truth, I never thought I'd see any of my old unit again. In fact, the little Irish guy that looked after me in the ambulance transport back to England said they nearly amputated the darned thing on the night it happened. It was only thanks to him they didn't. He told the major in charge he'd seen a worse one recover a few weeks earlier, so they decided to give me the benefit of the doubt. I've told him I'll buy him a drink if I'm ever in Dublin.'

Maeve's ears pricked up. 'Dublin you say. He was from Dublin, was he?'

Chuck nodded as he lowered himself into a chair by the window and rubbed his thigh. 'O'Rourke was his name and he looked as Irish as they come – red hair, freckles, the lot!'

Maeve drew in her breath sharply. 'And how old would he be, this O'Rourke fella?'

'Middle to late twenties – it's hard to tell. He said his mother wasn't too keen on him fighting England's war. His father was killed by the Tommies, as he called them, before he was even born, but most of his buddies joined up . . . Why do you ask, Mom? Did you know any O'Rourkes in your day?'

Maeve shook her head. It was ridiculous – there must be hundreds of O'Rourkes in Dublin, and half of them with red hair and freckles . . . But how many with a father killed by the British? That surely narrowed the field. 'Oh, not personally. One or two by name – you know how it is – shopkeepers and the like. I wouldn't know your friend's family though – my own family were always on the side of law and order. Your Grandfather Ballantine was a pillar of society.'

Chuck's fair brows furrowed. He was sure Kitty had once told him that her and Kieran's father was a real Irish rebel, as she had put it, who had taken part in the Easter Rising of 1916, and then been killed fighting for the cause. Who on earth could have told her that, he had no idea, for their mother never mentioned the subject. In fact, whenever Ireland was mentioned she usually clammed up altogether, so it was no use asking her to satisfy his curiosity now. 'Kitty was saying you might ask Aunt Katie over for a while to keep you company.'

Maeve's eyes took on a much softer, faraway look as the

picture of a small, flame-headed child filled her mind's eye. Dear, dear Katie ... 'Katie aroon,' she said softly. 'Yes, I just might do that.'

The letter reached Belfast several weeks later, to be opened by a small, stout, red-haired woman in her middle thirties. Katie Muldoon read, then re-read the words on the thin blue airmail paper, then sat down heavily at the kitchen table. 'It's from Maeve, in New York,' she said finally. 'She wants me to come over for a wee while. She's been really low since Frank died and the family think it would cheer her up to see me.'

'Why you, for God's sake? She hasn't exactly been in a hurry to come over here and visit us since she left.' Eamon Muldoon pushed the tepid cup of tea from him and got up to straighten his tie in the mirror on the window-ledge behind the sink. His work in the Fire Service absorbed almost all his energies and he was already a few minutes later than usual in leaving for the day shift. 'Anyway, how can we possibly afford the fare?'

'Maeve'll send it – she says so. It's all her money now, since Frank died. She's a wealthy woman, Eamon. She even says she'll pay for a housekeeper so you and the family don't suffer while I'm gone.'

'Holy Mary and Joseph! A housekeeper, is it? That'll be the day! We'll take the money, though. We're not that daft!'

'You'd have no objections to me going, then?'

He turned to face her. 'What about Mary-Agnes? Won't it cause ructions in that quarter that it's you and not her that's been asked?'

'Good God, no! Maeve and Mary-Agnes had no time for each other. If she ever came across here, it would be only me and Dermot that she'd visit, I'm sure of that. Apart from her own family, the Ballantines, of course.'

Eamon Muldoon nodded. 'They're the rich so-and-sos in Dublin, aren't they? Wasn't her father made a knight or some such piece of nonsense a few years back?'

'Aye, he was that. And he had to apply for British citizenship to use the title. It was Sir Charles, no less. But, if I remember rightly, the old man's either dead or retired from the business and it's young Charlie, Maeve's brother, that's running things.'

'If you ask me, Maeve'd not be short of a bob or two without her husband kicking the bucket. Some folk seem to have the luck o' the devil, while others like us work all our lives and still have nothing to show for it at the end.'

'We have our health, Eamon. Frank's dead, remember. A fat lot of good all that money did him.'

Her husband made no reply, but reached for his peaked cap off a hook on the back of the door and wedged it down over his thatch of greying hair. 'I shouldn't be that late back, barring anything untoward cropping up.' There hadn't been a bombing raid for some time and his shift work was assuming something akin to normality.

'I can say yes, then – to the letter?'

'Since when did you need my permission to do anything you really wanted to do?'

She watched him disappear out of the front door, then down the garden path, before mounting the bicycle that would take him the few hundred yards to the fire station. He wasn't a bad man really. They'd had their ups and downs, of course, who hadn't? But she still offered up a small prayer every time he set off on one of his shifts; the one night she had omitted to do so would remain etched in her heart forever. It was the night of the fifteenth of April 1941, and she could still remember it as if it were yesterday. She had been preparing for bed at around quarter to eleven when the sirens sounded. Old Pat McKenna, from next door but one, had been walking his dog at the time and called to her through the open window, as she'd gone to close the bedroom curtains. His son-in-law, one of the city's anti-aircraft gunners, had been ordered to 'stand to' at Castle-reagh, on the softly rolling hills that overlooked the great Harland and Wolff shipyards. 'It'll be the real McCoy tonight, sure an' it will, Katie, m'dear. 'Tis under the kitchen table you'll be spending the night, not in that comfy bed o' yours!'

A chill had run through her. Irrationally she had blamed herself for not bothering to say her usual prayer. She had had words with Eamon before he left for work and in her irritation she had neglected the prayer.

As the anti-aircraft guns began to fire, she had stood at the bedroom window and stared up into the night sky. A low humming in the heavens, rising above the anti-aircraft noise, that seemed to be heading in their direction from the hills of County Down in the south-east had turned her blood to ice water. The Luftwaffe was on its way and Eamon was out there, down in the shipyards, waiting for the inevitable. 'Dear God, protect him. Guard him now in this terrible hour . . . Help us all . . . God help us all in this city tonight.'

The plea had barely left her lips when the first wave of Heinkels and Junkers swooped low across the city spraying flares out of the darkness over its terrified citizens. They spread their blazing trail across the night sky, bathing the rooftops in a ghostly silver light. Then, before her eyes, the whole city lit up in a bright white and orange ethereal glow, more brilliant than anything she had ever seen.

Before the light faded, the next wave of bombers swept in from the Lough, raining their deadly cargo on to the sleeping streets. In their own area, in the north-west of the city, where the warren of narrow Victorian streets stretched from the York Road docks up towards the Antrim Road and Girdwood Park, the bombers headed onwards overhead, leaving a path of destruction that Katie and the other panic-stricken inhabitants could only guess at, until the grey dawn revealed the damage for all to see.

The girls, Deirdre and Bridget, joined her at the window, praying aloud throughout the bombardment. Only Kevin remained in his bed, doggedly determined that 'Jerry' wouldn't disturb his night's sleep, if he could help it. They had finally crawled into their own beds at a little after six, to snatch a few hours' sleep before the morning light revealed the trail of heartbreak of the night.

Jimmy O'Dowd, Kevin's best friend, had been killed along with his mother and sister when the great six-storey redbrick Victorian edifice of the Flax Spinning Company received several direct hits and crumbled into the dust, taking over forty houses in York Street along with it. And the full tragedy of the night had hit even harder when they heard that Eamon's youngest sister Eileen had been killed carrying her young baby to the safety of the vaults of the Clonard monastery, half-way up the Falls Road.

Yes, it was a night to remember, all right. Katie smiled grimly as she turned from the window. A night to forget, more like. It was times like that, and the others that followed, that made her wish she had emigrated to the States along with Maeve.

They had no idea what war was really like over there. Not a clue. Oh, it wasn't that she wasn't grateful for the food parcels that had been arriving from Park Avenue at regular intervals for the past few years. The supplies of tea, sugar and other essentials were a real godsend, no one could deny that. The tins of cooked rabbit had proved especially popular with the family, and caused Kevin to break into an Al Jolson type rendering of 'My bunny flies over the ocean', whenever another tin was extracted from the depths of Maeve's carefully packed cardboard box of goodies. But, in a way, the parcels themselves merely proved that they were hardly even suffering in that regard over there either. Not that she would wish Maeve and her family to be in the front line – anything but. In fact, in a curious way, she would rather suffer herself than know that Maeve was under any kind of stress. It seemed a cruel twist of fate that Frank should die now, before this awful conflict was over. It seemed only yesterday she had said goodbye to them on the way to their new life together across the Atlantic. She had wondered then how Maeve could ever bear to leave Dublin, that most beautiful and civilised of cities. In fact, the worst part of her relationship with Eamon had been the bit before their marriage when she had had to make up her mind if she wanted to leave her native city or not.

No, it hadn't been the easiest decision to come and live in Belfast, but on the whole she had never regretted it. Belfast to her would always be a sort of rebellious, rather uglier younger sister to her beloved Dublin, but despite – or maybe because of – its sprawling docks and surrounding mean little streets that had been home for so long now, she had grown to love it. All three of her children had been born here and most years she was able to spend at least a few days with her remaining family in the South.

Her remaining family, she thought wryly, meant Mary-Agnes and her lot, and Dermot, and that was about it. She knew what her sister's thoughts would be about the New York visit already, but Dermot would be pleased. Surely he would be pleased? They seemed to get on so well, him and Maeve, from what she remembered as a child. But after Maeve married Frank and emigrated back to the States with him, for some reason Dermot seemed to clam up whenever she mentioned them. 'Do you not like Maeve any more, Dermot?' she had once asked in all innocence, not long after they had gone, and she could still remember the look on his face. 'Only the foolish and the old live in the past, Katie, my girl,' he had said. 'I pray to God I'm not yet either one of them!' And with that the subject had been closed.

She folded the letter and placed it safely in her apron pocket. It was something to mull over as she went about her daily tasks and to talk over with the others when they got in later in the day. Funnily enough, almost more than her beloved Maeve, it was her young namesake Kitty she was really looking forward to meeting one day. They had started corresponding personally about ten years ago and the young girl had proved an avid recipient of all the tales her Aunt Katie could tell about Danny, her dead father, and others who had lived and died for the cause. And they were many – most of them gleaned, not from the family itself, but from others in the school playground who were also nurtured on the cause of Irish freedom and its dear, dead heroes.

But the Rising, and the men who had fought and died for the cause, seemed a lifetime ago now; as indeed they were. Things were different in this war. The bombs had seen to that, welding the people together, Catholic and Protestant alike, in a way that she would never have thought possible at one time. A verse from a currently popular song resounded in her head and she began to sing softly to herself as she set to to clear the table:

> 'On the Shankhill, on the Falls,
> You forget oul' Derry's walls.
> You'se run as the bombs begin to fall,
> Says good oul' Rule Britannia!'

No matter how catchy the tune, she knew these words would never have passed her lips a few years ago, but under attack from outside they were all Irish – just that, nothing more. Religious differences had been submerged in the fight against the common enemy. Although she was not fool enough to believe it could last. The gulf was too wide, the bitterness too deep to be bridged as easily as that. The past could not, must not, be forgotten and that was something that must be impressed on the younger generation at all costs.

Maeve's two younger children, Chuck and Maudie, she was ashamed to admit she had little interest in, but Danny's two – Kieran and Kitty, they were quite another matter. She had written personally to Kieran once, on his twenty-first birthday, but they had never corresponded privately again. For a young man, he seemed strangely indifferent to what his father had been, and Ireland in general. Instead he wrote about someone called Earl Browder and the cause of World Communism and peace, claiming the two to be inextricably linked. She had taken some heart in that, for Danny himself had been an avid reader of both Marx and Engels, but all this talk of pacifism defeated her. How could Ireland ever be free if no one was prepared to fight for it? Had England ever just given away any of its colonies? There might be an example somewhere in the history books, but she had never come across it. No, poor Kieran had the wrong end of the stick altogether, but thank God for Kitty . . .

Chapter 31

The man in the dishevelled bed rolled over on to his back as the young woman slipped from his grasp and got up and walked to the window. With a single jerk of her right hand, the slats of the blind twanged upwards and a stream of brilliant sunshine filled the room.

'Close it again, for Chrissake, it's blinding me!' Lee Finkelstein threw a protective arm over his eyes as the young woman ignored his command and instead pushed up the lower half of the window frame. 'Kitty – what the hell are you playing at?' His patience was beginning to run out.

She turned to him, her naked body startlingly white in the bright sunlight. 'I'm throwing some light and fresh air on our relationship, that's what I'm doing.'

Lee sat up on the crumpled sheet, then groaned and fell back again. Did she have to come all this heavy stuff every time they met these days? 'What do you want me to say? That I don't think we should go on seeing each other because we want such different things from life, is that it? That's crap, Kitty, it really is! This is wartime – there must be millions of couples like us just taking what happiness they can out of this god-awful situation. Who knows where any of us will be in five years' time?'

'I know where you'll be. In Palestine.' She kept her tone deliberately light, but there was that old accusatory light in her eyes as they glanced across and found his.

'You can come with me.'

'I'm not Jewish.'

'So?'

'So what possible interest do I have in fighting for a proper Jewish state thousands of miles away? If I was going to fight for anything, I'd fight for Ireland. Would you come there with me?'

'No.' It was the first time he had been so honest.

A bitter smile twisted her lips as she bent down and picked up his shirt that had been carelessly dropped on the floor in their haste to undress two short hours ago. She slipped it on and did up the bottom few buttons before running a hand through her rumpled hair. 'Your honesty becomes you.'

'Come here.' He stretched out a hand and she took it, sitting down on the edge of the mattress beside him. 'You know our trouble, Kitty Donovan? We're two of a kind – two stubborn, bloody-minded critters who are old enough to know better.'

She shook her head. 'No, Lee, we're two passionate human beings, whose only crime is caring too much for the history of our races. I reckon the Good Lord was in a really skittish mood when he ordained it that the two of us should meet.' Her mind suddenly drawn back to that first encounter, and the reason for it, she asked, 'How is your mother these days anyway?'

'Doesn't Maudie mention her?'

'Not to me.'

'She's fine – on top of the world actually. The show opens next week and all the signs are it'll be a smash hit. Well, as far as you can have such a thing in wartime. Do you fancy seeing it? I can get tickets.'

At first she looked shocked, then thought, why ever not? She'd never actually set eyes on Estelle, except in photographs, and it might prove quite an interesting experience. 'Do you know, I just might!'

'Great!' he grinned. 'We'll go together. Just say when. Come to think of it, it's ages since we've taken in any kind of a show. How about a movie? There's something on at the Trans-Lux on Broadway that I'd like to catch.'

'Right now, you mean?'

'Saturday afternoon's as good a time as any and it leaves us the evening free.'

Less than a hour later found them sitting in the darkened auditorium, their eyes glued to the screen. Kitty's hand reached out and found Lee's as the music started; stirring, heart-stopping waves of sound that sent icy fingers down their backs and made them sit up in their seats in nervous anticipation.

As Anatole Litvak's *The Battle for Russia* burst on to the

screen, she glanced across at him, suddenly anxious about what she had let herself in for. Until they reached their destination, she had completely forgotten that the Trans-Lux was a newsreel cinema and had been expecting something lighthearted. The posters outside had come as a shock when she realised that this was what he was so desperate to see.

She shifted uncomfortably in her seat in the darkness. Russian faces and landscape filled her vision – ravaged faces in a ravaged land. She felt him tense beside her. He was no longer here in central New York, but thousands of miles away on the steppes of the Ukraine. Come to think of it, it was understandable really; for hadn't his father's family all come from Russia, fleeing from the pogroms that had become a terrifying part of Jewish life beyond the Pale? Despite everything; despite all the hardships and their dreams of building a new Zion eventually in the Promised Land, to the end of their lives, he had told her, his grandparents had retained a love for this vast land and its people now so mutilated by Hitler's barbaric hordes.

Within seconds it became evident that this was no ordinary Allied propaganda piece, but the real thing; captured Nazi film showing in graphic detail the horrors being endured by their Russian ally. Accompanied by heart-tugging, mournful Slav music, the camera panned in on a row of young partisan girls slowly choking to death on a Nazi gallows; old women and children starving to death in the ruins of their homes. Millions had already perished; doubtless millions more would die. Here in the darkness, they too could feel the pain as the huddled forms of old men and women, their faces contorted with grief, searched through the mounds of bloodied corpses on the outskirts of their village, after the Nazis had passed through and slaughtered their children and their children's children.

They remained sitting in their seats for some time after the last broken chords of the Pathétique symphony had faded into the darkness and silence around them, signifying the end. Then, without a word, they got up and, hand in hand, they walked out into the late afternoon sunshine. It seemed grotesquely incongruous, obscene even, to so quickly become a part of this normal, bustling city once more.

A young man with an eagle lapel pin, showing him as

honourably discharged, stood behind a newspaper stall a few yards away on the sidewalk. Lee bought a copy of the *New Republic* and shoved it in his jacket pocket, while an old Jewish man, wearing the traditional Orthodox long black coat and hat, shuffled quickly past them towards the edge of the sidewalk.

Kitty glanced across at him; he had been sitting two rows in front of them in the cinema and had vaguely irritated her by loudly blowing his nose into an oversize handkerchief whenever the film reached a particularly harrowing part. For a moment he paused at the edge of the kerb, then with a cry in Yiddish that she could not understand, he dashed out into the road.

'Jesus!' The screech of several sets of tyres and brakes brought Lee sprinting out into the street, along with Kitty and several other passers-by. The black hat, now squashed beyond recognition, lay beneath the wheel of a yellow cab, while its owner sprawled, half-hidden beneath the wheels of a battered Chevrolet.

'He was in there, Lee! He saw the same film . . .' Kitty clutched at Lee's arm, as those nearer the tragedy shouted for a doctor and ambulance.

Gripping her wrist, and too choked to speak, he pulled her back to the safety of the sidewalk. It could have been his own grandfather. There were millions like him, Russians without a motherland, Jews without a Promised Land. His Grandpapa Itzak had once said he was the most privileged of men to have belonged to two such great peoples, but, in fact, he belonged nowhere. Wasn't that the reality? His jaw clenched as he shepherded Kitty through the congregating onlookers and on down the street. His desire to leave this place, to go to Palestine after the war and fight for Zion, for a Jewish homeland, hardened in his heart to a fierce resolve.

Kitty glanced across at him as she increased her pace to keep up with his determined stride. She knew what he was thinking, just as surely as if he had spelled out his thoughts in words of single syllables. She should be happy for him. How many young men knew by his age what their role was to be in this life? But somehow she could not rejoice. For how many young men would grow old never having known their own child?

The new life that was growing inside her was only weeks old, but already it lay heavy on her heart.

Maeve sat in the ornately gilded box and gazed down at the scene below her. There was no denying it, Estelle Finlay was a beautiful woman. Even in her best ermine wrap and shot silk gown, Maeve felt dowdy in comparison as her one-time rival cavorted about the stage in blood-red velvet and white chiffon. She had thought long and hard before agreeing to accept the free ticket for the opening night, but what excuse could she have possibly made to Maudie if she had refused? It was miracle enough that she had succeeded in keeping Frank's affair with Estelle from her for all this time – not to mention their previous marriage.

A grimace flickered across her face at the thought. How lucky it was that Frank had made it a policy never to talk about his past life, for consequently all their friends and relatives had followed suit over the years. It wasn't that she, personally, had determined to keep secrets from any of the children, but simply that there were certain areas in everyone's life, she believed, that they preferred to keep private. And that was how it should be, she was convinced of that. It was part of the creed by which she had been brought up – by which the Anglo-Irish had lived. Perhaps even more than the mainland English themselves, the Anglo-Irish had maintained the principle of the stiff upper lip over the generations. One simply did not expose one's innermost feelings to the scrutiny of others; painful episodes in one's past, like deeply-felt emotions, if they existed, were kept firmly below the surface, and this suited her just fine. A painful memory left a scar on the soul that could never be expected to heal if it was constantly picked over and exposed to re-examination by all and sundry. There was something disconcerting about the way the indigenous Irish had appeared to take real pleasure in displaying their emotions for all to see.

Even now, a whole generation later, a flush of embarrassment crept up her neck at the memory of the countless scenes she had borne witness to in the short time she had lived as Danny Donovan's wife. If it wasn't Mary-Agnes letting off steam about something, it was Danny himself. She leaned back in her seat and pondered on the differences in their natures. Perhaps that was one of the reasons that had attracted her to Dermot. He was so different from his fiery younger brother; he had kept such a tight rein on his own emotions when she first met him, she had begun to wonder if he had any normal feelings at all. And she had no doubt that in the years since she had left Ireland, like herself, he had not breathed a single word to anyone of what had gone on in his heart during those fateful months towards the end of the Great War.

And that was how it should be. What went on in the secret places of one's heart was not for discussing with others – no, not even with your own family. Especially not your own family. In fact, she had never knowingly brought up the subject of either Danny or Dermot with any of the four of her children. She knew that Kitty, for one, felt that this was because she was somehow ashamed of her past as the wife of an Irish rebel, but this wasn't the case. On the contrary, as a young girl, Danny's passion for the cause had been one of his main attractions. Politics had been a subject that had rarely come into the conversation in her own home. In fact, when she came to think about it, she had realised that the Anglo-Irish were a curiously apolitical people. They really didn't seem to give a damn who governed them, just as long as their money was safe and the trains and buses ran on time. And, if she were entirely honest with herself, that was exactly her own attitude when they first met. But what had happened that Easter in 1916 had sickened her of political zealots for life. It was one thing listening to your husband spouting wonderful political rhetoric about a free Ireland, but it was quite another thing witnessing him taking up a gun and actually killing for those beliefs . . . No, it was best that she held her counsel as far as Danny's part in the cause was concerned; her memories of that time were not happy ones, and no good would have come of besmirching his memory in the eyes of the younger generation. One got no satisfaction in scoring points over the dead.

That was not to say that she had ignored all those still living who had been an important part of her past. She was still in regular contact with her own family, the Ballantines, and she had never once in all these years failed to write at least once a month to Katie. Oblivious now to the music and dancing down below, a mercurial shiver ran through her at the thought that Katie would be here, God willing, within the next week.

Somehow she could never have agreed to her coming if Frank had still been alive, but now it was different. Over the past few months since his death, her thoughts had been returning more and more to Ireland. But not to the Dublin of her parents, and those grand houses and their equally grand inhabitants around St Stephen's Green, but to the Dublin of McIntyre Street, and the days of agony and ecstasy that had followed the Easter of 1916. Life had been hard then. For the first, and last, time of her life she had known poverty and the taste was still bitter in her mouth. Little could she have dreamt then, in that small kitchen, as she rocked Kieran to sleep in his wooden crib, that another world war later would find her sitting here in this grand box, in one of the finest theatres on Broadway, watching her own daughter on the stage.

As the music of another number swelled around her, her mind travelled back across the years to someone's else's daughter – to Cissie O'Rourke's. To Danny's other child. Where was she now, the thirty-year-old woman who was a half-sister to her own son? The story Chuck had told her before he had returned to his unit repeated itself in her head. Was it really possible she could have been carrying that child as Dermot said the final prayer over him, and they laid him to rest, to live on in the hearts and minds of the next generation of Ireland's sons to take up the fight? It was possible. Yes, it was that all right. But she would probably never know.

Maudie did not appear until the second half of the performance and Maeve had trouble picking her out of the host of other blonde young beauties who composed the brothel scene. Her heart swelled with pride nevertheless, especially when she stole a glance up in her mother's direction. She was her father's daughter, Maeve had no doubt about that, for there was nothing even vaguely reminiscent of the Ballantines about either of her Fullerton offspring. 'Goddam WASP!' she had once heard Kieran exclaim at his younger brother in a fit of temper and although she had been incensed at the time and made him apologise unreservedly, she had to admit that both

299

Chuck and Maudie were the archetypal White Anglo-Saxon Protestants, if ever she saw a pair.

At the end of the performance, she did not join the rush backstage to shower congratulations on Maudie and the rest of the cast. To come face to face with Estelle was more than she could bear. She preferred instead to slip out quietly with the rest of the audience, to hail one of the waiting cabs.

She had just edged into the rear seat of the fourth in line, when a young couple passed right by the window. The young man was tall and dark, with distinctive rather than good looks, but his companion . . . 'Kitty!' Her astonished exclamation was lost in the revving of the engine as the cab made its way out into the stream of traffic.

She craned her neck for as long as possible, to catch a better look, then sank back into her seat, with an incredulous shake of the head. Kitty had been at the show tonight, but had never even mentioned it to her beforehand. And who on earth was that young man? There had been no mention of a boyfriend since she had split up with Guy — and that had been ages ago!

A feeling of desolation swept over her. It was as if all her children had drifted so far out of her life there was no calling them back. Kieran had gone — for good probably — because of that row with Chuck, after Frank's funeral, and Chuck himself was back in the fray in Europe, with heaven only knew what consequences. As for Maudie, a bitter smile quirked the corners of her lips, Maudie was already half-way to Hollywood, she was certain of that. She had made no secret, over the past few weeks, that she had fallen completely under the spell of Estelle, and would be seeking a career out West just as soon as the show folded on Broadway. And now Kitty . . .

But Kitty herself was quite oblivious to the fact she had been spotted as she sat in their own particular corner of Yehudi's, their favourite kosher restaurant, on Broadway and 23rd, and toasted the success of *Madame Bovary* over a dish of milon btzlochit.

'You know there's talk of making a film of it?' Lee said, as he downed his first gulp of wine, then dug his fork into the melon.

'My father will be putting up the money once again, no doubt. He always was a sucker for my mother's sweet talk.'

'He's never married again, has he?'

'Nope. He prefers living with his ladies.'

'Will *you* ever marry eventually, Lee? Once you reach that Promised Land?'

He looked at her for a long time before answering. 'You mean will I ever want to find a good Jewish girl and settle down? Who knows?'

'You must have a picture of one in your mind – your ideal woman.' She knew she was playing with fire, but something drove her on. She had to know.

'I'll go one better than that,' he said, with a sheepish grin, as he reached into his inside jacket pocket. 'I've got one in my pocket, never mind in my mind!'

He handed across a faded sepia photograph of a young woman, in a high-necked blouse with leg o' mutton sleeves. She had a thick head of dark hair, frizzed into a fringe above the dark expressive eyes, and tied back at the nape of her neck. 'She's very beautiful,' Kitty said truthfully, before handing it back. 'Who is she?'

He smiled proudly as he replaced it in his wallet. 'Leah Finkelstein, *née* Rosenbaum,' he said. 'But I'm a couple of generations too late. My grandfather married her.'

'She's your grandmother,' Kitty murmured. 'She looks a very gentle person.'

'She was, but she had a will of iron. In some ways she was much stronger than him. One of the earliest Russian socialists . . .' He paused and then gave a dry laugh. 'Do you know she actually believed the revolution of the proletariat would take place in America before it ever happened in Russia? How wrong can you be! She regretted to her dying day that she wasn't there – back in the old country – when it happened.'

Kitty gave a wry smile. 'There must have been precious little over here to compensate.'

'She did try eulogising over Eugene Victor Debs for a while, I believe, but he never did measure up to Lenin!'

They exchanged grins. 'But she influenced your own political views quite a bit, didn't she?'

'Yeah – it's funny really, because she had absolutely no influence on my father – her own son. He was always far too influenced by the great American dream of becoming a self-made millionaire to bother with such trifles as world revolution! : . . Anyway, I seemed to make up for it and managed to show at least a sufficient glimmer of political activism to satisfy her before she died. I must admit, as far as this country goes, though, it's abated a mite over the past few years.'

'Really – why?'

He smiled wearily. 'There are far too many reasons to ruin a lovely meal by boring you with even a fraction of them . . . Let's just say, hearing Earl Browder declare, in Madison Square Gardens, that Trotsky, Bukharin and Zinoviev are all Nazi agents didn't help!'

Kitty nodded as she took a mouthful of the tangy melon mixed with fruit and nuts. She had heard Kieran get on his high horse often enough about that very same thing. The day the leader of American Communism got up before the Party faithful and fellow travellers and betrayed the cause of world revolution had left a bitter taste in the mouths of many on the far left. But they were straying far too far from the one subject that was filling her mind to the exclusion of all others. She toyed with her napkin as she glanced across at him and said hesitantly, 'Getting back to your grandmother, Lee, and her influence on you. She would have wanted you to marry a nice Jewish girl, wouldn't she?'

He looked surprised at the abrupt change of subject, but nodded uncertainly, then gave a much more emphatic nod. 'Yes, dammit, she would. She would've been less than true to her religion if she hadn't. And she was never untrue to anything she believed in.'

It was no more than Kitty expected. 'And of course, if you do get to that Promised Land – to Palestine – they'll expect it to be a Jewish girl you choose once you're over there. Isn't it frowned upon to dilute the sacred blood of the Jewish race by marrying outside it?' A bitterness she found it impossible to disguise came into her voice as she continued, 'If you ask me, I don't see much difference between that and the Nazi race laws. What Hitler propounds about preserving the purity of the

302

Aryan race, and what the Jews have propagated in that regard for thousands of years seem to me to be pretty much the same thing!'

A shocked look came into his face as the words sank in. How dare she – how dare anyone imply that!

'Well, it's true, isn't it?'

To his horror, he could not deny it. But a cold anger burned within him that it should have been Kitty of all people who had pointed this out.

She had the bit between her teeth now as she sensed he was on the defensive. All the bitterness she had felt of late as his love for her had paled alongside the real love of his life – his Judaism – welled within her and spilled over in the words that poured in an accusatory torrent from her lips. 'You Jews regard yourselves as God's chosen people – so where does that leave the rest of us? Are we simply the ones God doesn't give a damn about? The sub-humans – the *Untermenschen* of Nazi philosophy? What's the difference, Lee? What's the difference between the philosophy of your race and that of that goddam little Austrian corporal and his cronies who are tearing Europe to shreds right now?'

He stared across the table at her, his face draining of all colour, as his fists clenched. How could she say such things? How dare she compare the teachings of his race with those of that monster over in Europe who was slaughtering innocent millions? 'You bitch! You insensitive little bitch!' he hissed, through gritted teeth. 'If you were a guy I'd floor you right now!'

Instead, he got up and walked out of the restaurant and out of her life.

She stared after him until the tears blurred her eyesight and she could see no more. She did not regret what she had said. Not a single word of it. His love for his race would always be greater than his love for her, she knew that, and the thought turned a knife deep in her heart.

Chapter 32

'Kieran! Since when did you have to knock at your own door?' Maeve's delight at seeing her elder son again was tempered by her consternation that he should not have walked straight into the apartment as in the past.

'It's no longer my door, Mom.'

She let it pass, simply relieved that he had seen fit to return home for the first time in over three months. 'Come in, come in! Don't just stand there!' She took him by the arm and almost dragged him through the doorway.

She led the way into the drawing-room and he looked around in mild curiosity while she fixed two drinks. Nothing had changed, not a single thing, since Frank's death. Except his mother. Maeve looked better than he had seen her in years. His eyes travelled from the top of her smoothly rolled and curled dark hair, down past the short-sleeved, pale blue linen dress, to the sleekly stockinged legs and neat feet in the navy sling-backed sandals. The sight of her, and the gleaming apartment, which Sarah kept so immaculately that no speck of dust would even dare to enter, made him uncomfortably aware of his own appearance. He wished now he had at least changed his shirt. It was the second day for this one and a glance at the collar in the mirror on the wall opposite told him it was curling noticeably at the edges.

'What did you want to speak to me about?' He nodded his thanks as he accepted a Jack Daniels on the rocks.

Maeve looked pained. 'Do I really need a reason for you to visit?' His silence caused her to shrug her shoulders after a moment or two and give a sigh as she perched on the arm of the leather settee in front of the window. 'Actually it's about the will. There is well over two hundred thousand dollars just waiting for your signature.'

'I told you I don't want the damned money.'

'Don't be ridiculous! Nobody says no to that kind of money!'

'Well, I just have – for the second time – so you'd better get used to it.'

'I won't touch it, you know. No matter what you say now, it'll still be there waiting for you until I'm dead and gone myself.' She looked across at him imploringly as she took a sip of her gin and tonic. Really bloody-minded he could be sometimes, just like his father Danny. 'That reminds me – there was another thing I thought you should know – your Aunt Katie arrives from Ireland tomorrow. I've asked the girls to make sure to be here in the evening to welcome her and hope you'll see your way to coming too.'

He caught her glance, and the pale lashes flickered over the hazel eyes, before looking down into the golden liquid in his glass. Tomorrow – tomorrow of all days! He had promised Louie he'd go along and watch him take part in one of his body-building competitions in the Village.

'Please, Kieran. It means a lot to me. You're the only one of my children Katie actually knew. She thought the world of you as a baby.'

He sighed. It meant a lot to her, he could see that. 'I'll be here, don't worry.'

'Wonderful! I prayed you wouldn't let me down. Say seven o'clock shall we? I'll tell Sarah to fix the meal for eight. That'll give us plenty of time to all have a good gossip and give Katie a chance to get to know you all before we eat.'

'You'd better count me out for the meal. I – I promised a friend I'd . . .' his voice faltered, unwilling to give too much away. He took another swig of the drink, then continued. 'There's a function on Bedford Street I promised to attend.'

Maeve's well-plucked brows rose in curiosity as her brow furrowed. 'Really? What might that be that's more important than your aunt coming all the way from Ireland to meet you?'

A faint flush crept up his neck. He had never deliberately lied to her before – more circumvented the truth on occasions. But this time the devil was in his soul. Why on earth should he lie? It wasn't as if he was planning to rob Tiffany's or the like. 'Actually I'm going to a body-building contest. Purely as a spectator, of course!'

Now it was his mother's turn to colour. He had tried to make a joke of it, but she wasn't having it. Her suspicions were aroused, but she prayed silently she was wrong. 'Is one of your friends taking part?'

'Yes, yes, he is.' He deliberately avoided her eyes as he answered.

'Do I know him?'

'No, you don't. It's just a guy from the office.' He stood awkwardly in the middle of the room, feeling like a seventh-grader having to give an account of himself. 'Look, Mom, knock it off, will you? Let's just lay off my private life, if you don't mind. It's not something I care to discuss – not with my family, not with anyone.'

Maeve got up from the arm of the settee, the features of her face a frozen mask. 'And why would that be, Kieran? It's not something you're ashamed of, by any chance?'

He looked at her, long and hard. '*You* – *you* have the gall to ask that? And just who are you – who are any of you – to sit in judgement on me? You, who married a murderer first time round; then the second time married a man who made the bulk of his fortune out of armaments – blood money – that's what Frank's left you all, Mother, only none of you can see it! And your other son – precious Chuckie – is over there in Europe killing other mothers' sons right this minute . . . !'

Maeve's lips tightened as her eyes turned to steel. She could swallow her anger and take what he had to say about both Danny and Frank, but how dare he – just how dare he – insult Chuck like this! 'That's enough, Kieran! That's enough of that! I'll have no more of that kind of talk in this house.'

Their eyes locked in mute combat across the Persian carpet, then Kieran downed the remainder of his drink in one and placed the empty glass on a side table containing the radio. 'I reckon it's time I was going.'

She had gone too far, she knew that, and it was backfiring on her. She made a conciliatory move towards him. 'You'll be back tomorrow night, though – for Katie's sake . . .'

Ignoring her outstretched hand, he did not even deign to reply as he looked her straight in the eyes, then turned and stalked as resolutely from the room as his lame left leg would allow.

She watched him go, the words of her unanswered question hanging in the air long after she had heard the outside door close with a bang. Her very soul had turned to lead. It was true what Chuck had said – every word of it. Kieran – her own son – was a . . . a . . . No matter how she tried, she could not put a word to it. They were all so dirty. As dirty as the practices she knew he must indulge in with those body-building specimens he seemed to chose as friends. How could she have given birth to such a creature? How could she?

Fighting back the tears, she walked to the baby grand piano in the far corner of the room and picked up a framed photograph from its polished surface. Katie and her own children smiled back at her – all as normal as the day was long. 'She must never know,' Maeve vowed. 'Katie must never know.' That would be more than she could bear.

Kitty drew the brush through her hair for the last time, then fluffed out the curling page-boy roll that skimmed her shoulders. Stepping back from the mirror she took a last critical look at her reflection, her eyes concentrating on the slim white leather belt encircling her waist. She had had to let it out a single notch since the last time she wore this dress, but, apart from that, there was no outward sign of the new life growing within her. A sigh of relief ran through her. How on earth would her mother react to having to introduce an unmarried mother-to-be of a daughter to her Irish relative? Not at all well. But given a few months, there would be no avoiding it. She smiled grimly at the thought.

She had not even set eyes on her aunt yet. Katie had arrived this afternoon, while Kitty was still at the gallery, and Sarah had informed her 'the Irish lady' was having a lie down and a bath when she got back just less than an hour ago. Her mother had looked in once, about ten minutes ago, but was far too excited to be completely coherent. Maeve was also desperately worried that Kieran might not turn up and Kitty did her best to reassure her that he was not so insensitive as to stay away tonight of all nights.

'But you don't know – you can't imagine what was said – or

almost said,' her mother had wailed, peering from behind the net curtains into the street beneath.

'You're not making any sense, Mom,' Kitty had replied. 'It couldn't have been that serious. It wasn't you Kieran fell out with originally, after all, it was Chuck.'

'But that's just the trouble, Kitty,' Maeve had sighed. 'I alluded to it – to what Chuck implied that night!'

Kitty bit her lip at the memory. 'Yes, well, we'll not go into that, if you don't mind.' It was as unbearable to even think about as it was impossible to talk about. She had deliberately closed her mind not only to the conversation that had finally driven her brother from the family home, but also to the memory of that rippling-muscled young man she had met briefly in Kieran's own apartment over in Queens. Poor Kieran, poor sick Kieran. If it was true then God help them all. One thing was certain, though, there wouldn't be a whisper of it in the conversation tonight. Tonight belonged to Aunt Katie and to Mother Ireland. Her heart leapt at the prospect.

Maudie was already in the drawing room, sipping a drink in the corner of the settee, when Kitty entered a few minutes after seven. She raised a hand and reached over to switch off the gramophone, abruptly ending Glenn Miller's melodic rendering of 'String of Pearls'.

'Aren't they here yet?'

Maudie was looking a picture – the archetypal budding Broadway starlet – in a peach-coloured organdie creation, with matching open-toed shoes. She raised one immaculately shaved leg and smoothed an imaginary wrinkle from her left calf. 'Black market nylons,' she said, ignoring her sister's question completely. 'Five dollars a pair. I got the chance of three pairs today. Fancy buying a pair off me? I'm feeling peculiarly altruistic today.'

Kitty helped herself to a drink and glanced across at her sister. 'Don't tell me – it's a new boyfriend!'

Maudie's face lit up immediately, and, placing both feet together on the carpet in front of her, she leaned forward, her hands clasped around the glass on her knees. 'Well, he's not exactly my boyfriend yet,' she confided. 'Estelle only introduced us today, but I'm working on it. She's giving a party tomorrow night and he's going to be there – then zowieee!'

308

Kitty smiled indulgently. 'And just what makes you so sure this boyfriend-to-be will be there?'

Maudie looked suitably smug as she took a sip of her drink. 'Because he's her son, that's why, and it's Estelle's birthday tomorrow. He's bound to be there!'

Kitty stared at her, her heart turning over. 'Her son?' Her voice was little above a croak.

'Yes, that's right. She only had the one kid. He's a scientist working up in Massachusetts, but seems to get plenty of time off. I really go for him, Kitty. He's a real man – not one of those acne-infested kids I've been around with in the past. You'd like him, I know.'

'I'm sure I would.' Kitty put her drink back down by the soda siphon. She felt physically sick. Lee with her little sister – with Maudie!

She hadn't set eyes on him since that awful moment in Yehudi's restaurant when he had walked out of her life. Pride had stopped her getting in touch. After all, he was the one who had walked out on her, wasn't he? He was the one who had said that one day he might well find a nice Jewish girl to settle down with. But she was the one who was carrying his child – and not a single hour had passed since that day when she had not thought about him and what might have been, if they had not both been born so darned stubborn. If she had not had a life-long love affair with the land of her fathers, and he with his . . .

'Kitty . . . Maudie . . . I'd like you to meet your Aunt Katie!'

Both turned simultaneously towards the door, where their mother stood with her arm round a smaller, stoutish, red-haired woman. Her shock at Maudie's revelation momentarily submerged, the first thing that struck Kitty on seeing her aunt was how like Kieran she looked: the same colouring and freckles, although the latter was discreetly played down behind a thin film of powder. She was dressed quite plainly, in an apple-green crêpe blouse and dark grey skirt; a single string of artificial pearls adorned the Peter Pan collar of the blouse and her hair was cut much shorter than was currently fashionable, and had either been quite severely permed or was naturally very curly. Her bright, amber-coloured eyes positively danced as she came forward to clasp each one in turn.

To her embarrassment, as Kitty bent to hug the much smaller figure, the words of the old song, 'When Irish Eyes are Smiling', rang through her head, and she felt the hot rush of tears to her eyes. 'Oh, Aunt Katie, I can't tell you . . .' To her horror, and the evident amusement of the others, the tears ran down her cheeks in scalding rivulets as they drew apart, and she was forced to scrabble about in the pocket of her dress for a clean handkerchief.

'What'll it be, Katie?' Smiling indulgently at her daughter's surprising show of emotion, Maeve held up a bottle of Jameson's for her sister-in-law's approval.

But Katie shook her head. 'Sure and it's not Irish whiskey I'll be drinking here in New York, is it? Have you none of that home-grown fire water I've heard so much about back home?'

Maeve replaced the Jameson's with a shrug. 'If it's bourbon you're after – how about a wee drop o' Southern Comfort on the rocks?' She was aware of her speech having already dropped into a faint Irish lilt that it had not possessed for years and the change brought a peculiar satisfaction, as if she had somehow found something very precious that had been misplaced for a long time.

'That'll be champion,' Katie replied with a smile, as she settled herself on the settee between her two nieces.

When they had each been furnished with a glass, Maeve raised hers. 'I had thought Kieran would have been here by now,' she said, as a glance at her watch told her it had already gone seven-fifteen, 'but no matter. We'll drink a toast, ladies – to Katie, dear, dear Katie – and all those back in old Ireland who can't be with us on this happiest of occasions!'

As they raised their glasses, through the mists of memory, Maeve could see only one face before her. The face of a dark-eyed intense young man, wearing the dark robes of a Catholic priest.

Then, as if reading her mind, Katie's voice interrupted her thoughts. 'Let's drink especially to Dermot,' she said quietly, holding her drink aloft. 'I'm afraid he needs all your prayers at the moment.'

Chapter 33

'Dermot? And what's wrong with Dermot?' The question came
out much more abruptly than Maeve intended. But just hearing
his name spoken by another human being after all these years
brought the bare skin of her arms out in gooseflesh.

Katie took a sip of her drink and balanced it on her knee as
she looked up at her sister-in-law. 'We only heard quite
recently,' she said. 'From Mary-Agnes, actually – for the divil
would never let on himself that there was anything wrong . . .'

'But what is it, Katie? He's not ill, is he? It's nothing serious?'

'Oh, aye, he's ill, all right. Or at least, he has been of late. It
seems he spent some time in a sanatorium this summer and
none of us knew anything about it.'

Maeve's face paled. 'A sanatorium? You mean he's consumptive? He's got TB?' Her hand flew to her breast as she uttered
the words . . . Dear God, don't let it be true!

Katie nodded. 'It seems like it. He wasn't there long, mind –
only a few weeks. But it's right queer, so it is, for none of our
family have ever had such a thing – touch wood.' She leaned
across and skimmed the edge of the coffee table in front of her
with her fingertips, as she shook her head at the memory of
the shock she had felt when Mary-Agnes had written with the
news.

'But how is he? Is he all right now?' Maeve's voice was
insistent. Couldn't Katie see how important it was?

Katie shrugged. 'Well, he's back in the parish, but he's a
right sight for sore eyes – death warmed up on a shovel, an' no
mistake! I went down to see him just before coming over here
and, my God, he was never the healthiest lookin' o' specimens
to begin with, but now he's a sight to behold all right. His neck
was stickin' out o' his dog collar like a thrawn chicken's. I told
him he'll no' be long for this world if he doesn't take better
care o' himself. Not that he'll take a blind bit of notice of what
I say . . . Now you, Maeve, he used to listen to you . . .'

'Did he?' Maeve avoided her eyes, as the words twisted in her heart.

'Aye, he did that! But, as he himself put it, when I said that very thing to him — a lot o' water has passed under the bridge since then. And he's probably right. He sends his best wishes, though. He was real interested to hear I was coming over to see you all.'

Maeve's face had gone quite white, but she attempted to keep her voice level. 'He knows about Frank's death, then? He knows I'm a widow? . . . I didn't write to tell him.'

'Oh, aye, he knows all right. It seems your brother Charlie's daughter Emma married a Catholic and had to convert. Dermot was the one who gave her most of her instruction, just like he did for you yourself, I believe. They still live in his parish, by all accounts.'

Maeve listened, hanging on every word. She'd had no idea that it was a Catholic that Emma had married last year, let alone that it was Dermot who had given her the instruction. But then, Emma's conversion wouldn't have been something any of the Ballantines would have wanted to broadcast. They were probably still getting over her own defection to the other side a generation ago!

'Anyway, like I said, he sends his best wishes and wants me to bring some good photographs back with me. And, do you know, he asked if I'd make sure I got a decent one of Kitty!'

Maeve turned away, her face draining of all colour, as, oblivious of the impact of her words, Katie turned to the surprised young woman on her left. 'And just what makes you so privileged to get a special mention, young lady, I can't imagine!'

'Beats me!' Kitty said, with a smile and a shrug, feeling an absurd pleasure in the interest expressed by this unknown relative across in the old country. 'He was my father's elder brother, wasn't he, Mom?'

Maeve nodded, too choked to speak. To think he had actually asked for a picture of Kitty. For twenty-seven years the question that he had tried to wring out of her before she left Ireland for good must have festered in his mind. She stared down at her elder daughter. Could you tell just by looking whose child she was? Certainly the thinnish, sensitively drawn features and darker hair belonged to Dermot and not Danny . . .

'Did you hear me, Mom? This Dermot — he's my father's elder brother, isn't he?'

Maeve nodded dumbly. She had not spoken Dermot's name aloud to anyone for so long, it seemed totally wrong to be suddenly discussing him like this in front of the girls. 'Yes . . . yes,' she said quickly. 'He's the only male of the family still alive.'

'He had brothers, then, but they're dead?' Blissfully unaware of her mother's discomfort, Kitty was thoroughly enjoying this.

It was Katie who answered. 'I believe our Mammy lost one or two wee ones in the cradle, Kitty, and the only boys to survive infancy were Danny, Dermot and Willie-John.'

'Willie-John!' Maudie, who had remained silent until then, gave a sudden giggle. 'And who is Willie-John, may we ask?'

'Was,' her mother cut in sharply. 'Willie-John died during the Great War — killed by a bomb manufactured by another Irishman, not a German.' After all this time, the bitterness she had felt about the death was still evident in her voice.

Katie nodded, her face suddenly serious as the memory of her beloved Willie-John's shattered body crowded her mind.

'Did you know him, Mom? Was that in your time?'

'Aye, I knew him.' Maeve said quietly. 'I was there, with Kieran in my arms . . . I was the one who identified the body . . .' Her voice trailed off, as her thoughts took wing across the years.

As that awful vision on the pavement outside the pawnbroker's faded, for one searing moment, the vision of Willie-John wetting himself in Mary-Agnes's small, steam-filled kitchen filled her mind. And the agony of the remorse she had felt at her sister-in-law's jeer that she was the only one who would have him bit acutely into her soul. Even after all these years the memory was still as painful. Certain scars, she had learned to her cost, time did nothing to heal. They would remain, still as livid, still as painful, to the end.

Her discomfort was brought to a swift halt, however, by the sound of the door opening.

'Kieran!'

All eyes turned to gaze at the young man in the grey lounge suit and neatly brushed flame-red hair who stood, with a faintly embarrassed air, in the open doorway.

'Holy Mary and Joseph, if it's not Danny himself!' Katie jumped up from the settee, spilling part of her drink down the front of her skirt, as she stared in incredulity at her nephew. 'Is he not just the living spit of his father, Maeve?'

Maeve looked at her son, studiously avoiding his eyes. There was no denying it – in looks he was Danny's double. 'Yes, yes he is,' she agreed quietly. 'Kieran, I'd like you to meet your Aunt Katie.'

'It's a pleasure to meet you at last, Aunt Katie,' Kieran replied, extending a hand as he walked into the body of the room. He had a relaxed smile on his face that in no way reflected the turmoil within as the two shook hands. But outward appearances were all that concerned his mother at this moment.

Maeve breathed a secret sigh of relief as the two looked at each other at arm's length, then embraced. He had not let her down. In this, at least, he had not proved a complete disappointment.

'Well, how did it go?' Louie rolled from the bed and made for the icebox in the cramped kitchen of Kieran's apartment, extracting two bottles of beer as Kieran took off his jacket and threw it over the back of a chair. 'Is she just as you imagined – the Irish dame?'

Kieran unbuttoned his trousers and stepped out of them, before peeling off his shirt, and flopping down on the bed in his boxer shorts. Was she just as he imagined? His mind returned to the talkative, lively little redhead whose company he had to admit he had thoroughly enjoyed. 'Yeah, I suppose she is, in a way. She certainly yacked a lot, but then most Irish do, don't they? Anyway, my mother certainly seems happy to have her here.'

'Is she one of those bog Irish from the other side of the tracks, or is she from your Lord Fal-de-ral grandfather's side?'

'I've told you before, Louie, my grandfather ain't a lord – he was made a Sir, that's all. And no, she's no relation to him. She's my late father's sister. Bog Irish, if you insist.'

Louie prised the tops off both the bottles and handed one over, before taking a swig of his own. 'You know, you never did tell me what happened about your old man's will. Old Frank's, I mean.'

Kieran paused, the neck of the beer bottle at his lips. 'There's nothing to tell.'

'What's that supposed to mean? Are you getting your share of the money or ain't ya?'

'Yes and no.' He grinned across at Louie, but his friend was in no mood for playing around.

'What the hell's that supposed to mean?'

'Yes, I was offered my share of the money – and no, I'm not accepting it.'

'Not accepting it?' Louie shouted the words across at him. 'You loco, or something? How much did they come up with anyhow?'

Kieran shrugged. 'A couple of hundred thousand or so.'

A strangled gasp left Louie's lips as he stared dumbfounded at his friend. 'A couple of hundred grand? Holy Moses, have you taken leave of your senses? What d'ya mean, you're not accepting it?'

Kieran pulled himself up on the bed. 'It's quite simple. Old Frank left an unholy pile of blood money and I won't contaminate myself by touching it.'

'Jeeeezus . . . I don't believe it! I do not believe it!'

'Well, you'd better, buster, 'cause it's the truth.'

The two men stared at one another across the rumpled bed. They had made love there only a few short hours ago, just before Kieran left for Park Avenue, but now they seemed light years apart in thought.

Louie shook his head in disbelief. A couple of hundred thousand was more than he could expect to earn in a lifetime of shifting mail around the city for Hayes and Hamilton. It was more than most people could earn in a lifetime in this human cesspit.

'You know how much my Mom earned over on Grand Street, making lace for the likes of your goddammed Fullerton relatives? A dollar a day! One measly dollar a day! She died still sitting at her workbench. She used to see those darned bobbins in her sleep – what little of that she got!'

A nerve twitched spasmodically at the side of his clenched jaw as he stared down at the figure of his lover on the bed. At times like this he hated him, he really hated Kieran Donovan's privileged guts. What did he ever know about poverty? It certainly wasn't for the likes of him that FDR had come up with the New Deal! Those bastards on Park Avenue hadn't had a raw deal out of this country – no siree – it was the likes of his own folks, and the other poor suckers on the East Side who had suffered.

Kieran sat up on the bed, slightly perturbed by the look in the dark Italian eyes that bore down on him. 'Look, Louie, I'm sorry about your Mom. I'm sorry about all your darned relatives, if that makes you any happier. But I sure as hell don't see what that's got to do with my decision not to touch Frank's money.'

Real anger flared in Louie's eyes. 'Oh, you don't do you? Well, I'll tell you what it's got to do with my relatives, buster! It's got to do with my relatives because it's got to do with me! You're the one who's made all the running in this thing we've got going and up till now I've been happy to go along with it. But, let's just say, tonight I wised up, Kieran – okay?'

'And what's that supposed to mean?'

Louie took a swig of the beer and looked down at him, his eyes moving slowly from the top of Kieran's red head, down across the almost hairless, pale-skinned body, to the lame left leg that lay at an awkward angle on the crumpled sheet. It was thinner and slightly shorter than the right and the comparison between their two physiques could not have been more marked. There was an expression akin to contempt in his eyes as they began to move back up towards the striped boxer shorts. Then a feeling of superiority surged through him. The evidence was there before his very eyes. Kieran was becoming aroused. And the greater the contempt in Louie's eyes, the more aroused he was getting!

Louie sat down on the far edge of the mattress and took

another long draught of the beer, letting the neck of the bottle linger on his wet lower lip as he looked down at his friend.

Kieran's eyes were riveted on the neck of the bottle and on Louie's lower lip, as he shifted his position slightly. The young Italian had the most sensuous of mouths – curved like a girl's, almost, and a disconcerting habit of leaving it slightly parted.

The tip of Louie's tongue toyed with the mouth of the bottle as he rolled it thoughtfully across the wet pink skin. He was acutely conscious of the other's eyes on every movement of the green glass neck of the bottle. He was well aware of countless little ways to arouse his companion and his ability to exercise them at will, for his own benefit, whenever an opportune moment arose, gave him an innate sense of superiority in the relationship.

A gold crucifix glinted amid the tangle of dark hairs on Louie's chest and his hand moved to it and held it up towards Kieran as he said quietly. 'You see this, man? In Sicily, where the Carellis come from, we're true Catholics. And, to a true Catholic, sodomy is a sin. Do you know that, huh? Every time you commit buggery with me, I damn myself in the eyes of our Lord? That must be worth something, wouldn't you say? How much are you willing to pay for my immortal soul, Kieran?'

Kieran moved uncomfortably on the bed. 'You're talkin' crap, man. I'm a Catholic too, remember.'

A quiet smile crept around the corners of Louie's lips as with the fingertips of his right hand he lightly caressed the pale golden hairs of Kieran's right shin. 'I've learned a lot over these past few months,' he said quietly. 'I've learned there are others – richer bastards than you – who are willing to pay a helluva lot for what I give you for free. What would you reckon, Kieran, honey? What would you reckon Joe Soap would be willing to pay for the use of this ol' carcass of mine? A hundred bucks a time? Or maybe two? A grand even – if the old bugger in question was ugly enough?'

A bead of sweat formed on Kieran's upper lip. He was playing with him. The little bastard was playing with him and there wasn't a darned thing he could do about it. He was besotted by him – crazy about every square inch of the little Sicilian monster. He could no longer hide the evidence of his desire and the physical ache in his groin was becoming almost unbearable, as Louie's fingers reached his inner thighs, only to draw back again, as the pale flesh beneath them squirmed uncontrollably and Kieran groaned out loud. 'What is it you want, for Chrissake?'

'It's not what I want that matters most, man. It's what you want. What do you want, Kieran? What do you want more than anything right now?'

Desire pulsated through Kieran in great waves, drowning all sense of proportion and reality as the bronzed fingers started their upward journey once more. 'You – damn you! It's you I want!' Unable to bear it any longer, he lurched forwards to make a grab for his torturer.

But Louie was too quick for him. He deftly moved to one side and stood by the bed, hands on slim hips, looking down at Kieran's body sprawled across the tangled sheet. 'I'm yours for the taking, honey,' he said softly. 'I'll sell my immortal soul for you, Kieran Donovan. But at a price.'

Kieran's eyes were level with his friend's groin, as he lay on his stomach looking up at him. And Louie moved deliberately within touching distance. 'I'm all yours, Kieran,' he repeated softly. 'Every fuckin' part of me ... What's it worth? If I'm willing to sell my immortal soul to you, ain't this worth at least half of that blood money you talk about?' With one deft movement, he stepped out of his shorts and stood before him, naked and beautiful in the cold, autumn light from the window. 'Ain't it worth at least half of it, Kieran, honey?'

Kieran let out a groan that came from his very soul as his hand reached out for the object of his desire. 'Yes, damn you, yes! Two hundred bloody thousand times yes!'

Chapter 34

Kitty got up from her desk and made for the door to the washroom. Letting it slam behind her, she reached the hand-basin and leant over it, clutching the white porcelain sides, as her stomach heaved and retched. Having had no breakfast, bar a few sips of chilled orange juice, nothing came up, but it was a few minutes until the nausea subsided enough for her to return to her office.

She sat back down again in her chair with a sigh. Her face was chalky white and a thin film of perspiration gleamed on her brow. Just when she thought she was to be spared the agonies of morning sickness, it had descended upon her with a vengeance over the past week. She felt drained of all energy as she picked up her pen and attempted to address the work in hand. Her paperknife slit into the corner of a buff-coloured envelope, but got no further, as the ring of the telephone at her elbow jarred in the quiet morning air.

'Bellini Fine Arts . . .'

'Kitty, it's me – Kieran.'

She sat up on the edge of the seat, a frown creasing her brow. It was barely a week since she had seen him. But at least they had parted on the best of terms after Aunt Katie's welcome dinner. She fought to keep her voice cheerful as the queasiness churned in her stomach. 'Hi there! To what do I owe this pleasure?'

'I've got to see you, Kit – the sooner the better.'

The frown increased. He sounded worried about something. 'There's nothing wrong is there?'

''Course not. I just want your help, that's all. Are you free for lunch?'

She glanced down at the desk diary, running her finger over the page until she came to today's section. 'Uh-huh . . . I've got nobody due till two.'

319

'Great! How about twelve-thirty, then? Where do you fancy?'

She paused. 'How about Yehudi's on the corner of Broadway and 23rd?' It would be the first time she had been back there since Lee walked out on her, but now was as good a time to lay his ghost as any.

'Sounds fine by me. See you at twelve-thirty!'

She replaced the phone carefully in its cradle, her fingers lingering on the handpiece. She wished she felt better; it was bad enough having to run the gallery practically singlehanded without having to supply a shoulder for Kieran to cry on into the bargain. But wait — that was unfair. She had no evidence, except a certain tenseness in his voice, that he had a problem. She had problems on the brain. Life seemed suddenly full of them this summer.

'Hey, anyone in?'

She glanced up to see the face of Mary-Jo Brumsack grinning round the edge of the office door.

'I've got the watercolours you wanted to see,' the girl announced, heaving a heavy-looking portfolio into the room and propping it up against the nearest wall. 'Fancy having a look now?'

Kitty focused her eyes on the bulging article as another wave of nausea welled within her. 'Sure, Mary-Jo,' she sighed. 'I can't wait!'

Kieran was already seated in the restaurant, at a table for two by the window, when Kitty arrived at Yehudi's. She flung her shoulder-bag down on the floor by her feet and sat down with an almighty sigh.

'You look pooped.'

'Yeah, I guess I am. I'm sorry I'm late, I got held up. Everyone seemed to choose today of all days to bring their stuff in for my perusal.' She accepted a cigarette with a grateful nod and leaned over to reach the flame of the lighter in his outstretched hand. 'Thanks!'

'You're obviously a very popular young woman.'

She grimaced. 'Only when people want something.'

'Like me, for instance.'

320

'I'm sorry, Kieran – I didn't mean it like that.'

'I know.' He smiled across at her and picked up the menu and handed it over.

She gave it a cursory glance, then sighed. 'To be honest, I'm really not hungry. I'll settle for a plain omelette and a glass of sahlab.'

The waiter had appeared at their elbow and Kieran turned to him, with a nod. 'Make mine an omelette too, with French fries, zemino sauce and sauerkraut. And I'll have a glass of kvass with it and a coffee to follow . ... How about you, Kitty – fancy a coffee?'

'No, I'll take a rain check on the caffeine, if you don't mind.'

Kieran shook his head, as the waiter nodded politely before disappearing in the direction of the kitchens, then said with a grin, 'Only an omelette and a glass of cinnamon milk – and no caffeine ... Anyone would think you were pregnant or something!'

'Then anyone would be right, wouldn't they?'

He stared across at her, his mouth dropping open, so that the cigarette that had been dangling from his lower lip tumbled on to the clean damask cloth. 'Damn!' He flicked the burning ash off the white cloth with his napkin, as she sat watching, an amused smile on her face.

She hadn't meant to tell him. Not really. It had just seemed natural somehow. 'Don't look so shocked, brother dear. It does happen occasionally you know, when heterosexuals make love.'

'Ouch!'

The colour flared in her pale cheeks. 'God, I'm sorry, Kier – I didn't mean it like that!'

'Forget it.' He attempted a strained grin. In a way, her confession about the baby had made him feel slightly easier about his own request. 'Do I know the guy?'

She shook her head. 'No, you've never met.'

'You're going to have the kid, though, I take it?'

She nodded. 'I'm a Catholic, Kieran. Not a very good one – granted, but I try.' She took a long drag on the cigarette and let the smoke out slowly through her nostrils. 'Yes, I'm going to have it.'

'Will you marry him?'

'He's never asked me.'

'And if he does?'

'Then – no, I won't marry him.'

Kieran took a deep breath and leaned back in his chair. She was a funny one and no mistake. 'Do you love him – this guy whose kid you're having, but who you won't marry?'

'Yes, I love him.'

'Holy Moses, Kitty . . . are you out of your mind?' The last few words were hissed beneath his breath as the waiter returned with the order.

They sat in silence as it was served, then when he was quite out of earshot once more, Kieran leaned across the table, a deep frown etched across his brow. 'You'll be ostracised, you know, kid. People will crucify you – even people you once regarded as friends suddenly won't want to know.'

She gave a wry smile as she stabbed into the yellow cushion of egg with her fork. 'You sound like you speak from experience.'

Their eyes met across the few inches of space. This was no time for charades and both knew it. Finally, Kieran nodded slowly. 'Yes, Kitty, I do.'

The hazel of his eyes had clouded to a darker brown as he lowered them and impaled a French fry with his fork. She wanted to reach across, to touch his hand, to tell him she was sorry for everything that had gone before, for all the misery he must have gone through over the past few months. But the words would not come. Instead she took a sip of the sahlab and waited for him to speak.

'You may already have guessed – it's to do with Louie – the reason I asked you here today.'

She hadn't, but she nodded nevertheless.

'I – I would've asked Mom, but it's kinda difficult at the moment, with Aunt Katie there and all . . . It's about Frank's will, Kitty. I want my part of it.'

She stared across at him, a forkful of omelette halfway to her mouth. She replaced the portion, uneaten, on her plate. 'Well, this is a turn-up for the books and no mistake!'

He looked uncomfortable. 'Yeah, I know . . . And don't

bother repeating all I said at the time. There ain't a man alive who hasn't gotten indigestion from eating his words. I – I changed my mind, that's all.'

'Look, Kieran, there's no need to get all defensive with me. To be honest, I'm delighted you're taking it – for whatever reason. And I'd rather not know all the details of that, if you don't mind.'

In her mind's eye she could see Louie, that bronzed little muscle-man with the superior smile, and felt heart-sorry for her brother. It was funny really, she had never really thought of him as a weak person before. He had always just been Kieran, her big brother. She had envied him in many ways, in the way he had stood up to their parents and refused to be pigeon-holed like the rest of them had been at school – and now in the way he had the courage to speak out against war, when the whole world was cheering their boys fighting over in Europe. This guy Carelli had a hold on him, there was no doubt about that, but it was nobody's affair but his own. 'What exactly do you want me to do?'

He shrugged as he carried a forkful of sauerkraut to his mouth. 'Just have a word with Mom, really. Ask her if she can arrange for the money to be transferred into my personal account . . . I've got the details here.' He dug into the inside pocket of his jacket and extracted a white envelope which he handed over to her. 'Just give her this. If there's anything to be signed et cetera, she can give me a ring. Or if she doesn't want to do that, then her lawyer can ring. But I've got to have that money, Kitty – and soon.'

Kitty nodded as she bent down to slip the envelope into her bag. And, at that precise moment, the door opened. It was the shoes she recognized first – an old pair of well-worn brown suede shoes. She remained frozen, half bent beneath the table, as their owner escorted the wearer of the pair of beige, high-heeled court shoes to a table at the back of the room.

'You okay down there?' Kieran's freckled face peered down at her from above the frill of the tablecloth.

'Yes, of course!' She straightened up in her seat, her stomach turning over, as she threw a quick glance in the direction of the newly-arrived couple. Lee was sitting with his back to her, so she got a full-face view of his companion. Her first reaction was one of relief that it wasn't Maudie he was with, but the sight of the beautiful dark-haired young woman made her spirits sink to the soles of her feet. She was Jewish, there was no doubt about that. With her long mane of blue-black hair, pale olive skin and elegantly curved nose, above the well-drawn lips, it was as obvious as if she was marked out with one of those yellow stars that the Nazis were making them wear in Europe.

She dragged her eyes back down to her plate and made a valiant attempt to eat a mouthful of food. Why couldn't he have been with a blonde? Why was it a Jewess he was sitting there with? Somehow, someone of her own race would have been less of a threat.

She glanced back in their direction as a peal of laughter came from the lips of the young woman and she raised a hand to smooth a stray wisp of dark hair back from her brow. Dear God, she was wearing an engagement ring! The stones glinted in the light as she lowered her hand and reached across to clasp his.

'You sure there's nothing wrong, Kit? You look like you've seen a ghost . . . Sure you're all right?'

She nodded briefly as she avoided Kieran's concerned gaze and stared back down at her plate. She had seen a ghost all right. She had seen the ghost of a past love affair; a ghost that would haunt her for the rest of her life, every time she looked into the eyes of the child she was now carrying.

Ignoring the young artist she knew would be waiting for her back at the gallery, when she left Kieran outside Yehudi's at one-fifteen she remained behind, closeting herself in the crowded doorway of a bookstore across the street, to wait for them coming out. They obliged ten minutes later, their arms entwined around each other's waist.

White-faced, Kitty looked on, as they disappeared down the crowded sidewalk. He had never walked like that with her – not once. They had held hands, yes, but he had never put his arm around her in the street. It was a small point, but it cut to the quick as she replaced the book in her hands on to the laden trestle table and made her own way into the lunchtime throng.

The rest of the day passed in a haze of nausea attacks and visiting artists. It was hard to decide which gave her the most discomfort. All she longed for was to get back to Park Avenue and lie down, to make an attempt at putting her chaotic thoughts in some kind of order. But even that would not be easy, for she had promised Kieran to talk to their mother about the will. It was not a prospect she relished.

It was almost bedtime before she managed to get a word with Maeve alone. Her mother listened in silence until she had finished speaking, then said bitterly, 'Something's up, Kitty. I just know it. After the way Kieran talked about Frank's money – blood money he called it – in this very room, it would take something really incredible to make him change his mind.'

'Or someone.'

'Pardon?'

Immediately she regretted her words as Maeve's eyes cut into hers. 'Nothing, Mom, I just meant . . .'

'You said, "or someone", Kathleen. What exactly did you mean by that? Is anyone putting pressure on your brother to get at this money?'

Kitty threw up her hands in a helpless gesture. 'Honestly, Mom, I've really no idea! You make it all sound so dramatic. Dammit all, he is entitled to the money, after all, isn't he? It was left to him.'

Maeve's lips twisted into a bitter smile. 'Yes, Kitty, he's entitled to it, as you so rightly put it. But had Frank lived a day or so longer, Kieran wouldn't have got a cent – I'll tell you that for nothing.'

'Whatever do you mean?'

'Just what I said. Frank told me the night before he died that he was changing his will and cutting Kieran out.'

She threw up her arms in a futile gesture, then clasped them around her once more as she paced the space between the window and the settee. 'Oh, it might have been just talk, but Frank was never one for making rash statements. Something had happened between them that upset him deeply. The trouble is, he didn't live long enough to tell me about it . . .'

Her voice faded to a whisper as she looked across at her daughter. 'There was so much we never had time to talk about, Kitty, so much . . .'

'You loved him, didn't you, Mom? You really loved him?'

Maeve looked at her, her eyes suddenly vacant. 'Love, Kitty? What is love? He was my husband – and I wanted it to continue that way.'

She paused and turned to stare out of the window, at the sea of twinkling lights beyond the glass. 'You know, you never really appreciate what you have until you're in danger of losing it. I guess I never really appreciated Frank until Estelle came back on the scene. Can you understand that? Why should a man suddenly become much more desirable just because he's seeing another woman?'

She did not expect an answer, and for that Kitty was thankful. She understood what her mother was saying all right. She understood only too well. Life could not have been sweeter when she first started seeing Lee, for she could indulge her own fantasies of independence by declaring that she had no intention of ever tying herself to one man. But when one day he suddenly began agreeing with her, then the sweetness turned sour in her mouth.

Life had taught her a bitter lesson this summer – a lesson she would carry with her for the rest of her life, in the form of Lee's child. And, perhaps the greatest irony of all, was that this child that she now carried secretly beneath her heart, would be the first grandchild for both her own mother and the woman that Maeve hated more than anyone on earth – Estelle Finlay.

Chapter 35

Maeve stood outside the bathroom door and listened to the sounds within. The constant retching brought tears to her eyes as Kitty's agonies continued behind the closed door. Why couldn't she confide in her? Why couldn't she admit she was having a child? It was not the fact that her unmarried daughter was pregnant that brought the look of anguish to Maeve's face, but the fact that Kitty could not, or would not, share her secret with her.

She had suspected it for some time – since just after Katie's arrival, to be exact, and her lively sister-in-law was now coming to the end of her stay in New York. She had been with them almost a month. Perhaps she could mention it to her? Not that she believed in the old maxim – a trouble shared is a trouble halved. That was rubbish, Maeve thought – it had been more like a trouble shared is a trouble doubled, in her experience. But she might just tell Katie, nevertheless . . .

She moved on quickly down the passage as a sound from behind the door indicated that Kitty was on her way out.

'Mom – just a minute!'

Kitty's voice caught up with her as she was in the act of disappearing into the breakfast-room. She turned and was momentarily shocked at the gaunt white face that greeted her. 'Are you all right, Kathleen?'

'Yes, I'm fine. I just wanted to say I'll be late home tonight, so tell Sarah not to bother with dinner.'

'You're going out? You'll be having dinner elsewhere?'

Kitty looked pained. 'You're Irish, Mom, remember? Not one of those clinging Yiddisher Mommas!'

'I'm sorry, honey. I worry about you, that's all. You just haven't been looking yourself lately.'

Kitty made a brave attempt at a reassuring grin. 'You're only saying that because I haven't got my make-up on, that's all! . . . Remember now – no dinner!'

Maeve sighed wearily and watched as she disappeared back down the hall, her toilet bag slung casually over her shoulder. She was right of course, she shouldn't interfere. Kitty was a grown woman – but a grown woman with a problem that wasn't just going to go away by not worrying about it.

In search of a sustaining cup of coffee, she headed for the breakfast-room as Kitty paused at the door of her own room and glanced down the passage. Maudie was just coming out of her bedroom three doors down. The successful run the show was having on Broadway was obviously doing her good, for, in contrast to herself, her younger sister had never looked better. Her natural blonde hair had been enhanced by platinum highlights and was curled high at the front and sides in typical Betty Grable fashion. In fact, come to think of it, Kitty mused ruefully, there was more than a passing resemblance between the two.

'Morning, Kit! You're behind time this morning, aren't you?' Maudie's smile was dazzling as she presented a perfect set of straight white teeth to her sister. Almost five hundred dollars worth of cosmetic dentistry had recently removed two protruding eye teeth and had produced the perfect toothpaste advertisement.

In comparison, Kitty felt old and far from perfect, as she paused, with her hand on the knob of her bedroom door. 'Maudie . . . I never really got a chance to ask you, but did anything ever come out of that party – you know, Estelle's birthday shindig? Did her son turn up?'

Maudie threw up her eyes in mock horror. 'Oh, that! Yes, he turned up all right, but with another dame! I mighta known – the girls in the show all said he fancied himself as a real intellectual and wouldn't look at anyone in show business!'

'I take it this "other dame" wasn't an actress, then?'

'Good God, no! I got a chance to have a word with her later on and she was a typical blue stocking . . . Or, pardon me, I should say "brown", since she must be the only one wearing those awful lisle things these days, if what she says can be believed. Do you know she claims she hasn't worn silk stockings since Pearl Harbor? In fact, she swore she boycotts anything made of silk these days because it's almost certainly produced by . . . quote – Japanese imperialist silkworms!'

The look of indignant derision on Maudie's face was a picture as Kitty shook her head. 'But, for heaven's sake, almost everyone wears *nylons* these days – when we can get hold of them!'

'Say – that's right! I should've thought of that at the time. But I did give her one piece of good advice. I told her that most beauty parlours these days will paint your legs, and draw a line down the back, to make it look like you're wearing stockings for fifty cents a leg!'

Kitty smiled. 'Was she impressed?'

Maudie shrugged. 'She acted like she never even heard me. You reckon she was just trying to impress a dumb blonde? The bitch!'

'No, I'm sure that wasn't the case,' Kitty said soothingly. 'But she sounds a pretty interesting lady. Did she say what she does for a living?'

Maudie winced. 'It gets worse – she's taking a doctorate in bacteriology at Bellevue!'

'Whew . . . !'

'Her family came from Russia originally, I believe she said. Her grandfather helped found the Hebrew Immigrant Aid Society, to aid Jewish families through the agonies of Ellis Island, and get them settled into some kind of accommodation over here.'

The image of old Itzak Finkelstein and his beautiful wife Leah flashed into Kitty's mind. They would be pleased. Their grandson had found the perfect mate – a young woman that both the old man and, more importantly, his wife, Lee's beloved grandmother, would have approved of wholeheartedly. That it was that same young woman she had seen in Yehudi's she had no doubt.

'What's with the interest in that guy Finkelstein, anyway?' Maudie looked curiously at her sister. 'You fancy him yourself or something?'

Kitty opened the door to her room and gave an enigmatic smile. 'Let's just settle for the "or something", shall we?'

Maeve waited until both her daughters had left for work before she fixed herself and Katie another cup of coffee. She toyed nervously with the handle of her cup as she wondered how to word the questions that were causing her so much heartache.

'There's something on your mind, Maeve. You've been distracted about something for the past week. It's not the family, is it?' Katie could not hide the anxiety in her voice as she accepted the cup and saucer and sat down at the opposite side of the table. She would have to be blind or just plain stupid not to see something was wrong. And that, she prided herself in believing, she certainly was not.

'What else?' Maeve replied with a sigh. 'What else but family ever causes upsets in your life?'

'Would you like to tell me about it?'

'Oh, Katie, how can it happen? How can it happen, when you lavish love on them for a lifetime – give them the best that money can buy – that things never seem to turn out the way you hope?' She blurted the words out with much more vehemence than she intended.

'You mean why do so many parents believe they have failed their children somewhere along the line and vice versa?' Katie took a sip of her coffee and regarded the contents of her cup thoughtfully. 'I suppose, because they're not copies of us, Maeve my dear, and never can be. We are all individuals who must be free to make our own mistakes . . .'

'And, by God, they do that all right! At least, two of mine have with a vengeance!'

'The Irish two?'

Maeve gave a weak smile at the description 'Who else? . . . You know Frank once joked to me, at the time of Kieran's expulsion from school, that nervous breakdowns are hereditary – you get them from your children! I've come to realise there's a lot of truth in that! If you weren't here to talk to right now, I think I'd probably crack up.'

Katie shook her head emphatically. 'No you wouldn't. You're made of sterner stuff than that. And if one of your problems is Kitty's pregnancy, I wouldn't worry about it. She's perfectly capable of taking it in her stride. She's a very capable young woman.'

'She – she's told you?' Maeve looked at her sister-in-law in astonishment.

'Of course not! She doesn't have to – 'tis as clear as day, so it is! But it's her affair, Maeve, not yours.'

'"Affair" being the operative word, I suppose?' It was hard to keep the bitterness from her voice. 'The whole thing's a complete mystery to me. I'd no idea she was even seeing a man – although I did set eyes on her with someone at the premiere of *Madame Bovary* some time back. Whether he's the one responsible or not I've really no idea ... And what if she refuses to marry the father? Good God, Katie, I've probably never even set eyes on the guy!'

'Well, you can be sure it's not got there by immaculate conception. No matter how virtuous Kitty may be, this is no virgin birth. He's bound to exist and, whoever he is, his child will be your grandchild and you must welcome it into the family as such.'

'Poor little bastard.'

The two women looked at one another over the polished pine top of the table and Maeve sighed deeply as she topped up her coffee cup. 'It's not going to easy for her, bringing up a child on her own.'

'At least it'll be a heck of a lot easier here than back in Ireland! I remember when poor Eileen, God rest her soul, fell with Seamus – the things that poor creature got said to her because she wouldn't reveal the father's name!' Katie shook her head at the memory. 'We all reckoned it was a plater from Harland and Wolff's who lived a couple of doors down from the Muldoons, but I suppose we'll never know now, for the secret's gone to the grave with her.'

'But the baby – what about the baby?'

'Oh, Eamon's oldest sister Jessie's looking after him. One more mouth doesn't make much difference when you've already got five of your own. Anyway, she kept him before. Eileen worked as a machinist in a clothing factory on the Shankill Road before she was killed and gave her sister a couple of quid for looking after the baby while she was out.'

Maeve stared silently into her cup. Katie was trying to be some comfort but it didn't really help much. Ireland or America, an unmarried mother was an unmarried mother. And, as if she didn't have enough to contend with with that, there was

Kieran too ... She shook her head slowly as she looked up bleakly and sighed, 'So my elder daughter's to be an unmarried mother and my elder son's a homosexual.'

'He never is!'

'It's true, Katie. It's the God's truth. As if one blow from Kitty isn't enough, along comes a real knockout punch from Kieran that has completely floored me, I can tell you.'

'Who told you such a thing?' Katie's face had gone quite white.

'Nobody's *told* me – they don't have to. I'm his mother, Katie – I just *know*. And, what's more, he's just cashed all the bonds that Frank left him, after swearing he wouldn't touch a cent of the money. I think he's being blackmailed.'

'No!'

Maeve nodded bleakly. 'It's the only explanation.'

'But that's terrible. You must do something, Maeve. You must help him.'

'I know. But what? Tell me, Katie. I'm at my wit's end!'

They sat in silence as both pondered on the problem, then Katie said flatly, 'You must find out who this devil is that's doing it to him and try to put a stop to it. It shouldn't be too difficult.'

'You're joking? I can't just ring Kieran up and ask him, for heaven's sake!'

'Of course you can't. Whoever suggested such a daft thing? But this is America, isn't it? You have such things as private detectives here?'

'Hire a private eye!'

'Why not?'

They stared at one another as the idea took shape, then Maeve nodded excitedly. 'You're right, Katie! You're so right! Why didn't I think of that? I'll go this very afternoon. I'll hire someone and get him to find out who it is and put a stop to that blackmailing scum, if it's the last thing I do!'

Louie's eyes lit up as they moved around the well-appointed living-room. Two black hide sofas faced one another on either side of a low-line coffee table and a series of abstract prints in black, white and grey adorned the plain white walls. The doors had art deco fluting at the corners and the walls were covered in a soft grey hessian. 'Nice, Kieran, man . . . real nice!'

He walked across the grey wool carpet and threw open one of the doors on the far wall. He nodded his approval as he gazed slowly round the all-white bedroom. 'This'll suit me just fine.'

'The one next door's identical,' Kieran said. 'I figured it'd be better to get them both done out the same.'

'When do we move in?'

'As soon as we like. It's all paid up — everything signed and sealed.'

'I'm still keeping on my old place, though. You know that.'

'Yeah, I know that.' Kieran's lips tightened as he fought to hide his irritation. The fact that Louie was so adamant in keeping on his old apartment was a thorn in his side. There could only be one reason for it — he wanted somewhere private to go. But what for? He had everything here he could possibly want. Except other guys. Kieran felt sick to his stomach. There had been far too many other pretty boys hanging around recently. Of course Louie laughed them off — made a fool of him even, for being so jealous. But, in his heart, Kieran knew he actually enjoyed it — he actually enjoyed seeing him suffer.

Louie strolled back into the living-room and flopped down on one of the sofas. 'Know where I was this afternoon?'

'Working — the same as me.'

'Correct. But not only working, Kieran, old buddy! I also just happened to look into McCall Motors.'

Kieran's brows rose. 'Oh yeah?'

Louie was obviously enjoying this, for he leaned back on the deep buttoned cushions, a slow smile spreading across his tanned features, as he nodded emphatically. 'And guess what else I just happened to do?'

'Surprise me.'

'Just ordered the latest Chevy, in the most goddam beautiful pale blue you've ever seen in your life, that's all!'

Kieran stared at him. He was going through the money he had lodged in their joint bank account like water. 'You mighta said! You might have warned me! What the hell do you want with a new Chevy anyway? What's wrong with your old one, for Chrissake?'

'It's old, that's what's wrong with it!' Louie said, sitting up in indignation. 'You want me to ride around in an old beat-up thing like that? Is that it? You get some kinda kick outa seeing me riding around in that heap of rust?'

'It's only three years old, goddam it, Louie. My own one's older than that!'

'That's your problem, man! You never did have class, Kieran, you know that? Your old man may have had money, but you're a born slob! Well, that's okay. If that's your scene, man, then that's okay by me. Only don't expect to drag me down to your level! Your trouble is you have the bucks and no class and mine was that I had the class and no bucks – but that's all changed now.'

'You're like a kid, you know that, Louie? You're like a poor starving kid let loose in a candy factory. You think by stuffing yourself with all the goodies that money can buy it'll make you happy. But it won't, you know that? It'll only make you sick.'

'Quit sermonising! You ain't my keeper.'

'Ain't I? Ain't I, Louie boy? Ain't that just what I am?'

The cold anger that had appeared in Kieran's eyes made his friend get up from the sofa. He attempted a light shrug. 'Hell, no, honey child – you be ol' Louie's sugar daddy – that's what you be!'

Kieran's jaw tightened. 'Well, this sugar daddy's beginning to turn sour.'

'Aw, come on, buddy boy. You ain't mad with ol' Louie – I was only having a bit of fun!' Louie came over and wound his arms around Kieran's neck, nuzzling the soft stubble of his cheek with his nose. 'Who needs a stupid new Chevy, anyhow?' His lips moved up to Kieran's ear, tracing the outline with his tongue.

Kieran took a shuddering breath, then another, as his friend moved nearer, repeating the question with a soft huskiness that made the small hairs round his collar stand on end.

'Who needs a stupid new Chevy, Kieran, honey?'

'You do – goddam it, Louie – you do!'

'And who's getting a brand new Chevy, Kieran, honey?'

'You are, Louie. You are . . .'

Chapter 36

'It looks a terrible place. Do you think they all look like this?'
Maeve's heart sank as she grasped Katie's arm and stared up at
the grimy redbrick block of apartments, then down at the piece
of paper in her hand. 'It's the right address, all right.'

'It'll be fine — you wait and see,' Katie said soothingly. 'If
you ask me, I'd be more suspicious if it wasn't a bit seedy and
down at heel. If a private detective lived in too grand a style I'd
be asking myself where he got all his money from. At least this
is one who's not making a fortune out of his clients.'

'Let's hope you're right.' Maeve wasn't entirely convinced as
her finger reached for the bell and gave one long hard buzz.

The elevator that took them to Eugene D. Kelly's office-cum-
apartment smelt vaguely of urine that had been unsuccessfully
disguised with disinfectant and Maeve tried not to breathe too
deeply as they creaked their way up to the fifth floor. He had
been Katie's choice really — plumped for on the assumption
that having a good Irish name he could surely be trusted.

Their first sight of him, however, did little to dispel any
misgivings as he ushered them into the crowded front room.
He was a short, bald-headed man in his late fifties, with an
enormous beer-gut and horn-rimmed glasses that perched
precariously on a broad, stubby nose. 'Be seated, please, ladies.
And excuse the mess, will you. I've been outa town for a week
or so and things have sort of piled up lately.'

He was not exaggerating, for the room looked as though it
had not seen a good clean in weeks. Papers lay scattered on
every available surface and a collection of unwashed cups sat
stacked in a precarious pile on a side table. The smell of stale
cigarette ash hung in the air and a crumpled empty pack of
Lucky Strikes had been squashed on top of an overflowing
ashtray less than two feet from Maeve's nose. With great
difficulty, she fought the impulse to empty it into a nearby
wastebin.

She followed Katie's example and perched herself on a hard-backed chair in front of the paper-strewn desk and waited as the owner of this ungodly mess squeezed his great bulk into position for business by wedging himself between the chrome arms of a revolving chair.

'Now what can I do for you both?' A cigarette remained stuck to his lower lips as he spoke, and the vibration sent a shower of ash down the front of his shirt.

'Well, it's for me, actually,' Maeve said quickly, tearing her eyes from the ash-flecked cotton. 'I won't beat about the bush, Mr Kelly — my son's being blackmailed and I want you to find the culprit, so I can do something about it.'

Eugene Kelly's sparse brows rose behind the glasses as he reached for his pen. 'Now then, lady, I trust you have evidence of this. It's quite a serious allegation — you're aware of that?'

'Yes, I am,' Maeve said sharply. 'But I wouldn't be here unless I was pretty sure of my facts, would I?'

Eugene Kelly sighed and sat back in his chair, to Maeve's relief removing the cigarette from his mouth and flicking it in the general direction of the ashtray. He had a sharp cookie here, but he was ready for her. In thirty years of the business he had met them all. The secret was to let them have their head; that kept them happy, made them believe they were in charge. 'Well then, would you care to tell me about it . . . ?'

The two women glanced at one another, then Maeve cleared her throat. It wasn't going to be easy voicing her fears about Kieran, but she hadn't come all this way to back out now . . .

It took all of half an hour before she completely satisfied the man behind the desk that she had given every detail possible to aid his investigation. For the first ten minutes she had tried beating about the bush in every way possible, rather than reveal the fact that her son was a homosexual. But, surprisingly, the inscrutable Mr Kelly seemed to take the revelation rather well. He had a distinctly world-weary air that told them that nothing surprised him any more, he had heard it all before. But it would still be no easy task, he informed them as he showed them to the door. 'It's getting the proof, you see, ladies. That's the hard bit. It's getting the proof that will stand up in court.'

Maeve put him right on that point immediately. 'Quite frankly, Mr Kelly, I don't give a damn about satisfying the courts. All I want you to do is to find out for certain the name of this – this bloodsucker who had got his tentacles into my son and I'll take it from there.'

He looked at her over the top of his spectacles and shrugged. It never did much good to argue with a client. They paid the bills, after all, and he was already over two months behind on his car payments. 'You're the boss, lady.'

As they shook hands at the door, Katie, who had remained silent throughout the half-hour they had been inside, gave him an almost sympathetic smile and said, 'By the way, Mr Kelly, which part of Ireland would your family be from?'

'Ireland?' He gave a puzzled frown, then laughed out loud. 'They're from just outside Lodz, ma'm. That's in Poland, not Donegal!'

Katie looked startled. 'But – your name – Kelly . . . ?'

'It's short for Kulinski, ain't it?' He smiled, a great beaming smile, as he reached for the door handle. 'G'day, ladies. It's been real nice meeting you and there's no need to worry, just leave that to yours truly Eugene D. Kelly. As soon as I've got anything to report, I'll be in touch.'

The door closed behind them and Katie turned to Maeve with a sheepish smile. 'A Polish Paddy . . . life's full of surprises, isn't it?'

When Kitty heard what they had done after supper that evening her face paled visibly. 'But, Aunt Katie, that's terrible! Kieran will never forgive Mom when he finds out.'

'But he's not going to find out, is he?' Katie protested. 'Not unless you tell him. You won't, will you, Kitty?'

Kitty shook her head impatiently. 'Of course not. But I still think it's a stupid idea. A really dangerous idea, in fact. This could end Kieran's relationship with Mom for good, if he ever discovers what she's done. It's pretty precarious as it is, and has been ever since Chuck mouthed off far more than he should have after Frank's funeral.'

'Your mother had to do something, Kitty. She's at her wits'

337

end with worry, believe me. Why do you think she's away to bed with a migraine tonight?'

Kitty pulled her legs further up beneath her on the settee and stared down at the cup of coffee in her hands. 'To be honest, I find it a hard thing to come to terms with myself, but I won't sit in judgement on Kieran, Aunt Katie — not ever. Even if Mom's wrong and there's no question of blackmail and he's simply given all his inheritance to this Louie of his own free will, then it'll make no difference to me. He's still my brother and I love him dearly.'

Katie's fingers froze on the knitting needles as she stared across at her niece. 'Louie you say? And who may Louie be?'

Kitty caught her breath. 'Oh, nobody — just a guy Kieran knows.'

But her aunt was not to be put off. 'You think he's the one — the one who Kieran's been giving all this money to?'

Kitty shrugged helplessly, inwardly cursing her loose tongue. 'I've really no idea, Aunt Katie. Honestly I don't. If you must know I've hardly given Kieran a thought recently. I've had enough problems of my own to think about.'

'You mean about the baby?'

Kitty's face paled. 'Who told you that?'

Katie shook her head wearily. 'Nobody told me, Kitty, dear. Nobody had to. You can't keep a thing like that a secret for long — certainly not from close relatives like your mother and me. We're women too, remember. We've had children of our own, God help us.'

Kitty took a deep breath and let it out slowly. They knew — they both knew. She had a sudden unaccountable impulse to burst into tears, but succeeded in stifling it, as her aunt quietly voiced the question she knew to be uppermost in Maeve's mind, 'You'll not be making plans to get married, I take it?'

'No, I'll not be making plans.'

They sat in silence for a time, then Katie said quietly, 'I don't know the circumstances that brought you to your decision, Kitty, and I'd never ask. It's got nothing to do with anyone but you and the father of your coming child, but I admire you, I really do. You've got guts, just like your own father. He had guts too . . . Oh, yes, Danny had guts all right.'

Kitty's eyes lit up. 'What do you remember of him, Aunt Katie? Tell me. Mom never would talk about him and I suppose I never really liked to bring up the subject of Ireland much. Somehow it seemed to be some sort of a slight on Frank. But what was he like? What was he really like?'

'Well, he was no saint, I can assure you of that! But he was a bonnie fighter. Oh, yes, he was that and more. One of the bravest men ever to walk God's earth. I can remember as if it were yesterday when he marched off with Connolly and Pearse and the rest that Easter morning. His dearest pal, Con O'Malley, died in the Rising, but it didn't stop Danny continuing to fight for the cause. In fact, he was with John-Joe, Con's younger brother, when they were both killed fighting for the cause — somewhere in the Galtee Mountains, I believe it was.'

'I wish I were a man,' Kitty said softly. 'I wish I'd been born a boy. Instead of finding myself in this position, I'd be over there now carrying on where my father and the others of his generation left off. What's happened to them all, Aunt Katie? Where are the young bloods of the IRA today? What's happened to this generation?'

Katie shrugged and shook her head, putting down her knitting momentarily in her lap. 'Hitler happened, Kitty, that's what. I suppose that's the long and the short of it. I can't really speak for the Dubliners any more, but I'll tell you this, very few folk who lived through those awful April nights in Belfast, three years ago, have been able to just sit back and do nothing about it. When you're attacked you want to fight back, it's as simple as that. Those nights of the air raids and the days that followed will be with me till I meet my Maker. After the bombing it seemed like the whole population was on the move. Almost everyone around us knew someone who had perished. You can't imagine the horror of going out in the morning with all those fires still burning and great holes in the earth where houses had once stood. No wonder folk wanted to get away from it all. I can still see them now pouring in their thousands up the Shankill towards the hills above the city . . .'

'But where could they go?'

'They had nowhere to go, and that was the tragedy of it. The ditchers they called them, for that's where most of them ended up – sleeping in ditches, old barns, you name it – anywhere that was out of the target area of the bombs.'

'But what about you and the children? You didn't stay, did you?' Kitty knew her aunt lived within a stone's throw of the shipyards and the danger must have been appalling.

'Oh, we stayed all right. We could have gone to Dublin – thousands did. But somehow I couldn't leave Eamon. The poor man was out on his feet, as all the fire-fighters were, during that awful time and it seemed to me to be a terrible thing to do – to run out on him when he needed us most. I couldn't have done it, Kitty . . . Everyone was doing their bit and somehow you felt less helpless as a woman knowing you were supporting your man.' She paused, remembering the agonies over the decision to remain in Belfast with the children. 'It may seem strange to you over here that so many young Irishmen have joined up to fight for the British, but you'd only have to live through one of those raids to understand why. And most people lived through a lot more than that. Anyway, 'tis a terrible thing that's going on in Europe just now. That Hitler's the divil incarnate, if you ask me. And it's not just us that's suffered – they say the Nazis are doing terrible things to the Jews in the East.'

The mention of the Jews sent a shiver through Kitty. It had been weeks since she last saw Lee. And God only knew what she would do if she ever ran into him again, for there was little chance of disguising the fact now that she was carrying a child. 'It's ironic, isn't it?' she said quietly. 'Some actually say that the Irish are the real lost tribe of Israel, and certainly their history this century has been almost as troubled as that of the real Jews.'

'Can't say as I've ever met one face to face – a Jew, I mean,' Katie said. 'There aren't that many in Dublin, or Belfast, come to that. But then I believe New York makes up for it. In fact, your mother told me that Frank's first wife left him for one. He couldn't show his face in the golf club for weeks.'

Kitty sat up in the settee at the indirect reference to Lee's father. 'But that's terrible!' Surely anti-Semitism wasn't that rife here too – not amongst thinking, educated people? The thought appalled her.

'Well, I don't know so much about that. Not everyone seems to think it so terrible. The world's full of jealousy, m'dear. Folk look at their neighbours and think – why should they have all those thing if I can't? I think any minority who gets on too well in the world is resented – and the Jews most of all because their speciality seems to be making money. But from what I hear that Jewish fella should've been praised, not vilified, for he actually did Frank a favour in stealing his wife. He was much better off with your mother – not that I go along with divorce, of course . . .'

Kitty managed a weak smile. 'I guess it was still quite a shocking thing in those days. And it probably still is in Ireland. It must be hard for you with a brother in the priesthood. You must be terrified of straying from the straight and narrow.'

Katie drew another length of wool off the ball and smiled. 'Oh you wouldn't say that if you met Dermot. He's the gentlest of souls – too good for his own good, I've always told him. Chalk and cheese, he and Danny were – chalk and cheese.'

'He's a pacifist like Kieran, then?'

Katie looked puzzled, as if the thought had never really occurred to her. 'Do you know, I suppose he is. Come to think of it, that's probably one of the reasons why he joined the Church. It's very hard to be a Catholic male in Ireland, Kitty, round where we lived at least, and not join the cause. And somehow I could never imagine Dermot carrying a gun. He was always much more at home with his poetry and books. He could never bear to see suffering, in man or beast. Aye, he's the gentlest of souls and no mistake. I hope you'll get the chance to meet him yourself someday.'

'So do I. To be honest, he hardly even existed in my mind until you arrived. Mom certainly never talks about him.'

'Now that's a funny thing and no mistake, for the two of them were as thick as thieves before Maeve left Ireland.'

There was a momentary silence as Katie pondered on Maeve's reluctance to discuss Dermot with her daughter, then Kitty cut in, 'Did you ever think of joining it yourself – the cause, I mean?'

'Oh, I've done my bit one way or another. Lent support behind the scenes mainly. Most of the lads still feel it's not a

341

woman's place, where the action is. I thought it would be harder to keep in touch when we moved to Belfast and so it was at first, for all the orders still came from Dublin, but just before the start of the war they formed a Northern Command in Belfast.'

'There are others still active in Ireland, then? They haven't all died out?'

Katie laughed. 'Good God, no! In fact, one of the boys was killed in a shoot-out with the RUC just before I came over here.'

Kitty felt the blood course faster in her veins. 'What about your husband? Is he an active member?'

Katie sighed. 'It takes Eamon all his time being an active member of the human race! Oh, I'm not running down the poor soul, God love him, he's a good man at heart, so he is. And comes from one of the best IRA families into the bargain. But no, Kitty, he's never bothered taking the pledge himself.'

'Don't you mind?'

'Mind? Aye, I suppose I did in the beginning, but somehow as life went on it became less and less important Eamon opting out, for there were the children to think of – a new generation to carry the cross. You know, the older I get, the more convinced I become that it's the women that are the real backbone of the fight in Ireland. They are the ones that pass on the word, that light the flame in their young hearts, that tell them there is no greater love than that for one's country, no greater sacrifice than to give their lives in Ireland's cause.' Her eyes misted over and her fingers slowed to a stop as she paused, then softly repeated the lines that were now engraved on her own children's hearts and minds:

> 'Let me carry your Cross for Ireland, Lord!
> For Ireland weak with tears,
> For the aged man of the clouded brow,
> And the child of tender years;
> For the empty homes of her golden plains;
> For the hopes of her future, too!
> Let me carry your Cross for Ireland, Lord,
> For the cause of Roisin Dubh.'

Kitty stared down into the cold pool of coffee in the bottom of her cup. 'That's beautiful, Aunt Katie, really beautiful. I envy your children, having you for a mother. You must be very proud of them all.'

Katie smiled ruefully. 'You'll find out one day, Kitty my dear, that your children never quite turn out as you expect. But, yes, on the whole my three are not doing too badly. The girls were always a lot more politically aware than Kevin, though.'

'He's not a member, then?' Somehow the thought that a young man – a son of her Aunt Katie – was not a member of the IRA shocked Kitty to the core.

'Oh, he is now – and will probably be a much more enthusiastic one once he gets himself a steady girlfriend. It always takes some explaining why you're not playing an active role if your girlfriend's own brothers and other relatives are.'

'You really feel you can't be a true Irishman if you're not prepared to fight for the cause, don't you, Aunt Katie?'

'Aye, Kitty, I do.'

Kitty was thoughtful for a moment. 'Then how would you rate my mother's family in Dublin? I reckon they would take great exception to being regarded as not true Irishmen.'

Katie's face coloured. The last thing she wanted to do was to run down Maeve's relations. 'Well, I'd not deny anyone the right to call themself Irish who really wanted to, but let's put it this way, Kitty – you wouldn't call a cat a kipper just because it was born in a fish box, would you now?'

'But the Ballantines have been in Ireland for at least a hundred years.'

'They have that.'

'And it still doesn't make them true Irish?'

Katie looked down at her knitting. 'That's not for me to answer, Kitty my dear.'

'But it is for me.'

'Maeve!' Katie turned in astonishment. 'I thought you were lying down.'

Maeve closed the door behind her and made for the gin bottle on the drinks table. She poured herself a generous one and topped it up with tonic, as she said quietly, 'Where were we now? Are the Ballantines true Irishmen or not?'

343

Embarrassment flamed in Katie's cheeks. 'I'd never imply your family weren't true patriots, Maeve – never!'

Maeve took a sip of the drink and gave a wry smile. 'Patriotism? What is patriotism, Katie aroon?'

Katie glanced across at Kitty. 'Patriotism is the noblest of all human emotions. That's what I've brought up my own children to believe and, no doubt, that's what you'd have Kitty here believe too.'

Maeve looked from her elder daughter back to her sister-in-law, then said softly, 'No, Katie dear, not quite. Patriotism to me seems to be the most ludicrous of all emotions. What is it but merely the conviction that your country is superior to all others simply because you were born in it? To me there's nothing inherently noble about an accident of birth.'

Kitty's lips tightened. 'You mean there was nothing noble about my father giving his life for his country?'

Maeve looked across at her daughter. She could see the anger burning in Kitty's eyes, but could not understand it any more than she could understand what had motivated Danny. 'I won't defile Danny's name, Kitty – not to you, not to anybody, but there's one thing I couldn't understand then and still don't have an answer for to this day . . . Patriots talk a lot about dying for their country, but never about killing for it. It was the latter I couldn't stomach then and still can't. Danny died for his country, but he also killed for it. And the tragedy is that it was other Irishmen he killed. Convince me there is anything noble in that!'

Kitty shook her head and looked across at her aunt, but Katie was already gathering up her knitting. She, more than anyone, knew that Maeve had just asked the unanswerable question; the question that had plagued generation after generation on that green isle far across the sea. Was it right for Irishmen to kill other Irishmen in Ireland's cause? Does the end always justify the means used to attain it? Can the price ever be too high? She knew her own answer to that question. And she also knew from the set expression on her sister-in-law's face that her answer would never be the same as Maeve's. She attempted a conciliatory smile as she patted her niece's shoulder. 'Goodnight, Kitty, my dear. Goodnight, Maeve. God bless you both and sleep well.'

'Goodnight, Aunt Katie.'

'Goodnight, Katie aroon.'

Chapter 37

Kieran jumped up from the table in the window of Casey's Ice Cream Parlour on East 48th Street, and gaped through the plate glass. His eyes fixed on the shining automobile in the centre of the stream of traffic that ground to a halt directly opposite. The chrome on the pale blue Chevy gleamed in the autumn sunlight. But so it should for it was barely a month old. 'Jeee–zuz!'

Louie sat behind the wheel, cursing the slowness of the truck in front that had meant him missing the lights. But it was the young man in the seat next to him who held Kieran's attention. He had blond, curling hair and the blunt, even features of a comic-strip hero. His right arm was slung carelessly around the back of the driver's seat, his fingers playing absent-mindedly with the dark, curling hair at the nape of Louie's neck, as they waited impatiently for the lights to change. Kieran's eyes narrowed. It was him, all right. This was the third time now he had seen them together. Just let the little bastard deny this when he got back tonight!

Sick at heart, Kieran stumbled out into the sunlight as the signal changed to green and the row of traffic roared off down the street in a cloud of exhaust fumes. He stared after them, a deep emptiness filling his being. What could he do? What could anyone do when someone they loved started seeing somebody else?

Mechanically, he turned and started to walk in the direction of the subway, then stopped abruptly. A fat guy in a grey dog-tooth check suit and soft felt hat was standing in a doorway a few yards away. He held a newspaper up in front of his face as Kieran's eyes met his, but it was too late.

'What the hell are you playing at, Mac?' Kieran ripped the *New York Times* down the middle with one jerk of his hand, as he spat the words into the stranger's fat face. 'You've been tailing me for days. What the hell's your game?'

Eugene Kelly's eyes bulged behind the horn-rimmed glasses. 'Easy buddy, easy . . . I ain't never set eyes on you before!'

Kieran's hand grabbed his throat. 'Don't lie to me, mister! Just don't try it. Who the hell are you, anyway? Some private dick? . . . Who's paying you?'

His grasp tightened, causing Kelly's mouth to fall open as he gasped for breath. 'Lay off, will ya? Just lay off!'

'Not until you tell me! Who's paying you to put a tail on me?'

Kieran's irate voice had caused a small circle of interested onlookers to gather, including a Sergeant Hiram Gross. He knew Kelly of old: they had grown up on the same block on Green Street and Grand, over on the Lower East Side. A sinewy hand reached out and made a grab for the back of Kieran's collar. 'What's your game, buster?'

Kieran staggered backwards, attempting to brush the restraining fist from his neck. 'This guy's following me, officer! I want to know why.'

The sergeant raised a pair of shaggy brows and looked across at Kelly. 'Is that right, mister? You tailing this guy?'

Eugene Kelly backed out of the doorway, straightening his collar. His plump face had gone a delicate shade of puce. 'You know better than that, sarge.'

Hiram Gross nodded slowly. 'Yeah, you could say that I do . . .' He turned to Kieran. 'You got evidence against this citizen?'

'It's like I told you,' Kieran protested. 'The guy's following me. I want to know why.'

'He says he ain't – and you're causing an obstruction. You gonna move on, mister, or am I gonna charge you with causing a public nuisance?'

Kieran glared across at Kelly, who was now backing even further down the street, towards a yellow cab parked by the kerb. 'Looks like I don't have much choice, does it?'

'Too right, you don't.'

Saving his parting glare for the sergeant, he turned to the gaping crowd and called, 'The show's over, folks!', before limping quickly in the opposite direction to that he had intended to head. It had turned into one helluva day, and it was still only one o'clock!

It was exactly twelve hours later before Louie returned to their apartment. There had been no message from him – nothing to say that he would not be home for dinner. The tuna and mushroom pizza that Kieran had specially prepared and cooked for seven o'clock, the time they usually ate, lay cold and soggy on the worktop by the cooker. The bottle of white wine stood unopened beside it. He had not appeared at the office that afternoon, but that was nothing new. Often he was kept busy downtown delivering scripts or acting as their general dogs-body, going between Hayes and Hamilton and their associates. Kieran had taken his first drink at just after six – the time Louie usually got in. The second was half an hour later, as a slight nervousness began to creep into his mind. By midnight almost a whole bottle of Jack Daniels had been drunk and the freezer-box was long since bereft of ice cubes. The spirit ran pungent and neat over his throat, clouding all but the cold realisation that Louie, his beloved Louie, was not back.

The image of that blond, curly head, and those even, comic-strip features, filled his mind, and how the young man's fingers had played with the thick curling hair at the nape of Louie's neck. No casual acquaintance did that – and the knowledge seared his soul.

'Bastard! The little bastard!' Kieran lunged over to the window, yanking up the blind to peer into the darkness below. Half the lights were out in the block opposite. Half the damned neighbourhood were asleep. He should be too – with Louie, in the bed next door!

A bitter bile rose in his throat and he stumbled through to the sink in the kitchen and retched over the enamel basin, but nothing came up. He had had no appetite for food tonight; only the whiskey churned sickeningly in his stomach.

Why wasn't blondie in the army, for God's sake? How come the little bastard had escaped the draft? He looked all of twenty. Maybe he was like Louie, suffered from some indefinable illness, when the whole goddam world knew it was because 'the Family' had been at work on his behalf. 'What's the sense in coming from Sicily if you don't make use of it?' he had said often enough. A fistful of dollars, or a bullet, in the right direction worked wonders.

He had wondered often enough in the past why a guy like Louie stuck it at Hayes and Hamilton. With his Mafia connections he could be already well up in the Family ladder of success. But maybe he was already involved. They didn't exactly go around publicising their presence, did they? And certainly he had never been short of a buck, even before Kieran had halved his hand-out from Frank with him. In fact, Louie had a gun somewhere, he was sure of it.

Kieran got up, steadying himself on the kitchen table, and wove his way through to the bedroom. It was odd how his left leg never seemed to bother him half as much when he had had a drink.

Louie's tallboy stood on the far wall and he made for it, almost collapsing on the polished walnut top, as he pulled at the first drawer. There was nothing in there but a pile of underwear and he slammed it shut and yanked out the next, then the next, until a small yelp of triumph escaped his lips. There it was – he knew he wasn't wrong! It lay beneath a pile of winter sweaters – a small, pocket-sized automatic pistol.

Gently he removed it from its resting place and placed it in the palm of his hand, his fingertips caressing the cold grey metal. Then he tried it for size, pointing it at the life-size pin-up of Clark Gable that grinned down from the wall on Louie's side of the bed.

As he swayed unsteadily on his feet, the sleek dark hair of the film star became a head of blond, curling locks and the smooth, man-of-the-world features were transformed into the blunt, clean-cut ones of the young man in the car. He was laughing at him – the bastard was laughing at him!

'Shut your face! Shut your goddam face, will ya!' But still the grin leered back at him, taunting him, mocking him, asking him where he thought Louie was this minute. 'Lay off me, just lay off, buster!' The grin remained. He staggered back a few feet. He would wipe it off that smart-assed face! One shot rang out, then two, blowing two holes clean through the leering features of his tormentor.

'What the hell's going on?'

'Louie! My darling Louie! Come in!' Kieran waved the pistol in greeting at the figure in the doorway of the bedroom. 'Come in, you're just in time for the funeral!'

'What funeral?' Fear flickered momentarily in the brown eyes of the young man at the door and he took a defensive step backwards. 'What the hell are you playing at, Kieran? Put that gun away, for Chrissake – you're drunk!'

'You bet your sweet ass I'm drunk!' Kieran declared, waving the gun aloft once more. 'I'm drunk on power, Louie baby! I've finished him off! I've finished lover boy off, for good and all!'

Louie shot a glance at the blasted face of the film star. 'What are you talking about? What the hell's Clark Gable ever done to you? It's just a picture, man – it's just a goddam photo!'

'Wrong, my friend – my little, two-timing friend! It's lover boy I've just blown into next week – that little blond-haired asshole you thought fit to ride around town with in the Chevy this morning. The Chevy you bought with *my* dough!'

'You're crazy!' Louie's eyes remained fixed firmly on the pistol that Kieran now had aimed threateningly in his direction.

'You're right, Luigi, my little wop friend – you're so right. I'm crazy all right. I must've been outa my goddam head to ever trust a little double-dealing bastard like you! But no more, my friend – no more!'

'Put the gun down, for Chrissake, man. Put the goddam gun down!'

'Not until you've told me first where you've been tonight.'

'I ain't bin nowhere – seeing some of my folks over on Grand Street, that's all.' A bead of perspiration had formed on Louie's upper lip and he wiped it away, as his eyes remained transfixed on the gun.

'You're a liar – a goddam liar, Louie, old pal. Try again!' He made a move towards the now profusely sweating figure of the younger man, the pistol pointed directly at the pit of his stomach.

'Give me a break, Kieran, for God's sake. Put that thing away and I'll tell you. I'll tell you everything you want to know!'

But, for the first time in their relationship, Kieran had the upper hand and would not easily give it up. 'Too right you will, baby. You'll tell me everything – and you'll tell me NOW! Who is that little shit – and what were you doing with him tonight? I want the facts, lover boy – all of them! Every stinking little detail!'

A tremor ran through Louie's body and his eyes shot a look towards the bedroom door, as if to check that it had shut behind him. It had.

'Forget it, Louie. You ain't going anywhere. Not tonight – not ever – without my say-so! Get down on your knees!'

'What?'

'You heard. Get down on your goddam knees!'

White-faced, Louie sank to his knees on the grey wool carpet. 'You're sick man, do you know that, you're sick!'

'Not half as sick as you'll be if you don't tell me what's been going on between you and that yellow-haired fairy behind my back.'

'What d'ya want to know, for Chrissake? How many times we did it tonight, is that it? Will that satisfy your sick little mind?'

Kieran's blood froze. So it *was* true! The stupid little creep had just admitted it. The blood began to pulsate once more through his body as he stared down into the face before him. He had given his all to this man. And it wasn't just the money. He had given something much more than that – he had given away his pride in order to satisfy the ungrateful little bastard's craving for dough. But even that wasn't good enough.

His mouth twisted into the semblance of a smile as he moved a step nearer the kneeling figure. Nothing he could ever give would be enough for him. No amount of money – nothing. Not a goddam thing would ever satisfy him. He would simply use him up, then move on to the next poor sucker stupid enough to be taken in by him. 'You're nothing but a shit, do you know that, Louie? You're nothing but a greasy little Italian shit!'

'Then what does that make you? Tell me that, Kieran, baby? A pale-faced jerk, a cripple who can only get his kicks by buying the bodies of little shits like me! You've got no guts, man – never have done! I could take that gun off you right now, if I'd a mind to!'

A nerve twitched spasmodically at the side of Kieran's jaw as he hissed, through gritted teeth, 'Then do it, asshole. Just do it!'

Their eyes locked and the leer on Louie's face grew broader before he made a sudden lurch forwards, his right hand flailing the air in the direction of the pistol. The movement made Kieran stumble backwards, to land against the edge of the bed, as Louie toppled on top of him.

The crack of the gunshot was instantaneous and shook him rigid, as the man he had loved more than life itself clutched at his stomach and fell sideways on to the bedside rug.

'You got me, goddam it, Kieran . . . you got me . . .' Louie gasped the words out, a look of shocked surprise on his perspiring features as he stared up, wide-eyed, at his friend.

'No! Jesus – no!' Kieran threw the gun across the floor and slumped on to the carpet beside him. 'God help me, Louie, I didn't mean it! You came at me . . . It just went off!'

But Louie's eyes were already closing as the blood began to ooze out from between the fingers that clutched at his groin.

'No, man – look at me . . . Listen to me, Louie. I love you! I wouldn't kill you – not you, man . . . I love you!'

Tears welled in his eyes as he attempted to focus them on Louie's face, but somehow the features remained a blur. It was Jack Daniels who had pulled the trigger – not him. He loved every hair on the head that now lay motionless on the rug beside him. 'Speak to me, Louie, for God's sake, speak to me . . .'

But Louie was already dead.

It was almost three hours later, at half past three in the morning, when Kieran put the gun to his own head.

Chapter 38

'Noooo!' The word turned into a scream as Maeve backed away from the police officer in the hallway.

'There must be some mistake.' Even as she uttered the words, Kitty knew there was no mistake. Kieran was dead all right, and the other body found beside him, although the officer hadn't said it, she knew to be Louie.

'I only wish it was a mistake, miss. But they've both been unofficially identified by the landlord – a Polish guy who lives in the apartment below.'

By this time both Maudie and Katie had appeared in the hall, and even Sarah had arrived from the kitchen, alerted by her mistress's scream. 'It's Kieran,' Maeve informed them, in a peculiarly high-pitched voice. 'He's dead. Kieran's dead! He's been murdered!'

A frown crossed the officer's face. 'Now I never said that, ma'm. We've no evidence to that effect at the moment. It could be a double suicide, for all we know.'

'A suicide!' Maeve almost screamed the words back at him. 'What reason would my son have to commit suicide? The very idea!'

'Well, if you'll pardon me, ma'm, that's one of the things we'll have to find out. He wasn't in any kind of trouble, was he? Money problems, maybe?'

Maeve and Katie exchanged looks. Then Maeve shook her head vehemently. 'Of course not. I know that for a fact.'

'That's not true, Mom.' It was Kitty who intervened. 'I'm sorry, officer, but my mother's a bit overwrought. I believe my brother may have had money problems. We have reason to believe he may've been being blackmailed.'

The policeman's brows shot up. 'Really, miss? Would you care to expand on that?'

'No, she wouldn't!' Maeve cut in angrily. 'If there's any

information to be given out on my son, then I'll be the one to do it.'

A loud wail went up from behind them, as Sarah threw her white apron over her face and gave vent to her grief. She had been with the family for almost twenty-five years and Kieran had been as dear to her as any son of her own.

'Shut up, Sarah!' Maeve said sharply, but Sarah would not be silenced.

'It's Mista Chuck who done it!' she sobbed into the damp white linen of her apron. 'If he hadn't done gone said all those things after Mista Frank's funeral, Mista Kieran never would've left — never would've gone done such a thing!'

'Hold your wicked tongue, woman!' Maeve's face was quite white as she glared at her. 'We don't know what Kieran has or hasn't done — do we, officer?'

'No, ma'm, we surely don't.'

'You'll want someone to officially identify the body,' Kitty said quietly, and he nodded.

'There ain't a man in the family who could save one of you ladies the upset?'

He looked from one to the other, but Kitty shook her head, as she put a consoling arm around her mother. 'No, there isn't, I'm afraid. But, don't worry, I'll do it . . . Maudie, will you take Mom into the lounge and get her a drink.'

Ashen-faced, Maudie obeyed, and led her mother back down the hallway, as Kitty stayed behind with her Aunt Katie to get the details about the identification from the officer. 'I think a strong coffee would be more in order, Sarah,' Maudie said quietly to the still sobbing housekeeper. 'Bring it into the drawing-room, will you?'

Sarah shuffled off in the direction of the kitchen, as Maudie and Maeve disappeared into the drawing-room. Maudie beckoned to her mother to sit down, but Maeve chose to disregard her, choosing instead to pace up and down in front of the window, her arms clasped defensively around her shivering body.

'Are you cold? Shall I turn the heating up?'

'No. I'm not cold.'

Maudie sat on the edge of the settee, her hands clasped in

her lap. She should be crying – they all should, but only Sarah had found the tears impossible to control. She felt vaguely ashamed for the lack of emotion she felt, but was glad she had parted on good terms with her brother the last time they met.

'How could he do this to me?' Maeve's voice broke the silence. 'How could he?' She stared across at her youngest child, but Maudie could only shake her head. 'Didn't I give him everything? Didn't I give him the best that money could buy?'

'Yes, Momma, you did.'

'And this is how he repays me!' Maeve stared out into the darkening sky over Manhattan. 'It only leaves Chuckie. Do you realise that, Maudie? There's only Chuck left now, with your father and Kieran gone. And, God knows, there's no guarantee that *he'll* ever get back to us safely!' At that, she began to cry – dry, grating sobs that seemed to come from the very depths of her being.

Sarah brought the coffee in and placed the four cups and saucers on the table in front of the settee. 'Ah'm sorry fo' what Ah said out there, ma'm. Ah guess Ah jest got carried away. Mista Kieran he was mah favourite of all dem kids.'

Maeve looked up at her and took a shuddering breath, but could not bring herself to speak. How could Sarah say that? How could she have preferred Kieran, who had brought her and Frank so much unhappiness, to any of the others?

'That'll be all, Sarah, thank you,' Maudie said quietly. 'I'm sure Mom appreciates the apology.'

As Sarah made her way back to the kitchen, Kitty and her Aunt Katie joined them in the drawing-room. There was a peculiarly embarrassed silence as they all looked at one another. Then Katie said quietly, ''Tis an awful thing and him so young and all.'

She walked over to the baby grand piano in the corner and picked up a framed photo of Kieran as a schoolboy. The freckled face grinned back at her from out of the silver frame. 'He was so like his father, so he was,' she said softly. 'Sure an' it's enough to break your very heart.'

At that the phone began to ring, causing them all to turn and stare at the abrupt intrusion into their private grief. 'I'll get it,' Kitty said, hurrying across to the small side table and grabbing the handpiece. 'Hello . . . yes . . .' She listened in silence for several seconds as the caller on the other end stated his business, then, frozen-faced, she held it out to her mother. 'I reckon you'd better answer it, Mom,' she said quietly. 'It's a Mr Kelly, private investigator, to speak to you . . .'

They buried Kieran in the Fullerton family vault next to Frank. Despite medical evidence which seemed to suggest that Kieran in fact died after Louie, and the two deaths were at his hand, Frank's family connections succeeded in playing this down so that his stepson could be buried in consecrated ground with the rest of his American relations.

But Kitty felt a pervading sense of injustice as they lowered the coffin into the stone-lined tomb. He should not be lying here in this foreign land, next to people with whom he had no blood tie. He should be lying next to his own folk beneath the green Dublin turf. Even the words that were said by the priest over his grave seemed to bear no relevance to her brother. 'A good son and brother, who, had he lived, would have made a fine husband and father, but is now gathered into the family of God . . .'

Maeve had asked Father Donnelly for a poem to be read as they scattered the earth of the New World over her son. If it was to be America who would receive his body in death, then she wanted the farewell to be said in Irish words. She left the choice to him, feeling that, as a first-generation Irish-American, he would know what would be appropriate.

For the first time all afternoon, the wind seemed to drop and a thin beam of pale yellow sun pierced the bank of dark cloud above them, as she stooped to scoop up a handful of rich brown earth and let it trickle gently through her fingers on to the gleaming casket bearing the name of Kieran Ballantine Donovan. And the priest's voice carried clear and dramatically to the ears of all those gathered at the graveside, as in the words of Patrick Pearse, with a tragic irony, he declaimed:

'I have squandered the splendid years.
Lord, if I had the years I would squander them over again,
Aye, fling them from me!

For this I have heard in my heart,
that a man shall scatter, not hoard,
Shall do the deed of today, nor take thought
of tomorrow's teen,
Shall not bargain or huxter with God;
or was it a jest of Christ's
And is this my sin before man, to have taken Him at His
word?
O wise men, riddle me this: what if the dream
come true?
What if the dream come true? and if millions
unborn shall dwell
In the house that I shaped in my heart,
the noble house of my thoughts . . .'

Kitty's lips twisted bitterly as she took her turn in scattering the soil on the remains of her brother, now encased in the gleaming mahogany and brass coffin. Would he have felt he had squandered his years? Certainly he would have vehemently denied that there was anything remotely splendid about them. But there could have been . . .

Her eyes fell on her mother's drawn face and she felt a great sense of injustice well within her. They had never asked to be brought to this place, to leave Ireland. The decision had been thrust upon them, and now they had to live with the consequences. And what a consequence for Kieran . . . No, there had been nothing splendid about his short life, and there was nothing splendid about his death. It had been abrupt and squalid, and no amount of covering up could ever disguise that fact.

Declining one of the black limousines that lined the road at the bottom of the path, she chose instead to make her own way back from the funeral.

A fresh autmn breeze was eddying up from the East River a few miles away and it ruffled her hair beneath the black chiffon scarf. Above all she wanted to be alone, to make her own peace with the troubled soul who now lay at rest in the cold stone beneath her feet.

Some bushes of late-flowering roses bordered the plot and she stooped to pick two – one red for love, one white for honour. As she bent to smell their perfume, the wind carried some of the petals into the air. They were already dying, like the year itself, and soon they would be part of the never-ending wheel of things, the cycle of life, that had taken her father as a young man, and had now taken her brother from her.

She laid the two flowers side by side on top of the stone slab engraved with the Fullerton family crest and stood back to look at them. A few petals from the red rose lay scattered on the stone, and on its neighbouring bloom, like drops of blood. She gazed down at them, and tears stung her eyes as the words of one of Danny's fallen comrades came to her lips and she whispered them into the eddying breeze:

> 'I see his blood upon the rose
> And in the stars the glory of his eyes,
> His body gleams amid eternal snows,
> His tears fall from the skies . . .'

There had been too many tears in Kieran's young life, and very few of them of his own making. They had never under-stood him – none of them, her mother least of all. Maeve had wanted an all-American hero, like Chuck had turned out to be, for her firstborn, but Kieran could never be that. Kieran could only be Kieran. But for all his imperfections, and he had had no more than most, he was her brother and she had loved him. She still loved him. She would always love him. And if she gave birth to a son, in the coming spring, she would name him after him – Daniel Kieran Donovan. It had a good ring to it . . .

She turned slowly from the grave, her head down against the buffeting wind, her sight blurred with tears, so that she did not see the young man who was watching silently from behind a tombstone several yards away.

He waited until she had reached the cemetery gates before he made a move, then his tall figure strode quickly down the gravel path, to catch up with her as her hand reached the wrought-iron handle.

'Lee!' Her heart flew to her mouth as she gazed up into the dark eyes that looked down into hers. It had been months since she had set eyes on him, but the time between melted into nothing. He had not changed, not in the slightest. Not on the surface at least. 'What are you doing here?'

'I read about it in the paper,' he said quietly. 'It gave the funeral arrangements. I had to come, Kitty. I had to say how sorry I am. I know what he meant to you.'

She flushed and drew her coat closer around her body, thankful she had chosen a swagger style for the ceremony. It completely hid the growing bulk of her waistline. 'There was really no need. A card would have sufficed.'

He had on a heavy Harris tweed coat, and carried a pair of rabbit-backed leather gloves, which he shoved into his coat pockets as he took her arm and proceeded through the gates. 'I know that,' he said quietly. 'But I felt bad about the way things ended between us.'

Despite herself, her heart leapt. 'Really?'

'It was childish of me, storming out on you like that. I want you to know that.'

She glanced up at him, waiting for him to continue, to suggest perhaps they should give it another try, say how much he had missed her. She would play it coy at first, of course. It was only natural. After all, he had been the one who had walked out. 'I appreciate that, Lee. I really do.'

To her consternation he merely nodded and remained silent for several minutes so that she was forced to ask how his work was going. He was doing research into the production of plutonium, she knew that much, for she had seen a paper once, lying on top of his desk in his apartment. So keen had she been in learning everything possible about his life, she had even memorised the words. It had been to do with extracting plutonium by chemical means. The words had been typed in red ink on blue paper and said something about no isotopic separation being required. Then in his own hand beneath he had written that it might well give it a great advantage over U-235 as the material for the bomb that they were racing the Germans and Japanese to produce.

The information had burned its way into her brain, although the words meant nothing in themselves; they might as well have been in Greek. But he had been furious, nevertheless,

that she had even strayed into the vicinity of his private papers
. . . She still shuddered when she recalled the look in his eyes,
as he had gathered them up and shoved them back into his
briefcase.

'My work's going fine,' he said at last, bringing her back to
the present day. 'In fact, that's one of the reasons I wanted to
come personally – to say goodbye.'

'Goodbye?' The word caught in her throat.

He nodded. 'I've had the chance to go to New Mexico – to
Los Alamos – to work with Bob Oppenheimer and his team.
He's been my hero for years, Kitty. And he's a Jewish New
Yorker into the bargain. Our families knew each other way
back, but I never dreamt I'd get the opportunity to actually
work with him – to be part of his team. It's the chance in a
lifetime.' His eyes positively gleamed as he spoke. 'We're almost
there, Kitty. We've almost cracked it. We'll beat those Nazi and
Nip bastards to it and bring this war to an end before this rotten
world is much older, you wait and see.'

'And then, Lee? What then? What when you've made your
bomb? What happens then?'

His eyes took on a faraway, dreamy look that she had seen
all too often in the past. 'Then, Kitty, I go to Palestine – to build
a new world from the ashes of the old.'

Her heart froze. 'Does it ever occur to you, Lee,' she asked
softly, 'that you might just be partly responsible for reducing
this rotten old world to ashes by what you're doing? What's
the difference in what you're working on, in terms of potential
human misery, to what the Nazis are doing in Europe?'

He stared down at her, his hands gripping her upper arms,
so that his fingers dug into the soft flesh beneath the fine wool
of her coat. 'Jesus, Kitty! Can't we ever meet these days
without you branding me as a war criminal? I'm working my
butt off trying to end this goddam war – not prolong it! Every
day brings us a step nearer – and every day can save a thousand
lives or more . . . Maybe even your own brother's!'

The mixture of real anger and hurt in his eyes and voice
shook her and she drew in her breath sharply. 'I'm sorry, Lee.
I spoke out of turn.' She shook her head, inwardly cursing her

wayward tongue that always seemed to fail her at the crucial moment.

'No, Kitty, you're not sorry. Not really. You meant every word you said.' His eyes were puzzled now, puzzled and sad, as they looked down into hers. 'It's me who's the sorry one. I'm sorry for you. Sorry for the fact you can't see that I'm working for the good of humanity, not for its destruction. We're not in the same world, you and I – never have been I suppose, only I was too smitten to see it in the beginning.'

'And now, Lee, what about now?' Her voice was barely audible.

'Now my eyes are open. I see it could never have worked between us. We had something good going for us in the beginning – something real in our hearts, but our heads intervened. It was as well we found it out before it was too late.'

Too late? *Too late for what?* she wanted to shout. Was it too late to regret the new life that was growing within her? Too late to regret the fact that before he had invented his precious bomb she might already be the mother of his child?

Instead, she simply shrugged herself free from his grasp and held out her black-gloved hand. 'It was kind of you, coming to say good-bye,' she said softly. 'I appreciate it and wish you luck, both in New Mexico and after the war in Palestine.'

He did not shake her hand, but lifted it to his lips. 'Good-bye, Kitty Donovan,' he said softly. 'Good-bye, my wild Irish rose . . . May you find what it is you're looking for in this crazy world of ours. In many ways, I'm sorry it wasn't me . . .'

She watched until his tall figure had disappeared into the distance, then whispered, 'Good-bye, my love . . .' into the silence.

Her words were carried on the breeze that had already robbed the roses on the grave of their petals. And, as she turned up the collar of her coat against the chill autumn air, a soft rain began to fall. She turned her face to the heavens and the cold rain mingled with the hot tears that ran in scalding streams down the pale skin of her cheeks.

Chapter 39

Autumn dragged into winter and life in the Fullertons' Park Avenue apartment took on a sameness that brought a peculiar comfort to the women within. Katie left for home a few days after Kieran's funeral. She had already overstayed her proposed visit by almost six weeks and the family back in Belfast were getting restless, although the five-thousand-dollar cheque Maeve had wired to be deposited in the Muldoons' own bank account went some way to compensate. There had been a problem in getting such a large sum out of the country in wartime, but Frank's old associates on Wall Street had not made a living out of international finance for nothing. As with the hushing up of the true details of Kieran's death, there were ways and means round everything, providing you had the influence, which in New York meant money, and the Fullertons had plenty of that.

Katie's return to Ireland threw Maeve into a deep depression for days. She even toyed with the idea of going back with her to the old country for a time. It came to nothing, though. A whole generation – a whole lifetime in Kieran's case – had passed since she had last set foot on Irish soil, and one did not make such a decision without a great deal of thought. And the more she thought about it, the more nervous she became.

It would be wonderful to see Charlie and Amy, of course, and even the thought of seeing her mother again she no longer viewed with trepidation. Now the sole resident of the family home on Jubilee Avenue, Emily Ballantine had mellowed in her old age, devoting herself to good works on the many war relief committees that commanded her attention.

No, it was not her mother that caused her to think again; it was the middle-aged man who was now back at work amongst his parishioners in Dublin. It was the thought of seeing Dermot again that made the nerves clutch at her stomach and her mouth dry so much that she could not say his name out loud, even after all this time, without difficulty.

He had been back in her thoughts so much more since Katie's visit that she often wondered how she could possibly have become so overwrought over such a trifle as Frank's affair with Estelle last summer. It was odd how her life, both emotional and physical, seemed to have divided itself into two complete parts – the Irish part and the American. For each she had a completely different set of feelings; in fact, she had even had two completely different sets of children.

She often thought of Kieran these days and wondered if things might have been different; if she might have understood him better; if she could have prevented his life ending in that awful way. But she comforted herself with the thought that this was almost certainly not the case, for she had had as little influence over his father's life. There was nothing she could have said or done that would have made the slightest bit of difference to Danny's life, and it was surely the same with his son.

But Kitty – now Kitty was a different kettle of fish altogether . . . She had thought at one time that she might even have gone back to Belfast with Katie, for the idea of having her child born in Ireland was very appealing, but the commitments of everyday life in New York had weighed too heavily on her. The gallery demanded too much of her energy and there was no one she trusted enough to hand over the reins to for such a length of time. Instead, she had thrown herself into organising her autumn and winter exhibitions of up-and-coming artists, and spent what little spare time she had helping out at the local Democratic headquarters.

Franklin Roosevelt's continuation as President had come as no surprise to anyone and, although the Fullertons had been traditionally Republican since the days of the Civil War, when Frank's great-grandfather had been one of Abe Lincoln's strongest supporters, Kitty felt that a world war was no time to change political horses in mid-stream. Having been a staunch supporter of Dr New Deal in the depressed years of the thirties, she believed that, in his guise of Dr Win-the-War, the President was at least worthy of their continuing confidence as long as hostilities lasted.

Maeve had only once seen her dejected throughout the long autumn of political campaigning and that had been on returning home one very wet Saturday night, on the twenty-first of October. President Roosevelt himself had been touring the city all day and Kitty had been only one of his indefatigable band of supporters who had worked all out behind the scenes to make his four-hour New York tour an outstanding success.

As far as her mother was concerned, her daughter's moody silence was simply a by-product of driving herself too far in her condition and Kitty was only too happy to leave it at that. In fact, nothing on earth would have made her admit the true reason – a reason that became apparent within minutes of assuming her position as Jill-of-all-trades in the back office of the main campaign headquarters.

At first she did not notice the tall young woman, with the red bandanna wrapped around her hair, who was hammering at a typewriter in the back office, and it was only when she broke for coffee at eleven o'clock that they came face to face.

She must have stared much harder than she intended for her gaze brought a look of amused curiosity to the other's face. 'Do I know you? If you don't mind me saying so, you're looking at me as if I should.'

Kitty blushed. She would swear her life on it – this was the young woman in Yehudi's with Lee that day. 'I'm sorry. You – you look like an acquaintance of a mutual friend, that's all.'

The elegantly curved eyebrows rose beneath the red bandanna. 'Really? Who might that be?'

'Lee . . . Lee Finkelstein.' She had difficulty in saying his name.

'Oh, really? You know my husband?'

The colour drained from Kitty's face. 'Your – your husband?'

'We were married last week.'

For one awful moment Kitty thought she was going to faint. She backed against the desk and fought to control her breathing. 'Oh . . .' was as much of a response as she could manage.

'Yes,' the girl responded. 'I haven't really got used to it yet – calling myself Rose Finkelstein, I mean. It doesn't even feel like

I've got a husband – what with Lee being away in New Mexico now and all . . . I'm sorry, I don't think I caught your name?'

'I didn't throw it.' Why did she always resort to a stupid quip every time she found herself emotionally exposed? 'It's Kathleen,' she said, forcing a smile to her lips as she extended her hand. 'Kathleen Donovan – Kitty to my friends.'

'I'm Rose Finkelstein, like I said.' Her grip was warm and firm. 'I hope we can be friends. To be honest, I'd like a feminine shoulder to cry on now that I'm a grass widow, so to speak – especially now that I've given up work for my degree.'

'Really?'

'Yes. I was studying for my doctorate in bacteriology, but now I'm a married woman it's become a bit difficult. I'm hoping to move down to New Mexico to be nearer Lee by Christmas, so there really wasn't much sense in carrying on with it.'

She walked over to the drinks machine and brought back two paper cups full of the steaming brown liquid that passed for wartime coffee and handed one to Kitty. 'Did you know my husband well?'

Kitty took a sip of the coffee and swallowed hard. How did you answer a question like that? How did you tell a man's new wife that you were still madly in love with her husband and that you were at this moment carrying his child inside you? 'Fairly well. You could say we had a mutual passion for lost causes.'

'Lost causes?'

'A free Ireland and a free Jewish state.'

'But a free Jewish state's not a lost cause!' her companion protested. 'Have you never read the British Prime Minister Arthur Balfour's Declaration – his promise to all Jews?'

Kitty shrugged, unwilling to get into a discussion of English political rhetoric. 'The British promise the earth when it suits them – they don't always deliver.'

'Well then, it's up to the likes of us to make them, isn't it? And we will! When this war is over, Lee and I will be on the first boat out of New York heading for the Near East. We want to start a family right away. Lee wants his first child to be born in Palestine.'

Kitty had to bite back the retort, 'Then he's going to be disappointed, isn't he?' Lee Finkelstein's first child would be born right here in New York in approximately five months' time and there was no way he could do anything about it. 'Well, I hope you make it – to Palestine, I mean. Will you be sorry to leave New York?'

'No.' The answer was quite emphatic as Rose Finkelstein hoisted herself on to the edge of the desk and took a sip of her coffee. 'That sounds really unpatriotic and all that, doesn't it? I don't mean it to. It's just that I've never really felt that this was my home. And I know that Lee feels the same way. You know, fifty years ago or more, Pobedonostsev – he was the head of the Russian Synod – said of the Russian Jews that one-third would die, one-third would leave the country, and the last third would be completely assimilated. We reckon he got it exactly right – except for one thing. He should have added that part of that one third that left the country would finally reach the Promised Land. At least their descendants would . . .'

She took another sip of the coffee and paused, as if musing on the pronouncement. 'The Zionist cause owes so much to our forefathers, the Russian Jews. I remember my grandfather saying that the book that had the biggest influence on him – in fact, it turned him into a Zionist – was by a Russian contemporary of his, Peretz Smolenskin. *The Eternal People*, it's called. It's one of Lee's favourite's, too. Have you read it?'

Kitty shook her head. Her early nationalist readings were by such men as Tone, Emmet and Charles Stewart Parnell, not by Russians with unpronounceable names.

'Well, I still have it at home. He left it to me in his will and I still can't open it without being affected emotionally by it. I guess it's partly the knowledge that this passionate desire for a Jewish homeland has persisted for all these centuries – right through the long years of the Diaspora – and is still as deeply felt today by our generation. Did you know that it was a group of Russian students who were amongst the first of the Ashkenazim to settle in Palestine and lay the foundations of what is now almost a reality – a Jewish state?'

Kitty shook her head as the flood of words washed over her. Already she felt the gulf between her and Lee to be much wider than she had ever imagined. But in Rose he had surely found as great a zealot for a partner as he could ever wish. 'The Ashkenazim?' she ventured, acutely aware of her ignorance.

'The Yiddish-speaking European Jews,' Rose explained, her dark eyes gleaming, as she warmed to her favourite subject. 'The Russian students called themselves "Bilu" and started an agricultural settlement in Palestine towards the end of the last century, which was the forerunner for many more – Mikvei Israel, Rishon Le-Zion, to name but two that both my own relatives and Lee's emigrated to join.' Sensing a quickening of interest in her listener, Rose added, by way of explanation, 'Lee's paternal forefathers were Russian Jews, didn't he tell you? In fact, both our families were from Russia and if I feel anything other than Jewish, it would be Russian.'

'Despite the pogroms?'

Rose shrugged. 'In some areas they were bad, it's true, but they weren't the reason my family left. My grandfather simply believed the New World could offer his children a better chance in life than the old. It was probably true, for my father became a member of that most revered of all professions to Jewish mothers – a doctor. But who knows what he might have become if they had stayed.' She sipped her coffee and smiled ruefully. 'His family came from Yanovka, the same small Ukrainian village as Trotsky. In fact, the Bronsteins were close family friends. Just think of it, I could be the daughter of a revolutionary!'

Kitty managed a tight smile. 'You may well end up being one yourself if you insist on emigrating to Palestine to found a new separate Jewish state!'

Rose's face was suddenly serious. 'We've thought of that – both of us – and are prepared for it. We want our son to grow up in the land of his forefathers. Who knows he might even become the first President of the Promised Land – of Israel!' She glanced across at Kitty, her eyes gleaming. 'Gedaliah Finkelstein – President of Israel – it has a good ring to it!'

'You have a name for him already?'

Rose nodded. 'Gedaliah is an ancient Hebrew name. It means "God is Great". Lee reckons we couldn't have a more appropriate name for our son, when we finally get there. He will have fulfilled all our dreams.'

Kitty looked down into her coffee cup, unable to bear the look of sheer happiness and excitement in the other's eyes. Gedaliah Finkelstein ... It was a far cry from Daniel Kieran Donovan, but if he was ever born, he would be her own son's half-brother. 'It's a fine name,' she said at last. 'I'm sure he'll be a fine boy.'

Rose beamed. 'It's lovely having someone like you to talk to at last. Especially someone who knows Lee ... It's almost as if you were part of the family.'

She placed her coffee cup on the desk top and started to dig into her handbag, eventually extracting what looked like a white, postcard-sized piece of card. 'Look,' she said, handing it across, 'I only got it back this morning. Doesn't he look handsome? I feel so proud to be his wife — especially knowing he's doing all that valuable work for our country down there in New Mexico, while we're sitting here passing the time of day yacking and drinking coffee!'

Kitty took the white card and opened it out. It was their wedding photograph. Lee smiled back at her, as tall and handsome as she had ever seen him. A wave of anguish swept over her — a great swelling surge of regret for what might have been, if only, if only ...

Then, as she bent forward to hand it back, for the very first time she felt his child move within her.

'Are you all right, Kitty? You've gone quite pale.'

She nodded mutely, not trusting herself to speak. Then turned and rushed from the room.

She was met in the passage by a group of drenched, but jubilant party workers, one of whom grabbed her arm in delight. 'Come on, Kitty. You're just in time. The President's cavalcade is just arriving. You'll be able to meet him. He's promised to shake hands with all his party workers. Is this not just the proudest and happiest day of your life?'

She looked at him blankly, as her eyes filled with tears ... The stupid, stupid man!

Chapter 40

Christmas Day 1944 was like no other ever experienced in the Fullerton household. It was the first that did not include a man at the dinner table. As Maeve stood, glass in hand, to make the toast, before the carving of the turkey, the fact was not lost on her. Despite her resolve not to dwell on the misfortunes of the past year, tears filled her eyes as she raised the crystal wine flute and looked around almost all that remained of her family.

Maudie and Kitty moved uncomfortably beneath her gaze. Both would have given anything to be in a place of their own right now, but the two bereavements of the past six months had made any moves in that direction almost unthinkable, although Kitty was determined to find an apartment of her own once the baby was born, and Maudie was nursing a secret reason of her own for moving on. It could wait a few minutes longer, though, she decided as she raised her own glass together with that of her mother.

'It hasn't been an easy year for any of us,' Maeve began. 'First there was Frank, and then Kieran . . .' she paused once more, to look at the largest of all the family portraits in the room – a foot-high, tinted one of Chuck that sat in pride of place on the mantelpiece, 'and who knows where your other darling brother is right now. Who knows whether he has already, as we sit down to this meal, joined his father and brother in a far better place than this. Let us drink a toast to Chuck, girls. Let us pray that the Good Lord spares him to return to us in the coming year, and that 1945 sees an end not only to our own troubles, but also an end to this awful war itself.'

'To Chuck!' Maudie and Kitty rose as one and leaned across the table to touch glasses with their mother, then with each other.

All three sat down together and waited in silence for the bird to be carved. Then once more the past impinged bitterly on the present. It had always been Frank's job, but he was no longer here. There was no man here to do the needful. They had not noticed it at Thanksgiving, for Maeve had deliberately instructed that no special meal be laid on, claiming there was nothing this year to give thanks about. Kitty had felt the statement to be almost blasphemous, but could understand it and had made no comment.

'Sarah, would you care to carve?' The question was purely rhetorical as Maeve turned to the buxom, white-clad figure of the housekeeper standing by the door.

Sarah looked from one to the other, but Kitty's and Maudie's eyes were both fixed firmly on the table. 'Ah sho' will, ma'm.'

She came forward and, wiping the palms of her hands on her apron, she set to to carve the gleaming golden carcass of the bird. Within minutes all three plates were filled with ample helpings of brown and white meat from the turkey, chestnut stuffing, roast potatoes, green peas, carrots and Sarah's special gravy, accompanied by two dollops of cranberry and bread sauce.

'Thank you, Sarah, that will be all.'

All three pairs of eyes watched as the servant left the room, closing the door quietly behind her. Then, to the astonishment of the other two, Kitty said, 'We should have asked her to join us. She feels this just as much as we do, you know. She's suffering too. It doesn't seem right somehow that she should have to eat all alone in the kitchen today.'

Maudie looked at her mother, as Maeve's lips tightened. 'She wouldn't want that, Kitty,' Maeve said stiffly. 'Good servants know their place – and Sarah is one of the best.'

'But she's more than a servant, Mom,' Kitty protested. 'You know that. She's practically one of the family.'

Maeve's head bent over her plate and in the embarrassed silence that followed Maudie intervened. 'Don't upset Mom, Kitty. You know it ain't a fitting thing to suggest. She's only doing what's right . . .'

'There's no need to defend me, Maudie,' Maeve cut in brusquely.

But there was, and she knew it better than anyone. In her innocent request to let the servant eat with them, Kitty had unconsciously touched a raw nerve in her mother's psyche. A picture of Mary-Agnes appeared. Mary-Agnes taunting her for not having the guts to take Willie-John into her own home. Two very different incidents, a whole generation apart, but the feeling she was left with was the same; a feeling of having less than the courage of her convictions to do what she knew in her heart to be right.

They ate in silence for several minutes until, unable to bear it any longer, she looked up and said brightly to Maudie, 'How have things been at the Academy since the show closed, honey? It must be pretty galling going back to being just a student again.'

Maudie's fork paused over a slice of carrot. She hadn't intended to raise the subject until their after-dinner drinks, when her mother was sure to be in a more mellow frame of mind after one or two gins. But there was no backing out now. 'Actually, Mom, it mightn't be for much longer – me being a student, I mean.'

Maeve's eyebrows rose. 'Really?'

Maudie shifted uneasily in her seat as she toyed with her food. 'Yes. There's talk of . . .' She paused – that was wrong; it had gone much further than that and there was no use lying. 'I've been asked to travel out to Hollywood to test for a movie.'

'What?' Maeve and Kitty chorused the word in unison.

'Yes. Estelle's fixed it up for me. It's with her ex-husband's company, Phoenix Films.'

Maeve's lips tightened, as she took a sip of her wine. 'And what is this movie to be about, may I ask?'

Maudie shrugged. 'I'm not quite sure, but Estelle says she can guarantee I get a decent-length talking role and a good mention on the credits – providing my film tests go okay.'

'Estelle seems to be guaranteeing an awful lot, if you ask me . . . But then you never do these days! Does she also guarantee you a place to live in Tinsel Town?'

Maudie nodded, her eyes shining. 'With her in Beverly Hills – to begin with anyway!'

'Good God!' Maeve looked from her younger daughter across to Kitty. 'What do you think of it?'

'Don't bring me into it.'

'Oh come on, Kitty!' Maudie protested. 'Surely you agree with me that it's the chance of a lifetime? I'd be really stupid to turn it down. You're doing what you want in life, after all, by having this baby, so why should you deny me the same chance?'

Kitty stared at her. Was that really what she believed? Was that what they all believed — that she deliberately chose to get pregnant, to have this child, and not marry its father? She looked across at her mother. Maeve's eyes were concentrated firmly on her food but the set expression of her mouth said it all.

'Well, Kitty, isn't it true? And isn't it right that I should get the chance to live my life the way I want to, too?'

'Yes, Maudie, of course you should.' Kitty attempted a reassuring smile as her eyes found those of her sister, but their mother's ominous silence hung like a suffocating blanket over their spirits.

Both her daughters looked across at her and thought their own private thoughts as they finished their meal. Just who was she, this woman who had given birth to them? What were her real thoughts as she sat there with that inscrutable look on her face? Had she never been a young woman? Had she never wanted something, or someone, so much that it hurt — physically hurt? Or was she always like this — a beautiful woman grown old before her time; a woman whose passion, if she ever possessed any, was long since spent?

Had they but asked, Maeve could not have told them. She could admit to no one, least of all her own daughters, the flame that had once burned in her heart for a man who had loved his God far more than he could ever love her . . . A man whose face still haunted her dreams in the wee small hours of the night, when the city slumbered beneath her, and her eyes fixed on a single star in the blue-black heavens and she wondered if he might also be looking at it; if it might be shining from an Irish heaven — a heaven that she would probably never see again . . .

But Dermot had been out of her life for almost thirty years now, and, in his own way, he was as dead to her as Frank and Kieran now were. There was only her daughters left, for she could not bring herself to believe that Chuck would ever come back. And now one of the girls was leaving. She looked across at Kitty and forced a smile to her lips. 'We'll be alone soon, you and I, Kitty, my dear. Two husbandless females rattling around this old apartment on our own.'

'Not quite, Mom. There'll be someone else to keep us company soon, don't forget.'

Maeve raised her eyebrows over the top of her wine glass. 'Really? Who?'

'Your first grandchild, of course.'

Maudie left for Hollywood six weeks later, on 3 February 1945, the day that Roosevelt's and Churchill's planes touched down on the snowswept Saki airfield in the Crimea.

But Stalin's meeting with his two Western counterparts was the furthest thing from both Maudie's and Kitty's minds as they made their way up to Estelle's Fifth Avenue apartment. Maudie was to travel with Estelle to Los Angeles that afternoon, but she was far too nervous and excited to consider going over there alone.

She knew there was no question of her mother accompanying her, for Maeve had at last found the courage to talk to her younger daughter about Frank's first marriage and Maudie agreed it was best if the two women did not meet. Not that Maudie believed that Estelle would have anything against meeting her ex-husband's second wife, she was far too much a woman of the world to be as small-minded as that, but she knew that her mother wouldn't care for the experience, so it was to Kitty that she turned.

As they stepped out of the elevator, to be ushered into the Finlay apartment by a white-coated Negro butler, Kitty experienced an uncomfortable feeling of *déjà vu*. Lee's old home was the last place she would have chosen to visit, and the memory of their first meeting on this very doorstep came rushing back to her as they proceeded through the elegant hall and on into the lounge.

'Miz Estelle will be right with you,' Washington, the butler, pronounced with a perfectly executed bow before taking his leave, and the two young women thanked him with a perfunctory nod.

'Oh, Kitty, just look at this, will you?' Maudie could barely disguise her admiration as she made a beeline for the huge oil portrait of Estelle that dominated the room. 'Isn't she perfectly beautiful?'

Kitty murmured her agreement, as her own eyes fell on a much smaller, but much more emotive picture. The wedding photograph of Lee and Rose stood on the mantelpiece, by the side of a beautiful display of red roses. It was the same one that Rose had shown her, but bigger. She picked it up and looked closely at the face with the dark eyes that had so often looked into her own, with that same familiar, slightly crooked smile. Had he thought of her at all that day? She was not even sure what day it had been, but perhaps it was just as well. The date would brand itself on her memory, so that every year, in early October, she would look at the calendar and remember, and the pain would begin again . . .

'A good-looking couple, huh?'

The unfamiliar female voice made her look round to find Estelle standing in the doorway and she replaced the picture quickly, only to have its owner walk across and pick it up herself and gaze down at it fondly.

'That's my son Lee and his new bride. Do you know I learned only this morning that I'm to be a grandmother? Isn't that something?'

'Why, Estelle, that's wonderful!' It was Maudie who rushed forward and clasped her idol by the hand. 'That's simply wonderful! . . . Isn't that wonderful news, Kitty?'

Kitty's lips moved into an automatic smile as she nodded her agreement. 'Yes . . . Yes it certainly is.'

'Estelle; I'd like you to meet my sister Kathleen . . . Kitty this is Estelle Finlay.'

'Hello, Maudie's sister!' Estelle replaced the picture on the mantelpiece and held out a soft, beringed hand in Kitty's direction. 'Are you in the business, too?'

'The business? . . . Oh, no, I'm no actress. I'm in the art world, actually. I run a small gallery — the Bellini Gallery on . . .'

374

'An art gallery – how wonderful!' Estelle interrupted, removing her hand. She smelt faintly of Ashes of Roses and seemed to move on a pink cloud all of her own as she wafted across to the drinks table. 'I once considered studying art myself, you know. In fact, my folks sent me across to Europe to do the Grand Tour – you know Florence, Rome, the works . . .' She poured three large glasses of champagne and handed two out with consummate grace, before lifting her own.

'What happened to stop you continuing?' Kitty asked, taking her first sip of the sparkling liquid.

Estelle's long lashes fluttered momentarily, then smiling sweetly she said, 'A little – well, I really should say a *big* matter of marriage – to Maudie's father . . . It really is the smallest world. If things had worked out between Frank and me, you two girls – well, Maudie at least – could be my own daughter . . .'

She turned to Maudie, with an incredulous shake of her platinum head. 'Just think . . . Lee there could be your brother, honey. But I can't say I'm sorry things turned out the way they did, for Art gave me the finest son a mother could ever wish for . . . Isn't that right, sweetness?'

'If you say so, sweetheart.'

The strongly masculine voice made both Kitty and Maudie swing round in amazement, to see a tall, darkly handsome man, in late middle age, standing in the doorway.

'Girls, I'd like you to meet my former husband, Art Finlay . . . Art, you've already met Frank's girl, Maudie . . . This other young lady is her stepsister Kathleen.'

Kitty caught her breath as the dark eyes bore down on her, and Art Finlay crossed the room in half a dozen long, easy strides. He was Lee in twenty-five years' time, a more mature, in many ways better-looking Lee, but Lee all the same . . . 'It's Kitty – please call me Kitty,' she found herself saying, as his hand took hers. 'Kitty Donovan.'

'Well, Kitty Donovan, the pleasure is entirely mine.'

She had read of electric shocks when skin met skin, but had never experienced it until shaking hands with him. He held on to her hand for far too long, and out of sheer embarrassment she was forced to extract her fingers as unobtrusively as possible, from beneath his amused gaze.

'Art's travelling out to Los Angeles with us today,' Estelle informed her, as she poured another drink and handed it across to him. But Art Finlay merely shook his head.

'Oh, didn't I tell you, honey? Something's cropped up here in New York that I've got to see to. But I'll be following you out there as soon as possible.'

Estelle raised her eyes to the ceiling and gave an exasperated sigh. 'Oh, Art, really! What can possibly have turned up so suddenly that can be so important?'

Kitty glanced across at him and for a fleeting second their eyes met. And immediately, incredibly, she knew . . .

Chapter 41

Kitty embraced her sister at the door of the Finlays' apartment. 'Take care, Maudie . . . Remember we love you and California's not so very far as all that . . . Mom and I are only ever a phone call away.'

'I know . . . Tell Mom I'll write as soon as we get there. And tell her to give my address to Chuck when she next writes. He'll be so happy for me.'

'We all are. You're going to be a big star. Just wait and see!' They hugged again, before Maudie pulled away to return to Estelle who was waiting in the lounge.

'Did you come in your own car?'

It was Art Finlay who spoke. He had accompanied them to the door and, to her embarrassment, Kitty found herself colouring. 'No, actually, we came by cab.'

'Good. In that case I'll take you back.'

'There's really no need . . .'

'I know that.'

There was something in his voice and about the way he looked down at her that made argument impossible. She could only nod her head as he turned to her sister who was now half-way back down the hall. 'Maudie, would you tell Estelle to let Washington know I'll not be back for lunch, and not to bother keeping anything for me, I'll make my own arrangements today.'

'Sure thing!'

The apartment door closed behind them and he took Kitty by the arm as they headed for the elevator. 'You know you're joining me, don't you?'

Incredibly she found herself nodding. She had never doubted it, although not a single word to that effect had passed between them.

His fingers squeezed hers in silent response, as they stepped inside the plushly carpeted elevator. 'I know a great little place over on . . .'

'Don't tell me – the corner of Broadway and 23rd!'

He let go her arm and stared at her, dumbfounded. 'How in tarnation did you know I was going to suggest Yehudi's?'

She gave a secretive smile. 'I'm Irish, remember, Mr Finlay . . . Some of us are known to have the gift of second sight!'

She expected him to have a classy car waiting, but the silver-grey Rolls Royce, with the black leather upholstery, momentarily took her breath away as she took her place in the passenger seat next to him. 'I bet you're not used to this – having to drive yourself around. I bet you have a chauffeur out in Hollywood,' she chided, as they swung out into the late morning traffic.

'True. Is that your second sight at work again?' He threw her a grin as they moved smoothly along Fifth Avenue towards its junction with Broadway.

He was easier to talk to than Lee. Less spiky. Perhaps it was a self-assurance that came with age – or with power and success – for he had both of those in abundance. Whatever it was, she liked it and felt instantly at ease with this undeniably attractive man.

When she felt he was concentrating on the traffic, she stole a few furtive glances at him and liked what she saw. Like his son, he had an angular, sensitive face, the only perceptible difference being that Art's jaw-line was the more positive of the two – verging on stubborn, almost – and his dark hair was flecked with silver at the temples. And when he laughed, which seemed to be often, the skin at the corners of his eyes creased into beautifully etched laughter lines that fanned upwards towards the straight dark brows just like his son's. It was hard to believe she was young enough to be his daughter. In no way could she ever think of him as a father figure!

The restaurant was almost empty when they arrived, for it was not yet midday, and, thankfully, they sat at a completely different table to any at which she had ever sat with Lee. But it was an uncanny feeling to be sitting there next to a man who was so like him – who was in fact his own father. She had no appetite for food, but he succeeded in persuading her to accept a dish of shakshouka, which she dutifully picked at as he tucked into a steak and talked of the film he was about to make with Estelle and her sister on the West Coast.

He was at great pains to point out that Maudie would be in good hands – he would see to that. 'Not all those stories you read about the going-ons over there are true, you know, honey. Some of them – yes; even I have to admit that. But not all.'

His eyes smiled into hers across the table as her mind flew back to all those stories she had read over the years of his succession of affairs with the movie capital's most glamorous names. It was not difficult to see what they had seen in him. The only puzzle in her mind was what on earth he could see in her. And, as the meal wore on, the more convinced she became that it wasn't just her imagination. All the time he spoke, she was aware of an underlying current beneath the small-talk, a chemistry between them that they were both acutely aware of, until finally he laid down his knife and fork and looked her straight in the eyes, and said softly, 'I'm about to be a grandfather, you know, Kitty. I'm one helluva lot older than you. Does it matter?'

Her heart pounded mercilessly in her breast as she shook her head. It was crazy, grotesque even, she herself was eight months pregnant – with his grandchild! But something – some wild, impossible impulse told her it didn't matter. Nothing mattered but the fact that they were here together and enjoying every minute – every single second – of each other's company.

Towards the end of the meal, he took her hand in his. 'I want you to know, Kitty Donovan, I don't make a habit of dating unmarried young ladies who also happen to be heavily pregnant.'

His voice was soft, his eyes very gentle, but she blushed fiercely nevertheless. 'You noticed.'

'It's pretty difficult not to.'

She glanced down at her bump and gave a rueful grin. 'I guess you're right.'

'I don't see a ring, so I take it you don't intend to marry the guy.'

She nodded. 'I don't intend to marry him.'

'Good.'

His reaction sent her pulse racing and she was not entirely certain why. All she *was* certain of was that there was no way she could even hint to Art that his son was the father of her coming child – not when Lee himself wasn't even aware of the fact.

'He's married, huh?'

'He's married.' A shiver ran through her. The truth still hurt.

His fingers were stroking hers – long, tanned, capable fingers. She stared down at them, as his voice caressed her hearing. 'I want you to know, Kitty, that whatever happens between us, I'll never ask . . . If you ever want to tell me, then that's fine. But it has to be your decision and yours alone.'

She nodded mutely, not knowing quite how to respond. What was he saying to her? He spoke as if he had taken it for granted that they would see each other again – see a lot of each other. She found herself deliberately avoiding his eyes, for to meet them was to set her heart pounding beneath the green plaid of her dress. But she was aware of his eyes on her. She had been only too aware of that ever since he had entered the room back in Estelle's apartment.

When the meal was over, she expected them to head back towards Park Avenue, where her mother was waiting. But instead he headed off in a completely different direction. 'Ever been to Brooklyn Botanic Gardens?'

'Not recently.'

'Well I can only think of one place nicer than their hot-houses on a freezing day like this. But I'm not going to suggest it . . . being the gentleman that I am!' He grinned across at her, forcing her to respond in kind. She knew exactly what he meant.

After he had parked the car, she stayed at a deliberate arm's length as they entered the verdant humidity of the Gardens, but when, after a few minutes, he held out his hand and she took it, it seemed the most natural thing in the world.

As they walked, hand in hand, through the luxuriant greenery of the hot-houses, he told her of his childhood here in New York, and of his parents' disappointment when, scorning his studies, he went West to get into the infant motion picture industry. As he spoke, her mind went back to that old sepia picture of a beautiful young woman, Leah Finkelstein, *née* Rosenbaum – his mother, and Lee's beloved grandmother.

'It hit Momma hardest,' he said quietly. 'I guess either a rabbi or a doctor would have sufficed nicely – but a film producer!' He threw up his hands in mock horror.

They landed on her shoulders, and he tilted her chin up to look at him, with his right index finger. 'You know, when I first set eyes on you this morning I had the most strange feeling – almost like I'd known you all my life. And now I think I understand why. You remind me of her, you know that? You remind me of her.'

With any other man she would have been mortally offended to be told that she reminded him of his mother. But not with him, not with Art. She had seen her – she had seen Leah, and she could think of no greater compliment. 'Thank you,' she said softly. 'Thank you, Art.'

When the time came for him to let her off at her door, he parked the car and walked with her to the main entrance of the apartment block. As they stood side by side on the snow-covered sidewalk, he took both her hands in his and raised them to his lips. His breath rose in a white icy cloud as he kissed each finger in turn. 'You've got to help me, Kitty Donovan,' he said quietly. 'I'll be no good for you, girl. I'm much too old and much too busy to ever make you really happy . . . You've got to help me fight this thing . . . Will you do that? Will you help me?'

She looked up at him; his eyes were very brown as they looked down into hers. What if she didn't want to? What if she didn't mind the fact that he was old enough to be her father? What if she might actually fall in love with him? 'I – I'll help you, Art,' she whispered.

His fingertips touched her cheek. 'I'm leaving for Hollywood tomorrow,' he said quietly, 'and I'll be tied up there for at least three months. What do you say we put whatever we might have going for us on ice . . .'

'Ice melts with the springtime, Art,' she answered softly. 'Come back then and I just might be around . . .'

* * *

381

Maeve could not understand the reason for her daughter's high spirits as Kitty came sailing into her bedroom, to waken her from her afternoon nap. 'Why, Kitty, I was just getting really worried about you!'

'No you weren't — you were fast asleep!' She sat down on the edge of the bed and took her mother's hand.

Maeve pulled herself up on the pillows and looked at her curiously. 'What in heaven's name's got into you? You look like the cat that got the cream!'

'Nothing,' Kitty shrugged. 'I saw Maudie safely to the Finlays' apartment, that's all.'

Maeve's smile faded. 'And met the lovely Estelle, I've no doubt.'

'And her ex-husband.'

Interest flickered in her mother's eyes. 'Really? Which one?'

'Art Finkel . . . Finlay.' She corrected herself in time.

'Well, well, well . . . You met the great producer himself, did you? And what did you think of him?'

Kitty's pulse raced faster. 'He — he seems a nice enough guy.'

Maeve gave a dry laugh. 'A nice enough guy! Well, that's a new one on me. I must say I've never heard of him referred to quite like that before!'

'And why not, may I ask?' It was hard to keep the indignation from her voice.

Maeve sighed. 'Honey, Art Finlay is one of Hollywood's biggest producers. But, more than that, he's also head of one of its most successful film studios. You don't become a movie mogul of that dimension by being a "nice enough guy"!'

Kitty got up from the bed and walked to the window. A light snow was falling from a white blanket of a sky, and icicles, like long glass fingers, were pointing downwards from the window-frame to the sill beneath. What did she care about his past? The past was dead, long dead, like the old year. The present was all that mattered. The present and the future. 'Ice melts in the springtime,' she said softly, and her heart leapt at the prospect.

As February moved its slow, frozen way into March, Kitty found her enthusiasm for spring and what it might bring begin

382

to wane. It was difficult to remain enthusiastic about anything when your own body became a shapeless bulk that you could only move around with difficulty.

She kept on with the gallery as long as possible, but finally at the end of the month she admitted defeat and put a printed sign in the window saying, 'Closed. Open in Spring.'

Art never got in touch. Not that she expected him to, she kept telling herself. After all, that wasn't part of the bargain. But she eagerly read all the newspapers and movie magazines for any detail, no matter how small, that might give some indication of what he was doing.

Maudie wrote regularly, of course, but her letters were filled mainly with gossip about the hectic social life that she seemed to be engaged in. She was no longer living with Estelle, but had moved into a small apartment, with two other girls, on Sunset Boulevard. Her movie, provisionally named *Reveille*, seemed to be a frothy musical based on an army camp. Just the type of thing the government was demanding to keep up morale in what everyone hoped would be the last year of the war.

Maeve had pinned a large map up in the kitchen on which she tried to plot the daily progress of the war in Europe. Chuck and his unit were somewhere on the Rhine, they knew that much, but it was almost impossible to keep entirely up to date. Letters were infrequent, and, because of censorship, said very little from which they could gain a clear idea of his exact whereabouts.

On 7 March they got a letter from Belfast, enclosing a wedding invitation, written out in Katie's familiar upright script. Her eldest daughter Deirdre was marrying a young man by the name of Seamus Heaney, on Friday the 23rd in the local registry office. Katie's accompanying note informed them that he was a Catholic, but the families could not bring themselves to agree on which church to settle for. They were all invited, of course, but both Kitty and her mother knew it was only a formality. Katie was well aware that neither would be making the long journey across the Atlantic.

As they finished their morning coffee and Maeve headed for her own room to pen her reply, before making plans to go downtown and choose a suitable wedding present for her niece, Kitty felt an unfamiliar tightening in her stomach. At first she dismissed it as a natural product of the too energetic breathing exercises she had indulged in on the bedroom floor before breakfast. But when it happened again half an hour later, she knew it was time she roused her mother from her letter-writing.

'Mom! I think it's time we called the doctor!'

Chapter 42

At a little before three o'clock, on the afternoon of Wednesday 7 March 1945, a detachment of the United States 9th Armored Division drew to a halt on the brow of a hill overlooking the small town of Remagen on the Rhine. The men, who included a young captain by the name of Chuck Fullerton, were mystified. They had been informed by other Allied units to reach the river before them that all bridges over the Rhine had been destroyed by the Germans in an effort to halt the enemy advance into the Fatherland. But there she was, as plain as day – the great Ludendorff Bridge at Remagen was still intact. Not only had the Germans not yet destroyed it, they were streaming over it in their hundreds, in their eagerness to escape the advancing Americans.

As Chuck and his men watched, a platoon of American tanks trundled up towards the great stone towers that marked the western side of the structure. Before their horrified gaze, as the leading tanks got within a few yards of the parapet, there was an ear-shattering explosion and a volcano of stones and dirt flew into the air, scattering debris over everything within fifty yards.

Amid the noise and confusion the tanks pulled back, expecting the whole edifice to topple into the Rhine, but incredibly only the western entrance had been touched – and that not enough to prevent entry.

A German officer, whose job it had been to blow up the bridge, lay flat on his face amid the rubble at the eastern approach, knocked completely unconscious by an exploding shell. An eerie armistice lasted until he came to, when he was given immediate orders to try again to blast the bridge into the river.

He did, but this time nothing happened at all.

As the Americans watched from the other bank, unaware of the consternation among the enemy, the German commanding officer called for a volunteer to go on to the bridge itself and attempt to ignite the primer cord of the dynamite by hand. A sergeant responded and, bent double to avoid the ensuing American machine-gun fire and tank shells, he made a dash on to the bridge and carried out his task, before making it back to safety.

Watching from the hilltop, Chuck couldn't but admire the courage of the man, as he waited with his own men, and the enemy on the other bank, for the ensuing explosion. It followed within minutes. A great shuddering roar sent part of the wooden structure flying into the air, and the bridge itself visibly rose before their eyes. But, to their amazement, when the dust cleared, several seconds later, the bridge was still there, although great holes had been gouged from the planking over the railroad tracks.

For those Americans nearer the scene of the action, an immediate decision was called for. Orders had been given to take the bridge and, since it was still there, an attempt must be made before the Germans tried again – more successfully next time. Luckily, although great holes had been blown in the rail tracks running down the middle of the bridge, the footpaths on either side were still intact, and the leading contingent made for these, ducking and weaving their way from one metal girder to another to avoid the hail of German fire that opened up around them.

Chuck stared down at them all, now swarming like ants over the great wounded edifice. A low whistle escaped his lips. Just a handful of men, that's all it took – just a handful of men, with the guts to go first, and thousands would follow. But, hell, this was what they were here for, wasn't it – to take chances? No one was gonna win this war who was yellow-bellied about taking a darned bridge. It had been there for the taking – and they had done it. They had opened a main artery into the still beating heart of Germany itself. Pride welled within him.

'Come on, guys, what are we waiting for!' he yelled above the noise from below to the man in the driving seat beside him. 'Let's get in there with 'em! Step on it, buddy!'

'Hold on to your hats, guys!' The driver spat a wad of tobacco into the grass verge as he pressed his booted foot on to the accelerator and the jeep shot forwards down the hill and headed at full speed towards the western entrance to the bridge.

They abandoned their vehicle behind the tanks lined up about fifty yards behind the rubble-strewn approach and joined the other men now forming squad columns to make the dash to the other side.

Once on the bridge, it was every man for himself as the German machine-gunners kept up their relentless fire. Running head down, bent almost double, no one could be quite sure where exactly he was, as they followed one another in single file, in the zig-zagging footsteps of the man in front. All that mattered was getting to the other side in one piece.

Once across, the men scattered immediately into several of the bomb craters that had been gouged out of the eastern bank of the river, and it was only then, as he half-collapsed inside the temporary refuge, that Bill Brodie, a fair-haired young corporal, noticed that one of their number was missing. 'Where the hell's the Captain? Where's Chuck?'

The other three men crouching beside him looked round in mystification. 'He came after us,' the young man protested. 'He was covering our tail ... He yelled at me to keep my head down as we skirted the bastards in the towers back there.'

All eyes moved to the great stone stanchions less than twenty yards away. Over a piece of blasted concrete, about fifty feet away from safety, an American soldier hung at a grotesque angle. A hole in his left temple told them that their captain, Chuck Fullerton, would not be joining them in their victorious march into Germany's heartland. He would be taking no more bridges. For him the war was already over.

At the moment his comrades hauled Chuck's lifeless body into their rudimentary shelter, oblivious to all but the pain that racked her own body, his sister lay in the St Bridget Nursing Home in New York City, and prayed out loud that the agony would soon end.

Beads of sweat stood out like diamonds on Kitty's pale brow as a young nurse implored her to breathe more regularly. 'It'll help, Mrs Donovan, honestly.'

'Miss . . .' Kitty corrected needlessly, gasping the word out as her insides were torn apart. She had an uncontrollable impulse to sit up. It was defying the laws of gravity to lie here on her back like this. She had to sit up. It became vitally important.

She struggled to haul herself up on the hard bed, only to incur the wrath of the nurse. 'Now, Mrs Donovan, that's not helping at all!' Firm hands pushed at Kitty's shoulders, forcing her back down on the mattress.

'Stop it, damn you, stop it! I want to sit up!'

'You mustn't, it's against orders.'

'Whose goddam orders?' She shouted the question as, red-faced, she lashed out at the attendant.

'My orders, Mrs Donovan.' The answer came from the buxom, white-uniformed figure of the matron, who entered the room with Maeve at her side. 'If you need more painkillers, we'll supply them, but you must obey hospital procedure.'

To hell with hospital procedure, Kitty thought in despair. All she wanted was for this awful pain to go, for her body to be rid of its terrible burden. 'Hi, Mom . . .'

Her voice was so faint that Maeve saw only her lips move, as she neared the edge of the bed and took her daughter's damp hand in hers. 'They say you haven't got much longer, honey . . . Half an hour at the most . . .'

Kitty nodded weakly and passed her free hand through the damp strands of hair that clung to her brow. 'They don't warn you, do they?' she said faintly. 'Nobody tells you it's going to be like this . . .'

Maeve gave a wry smile. 'If they did, I expect the population growth of the world would come to a speedy halt!' Her eyes moved over her daughter's face as Kitty's eyes closed in a moment of respite between the pains. Her mind went back to Kitty's own birth in this very hospital so many years ago. She was so like her father, so very like her father. The moment the nurse had handed her daughter to her Maeve had immediately recognized the tiny, red-faced creature as Dermot's child.

'A drink . . . please . . .'

Maeve leaned over and held a glass of water to her daughter's lips. 'Sip this . . .'

Kitty's lips were covered with the obligatory smear of Vaseline and the taste of the grease mingled with the water on her tongue. She grimaced and pushed the glass away.

'Have you thought of a name for him — or her?' Maeve asked, anxious to keep Kitty's mind off the approaching contraction.

'Y—e—s . . .' The word came out with difficulty as her insides were once more gripped in a vice that seemed to squeeze the very breath of life out of her. She wanted to scream, but her mother was sitting there with those fearful, anxious eyes. 'Go now, Mom . . . Please . . .'

A fleeting look of consternation passed over Maeve's face as Kitty's eyes met hers.

'Please, Mom . . .'

Then she understood. There was nothing dignified about giving birth. Her daughter wanted privacy for her agony and she was entitled to that; every woman was. She got up and bent over and kissed the damp brow. 'All right, honey, I'll go . . . But I'll be right outside if you need me.'

Kitty shook her head. 'No, don't wait . . . I could be here all night . . . Go back home. I'll tell them to ring as soon as he arrives.'

'You're very sure it's going to be a son.'

Her daughter nodded and managed a weak smile. 'I'm very sure . . .'

Kitty watched her mother leave the room, closing the door softly behind her. She was on her own now. Alone but for her child — Lee's child — who was putting her through more hell on earth than she believed it was possible for one human being to endure . . . She would never have another. She was sure of that.

'Aaaaah . . .' Her right hand reached out and fumbled for the buzzer on the bedside cabinet. 'God help me . . . Somebody help me . . . !'

Maeve was barely inside the front door of her apartment when the telephone rang to say her first grandchild had fought his red-faced way into the world. 'Sarah!' She replaced the receiver with an enormous sigh of relief. 'Sarah!'

The housekeeper's white-aproned bulk appeared at the open door of the drawing-room. 'Yus'm?'

'I'm a grandmother, Sarah! I'm a grandmother!'

The two women embraced, spinning round on the Indian carpet in a grotesque dance of glee, as tears of happiness and relief flooded down Maeve's cheeks. A grandson! She and Dermot had a grandson, and she was sobbing unashamedly, like a small child, into the starched cotton comfort of Sarah's ample shoulder.

The housekeeper made little understanding noises as she patted her mistress's back. She was a grandmother herself and understood.

Daniel Kieran Donovan weighed in at seven pounds nine ounces – over half a stone of pink, wrinkled flesh that screamed its way through all the weighing, washing and powdering before finally being placed in his mother's arms.

Kitty looked down in wonder at her baby son. She had expected a familiar face – a combination of Kieran and Lee, perhaps . . . But this small scrap of humanity was a stranger to her; a stranger with tightly screwed-up eyes and a beautifully shaped head of dark hair. She stroked the tiny, tightly curled fist with her finger and he reached out and gripped it. 'It's just you and me, kid,' she whispered. It was a daunting thought.

Maeve was not prepared for her own reaction when she first set eyes on her grandchild, for a great surge of love welled up within her towards the tiny creature in the cot by the side of his mother's bed. She looked down at him, then across at her daughter. Kitty looked so frail, so very vulnerable, lying there on the white pillow. Far too vulnerable to raise a young son on her own. Thoughts of Kitty's own birth flooded through her head. It had been a crime – unavoidable, but a crime, nevertheless, that a man should have been denied the chance to acknowledge his own child . . . Finally, she could contain herself no longer. 'It's not fair, you know, Kitty. It's not fair at all bringing him into the world without a father. A child needs a father.'

'He has me.'

Maeve shook her head impatiently. 'It's not enough, honey. It's just not enough. He has a right to know his own father.'

'I never knew mine.'

She meant Danny, Maeve knew that, but the words struck home. God forgive me, she thought in despair, and God forgive Dermot . . . Her voice, when she spoke, seeemed to come from a million miles away. 'That was different . . . You know all about your father's side of the family – and mine.' Her eyes searched her daughter's for understanding. 'You know all about all the family still in Ireland. In fact, a letter came from your grandmother in Dublin asking about you this very morning. A child needs a father, Kitty . . . He needs grandparents, too.'

'He has you.'

'Yes, that's true. But what about his other grandmother? Shouldn't he know her, too?'

Kitty's lips twisted ironically as she avoided her mother's eyes and gazed past her out of the window. She could not trust herself to speak. What, oh what, would she say if she were told the truth – that her beloved little grandson's other grandmother was, in fact, Estelle? The whole thing seemed to have become a perverse joke. But no one was laughing. Least of all herself.

'Of course, we can't help Danny's death, or even Frank's, God rest their souls,' Maeve's voice continued, 'but that's all the more reason for him to be in touch with his other grandfather. He ought to know him, Kitty. He certainly ought to know him.'

The image of Art flashed into her mind. She could not – she would not think of him as her son's grandfather. It seemed wrong – very wrong, somehow. But she was spared the effort of replying to her mother's question by the arrival of a bright-eyed young nurse carrying what was the most enormous bouquet of spring flowers she had ever seen.

'These have just arrived,' the girl said, depositing her fragrant burden on the edge of the bed, and handing Kitty the card.

Maeve watched with barely concealed curiosity as her daughter opened the small white envelope and extracted the florist's gilt-edged card.

'Who's it from, dear?'

Kitty ignored this question, too, and gazed down at the card in her hands, as her heart missed a beat. The message was typed, for its contents had been dictated by phone from the other side of the country barely an hour before.

Have just heard the good news – Congratulations – and may these few flowers prove to you that the ice is melting and spring is just around the corner.

There was no signature. There didn't have to be . . . Art – it was from Art! Kitty's whole face lit up as she read, then re-read the words. How on earth had he got the news so quickly? She could feel the hot rush of blood to her face as she leaned back against the pillow and closed her eyes. She had tried to put all thoughts of Lee's father out of her mind over the past few weeks and had not reckoned on the effect hearing from him again would have on her.

'May I see?' Unable to contain her curiosity any longer, Maeve plucked the card from her daughter's fingers, her brows furrowing as she read the neatly typed words. They didn't make any sense. She read them again, just to make sure, then shook her head. It was obviously some sort of coded message. But the fact that Kitty had actually received the flowers brought a genuine, although puzzled, smile to her face.

'Have you, by any chance, already phoned Maudie in California, Mom?'

'Sure – I called a couple of hours ago, as soon as I heard the news.'

Kitty closed her eyes again, a quiet smile lighting the corners of her lips. So that was how he knew!

'I presume these are from his father?'

'What . . . ? How . . . ?' Kitty's eyes flew open. How on earth did she know about Art? Then realisation dawned – by 'his father' she could not mean Lee's; she could not possibly mean Art.

Maeve plucked a daffodil from the middle of the bouquet and stroked the bright yellow trumpet with her forefinger. 'Well, at least, it shows the little soul's got a father – now that he's bothered to send these.' She made a gesture towards the other flowers with the bloom in her hand. 'But heaven only knows what that peculiar message is supposed to mean! I presume it makes some sense to you?'

'Yes, Mom,' Kitty smiled. She had the wrong end of the stick altogether, but thank God for that. Her secret was safe. Art had not forgotten her. And no one else, not a single other living soul had any idea what that meant to her. Her smile grew broader as she leaned back on the pillow and closed her eyes once more. 'Yes, Mom, I know only too well what it means.'

Kitty's secret lasted only four months, until 16 July 1945, for Art insisted on being present at her son's baptism.

After the initial shock, Maeve took the news very well, although she could not bring herself to believe that this man was actually the father of her first grandchild. Kitty said and did nothing to enlighten her on the subject and Maeve had for too long been an avid guardian of her own privacy to pry any further into her daughter's. If Kitty wanted to tell her the truth about Danny's paternity one day, then she would, but in her own good time. When it came to her private life, Kitty Donovan was as much a Ballantine as she was herself. Her private life meant exactly that.

Maeve obtained a curious comfort from the thought. It was almost as if she had passed an indefinable burden from her own shoulders on to those of her daughter. The spotlight had moved on from her to the younger woman. The present belonged to the new generation. She had moved, along with the Great War, into the past. It was as if, in assuming the role of grandmother, she had moved beyond the old hurts of yesteryear. Frank was dead now; so many of them were dead . . . Frank, Danny, Kieran, Chuck . . .

Now there was a new generation to look to. She had a grandson. She and Dermot had a grandson. The knowledge filled her with more love and pride than she believed it possible for one woman to experience.

The ceremony was held on the terrace of their summer house on Cape Cod and she had enjoyed every minute of the planning and preparations she had indulged in with Sarah. And now, seeing everything go so smoothly, a great feeling of satisfaction welled within her, as she took the lace-robed child from his mother's arms and cradled him in her own, before laying him in the cradle that had sheltered her own children in their turn throughout their infant years.

It had been Kitty's own decision to delay the christening until now. Somehow it had seemed wrong to commit her son to God when she still felt a great bitterness in her heart towards Him for the death of Chuck. For her brother to die only weeks before the death of Nazi Germany itself was bad enough, but for it to be on the very day that her son made his entry into this troubled world, was almost more than she could bear.

In his honour the name Charles was added to his given names. Daniel Kieran Charles Donovan – it was a lot to live up to, all these men she had loved. Only two other names were missing – those of his father and grandfather. But what would the man standing beside her at this most special moment think if the priest read out the names Leon Arthur along with the others?

After the ceremony, with Danny sleeping soundly in the crib by his grandmother's side, Art took Kitty's arm as they walked out into the fresh sea air.

A pale sun gleamed above them in an azure sky; its rays seemed to point like ethereal fingers towards the man and woman on the deserted terrace, bathing them both in its glow. No words passed between them as, hand in hand, they gazed out over the shining blue water of the bay. Kitty was aware of being as happy now as she had ever been in a long time. But how long would it last? The whole world was in a state of flux. The war in Europe was over, it was true, but Japan had still not surrendered. And who knew when that would happen?

One man among a privileged few knew. One man who, for the past eight months, had lived and worked in the desert heat to perfect a device that would change the world from that moment on.

As the woman he had once loved, and his father, stood in the tranquil peace of the East Coast retreat, in a remote outpost of the Alamogordo Air Base, in the New Mexico desert, the first full-scale test of his life's work took place. The first atomic

394

bomb in the history of mankind was detonated into the atmosphere of the clear summer morning.

As the enormous mushroom cloud rose to the heavens, an awesome fear swept over him and he turned to the man who had led their team, his beloved Bob. But J. Robert Oppenheimer was oblivious to all but the enormity of their creation. He had tears in his eyes, as he whispered the sacred words from the Bhagavad-Gita:

'If the radiance of a thousand suns were to burst into the sky, that would be the splendour of the Mighty One . . .
I am become death, the shatterer of worlds.'

A cold hand touched Lee Finkelstein's heart. If he were to have that son he longed for, what kind of world had he created for him?

At that moment Daniel Kieran Charles Donovan, his first-born son, was sleeping peacefully in his cot many miles away; an innocent hostage to fate. Only time would answer his father's unspoken question.

BOOK THREE
The red-gold flame

Who fears to speak of Easter week
Who dares its fate deplore?
The red-gold flame of Erin's name
Confronts the world once more . . .

Rebel song to tune of
'The Men of '98'

Chapter 43

The sky above the Annam highlands exploded into a blaze of flame as the US helicopter plummeted to the ground. Screams rent the air; blood-curdling screams that signalled the approach of death for the men aboard. The oldest was only twenty-two. He had been waiting for – dreading – this moment for two years; the whole two bloody years he had been here in this God-forsaken land. Heat and pain, he could not tell the difference, seared through him as the chopper made impact with the earth, shearing the foliage from the trees in its blazing path. Then nothing . . . Second Lieutenant Danny Donovan lay sprawled on his face alongside a shattered piece of rotor blade, unaware of the carnage around him, or of the blood seeping from his gut, through the mottled green of his combat trousers, to stain the dry earth a deeper brown.

Oblivion brought relief. Relief from the sight of his friends being parcelled up, like pieces of bloodied butcher meat, and thrown into the green standard-issue plastic bags that the Administration had supplied to bring back what was left of their young men from the battlefields of Vietnam.

They held a service for them the following morning, these bits and pieces of American manhood who had fought beside him for a cause that was not theirs, in a land they did not know, for a people who did not want them there. Gary, Raoul, Carl, Fatcat . . . all gone. He watched from a stretcher wheeled out specially, as the strange ritual was enacted once again in the grey dawn at the US base of Dak To, from where they had set out less than twenty-four hours before. Fatcat, his round babyface sweating beneath his helmet, had made a joke as they had taken off about being brought back in a plastic bag; they had seen it so many times. A few had laughed. Bravado came cheaply at a time like this. But the joke was over – for him and the others.

A skinny corporal from Nebraska lowered the Stars and

Stripes to half-mast, and the onlookers stood in mute contemplation, as their chaplain read from the Bible a sermon that Danny could not listen to. He stared instead at the empty boots. Had they not yet realised that God no longer existed?

The voice droned on in his head, speaking of courage and sacrifice, as he continued to stare dully at the boots of the dead men. They had been collected from the severed limbs and polished until they shone, then carefully arranged in a semicircle in front of their dead owners' remaining comrades. He started to laugh hysterically. Who gave a damn about polished boots? Not old Fatcat – not Gary or any of the others. And certainly not Sol, his only buddy to survive. No, certainly not Sol. Sol had no legs left, let alone feet . . .

The laughter grew louder and louder, until it became a scream and Danny awoke, breathless and bathed in sweat, to switch on the light, squinting through the sudden brightness at the clock by his pillow. Half-past two. It was improving – usually he managed only a couple of hours' sleep before the nightmares brought him tossing and turning back to consciousness on the dishevelled bed.

He poured some water into a glass, from the jug on top of the bedside cabinet, and gulped it down, his eyes falling on the small brass perpetual calendar next to the alarm clock. Tuesday 12 March 1968 – it was six long months since his discharge, since he had been flown out of Nam along with Sol and the others lucky enough to be making it back to sanity. But was this sanity?

His lips twisted bitterly as he replaced the glass and sank back on the damp pillow. He could go back to college, they had told him yesterday. 'Ease yourself back into it gradually, Dan,' the doctor had said. 'Don't push things too quickly. That old carcass of yours has taken quite a pasting.' Internal injuries, they had told him in the Hercules transport that had taken him back to the main base to be operated on. All he knew was that his gut hurt – hurt so much that for weeks he could not eat a light meal without feeling afterwards that someone was pulling his insides out.

It was worse for Sol, though. Sol's world now had two wheels and was battery powered. But how could you – how could anyone – ever come to terms with life in a wheelchair? Especially with a wife like Shiralee . . . Shiralee Bernson, Sol's wife – the wife the young former electronics engineer had known for barely ten days before they married three years ago. Danny's eyes clouded as he stared up at the ceiling. He had known her much longer. Since they were seven years old, to be exact. Shiralee Doyle she had been then.

'Jee . . . zuz God . . . !' His fists clenched and beat the satin bedspread in a combination of anger, frustration and despair. The gooks should've killed him back there – finished him off. He would have deserved it; deserved it more than those poor guys that didn't make it back. Surely there could be no lower scum on the face of this earth than a guy who would make love to his best friend's wife behind his back; especially when that friend was no longer capable himself. 'God . . . !'

Kitty Donovan sat up in her bed and glanced through the darkness at the fluorescent hands on the clock by the bed. 'Not even three,' she sighed; it was not even three o'clock and Danny was still not asleep. Either that or he had had one of his nightmares again. It was the same story almost every night. She had even thought of moving her bed into the spare room, for the dividing wall between her room and her son's was far too thin to allow her to sleep through his troubled nights.

She had even thought of going to the doctor herself and telling him about it, but he had hundreds of Dannys on his list – young men who had come back from Vietnam with problems far more serious than this. He had had very little discomfort from his stomach for weeks now and these night-time trials would surely pass; after all, he'd only been back six months.

As usual, it was not mentioned at breakfast, as she fixed his scrambled eggs and coffee before leaving for the gallery. 'Sleep well, honey?'

'Sure, Mom.' He lifted the copy of the *New York Times* from the table-top and flicked through it. Deliberately avoiding the war news, he moved to the sports pages and tried to work up some enthusiasm for his old passions.

'Got any plans for today?'

'If you mean, am I going down to see the Principal about re-enrolling today, then the answer's no.'

Kitty passed a hand over her smoothly bouffant hair and sighed audibly. 'Well, far be it for me to tell you how soon you should be getting back to your studies . . .'

'But?'

'But I can't help thinking at least it would give you something to occupy yourself with. It really can't be doing you much good moping around here all day.'

'I won't be moping around here all day.'

Kitty's face brightened. 'Really? Are you planning on going somewhere special?'

'Nope. Just round to Sol's.'

'You seem to spend quite a bit of time around there. Shouldn't he be at the rehabilitation centre most days?'

Danny's head jerked round. How in heaven's name did she know that? She didn't suspect, did she? . . . No, it was impossible.

'Oh, I don't take up much of his time – just stick around long enough to have a beer and chew the fat for an hour or so.'

'How's that little wife of his? Shiralee, isn't it? Is she taking part in the St Patrick's Day parade this year?' As an active member of the city's Irish community, Shiralee had been introduced to Kitty once during the post-march celebrations, and she had quite taken to the young woman she already knew to be an old classmate of her son.

Danny reached out for the plate of eggs on toast, then piled a lump of the thick, yellow mass on his fork. As a second generation Irish-American, Shiralee had never missed any of the parades through the city on 17 March in all her twenty-two years. 'I guess so. I haven't asked.'

Kitty poured the coffee and looked thoughtful. 'It must be awful for her – what happened to her husband, I mean. You have to have a real inner strength to cope with something like that.'

Danny nodded but said nothing. Shiralee had that all right – determination would be a better word for it. Ever since first grade she had been getting her own way – getting exactly what she wanted out of life, and the crazy thing was that everyone who knew her was more than glad to agree to it, including him. There was something about the petite figure, with the dark elfin-cut hair and almond eyes, that brooked no refusal, no matter how unthinkable the request. Not that she had ever requested he make love to her. She was much too subtle for that. No, she had simply made it clear in other more intimate ways. Even now in his mother's bright airy kitchen his skin broke out in a sweat even to think about it . . .

'By the way, Danny, your grandmother rang this morning. She'd like you to call by sometime. And don't ask me what it is she wants – she didn't say.'

Danny grinned as he took a swig of his coffee. 'Don't worry, I'll find out soon enough and let you know.'

Kitty's cheeks coloured beneath her make-up as she poured herself a glass of fresh orange juice. 'Am I really so nosy?'

He nodded, grinning across the table at her, but ignored the question. 'Is Art due back this weekend?'

His mother shrugged. 'He hasn't called, so I doubt it . . . Not that that ever stopped him jumping on a plane in the past, though!' She smiled fondly as she downed the last of the orange. Who would ever have thought that even after more than twenty years she could still get that same old tingle at the knowledge he would be winging his way back from California any time now to see her? But perhaps that was why their relationship had lasted so long – why it had retained its freshness and excitement for them both – the fact that they lived apart for so many months of the year. Yes, maybe living in sin, as the priest would term it, might well be the reason for their continuing love affair. They had never married, Art preferring to keep his main base in Hollywood, knowing full well she would never leave New York and her beloved gallery. But both his elegant mansion in Beverly Hills and her apartment here on Fifth Avenue bore the marks of both their very individual personalities, and even Danny had grown up to think of both homes as his own. She had never told him that Art was his grandfather. In fact, not another living soul knew that Lee Finkelstein was Danny's father. The fact that she had been able to keep her secret for twenty-two years still never ceased to amaze her. But, incredibly, since early childhood

Danny had never asked, and Art had kept to his promise to her in Yehudi's on that very first day not to ask questions she might not wish to answer.

'Well, that's it, Mom! I'm off!' Danny got up from the table, interrupting her train of thought. 'I'll call in and see Gran sometime this afternoon.' He slotted his used crockery and cutlery into the dishwasher, then leaned over and kissed his mother on the cheek. Already his heart rate was increasing at the thought of seeing Shiralee in less than an hour . . .

He was not in the habit of visiting the Bernsons on a Saturday morning, but Shiralee had called last night to say that Sol would be visiting his parents over on the lower East Side for most of the day, and anyway, there was something important she wanted to talk to him about. The last remark had puzzled him, for it was delivered in a none-too-casual voice. It was with an even more racing pulse than usual that he climbed the stairs to the Bernson apartment at a little after ten.

There was no response to his first ring at the bell, nor his second, and he was just on the point of retracing his steps back downstairs when the sound of running footsteps halted him on the top step.

'Danny! I'm sorry I'm late. Have you been waiting long?' Shiralee's face was flushed as her high heels clattered up the last few concrete steps. She planted a kiss on his cheek before delving into her bag for the key.

'Been shopping?'

She shook her head as the key was pushed into the lock and she preceded him into the narrow hallway beyond. 'Just go through, will you? I'll hang my jacket up and be right with you.'

He walked on into the cramped living room. A Bob Dylan album cover lay on the arm of a chair by the hi-fi, the record from which was still going round soundlessly on the turntable. Whoever had left the apartment last hadn't even bothered to switch it off. Somehow he could not believe it was Sol. Of all the guys who shared their accommodation out in Nam, he was the one whose kit was always immaculate and who never ran out of toothpaste or shaving soap. But Shiralee now, she was a different matter altogether. There was no way she was ever going to win the Housewife of the Year award.

'Fancy a drink?' She appeared at the door dressed in a pink satin, wrap-around housecoat and held out a glass of Budweiser. He took it with a nod of thanks. The white froth ran down the sides of the glass and made a dark stain on the denim of his jeans as he sat down and balanced the beer on his knee. 'You're probably wondering why I called last night . . .'

'It did cross my mind.' He looked across at her quizzically, feeling the familiar knot of nerves in his stomach as their eyes met. Even this greeting made him uneasy. On a normal visit, with Sol absent, they usually lost no time in heading for the bedroom, but to be handed a beer out here in the living-room . . .

Shiralee sat down on the chair opposite and lit a cigarette. She crossed her legs, allowing the pink satin edges of the wrap to slip open, revealing the stocking tops of her black nylons as she leaned back and drew deeply on the cigarette. She was trying to compose herself, he could see that, and it wasn't like her to be nervous about anything . . . 'We've known each other a long time, haven't we, Danny?' Her voice was soft, almost childlike.

'Just about all our lives.'

'And I've only known Sol for a few years.' He nodded, as she smoothed an imaginary wrinkle from the pink satin on her thigh. 'In a way, I'm really closer to you than I've ever been to him . . . with us being childhood sweethearts for so long and all . . . Why, if it wasn't for the fact you stood me up at our graduation prom, it would most likely have been you I married and not him.'

'Correction – you were the one who stood me up, remember? You were the one who accepted two invitations and chose that creep Headley to go with, not me!' Even after all this time, it was hard to keep the bitterness from his voice.

She shook her head impatiently. 'Remember it any way you want – the fact is, we've always loved each other, haven't we? Making love together over the past few months has only been a natural result of all those years when we should have been together. Why, if Sol hadn't had this awful thing happen to him, I never would've had to stay here, would I? I would've put in for a divorce to marry you.'

'What's all this leading to, Shirl? You don't have to justify what's been going on between us to me, you know that.'

She got up from the chair and walked to the window. Her movements were jerky as she ran a hand through her hair and puffed nervously on the cigarette. A sense of unease filled the room. He got up to join her and she avoided his eyes as he placed his hands on her shoulders and said quietly, 'Listen, honey, no matter how much we may attempt to justify it, we both know what we've been doing ain't right. In fact, if you must know, I've felt the most low-down dirty piece of vermin you can imagine over these past few months. If you're asking if I love you, then the answer's probably yes – if love means that I crave you more than any amount of hash or any drug you care to mention . . . But don't ask me to condone what we're doing. Don't ever do that. The memory of this affair – the guilt – is something I'll just have to live with. I just pray to God that Sol never finds out.'

'It's too late for prayers, Danny. Much too late.'

'What the hell is that supposed to mean? He doesn't know, does he?' The thought appalled him.

She shook her head. 'No, not yet.'

'Not yet! You mean you're going to tell him?' His voice rose to a shout as his fingers increased their pressure on her shoulders.

She winced. 'I won't have to,' she yelled back. 'He'll see for himself soon enough. I'm pregnant, Danny. I'm going to have your baby!'

Chapter 44

'Pregnant! You've got to be joking! You *are* kidding, ain't you?'
But Danny already knew the answer from Shiralee's defiant
face.

'I'd hardly make a joke of a thing like this. I can think of
funnier subjects, can't you?' She shrugged herself free from his
grasp and stubbed her cigarette out in a nearby ashtray. 'Where
do you think I was this morning?'

He stared at her dumbly, unable even to shake his head.

'I was at the doctor's, that's where! I went for a second
opinion. I wanted to make sure before I told you, although my
own doctor was pretty certain when he confirmed it yesterday.'

'But we've been so careful.' He let out a long slow breath
and shook his head in confusion.

'Obviously not quite careful enough!'

'But you kept a chart, didn't you? You told me you kept a
goddam chart showing the safe period to do it.' She looked past
him, staring blank-faced out of the window. 'Answer me, Shirl,
you kept a chart, didn't you?' But still she remained silent.

He reached out and grabbed her arm. 'Show it to me! Show
me that chart!'

She pulled away from him once more, tears springing to her
eyes. 'Stop shouting at me . . . It's not just my fault, you know.
This baby didn't get where it is by my wishing it here!' Her
eyes were defiant as they glared back at him.

'You're not having it, are you? For Christ's sake, Shirl, we
can't do this to him – not to Sol!'

She backed away from him. 'I'm having it, Danny. I'm
having this baby, all right. I'm having *your* child – got it? *Your*
child! And you're in this just as deeply as I am. You're just as
guilty as I am. We're having this baby, you and me together!'

'But Sol . . .' He felt sick to the pit of his stomach.

Shiralee's face softened as she reached out for his hand. 'Sol
won't be an obstacle, honey . . . Oh, sure, he'll be upset to

407

begin with – what man wouldn't be? But he'll get over it. He'll give me my divorce. There'll be nothing to stop us being married before it even shows!'

'Jesus Christ! Jesus bloody Christ!' He jerked his hand free of hers and stared across at her. 'This was no accident, was it, Shiralee? This was no goddam accident! You planned it all. You planned it from the beginning.'

Her face went white. 'No – no, of course I didn't! How could you say such a thing!'

'Because it true, that's why! Because it's true! You couldn't do it on your own, could you? Plucking up the courage to leave a husband who's a paraplegic war hero took the kind of guts – or callousness, take your pick – that even you didn't possess. But it's quite a different matter when that guilt is shared. You can be the poor little innocent – the wife who was seduced by the husband's best friend, his old war buddy, for good measure . . . Jesus, what a fool I've been!'

'No, that's just not true! You make it sound dirty – something to be ashamed of. You make it sound like I used you and that simply isn't the case. We love each other, don't we? You love me, Danny. You love me! We've always loved each other!'

'Don't use that word!' There was real hate in his eyes as he turned from her and stared out of the window. 'We had an affair, Shiralee – a messy little affair. Don't try to make it out into the great love story of the twentieth century. It was never that – and never can be now. Surely you can see that?' He turned back to face her as she shook her head violently.

'No, I can't see that! You're shocked, that's all. But you'll get over it. We'll be happy, Danny – real happy. Just wait and see!'

'Wait and see?' He shook his head in incredulity. 'Nobody's gonna do any waiting around here. These things can be fixed. It'll have to be fixed . . . Dear God, Shiralee, this will finish Sol off. You'll have to get rid of it. There just ain't any choice in the matter.'

'You're telling me to kill my own child – your child?'

'I'm telling you to see someone who can perform a simple little operation. A few minutes, that's all it'll take – two goddam minutes, and Sol will be spared all that misery.'

'It's impossible.'

'Why? Give me one good reason.'

'I'm a Catholic.'

'So am I. I'm a Catholic, too, remember. But I'm not a fool . . .'

'That's where you're wrong, Danny Donovan. You are a fool – and a bigger one than I took you for, if you really believe that I'm going to get rid of this child. You got me into this – and, by God, you'll get me out!'

Her words still rang in his head as an hour later he stepped out of the elevator and walked the few steps to his grandmother's front door. He felt drained of everything – emotion, energy; it was a mere empty shell of his former self who kissed Maeve's cheek, before following her through into the familiar drawing-room.

'It was good of you to come so quickly, Danny dear. Did your mother tell you I wanted to see you?'

'Yeah, she said you called.' He flopped down on the settee by the window and looked across at her expectantly. He wished she would just get on with it and let him get out of here – back to his own home to think things out.

Maeve sat down at the opposite end of the settee from him and leaned across and took his hand. She gazed down at the back of it as her fingers stroked the smooth skin; it was pale and covered in tiny freckles beneath the light down of gold hairs. It was identical to both Danny's and Kieran's. Having a grandson who was the living image of her late husband, and son, produced a peculiar mixture of emotions in her. The fact that she had doted on him from the moment of his birth seemed curious, for she had never loved his namesake, her first husband, or Kieran, her own son, this way. But maybe that was why she now felt as she did; maybe in some way she was making up in double measure in the third generation for the love she had denied the first and second. And there was something else, something that no one else on this earth knew for certain, Daniel Kieran Charles Donovan was Dermot's grandchild. And that fact alone made him the most treasured of beings.

She released his hand and carefully smoothed the soft

cashmere of her dress over her knees, before clasping her hands in her lap and looking across at him. 'Things have been pretty awful for you these past couple of years, haven't they, Danny?'

He started to protest, but she silenced him with a reproving gesture of her hand. 'Don't think I don't know. Living here alone, apart from old Sarah, in this mausoleum of an apartment gives me time to observe things and make my own judgements. You've been coping pretty well on the surface with your convalescence, but it's taken an awful lot out of you. That old sparkle has gone and something's got to be done about it before it's lost forever. What you need more than anything is a complete change – a change of scene, a change of people . . .'

She paused, carefully choosing her words. 'I think the world of all three of my grandchildren, as you know. By rights, Jeff and Jaynie, your Aunt Maudie's two, count for just as much in my book . . . But, well, I don't have to tell you that you have always been extra special to me. Not only because you're the first grandchild, but also because you remind me so much of . . .' Her voice tailed off, unable to speak the names of any of the other men who had played such a great part in her life. There was no doubt about it, he had his grandfather Dermot's gentle nature combined with the fiery, flame-red looks of both Danny and Kieran. How could he be anything other than special? 'Well, I guess what I'm really trying to say is that you mean a great deal to me and that's why it's you I want to accompany me and not the other two.'

'Accompany you where?'

'To Ireland, Danny. I'm going back to Ireland – and I want you to come with me.'

'To Ireland?' His mouth dropped open. His grandmother had never been back to the land of her birth since she had left during the Great War. 'For ever?'

'My goodness, no!' The thought obviously amused her. 'At least, I've no plans to stay there for ever – although it's quite tempting to think of myself ending my days on the oul' sod, before being laid to rest beneath it!'

'How long then? How long do you intend staying?' The idea was slowly beginning to have possibilities.

'Oh, a month or so. We'd be in no hurry, would we? There's

410

nothing much here worth dashing back for at the moment, is there?'

His mind flew back to Shiralee. No one had ever spoken a truer word. 'Well . . .'

'Oh, you don't have to make up your mind right away,' Maeve put in quickly.

He grinned. 'You mean two minutes from now will suffice?'

Maeve laughed. He obviously knew her only too well. 'All right, I've never been known for my patience. But I would appreciate it, Danny, really I would. And I know you'll love Ireland as much as I do – it's so green, so peaceful. It'll be such a change for you after Vietnam.'

'You mean you've no IRA any more to liven things up? You disappoint me, Gran!' His grin broadened, but her face became suddenly serious.

'You'd have to ask your Great-Aunt Katie about that. But, as far as I'm concerned, the less you have to do with that lot the better. Anyway, I would've thought you've seen enough of fighting lately to last a lifetime.'

'You can't compare the two,' he said quietly. 'Nam wasn't my fight, nor was it the fight of any of those poor guys I knew who never came back. But you can't say that about the boys fighting for the cause in Ireland, can you? That's their fight all right, just as it was my grandfather's fight all those years ago.'

Maeve looked across at him with a sinking heart. There was a strange light in his eyes that she had seen once before – in another time, another place, a long, long time ago. It was the same light she had seen in the eyes of another Danny Donovan – her husband – fifty years ago. A whole half-century – she could hardly believe it.

He lifted her hand to his lips and kissed it lightly. 'Hey, cheer up! I'll come with you – just try and stop me!' He had mistaken her sudden change of expression for anxiety that he might not come.

Maeve forced a smile to her lips as a great nervousness welled within her. She should tell him – tell him now, before it was too late, that his mother's romanticised stories of Ireland were not the reality. There was nothing glamorous about young men sacrificing themselves for political ends. Oh yes, it

411

made stirring tales for the telling to the following generation, and exciting reading in the pages of the history books, but from both those accounts something was missing. The agony was missing. The heartbreak of identifying the body, then burying a beloved husband, son or brother. She should tell him all that, before they took the matter any further . . .

'Well, Gran, just say the word. When do we leave?'

She withdrew her hand and avoided his eyes as she got up from the settee and drew a hand over her hair. 'Just as soon as I can get it fixed up, Danny dear.'

Kitty could not disguise her surprise when she got back from the gallery that evening and he gave her the news. 'I just don't believe it – not after all this time! What on earth's got into her? There must be something – some reason that's prompted her to go now.'

Danny shrugged. 'If there is, she didn't confide in me.'

'And you really want to go?' She slipped off her jacket and tossed it over the back of a chair, before switching on the coffee percolator.

'Yes, I really want to go. Wouldn't you?'

'You bet your sweet life I would!' She lit a cigarette and drew on it deeply. 'God, it's been my lifetime's ambition to get there!'

'Then why didn't you?'

It was a simple enough question that she had often asked herself. 'I really don't know the answer to that, Danny, and that's the truth. Maybe it's a bit like being a little kid who has a sneaking suspicion that Santa Claus doesn't really exist, but won't admit it to himself. He prefers to go on believing in the dream.'

'You mean it might not have lived up to your expectations?'

She laughed. 'Even for Mother Ireland that would have been an impossibility! To me the Emerald Isle is the heaven on earth that's always out there somewhere waiting for me. And when things get just too hectic, too unbearable here, then some day I'll simply up and fly away . . .'

'And where will you be flying to, may I ask?'

The deep, masculine voice from the door made them both look round as Art Finlay walked in, tossing his briefcase on to

412

the table. Kitty's face immediately lit up as she ran across to embrace him. 'You old devil, you might have phoned!'

'You're right, I might have, but there was a very good reason why I didn't!' He planted a kiss on her brow, then disentangled himself and delved into his jacket pocket.

'What's that? Why couldn't you call?' Kitty impatiently made a grab for the blue envelope he extracted, but he held it aloft out of her reach.

'All in good time! A coffee first, woman, then – and only then – do I spill the beans!' He sat down at the table as Kitty set about pouring another coffee and looked across at her curiously. 'Anyway, what was all that I heard a minute ago? Where are you intending to be flying off to?'

'Not me, unfortunately,' Kitty laughed. 'We were talking about Ireland. Mom's asked Danny to accompany her on a trip back home.'

Art's shaggy silver brows shot up. 'And you're going? You're going to Ireland with her?' He looked across at Danny who nodded. 'Well, well, well – ain't that something! Old Maeve's finally going home!'

Kitty handed him his coffee. 'She sure is.'

'And you're green with envy, ain't you, honey? Go on – admit it!'

'All right it, darn you, I do! I'd give anything for a break right now . . . Just to fly off somewhere into the deep blue yonder – but fat chance I've got to do that, with you so busy!'

Art took a gulp of his coffee and sat back in his chair, a curiously smug expression on his face. 'That's where you're wrong, honeychild! When this movie I'm finishing is finally in the can next week, we're taking off, you and I . . . Yep, we're taking off all right!'

'But where . . . What are you getting at, Art Finlay? You've got something up your sleeve. I know that devious look only too well! Is it something to do with that letter you've so carefully hidden back in your pocket?'

'Correct!'

'Who's it from? Tell me, for heaven's sake, you know how much I loathe surprises!'

He shot a grin across at Danny, as he took the envelope from his inside pocket and tossed it across the table at her. 'It's from Lee,' he announced proudly. 'He's just been made a general in the Israeli army and we're invited across to the celebration party!'

'Lee!' The colour drained from Kitty's face as she stared down at the familiar writing on the pale-blue airmail envelope. 'You mean you're going to Israel and you want me to come with you?'

'That's exactly what I mean,' Art said firmly. 'And, this time, there's absolutely no way you're getting out of it! In fact, Lee is quite adamant that you come with me. He says it's now far too long since you two met and your excuses for not accompanying me whenever I fly out there are beginning to wear a bit thin. How long is it since you last saw each other, anyhow?'

Her mind flew back to that windy afternoon in the graveyard where they had buried her brother. 'It was 1944,' she said softly. 'A whole lifetime ago.' Her eyes met those of her son as she said the words, but neither he nor his grandfather knew how very apt they were.

Chapter 45

Kitty sat at the dressing-table mirror and drew a brush through her hair. After more than twenty years of making excuses, there was finally no way out of it, she would have to meet Lee again. After all this time, they would be coming face to face. A shiver ran through her and she glanced over her shoulder in the mirror, but Art had not noticed. He was too engrossed in the late movie on the small portable television at the foot of their bed.

He had already made several trips out there to Lee's and Rose's palatial ranch-style house just outside Tel Aviv, beginning with the visits to mark the births of both his Israeli grandchildren. She smiled wryly at the thought as she dipped her fingers into the jar of cleansing cream and rubbed a blob over her cheek. Little did he know that his firstborn grandchild was not the twenty-two-year-old Ruth, but her own son, Danny, now asleep in the next room. It was ironic that Lee had not got his wish for a son with Rose first time round, but Ged had been born less than two years after his sister and the two tall, dark-haired, clear-eyed young Israelis whose pictures now adorned the mantelpiece in the drawing-room would be a credit to any parent.

It was silly really, this reluctance to come face to face with Lee again. It wasn't that she was afraid of the deeply buried emotions a visit might expose. Too much had happened since then. It was simply that meeting the father of her son would underline for her the guilt she had carried for all these years in keeping the truth of Danny's parenthood a secret from the three men who had more right than anyone else to know — Danny himself, his father Lee, and his grandfather Art. Her eyes moved once again to the figure in the bed, less than ten feet away. Although they had never gone through any official ceremony, he had been as good a life's companion to her as any man could ever be. She had never thought of him as a generation older than her, and still didn't. Art Finlay was as vital as any man thirty years younger.

'Come on, honey, you'd enjoy this!'

The voice from the bed interrupted her reverie and she responded immediately by speeding up her cleansing ritual. 'Have you decided exactly when you want to fly out to Israel?'

'Oh, in about three or four weeks, I reckon. That would give me time to finish my work on the West Coast and the middle of April seems a pretty good time to be arriving. From what Lee says in his letter, they plan to have their celebration around then. It's not every day you're made a general, after all!'

'It's certainly not.' She slipped into bed beside him and nestled down in the crook of his arm. He smelt of his favourite brand of pine aftershave as his lips nuzzled a welcoming kiss into her hair. He was watching *Adam's Rib*, one of his favourite old movies, but no matter how fond she was herself of the Hepburn–Tracy partnership, she could concentrate on nothing but the thought of Lee in the uniform of an Israeli general.

Morning dawned fine but breezy – a typical mid-March day and she was up at eight to fix a quick breakfast for Art before he disappeared downtown on business. He was meeting with his Madison Avenue advertising company to supervise the publicity for his latest film. 'I won't be back for lunch, honey,' he warned her, as he downed his coffee on his feet. 'Why don't you give your Mom a call and have her over? There's bound to be a lot to talk about with both of you now planning trips abroad.'

'You know I might just do that!'

Maeve was delighted with the idea when Kitty called half an hour later. 'I'll be right over just as soon as I've finished with the hairdresser. I've an appointment for ten, but should be out just after eleven. That means I can be at your place around twelve.'

'Sounds fine by me.' She had just replaced the phone in its cradle with a satisfied smile when Danny made an appearance at the kitchen door. 'Well, well, you're up bright and early! Got any plans for today?'

He shuffled in, his feet still damp, in thonged Jesus sandals, and clad only in his underpants and a towelling robe. His hair

416

was still wet from the shower and he rubbed it with a small handtowel as he sat down at the table and poured himself a coffee. He had made up his mind during the night to see Shiralee again this morning, to try to talk some sense into her, but there was no way he was going to tell that to his mother. 'Naw, nothing special.'

'Will you be back for lunch? Your grandmother's coming over.'

He shook his head. 'I guess you two can find plenty to talk about without me being present. She'll be real surprised to hear you and Art are heading off to Israel so soon. Real bad timing that is!'

'I beg your pardon?'

'Bad timing, that's what it is – your Israeli visit clashing with the Irish trip.'

'How do you make that out?'

'Well, I'd have come with you, wouldn't I?'

'To Israel?'

'Yeah, why not? I've always fancied seeing the Middle East.'

Kitty put down her cup in the saucer and stared across at him. The thought of Danny accompanying them had never even entered her head. The thought appalled her. How on earth could she have coped seeing him with Lee – his own father – and neither of them knowing? 'Well now, I'm sure you would have been very welcome to come, honey. It's just a pity, like you say, that the plans for the two trips have come at the same time.'

Danny finished his coffee and stood up, tossing the damp towel on to a radiator. 'Well, don't make it sound so final. Nothing's decided yet, is it? I mean, maybe Gran doesn't plan on going over till the summer. Ask her today, will you? And, if that's the case, then I'll be able to join you. You don't mind, do you?'

Kitty's face had gone quite white. 'Of course not, dear. I don't mind in the least!'

It seemed an eternity to Kitty until her mother arrived. She almost pulled Maeve in through the front door of the apartment, causing the latter's high heels to slip precariously on the polished parquet flooring. 'Hey, steady on, Kathleen! I'm an old woman now, you know!'

'You'll never be that.' Kitty meant it too, she could never think of her mother as an old woman, and certainly nothing in Maeve's appearance this morning justified the label. Her grey hair was rinsed a fashionable bluish-silver and styled in a soft bouffant around her face, which was curiously unlined for a woman of her age. She had on a matching dark blue corded velvet coat and dress, and she slipped off the coat and handed it to her daughter as they made their way into the L-shaped dining-kitchen.

'I can't tell you how excited we all are at your news, Mom,' Kitty called as she hung the coat on the hallstand. 'And it's a really wonderful idea to take Danny. I'm sure it's just what he needs right now.' She walked through to join her and switched off the bubbling percolator. 'To be honest, the thought of him going through even another month in this depressed state would have been just too much to bear. Your trip has come at exactly the right time for us all.'

Maeve reached forward to take the proffered cup, her brow furrowing. 'Well now, Kitty, I think you may just have got hold of the wrong end of the stick. I never said any specific date to Danny when I spoke to him about the trip yesterday.'

'But – but there's nothing stopping you is there – from going right away, I mean?'

'I'm afraid there is, my dear. I was on the phone to Ireland last night and I'm afraid there are quite a few things stopping me from going right away.'

Kitty went quite cold as she stared across the table at her mother. 'Such as, may I ask?'

'Well, for a start, Katie's going into hospital for a gall bladder operation next week, so I wouldn't want to put upon her for at least a month or so. And we can't even go to my mother's in Dublin, for she's over in Ballinalea visiting your Great-Aunt Maud, who's been confined to bed with a slight stroke. I spoke to Amy on the phone last night and she said Mother's planning to come back in about six weeks, so it looks like I'll be planning my trip for around that time. You don't mind me going then, instead of now, do you?'

Kitty's lips froze in the semblance of a reassuring smile. 'No, of course not, Mom. Why ever should I?' She took a sip of her coffee and attempted to keep the conversation going in a cheerful mood. 'Whatever made you decide to take the plunge and go back, after all this time, anyway?'

Maeve looked down into her coffee cup as a faint blush crept up her neck to her carefully powdered cheeks. 'Would you laugh if I told you it was a dream?'

'A dream!'

Maeve nodded, looking slightly abashed at her confession. 'Yes, I've had it quite a few times recently. I dreamt that Dermot had died without me ever having the chance to say goodbye . . .' Her voice trailed off and to her embarrassment tears sprang to her eyes.

'He – he meant a lot to you – the priest?'

Maeve avoided her eyes – they were so like his, so heart-breakingly like his at times. 'He was . . . he is a good man, Kitty . . . The best . . .'

'Has he been ill recently?'

Maeve shook her head. 'Not really, that's the silly part of it all. Oh, he's had his share of illnesses over the years – TB and the like, but he's been keeping fine of late, so I believe.'

Kitty forced a smile as she lifted her coffee cup. 'You're afraid it's that old Irish second sight, aren't you?'

Maeve sighed and gave a mirthless laugh. 'Let's just say, in going over there at long last, I'm hedging my bets . . . It'll be strange though, seeing all those people I haven't seen in half a century. Can you imagine what it'll be like? What are the first words you say to someone you haven't seen for a whole lifetime?'

Kitty's hand froze with the cup halfway to her lips, as her thoughts raced forwards to that first meeting in Israel only a few short weeks away. 'I really can't imagine, Mom, and that's the truth!'

As his mother and grandmother finished their coffee, Danny was entering Giacopazzi's Coffee Shop on West 42nd Street. He could not bear to return to Sol's apartment, feeling as if he had irreparably contaminated it in making love to Shiralee there – by making his friend's wife pregnant under his own roof.

Shiralee was already there, sitting in a corner booth at the far end of the long room. She gave no indication of having seen him as he walked quickly down the aisle towards her. She had obviously been there for some time for there was an empty coffee cup on the table in front of her and a pile of cigarette stubs in the ashtray.

'Two coffees, please, and a couple of Danishes,' he called across to the waiter who was wiping the table in the booth next of them.

'I hope one of those Danishes wasn't for me – I'll vomit it right up!'

'Well, how's that for a pleasant little greeting!' Danny wedged himself into the bench seat opposite. 'I'm not exactly well up on expectant mothers, but I would have figured it's a bit early in the proceedings to be suffering morning sickness.'

'Not for me it isn't.'

He sighed and reached into his jacket pocket for his cigarettes. This meeting wasn't going to be easy, he could see that. 'Want one?'

She took one and he lit it, then lit one for himself, as she said quickly, 'I haven't got long. I told Sol I was just going out for some shopping.'

'I hope that's all you told him.'

Shiralee grimaced and blew a thin stream of smoke into the air. 'I haven't told him about the baby yet, if that's what you're getting at. I trust I'll have your support when I do that.'

'Like hell you will!' Danny glared across the table. 'That's what I've come to tell you, Shiralee. I won't be here to dance to your tune at all very soon. I'm going abroad.'

'Abroad?' She almost shouted the word, as the waiter appeared with their order. She waited until he had left before continuing, through gritted teeth, 'And just where are you running off to, may I ask?'

'You may ask, but I don't have to tell you . . . I thought you should know that I'm going, though. I just ain't gonna be around, Shirl, so whatever you decide about the baby, you're on your own.'

'You mean you'll walk out on your responsibilities – just like that!'

He looked around in embarrassment as her voice rang out above the canned music. 'I may be a low-down bum, but I haven't quite reached that depth yet! If you really intend going through with it and having this kid, then I'll see you're all right.'

'And just what is that supposed to mean?'

'It means I've got the money – my grandmother saw to that when I was born – and the kid will be well taken care of.'

Her eyes narrowed, as she drew deeply on the cigarette. 'How much does "well taken care of" mean?'

'We'll let an attorney decide that.'

Shiralee sat back in her seat and regarded him scathingly through a cloud of smoke. 'You really mean it, don't you, Danny? You really want me to get rid of this baby. There's no way you'll stand by me when I have it.'

'There's no way I'll stand by and let Sol be destroyed by seeing you have my child.'

'But you'd destroy that child!'

He flicked his ash in the general direction of the ashtray and regarded her coolly across the table. 'Quit the melodrama, Shirl. You're not exactly Mother Earth. You're using this pregnancy for your own ends. Why you didn't just have the guts to say to Sol it was all over, I'll never know.'

'Because I loved you, that's why.'

'Crap. You never loved me – you used me and actually thought I'd be fool enough to fall for it. But even I'm not that much of a fool. Name your price, Shirl, and I'll pay it – but just don't ask me to be part of prolonging this charade.' He reached into the breast pocket of his denim jacket and pulled out a piece of paper and handed it across to her. 'That's my folks' lawyer's name and address. I'll tell him to expect a call from you.'

She took the paper and slipped it into her handbag without looking at it, as Danny rose from the table and began to head for the door.

'Hey, lover boy, you forgot something!' Shiralee's irate voice assailed his ears as a Danish pastry came flying through the air past his right ear, to be followed by the second which landed at the feet of the astonished waiter.

Danny picked up the remains of the two cakes and placed them on the waiter's empty tray, along with a five-dollar bill. 'Sorry about that, Mac. I guess the little lady's lost her appetite.'

Chapter 46

Kitty fumbled in her handbag and removed her sunglasses as the plane circled in the brilliant azure sky above Lod Airport. Twenty minutes – that was about all it would be until she was face to face with Lee again. Art was convinced he would be at the airport to meet them. She glanced across at Danny in the seat opposite. Never in her wildest dreams could she have imagined a meeting like this: a father and son meeting for the first time, both oblivious of their relationship. She sighed deeply and leaned back in the seat and closed her eyes. Her deception weighed heavily on her heart.

'Tired?' Art mistook the sigh for travel fatigue and she did not enlighten him.

'A little. I'll perk up once we land, though.'

It took ten minutes for the plane to touch down and a further twenty for them to get through the formalities of Israeli customs and passport control. 'I told you you should never have grown that beard,' Kitty hissed at Danny, as he was picked out for a complete baggage search. He looked like the archetypal terrorist now, with his shoulder-length red hair and beard. She wondered what Lee would make of him, and somehow it mattered very much.

'There's Rose and Ruth! Look Kitty, over there!'

Art's excited shout made her turn and stare in the direction of his pointing finger. At the other side of the barrier, about sixty feet away, a middle-aged woman in a multi-coloured kaftan stood next to a startlingly beautiful young woman in jeans and a T-shirt. Rose raised her right hand and gave a hearty wave, then said something to the girl, who raised hers.

Art took Kitty's arm as they crossed the marble tiles to greet them. 'Rose, my dear! And Ruth ... Well, well, well ... Haven't you turned into quite a young lady!'

'Not in those clothes, she hasn't!' Rose quipped, as grandfather and granddaughter embraced. 'Kitty, my dear, how marvellous to meet you again at last!'

The two women hugged, then Kitty introduced her son to Rose and Ruth. A curious foreboding ran through her as the two young people shook hands. Danny, she knew from long experience, was not averse to feminine charms and Ruth had to be one of the most attractive young women she had ever set eyes on.

'I'm sorry Ged can't be here,' Rose said, as they made their way to the waiting car. 'He did hope to get a few days off to join us for the party tomorrow night at least, but you know the army . . .'

'Does he plan on making it his career?' Kitty asked.

'Heavens no! He reckons the time spent on military service is quite long enough!'

'He's not overly impressed by his father's exalted rank then, I take it?'

Rose laughed. 'You could say that. Although, to be honest, he was real proud of the part Lee played in the war last year.'

'Ged wasn't in it himself, was he?' It was Danny who cut in, curious to know if the young man he regarded as his Israeli opposite number in the family had also actually taken part in armed combat.

'No, thank God! He just missed it by weeks, but was called up straight afterwards in July. Some of his best friends weren't quite so lucky, though. He knew quite a few who didn't come back.' Rose's relief at what she considered her son's good fortune in missing the war was obvious on her face, as she opened the car doors and got into the driver's seat. Art took the front seat alongside her, leaving Kitty to get into the back with Danny and Ruth.

The Finkelsteins' single-storey, ranch-style house was on the outskirts of the city, in the northern, wealthier part of Tel Aviv, and stood back at the end of a long drive shaded by eucalyptus trees. Kitty glanced curiously at the poker-worked sign, 'Ein Gev', on the main gate, and Rose commented, 'It's a far cry from the kibbutz where we began life out here,' in reply to her murmurs of approval, as the car slid to a halt in front of the main door.

'But it hasn't made you any happier, has it? This can never

424

compare to Ein Gev,' Ruth insisted. It was the first time she had spoken since leaving the airport.

'Ruthie is a real kibbutznik,' Rose declared, throwing a smile at her daughter in the back seat, as she pulled on the handbrake and switched off the ignition. 'She works on one not far from here as a children's nurse and can't wait to get back and away from all this bourgeois decadence!'

'You are staying for the party though, aren't you, Ruth? It's not every young lady whose father is made a general.' It was her grandfather who spoke, and Ruth threw him a dazzling smile.

'Of course, Grandpa. But I reckon there will be more than enough people to congratulate Daddy tomorrow night. I doubt very much if I'd even be missed!'

Art looked reproving. 'Come on now, I'm sure that's not the case! Your father would be real put out . . . Anyway, where is that no-good son of mine? I half expected him to be at the airport to meet us.'

Rose sighed as she held the door open for Kitty to get out. 'Being a general seems to be a twenty-four-hour occupation these days. I swear I saw more of him in the early years when he was part of the Haganah!'

'What's the Haganah?' Danny looked enquiringly at Ruth, as they got out of the car, into the bright spring sunshine.

'It was the old underground military arm of Israel before it became a state. Daddy was a leading member.' It was impossible to disguise the pride in her voice.

'You mean it was the Jewish equivalent of the IRA?' Danny looked impressed, but now it was Ruth's turn to look confused.

'Whatever's the IRA?'

Art laughed aloud as the two young people stared at one another. 'I guess you young folks have quite a lot of learning to do about each other's respective homelands!'

'Not really,' Ruth said, with an emphatic shake of her head. 'I bet I know as much as any New York kid about American history.'

'So you might, young lady, but I wasn't referring to the States. I meant Ireland — that's where the Donovans come from. And I bet you know precious little about that!'

Ruth gave a shrug of her shoulders. She hated admitting defeat in anything. 'I can always learn. Care to teach me?'

The question was directed at Danny, whose face broke into a smile. 'Sure – why not? Where is your father anyway? I'd sure like to discuss a few things with him, too.'

Ruth glanced across at her mother, who gave a long-suffering sigh. 'He should've been here today but got called away last night. But he *has* promised faithfully to be back by tomorrow at the latest. You know he's really looking forward to it – and especially to seeing you again, Kitty – and Danny. He told me so before he left!'

Kitty managed a strained smile. 'That's real nice to know, Rose. I'm sure both Danny and I are looking forward to meeting him.'

Ruth showed them to their respective rooms where there was time for a leisurely shower and a rest before supper. Art showered first and was waiting on the bed for her to return dripping and squeaky clean from the cubicle in the far corner of the room. 'Come here, Kitty Donovan!' That old light was in his eyes again and she pretended not to have heard as she walked to the dressing table and began towel-drying her hair. She glanced at his reflection in the glass and her lips broke into a broad smile as he raised a finger and beckoned her towards him.

It was almost three months since they had made love. When he was in the middle of making a movie he seemed to need to preserve all his energies for that, but now it was over . . . Well, that was a different matter entirely.

They made love slowly, tenderly, on the white cotton sheet. After so many years their bodies moved in perfect, effortless unison. The frantic passion of twenty years ago had made way for a gentler, more satisfying expression of their feelings for each other. 'Know what, Kitty Donovan, I've got an idea.' His voice was intimately soft in her ear.

She rolled over in the bend of his arm and ran her fingers through the thick mat of curling hair on his chest. 'I'm listening. Does it concern me?'

'Who else?'

'Well . . . ?'

426

'What do you say to us getting married?'

'Married!' She disentangled herself from his arms, to sit up on the bed and stare at him in astonishment — only to be pulled back down beside him.

'You heard!'

'When . . . ? How . . . ?'

'Right here in Israel — as soon as it can be arranged. What do you say, Kitty?'

Their eyes were less than a foot apart as she said softly, with a coy little smile, 'But this is so sudden, Art honey . . . Do you think we've known each other long enough?'

'No, I don't . . . If I knew you forever, Kitty, it would still not be long enough. I need all for ever to love you in . . .'

He reached out and touched her cheek, his hand sliding up round the back of her neck to bring her gently towards him. As their lips met and they rolled over on the mattress, her eyes were in direct line with the huge plate-glass window. The sound of laughter met her ears and through the venetian blinds she saw Danny and Ruth walking together at the bottom of the garden. To anyone who knew no better, they looked the perfect young couple. Danny had his arm slung casually around Ruth's shoulders, then slipping from his embrace, she started to run towards a hedge of magnolia bushes. She held out her hand and he took it, before they disappeared from view into the green of the shrubbery. Kitty shivered as a cold wave of foreboding swept through her and tears sprang to her eyes, hot, bitter tears for the deceit in which she had lived her life. A deceit that could only devastate those closest to her — those she loved the most.

'Hey, Kitty, honey . . . When two people decide to get married it's a time for celebration, not tears. Unless they're tears of happiness that is!' Feeling the dampness against his own skin, Art pulled himself up on the mattress and looked down at her in concern.

'Of course, Art, darling. Of course that's what they are!'

As his mother tried in vain to control her emotions, Danny glanced down at the young woman by his side. This was a bonus he had not bargained for on the trip to Israel. He had paid very little notice to the photographs that had arrived at yearly intervals from Tel Aviv and the one on the mantelpiece back home was at least three years out of date. In fact, he had not seen any more recent photographs since being drafted to Vietnam two years ago. Ruth had still been at college then, still a kid. But now . . .

She let go of his hand and ran on ahead of him through the shrubbery. The scent of the flowers seemed to waft over them in the still air, heightening his senses as he watched her dart between the luxuriant foliage. She had a light, easy grace and long, waist-length dark hair that contrasted dramatically with her almost boyish figure. His eyes were riveted to her as she turned to throw him another of her dazzling smiles. 'Fancy a swim?'

'What?'

'A swim, do you fancy one?' She stood, hands on hips, smiling across at him, in front of a thick wall of greenery.

'Sure . . . But where?'

With a toss of her head, she pushed the trailing foliage apart to reveal a sparkling glint of blue water.

'You've got a pool!' Danny followed her through the bushes to stare in delight at the rectangular, shimmering blue expanse of water, bordered on all four sides with ornamental, wrought-iron tables and chairs.

'It was a present from Grandpa. Mom and Dad do most of their entertaining out here,' Ruth announced. 'There is an easier way to get here, of course. We were just stupid enough to choose the wrong way in!' She turned to glance down at the sparkling water. 'I spend most of my time here when I'm at home. I've been waiting all day to get in there! Are you coming?'

He looked across at her, a slight sweat breaking on his upper lip beneath the red moustache. 'Sure . . . But I haven't unpacked yet.'

Amusement glinted in Ruth's dark eyes as they looked straight into his. 'What do you need to unpack for?'

'Well . . .' The little bitch was deliberately trying to embarrass him. 'Well, no reason . . .'

'Don't they go in for skinny-dipping in the States?' She was looking straight at him, daring him to refuse.

'Sure they do! It's the only way to swim, ain't it?'

'After you!' She stepped back and stood, hands on hips once more, smiling at him, daring him to go first.

A pink flush crept up Danny's neck and cheeks beneath the red whiskers. He had never been put on the spot by a little bit of a girl like this before, but there was no way she would get the better of him. Looking her straight in the eyes, he began to peel off his clothes. First his denim jacket, then his T-shirt, then his jeans were cast aside, until he stood only in his red cotton underpants. She was still looking at him, a broad smile now forming on her lips as his fingers hooked into the elasticated sides of his remaining garment. His first impulse was to half turn from her before stepping out of them, but that would simply be a victory for the female of the species. There was no way he could allow that to happen.

'Here, bitch, catch!' With a flourish the pants were removed and thrown across the few feet of space at her, before he ran down to the poolside and executed a perfect swallow dive into the water.

He had barely surfaced when a noise at the other end of the pool made him turn round to see Rose pulling a large white cloth off the longest of the tables to reveal a mouth-watering spread of salad dishes. 'Why, Danny, this is a novel arrival! Did Ruth tell you supper's ready and we're all eating out here tonight? Your folks will be down in a couple of seconds. I've just called them.'

Thank God, she was too busy with what she was doing to realise his predicament. He turned back in consternation to where he had left Ruth, but she had already vanished, along with his clothes. 'All right, Miss Smarty-pants,' he hissed, under his breath. 'Just wait! Just you wait!'

They were seated across from each other at the supper table and incredibly, in the few minutes she had had to change, Ruth had been transformed from the boyish figure in T-shirt and jeans, to an elegant young woman in an off-the-shoulder, wraparound dress of crimson silk. Her long mane of hair was swept to one side and hung, dark and gleaming, over her bare shoulders. She looked the picture of perfect innocence and decorum and he wondered if she had any idea of the embarrassment he had suffered in making the dash back into the house completely naked, in the odd minute that Rose's back was turned. He had been certain he would run straight into his mother and Art, but thankfully that wasn't the case. It did not, however, stop him from wanting to murder the young woman in front of him.

It was half-way through the meal when he first felt the toe of the high-heeled sandal find its way beneath the bottom of his Levis. At first he thought it was simply an accident – that he had had his feet spread too far across the narrow space beneath the table. But when it happened a second time and then a third, each time the toe working its way further up his shin, he could only take a deep breath and contemplate on what the rest of the night might bring.

But it was Rose who proved the catalyst and not her daughter, for they had just reached the coffee stage when she turned to Ruth and said lightly, 'Ruthie, dear, I'm sure Danny would rather have a beer. Why don't you two young folks go and help yourself to what's in the icebox and take a walk around the gardens? It's a lovely night, it seems a pity for you to waste it in sitting here yacking with us oldies.'

Kitty's cheeks paled as she looked from one to the other. 'Oh, I'm sure Danny would just as rather stay right here and join in the chat, wouldn't you honey? There'll be plenty of time for sightseeing around the garden in the morning.'

But it was too late. Ruth had already stood up and was holding out her hand across the table. To his mother's dismay Danny got up out of his chair and took it, and the two went off, hand in hand, into the gathering dusk.

Kitty looked across at Art, only to find him smiling indulgently. 'They sure make a good-looking couple, don't they, honey?'

She could only nod mutely as she downed her drink in one long gulp. She was going to need a few more of these before the night was through . . .

Chapter 47

'Do you know we're only half a mile from the sea here?' Ruth turned to Danny as they skirted the far edge of the swimming pool.

He had an almost uncontrollable urge to throw her in – to get his own back for the trick she had played on him earlier in the evening. 'So?'

'So I've never had that swim yet.'

'There's a pool right there. What's stopping you?'

She shrugged and glanced back at the others still sitting at the far end, as a coy smile broke on her lips. 'They might not approve.'

'You mean you only swim in the altogether?'

'Not always. But I much prefer it. Don't you?' She lowered her lashes as she looked at him, her lips parting slightly as she waited for his answer.

He had met her type before, he decided. Every high-school class had them – the guys had a name for them too, but he was still too much of a gentleman to use it on her, despite the provocation. 'Whatever turns you on, kid!'

A sudden anger flamed in her eyes. 'Less of that if you don't mind! I'm no kid, Mister High-and-Mighty War Veteran! I've had to face bullets and bombs, too, you know. It was no picnic living on a kibbutz less than a mile from the border when the war broke out last June!'

'I thought your mother said you worked not far from here.'

'That's now. Dad insisted I move after Becky, an American girl I worked with, got her leg blown off by a mortar.'

Danny's eyebrows rose slightly as they continued their walk towards the drive. 'I bet you weren't too happy about that – your old man laying down the law, I mean. You don't strike me as the type who likes being bossed around.'

'Too true! In fact, I regard it as an ungodly cheek – especially after what he let my mother go through when they first arrived out here. See that sign there?' She indicated towards the house sign on the gate. 'Ein Gev was the kibbutz where they started life when they arrived out here after the war. At least, Mom lived there with Ged and me — Daddy was away most of the time working for the Haganah. It couldn't have been much fun with a couple of tiny kids, when the worst of the fighting broke out between us and the Arabs after the Israeli state was proclaimed.'

She paused and turned to look at him, as if to check she had his full attention. 'The worst attack occurred on Mom's twenty-sixth birthday — 10th June 1948 — and every man, woman and child able to fire a gun had to do just that.' She gave a wry laugh. 'Ged says it's his first memory — firing at the Syrians, but since he was only two, and I can barely remember it myself, I take that with a mighty big pinch of salt!'

They continued to walk in silence for several minutes and, as they neared the sea, a light breeze came eddying off the moonlit water. She walked a few feet in front of him and the wind pressed the silk of her robe even closer around her lithe figure. He had never met anyone quite like her before; there was something mercurial about her. He felt if he was to reach out and touch her she would suddenly vanish.

'This is where I usually come,' she called behind her, pointing to a clump of stunted palm trees that seemed to skirt the very edge of the water. 'It's too far out for tourists, and the locals don't use the beach here at this time of night.'

He did not answer, but merely stood there looking at her. It was as if they were going through some elaborate routine, a courtship dance almost, where she was the main protagonist. But this time there was to be no playing games; she had already tested him on that one. He could feel his pulse quicken, nevertheless. There was an electricity in the air — a chemistry between them that was almost tangible, and brought the skin of his arms out in gooseflesh as their eyes met and held.

He stood quite still, his eyes locked with hers, as very slowly she began to unwrap the silk robe around her body, to reveal a totally naked form that gleamed a silver-white in the bright moonlight. His breath caught in his throat and from the ghost of a smile that flickered at the edges of her lips, he knew she was well aware of the effect she was having on him. Her hair fell forward over the small, firm breasts as she carefully folded the robe and laid it on the ground, then turned and walked slowly towards the water's edge.

For a moment he was totally dumbstruck. It was no more than he had been expecting, but it shocked him nevertheless. And the knowledge that she had this ability to shock him disturbed him deeply. His whole body was covered with a film of nervous perspiration as his hands tugged at the buttons of his sports shirt. It landed on the dry sand beside her robe, then his trousers joined it, followed by his underpants and sandals. He glanced down at his body and did not like what he saw. His skin was startlingly white, his upper torso covered with tiny amber freckles, as if someone had flicked a paint brush at him, and the whole was covered in a golden down of fine hairs. But more embarrassing than that, the effect she was having on him was there for all to see – for *her* to see. Was there to be no end to his mortification tonight?

At first he attempted to emulate her and walk sedately into the water, feigning a calmness that he did not feel, but after a few steps the evidence of his desire proved too embarrassing a handicap and he began to run. But she was not watching him, anyway. She was at least twenty yards out into the Mediterranean and doing a slow crawl away from the shore.

Taking a deep breath, he waded into the black water and broke into a crawl himself. He wondered whether he was expected to join her, then decided against it. But after almost five minutes of being ignored, he called out, 'Hey, Ruth, you had enough yet?'

She swam back towards him, stopping about ten feet away. The water lapped around her shoulders, which gleamed in the moonlight, as she squeezed the water from her hair and tossed it back behind her head. She was tantalisingly close, almost within touching distance, but not quite. 'Something wrong? Aren't you enjoying it?' There was a faintly mocking smile hovering round the corners of her lips as she spoke.

'Sure I am.' He was on the defensive once again and they both knew it.

'Well, there's no point in lying on the beach back there. It's a bit late in the day for getting a suntan. Unless you had something else in mind?' She bent her head to one side as she smiled across at him.

The little bitch was at it again! But he could only take so much . . . He took a deep breath and made a dive towards her. His fingers reached her arm, but she succeeded in slipping his grasp and, with a peal of laughter, made a dash for the shore. She moved like lightning up the beach, grabbing at her waiting robe before he was half-way across the sand. She had it wound around her soaking form before he had even reached his clothes.

'You're a bitch, you know that, Ruth Finkelstein! A regular little bitch!' A mixture of anger and frustration burned within him as he scrambled into his pants, acutely aware of her eyes on his every move.

'No I'm not,' she said defiantly. 'All I did was suggest we go for a swim. We do it all the time on the kibbutz – girls and boys alike. We have done since we were kids. It's different here, you know. It's not like the States. We're not all hung up on sex like you Yanks!'

'So who's hung up?' He glared at her as he pulled a comb through his soaking hair.

'You are. I could tell by the way you looked at me when we first met.'

'I don't believe this . . . I *do not* believe this!'

'Deny it, then. Go on, say I don't appeal to you?' Her chin tilted defiantly as her eyes challenged him, then she started to walk slowly across the sand towards him. She stopped less than a foot away and lifted her face to his.

He could feel his pulse quicken, as she looked up at him. Her eyes seemed enormously large and luminous in the moonlight, her wet lashes forming a spiky dark frieze around the dark, gleaming orbs, as they held his gaze. 'What is it you want, Ruth? What is it you want, for God's sake?'

Her lips crinkled into a broad smile. 'Just a bit of fun, Danny, that's all.'

His arm reached out and grabbed hers. 'You're a silly little bitch. Do you know that? I ain't one of those kids from the kibbutz that you're used to playing around with, you know.

I'm too old for that kind of crap. You're playing with fire, Ruth, and kids who do that get burned!'

She wrenched herself free and jerked round, staring out to sea. 'I've told you before, I'm not a kid. And I'm not the silly little bitch you think I am. I'm no little innocent, Danny Donovan, if that's what you think!'

'Oh, so you're no virgin. What a surprise!'

She glared at him. 'Scoff if you like! You men are all the same!'

'Do I detect a hint of bitterness there? It couldn't just be that you're on the rebound, could it? And I'm the first poor sucker you've had a chance to bounce off? . . . Who was he, Ruth? Was he married, was that it?' He made a move towards her, but she fought him off.

'Keep your sympathy! I don't need it.'

'I didn't offer it.'

The breeze from the sea was chill now on her damp skin, and she shivered. 'What is it you want of me?'

It was his turn to smile now. 'I think I just asked that same question a few minutes ago.'

He put out his hand and she looked at it for a moment, then took it, and they walked slowly back up the beach. When they finally reached the garden of Ein Gev there was no one in sight, but music and laughter were coming from behind the closed blinds of the lounge window. There was a small gazebo at the far end of the pool and Danny gestured towards it. 'Fancy sitting down for a while before we call it a day?'

She nodded and they walked hand in hand into its carved wood interior. A pile of candy-striped beanbags lay on the floor and they sat down side by side. Her hair was still wet and he reached out and smoothed a soaking strand back from her cheek. 'You were right, you know – what you said back there about me fancying you. But I doubt if you'd have bothered to mention it if the feeling hadn't been mutual.'

She looked at him in astonishment, then began to laugh. 'You could be right, who knows?' she said softly. 'But on that cue, I reckon it's time I said good night!'

He held on to her arm as she attempted to rise. 'Don't go, Ruth . . . Not now . . .'

435

She shook her head. 'I'm not ready, Danny – not for that kind of relationship.'

'You'd have made love to me, though, wouldn't you – out there on the beach?' His voice was harsher now.

She shook her head, then nodded. 'Maybe . . . I don't know . . . It could've happened, I guess. But that would've been different . . . It would've been a purely physical thing. Free love, isn't that all the rage in the West just now?'

'Yes, except it's never free – and it's never love.' His voice was bitter as his thoughts flew back to Shiralee. 'It always has to be paid for, Ruth, in one way or another. And I think you know that better than anyone.'

A sigh shuddered through her. He was speaking the truth and he was right, and she *did* know that better than anyone. Amos Liebel had taught her that. But he was now back in his apartment on the Jaffa waterfront with his wife and two small boys . . . 'I – I think it might be best if we didn't see too much of each other alone in future.'

She stood up and walked to the doorway, leaning back against it as she looked down at him. 'I'll go back to the kibbutz straight after the party tomorrow . . .'

He got up to join her and his voice was husky, almost harsh, as he looked down at her. 'You'll be running away, Ruth. You know that, don't you?'

She nodded bleakly, unable to meet his eyes. 'Don't make things difficult for me, Danny,' she said softly. 'Don't let's complicate our lives by doing or saying anything silly . . . Things we might regret later.'

'Things like making love?'

She shook her head. 'Things like falling in love.'

He watched her as she ran back down the path towards the house and disappeared in through the back door. 'Jeez . . . !' His fist crashed into the wooden upright of the door in frustration.

He reached inside his trouser pocket for his cigarettes and lit one, filling his lungs with the white smoke. He could feel his heart beating beneath the damp cotton of his shirt. This was the last thing on earth he had wanted, or expected, when he flew out here with his mother and Art. He had quite enough problems with Shiralee at the moment. It was the last thing his mind wanted, he thought bitterly. But his body was still telling him quite the opposite.

It was ten minutes before he joined the others in the house. His mother, Art and Rose were all seated in the lounge, talking quietly over a drink, as he came in, but there was no sign of Ruth.

'Has Ruthie gone to bed, Danny?' Rose enquired, from the depths of a leather armchair, and he nodded. 'Do you fancy a drink yourself?'

'No, thanks all the same. I guess I'll just turn in, too. It's been a long day.'

Kitty gave a strained smile in response to his goodnight wave. She had heard running feet pass the lounge door a few minutes earlier and knew it must be Ruth. What on earth had happened out there tonight? She glanced across at Art, but he was totally oblivious to the turmoil within her. She wished with all her heart that she could confide in him, but it was impossible. To admit the truth now would be like setting off an emotional bombshell in the household. She wished she had never agreed to come in the first place. It had been a crazy idea. And bringing Danny had been doubly so. 'I – I think I'll turn in, too, honey, if you don't mind.'

She leaned over and touched Art's knee, then got up from her chair and smiled her apologies at Rose. 'It was a lovely supper, Rose. I'm sure I'll sleep like a log after it!'

'Sleep the sleep of the just, honey. You do that every night,' Art smiled. 'I wish I could say the same, then I wouldn't have to pay through the nose for all those pills it takes to guarantee a little shut-eye!'

The sleep of the just ... The words rang ironically in her head as she went out and closed the door quietly behind her.

Chapter 48

'Honey, you look fantastic!' Art's eyes registered his approval as Kitty turned critically in front of the dressing-table mirror in her new evening gown.

'Mmm, thank you, kind sir.' At five hundred dollars it had seemed like an enormous extravagance at the time, but she had no regrets now. Around the swathed bodice, the white chiffon clung to her body like a second skin and the flowing skirt whispered seductively around her ankles as she moved.

'Come here!' She obeyed his command, winding her arms around his neck as his eyes smiled down into hers. 'Got used to the idea of becoming Mrs Finlay yet?'

For a split second her smile froze. The words, so innocently spoken, triggered a distant echo in her mind of similar words spoken a very long time ago . . . spoken by the man she knew was already waiting downstairs to meet her. She had heard his car drive up half an hour before and, although she had not dared to go to the window, Art had confirmed that his son had arrived home.

'When do you reckon we should make the announcement – right at the beginning, or half-way through the evening?'

'You – you intend telling everyone tonight?' Somehow the thought had never occurred to her.

'You bet your sweet life I do!'

She untangled herself from his arms and took a last look in the mirror, fiddling nervously with a kiss curl at the side of her cheek. 'It – it's up to you, honey. I really don't mind when you tell them.'

'Your enthusiasm for the idea knows no bounds!' He grinned across at her as he held out his arm for her to take. 'I can see getting you to the altar may prove no easy matter.'

She squeezed the dark-blue velvet of his sleeve. He knew better than that.

Music and voices greeted them from the end of the passage

as they emerged from their room and Kitty clung tightly to Art's arm as they passed through the open door of the lounge. It was packed with people and beyond the open french windows the patio area around the pool was equally crowded. She spotted Danny and Ruth at the far end by the gazebo, but gave it little thought. Right now her mind was on a much more pressing subject.

'I can't see him, can you?' Art's eyes narrowed as he looked around him. 'But it's almost impossible to recognise your own reflection in a crowd like this!'

'Pop!' The masculine voice from their right gave Kitty no time to reply, as the tall figure strode across the room towards them.

'Lee – you old son of a gun!' Art dashed forwards to embrace his son, whose eyes looked over his father's left shoulder straight at Kitty.

Her heart turned a somersault beneath the swathed chiffon. The hair was greyer, it was true, but the eyes – those incredible dark brown eyes – had not changed at all. The whole room and everyone in it faded to a multi-coloured blur as she stood rooted to the spot.

'Lee, you know all about Kitty . . . And I know you two actually met each other at some point during the war . . . The Second World War, I mean. I reckon I've got to qualify the word "war" now, after that skirmish you took part in against the Arabs last year!'

Lee reached out and took her hand, his touch making her catch her breath, as he said softly, 'Yes, that's true. We did know each other a long time ago . . . How are you, Kitty?'

'Fine . . . I'm real fine, Lee, thank you.' Her mouth and throat had gone dry and the words came out with difficulty. 'But I knew Rose too, Art, remember.' Her protest sounded needlessly defensive as she turned to her husband-to-be.

'Sure you did, honey . . . By the way, speaking of our hostess, I want to have a quick word with Rose. Why don't you look after Kitty for me for a moment, Lee, while I go look for your lady wife? I'm sure you two have lots to catch up on.'

Kitty put out a restraining hand – the last thing she wanted was to be left alone with Lee so early in the evening, but Art had already disappeared into the throng of guests.

'A respectful son must always obey his father.' Lee smiled down at her, as he offered his arm. 'How about a wander in the garden – it's a lot less crowded than in here.'

'Only marginally so, by the looks of it,' she murmured as they headed for the open glass doors. There seemed to be people everywhere. They wandered slowly around the front of the house which was amazingly bereft of guests, although the driveway was totally blocked with parked cars.

'You certainly have a lot of friends,' she commented drily, as they paused by a bower of bougainvillaea. Its scent hung heavy in the air as she leaned back against it and looked up at him. She had expected him to be in uniform and was vaguely disappointed to find him in merely a white tuxedo and charcoal slacks.

'Acquaintances,' he corrected. 'Real friends, like lovers, are pretty thin on the ground for the majority of us in this life, Kitty. That's something you learn to your cost as you get older.'

A pink flush crept up her cheek. Was he deliberately trying to embarrass her? 'I take it congratulations are in order,' she said, quickly changing the subject. 'I hear you're a general now. I somehow never imagined you as a military man.'

'It doesn't surprise me,' he said quietly. 'We never seemed to quite get through to one another in the things that really mattered, did we?'

She felt a hot flush break out on her skin, but pointedly ignored the remark and passed on, curious to fill in on the missing years. 'How and when did it come about? What on earth made you give up science?'

He tensed visibly, although he attempted to make light of her question. 'Let's just say, after Hiroshima and Nagasaki my enthusiasm for nuclear physics took a nosedive, and leave it at that, huh?'

'That still doesn't answer my question.'

He shrugged. 'There's not a great deal to tell. After the war I was asked by Ben-Gurion to join the Haganah Mission in the States. He was adamant that the destiny of Palestine would ultimately depend on the outcome of an armed struggle, first

440

against the British and then the Arabs, and succeeded in persuading around forty of us to help him prepare for it.' He gave a short laugh. 'Not that it took much persuading! Ya'akov Dori, who went on to become the Chief of Staff of our defence forces out here, was appointed to head the New York mission and we were each designated our own particular task. They set up various units – "Land and Labour for Palestine" and that sort of thing.'

'And what was yours?' She was genuinely interested now – eager to know what he had been doing when she was coming to terms with her new role as a single parent.

'Well, it wasn't all above board, I have to admit that,' he said, with a wry grin. 'The Truman administration had placed an embargo on the export of war materials and on recruiting guys to serve as soldiers in foreign countries, but there are ways and means around just about everything if you're determined enough. And we were. We succeeded in recruiting plenty of American volunteers and sent them to Palestine as agricultural labourers, which the government had no objection to at all, then when they got over here they simply stepped into the jobs of the Jewish guys already here – so releasing them for the armed forces.'

'Clever!'

'We thought so. But, I must admit, the exporting of actual war materials wasn't quite such a dawdle.' He gave a quiet laugh, as his mind travelled back over the years. 'I remember the job we had managing to purchase aircraft . . . After one heck of a negotiation we succeeded in buying four Constellations from army surplus for fifteen thousand dollars each and felt very proud of ourselves, but only one ended up ever reaching Palestine. One was cannibalised for spare parts, two were impounded by the FBI for the US Treasury, and the fourth only reached Israel when the fighting was over. But that one, I'm proud to say, became the foundation of El Al, our national airline!'

She was impressed. 'I bet you could write a book about it all.'

'I could, but no one would ever believe it. Anyhow, I'm much too busy living my life to waste time sitting down and putting it on paper. This has been the most incredible twenty years you could imagine, Kitty. To be in at the birth of a new nation is privilege enough – but to be in at the birth of Israel – to actually be a part of what our forefathers have only dreamt of for generations!' His eyes were gleaming now, gleaming with that same light she had seen so often, so many years ago. 'I tried to tell you once – to explain to you what it meant to me. But you wouldn't listen. I just couldn't seem to get through to you.'

'That's just not true! In fact, our trouble was we got through to each other only too well!'

Her sudden outburst brought a quiet smile to his face. 'You mean it wasn't all physical passion?' Even in the moonlight he could detect the quick surge of colour to her cheeks. His hand reached out to touch the flaming skin. 'You're still a very beautiful woman, Kitty Donovan.'

'And I am also practically your mother-in-law! Art and I are getting married, Lee. Soon.' She drew back from his touch and glanced up to see the effect of her words.

'It doesn't shock me, if that's what you intended. You've been living together for as long as Rose and I have been married, just about, haven't you?' She turned from him, taken aback by the accusatory tone in his voice, but his hand gripped her upper arm, whirling her back to face him. 'It could have been me, you know, Kitty. If you'd played your cards right and not been so damned bolshie all the time about my desire to go to Palestine, then it could have been me you got and not the old man.'

'Don't call him that! Don't you dare refer to your father in that way! He's more of a real man than you'll ever be!'

'Oh ho, so it's "let's draw comparisons time", is it? Do you expect me to retaliate? Is that my cue to say that Rose fulfilled me in ways you never did? If that's so, then it's true – for she gave me the one thing you never would. She gave me the one thing I desired more than any other – a son for Israel!'

'Really, Lee? You're absolutely sure of that, are you? Even big-shot generals can be pretty dumb at times, you know!' The moment the words were uttered she regretted them.

'What the hell is that supposed to mean?'

Unable to bear the close scrutiny of his gaze, and no longer able to trust her own tongue, she swung round to make her way back to the house, then pulled up sharply before she could attempt a single step. Danny and Ruth were on their way across the lawn towards them.

Lee's hand gripped her arm. 'What the hell did you mean by that last remark, Kitty? Tell me!'

But it was already too late. 'Daddy, I want you to meet Danny!'

'It's an honour to meet you, sir.' Danny held out his hand to the older man, while Ruth stood smiling at his side.

Although they were no longer touching, Kitty could feel the tension in the man next to her, and the pain where his fingers had gripped her forearm remained as he extended his own hand to be shaken. 'The pleasure's mine . . . Danny.'

He had almost said 'son', but corrected himself in time. Kitty had never been more sure of anything.

'I'd no idea you were coming on the trip till Rose told me you were here,' Lee said. 'It's real nice you decided to tag along.'

'It's a belated birthday present,' Kitty cut in. 'Danny was twenty-three on the seventh of March.'

Danny threw her a puzzled look. It was the first time he had heard of it as that. He had already been given a new Rolex watch for his birthday to replace the one lost in Vietnam. But his mother was oblivious to the puzzlement caused by her white lie. Her eyes were fixed firmly on the face of the man by her side. A look of consternation had crossed Lee's features for a fleeting second. It had been noticed by no one but her. He had calculated nine months back from the beginning of March '45 to the summer of '44, she was certain of it. But within seconds the affable exterior had reasserted itself. 'Rose tells me you've been out in Vietnam and got pretty cut up into the bargain.'

'You never told me that!' Ruth turned accusingly to Danny. 'You never told me you were badly wounded.'

'It's a failing of the Donovans, I'm afraid, my dear,' Kitty cut in, with a quiet smile. 'The Irish cherish their secrets.' Her eyes

443

flicked across and caught Lee's, but there was no answering smile on his lips.

All four walked back together towards the house to be met by Art and Rose on the patio. 'Here you all are,' Rose called. 'We're ready for the toasts now. The champagne is all on ice and just begging to be let out of the bottles. Pop, would you do the honours and uncork them?'

Art was only too happy to oblige and opened the bottle handed to him from the silver ice-bucket as, on a signal from Rose, two white-coated waiters moved silently among the assembled guests dispensing countless crystal flutes filled with the sparkling wine.

After all those assembled had been served, Lee was forced to endure the eulogies delivered to himself by both Rose and two of his fellow generals. Then it was Art's turn. Taking Kitty by the arm, he raised his hand to silence the murmur of conversation that had broken out and declared, 'Friends old and new, my beloved family . . . It is with enormous pleasure that I can inform you that the lovely lady who has brought me more happiness than an old critter like me deserves over the past twenty years has finally agreed to make our relationship permanent! I give you my darling Kitty – the future Mrs Arthur Finlay.'

An enormous cheer went up from the surrounding company, but among all the smiling faces that surrounded her, Kitty was acutely aware that one face was not smiling. Their eyes met for a fleeting second, then Lee turned and walked quickly back into the house.

'Come on, honey, you haven't touched that champers yet!' Art said reprovingly. 'I've already downed my second.'

To please him she swallowed the whole glass in one go, then reached for another. Tonight should be one of the happiest of her life, but it was turning out to be one of the worst. By the time Lee reappeared she had already emptied four champagne flutes and the party was at last beginning to take on a decidedly rosy glow.

'May I borrow your intended, Pop? I haven't had the pleasure of a dance with my future mother-in-law yet.' Lee's hand was already on Kitty's arm before the words were spoken.

'Sure, son. Be my guest!'

She preceded him on to the stone-flagged terrace where a selection of Beatles hits was filling the night air from strategically placed loudspeakers. His hands slid around her waist, forcing her to twine hers around his neck as they began to move in slow, swaying time to the music. 'You've got to tell me, you know, Kitty,' he said softly. 'I'll ask Danny myself otherwise.'

'You can't!' She pulled back from him aghast.

'I darn well can – and will!'

'You can't!' she protested, her eyes darting around her anxiously for possible eavesdroppers. 'He – he doesn't know himself.'

'What?' He stared down at her in disbelief. 'You mean he's reached this age and you've never told him who his father is? I don't believe it. I just don't believe it!'

She shrugged her shoulders in a helpless gesture. 'It's true,' she said miserably. 'Believe me, it's true.'

'Has he never asked?'

'He did – quite a few times when he was younger, but he saw how it upset me and – well, I guess he just stopped asking . . . He knows I never married and I think he believes his father was killed in the war and it's just too painful for me to talk about.'

'Convenient – but despicable on your part!'

They had stopped dancing now and were standing facing each other against the wall of the house. 'You don't understand,' she began. 'How – how could I possibly tell him – tell anyone – once I was living with Art?'

The complication of his father had obviously not occurred to him and he drew in his breath sharply. 'But why didn't you tell me? For God's sake, why didn't you tell me?'

'I might have,' she confessed truthfully, 'if I hadn't met Rose and learned very soon afterwards that she was not only your wife but was also expecting your child.'

'You must have hated me then.'

She shook her head. 'No, Lee, I've never hated you. I could never do that.'

He reached out and touched her hair. 'I loved you, Kitty

445

Donovan, do you know that? I loved you so much that I also hated you. I hated you for making me love you so much and forcing me to choose between my beloved Palestine and you.'

'It was always no contest, Lee,' she said softly. 'No woman – especially a *shiksa* like me – could expect to compete with a thousand years of longing . . . a longing that you have been privileged to see fulfilled in your own lifetime.'

'You're a very special person, Kitty. You know that, don't you? And I will always love you.'

'And I will always love you.' Her voice was barely audible as she whispered the words. But they were true and had always been true, she knew that now.

'I want to reach out – to touch you – to kiss you one last time.' His voice had a husky intensity that sent a bolt of quicksilver down her spine.

She pressed herself against the rough wall of the house as she shook her head wildly. There were too many people – far too many people. And what of Rose and Art? His eyes were burning down into hers, their message unmistakable. It was wrong – so very wrong, but her heart was racing uncontrollably now. His lips were only inches from hers as she attempted to maintain her hold on reality.

Sensing her anxiety, but aware that the feelings that were stirring within him were reciprocated in full, his hand reached out and took hers and drew her round the corner of the house, so that they were partially hidden in the thick foliage of a magnolia tree. Then his fingers froze in hers as he took a sudden sharp intake of breath. 'God, no . . . !' His eyes were staring at something, or someone, just beyond her left shoulder.

She turned to follow his gaze, then a gasp of horror escaped her own lips. Danny and Ruth were less than twenty feet away locked in an embrace.

Chapter 49

'God Almighty, that's all we need!' Lee stared in horror at the sight of his daughter in the arms of his son. He turned to Kitty. 'You've got to stop this! Jesus,.Kitty, you've got to tell him!'

Panic welled within her. What a mess she had made of everything – what a ghastly mess. 'He – he might not believe me.'

'What do you mean he might not believe you? Of course he'll believe you. Why, in heaven's name, would you make a thing like that up?' There was real anger in his eyes as he stared down at her.

'But what of Art? What if he finds out?' She couldn't bear that, she really couldn't.

'Then it's just too bad, isn't it? That's something you should have thought of a long time ago. It's been the most ludicrous deception, keeping this to yourself for all this time.'

Now it was her turn to get angry. 'I didn't do it for myself, you know! There were the feelings of other people to think about – Rose, your wife, for a start! The pair of you had always made such a big deal out of having a son for Israel, what if I'd just come along with my little bombshell and dropped Danny right into your arms, while she was still pregnant? How would she have liked that? And how would you have come to terms with the fact that your firstborn son wasn't called Gedaliah Finkelstein, but was a half-Irish *mischling* with red hair and freckles, called Daniel Kieran Charles Donovan?'

A nerve twitched at the edge of his jaw as he clenched his teeth and looked back over his shoulder in the direction of Danny and Ruth. He could not answer that question. He could not even bear to think about it right now. 'Look,' he said, through gritted teeth. 'We'd better get back to the others or they'll suspect something's up. It's useless trying to tell Danny now – Ruth would only get curious and there's no way I want her involved.'

'What do you mean – there's no way you want her involved? You mean I've got to tell Danny, but you've no intention of telling her?'

'Got it in one! This is a big enough mess as it is, Kitty, for God's sake. Why involve more people than need be?'

'You mean, it's to remain a secret between you, me and Danny?' Somehow, despite her determination not to hurt Art, it didn't seem right. It seemed as if he was denying his own child, refusing to admit his paternity to those others who really mattered.

'You got a better idea?'

She shook her head. She hadn't and he knew it.

'Come on, then. Let's get back.' He forced a smile to his lips, as they headed for the dance area. 'Fancy a twist?'

An old Chubby Checker record was blasting out of the loudspeakers, but she had never felt less like dancing. 'I fancy a drink,' she said faintly. 'A good strong one!'

Danny and Ruth watched them make their way back through the dancers to the table with the drinks. 'They seemed to be having a pretty heavy discussion about something,' Ruth mused, as she partially disentangled herself from his arms.

'Maybe your old man doesn't fancy her as a mother-in-law,' Danny joked. 'It is kinda weird having one who's younger than you, you've gotta admit!'

Ruth nodded. 'I guess it must have been funny for you having to think of Grandpa as your father – with him so old and all.'

'Not really – he was always just Art . . . A real nice guy who was sometimes there and sometimes not. It also made me one up on the other kids when I was younger, having a stepfather who was a big shot in the movies!'

'I've never been to Hollywood,' Ruth said wistfully. 'In fact, I've never been to the States even.'

'You'd really like to go, huh?'

'I'd like to go everywhere and do everything! There's a whole world out there that I've never even glimpsed. I even envy you going on to Ireland after this!'

He was silent for a moment, then said quietly, 'Is that true, Ruth? Do you really envy me going to Ireland?'

'Of course I do! Particularly after all you've told me about the IRA and all that! I've always envied my parents for all the excitement they had when they were young and fighting for the freedom of their country – and to think that you're leaving here soon to go to a country where the youth are still doing exactly that!' She clutched hold of his arm. 'Take me with you, Danny! Take me with you – please!'

He looked at her quietly for a second, then a smile broke on his lips. 'If that's what you really want, Ruth honey, then yes – yes, I will!'

She flew back into his arms, covering his face with kisses. 'I'll drive out in the morning and tell them on the kibbutz that I'm taking a few weeks' leave of absence!'

'Your folks won't mind?'

'Mind? Why on earth should they? You're practically family, after all!'

For the remainder of the evening Kitty could not relax. Her eyes followed Danny in every move he made. What she would do if he and Ruth disappeared, she really couldn't imagine. But, thankfully, as the night wore on he seemed content to remain within sight, spending most of the time on the dance floor with Ruth. By one o'clock in the morning, however, Kitty had had enough of her seemingly endless vigil. Her legs would support her no longer and she turned to Art, who was himself slumped half-asleep in a chair. 'I think I'll turn in for the night, honey. Coming?'

He grunted, then after she had repeated the question, he nodded wearily. 'Sounds like a pretty good idea to me!' He pulled himself out of the chair. 'I'll go and say goodnight to Rose. You can maybe do the same to Lee for me – he's right over there.'

Kitty turned in the direction he had indicated, to see Lee leaning against the open door of the french windows. He had almost disappeared from view for most of the night after their conversation and his face still wore that numbed, set look it had when she left him a few hours ago. He raised his eyebrows as she approached, but did not smile. 'I – I just came over to say goodnight,' she began.

'I'd hardly call it that, would you?'

'Please don't make it any harder for me, Lee,' she sighed. 'Don't think I don't feel as badly about this as you do.'

'How can you?' he scoffed. 'How can you possibly? You've had over twenty years to come to terms with this – I've had less than three hours! And, to crown it all, not only do I learn I have another son, but he's been making love to my daughter for half the goddam night!'

'That's not true and you know it!' She glanced back towards the dance floor, where Danny and Ruth, arms entwined around each other's necks, were slowly swaying to the strains of 'Release Me'. 'Exaggeration isn't going to help anyone at a time like this.'

'You will admit they're a mite too friendly for brother and sister, though?'

'Half-brother and sister.' But the correction seemed pointless. He was speaking the truth.

'You will tell him tonight, won't you, Kitty? For all we know they could have made plans for first thing in the morning – then, God help us, anything could happen!'

He was worried, desperately worried, and she could only nod her head bleakly. 'If it means staying awake half the night, I'll tell him.'

Art fell asleep as soon as his head hit the pillow, leaving Kitty lying listening to the sound of the music far into the night. On and on it went. Esther and Abi Ofarim's 'Cinderella Rockefella' was blasting forth at just after three when, finally, she could bear it no longer and got out of bed. Prising the blinds apart with her fingers, she stared out into the darkness. Almost all the guests had left, leaving only a handful scattered around the pool, with only one couple actually dancing. But there was no sign of either Danny or Ruth. A cold shiver ran through her.

Quickly, she snatched her satin wrap-around from the chair by the bed and put it on, knotting the belt tightly around her waist, as she slipped her bare feet into the matching mules.

There was nothing else for it, she would have to go looking for them.

The house seemed deathly quiet compared to the din still going on outside as she padded down the passage. Ruth's and Danny's bedroom doors were both closed, with no light showing beneath either. With a bit of luck they were both in bed and fast asleep by now. It would do no harm to check, though, she decided. And, after all, she had promised Lee she would speak to Danny before morning. She paused by his door and tried the handle. It was locked, but a faint noise came from inside. She tried again, rattling it harder this time, as she called softly, 'Danny, are you awake? I want to talk to you.'

The noise inside had ceased but there was no response to her question, so she tried once again, knocking this time on the panelled wood. 'Danny – open up! I want to talk to you. It's very important.'

At last there was movement from within – a shuffling sound that ended with the gruff question, 'What do you want?' from behind the closed door.

'I want you to open this door. I've got to talk to you, Danny, it's important – very important!'

'It can wait till morning.'

'No it can't!' she insisted, her hand rattling the handle again. 'I've got to talk to you now.'

There was a moment's silence, then his voice muttered, 'I'll come out. You wait there.'

She stood back from the door, tapping the rubber sole of her mule on the tiled floor, as he fiddled with the key in the lock. Then finally he appeared, barefoot and clad only in his trousers. 'What is it, Mom? Don't tell me it couldn't wait till morning!'

'No, Danny, I'm afraid it couldn't. But we can't talk out here.' She made to push past him to enter the bedroom, but he shot out an arm to stop her. 'Let me in, Danny, for heaven's sake. You don't expect me to talk out here in the passage, do you?' It was hard to keep the irritability from her voice and she was not to be deterred. Ducking out of reach of his restraining arm, she switched on the bedroom light, then gave a gasp of horror. 'Ruth!'

'Kitty . . .' She was sitting on the edge of the bed, fully

451

clothed, but looking distinctly dishevelled. She got up immediately, blinking her eyes against the bright light. 'I – I'll see you in the morning, Danny,' she said softly, as she backed out of the room, squeezing past them in the open doorway.

He watched her disappear back down the passage in the direction of her own room, then turned in anger to his mother. 'Well, thank you very much! That was the height of diplomacy, I must say!'

'That, Danny, was exactly why I had to talk to you . . . Why it was so important I saw you right away.'

'What's that supposed to mean?' He slammed the door shut behind him and reached for a cigarette from a pack on the bedside cabinet. 'What has Ruth got to do with anything?'

Suddenly words left her and she stared at him blankly. This was not how she had imagined it would be at all. Not only was she having to divulge the identity of his father, but she was having to tell him that the young woman he was falling in love with was his half-sister.

'Well, out with it! What was so darned important that you had to come barging in here like this?'

'Let's sit down, honey.' She put out a hand and gestured towards the edge of the mattress.

They sat down side by side as she struggled to find the right words. 'Danny . . . this is not going to be easy for me. In fact, it's the hardest thing I've ever had to do in my entire life.'

He stared at her, a deep furrow etched between his brows. There could be only one subject as important as this. 'It's not about my old man, is it? You haven't chosen now of all times to tell me about *him*?' This was really going too far. She must have drunk far more than he realised.

'Yes, Danny, that's exactly what I want to talk about.'

'And what if I don't want to know?'

'Then I'll tell you anyway, to stop you making a fool of yourself.'

'Come again?'

'You heard. You mustn't see her any more, Danny – not like that. You mustn't see Ruth . . .'

'Why the hell not?' He jumped up from the bed and glared down at her. This was really going too far. 'What's the hell's

452

wrong with her? Are you telling me she's got the dreaded plague or something? Or VD maybe – is that it? Are you telling me she's got the clap? If so, then forget it, Ma – I've had worse things to deal with than that in Nam!'

She shook her head in despair as she got up and faced him. 'No, honey, I'm not trying to tell you that. I'm trying to tell you that she's your sister. Ruthie is your half-sister, Danny . . . God help me, Lee Finkelstein is your father!'

Chapter 50

'You're kidding!'

'I only wish I were.'

Danny sat down on the edge of the bed and stared blankly at the far wall. 'Lee Finkelstein my father . . .' He shook his head, as if to negate the truth of what he had just heard. 'How . . . ? Why, Mom, for God's sake, why?'

'It was all a long time ago, Danny. A very long time ago.'

His head continued to shake, as he ran his fingers through his hair. 'And all this time I never guessed – I really never guessed!'

'There was no reason why you should.'

He gave a mirthless laugh. 'You know, when I was a kid I went through a period of believing that Art was my father, but I couldn't figure out why the pair of you didn't tell me. It never crossed my mind that he could have been my goddam grandfather! Why the hell didn't he ever act like one? Why treat me any differently from the other two?'

She could not bear the accusatory look in his eyes and sat down on the edge of the mattress beside him and stared at her hands. 'Because he doesn't know, Danny. I've never told him, that's why.'

'You've never told him!' He looked across at her in disbelief. 'Then who the hell *did* you tell?'

'Nobody,' she answered truthfully. 'I never told a single soul – until tonight.'

He took a deep drag on his cigarette. 'And just who has been privileged to receive this information tonight, apart from me, may I ask?'

'Just your father. Just Lee.'

His jaw clenched and for the very first time she could see a likeness between father and son. 'Because of Ruth.'

She nodded mutely, her fingers fiddling nervously with a cameo ring on her left middle finger. 'Yes, because of Ruth,'

454

she admitted finally. 'I – I don't know quite how far things have gone between the two of you . . .'

He got up from the bed and stubbed the cigarette out roughly in a nearby ashtray. 'Let's put it this way, Mother *dear* – if you had been a few minutes later tonight in knocking at that door to tell me this, I wouldn't be standing here taking it as calmly as I am now!'

A wave of relief swept through her. 'You mean . . .'

'I mean things were moving pretty damned fast between us and if you'd waited till morning to tell me this . . . Well, I guess I wouldn't have been responsible for my actions! In fact, right now I feel pretty goddam sick about it . . . She's coming to Ireland with me, you know that?'

'No! You'll have to stop her.'

'How? Tell her if she comes we'll have to have separate bedrooms because she's my goddam sister?'

Kitty looked up at him in despair. 'She can't go with you, Danny – she mustn't. Can't you see that? It's only asking for trouble, knowing how you feel about each other. Ruth's still a child in many ways compared to you. It's up to you to be the strong one.'

'How? Tell me that. What do I say? Sorry, kid, I just don't fancy you any more – I'd rather go by myself.' He shook his head. 'She just wouldn't wear it – and can you blame her?'

'She must. Your father doesn't want her to know the truth.'

'Don't call him that! Don't you ever call him that! Lee Finkelstein's not my father – he's Ruth's, and her brother's. He's the man who went to bed with you before I was born, that's all. And that's all he'll ever be to me.' He paused, a small pulse throbbing at the base of his neck as he clenched and unclenched his fists. 'And why the hell doesn't he want her to know the truth? He's not ashamed of having fathered me, is he?'

'Don't be silly, Danny. Of course he's not. There's no question of that. He simply feels there will be too many people hurt by the disclosure, that's all . . . His wife, for a start, and Art . . .'

'Art doesn't know, you say?'

She shook her head. She wasn't proud of the admission.

'Will you tell him?'

'I don't know. I really don't know.'

'What a mess! What a goddam mess!' He kicked at a sandal that was lying on the floor at his feet. It skidded across the tiles and bounced off the leg of the dressing table. He continued to stare at it for a moment, then said quietly, 'There's nothing for it, is there? I'll have to leave tonight.'

'Leave?' She looked up at him in alarm. 'But where will you go?'

'Ireland, of course. Being a few weeks early won't make that much difference. If I can't find a relative to put me up, I'll simply stay in an hotel. I take it they have such conveniences for travellers over there?'

She managed a strained smile. 'What on earth will I say to the others?'

'That's up to you, Mother dear, isn't it? As the saying goes – you got us into this mess, and you can darned well get us out of it!' She watched in silence as he pulled his case down from the top of the wardrobe and started throwing clothes into it. 'It's just as well I'm a lazy bum, isn't it? Otherwise I'd have had all this unpacked by now and would have given myself double the work!'

'How will you get to the airport?'

He gestured with his head to the phone by the bed. 'I take it this country's not so goddamn new you're not able to call a cab in the middle of the night?'

'Oh.' A feeling of panic set in. She should say something meaningful – tell him this wasn't how she planned it; that she had intended telling him everything one day; that she hadn't meant it ever to happen like this. 'Will you write?'

He shrugged. 'I guess so. Don't count on it, though. I never was much good at keeping in touch.'

She wanted to reach out and touch him, cradle him in her arms as she used to do whenever he hurt himself as a little boy. And he was hurt now. Oh God, how he was hurt now. And she was responsible. She was the one who had caused it. 'I – I'd better be getting back to bed . . .' Her voice was barely audible.

'Yeah, I guess you had.' He did not look at her, but continued to throw things into the case.

She walked to the door and stood with her hand on the door knob. 'Take care, Danny aroon . . .' She had heard her mother use that word when she was a small child and though she had no idea what it meant, she knew it was something special. It was the nearest she had ever come to telling him she loved him; to telling him that she was sorry. So very, very sorry.

'Goodbye . . . Mom.'

Art was still fast asleep, snoring in their double bed, when she got back to their room, so he was not aware of the hot, bitter tears that flowed down her cheeks as she stood for over an hour at the window, gazing out on what was left of the night. Danny's taxi arrived after a wait of about half an hour, and although she did not see him get into it, she listened to the soft purring of the engine as it idled at the gate for a minute or so. He must have gone down there to wait for it, for no one came up the drive to ring the bell, and for that she was grateful.

When morning came her eyes were still swollen with crying and she spent a good half-hour bathing them with cold water before Art woke up. How she was going to explain Danny's absence she had really no idea. And by the time they were ready to go down to breakfast she felt almost sick with nerves.

Happily, there was only Rose in the kitchen. It was not a household that gathered for communal meals. 'I guess it'll be almost afternoon before we see anything of the young ones,' she smiled as she dished out the cereals and orange juice. 'They were almost the last to turn in after the party.'

Kitty made an appropriate noise as she took her place at the table opposite Art. 'This is lovely, Rose.'

'Help yourselves to toast and honey – and there's coffee in that pot over there.' Rose sat down herself and looked enquiringly at her father-in-law. 'Got any plans for this morning?'

'I just might at that!' A light came to his eye as he stole a glance at Kitty. 'I reckon the bride-to-be needs a proper engagement ring, don't you, Rose?'

'Oh no, honey, really!' Kitty cut in. 'That's not necessary!'

'Maybe not to you it ain't, but it sure is to me!' He laid down

457

his spoon and took her hand across the table. 'Kitty, honey, these two days are gonna be just about the happiest of my life and I want them to be just the same for you!'

Borrowing Rose's car, they headed downtown directly after breakfast and made for the best jeweller on Ben Yehuda Street. Art took her unusually quiet mood for tiredness after the party, combined with delayed jet lag. 'Don't worry, honey,' he murmured, as the dapper little man behind the counter brought out the third tray of gems for their inspection, 'one of these little rocks is guaranteed to cheer any female up!'

She looked at them dully, trying them on mechanically as Art picked out whichever ones took his particular fancy. They finally settled on a diamond cluster with an enormous emerald set in the centre. 'I guess I should've known. It couldn't be anything else but an emerald, could it?' he said with an indulgent smile as they left the shop arm in arm. 'Not with a name like Kitty Donovan!'

They had lunch in town, only returning to Ein Gev at a little after three, to be met at the door by a white-faced Rose. She looked quite clearly uncomfortable as she led them through into the lounge and set about pouring stiff drinks all round. Ruth was sitting in the far corner with a fixed expression on her face as she stared out of the window. She gave no indication of having noticed Kitty's and her grandfather's arrival, nor the drink that her mother placed in her hand.

'Has something happened, Rose? Has Lee, or Ged, had an accident?' It was Art who broke the tension first.

Rose did not answer, but reached inside the pocket of her skirt and took out a scrap of paper. She walked across and laid it in Kitty's lap. 'We just don't know what to make of it – none of us.'

Kitty stared down at the familiar scrawl:

Dear All – Have taken off for Ireland. Just couldn't wait to see the land of my fathers,

Danny

The land of my fathers – Kitty mentally re-read the words. He had chosen that phrase with care all right. She handed it across to Art without a word.

'What in tarnation is this supposed to mean?' He looked up from the note at Kitty, then at Rose. Both women shrugged their shoulders. 'What about you, Ruth honey? What do you make of it?'

Instead of receiving an answer, he could only watch in astonishment as his granddaughter got up from her chair and ran from the room.

'She's taking it particularly hard,' Rose said. 'She seems to have become real fond of Danny in the short while you've been here . . . I guess she thought the feeling was mutual. She told me this morning they were making plans to go to Ireland together . . . Then this . . . What on earth do you make of it, Kitty? You know him best.'

'I blame Vietnam!' Art cut in. 'Isn't that right, honey? He's never been the same since he got back from that place. None of them are. If you ask me the government should pay for every last one of them to see a shrink when they get back to this side. It would do them a darn sight more good than a truckload of those Purple Hearts they dish out!'

Kitty nodded, relief flooding her face. 'Yes, that's it,' she said softly. 'He's never been the same since he got back from there.'

Rose took a deep breath and shook her head. 'Well, if it's any consolation, I took the liberty of phoning the airport and he's on his way to Ireland all right. In fact, his flight left almost four hours ago.' She glanced down at Kitty, slightly embarrassed at the admission. 'I wouldn't have interfered, but Ruth was all set to drive to the airport herself when she read the note.'

Kitty managed a strained smile. 'That was kind of you, Rose. I'm sorry about this, really I am.'

'Goodness, don't apologise to me! I've had kids too, remember! And don't think we haven't had our fair share of problems with our two. In fact, Ruth moved her things out of here, lock, stock and barrel, only last month when we discovered that the guy she was seeing was married. She wasn't too amused at hearing it from us and not from him, I can tell you. But, as Lee said at the time, you often have to protect them from themselves, don't you?'

Kitty nodded automatically, but knew that Danny would be the last person to agree with that. As far as he was concerned, it was parents kids needed protection from — no one else!

Chapter 51

Danny stood in the telephone booth at Belfast Airport and flicked through the dog-eared pages of the directory. The fact that he had flown here without having a note of his Great-Aunt Katie's address reflected his confusion. Once he had got to Lod Airport last night he had even considered catching the next plane back to New York, but the thought of explaining his sudden arrival to his grandmother had proved sufficient deterrent. And quite apart from that, there was the thought of Shiralee. The last he had heard from the family lawyer was that she had submitted a claim for twenty thousand dollars once the baby was born, a thousand dollars a year in child maintenance, plus an interim payment of five thousand dollars for medical expenses throughout the pregnancy. But it wasn't the money that bothered him, it was the fact that she had probably told Sol by now. There was no way he was in a fit state emotionally to handle that.

His finger ran down the column of Muldoons. Thankfully there weren't that many, and only one Eamon Muldoon. 'Twenty-seven Hamilton Street,' he murmured, scribbling the address along the top of a day-old copy of the *New York Times* he had bought at London Airport a couple of hours ago. He should really call first; it would be the height of bad manners just to turn up on their doorstep, but somehow he could not lift the phone. What if the voice at the other end was less than welcoming? What if there was no one at home? No, it would be easier just to take a taxi there and hope for the best.

It took him completely by surprise to find that the taxi driver he chose was personally acquainted with his aunt and uncle. 'So it's a relation of ould Eamon you are, is it?' the elderly man said, as he swung the cab out into the main road. 'You'll know his missus has been into hospital, then?'

'Yes – my grandmother did mention it. She's to have an operation, I believe.'

461

'She's had it!' the driver declared, relighting the dog-end of a cigarette from a lighter on the dashboard. 'Got out the other day, so she did. Deirdre lives two doors down from us on Nelson Street. You'll know Deirdre . . . ?'

Danny searched his mind for the last photograph he had seen of his Aunt Katie's eldest child. It must have been at least five years ago. She would in her middle to late forties by now. 'No – no, I've never met any of my Irish relatives before.'

'So it's your first time in Ireland, is it? Well, well . . . They'll be expecting you, though?'

Danny began to feel as if he'd been picked up by a remnant of the Spanish Inquisition. But maybe the guy was only trying to be friendly. 'Well, I'm a bit earlier than they expect, but I can always go to an hotel if they can't put me up.'

The man laughed and rubbed the greying stubble of his chin. 'Sure with all the relations the Muldoons have got in this city, I doubt very much if that'll be necessary! Deirdre herself has been known to take in the odd lodger, ye know. But that's only when her man takes it into his head to go walk-about over in England. He's at home just now though, but for how long, God only knows.'

Danny stared out of the window at the passing landscape. There was something unnerving in having a perfect stranger fill you in with details of your own family, and he was not quite sure how to respond. He lasped into silence for the next ten minutes, until finally the cab drew up in front of a neat semi-detached house.

'Here we are, then. That'll be twelve and six.'

'I beg your pardon?'

'Twelve shillings and sixpence,' the man said, articulating the words as he would to a child. 'The fare – it's twelve and six.'

Danny flushed. 'Of course!' He dug into the pocket of his jeans and extracted a crumpled pound note. 'Keep the change.'

'Well, thank you, son!' The hefty tip quite obviously found favour, for he insisted on carrying Danny's case up the short garden path to the front door. 'Remember me to your Uncle Eamon now. We joined the Pioneers together, so we did, but I reckon he's kept to his pledge a lot better than I have to mine!'

Danny's pulse quickened as he smiled his goodbye and the black hackney cab disappeared back down the road. The Pioneers – they must have been in some special unit of the IRA together! It was a new one on him, but no doubt he'd learn plenty more new facts about his grandfather's organisation before this visit was over.

The door was opened, in response to his ring, by a teenage girl in a red miniskirt and white polo-necked sweater. Her dark auburn hair was cut in a long fringe and hung in two straight curtains to just below her shoulders. She had a roundish, pretty face and was probably no more than about seventeen, he decided, as she looked suspiciously at the case by his feet. 'We're not needing anything, thank you.'

'Beg your pardon?'

The door was half shut in his face as the girl repeated her statement. 'Nothing today, thank you.'

Danny glanced down at his case, then back at her as a grin broke on his face. 'Now wait a bit – I'm not selling anything!'

'You American?' The door was opened slightly.

'I'm your cousin Danny.'

'Cousin Danny?' The girl repeated the words as if they belonged to some foreign tongue, then her brow wrinkled. 'You – you're not from New York, are you? You're no relation to the Donovans?'

'I'm Danny Donovan.'

'Holy Mary and Joseph!' Without a further word she disappeared back into the house, leaving him standing open-mouthed on the step. She had obviously gone for reinforcements and there was nothing for it but to wait and see what transpired next. Who exactly she was, he hadn't a clue, and could only surmise she was one of his great-aunt's grandchildren. That would make her a sort of second or third cousin, he wasn't sure which, but he wished fervently he had taken more notice of all those Irish family letters and photographs that had crossed the Atlantic over the years.

He had little time for reflection, for within a few minutes the door was flung wide open and an older version of the girl stood on the step in front of him. 'Marie tells me you're Danny Donovan.' The woman's eyes travelled from his bearded head, down over his denim jacket and jeans, to the canvas sneakers on his bare feet. She had a harder face than the young girl who now stood at her shoulder, but it was a hardness that he felt had come through hardship, not through a defect of character. She wore more make-up than the young woman, too, and her hair was dyed a raven black and piled on top of her head in a cone of back-combed coils. 'I'm Deirdre,' she said, in a peculiarly formal voice, as she extended her hand to be shaken, 'and this is my daughter Marie.'

They shook hands, then Danny leaned forward to do likewise with Marie, before picking up his case and following them in through the narrow hallway into the kitchen at the far end of the passage.

'You'll excuse the mess, but we weren't expecting visitors.' Deirdre gestured with her head at the pile of ironing waiting to be done on the small Formica table and the remnants of a lunchtime snack that lay on the side of the draining board by the sink. 'We don't live here, you see. I'm just popping over during the day to give Mam a hand. She's upstairs, still recovering from her operation. It's funny, she told me you and your grandmother were coming over in a month or so . . .'

Danny shifted uncomfortably. 'Yeah, that was the idea, but I'm afraid I've jumped the gun a bit.'

'Your grandmother's not arrived, then? It's only you?'

'It's only me.'

The two females looked at one another, then Marie said, 'Well, he'll just have to stay with us, won't he, Ma?'

Deirdre looked taken aback for a moment, then agreed. 'Yes, you'll just have to stay with us. Mam and Dad have got two spare rooms here now, but until she's on her feet again you'll be better off with us.'

Danny was truly embarrassed by now at the obvious upheaval he was causing. 'It's very kind of you, but there's really no need. I can perfectly well go to an hotel.'

'An hotel!' Deirdre exclaimed. 'Sure an' you'll do no such thing! The very idea! Marie run upstairs and see if your Granny's awake and let her know who's here, while I put the kettle back on. I take it a cup of tea will suit you fine, Danny?' She turned to the kitchen cabinet on the far wall. 'Or we

464

should have some instant coffee somewhere if you'd prefer that?'

'No, no – thank you. Tea would be just fine.' Moving his suitcase out of the way to let Marie squeeze past, he perched himself on the edge of a chair and reached inside his jacket pocket for his cigarettes. 'Smoke?'

It was a packet of Israeli cigarettes he had picked up at Lod Airport during the night and she looked down at it in curiosity. 'Are they Arabic?'

'Israeli,' he said, leaning across to light hers before lighting one for himself. 'I've just been out in Tel Aviv.'

Deirdre's brown eyes widened. 'Tel Aviv! My, my! I wouldn't even know how to spell it, let alone get there! Have you got friends out there?'

Danny shifted uncomfortably on the chair. The last thing he felt like doing was discussing the Finkelsteins. 'My Mom and stepfather are on holiday out there just now. I joined them for a couple of days, but decided to fly on here a bit earlier than I intended.'

Deirdre gave an uncomprehending shake of the head. 'I can't think what possessed you to go and do a daft thing like that for . . . Oh, it's not that we're not glad to see you and all – it's just that I wouldn't have thought Belfast has anything to compare with all that sun and sand they've got out there. Your mother's married to that Hollywood producer, isn't she?'

There was a undisguised hint of awe in her voice as she asked the question and Danny smiled. 'Yes, Art's in movies.'

Deirdre switched on the electric kettle and shook her head. 'It all seems a bit unreal to us over here – Hollywood and all that. I expect the likes of you is used to that type of thing, though – living next door to Paul Newman and all that kind of folk.'

He gave a short laugh. 'If I remember rightly, the Newmans don't live anywhere near LA for most of the year . . . And no, I'm not really all that blasé about it. I still get quite a kick out of going over to the West Coast. Our Beverly Hills house is real nice and the weather's better there than in New York.'

Deirdre was listening attentively. 'We collect all the American film magazines we can – you know, *Modern Screen* and

Photoplay and that type of thing, in case there are any articles on your Aunt Maud in them.'

'She's just about retired now, but her daughter Jayne's made a couple of films recently.'

Deirdre's face lit up. 'Oh, we know that! We've all seen them – at least most of us have. My eldest girl Elaine doesn't go in for that type of thing.' She looked slightly embarrassed for a moment, then added, 'She's at Queen's – the university here,' by way of explanation. 'You'll meet her tonight. She's due round with her dirty washing. Women's Lib doesn't stretch to doing your own yet!'

'Gran says to send Danny right up!' Marie appeared in the doorway and beckoned to Danny. 'She's in the room directly in front of you at the top of the stairs.'

He looked around at Deirdre. 'Do I go up on my own?'

'Sure and whyever not? You're hardly little Red Riding Hood and it's not the wolf we've got dressed in a winceyette nightie in the bed up there! 'Tis only me ould Mam.'

He grinned sheepishly and, after stubbing out his cigarette in the tin ashtray on the table, he squeezed past Marie, to climb the narrow stairs two at a time and knock gently on the closed bedroom door.

Katie was sitting up in bed, in a lacy woollen bed-jacket; a book lay open on the candlewick bedspread in front of her. She looked older, and much smaller and frailer than Danny had imagined, but her smile was welcoming, as she took off her reading glasses and put out her hand in greeting. 'Danny, my dear, this is a great surprise!'

He bent to kiss her cheek. 'I'm sorry to turn up out of the blue like this, Aunt Katie. I've told Deirdre I can go to an hotel. I really don't want to be any bother to anyone!'

'An hotel indeed! Who ever heard of such a thing! You'll stay right here with me!'

He looked uncomfortable as he sat down on the edge of the mattress at the foot of the bed. 'Actually Deirdre says I'm to stay with them – until you're up and about, at least.'

'Well that'll be soon enough and no mistake, for to tell the truth I'm fed up to the back teeth with being bossed about in me own home. She's a terrible woman, that one!' But her eyes were smiling as they glanced towards the open door. 'I take it your grandma's not with you?'

'No, in fact she doesn't know I'm here. She'll probably have a fit when she finds out.'

'Then let me tell her. We're on the phone, you know. We had to be with Eamon's job – although he's been retired these past three years.'

'He's out just now, I take it?'

'That he is. He takes a walk down to the bowling green most fine afternoons. He doesn't play much himself; he hurt his back in the Service and it plays him up from time to time, but he likes to have a crack with his old pals. But enough about us – how's your dear mother, how is Kitty these days?'

'She – she's fine. I was telling Deirdre, I left them out in Israel. She's out there with Art visiting his son – Lee Finkelstein.' His voice faltered on the name.

'The general! My, my! Sure and Maeve had told me all about him being made a general. A real hero, she says he was in that war they had out there last summer. What is it they're calling it now – the Six-Day War, or some such thing?'

Danny nodded. 'That's right. The media love to stick labels on things. I don't know much about it myself though, to tell the truth. I was still out in Nam when it was going on.'

'Nam?' Katie looked puzzled for a moment. 'Oh – Vietnam! Of course you were! Maeve's letters were full of nothing else at the time. You're her pride and joy, do you know that, Danny?'

He gave an embarrassed shrug. 'Oh, I don't know.'

'No, it's true! You're someone special and I know now that I've seen you in the flesh it's not just because of your name. No, it's not only because you're your grandfather's namesake – you're also his living incarnation, as sure as God, you're his spitting image!' She leaned forward in the bed and pointed with her glasses to a small mahogany dressing chest beneath the window. 'Open the top drawer, would you, and bring me out the box that's lying among the hankies in there.'

He obeyed her request and brought across a heart-shaped chocolate box and laid it in her lap. It smelt of the lavender sachet that had been lying in the drawer with the neat piles of white linen handkerchiefs.

She opened it carefully, as if this were a special ritual to be carried out with due reverence, and laid the lid down on the bedspread beside her. It was full of old photographs, many of them sepia coloured and of unfamiliar faces with stoical looking expressions. Her fingers rifled through them, finally extracting one and gazing down at it with a triumphant smile. 'Here we are. It's my proudest possession!'

She handed him across a picture of a young man in his early twenties who could have been himself in fancy dress, minus the long hair and beard. He was wearing what looked like working clothes, but had on an official-looking armband and had a bandoleer strapped to his chest. He was carrying a rifle in his right hand. 'It's your grandfather, Danny – the first Danny Donovan himself. It only came into my possession a few months ago,' Katie said. 'Old Mrs O'Malley whose husband had the photographer's shop over on York Street brought it round herself. She was clearing out after the old man died and came across it. Their son was a great friend of your grandfather's – Con, if I remember rightly, his name was. It seems the old man took pictures of both him and Danny before they set out that Easter Monday morning.'

'The morning of the Rising? This was taken the morning of the Rising?'

'It was. The photos the old man O'Malley took were the last to be taken of him and his friend Con, God rest their souls. She brought me Con's to look at too, and, to be honest, we had a wee bit of a cry together, for he was killed along with Connolly and Pearse and the others.'

'My grandfather survived the Rising though, didn't he?'

'That he did. And went on to do some sterling work for the cause before he was gunned down by some gun-happy Prod in the Galtee mountains.' She shook her head at the memory. ''Twas a sinful waste, so it was.'

He made to hand it back, but she waved it away. 'It's yours now, Danny. Take good care of it. It does my eyes good to see you here with us. Sure and it's as if he'd never gone – as if

Danny Donovan had never died in his country's cause! You believe in it too, don't you, son?'

'Of course I do.' He glanced down at the picture once more, then carefully placed it in the left-hand breast pocket of his denim jacket. 'Quite honestly, I can't wait to learn all there is to know – not only about my grandfather but about all those men who gave so much.'

'Not only men, Danny. Never think that. Women too have played their part – and are still playing it. Just wait till you meet Elaine. She'll put you right on everything you want to know on that account!'

'She's your granddaughter, isn't she?'

Katie sat back on the pillows with a satisfied smile. 'She's not only my granddaughter, Danny. She, and others like her, are our hope for the future. Like you can be. Like you must be if your name means anything at all to you. And it does, doesn't it, Danny boy?'

'Yes, Aunt Katie, it does.'

Chapter 52

'So you're our rich relation, are you?' The young woman took off her jacket and threw it over the back of a chair as she let her eyes roam critically over the young man in front of her.

'Elaine — really!' Deirdre, her mother, looked up askance from the frying pan, where she was pushing a dozen sausages around in the sizzling fat with a fork. 'That's no way to greet your cousin. Danny's come all the way from Israel to see us.'

'Israel? What were you doing out there — signing on as a mercenary for Moshe Dayan in their next war?'

He grinned. 'Nope, I've had a gutful of fighting other people's wars. Literally — I'll even show you the scars if you want me to!'

'Danny's not long back from Vietnam, Elaine, remember!'

'You'll be pretty well up on guerrilla warfare, then. But I can't say that it did you much good. The gooks, as you Yanks liked to call them, gave you a pretty good hiding — and it was no more than you deserved!'

'Elaine!' This time her mother had had quite enough. 'That'll be enough of that! Good God, girl, you're not in the door and you're on your soap box. Heaven only knows what kind of folk Danny'll think he's landed amongst!'

'Mighty interesting, if you ask me.' He threw a grin back in Elaine's direction. 'Are you always so hard-hitting?'

'Truthful, you mean. What are you doing here, anyway?' She sat down in the chair opposite him and began to butter herself a slice of bread.

He narrowed his eyes as he leaned back in his seat and looked across at her. Unlike her sister Marie, she had light-gold hair cut short like a boy's, which flew totally in the face of every fashionable trend of the moment, and her black sweater and blue jeans were not exactly the last word in high fashion either. Only in her make-up had she paid any heed to her appearance, for her grey-green eyes were outlined in black

470

eyeliner and the lashes were heavily mascaraed. There was a scattering of freckles across the bridge of her nose that her make-up had not succeeded in disguising. She was pretty rather than beautiful, he decided. Yes, Elaine Heaney was quite definitely pretty.

'Danny's come to visit us, Elaine,' her mother informed her. 'And we're all very glad to have him.'

Her daughter chewed thoughtfully on the bread and butter as she looked across at him. 'You crazy or something? What on earth makes you want to come to a place like this?'

'Ireland sounds a very romantic place from across the Atlantic.'

'Distance lends enchantment!'

'Your grandmother tells me you're the one to enrich my knowledge on the subject. Do I sit at your feet after tea?'

'I wouldn't advise that,' Marie cut in. 'They're as black as the ace of spades! Just take a look at them, Mammy. Are they not a disgusting sight?'

'Shut up, shrimp!' Elaine said, glaring round at her sister, who was slicing a fruit loaf by the draining board. 'If you'd been where I've been all afternoon, you'd be pretty damned mucky too!'

'And where have you been, may I ask?' Deirdre divided the sausages on to three plates and added a spoonful of potatoes and one of baked beans, before handing them out. 'Not that you've any intention of telling me, I've no doubt! If you spent half as much time on your studies, my girl, as you do playing toy soldiers, you might just end up with a decent degree, and a decent job at the end of all this!'

Elaine glared across at her. She had heard it all so many times before. 'Got any plans for tonight, Danny?'

'Well, no . . .'

'You can come out with me if you like.'

'And where might you be going, may I ask?' her mother intervened.

'You may ask – and I *may* tell you, if I've a mind to! Actually I was only intending going as far as Smokey's – that's the students' local café,' she informed Danny. 'We can call round to Des's on the way and see if he's thinking of going out.'

'Des?'

He thought he could detect a slight colouring beneath her freckles as she shrugged lightly and said, 'Oh, he's just a guy on the same course as me.'

'And what might that be?'

'Political science.'

'Need you have asked?' her mother cut in. 'She lives, eats and sleeps the subject just now.'

'Don't tell me you weren't the same when you were my age,' Elaine said indignantly, through a mouthful of sausage. 'According to Gran you were the worst of the lot!'

Deirdre sighed as she pressed the baked beans on to her fork. 'Well, that's as may be, but it hasn't got me very far, has it? A tiny two-up, two-down bit of a house and a husband who's more often out of work than he's in!'

'But that's the whole point, ma, can't you see? The reason you're still stuck here and Dad spends half his life over in England looking for work is because your generation never got off your backsides to do anything about it!'

'When I was your age, my girl, there was a world war on – don't forget that! We had a few more important things to think about here in Belfast than protesting about living conditions. Like surviving the bombs, for instance, and just staying alive!'

There was a moment's silence, then Elaine said quietly, 'Yes, well, things have changed since then. We've got our welfare state, for what it's worth, and now we want our civil rights.'

'Civil rights?' Danny queried.

'Yes. You know all about them in the States!'

'Sure we do. But they're for equal rights for the blacks. You haven't got a colour problem here. At least not that I've seen. I don't believe I've even seen a single black face since I've been here!'

'No – 'cause we're the niggers in this country! Us – the only true Irish. We're the niggers in our own land here in Northern Ireland!'

He shook his head. This was all getting quite beyond him.

'Don't you know?' Elaine said. 'Didn't you know that? Didn't you know the Catholic population is discriminated against in almost every field of civil rights you could mention – housing, jobs . . .'

'But who's doing this discriminating – the British?'

The three others round the table looked at each other then laughed. 'The Prods!' Marie informed him. 'In theory, we're all British here in Ulster.'

'She means the Protestants,' Deirdre explained. 'They're in the majority here in the North and hold all the reins of government, at both local and national level.'

'And they positively discriminate against the Catholics?' This was a bit hard to take. He looked across at Elaine. 'How can that be allowed in a democracy like Great Britain?'

'There, my dear Danny, you have just asked the 64,000 dollar question!' She leaned across to reach the tomato ketchup bottle and shook a large blob on to the edge of her plate. 'What was it you were doing at college, before you were drafted, anyway?'

'Accountancy and English.'

She nodded thoughtfully, as if it was exactly what she was expecting him to say. 'Of course – the almighty dollar . . .'

'I actually preferred majoring in English,' he interrupted, before she could go off on her high horse again. 'I did my thesis on T. S. Eliot. Know anything about him yourself?'

She thought for a moment. 'It's an anagram for toilets.'

'Elaine, really!' By this time her mother was getting quite hot under the collar at the impression her elder daughter must be making on their guest.

Had she but known, Danny was not in the least bit put out – merely intrigued. 'How about you, Marie?' He turned to the younger sister now carefully laying the slices of fruit loaf on to a plate. 'What's your favourite subject?'

'Oh, I wouldn't bother asking the shrimp,' Elaine said, swallowing a mouthful of sausage. 'She's bored by school. It's the simpler things in life she goes for – like men!'

Marie slammed the bread plate down on the table in front of them and looked despairingly at her mother. 'She's at it again, Mam! Say something, will you?'

But Deirdre could only shake her head and wish, for the

umpteenth time, she'd had the gumption twenty years ago to enter a convent like her best friend Eilis.

After tea Danny was shown into the spare room, which was the other front room on the lower floor of the house, on the opposite side of the small entrance hall to the sitting-room. It had been Elaine's room before she moved into a flat with several other students, and it was now let out to various lodgers. Happily, it was empty at the moment. 'Where do you sleep when you come home?' he asked, as she followed him in with his case.

'Oh, I bunk down upstairs in Marie's room.'

'Doesn't she mind?'

'She minds like hell, but has very little choice most of the time. We need the money this room can bring.'

He dumped the case on the bed and sat down beside it, letting his eyes roam over their surroundings. It showed very little sign of ever having been a girl's room. The faded wallpaper was a dingy buff colour, patterned with dusky-pink overblown tea roses. A garishly-coloured picture of the Madonna and Child hung over the tiled fireplace, the grate of which looked as though it had never seen a fire in years. The whole house had a damp, dingy feel to it which contrasted strongly with the vibrancy of its occupants. In fact, the whole place and life style contrasted dramatically with what he had been used to back home in the States. And, the worst thing was, he wasn't prepared for it. He wished his grandmother had warned him that the Donovan side of the family lived in what was to him such dire straits. With her deliberately avoiding talking about Ireland, and her people there, he had taken it for granted that the Donovans lived in much the same style as the Ballantine side of the family down in Dublin. The fact that they so obviously didn't made him feel unbearably guilty for having descended on them out of the blue like this and imposing himself on their hospitality.

'It's not exactly what you'll be used to back in the States,' Elaine said quietly, as if reading his thoughts.

He shrugged and attempted a reassuring smile. 'There wouldn't have been much point in coming if it had been exactly the same, would there? Half the fun of a holiday is discovering other ways of life.'

'Seeing how the other half live.' It was hard to keep the bitterness out of her voice.

'If you like.' There was no point in denying it. 'You know, Elaine, I really had no idea how things were over here . . . You know, that stuff you were telling me at tea-time. I guess it was kinda stupid of me, but I still had a romantic vision of Ireland – all Irishmen together up here fighting for the overthrow of British rule. This religious thing complicates the issue. I presume the Protestant majority don't want Home Rule?'

Elaine grinned. 'Sure and that's a lovely old-fashioned phrase, if ever there was one! But you're dead right they don't. And, to be honest, neither would I, the way things are in the South. The Prods are always shouting about "No Popery" and reckon if we were to be ruled by Dublin we'd be under the thumb of the Vatican – and they're right.'

'You mean you don't want to be ruled by Dublin?' This was all getting quite beyond him.

'I want a free, united, socialist Ireland – and when I say free, I mean free from the shackles of Rome as well as London.'

'Is that possible?'

'We think so.'

'We?'

She walked to the window and looked out into the grey drizzle of the evening. 'There are a few of us, from Queen's mainly, who believe it's possible.'

'How?'

'By direct action.'

A chill ran through him. 'Is that what your mother referred to as playing toy soldiers?'

Elaine gave a dismissive shrug. 'She scoffs, but she's with us really. She worries, that's all.'

'I'm not surprised. Terrorism is hardly the occupation for a well-brought-up young lady!'

Elaine turned to glare at him. 'One man's terrorist is another's freedom fighter, Danny. I'd have thought you'd have known that. I'd have thought Vietnam would have taught you that! No one – not Britain, not America – no one has the right to impose their will on another people. Only they have the right to decide what political path they will follow. How can we be terrorists in our own land?'

He made a helpless gesture with his hands. 'It's crazy, but these past couple of years I've spent in Nam, I might just as well have been on another planet. I've landed back in a world of revolution – student revolution all over the place. But, I must admit, it was the last thing I expected over here.'

'Oh, it's not just here. It's happening all over the place – in France, in Germany, in London even, young people are wakening up to the fact that this is a dirty unfair world.'

'And they're willing to use dirty, unfair methods to change it.'

'God, you're a bloody little reactionary! Just because you've had it so damned easy all your life – just because you happen to have been lucky enough to have been born on top of the heap, you don't give a shit for them down below! Your type make me sick, you know that, little rich boy? You make me sick!' Her eyes flamed as she glared across the few feet of space at him, then gathering in her cheeks, she spat out her distaste of him and his kind, before whirling round and making for the door.

The globule of saliva landed on the case lid and he stared down at it for a second before jumping to his feet. 'Hey, hang on a minute! You've got it all wrong!' He grabbed her by the arm and pulled her back into the room. 'I was just explaining, dammit, this is all new to me, Elaine. It's not that I disagree with anything you say – I just haven't really given it much thought in the past, that's all!'

She looked straight at him, her grey-green eyes examining his face for any sign of cant. But she found none. She had never met anyone quite like him before. Someone from so privileged a background that politics had never been a part of his life. Someone who could go half-way across the world to kill people of another race, without apparently any real thought as to why he was there. 'What *do* you believe in, Danny Donovan?'

He stared back at her. He had never been asked such a question before. Then suddenly the picture of his Aunt Katie lying in that little bedroom over on Hamilton Street came into his mind. 'Ireland,' he answered quietly. 'I believe in Ireland, Elaine.'

She looked at him sceptically for a moment, then shrugged, as if she thought she might as well give him the benefit of the doubt. 'You might be able to say that with a little more conviction before you leave here,' she said quietly. 'I'm going out now. Are you still coming?'

'Just try to stop me!'

Chapter 53

'Are you here for long, then?' Des Devlin accepted one of Danny's cigarettes and sat down again on the small stool by the brass fender of his mother's living-room. His grey eyes surveyed the other critically.

Danny shrugged as he sat back down in the corner of the horsehair sofa. 'It depends.'

'On what?'

'On how long they'll put up with me as much as anything!' he grinned, glancing across at Elaine, who merely looked non-committal. He had the distinct impression she was somehow ashamed of him here amongst her own kind. There were three other people in the room, apart from her and Des. A quiet, dark-haired girl, introduced as Tricia, in a black sweater and blue denim miniskirt, sat on a chair by the window, and glanced out through the flounced net every time he caught her eye. On high-backed chairs opposite the fireplace sat two young men, Gerry and Sean, the former red-haired and bearded like himself, but much taller and thinner; the other smaller and dark-haired, with a Zapata moustache and a nervous tic in his right eye. Mrs Devlin, Des's widowed mother, came and went at intervals, with liberal supplies of coffee and a sticky dark gingerbread, cut into well-buttered wedges. They appeared to be waiting for someone, but Danny could not be sure who, until, at a little after eight, an old man, introduced as 'Des's Uncle Pat' came in. Des immediately got up and offered him his seat, squeezing himself into the settee in between Danny and Elaine.

Once fortified by a mug of tea and plate of gingerbread, Uncle Pat looked across at the new face. 'You're American, so I hear.'

Danny shifted slightly in his corner of the settee and nodded. 'That's right – from New York.'

The old man nodded, as if in approval. 'We've always done

478

better from the likes of New York and the East Coast than the West. One of our best sources of funding New York has been.'

Danny nodded. He presumed he was talking about funding for the cause, but personally knew next to nothing on the issue. He bitterly regretted not having attempted to learn more before leaving the States. While his grandmother would certainly not have discussed it, his mother would have gladly shared all she knew on the subject . . . His mother – he had not given her a thought since arriving here this morning. Israel and all that had happened out there seemed a whole world away, which indeed it almost was. He had not even given Ruth more than the occasional thought, which was even stranger, for she had made such an impression on him at the time.

'Have you done much work for the cause yourself, before coming over here? The boys of the Clan na Gael over there did a grand job in supplying us with arms when it mattered in the past.' The old man's voice broke into his thoughts.

'No, no – I'm afraid not. It's not too late to start, though!' What made him say that he had really no idea, for he had not completely made up his mind that he was even going to remain here in Belfast for that much longer.

'Well, we can do with every good man – and woman – we can lay our hands on, there's no denying that. You're staying with Mrs Heaney, I believe.'

Danny nodded.

'Well, you'll be ideally positioned for Elaine taking you under her wing. You could do worse.'

Elaine gave a quiet smile. From Pat Devlin that was a compliment of the highest order.

'You've been in the IRA long, sir?' Danny ventured.

Pat Devlin wiped the crumbs of the gingerbread off his jacket lapels and took out his pipe. 'We'll forget the "sir", if you don't mind, son. We're all equal here . . . Let's just say, I've been active in the cause for most of my natural life.'

'Uncle Pat's seen it all,' Des said proudly. 'Tell him about the killing of Frank Skeffington, Uncle Pat.'

'Sure and our American friend here's not interested in ancient history!'

479

'Oh, but I am – if it's Irish history. I've felt more ignorant by the minute on that account since arriving here this morning.'

'Well . . .'

'He'll do it with a wee bit of fortification,' Des declared, rising from his seat in the middle of the settee and going over to the sideboard on the back wall. Opening one of the doors, he extracted a bottle of whiskey and poured a generous amount into a glass and brought it across to his uncle. 'Here ye are, ye old divil – never say we're not good to you!'

'That's right civil o' ye, Des boy.' The old man lit his pipe with a taper from a jar by the fire and a silence descended, as all eyes in the room fixed firmly on him. After placing the glass carefully on the brass fender at his feet, he puffed the shag tobacco into life. Its pungent aroma filled the air as he settled back on the stool and, with half-closed eyes, began to cast his mind back over the years.

'Och, I was little more than a boy at the time. I'd gone to Dublin on that Easter Monday with me father and Uncle Ned to deliver some rifles – Italian ex-army ones they were, if I remember rightly, for Jim Connolly's Citizen Army boys to use. To tell you the honest truth, we had no idea that the Rising was still on, for the last we'd heard it'd been called off. Eoin MacNeill had published a proclamation saying so . . . But be that as it may, there we were that Monday morning in front of Dublin Castle, with Uncle Ned's furniture wagon. We'd used that to ferry the guns, for it looked innocent enough, especially with a kid sittin' up top. Anyway, there I am standing at the foot of Cork Hill when the attack on the Castle begins and Uncle Ned points out the man next to me as Frank Sheehy-Skeffington. I must admit, green behind the ears though I was, I was a bit in awe of the man, for Father had read out his writings in the *Irish Citizen* to us, and most of his various pamphlets for the cause. We all knew he had the makings of a great leader.'

'The greatest,' Des interrupted. 'He'd a far better political brain than Pearse or any of them.'

'Bar Connolly and probably Clarke,' the dark young man with the moustache put in.

'Will you hold your tongues, boys, and let him finish!' It was Elaine who put a stop to the argument.

'Well, as I was saying, there I stood, not able to move a blessed inch for the volleys of gunfire seemed to be coming from all directions, when a British officer – a Captain Pinfield, I believe his name was – was shot and fell seriously wounded by the Castle gate. The man lay there moaning, as the pool of his own blood got bigger and bigger and not one of us in the crowd dared move an inch. But Frank Skeffington did. He ran through the hail of bullets to find a chemist to help the man. The two of them returned through a barrage of gunfire that had me wettin' meself, I'll tell you that for nothing!'

'What happened then?' Danny's eyes were riveted on the seamed face as it puffed thoughtfully on the pipe.

'They were too late – that's what happened. By the time they got back some British soldiers had dragged the injured man away.' His eyes positively gleamed as he stabbed the pipe at Danny. 'But Frank Skeffington risked his life for that man, son! He risked his own life for that of his enemy. For one of those who, the very next day, arrested and then murdered him, without trial, in the name of the British army!'

'He was murdered by the British army?'

'That he was! His murderer was another British army captain, by the name of Bowen-Colthurst!' The stem of the pipe was stabbed at him once again to emphasise the point.

Danny tensed in his seat. 'And what happened to him – to the murderer?'

'You may well ask! After the cold-blooded murder of Frank Skeffington, and two of his journalist pals into the bargain, Pat McIntyre and Tom Dickson, that bastard Bowen-Colthurst tried to conceal the whole thing by secretly burying the bodies within the walls of Portobello army barracks and then repairing the wall that they'd been taken out like dogs and shot against. The divil then conducted a violent raid on Frank's home and placed his wife and seven-year-old son under arrest.'

'Were – were they active Republicans, the Skeffingtons and the other two journalists?' Danny asked, bemused. Surely it was the only explanation.

'Were they hell! Poor Tom Dickson and Pat McIntyre had no

481

Nationalist connections whatsoever, and Frank and his wife Hanna were both pacifists and socialists. Acts of violence, in whatever cause, they'd have no truck with.'

'There must have been a God-awful stink about it, surely?'

The old man sucked his pipe and gave a bitter laugh. 'Not a bit of it! The Brits did their best to hush the whole thing up, but didn't succeed. The public wouldn't hear of it. They wouldn't let the matter rest, so the Brits had no choice but to court-martial that bastard Bowen-Colthurst. It stuck in their gullets, but there was nothing else for it.'

'Was he hanged?' A ripple of laughter went round the room at Danny's innocent question.

'Was he hell! You'd think the very least he'd deserve was that he'd be taken out and shot like a dog against a wall like he'd done to those innocent men, wouldn't you – but not a bit of it! Oh, they found him guilty of murder all right, there was no way round that. But he served only twenty months. Can you believe it, Danny boy? Twenty months!' he repeated the words, with a shake of his head. 'You'd get more for pinching a bag o' sweeties out o' Woolies! And then what do you think happened to him when he was set free after that measly sentence?'

It was Danny's turn to shake his head. 'I've really no idea.'

'He emigrated to Canada, that's what. To live happily on a British army pension until his death three years ago. That's British justice for you!'

'It's not a pretty story.'

'No, but it's a true one. It's the God's truth, as sure as I'm sitting here . . . Of course the British Prime Minister Asquith and his cabinet tried to buy Frank's wife's silence with ten thousand pounds, if she'd forgo an enquiry into the affair. Blood money – that's what it was! Hanna Skeffington would have none of it!'

A silence fell for several seconds as each person in the room contemplated what he had just heard, then Elaine said quietly, 'No, like you say, it's not a pretty story, Danny, but there are hundreds more where that one came from!'

'Aye, there was blood – Irish blood a'plenty on British hands that Easter, Danny. But the dream lives on . . .' The old man looked down at the pipe in his hands, then picking up his glass from the fender, he raised it in silent salute and very softly, as if to himself, he began to recite:

> 'Their dream has left me numb and cold,
> But yet my spirit rose in pride,
> Refashioning in burnished gold
> The images of those who died,
> Or were shut in the penal cell.
> Here's to you, Pearse, your dream not mine,
> But yet the thought, for this you fell,
> Has turned life's water into wine.
>
> Here's to you, men I never met,
> Yet hope to meet behind the veil,
> Thronged on some starry parapet
> That looks down upon Innisfail,
> And sees the confluence of dreams
> That clashed together in our night,
> One river, born of many streams,
> Roll on in one blaze of blinding light.'

As the old man's voice quavered into silence, to his embarrassment Danny felt the hot sting of tears in his eyes. He stared down at the empty teacup in his lap, hoping that the others wouldn't notice, when the door suddenly opened.

'Oh, Jesus – another bloody Shinner convention!'

'Uncle Willie!' Des turned to the middle-aged man in the doorway. 'Would you be after a cup o' tea?'

Willie Campbell, Des's mother's eldest brother, came in closing the door behind him. 'That would go down a treat, Des boy.' He looked down at the old man on the stool by the fire. 'How are ye, Patrick, ye old bugger? I see *you're* doing all right for yersel', wi' a drop o' the hard stuff!'

'Well, there'll be no more of that dished out in this house tonight!' Maggie Devlin, Des's mother, stood in the doorway with a clean cup and saucer for her brother. 'I've gone through a whole bottle in the past week and that's more than a widow's pension can stand.'

'Now who's asking for it? Certainly not me,' Willie Campbell pacified his sister. 'Total abstinence may be the thin edge of the

483

pledge, but I'm all for it, Margaret me girl! Particularly where the likes o' that ould rascal sitting down there's concerned!' He nodded towards old Pat, who was eyeing him suspiciously over the top of his glass, then turned once more to his sister. 'How are you anyway, Maggie? Worn out playing lady bountiful as usual to your bloody Republican tribe, no doubt.' As a Protestant born and bred, he still had not come to terms with his favourite sister having married into an ardent Catholic Republican family.

'We'll have less of that, Uncle Willie, if you don't mind,' Des put in. 'Can decent folk not have a quiet cup of tea without it bringing a load of Proddy insults down on their heads?'

'There's nothing landing on your head that's no more than you deserve, young Desmond! And speaking of things landing on folks' heads — that's exactly what you remind me of — bloody, blind Samsons attempting to pull down the pillars of social order in our country! Well, decent, law-abiding citizens like us won't allow it — be warned of that! We'll not stand idly by and let you destroy our liberty, just to exchange it for the Papist rule of that lot down South!'

He paused in his rhetoric to allow his sister to pour him a cup of tea, then raised the steaming cup in front of him. 'If that old divil, Pat Devlin, sitting down there, can drink a toast to yon Fenian scum in the home of a good Protestant like my sister Maggie here, then sure an' I'll repay the compliment with one of me own!'

Danny could feel Des tense in the seat beside him as his uncle pulled himself up to his full height of five feet six and raising his cup even higher began:

'Here's to the glorious, pious and immortal memory of the great and good King William, not forgetting Oliver Cromwell, who assisted in redeeming us from popery, slavery, arbitrary power, brass money and wooden shoes. May we never want a Williamite to kick the arse of a Jacobite! And a fart for the Bishop of Cork! And he that won't drink this, whether he be priest, bishop, deacon, bellows-blower, gravedigger, or any other of the fraternity of the clergy, may a north wind blow him to the south, and a west wind blow him to the east! May he have a dark night, a lee shore, a rank storm and a leaky

484

vessel to carry him over the River Styx! May the dog Cerberus make a meal of his rump and Pluto a snuffbox of his skull! May the divil jump down his throat with a red-hot harrow, and with every pin tear out a gut, and blow him with a clean carcass to hell! Amen!'

There was a complete silence when he had finished and Willie Campbell looked triumphantly round the room before taking a loud slurp of the hot tea. 'So none of yez will drink wi' me, will ye not? Ye should away back to Dublin, every last one o' ye! You're a blight on Queen and country, the whole damned lot of you, so you are!'

'Now, Willie, don't go getting yourself all heated up. You know what the doctor said!' Maggie Devlin looked imploringly at her brother. Heart trouble ran in their family and Willie's cheeks were already an unhealthy ruddy colour. 'Heaven only knows what our young visitor there, from America, is going to think of us all. In all probability he doesn't give a traneen about us and our stupid religious bigotry. Is that not right, Danny?'

Danny looked about him helplessly. All eyes were on him. 'To be honest, Mrs Devlin, the whole situation still confuses me, I must confess. I guess I can't quite figure out what it is that everyone wants exactly. When I arrived here I thought it was simply the Northern Irish fighting the occupying British for their freedom, but now I'm here it turns out that the Protestant majority up here in Ulster don't want Irish freedom at any price.'

He glanced along the settee at Elaine, remembering her words in the bedroom earlier. 'And it seems like some of the Catholic Republicans don't want union with the South, under this present Dublin government either . . . What I'd really like to know is what exactly the likes of yourself wants – someone with a foot in both camps, so to speak.'

Maggie Devlin sighed. 'Oh, Danny boy, what I want – and pray to God every night for – is just to be left in peace! But in this poor troubled land of ours, even that seems too much to hope for. I can't even guarantee it in my own home, wi' silly beggars like this lot around!'

Chapter 54

'Waken up, Danny, I've got some news for you!'

Deirdre's voice, at his shoulder, forced him to open his eyes, blinking at the cold morning light that filtered in through the net curtains from the street beyond. 'What – what is it?' He pulled himself up on the bed. 'Wha – what time is it?'

'It's gone eleven. I'm just back from Ma's.' As if to emphasise the point, she was still in her outdoor clothes of a red-checked jacket and black miniskirt. 'I've got news for you!'

He yawned and ran a hand through his hair. 'From Elaine?'

'Good God, no! *She's* busy swotting for her exams today – or so she said when she left this morning. No, it's from your grandmother!'

'From Grandma!'

Deirdre nodded, making the most of the suspense, until she could contain herself no longer. 'She's arriving tomorrow!'

Danny was wide awake now. 'But she can't be! She told me – she doesn't intend coming over here for at least a month.'

'Well, she's changed her mind. Ma phoned her last night to tell her you'd arrived here safely and . . . Well, you can imagine the rest! With you already over here nothing was going to stop her and, of course, Mam gave her every encouragement to grab the next plane. To tell the truth, from what Ma says, I think she's been feeling a wee bit lonely on her own there in New York – what with Maudie and her family on the West Coast and your mother still over in Israel.'

Danny nodded. He could believe that. 'But your mother – she's not fit to cope.'

'Just try telling Ma that, when she knows that Maeve's on her way!'

'She'll be staying over there then, with Aunt Katie?'

'So it seems. I can't say that I'm exactly happy about it, but both her and Dad seem to think they can cope.' Seeing his troubled expression, she hastened to reassure him. 'Now there's nothing at all to worry about. Maeve will stay over there and you'll stay right here with us. You're quite comfortable, aren't you?'

He nodded quickly. 'Of course. But – but Elaine, what if she wants to come back home to study? She said something about her exams being in the next few weeks.'

'So they are, but that's never brought her back home yet. No, she's quite happy where she is in her little flat over on Newtonards Road.'

'I – I'll pay you for my keep, of course. It's the very least I can do.'

'You'll do no such thing! If we can't offer hospitality to our own, who can we offer it to, may I ask?' She shook her head as she made for the door. 'There's a fresh pot of tea waiting downstairs, if you fancy it. Marie's not at school today and has made it for us.'

'Yeah, sure – thanks. I'll be right down!' He shot her a smile of thanks, as he swung his bare legs out of the bed and gave his beard its first good scratch of the morning. What he wanted more than anything right now was to dive into a shower, but there could be no question of that. He didn't even like to ask for a bath, for that meant lighting the fire in the living-room specially to heat the water.

Grabbing his towel out of his case, he wrapped it around his middle, taking care not to tuck it too tightly around the scar tissue, which ran from his navel down towards his groin and was still red and livid, even after all these months.

'Well, good morning!' Marie greeted him in the passage as he opened the door and stepped out to make his way up to the bathroom. 'I thought you might like this in bed.' She glanced down at the cup of steaming tea in her hands, before her eyes moved on to his half-naked torso.

'Well, thanks . . .' He gave a helpless shrug. 'What do I do – dash up now and have a quick wash or come back in and have it?'

'It goes cold awful quickly.'

'Right, in that case, it's back to the bedroom!'

She smiled and led the way back into the room and placed the cup on the bedside cabinet. 'Did you sleep well?' Her eyes followed his every move as he sat himself back down on the edge of the bed and took his first sip of tea.

'Yes, thanks. Very well.'

She nodded and smiled, as if the answer really pleased her. 'Did you enjoy yourself last night with Elaine?' She looked straight at him, waiting for his reply as if the answer really mattered to her.

'It was an interesting evening.' It was the most truthful answer he could give.

'We're not all like that over here, you know. We're not all going around wrapping ourselves in the Plough and Stars and mouthing off about revolutions.'

He gave a wry laugh. 'I was beginning to wonder.'

Taking that as a sympathetic response, Marie continued quickly, 'To be honest, they make me sick, the lot of them. It's all hot air, you know. I'm convinced of it. Oh, sure she comes back here some nights with muddied shoes and clothes and all the rest of it, but it's all for show. If you ask me, that mud comes from the long grass round the edges of Ormeau Park, where her and that Des Devlin go to have it off, when they're supposed to be fighting for the cause, as they like to put it. The only cause they're interested in is their own image!'

The outburst made Danny look up at her curiously. Until now she had seemed almost a shadow of her elder sister – a darker, quieter version, with not a great deal to say for herself. 'I take it you're not an avid Republican, then?'

She shook her head. 'Oh, I believe in civil rights and all that. Who wouldn't? But as for the rest of it – they can keep it. That type of carrying on is okay for the mischief makers, like that Des Devlin and our Elaine, but they're just asking for trouble, if you ask me. Are you going out with her again tonight?'

'Well, we never made any plans.'

'Would you like to come out with me, then? There's a dance on over in York Road, at Groucho's. You'll enjoy it.'

'I'm sure I would. Thanks, Marie. I'd like that just fine.'

Her eyes smiled down into his, before she turned and walked quickly from the room, leaving him looking after her with a slightly bemused expression on his face.

By the time he had washed and dressed and wandered

through to the kitchen for a bite of breakfast, Marie had disappeared uptown to do some shopping, but a strange man was sitting at the small Formica-topped table finishing a plate of cornflakes.

'You must be Danny. I'm pleased to meet you, son.' He stood up and offered his hand across the table-top. It felt hard and calloused, as if it had seen more than its fair share of hard manual work. 'I'm Deirdre's old man, Seamus.'

'Pleased to meet you, sir.' Danny pulled up a chair as Deirdre herself appeared at the back door, with an empty washing basket in her hands.

'Oh, you're up, Danny. Help yourself to cereal and some toast, would you? And the tea's still fresh in the pot.'

'Marie's not in, I take it?'

Deirdre shot a glance at her husband, then gave a short laugh. 'She tells us you're going to Groucho's with her tonight. That's made her upside down with Elaine and no mistake. She's off to the shops to get herself a new rig-out, so you can expect to be dazzled when eight o'clock, or whenever it is, finally comes round!'

Danny scattered a spoonful of sugar on top of his flakes and gave a wry grin. 'Shouldn't she be at school?'

'Aye, she should that!' Seamus agreed. 'But you try telling her! We keep trying to persuade her to stick it out and get her university entrance, but at the least little excuse she's taking the day off. And at the moment you're a big enough excuse in her book to warrant a whole week off!'

'Lord, I wouldn't want to mess up her chances of getting into university!'

'Oh, you won't, don't worry,' Deirdre assured him. 'She's eighteen years old and, in many ways, is every bit as bright as Elaine, but is even more bloody-minded. To tell the truth I think she fancies herself as an actress, but how she gets into that business in Belfast, God only knows! Ever since she's been a little girl she's collected pictures of your Aunt Maudie – and now, of course, Maudie's own girl's doing so well in films . . . Well, you can imagine how she envies her.'

'Marie's an extremely attractive young lady,' Danny said truthfully. 'She'd have no trouble getting work in the States.

Especially now, since the Beatles have made everything and everyone British the height of fashion. She could be the Julie Christie of the seventies!'

'Holy Mary and Joseph, don't tell her that, for pity's sake, or you'll never get rid of her!' Seamus laughed. 'She'll be clinging to your coat tails when you finally get on that plane back to America!' But Danny's remarks pleased him enormously. Of his two daughters, he had always had a softer spot for the younger one. Elaine's more strident, political character could be wearing on the nerves when you'd just arrived back from a couple of months working in England, and all you wanted was a few days of peace and quiet with your family.

'Will you be gone for long, sir?' Danny looked up as the older man got up from the table.

'Seamus, if you please, Danny. And aye, I'll be gone the best part of a month.'

'I'll not see you again, then.' He stood up and offered his hand. 'I wish we could have had the chance to get to know one another better.'

'So do I, son. So do I.' Seamus clasped Danny's hand warmly in both of his. 'But I've no doubt I'll be kept informed from Deirdre here how you're getting on. I understand your grandmother's due to fly over tomorrow.'

'Good God, so she is!' He had completely forgotten the news that he had been woken up with.

'Well, give her my best and tell her I'm sorry I missed her.' He turned to his wife. 'Well, love, it looks like it's time again . . .' He picked up his case and carried it out into the front hall. Deirdre followed him, but Danny remained in the kitchen. Farewells between husband and wife were no place for a third party.

It was fully fifteen minutes before Deirdre came back into the kitchen, and by that time he had finished his breakfast and was busy with the dishes at the sink.

'Oh, Danny boy, there's no need for that. That's woman's work!' Her eyes were red and slightly swollen with tears.

'Don't let Elaine hear you say that!'

She laughed. 'She's a rum one, that one. But her heart's in

the right place. She's determined that she'll leave this world a better place than when she came into it, that's for sure.'

'Will she succeed?' He placed the last dripping cup on to the draining board and emptied the plastic bowl into the sink.

Deirdre sighed and picked up the teacloth from a hook on the back of the door. 'I wish I could say yes to that question, I really do. But this is Ireland, Danny – and Northern Ireland at that.' She gave a bitter laugh as she lifted a wet plate from the pile and began to dry it. 'You know, my Dad once said, "Place an Irishman on the spit and you'll always get another Irishman to turn the handle." He was not far wrong!' She looked across at him, with a wry smile, and gave a despairing shrug of her shoulders. 'That's about as near as I'll ever get to answering your question.'

He thought about their conversation a lot over the next few hours as he wandered around the city, trying to get some sense of place and people. He had imagined he would feel instantly at home, but he felt as much a stranger here as he had ever done in Vietnam or Israel. To be sure, with his flame-red hair and stocky build, he didn't look out of place, but he could not shake the terrible feeling of naïvety that had plagued him since arriving yesterday morning. Until now he had not realised, Vietnam apart, how sheltered a life he had actually lived. To have spent the best part of his young life commuting between New York and the West Coast had seemed a perfectly normal existence, and to have the money to do it was simply taken for granted. As for things like religion and politics, they had never entered into the scheme of things at all. He knew that by birth Art was Jewish and his mother was Catholic, but neither made a big deal out of it. And, as for politics, he had heard sometime that his mother had once done some work for the Democratic Party, but what either she or Art had actually voted at the last election, he really had no idea. One thing was for certain, though, they had not supported the escalation of the Vietnam war under LBJ.

By the time he found himself outside the Heaney home, at a little before five o'clock, he was still no nearer understanding his ancient motherland, and felt vaguely guilty for having come to no firm conclusion about it. In a way, it was a relief to know that Elaine would probably not be round here tonight, because he knew that something in him would drive him to want to impress her with his enthusiasm for the cause, and right now he had barely enough energy to ring the front-door bell.

The door was opened by Deirdre and the smell of frying bacon reached him from the kitchen. 'Come in, Danny. There was no need for you to ring the bell. The door was open. Tea will be on the table in a couple of minutes.' She left him at the door of his room to disappear back to the frying pan.

Feeling the need of a quick wash and brush-up, he climbed the stairs to the small bathroom on the top landing. The smell of the bacon had even penetrated up there and made his mouth water as he reached for the door handle.

'God, I'm sorry!' He stood in the open doorway, rooted to the spot, as through the haze of steam, his eyes met those of Marie.

She was standing, pink and glowing from the hot water, on the blue tumbletwist mat in front of the bath. She had been in the act of reaching for the towel on the back of the door when it had been snatched out of her grasp as it was pushed open by him. 'Danny!' Her hands flew to the appropriate places to cover her embarrassment as her cheeks flushed an even deeper pink.

He knew he should be a gentleman and back out immediately, but there was something about the look in her eyes that held his.

'Could you pass me the towel, please?'

He stepped further inside and lifted the blue bathtowel from its hook, then held it out towards her.

'Which hand do you suggest I use to take it?' she asked with the hint of a smile.

He walked towards her and draped it around her shoulders, lifting her thick dark curtain of hair to adjust it around her slim neck. She smelt sweet and clean as she lifted her face to his. Without make-up she looked even younger and more vulnerable, but also more womanly somehow. She raised her eyes to meet his and for the first time he noticed how deep a blue they were in colour and how long were the eyelashes that curled upwards to meet the delicately winged eyebrows. 'I got a new dress for tonight,' she said softly. 'You'll like it.'

'Not half as much as what you're wearing right now,' he said with a quiet smile. And meant it.

Chapter 55

When Marie had gone from the bathroom, Danny stood for a moment staring at the closed door. Their confrontation had lasted no more than a couple of minutes, but had left him strangely unsettled. Yesterday he had thought of her as no more than Elaine's kid sister, but now . . .

He turned and stared at his face in the mirror above the sink. The hazel eyes that stared back at him narrowed slightly as they studied the shaggy red moustache and beard. He had worn them since his return from Vietnam, but now they seemed wrong, completely out of place somehow. In New York, amongst all the Flower Power children, they felt right, but here, where life consisted of far more than smoking pot and handing out flowers to passers-by, they made him look and feel so much more than his twenty-three years. So much older than her . . .

His toilet bag was sitting on the edge of the bath and he lifted it up and reached inside for his shaving soap and razor, then very tentatively at first, he began to shave off all his facial hair. It fell into the porcelain bowl of the sink in curling red wisps and when he had finished he collected it up and flushed it down the lavatory. He went back to the mirror and stroked his clean chin and cheeks with his fingertips. The fresh-faced youth that looked back at him gave a grudging nod of approval. He would have had to do it sometime and now had been as good a time as any.

When he appeared downstairs for tea a few minutes later, Deirdre let out a yelp of surprise as she lifted the crisp rashers of bacon into the waiting rolls. 'Good God, what have you done to yourself?'

'Don't you like it?'

She took a pace back and moved her head to one side as she looked at him critically. 'Aye — aye, I do. You look younger. Will you be taking the scissors to the rest of it next?'

He gave a sheepish laugh and shook his head as he sat down at the table. The flame-red hair that curled down to almost shoulder length was a different matter altogether. 'Afraid not,' he said. 'After those years of being scalped in the Marines, no one's touching this!'

The rolls and tea tasted good and when he had reached his second cup he wondered aloud what had happened to Marie.

'Oh, she'll not be down until she's all dolled up,' her mother assured him. 'This is a big event in her life, you know, Danny – going out with you.'

'You're kidding.'

'No, I'm not,' she insisted, cutting herself a slice of currant loaf. 'You're a real big deal around here, whether you realise it or not. Most of the young men the girls here have to choose from are either unemployed or are in really mundane jobs, but you represent a different world entirely.'

'It doesn't seem to cut much ice with Elaine.'

'Oh, well, she's a different kettle of fish altogether.'

'New York, Hollywood, and all those places seem to leave her quite cold.'

Deirdre sighed. 'I'm afraid the gospel according to St Marx is the only thing that cuts much ice with Elaine at the moment. If your stepfather were Secretary-General of the American Communist Party, if such a thing exists, that would impress her a good deal more than Art being a Hollywood tycoon.'

'A Hollywood tycoon . . .' He grinned at the words. It was funny, he had never thought of him in those terms before. He was just Art. Labels put on by other people turned those you loved into something else entirely. 'How did you really think of us, Deirdre – you know, all your American relations?'

She flushed slightly, then laughed. 'Oh, we've always been a wee bit in awe of you all, I suppose. Well, a big bit in awe of you, actually. You all seemed so unreal – leading lives that we could only follow at a distance from the newspaper columns, or film magazines. I can't really blame Marie for being carried away just now.' She paused, pushing at a stray currant on her plate for a moment with her fingertip, before glancing up to meet his eyes once more. 'I ask only one thing of you, Danny.

Don't hurt her – don't hurt Marie. She's young yet, for all her make-up and fancy clothes. She's very young.'

A noise came from the door behind them, causing them both to look around. Marie was standing in the doorway, but had apparently heard none of their conversation. She was wearing a white lace minidress and had a white satin bow in the back of her hair, that matched her high-heeled satin shoes.

Danny got up from the table and held out the chair next to him. 'You look lovely, Marie. Real pretty.'

'Thank you, Danny. You look pretty good yourself. I prefer you without the face fungus.'

He smiled his appreciation as she took her seat beside him, then glanced across at her mother.

'Yes, you look really nice, dear,' Deirdre agreed as she looked from her daughter back across the table to Danny. His eyes had suddenly brightened rather too much for her liking. And what was more, she had received no answer to her plea. 'You did hear what I said a moment ago, Danny,' she said quietly, as she leaned across to fill Marie's teacup.

'Yes, Deirdre, I heard.'

Groucho's was in full swing when they finally got there at a little after nine. They had stopped off for a couple of drinks first, which mellowed the mood beautifully, and Danny felt more relaxed than he had done all day, as they took the floor to Gary Puckett's 'Young Girl'. The lyrics seemed embarrassingly appropriate, he found himself thinking, as they swayed slowly round the dance floor, locked in each other's arms. It wasn't that he was that much older than she was, but her mother was right – she was very young in the ways that counted. He even doubted if she had ever had a serious boyfriend before. And, try as she might to disguise her innocence, she seemed light years away from . . . from . . . He found himself tensing as his mind went back to Shiralee and Ruth. What were they doing right now, apart from cursing him for running out on them both like that? He closed his eyes and held Marie that bit tighter. The other young women in his life seemed a mere figment of his imagination now; they belonged to other worlds which he had left behind long ago.

'Will you be returning to New York soon, Danny?'

The whispered question in his ear seemed incongruously appropriate as Marie pulled herself back slightly to await his answer. Her fingers toyed with the lapels of his white sports jacket as he shrugged his shoulders. 'I don't have any plans at present. Trying to get rid of me already?' he grinned down at her.

'Oh, no – never that!' She looked totally aghast at the suggestion.

He pulled her closer, nuzzling his lips into the side of her neck, when suddenly she tensed in his arms. 'What is it, honey? What's wrong?'

'The bitch! The bitch! She couldn't bear it. She just couldn't bear the thought of me having you all to myself tonight!' Her eyes were staring somewhere over his left shoulder and, loosening his hold on her, he turned in the direction of her gaze.

'Elaine!'

She was standing in the doorway, wearing a duffle coat and jeans. Her eyes looked straight into his.

'Ignore her! Just ignore her!' Marie tugged at his sleeve, in an attempt to break his gaze.

'Don't be silly! She wouldn't have come here if it wasn't important.' His eyes were still locked with Elaine's.

'No! You don't know her! She's jealous, that's all. Ignore her, Danny, please!'

'Wait here!' Wrenching his arm from hers, he strode across the dance floor towards the doorway.

'I didn't expect to see you tonight!'

'Obviously.' Elaine glanced over his shoulder to where her younger sister still stood in the middle of the dance floor.

'Care to join us?' It was all he could think of saying. Just seeing her standing there like this made him feel unaccountably guilty, as if he'd done something to be ashamed of – been unfaithful to her almost. But that was absurd.

'I was just going to ask you the same thing.'

'Pardon me?'

'There's something on tonight, Danny. I thought you might like to join us.'

He looked at her in confusion. 'You – you don't mean an IRA thing?'

She gave a scornful laugh. 'Wise up, Yank! Whoever told you we're in the IRA? We've moved beyond that.'

'Look, whatever you call yourselves – Trots, Maoists, or whatever the fashionable thing is at the moment. To tell the truth, Elaine, I wasn't figuring on getting involved in world revolution tonight.' He glanced back over his shoulder towards the dance floor. 'Marie's enjoying herself – it wouldn't be fair.'

'Sorry I asked!' She made to turn back towards the door, but he grabbed her arm.

'Don't go – not like that.'

'What do you want me to do – stand here and watch you make up to my little sister?'

He ignored the jibe. 'Look, any other night – except maybe tomorrow night 'cause my grandmother's due to fly in tomorrow – but any other time at all . . .'

'Sure, Danny, sure . . . We'll fix up the next job to suit the dates in your diary!' She wrenched her arm free of his grasp and made for the door.

He made to go after her, but Marie's voice halted him in his tracks.

'Danny – no!' She ran panting at his elbow. 'Let her go, Danny. Whatever she wanted – let her go!' Tears of anger were sparkling in her eyes. 'It's been like this all our lives. Honestly it has. Whenever I got something new, she had to have it too!'

He put his arm around her shoulders and said soothingly, 'Come on, honey, you've got it all wrong. Elaine's not interested in me. She was trying to be sociable, that's all.'

Marie pulled herself away, to look up at him in incredulity. 'If you believe that, Danny Donovan, then you're a fool! I know her better than anyone, and she's got more than revolution on her mind when you're around, I can assure you of that!'

He pondered on her words as they walked back to the dance floor, but could not really bring himself to believe them. Nevertheless, the unexpected appearance of Elaine had cast a cloud over the evening that refused to lift, despite his valiant attempts to inject some humour into their conversation. In his arms she felt stiff and unyielding, as if waiting for him to give some further assurances of his feelings towards her before she allowed the intimacy she had so freely given before. But the words would not come. Her mother's plea rang in his ears. She was very young. And she was vulnerable. To take advantage of those things would be more than even he was prepared to do. He had landed himself in quite enough trouble with the opposite sex recently.

On the way home, he slipped his arm round her shoulders as they walked through the lamplit streets and tried to pretend he had not noticed her obvious unhappiness. When they got inside the front door, he asked if she'd like a coffee, but she shook her head, determined not to be pacified. He gave a resigned shrug of his shoulders and bent down to kiss her tenderly on the forehead. 'Goodnight, Marie, honey. Despite everything, it's been a real nice evening.'

He watched her walk slowly upstairs and disappear into her room, before he opened his own door and went inside with a sigh. He flung his clothes on to the chair by the bed and, dressed only in his underpants, lay down on top of the bedcovers and lit a cigarette. He had only been here a couple of days, but already he felt as if he had been embroiled for a lifetime in family rivalries. He could not really believe what Marie had said about Elaine's feelings towards him, but the idea that it might just contain a grain of truth gave him a curious thrill. Not that he had any romantic intentions towards her, he told himself. He had had enough of those to last him for long enough of late. And anyway, his grandmother was due here tomorrow. He smiled to himself through the haze of cigarette smoke. He was actually looking forward to that.

The room was in total darkness and he had no idea how long he had been asleep, when the whisper in his ear brought a groaning response of 'Wha'sat . . . ?'

'It's just me, Danny – Marie.'

He rolled over on the bed so that his eyes were directly in line with hers. 'Marie, honey, what are you doing here?' He reached out a hand towards the bedside light, but she stopped him immediately.

'No, don't do that, please . . . I – I couldn't sleep, so I came downstairs to make myself a cup of coffee. I thought you might like one.'

He heard the soft clink of a mug being placed on top of the cabinet beside the bedside light. 'What time is it?'

'It's gone one,' she said, in a hushed voice.

'Look, that was real nice of you, Marie, but I can't drink the stuff if I can't see it.' Ignoring her restraining hand, he reached over and switched on the light, blinking his eyes at the brightness that flooded the room. He could see now the reason for her reluctance. She was wearing only a pair of pink nylon baby doll pyjamas.

'I wanted to apologise for my behaviour tonight,' she said quietly. 'It was childish of me, sulking like that. It's just that I can't bear to think of you preferring her to me, that's all. I – I've never met anyone like you before, Danny . . .' She reached out and tentatively touched his forearm, then sensing he did not object, her fingers continued to caress the lightly freckled skin.

'There's no question of that, Marie,' he said softly. 'You're a great girl . . .'

'Do you really think so, Danny?'

'Of course I do.'

'Then show me . . . Show me you care . . .' Before he could reply, she had slipped on to the bed beside him, her right hand sliding up behind his neck, to draw his face down to hers. Her right leg entwined itself round his, so that he was pulled down on top of her.

She felt incredibly soft and fragile beneath him, as her body moulded itself to his, but this was the last thing he wanted right now. He was barely even awake. 'No, honey . . . No, Marie . . .'

'Kiss me, Danny, properly . . . Just once and I'll go. I promise . . .' Her voice was huskily insistent, her breath warm on his face, as her lips found his.

'Jesus bloody Christ!'

The exclamation from the doorway brought him jerking upright on the mattress. 'Elaine!' He scrambled off the bed, to stand, clad only in his underpants, on the bedside mat. 'I – I didn't expect you back tonight.'

500

'Obviously!' She threw a contemptuous glance at the half-naked figure of her sister on the bed. 'Get out of here, you little whore, and get up those stairs!'

'You've no right,' Marie began. 'You've no right to come barging in here . . .'

'I've every bloody right!' Elaine cut in. 'What am I supposed to think when I get home and find you not in your bed at this time of night and your clothes lying in a heap on the floor? If you're not capable of looking after yourself, then somebody has to!'

'But not you! You're not my keeper. You've no right – no right at all!' Tears were glistening in her eyes as she clambered off the bed and stood facing her sister. 'Tell her, Danny, tell her just to go and leave us alone!'

He shook his head. 'No, she's right, Marie. Just go back to bed, honey. We'll talk about this in the morning.'

'You – you're not staying here with her?'

'Of course not.'

Very reluctantly, Marie edged past him and then past the glaring figure of her sister to reach the door. 'I'll see you in the morning then – promise?'

'I promise.'

She slipped out through the door, deliberately leaving it open behind her. Elaine kicked it shut, with a sharp backheel of her shoe. 'You bastard!'

Danny reached towards her. 'Honestly, Elaine, this may sound like the lamest excuse of all time, but it wasn't like it looked. Marie doesn't mean a goddam thing to me!'

'Jesus! That's supposed to make it all right, is it? You attempt to rape my little sister and then tell me you don't give a damn about her and that's supposed to make me feel better! What are you – some kind of nut?'

Feeling far too exposed for the circumstances, he grabbed for his trousers and pulled them on. 'You know maybe you're right! Maybe I must have been some kind of nut to come here in the first place to this crazy country! I don't understand you, Elaine. I don't understand any of you, and that's the goddam truth.' He sat down on the edge of the bed and shook his head. 'I had this crazy romantic notion about Ireland when I flew out here, but it was a dream, it was all a goddam dream. That Ireland doesn't exist in reality. It's all in the mind, Elaine – it's all in the goddam mind!'

She stared down at him for a long time without speaking, then said softly, 'You're right, of course. It does only exist in the mind. But as long as it exists in the minds of people like us who are willing to make it a reality, then there's still hope for us. It's when it ceases to exist in the minds of the people, Danny, that's when the end of the dream will have come.'

Danny looked up and met her eyes, then reached out and lifted his coffee mug from the bedside cabinet. 'Here's to you, Pearse, your dream – not mine,' he said softly, repeating the only words of old Pat Devlin's poem that he could remember, as he raised the mug in silent, ironic salute.

'It can be *your* dream too, Danny, if you let it.'

Their eyes met and held, and he nodded slowly, then downed the coffee in one. 'I'm through with making commitments I can't keep, Elaine. Let's just take each day as it comes from now on, huh?'

'I wouldn't have it any other way.'

She remained standing just inside the closed door, looking down at him. He felt she was waiting for him to make the next move, to say something . . . 'You intend going on working for the cause yourself, I take it – despite your exams and all that.'

'*Arbeit macht frei*, Danny.'

'You really believe that?'

'Sure – you've got to go on working for freedom – and it'll come some day. If I didn't believe that, I'd either go bloody mad or emigrate! But until then you've just got to get on with life here in Northern Ireland. This is our prison camp – we're the poor bloody Jews of England's swinging sixties! Do you know what my Da has stamped on his card, when he goes looking for work over on the mainland? Political suspect, that's what! And I'll tell you this for nothin' – he's never been a member of any political organisation in his life, legal or illegal. He's been too busy looking for work over in England that the bloody British government can't, or won't, supply here. Political suspect!' She repeated the words with a contemptuous laugh. 'Yes, it might as well be a yellow star they stamped him with, for it amounts to the same thing – discrimination. But our generation won't stand for it like his has, Danny. We won't be treated like second-class citizens in our own country any longer – if there's going to be another holocaust, then it's not going to be us who are exterminated!'

'I wish you luck.'

'We need more than that. We need your help. You're Danny Donovan's grandson. Doesn't that mean anything to you?'

He thought of the photograph that still lay in the breast pocket of his denim jacket. 'Yes, Elaine, it does. And I won't let him down.'

'That's all I wanted to know.' She gave a quiet smile and went out, closing the door gently behind her.

Chapter 56

Danny swung the new Cortina out of the Hertz forecourt and headed in the direction of Hamilton Street. Finding that none of the close relatives that he had yet met in Belfast had a car had come as a surprise to him, and his suggestion of hiring one for his stay in the city had been greeted with enthusiasm by Deirdre at breakfast. Apart from anything else, it would save hiring a taxi to bring his grandmother from the airport tonight.

It was a bright, sunny morning and he hoped the change in the weather would signify a change for the better in the atmosphere in the Heaney household when he returned tonight. To his surprise, Marie had been nowhere to be seen when he appeared for breakfast and he was informed by Deirdre that she had, in fact, already left for school. 'Don't ask me why, Danny. That girl's a mystery to herself,' she had informed him, as she prepared to leave for her mother's house. 'She just turned up at the table in full school uniform at quarter-past eight and helped herself to a cup of tea. But neither she nor Elaine as much as looked at each other before they left the house.'

'Elaine's gone too, then?' he had asked.

'Oh, aye. To tell the truth, I got the shock of my life to see her here this morning. She must have arrived long after I'd gone to bed last night. And I've a good idea why – take a look at this!'

She had handed him a copy of this morning's paper, pointing her finger at the inch-high, black headlines: 'LOCAL ARMY DEPOT PETROL BOMBED. An army depot in the north of the city was the target for a petrol bomb attack late last night. The attack set fire to the kitchens, although no one was hurt. A spokesman puts the damage at several hundreds of pounds. No one was apprehended in connection with the incident, which is the fourth of its kind this month in the Province. Police have several leads, however, and are said to be pursuing their enquiries. Security is to be stepped up in those areas considered vulnerable.'

'You don't seriously think Elaine had anything to do with this, do you?'

'I don't *think*, Danny. I know! Every time she's appeared here in the middle of the night recently, there's been some incident in the paper next day. It scares me silly, so it does.'

He handed the paper back and said soothingly, 'I wouldn't worry about Elaine, if I were you. She's got a good head on her shoulders.'

'Aye, and that's what worries me! How much longer will it be on her shoulders if she carries on like this?'

'It's funny, you know. Aunt Katie said that of all her children, you were the most militant yourself when you were young.'

Deirdre paused momentarily, as she tightened the knot in her headscarf in the small mirror by the sink. 'It was different in those days,' she said. 'There was a war on and we contented ourselves in keeping the Home Rule fires burning by writing and issuing leaflets and that type of thing – until it was put a stop to. Sedition, they called it, but it had been going on since the days of Wolfe Tone – and before that even. We never actually caused any material or physical damage, though. God only knows what'll happen if someone gets hurt one of these fine days and they catch who did it!'

'She's obviously aware of that risk,' Danny said quietly. 'She must consider it worth running.'

Deirdre looked despairingly at him as she made for the door. 'Would you, Danny? Would you think it a risk worth running?'

He thought of the look in Elaine's eyes last night as she had sworn her generation would no longer be the Jews of England's Swinging Sixties. 'Do you know, Deirdre, I think I just might.'

It was not the answer she was looking for, as she made her way out of the house and down the street in the direction of her parents' home, but it was the only one he could have given. He had fought for another country's freedom over the past few years, or so they had told him, only to discover that the population of Vietnam did not want what their American 'saviours' had to offer. All they wanted was to be left alone to decide their own future and to live in peace. But it was different here. This was the land of his forefathers. Danny Donovan, his own grandfather, had laid down his life for Irish freedom – could he, his only grandson, do any less? It was a question he still had not yet fully resolved when he set off, half an hour later, to head for the car hire company.

His Aunt Katie was up and sitting in the kitchen, in a blue woollen dressing gown and furry blue slippers, when he appeared at the door at a little after ten o'clock. Her husband Eamon opened the door and Danny immediately warmed to the grey-haired man with the slight stoop to his back.

'Come away in, son. It's good to see you!' He led Danny through to the kitchen, where his aunt was reading the morning paper.

She put down her glasses as Danny took a seat at the opposite side of the table. 'Deirdre's just been telling us you're hiring a car to pick your grandmother up.'

'It's sitting at the door,' Eamon informed her. 'And real nice it looks too.'

'I thought it would be better than taking taxis everywhere,' Danny said. 'Although the guy that brought me here in his cab was real nice. I believe he's a friend of yours, Uncle Eamon. He said something about you being in the Pioneers together. Was that a branch of the IRA?'

'God love ye, no!' Eamon laughed, as he took a bottle of stout from the back of the kitchen cupboard and handed it across to Danny. 'It's a temperance organisation! That'll be old Tim Pat O'Hanlon you'll have been speaking to – the old rascal kept his pledge for about a six-month, if I remember rightly, and has made up for the half-year's drought ever since!'

'Speaking of drink,' Katie said. 'We might have told Deirdre to get a bottle of wine for the meal tonight, before she went out to the shops. Maeve always had wine with the meal in New York when I was there, even though it *was* wartime. And I bet she does to this day, isn't that right, Danny?'

Danny prised the top off the bottle of Guinness and poured it carefully into a glass. 'I guess so . . . but that doesn't mean she can't live without it. I bet when she was married to my grandfather they didn't have wine with every meal.'

Katie gave a hoot of laughter. 'You're right there, son! In those days in Dublin we thought ourselves lucky if we had food on the table, let alone wine! But times have changed a lot since then – a lot of water has flowed under the bridge and no mistake. I only wish you could have known some of them – some of the family that have gone . . . your grandfather, Danny, and dear daft Willie-John, God rest their souls . . .' Her voice faded as the hint of tears sparkled in her eyes, then suddenly she smiled again. 'But Dermot's still with us – your grandmother will want to meet him again.'

'Dermot?' He was sure he knew the name, but couldn't quite place it.

'My oldest brother,' Katie said. 'He's been a priest in Dublin these past fifty years. Maeve was real fond of him, so she was. But then so were we all, for a finer man never walked God's earth.'

'He was my grandfather's brother?'

'Aye, he was Danny's brother all right. But you never would have known it, either by looks or temperament. A real little scrapper Danny was – a born fighter, but Dermot was always the dreamer of the family, a gentle soul if ever there was one. It was funny really, but your Uncle Kieran, God rest his soul, seemed to have a bit of both of them in him. He had Danny's looks, but Dermot's gentle character.'

'I never knew him,' Danny said quietly, knowing they were now treading on sensitive ground, for neither his mother nor his grandmother liked to discuss the uncle who had died in suspicious circumstances during the war. 'But who do you think I resemble, Aunt Katie? Who would you say I take after?'

She looked at him long and hard across the kitchen table, then said thoughtfully, 'Well, you've got Danny's looks, there's no doubt about that – but as to your character, Danny boy, you'll have to ask me that in a few weeks' time.'

Danny gave a sheepish grin. 'You mean you'll be keeping your beady eye on me while I'm here and judging me accordingly, is that it?'

'Son,' Eamon said, 'she does that with everyone. She has us all summed up, that one! Even the poor blighter who comes round on a Thursday night to collect the pools coupon has had

507

his character marked out of ten in your Auntie's mind for years! Is that not right, Kathleen?'

'And what do you have to do to rate a ten, may I ask?' Danny said, taking a swig of the beer as he looked up at Eamon.

The elderly man thought for a moment. 'You have to be James Connolly himself,' he said emphatically, 'or God Almighty – take your pick!'

The Comet bringing Maeve from London into Belfast Airport was ten minutes late in arriving and Danny paced the terminal building impatiently as the passengers began to trickle through the barriers. 'Grandma!' There was no mistaking her as she strode towards him, proud and erect for all her seventy years, her grey hair rinsed a soft bluish-silver.

'Danny!' Her face lit up at the sight of him and she raised a gloved hand in greeting.

'I've got a car waiting outside,' he said, as they embraced. 'Unless you fancy a coffee first?'

She shook her head. 'Let's just get going. I feel I've already been travelling for months!'

They collected her cases from the luggage belt and he carried them out to the waiting Cortina. He held the door open for her and she slipped into the front passenger seat. 'I had one heck of a job getting an automatic,' he commented, as he switched on the ignition and eased the car out of its parking space. 'They seem to all go in for gear sticks over here.'

Maeve gave a quiet smile to herself. 'I reckon that's not the only thing you've been finding strange across here,' she said quietly. 'Ireland is not America, Danny – and nothing like it.'

'You can say that again!'

'What made you cut your trip to Israel short, anyway? I could get no real sense from your mother when I phoned her.'

His grip tightened on the steering-wheel. How honest should he be? 'Let's just say things got a bit too hot to handle out there, Gran. And I don't mean the weather!'

Maeve sat up in her seat and glanced across at him. 'You didn't fall out with anyone, did you? You didn't have an argument with the Finkelsteins?'

'No,' he said patiently. 'I didn't fall out with the Finkelsteins.'

'Your mother, then? It must have been your mother!' She was obviously not going to be put off.

He sighed, as he drew the car to a halt at a set of traffic lights. 'Yeah – if you must know – Mom and I didn't quite see eye to eye on a certain subject.'

Maeve drew in her breath sharply. There could only be one subject that could cause that type of rift. 'It – it wouldn't have anything to do with your . . . your . . .'

'My birth?' He finished the sentence for her. 'Darned right it would.'

Maeve's face paled as she glanced across at him. 'Did she tell you? Did she tell you who your father is?'

'Yeah, she told me.'

A multitude of questions tumbled through her brain, but she bit them back. It wasn't her place to ask. If he wanted her to know, he would tell her himself.

'Aren't you going to ask me who he is? Or isn't that necessary? Maybe you already know. Maybe the whole darned world knew but me!'

'No, Danny, that's not true. Kitty never said a word to me – not a single word over all these years – and I never asked.'

'You must have made some guesses, though.'

She gave a helpless shrug. 'In a city the size of New York, where do you begin? I guess the only front-runner, if you want to put it like that, was Art, but I discounted him pretty early on.'

'You were quite right to – he's my grandfather.'

'What?'

'You heard.'

'Good God!' She sat back in her seat and let out a low whistling breath. 'Lee Finkelstein's your father?'

'The same.'

'I don't know what to say.'

'You can guess what I felt like, then.'

'Pretty sore, I would guess.'

'Correct. Can you imagine what it's like being introduced to a stranger and finding out a few hours later that he's your father?'

'Is it her keeping the truth from you for all these years that hurts the most?'

'Yeah, that's partly it. If there's been no truth, no openness, between your own mother and yourself, then that relationship isn't worth a damn.'

Maeve's gloved hands clasped tightly in her lap. 'Don't be too hard on her, Danny.'

'But it's true, isn't it?' he insisted, as the lights changed to green and the car drew away slowly in the line of traffic. 'How would Mom have felt herself if she suddenly discovered, after all these years, that my grandfather, that Danny Donovan, wasn't her father — that you'd been lying to her all her life? How would she have felt, then? What would that do to your relationship? Answer me that, Gran. Just answer me that!'

A cold film of nervous perspiration broke out on Maeve's skin, beneath the smart travelling suit, as her throat went dry. She could not answer it. It was the one question she had been dreading for fifty years.

Chapter 57

Maeve stood at the open bedroom window and took a deep
breath, then another, filling her lungs with the cool night air.
It had been a long evening. She had sat up till well after twelve
with Katie and Eamon, catching up on all the news that had
escaped capture on the flimsy blue airmail papers that had
flown backwards and forwards across the Atlantic over the
years.

It was the first time she had met Eamon and already she had
formed a great respect for the quiet, grey-haired man who had
been Katie's husband for the past forty-four years. But, as for
Katie herself, she had been shocked at the change in her. Only
the eyes had remained the same since they had last met. They
still sparkled with that same amber, almost golden, light that
they had when she was a small child all those years ago in
Dublin, and had still retained, to a great extent, during her
wartime visit to New York. Oh, it was true her operation had
been a serious one and had taken a lot out of her, but she had
seemed shrunken and so much older and greyer than Maeve
had expected. Seeing her like this had made her almost
ashamed of her own well-preserved figure and vitality. No,
there had been no alternative, she had had to say that she
would be going straight on to Dublin tomorrow and would be
back in a week or so. It would give Katie a few more precious
days to get her strength back.

They had both seemed disappointed, of course, and had told
her they were planning a big family party for her at the
weekend, but that had only made her more determined than
ever to head on for Dublin as soon as possible. A party required
a lot of energy and that Katie just didn't have at the moment.

She had called her brother Charlie after supper and told him
she would be arriving tomorrow afternoon and both he and
Amy had been delighted. She would stay with them for one
night initially, she had said, then she intended to move into

511

her old family home in Jubilee Avenue. She was quite firm about that. She could get it ready for her mother coming back and, besides, she needed time to get used to things again, to collect her thoughts after the past hectic few days. Her mother was due back from her Aunt Maud's at the end of the week and she would enjoy the few days' peace in the familiar surroundings of her childhood, just getting to know her old home town once again and seeing old friends . . .

Old friends . . . A shiver ran through her. Those words meant one thing – one man. Dermot.

She got into bed and pulled the blankets up round her chin. She felt like a small child again, savouring the thought of a delicious treat, such as a coming Sunday school picnic. But it was much more than that. Soon she would be seeing again the only man she had ever really loved; the father of one of her children; the grandfather of her favourite grandchild . . .

'Danny,' she spoke the name aloud, as she opened her eyes and stared into the darkness. Their conversation in the car earlier this evening had left her with a cold, sick feeling in the pit of her stomach. What would he think of her if he knew that she was as guilty as his own mother – as Kitty – of such a deception? Guiltier even, for she had let Kitty – let everyone – believe that Danny was Kitty's father, when only she knew the truth. Only she and perhaps Dermot . . . Yes, she was certain that he knew, although she had never admitted it, not even to him. 'God forgive me,' she whispered. 'Dear God, forgive me . . .'

As Maeve closed her eyes and drifted into a troubled sleep, Danny drove the Cortina slowly up and down the almost deserted street in front of Elaine's second-floor flat in Newtonards Road. Why he was here, he did not know. She was probably inside right now, with her head stuck into one of her political tomes, if she wasn't already asleep.

He glanced at the clock on the dashboard. It was twenty past twelve. He had been driving around aimlessly since he left Katie's and Eamon's house almost half an hour ago. His eyes peered up again at the flat. There was a light still on. What if he were to park the car and go on up – say he was just passing and called in on the off-chance that she was still up?

As he slowed the Cortina to a crawl at the edge of the kerb, his breath caught in his throat. A slight figure was walking towards him in the middle of the pavement. In the pale yellow glow from the street lights he could make out the duffle coat and blue jeans. He would recognise them anywhere. 'Elaine!' His foot hit the brake pedal, as his right hand began to wind down the window. 'Elaine! Over here!'

She came to a full stop about twenty yards ahead of him, her brow furrowing as she stared at the unfamiliar car. But there was no mistaking the head sticking out of the window. 'Danny!' She began to run towards him.

He leaned across and threw open the passenger door. 'Get in!'

'What on earth are you doing here at this time of night?'

'Just passing!' He grinned across at her. 'How's that for a lame excuse?'

She settled back in the seat as he switched off the engine and turned to face her. 'You were looking for me,' she said quietly. The knowledge brought a quiet smile to her lips as she met his eyes. 'Why?'

'Must there be a reason?'

'It makes for more exciting listening.'

'What would you like me to say – that I missed you so much I simply had to spend the whole night kerb-crawling outside your apartment praying for a glimpse of you?'

'That'll do for starters!' She grinned across at him and curled her legs up beneath her on the seat. 'You were at Gran's tonight – Mam told me. How did it go? Did your grandma arrive safely?'

He nodded. 'She seems in good shape. She's leaving tomorrow, though – for Dublin, but she'll be back in a week or so.'

'You're not going with her, are you?'

'Well, no, not right away.' The anxious look on her face pleased him.

'Good.'

'Why good? Got any plans for me here?'

513

'I might have. They're planning something for Saturday night. Another hit.'

He felt a momentary stab of disappointment. He had not necessarily meant that type of plan. 'You want me to take part?'

She ignored his question, but continued, 'Des was supposed to be in on it with me, but he'll be at his Uncle Pat's wake. He dropped dead on the way home from his Ma's the other night.'

'You mean the old man who recited the poem – he's dead?'

'As a doornail. Des is pretty shook up about it. Pat was a cantankerous old bugger, but we all liked him. Gerry called him our guru. He wasn't far wrong, for the old boy had forgotten more about the cause than we'll ever know.' She looked past him, out through the windscreen into the lamplit street beyond, as her voice hardened. 'It seems there's as little justice in death as there is in life, with that old windbag Willie Campbell still walking around when old Pat's already met his Maker. Mind you, I said as much to Des and he disagreed with me. Said his mother would go to pieces if anything happened to his Uncle Willie . . .'

'So Des can't go with you on Saturday,' Danny cut in. 'Does that mean you'll have to go alone, if I don't come?'

'I don't mind that!' Elaine said defensively. 'It'll not be the first time.'

'It'll not be the second time either,' Danny said softly, 'for I'll be with you.'

'Are you sure?' It was impossible for her to keep the pleasure out of her voice.

'Just try and stop me!'

She smiled across at him and reached out and touched his arm. 'For a Yank, you're not a bad bloke, you know.' Her eyes, though a light grey-green in the daytime, were dark and shining in the darkness.

'You're not so bad yourself, Irish.' He wanted to reach across and touch her, to smooth the tiny furrows in the skin that seemed to permanently mar her brow, even when she was smiling. But something held him back. It had never happened to him before – this reluctance to take the first step. Even with Shiralee, for all his guilt about Sol, he had needed very little

514

encouragement to become physically involved. As for Ruth, she was already assuming the proportions of simply a rather special one-night stand. No, this time it was different. But maybe it was just Elaine that was different from any other young woman he had ever known. He moved back round in his seat, so that he was no longer looking at her, but staring straight ahead over the top of the steering-wheel. 'This guy Des – you've been seeing quite a bit of him for a long time?'

'I've been seeing *all* of him for a long time!' she grinned, then sensing he didn't appreciate the joke, she said quietly, 'About eighteen months, actually. I met him when I started at Queen's. He's on the same course.'

'You think a lot of him, huh?'

'You could say we're in tune politically. We both want the same things out of life . . . What is this anyway, the third degree?'

He shifted uneasily in his seat. 'Hell no, Elaine. I'm just curious, that's all.'

'What you really want to know is – do I sleep with him?'

He turned back towards her and gave an embarrassed laugh. 'You don't believe in beating about the bush, do you?'

'Life's too short to play games, Danny. And the answer to your question is – yes, yes I do.'

'Whew . . .' He slumped back in his seat, staring out through the glass of the windscreen.

'What did you expect – that we sit holding hands all night, discussing Marx's theory of surplus value, or Engels' *Anti-Dühring*?'

'No – no, of course not!' He felt like he'd been kicked in the solar plexus, yet it was no more than he had expected.

'Danny Donovan – I do believe you're jealous!' She grabbed his arm and pulled him round to face her.

'That's bull!'

'No, it's not . . . But there's really no need to be. Just because we're sleeping together doesn't mean I'm tied to him for the rest of my life. I wouldn't be tied to any man for that long.'

He had heard plenty of other females back home at college, before he was drafted, mouthing off about Women's Lib, but he could bet every last one of them had swapped their loudly proclaimed ideals for a permanent lunch-cheque and was now married, to a regular nine-to-fiver, with a couple of kids. Elaine wouldn't, though. He was certain of that. She was speaking the truth. 'I do believe you mean that.'

'You'd better believe it.'

Their eyes met. 'Would you ever consider living in America, Elaine?' The words came out with difficulty.

'No.'

The short, emphatic answer was like a slap in the face. 'Why the hell not?'

'Because I'm not into your American Dream, that's why not!' She moved round in her seat so that she was looking straight at him. 'You know what's wrong with you Yanks, Danny Donovan? You think the whole damned world is longing to become part of your Great Society. You think we're all longing for a piece of Mom's apple pie. But we're not – and when you discover we're not you retire all hurt and confused. Look what's happening in Vietnam. All those poor kids just out of high school, like you were, are told that you've got to go out there and save those poor Vietnamese for the "Free World" – only to discover that they've never heard of your so-called "Free World" and only want you to go home with your bombers and napalm and stop blowing them all to smithereens!' She shook her head at the futility of it all. 'Well, it's true, isn't it?'

'Yeah, it's true . . . "Join the army, meet interesting people, and kill 'em" – that about sums it up. Telling all those poor bastards out there that they're fighting for peace is about as big a con as going to an orgy and saying you're screwing for chastity's sake . . . But that still isn't any reason not to give the States a chance.'

'I just don't fancy it, Danny, that's all. Not that I think this place is paradise on earth, far from it!' She gave a wry grin. 'You know, Des once said if the Good Lord wanted to give the world an enema, he'd stick the tube in Belfast!'

He grinned back. 'You could say the same about New York, I guess, but I'd still rather live there than anywhere else.'

'I take it you'll never be emigrating to the Emerald Isle, then?'

'Never is a long time, Elaine. Who knows what even next week will bring?'

'I know what next week will bring,' she said, screwing up her face. 'It'll bring my first exam.'

'Shouldn't you be getting down to some work, rather than going out on this thing on Saturday night, then? I bet your mother doesn't know they're so close.' There was real concern in his eyes as they searched hers.

She sighed. 'She worries far too much – wants me to have the chances she never had and all that crap. But you're right, she thinks they're another couple of weeks away yet. She'd go mad and lock me in the house if she realised they started so soon.'

'Will I see you before then – before Saturday?' It was a complete contradiction of everything he had just said, but he couldn't stop himself asking the question.

'Do you want to?'

'Yes.'

She leaned across and kissed him chastely on the side of his cheek. 'That's nice to hear because I'm afraid the answer's no. I'm definitely going to stay in every single night and bury my head in a book. It'll be early to bed every night for me from now on.'

'Without Des.'

'Sans Des – sans everything, except those blessed books!' She got out of the car before he realised it and bent down to smile at him through the open door. 'Dream about me tonight, Danny Donovan,' she said softly.

He stared after her in the darkness as she ran across the pavement and disappeared into the front door of the house. 'Dream about you . . .' he said softly. He'd done nothing else for the past two nights . . .

He threw back his head and let out a long, whistling sigh. Dames! He needed to get involved with another right now like he needed a hole in the head. He grimaced wryly. If he wasn't careful that's probably what he'd end up with – a hole in the head – if he let her talk him into too many of these damn-fool escapades like this Saturday night thing she had lined up! But what else could he have done but offer to go with her? If he hadn't she'd only go alone and there was no way he was going to let that happen. She was her own woman, just like he was his own man. Or was he? He frowned in the darkness, drumming the fingers of his right hand against the black plastic of the steering wheel. Certainly he had always liked to think he was. Wasn't he the one to walk out when that little bitch back in New York, Shiralee, came on with the heavy stuff about being pregnant and confessing all to Sol? And wasn't he the one to walk out on Ruth out there in Israel? Okay, it wasn't exactly his choice and it could even look like running away — but, hell, he defied anyone to tell the difference between the two, walking out and running away.

Nothing in this life was black and white any more. There weren't even any good guys and bad guys. He'd discovered that much out there in Nam. Everything was a lousy shade of grey. He remembered a book of poetry Sol used to keep in his locker back at base. He was never much of a one for Auden's poetry himself, but two lines his buddy had underlined still stuck in his head:

> If they should ask you why we died
> Tell them because our fathers lied.

And it was true, goddamit, it was true. And how was he to know it wasn't only true in Nam? How did he know that it wasn't equally true right here in Ireland? Sure, his grandfather had died for the cause, and now Elaine and a new generation were willing to lay down their lives if need be, but who was to say that they hadn't been fooled in just the same way? What if the majority of Irish people didn't *want* to be saved — didn't want to be freed of the yoke of British imperialism, just like the majority of Vietnamese hadn't wanted to be 'saved' by American imperialism?

With an impatient stab of his left hand, he threw the selector into drive and sped off into the darkness. The army would make a man of you, the little jerk of a drill sergeant had said as they paraded before him every morning. Tell that to his buddies who never made it back from the God-forsaken place! Tell that to Sol, who stared into the future with only half a body

518

functioning! Tell it to the whole damned Marine Corps! But most of all, let them convince himself. More than ever he wanted to feel he had got it all together right now. He wanted to have all the right answers when Elaine posed all the wrong questions. He wanted to stand head and shoulders above that little creep Des and his like. Hell, he was the one who had already seen it all — who had experienced a *real* war, wasn't he? He was the one who Elaine should be turning to for advice.

His teeth gritted and his fingers tightened on the wheel. It was all a con. The whole damned world was a con. He had learned that much if he had learned anything from the past few years. But he had also learned that to survive in it, you had simply to learn to be an even bigger con-man than the next guy.

Yes, he would go with Elaine on Saturday. He would prove to her that he was the right guy to have by her side. If he was really honest with himself, the cause, as they called it, was irrelevant. After all he'd seen and done in the past few years, every cause would be irrelevant from now on. He knew that now. But not people. And certainly not Elaine. Godammit, certainly not Elaine . . .

Chapter 58

'Kitty!' Maeve could not believe her eyes as she passed through the ticket barrier at Dublin's main railway station. 'What on earth are you doing here?'

'I thought it would surprise you!'

The two women embraced and Kitty took her mother's arm as she shepherded her towards the waiting Rover. 'It's Uncle Charlie's,' she said, as she opened the passenger door and Maeve lowered herself into the plush leather upholstery. 'I'd better be careful I don't run into any oncoming lamp-posts!'

'Never mind the lamp-posts!' Maeve said impatiently. 'What on earth are you doing here in Dublin? I thought you were in Israel with Art.'

'I was in Israel until last night,' Kitty said, throwing the car into gear and moving out into the road. 'But things got, shall we say, rather difficult after Danny left, so Art and I felt it diplomatic to cut the visit short.'

'He's here with you?'

'No, he arranged to send himself a telegram requesting his presence in New York immediately. He flew out from Lod an hour before I did yesterday evening.'

'It must have been quite a little "difficulty", as you put it, to necessitate that type of subterfuge? Is it what I think it was about?'

Kitty's fingers tensed on the wheel. 'And what might that be, pray?'

'Danny told me, so we needn't beat about the bush. He told me you'd confessed to him that Lee Finkelstein is his father.'

Kitty gave a dry laugh. 'Confessed to him, did I? You make it sound like I had to do a dozen Hail Marys into the bargain! . . . But yes, yes I told him that Lee is his father. It became necessary – he and Ruth were getting rather too close for comfort.'

'He didn't tell me that.'

'I'm not surprised. He took it quite badly – naturally.'

'Did you tell her? Did you tell Ruth the truth?'

'No. It was Lee's decision not to. Neither she nor her mother know – he prefers it that way, and I respect his decision.'

'You told Art, though, I take it?'

Kitty's jaw tightened. 'I didn't see that I had any choice. I should have told him years ago, but just didn't have the courage, I guess . . . How do you tell the man you live with, and love dearly, that you once had an affair with and a child by his son?' She shook her head. 'It wasn't easy.'

Maeve took a deep breath. She could well believe it. 'How did he take it?'

'Very well under the circumstances. He didn't rush out and floor Lee, if that's what you mean. He appreciated it was already all over before we even met . . . We were to be married out there, you know – in Israel, but the wedding is – let's say – postponed for the time being.' There was a tightness in her voice as she said it, despite an effort to keep her tone light.

'I'm sorry.' It was a totally inadequate response, but it was all Maeve could think of to say.

'Don't be. There's really no need. I guess it's divine retribution for not coming clean right at the beginning. I can't blame Danny for reacting like he did either. I'd feel the very same if you were to suddenly tell me that a man I'd only just met was my real father.' She glanced across at her mother. 'But then you'd never be so dumb as to get yourself into a mess like that in the first place.'

Maeve's mouth went dry. Now was the time to say something meaningful – something that would smooth the way for whatever confession she felt might be appropriate before too long. But no words would come.

Kitty took her silence to be an endorsement of what she had just said and, with relief, changed the subject. 'I must say, Uncle Charlie and Aunty Amy have a nice place. And they really seem to be in the social swing here – you know, bridge parties, cheese and wines, and that type of thing every other night.'

'Amy always did love a social life, even when she was engaged to Willie Lovett.'

'Who?'

'Oh, no one you'd know,' Maeve said wistfully. 'One of the lost generation, that's all . . . That's what they call them these days, I believe.'

'Are you intending staying with them long? Aunt Amy said just the one night, to begin with, and then you might come back for a week or so later on in the month. What I'd like to know is where you intend going in between! You haven't got an old boyfriend stashed away round the back of St Stephen's Green, have you?'

Maeve's stomach turned over as her eyes darted to Kitty's face. But no – it *was* purely a joke. 'She never listens to anything you say, Amy doesn't,' she sighed. 'I told her I'd move into your grandmother's place for a few days. She's due back from Aunt Maud's soon and it'll be good for both me and the house. It'll give it an airing and let me catch my breath. I'm not as young as I was, you know, Kathleen, these past few days have taken a lot out of me.'

Kitty threw her a wry glance as the car made its way slowly through the city traffic. 'Snap!'

Amy was waiting in the bay window of the lounge for them to arrive. Before Kitty had locked the car doors, she was already running down the front steps. 'Maeve! Oh, Maeve!'

They hugged each other for so long on the pavement that Maeve was forced to pull herself free and exclaim, 'Why, Amy, anyone would think we hadn't seen each other for half a century!'

Amy looked at her in confusion, then giggled. 'It's incredible, isn't it? It really is that long! But you haven't changed, Maeve, not one little bit!' She held her old friend at arm's length and nodded emphatically. 'No, not one little bit!'

'Och, away with you!' Maeve laughed. 'I'm seventy years old, Amy dear! That's not saying much for how I looked when you last saw me at eighteen, is it now?'

Amy giggled as, arm in arm, they followed Kitty up the steps and into the house. 'Charlie's in his den,' she said. 'He told me to give him a shout when the car appeared.'

'No, he's not! He's right here!' The voice came from the top of the staircase.

'Charlie!' Maeve's eyes filled with tears as she looked up into the grey-blue eyes of her brother.

He came down the stairs slowly, taking one step at a time, his walking stick clasped firmly in his left hand. His tall figure was stooped now, whether from his old war wounds or simply age, Maeve could not tell, and his once lean frame had filled out to a stoutness that reminded her of their late father. But his face – his face was still the same dear old Charlie, give or take a wrinkle or two.

They hugged in silence, as the tears flowed freely. There was so much to say, but all that could keep till later. It was enough to be here, at long last, with those she loved . . .

The evening passed in a warm, mellow haze induced by a combination of Irish coffee and reminiscences. Maeve was glad that Kitty was there as they recalled old times, old places, old friends. It somehow made her daughter a part of her own world – a world that had remained a closed book for so many years. What was really surprising was how many of their old friends had remained in Dublin. 'You're the exception, you know, Maeve,' Amy insisted, nodding her elegantly coiffured head over the top of her Irish coffee. 'Everyone here regards you as the one that got away; the one that had the guts to go out into the big bad world and lead the kind of life we only read about in the newspapers or books. Why, even marrying Danny Donovan was the most outrageous thing to do – putting you on a par with Constance Markiewicz and Maud Gonne!'

'Hardly!' Maeve laughed. Comparing her with Ireland's two most revolutionary females this century was surely a bit of an exaggeration, but Amy was insistent it was true.

'Who could have guessed when you yourself married a revolutionary that one of his staunchest comrades that Easter Monday would turn out to be our century's greatest politician – Eamon de Valera! If only the generation that threw up its hands in horror at you then had all lived to see history take its course!'

'I guess we've all been reinstated now,' Maeve said, with a quiet smile. 'All of us black sheep. But I doubt if the likes of Mother would agree with you. Even at my respectable, advanced age of seventy she still sees me as a perfect example of wayward youth! I remember her once saying to me that parenthood seemed to consist of nothing but feeding the mouth that bites you. I don't think she ever revised that opinion!'

Amy gave a rueful smile. 'She's a remarkable old lady. How old is she now – ninety-four, ninety-five? To think that she can still find the energy to go traipsing off to look after your Aunt Maud. Why, until recently she still insisted on taking charge of every single church fête! "A fête worse than death", you used to call it when Mother was in charge, didn't you, Charlie dear?'

Her dozing husband grunted his agreement from the depths of the armchair nearest the fire.

'Do you know I've never even met my grandmother yet,' Kitty said. 'Who does she resemble, Aunt Amy – Mom or Uncle Charlie?'

'Don't answer that, Amy,' Charlie snorted, sitting up in the chair and reaching for his glass. 'I'll tell you the only thing your dear grandmother resembles, Kitty m'dear – a Russian war memorial! A great big rock-solid edifice built to last for a thousand years.'

'Charlie – really!'

Kitty stifled a giggle. 'It only makes me all the more eager to meet her,' she reassured her aunt. 'In fact, along with you and Uncle Charlie, my grandmother was the person I've been looking forward to meeting the most – apart from Uncle Dermot, of course.'

'Uncle Dermot?' Amy's carefully pencilled brows furrowed.

'My father's brother.'

'Oh, of course – the priest. How silly of me! It's such a pity – he was such a nice man.'

'Was?' Maeve interrupted, her heart in her mouth. 'What do you mean he *was* such a nice man? There's nothing wrong with him, is there? He – he's not . . .'

'Dead, you mean?' Amy finished the sentence for her. 'To be honest with you, Maeve, I just don't know. I did hear from Emma that he was in hospital around Christmas and wasn't expected to last until the New Year, but I can't say that I've read an actual report of his death. Not that it would be guaranteed to be in the *Irish Times*, you know. More than likely it'd be one of those Catholic papers which we never see. You haven't heard, have you, Charlie — whether that priest, Father Dermot, died or not?'

They were discussing Dermot's death as they would the weather ... 'Can you remember, Charlie, whether it was fine on Tuesday or not?' Every muscle in her body tensed as Maeve stared into the dying flames of the fire and clutched the glass containing the remains of the Irish coffee to her breast. Suddenly she felt tired, very tired. She wanted to get out of here ... Go for a walk in the cool night air and put her chaotic thoughts in order. What if he *was* dead? What if Dermot was dead? It was just conceivable that something had happened and they had kept it from Katie, knowing how ill she had been herself lately. Or maybe Katie had kept it from her ... Her mind reeled.

She got up from the settee with a jerky movement that made her reach down and grip the padded arm to steady herself. 'It's either the whiskey in the drink or just old age,' she joked, but her lips refused to form themselves into the expected smile.

'Let me give you a hand.' Kitty made to get up and help her, but Maeve waved her away.

'I'm not that decrepit.' She turned to Amy and Charlie who were looking on in concern. 'It's been a lovely evening,' she assured them. 'You'll not mind if I take a wee turn around the block to clear my head? It looks such a lovely clear night out there.' Her eyes moved to the big bay window, where the curtains were still open, showing a sky full of stars.

'Would you like me to come with you?' Charlie asked, reaching for his stick, but Maeve wouldn't hear of it.

'You'll do no such thing. Just you sit there, the three of you, and let an old woman have her way. It's been a long time since I've breathed the air of a Dublin night like this.'

They watched her walk from the room, carefully placing one foot in front of the other as she made her way across the Axminster carpet. 'Do you know, Charlie, I do believe you overdid it tonight with the whiskey in that Irish coffee,' Amy said, giving her husband an admonishing look.

It was the last remark Maeve heard before heading for the cloakroom and lifting her coat from the hallstand. She looked at herself in the mirror on the back of the door, as she buttoned the collar up around her neck and tied a silk scarf around it. Her face looked drawn, her mouth set, and she practised smiling, forcing her lips into what appeared as little more than a grimace, before she shrugged hopelessly and made for the door.

It was a long time – a very long time – since she had walked these streets, but she still knew the way to the presbytery as if it were only yesterday that she had been there. The night air was cool in her lungs and she practised breathing deeply at regular intervals as she walked on along the grey pavements. The sharp click-clicking of her high heels on the stone flags had a curiously pacifying effect, so that she found her energy returning as the yards disappeared beneath her feet.

When, at last, she came to the high stone wall that marked the boundary of the presbytery gardens, she came to an abrupt halt, as memories crowded in on her. She walked on slowly up the road towards the tall wrought-iron gates. They were shut, and so they should be, for it was gone midnight. But a light still burned at one of the windows on the second floor. 'Please let it be him,' she whispered into the darkness. 'Dear God, please let it be him . . .'

Chapter 59

Maeve rose at eight and breakfasted in the sunshine of the morning-room with Amy and Kitty. Charlie, clad in his gardening clothes, was pottering around in the conservatory while the women made their plans for the morning over coffee and wholemeal toast. Amy already had a standing engagement to serve behind the counter at the local Oxfam shop on a Friday morning and Kitty decided she could be most usefully employed writing a long letter to Art.

'What about you, Maeve?' Amy asked, as she rose from the table and brushed the toast crumbs from the front of her plaid skirt. 'I know you're intending moving into Jubilee Avenue sometime today, but not this morning surely?'

'No, I think I'll leave that till this afternoon,' Maeve replied, pushing her cup from her. 'Charlie has kindly offered me the use of the car to take my things round after lunch.'

'Then what about this morning? You're welcome to come down to the shop with me. We're always glad of an extra hand.'

Maeve smiled. 'It's a kind offer, Amy dear, but I thought I'd like to spend the morning just having a wander around some local haunts ... You know the type of thing – having a good wallow in nostalgia.'

'Well, you needn't bother looking for McIntyre Street, for you'll not find it!'

'You mean it's gone – the whole street?'

'Every last stone. They've built a ghastly council block where your old house used to stand and rehoused some of the original inhabitants of the street in that – but it's not a pretty sight, I can assure you.'

Maeve rose from the table. 'Well, I suppose that's progress,' she said, with a sigh. 'But it would have been nice to have a last look at the old place.'

'How about Uncle Dermot, Mom, weren't you going to see

what's happened to him?' Kitty looked up at her from behind a copy of the *Irish Times*.

Maeve flinched inwardly, as she always did at the mention of his name. That was the most important thing on her agenda this morning, but she certainly wasn't letting on about it. 'Oh yes, I might just take a wander round there, providing I don't get waylaid by any other old acquaintances.'

'Well, if he is still alive, tell him I'll pop round myself sometime – tomorrow most probably.'

Maeve stared down at the top of her daughter's head, only just visible behind the open newspaper. Just like that! If – please God – he was still alive, she was to say, just like that, 'Oh, by the way, Dermot, Kitty might pop in tomorrow.' Her heart quailed at the prospect.

She dressed with special care, choosing nothing too flashy; a simple duck-egg-blue cashmere dress, set off with a pale cream scarf at the neck, which matched her plain court shoes. On top of it she slipped a cream wool, three-quarter-length jacket which matched her handbag to perfection. Then she paused in her critical examination in the dressing-table mirror and a fleeting frown crossed her face. She removed the scarf and tied it instead to the strap of her handbag. It had totally obscured the most important part of her ensemble – the small silver crucifix he had given her on her departure for America; his last present to her.

Her fingers touched it gently, making sure it was resting perfectly on the soft wool of the dress. It glinted in the late spring sunshine that streamed in through the tall window behind the mirror. She could feel her heart begin to beat much too fast and was tempted to reach inside her handbag for one of the tranquillisers her doctor back in New York had prescribed for just such an occasion. But she shook her head defiantly. 'It's mind over matter,' she told herself, speaking the words aloud in the silence of the room. There was nothing – absolutely nothing – going to interfere with any of her senses today; she would not even have a nerve-steadying drink. If, God willing, Dermot was still alive, then she would walk up to him with none of her faculties impaired. This would be the moment she had waited over fifty years for – the moment she must savour, for it would live in her memory for the rest of her life.

Her good intentions almost crumbled once she was out in the fresh air and on her way across the city to Dermot's old home. The pubs she passed looked irresistibly inviting and it needed all her resolve to pass the doors and continue on her way, without the Dutch courage a glass of gin and tonic would provide.

When she finally reached the tall wrought-iron gates, she paused outside them and gazed up at the windows. There was no sign of life, but that did not mean anything, for even if Dermot were no longer there, the place would be occupied by his successor. Her eyes wandered around the large garden and her heart leapt to find that even that was exactly as she had remembered it. The huge bank of rhododendrons to the left of the house was still there, ablaze in all its dazzling pink glory, and the laburnum trees that overhung the wall still trailed their golden tendrils down the moss-covered stones. Yellow Welsh poppies danced in the slight breeze beneath the latticed windows, their small heads reaching to only half the height of their taller companions, the lupins, which would provide such a colourful display later on in the summer.

Her hand found the handle of the gate and, taking a deep breath, she pushed it open. It creaked loudly on its hinges. It was getting on in years, like herself, she thought wryly, as she continued up the gravel path.

Ignoring the bell, she gave three loud raps on the knocker and stood back, with a thumping heart, on the broad stone step. When, after a couple of minutes, there was no sound of movement from inside, she was on the point of knocking again, but the door was pulled open. A woman of about her own age stood on the step. Her white hair was done in a bun at the nape of her neck and she leaned heavily on a walking stick, as she peered at her through a pair of butterfly-winged glasses. 'Yes, can I help you?'

'I – I'm looking for Father Dermot Donovan,' Maeve said, with great difficulty. 'He used to live here many years ago.' Her hand clutched at the iron handrail at the edge of the step. Her heart was thumping so hard she thought she was going to faint before she could hear the answer.

'Father Dermot doesn't receive visitors in the morning. It's doctor's orders, I'm afraid.' The tone was quite emphatic and brooked no argument.

'He — he's in there?' It was a stupid thing to say, but the relief was enormous.

'He's allowed down to his study after breakfast for an hour or so.'

'May I see him — please. Just for a moment.' She was begging now. She would get down on her knees if need be.

'Are you a friend of his?' The housekeeper looked at her suspiciously through the bifocal lenses.

'An old friend,' Maeve assured her. 'A very old friend.'

The door was reluctantly opened a fraction more. 'You'd better come into the hall. I'll have a wee word with him. I'm not promising, mind. The Father's not a well man — you're aware of that?'

The housekeeper made to turn back into the house, but Maeve caught her arm. 'Actually, I've only just heard that he's been ill. It — it's not serious is it?'

The woman looked at her with an almost pitying expression. 'It's cancer,' she said flatly. 'That's always serious, isn't it?'

Cancer! Maeve followed her into the hall, the word resounding in her head. She wanted to run, but in which direction she had no idea. Did she run and throw her arms round him, or run back out the door?

'What name do I give?'

The question brought her back to reality. 'Fullerton,' she said quickly. 'Maeve Fullerton.'

The housekeeper looked at her curiously for a moment, then hobbled off in the opposite direction, leaving her standing on the threadbare rug just inside the door. She could not believe she was actually here. How would he take it? Could he stand the shock? She started to sweat. First the palms of her hands, then a thin film of perspiration broke on her brow, until her whole body grew damp and sticky and she hurried over to the tiny mirror on the hallstand to peer anxiously into the discoloured glass. Her face was flushed and glistening, her eyes standing out in her pink face like two blue beads. She ran her tongue over her lips in a desperate attempt to unfreeze them, as a shuffling sound from the other end of the hall made her whirl round to see the housekeeper on her way back. But this time, instead of the detached demeanour of a few moments ago, the woman was staring at her in a way she found quite unsettling.

She nodded for Maeve to follow her, and she did so, walking a couple of paces behind her stooped figure, as she led the way through a door at the back of the hall to a closed door next to the kitchen. Maeve stood back while the woman opened it and slipped inside, then held it ajar for Maeve herself to enter.

'Thank you, Cissie.'

She heard his voice before she saw him and her heart turned somersaults in her breast. She would have recognised it anywhere. She jerked round in the direction from which it came. He was sitting in an old leather armchair next to the gas fire, with a tartan rug over his knees. His face was skin and bone, his hair snow-white, and there were tears glistening in the dark eyes as they looked up into hers.

'Maeve . . .'

She ran blindly towards him and threw herself down on the rug at his feet, clasping his hand in hers. She could not look at him, for tears blinded her own vision, as she buried her face in his lap. With his other hand, he stroked her hair, as he had done so often, so very often, in years gone by.

It was several minutes before she felt composed enough to sit up and meet his eyes. Her hand went out to touch his face. His skin felt dry and brittle, like the most fragile tissue paper.

'Maeve . . . My Maeve . . . You came back . . .'

In her head she heard the words *just in time*, although he did not utter them. She nodded mutely, not trusting herself to speak. Instead she clung on to his hand as her eyes explored his face. It was as if the skin had fallen from the bones, leaving only a transparent covering on the fine contours. But his eyes, his eyes had not changed. They still burned with that same light she had known so well when they were young . . . And they had been young, so very young . . .

'You came back,' he repeated softly. 'Did they tell you?'

She shook her head. 'No . . .'

A wistful smile flickered in his eyes. 'My poor Maeve . . . What a shock . . . You come all this way and instead of the man you remembered, you find a decrepit old wreck.'

A momentary anger flared in her eyes. 'No, no – not that! Never that!'

He shook his head, as his eyes smiled indulgently into hers. 'Go on believing that, my Maeve.'

'I will, Dermot, always!' Her promise was made so fiercely that she was taken aback at her own vehemence.

His fingers touched the small silver crucifix around her neck. 'God gave us memories, Maeve, so that we may have roses in December . . . We never needed more, did we?'

She shook her head. 'No, Dermot, never . . .' She knew now, she had never loved Frank. She had never loved another human being – no, not even Kitty – as she had loved him.

There was so much she wanted to say. So much that was in her heart, that had been in her heart for all these years, to unburden. But it was impossible. This was not the time and he had not the energy to listen. Even if he thought he had, she could not do it to him. 'Does she look after you – your housekeeper?'

'Cissie's a good woman. She has seen to my every need for forty years.'

'Mrs Shea . . . ?'

'She died a dozen or so years after you left.'

'Forty years is a long time.' She was overcome with a sudden and passionate jealousy for the woman with the stick.

'Longer than most marriages. Longer than God granted you and Frank, I believe.'

The name of her late husband bit into her soul. If she had never met Frank Fullerton she would have stayed here in Dublin, next to him. She could have taken Mrs Shea's job . . . If . . . If . . .

'Will it be a cup of tea you're wanting, Father?'

The housekeeper's voice from the doorway made her whirl round, her hand flying to her wet cheeks.

'Are you sure you've got time, Cissie, my dear? I thought

you'd want to be away early this morning and Caitlin was to come in?'

Cissie ... Caitlin ... The names rang in Maeve's head. Names that had once pierced her heart a very long time ago. It couldn't be, could it? It couldn't be that woman – the one had borne Danny's child? She couldn't have moved into Dermot's life after his brother died?

'I – I didn't quite catch your name when I came in,' Maeve said, rising to her feet and addressing the other woman, before she had a chance to answer Dermot's question. 'It – it wouldn't be O'Rourke, by any chance?'

'No, Mrs Fullerton, it wouldn't. My name's O'Brien. Cissie O'Brien.'

A wave of relief swept over Maeve. She was overwrought, that was all, imagining things and situations that didn't exist. Cissie was a common enough name, and there must be dozens of Caitlins in Dublin. She glanced down at Dermot, to find he had a tense, tight look to his mouth as he said, 'About that cup of tea, Cissie – are you sure now you have the time?'

There was a tangible bond between Dermot and this woman, Maeve could feel it. It was in the very air they breathed. 'I – I'll not bother with the tea today, if you don't mind, Dermot. It's time I was getting back. I promised Kitty.'

'Kitty?' He straightened up in the chair and stared up at her. 'Kitty's here in Dublin?'

In her haste to invent an excuse, she had dropped their daughter's name. She could have kicked herself. 'Yes,' she said hesitantly. 'Kitty's here.'

'That'll be all, Cissie, my dear. Away home with you now. I'll be fine.'

Cissie O'Brien backed out of the door, closing it behind her, as Dermot looked searchingly at Maeve. 'Does she want to see me? Does Kitty want to see me?'

Maeve nodded, avoiding his eyes.

'Did you ever tell her, Maeve? Did you ever tell her the truth?' He knew. He had always known.

She shook her head, as tears filled her eyes. 'I couldn't, Dermot. I never had the courage.' It was the first time she had ever admitted the truth.

533

He sat back in the chair and closed his eyes. 'I can't acknowledge her then, can I? I can never make my peace.'

'Do you want me to tell her?' She whispered the words.

He shook his head. 'I'm being a selfish old man. I've already had more than my fair share of love in this life, Maeve. Cissie has been more than a housekeeper, she's been like a wife to me, and Caitlin more than a mere niece, she's been like my own daughter. They have been my family, these forty years.'

Maeve stared at him, her face draining of all colour. 'More than a niece?' she breathed. 'You said she had been more than a niece? . . . But that woman denied her name was O'Rourke. She told me it was O'Brien.'

'And 'twas the truth she was telling. She's been Cissie O'Brien getting on for fifty years now. She married a lad from Ballsbridge, Sean O'Brien, in the early twenties, but he was killed by the Black and Tans not three months after their wedding.'

'And she's looked after you all these years?' Her whole world was falling apart, as a jealousy such as she had never known consumed her.

'More than an old sinner like me had the right to expect.' Then seeing the look on her face, he reached out his hand to take hers. 'It doesn't upset you, does it, Maeve? You weren't there . . . You were three thousand miles across the sea. You walked out of my life that day and took my child with you.'

A shiver ran through her as her whole life, all those wasted years, passed before her eyes – years when another woman had been here, tending to his every need, caring for him . . . Roses in December, he had said. God gave us memories so we could have roses in December. He could have added that roses have thorns. And those thorns were now piercing her very soul . . . It should have been her. Oh God, it should have been her . . .

Chapter 60

Maeve stepped out of the taxi at the gates of Sundrive Park, clutching a bunch of pale cream roses to her breast. She reached inside her handbag and handed the driver a pound note. The fresh breeze blew the hem of her dress up around her knees, as she waved away his half-hearted attempt to reach for change. 'Keep it!'

She watched as it pulled back out in to the traffic, in a belch of blue exhaust fumes, and drove off down the road. She had no idea why she had come here instead of going for a bite of lunch. It certainly wasn't to sit in the park and watch the grass grow, or to smell the flowers. She intended to walk on beyond the park to the small graveyard that bordered its verdant perimeter. A graveyard that she had often thought of in the intervening years, for it contained the body of the young man who had set her life on its course by introducing her to his brother . . .

As if of their own accord, her feet started to walk in the direction where she knew her dead husband lay. She had not visited Danny's grave since the day after the funeral, when she had come up here alone to make her peace with the man whose ring she had once worn. Why she felt the compulsion to come now, only minutes after leaving Dermot, she could not say.

She had difficulty in finding his grave, for when she was last here there had been no marble cross erected at the head of the small plot. She had arranged for that to be done after she had left for America. She stared down at the inscription:

**Daniel Kieran Donovan
born 23rd November 1895
died 3rd October 1916
beloved husband of Maeve Ballantine
and father of Kieran**

AT PEACE WITH THE LORD

She gazed at the words etched in the shining grey stone. For anyone acquainted with them as a family, there was one glaring omission. Kitty's name was missing. Somehow she could not bear to send the instruction to have it added. It would seem a reasonable enough oversight, she had told herself. There she was, thousands of miles away across the ocean, with a new husband when her second child was born. But that was not the real reason. Dermot would be the only one who would have known that.

She stooped to pick up the flower vase at the foot of the grave, then drew back as if stung. There were already fresh flowers there; fresh spring flowers that tossed their heads in the midday breeze; as she stared down at them. Dermot couldn't have put them there, she was certain of that. And neither would Mary-Agnes, for her own parents' grave, including that of Willie-John and the brothers and sisters who had not survived into adulthood, was right next to Danny's and it was totally devoid of flowers. In fact, compared to the immaculate condition of Danny's plot, it looked as if it had not been tended in decades. Moss covered the inscription, almost obscuring the names, and the flower container was chipped and rusted. It must have been her – Danny's fancy-woman, Cissie O'Rourke. No matter how often she denied that was her name, Maeve knew she could never think of her as anything else. Yes, it was either her or the child she had borne for him, Caitlin.

A cold, sick feeling welled within her as she turned from the grave. It was as if this woman had been waiting – waiting for her to leave to step into her shoes. Not content with taking her brand-new husband – once Danny was dead she had moved into Dermot's life.

'Over forty years,' Maeve breathed the words. That was what he had said, wasn't it? Over forty years she had been with him, tending to his every need, doing the things only a wife should do for a man. The personal, little everyday things that she, Maeve, should have done. All those decades when she should have been here, she had been thousands of miles away in New York, acting out her life as Frank Fullerton's wife. The wife of a man who had not brought her the happiness she so desperately sought throughout all those decades since she had left this green and pleasant land . . . They all rolled before her, in one great wave – the Twenties, the Thirties, the Forties, the Fifties, the Sixties – as tears filled her eyes and she sank to her knees in front of the marble cross.

She had chosen marriage to Frank as the easy option. To have stayed here as a young widow, in love with and carrying the child of a Catholic priest, was almost unthinkable. But it could have been done. She knew that now. That woman had proved it. She could have done what Cissie O'Rourke so cunningly did. She could have simply moved in as Dermot's housekeeper. No one could have objected to that.

A burning jealousy consumed her as she closed her eyes and hot tears squeezed beneath her lashes, to stream down her pale cheeks. All she could think of was the unthinkable itself. Had she – had that woman been more to him than a housekeeper? She had to know. She could not rest till she knew. But who could she ask? Certainly not Dermot.

She rose unsteadily to her feet. There was only one person in this city who would know the truth. Mary-Agnes. But how would she find her? Hadn't Amy said this morning they had pulled down McIntyre Street – bulldozed it into the ground? She started to walk back towards the gates, her mind racing ahead of her. They had to do something with the inhabitants. And it had been a close-knit community. They had put up high-rise apartments in its place. Amy had said so, and had said that they had housed some of the inhabitants there. She would go there now. Someone must know. If Mary-Agnes no longer lived there, someone would know where she could be found.

It took the best part of an hour for her to make her way to the small landscaped area that was once McIntyre Street. Amy was right; she wouldn't have recognised the place. She narrowed her eyes as she looked up at the twelve-storey block that now stood where her old house used to be. If luck was with her, Mary-Agnes would be in one of those, would be behind one of the frilled net curtains that decorated the rectangular rows of plate glass that blinked down at her in the spring sunshine.

The first person she stopped to ask was a young girl carrying a baby, but she merely shook her head. 'Sorry, missus, I don't know no Kellys. I've only just moved in here myself.'

Maeve's face clouded. It wasn't going to be like this with everyone she approached, was it? Her eyes fell on an old man sitting on a wooden bench near the main door and she walked over to him and gave a nervous cough. 'Excuse me, I'm looking for a Mrs Kelly – a Mary-Agnes Kelly. She would be in her late seventies by now and used to stay over there, before the houses were pulled down,' she nodded towards the freshly landscaped area where Mary-Agnes and her family once lived.

The old man scratched the greying stubble of his chin and tilted his bonnet back on his head. 'Kelly, you say? Now would that be old Liam Kelly's missus?'

Maeve's eyes brightened. 'Yes, yes, that's her! Do you know where they live now?'

'Not they,' the old man corrected. 'Liam's been gone these five years. But Mary-Agnes is still hereabouts, as far as I know.'

'Here in this block?'

He squinted up towards the grey concrete that towered behind them. 'You could try the second floor. I think it's around there she gets out. I haven't seen hide nor hair of her for a good six month, though.'

'Thank you. Thank you very much.'

Buoyed up with this information, Maeve set off nervously for the main door. The interior of the entrance felt dank and cold, and the lifts had names scrawled on them in black aerosol paint. She decided to forgo them and headed for the stairs. Two flights up was just about manageable.

When she reached the second floor, she paused for breath, and let her eyes wander down the long expanse of blue-painted doors. Please let her be inside one of those, she prayed, as she took a series of deep breaths and attempted to calm her rapidly beating heart.

Sullivan, Tierney, Fitzgerald ... the names behind the narrow plastic nameplates stared back at her as she made her way along the row. Then, at the very last door in the passage, her heart leapt. 'Kelly!' she burst out in delight.

She took another deep breath as she raised her hand to ring

the bell. It had rung twice before the door was finally opened and she stared into the faded brown eyes of Mary-Agnes.

'Yes?' Mary-Agnes looked up at her from her wheelchair, a shrunken caricature of her old self. 'Can I help you?' She quite obviously had no idea who it was.

'Mary-Agnes, don't you recognise me?'

Mary-Agnes stared up at the well-dressed, elderly woman, with the elegantly coiffured silver hair, and shook her head. 'I'm sorry . . .'

'It's Maeve, Mary-Agnes. Maeve . . .'

'Maeve . . . ?' Mary-Agnes repeated the name, as if it still meant nothing, then she said it once again, much louder this time, 'Maeve – Maeve Ballantine?'

It was over fifty years since she had been referred to by her maiden name, but she nodded. 'That's right.'

'But you've been in America these past fifty years.'

'I know, but I came back this week, for a flying visit.'

Mary-Agnes continued to stare at her, as if seeing a ghost, as she shook her head slowly. 'I – I can't believe it. But why – why come to see me? What can you possibly want with me?'

The words were spoken with an almost wistful air, making Maeve want to reach out her hand and touch the older woman. And only then did she realise that she still had the bunch of roses clutched in her left hand. 'Here – here, Mary-Agnes,' she said, thrusting them forward. 'These are for you.'

Mary-Agnes looked down at them in her lap, then picked them up and buried her face in the pale cream petals. 'Peace – they're Peace roses,' she said softly. 'No one has ever given me roses before . . . not once in seventy-seven years.' She backed the wheelchair into the narrow hallway. 'You'd better come in.'

Maeve followed her into the flat and through into the neat living-room. It was a far cry from the interior of her last house. Everything was as neat and shining as a new pin.

'I've a home help comes in every morning to give me a hand,' Mary-Agnes said. 'And of course the family are always popping by.' She manoeuvred the wheelchair over to the sideboard and reached inside for a bottle of sherry. 'You'll join me in a wee tipple. It's not every day you drop in now, is it?'

Maeve laughed. 'It certainly isn't! And yes, yes, I'd love a sherry.'

'What'll we drink to?' Mary-Agnes asked, as they raised their glasses a couple of minutes later.

Maeve dropped her eyes, then said quietly, 'How about Dermot's health?'

'You've been to see him?'

'This morning. It came as a shock.'

'So it did to us all.'

'He – he's not expected to live, is he?' The words almost stuck in her throat.

'It's in God's hands,' Mary-Agnes said quietly. 'But Cissie sees he wants for nothing. Although, with her own ailments to contend with, it's only her love for him keeps her going.'

Maeve's fingers tightened around the stem of the glass. 'Has she family that can help her out?'

'Well, there's only Danny's two, Caitlin and Kevin. She had none by that poor fella that was finished off by the Black and Tans . . . Caitlin lives here in Dublin and takes a good deal of the workload from her, but Kevin's been over in England, Liverpool I believe, since the end of the last war. Teaches history in a Catholic school, if I remember rightly.'

The information was given so casually – as if it was taken for granted that the whole world knew – that she knew, as Danny's wife, that another woman had given birth to not one but *two* of his children. Her mind reeled.

'Are you feeling all right, Maeve? The sherry's maybe a wee bit strong for you? It's not the best quality, I'm afraid. It's not what you'll be used to.'

'No, no, the sherry's fine . . .' Her voice trailed off. There was so much she wanted to ask, but every new piece of information was like a knife in her heart. 'You haven't told Katie about Dermot, have you?' she asked quietly, veering the subject away from Cissie O'Rourke.

'No. I feel bad about that, but she's in a bad way herself at the moment. It's no use upsetting folk before there's a need to . . . Anyway, it was Dermot's decision really. He was adamant that no one should be told. He's a stubborn old devil when he sets his mind to it.' She took a sip of the sherry and looked at

Maeve curiously. 'You always had a soft spot for him, didn't you? I could never understand why the pair of you never wrote.'

'Couldn't you?'

The two women looked at one another for a long time, then Mary-Agnes said softly, 'Well, maybe I could, maybe I could . . .' She shook her head sadly. 'He always knew, you know, Maeve. Danny always knew . . .'

Maeve did not have to ask to what she was referring. 'No,' she said faintly, shaking her head. 'He couldn't . . .'

'But he did. He knew before he even married you. It would have taken the biggest fool in all of Dublin's fair city not to see what you and Dermot felt for each other – and Danny was certainly never that.' A real sadness welled in the faded brown eyes as she looked across at the elderly woman for whom she had once felt so much hate. 'It wasn't only because you were from the toffs around St Stephen's Green, you know, Maeve, that I could never accept you as one of us. No, 'twas never that . . . I saw what you did to them – to both of them – the two people I loved more than anyone in the world . . . Aye, more even than Liam.'

Maeve stared at her, her mouth had gone dry and there was a tight, knotted feeling in the pit of her stomach. Everything she had said explained so much. But it had never been quite like that. She had never meant to fall in love with Dermot. Surely she could see that?

She opened her mouth to attempt to say something, but Mary-Agnes shook her head, and held up an arthritic hand. 'No, Maeve, too much water has run under that old Carlisle Bridge since then. Those days, like so many of those we loved, are gone now . . . It was a touching gesture bringing me the Peace roses. I'll not forget it.'

God gave us memories so we could have roses in December . . . Roses . . . Memories . . . The words whirled in Maeve's head. There were so many memories flooding back as she sat there looking at the shrunken figure of the woman who had once been her sister-in-law, Mary-Agnes Donovan. It was as if she had never gone away; as if she had never left here and spent half a century across the sea. Tears sparkled in her eyes. This was where she belonged. These were her people . . .

'Will he forgive me, Mary-Agnes?' she whispered. 'Will Dermot ever forgive me?'

''Tis not forgiving *you* that's Dermot's problem, Maeve,' she said, with a quiet sigh. ''Tis forgiving himself. And if for fifty years he hasn't been able to do that – to grant himself absolution – how can he ever ask his God to do it?'

Chapter 61

'It came this morning, addressed to you care of Mam,' Deirdre said, handing the pale-blue airmail envelope to Danny. 'She gave it to me just before I left.'

'It's from Art.' Danny looked down on the familiar scrawling handwriting. 'He must be back in New York.' His brow creased beneath the fall of red hair. He had expected them to be still in Israel. What on earth had happened after he had left? He ripped open the thin paper envelope, as Deirdre put the kettle on, and began to read:

Dear Danny,
I expect you're wondering why I'm writing this from New York. The fact is your mother and I decided it would be more diplomatic under the circumstances to cut short our visit to Tel Aviv. Rose and Ruth still know nothing of the true reason and we feel that no real harm has been done. Apart from yourself, for whom the whole thing must have come as a great shock, it is your mother I really feel for. We should have been on our honeymoon by now and instead, here I am on the other side of the Atlantic, while she is in Ireland with you. I must do my best to make it up to her and have decided to fly over to join her in Dublin at the weekend. What could be nicer than a honeymoon in Killarney – if she'll still have me?
I have enclosed a letter that arrived yesterday, addressed to you. Look after your mother for me till I get there,

All my best,
Art

Danny folded the sheet of paper, with a quiet smile, then looked back inside the envelope and sure enough there was another one tucked inside. He pulled it out, his brows furrowing at the unfamiliar writing. The postmark was New York, which made it even more odd.

'Everything all right?' Deirdre asked, as she poured the boiling water from the kettle into two mugs of instant coffee.

'Yeah, sure. Art's planning on coming over here this weekend . . . Well, to Dublin actually. Seems like my mother is already there.' He ripped open the second envelope as Deirdre placed his coffee mug carefully on the kitchen table at his elbow.

'You got two for the price of one, I see? Is that one from anyone interesting?'

He glanced down at the address at the top of the page and gave an inward groan. 'No – no one interesting at all,' he said through clenched teeth. What the hell was Shiralee doing writing to him like this?

Dear Danny,

I feel I must sit down and write to you, as I can get no reply to my phone calls and no one seems to be at home in your apartment when I call. I have admitted to Sol about the baby and, as you can imagine, he is taking it very badly. He does not want a divorce, however, and that is fine by me. Being a Catholic (O.K. not a very good one!) I can't find it in myself to get an abortion, so I am going ahead and having the baby. We are arranging for my sister Peggy-Jean and her husband to adopt him as soon as he's born in the Fall. They have waited so long for one of their own, it seems the best solution all round. I just know he's going to be a boy and will look exactly like you. I hope he forgives you for what you have done, for I never can.

Shiralee

'Not bad news, is it?' Deirdre looked across in concern at the set expression on his face.

'No . . . No, everything's fine.' He shoved the letter back into the envelope and stuck both letters into the back pocket of his jeans. 'Thanks for the coffee.'

'Marie tells me you're going out with Elaine tonight.' It was put almost as an accusation.

'Well, yes . . . You don't mind, do you?'

'I don't – of course not, but Marie's a different matter.'

He sighed and toyed with the handle of his mug. 'I feel real bad about it, honestly I do, but . . .'

'I know, you can't live your life according to the whims of a teenage girl. But first love is tough, Danny, really tough. Maybe you could just go easy on the seeing Elaine bit, eh? I mean it's not as if she didn't have a boyfriend of her own. Des is a nice lad and I'd hate to see him upset by her playing around with you.'

Danny's lips quirked into a wry smile. 'You reckon that's what she's doing, is it — playing around with me?'

Deirdre's cheeks coloured beneath her make-up. 'Well, I wouldn't put it quite like that . . . But you know what I mean. It's not as if you're fond of her or anything. It wouldn't make the slightest difference to you whether you went out with Elaine again after tonight or not. Would it now? Come on, be honest.'

He looked her straight in the eyes. 'All right, Deirdre, I'll be honest. Yes, yes it would.'

'Oh God . . .'

His admission to her mother brought an uncomfortable atmosphere to the house for the rest of the day. It wasn't as if Deirdre was against his growing relationship with Elaine, he was sure of that, it was simply that she was concerned for her younger daughter in the anguish she was now going through. Marie, for her part, was doing her best to avoid him by staying in her room, playing her favourite Beatles albums at full blast. He tried escaping into the countryside, driving out as far as Larne, but after a lonely bar lunch at a pub on the outskirts of the small town, he headed back for Belfast and lay on his bed smoking for the rest of the afternoon.

Shiralee's letter had unsettled him. He hated the idea of Sol knowing about his affair with his wife. But even more, he hated the idea of his child being brought up by virtual strangers to him. He had only once met Shiralee's sister Peggy-Jean and her husband, and had only the vaguest memory of a thin, tight-lipped woman married to a sweaty-handed bank official from Syracuse. In fact, the more he thought about it the more adamant he became that it must not happen. If Shiralee was really serious about going ahead and having the kid, then he would fight for its custody, rather than have it brought up by old Tight Lips and Sweaty Palms. He sat up on the bed as the resolve hardened within him. Yes, he would fight it all the way to the Supreme Court if need be. He had the money – and if his own ran out then Art and his mother would help, he had no doubt about that.

'Art!' He was arriving this weekend. He could be in Dublin by now. It had been a shock to read that his mother was already over here. Maybe he should phone. He glanced down at his watch. It was just gone five. He'd tell Deirdre not to bother with tea and jump in the car and head on round to his Aunt Katie's and call from there, then call in at a café for a Coke and hamburger before picking up Elaine.

Katie and Eamon were delighted to see him again, and Katie was especially delighted to hear that Kitty was now in Dublin, with Art due over at any moment. 'They'll be heading on up here soon, won't they, Danny? You be sure to tell them now. I'll be mortally offended if they don't, so I will. You see you tell them that now!'

They closed the living-room door and left him in the privacy of the small hall, where the telephone sat in all its black splendour on a wrought-iron shelf. Luckily his grandmother had left the Jubilee Avenue phone number with Katie before she left, and that was the one he rang, as he puffed nervously on a fresh cigarette. To his surprise, the phone was picked up almost immediately by his mother.

'Mom?'

'Danny!' Kitty almost shouted his name into the receiver. 'How are you? It's lovely to hear from you . . . I just can't tell you! How are you, honey? Are you all right?'

'I'm fine,' he assured her, relaxing himself at the obvious warmth in her voice. 'And how's Gran?'

'She's fine, too. In fact, it's lucky you called now as we're heading off to visit Uncle Dermot later on this evening.'

He smiled into the phone. Things seemed to be going fine. 'You'll be having a visitor yourself before long.'

'Really? You're coming down – but that's wonderful!'

'Not me, Mom – Art!'

'Art?' Kitty gasped. 'But he's in New York. How – how can you possibly know that?'

An awful thought occurred to him. 'Oh, Gawd, I hope I'm not letting the cat out of the bag . . . I mean, he didn't say it was to be a secret, or anything like that . . .'

'Get on with it, Danny! How do you know Art's coming over?' It was impossible to disguise her impatience.

'I got a letter from his this morning, that's why.'

Kitty gave an audible sigh of relief on the other end of the line. 'He – he sounded all right in the letter, then? He's not still uptight or anything?'

'He sounded just fine to me. In fact, I reckon you'll have to get that wedding ring out again!' He could almost feel the relief and excitement coming over the line.

'Oh, Danny, that's wonderful . . . I can't tell you.' There was a long pause and he was just about to question if they had been cut off, when Kitty said quietly, 'I've been thinking a lot about what's happened and what was said and unsaid between us out there in Israel, and I want you to know, Danny, that I feel really badly about it all. I was entirely at fault – and have been for the past twenty-three years. A child must know who his natural father is. He has a right to know.'

Her voice broke with nerves, and she cleared her throat noisily, giving an attempt at a light laugh. 'You know, this is even more difficult on the phone than face to face . . . But I want you to know that Lee and I both feel terrible about the abrupt and cruel way things happened out there in Israel. It must have been the most awful shock for you – just as it was for him. I want you to know that, Danny – that it was just as bad for him. We talked about it a lot after you left and both agree that what's just as important as the child knowing his own father, is that a father must know about and acknowledge his own child . . . If anything, that's the most important thing of all . . . Lee certainly feels that way and wants you to know it. It wasn't his fault, Danny. I kept him in the dark just as I kept you and I realise now what a terrible thing that was for both of you.'

She paused again, as if struggling to find the right words. 'I don't expect you to understand this yet, Danny – how he feels. You must be a father yourself to know what it means to a man to have had a son and not to have known of his existence for

547

the whole of that child's young life. Could you imagine if you had a son of your own and you never set eyes on him until he was grown-up? You wouldn't let that happen if you could possibly avoid it, would you?'

His jaw clenched as he gripped the phone, his knuckles showing white through the freckled skin. The vision of Tight Lips and Sweaty Palms flooded his mind. 'No, Mom, I wouldn't let that happen.' He was certain of that.

When he hung up a few minutes later, Katie and Eamon were eager to find out how everyone was down in Dublin, and when Danny let slip that his grandmother had dropped in on Mary-Agnes the previous day, his aunt's jaw dropped open. 'Never – I just don't believe it! D'ye hear that, Eamon? Have you ever heard of such a thing?' But by her smile, it was obvious she was clearly delighted. 'For all Mary-Agnes's huffin' and puffin', she'll have been tickled pink that Maeve took the trouble to look in, I can vouch for that!'

'Mary-Agnes always was a stubborn old woman,' Eamon agreed. 'But there was a warm heart hidden somewhere beneath the icy exterior. She saw you through your childhood, Katie, lass.'

'Aye, and she would've done her best by Willie-John for the rest of his natural life, had he lived. Her arthritis is a fine reward for a lifetime's hard work, so it is.'

'Well, enough of this!' Eamon got up from the armchair by the fire. 'You'll be having a drop of tea with us, Danny boy – and we'll not take no for an answer!'

Danny glanced across at Katie who nodded emphatically. 'It's only colcannon,' she said, with a smile of apology. 'But it's good and wholesome – and what's more it's been in the oven this past half-hour, so should be ready for the serving.'

'Sounds great by me.' The great steaming plates of potatoes and cabbage done together in the oven was already a firm favourite.

It was almost seven o'clock by the time he left Hamilton Street, but as he had not arranged to pick Elaine up from her flat until around half-past, he was in no great hurry. He reached

Newtownards Road about ten minutes later and had just signalled to pull in at the side of the road opposite her flat when the sight of someone coming out the door caught his eye.

'Jesus – Des!' The sight of the young man in the faded anorak and patched jeans brought a knot to his stomach. What the hell was he doing here? Wasn't he supposed to be at his Uncle Pat's wake?

He brought the car to a screeching halt at the kerb as Des walked off in the opposite direction towards Albert Bridge Road, oblivious of all but what was on his own mind – the safe delivery of his morning's work. He hadn't intended coming round to Elaine's place today, but having to attend his uncle's funeral had meant he was behind in getting the needful ready for the job tonight. The relief when he had handed over the plastic bag to her safekeeping had been enormous. He just hoped that Yank she was insisting on taking along with her was up to it.

Danny glanced up at the window he knew to be Elaine's room, as Des disappeared round the corner in the distance. The curtains were half-drawn and there was no one to be seen. At least she hadn't thought it necessary to watch lover-boy until he was out of sight, he thought, with a grim satisfaction.

She opened the door immediately, in response to his impatient ring at the bell. 'Danny – you're early!' She was wearing only a thin cotton wrap-around housecoat, which she clutched defensively to her as she stepped back to allow him to enter.

He walked on down the narrow passage into the living-room beyond, where he looked scathingly at her as she followed him in. 'Do you usually entertain your men friends dressed like that, or is he singularly privileged?'

'Oh, that's it, is it? That's it! You saw Des leave!'

'I though he was supposed to be at old Pat Devlin's wake.'

'So he was.'

'Then what the hell was he doing here?'

Anger flared in her eyes. 'Since when has that anything to do with you?'

'Since now, godammit Elaine! Since now! Why the hell do

549

you think I'm willing to risk my life tonight? Why do you think I agreed to come with you on this crazy escapade?'

'Crazy escapade?' Elaine gasped. 'Crazy escapade? I hope you're coming with me because you believe in the cause just as much as I do.' He turned to look out of the window, avoiding the anger in her eyes, but she grabbed his arm. 'You *are* coming because you believe in it, too, aren't you? Say it, Danny, damn you, say it! Tell me the truth – why are you here tonight?'

He turned to face her. Suddenly the time for honesty had come. Honesty with himself and with her. 'I'm here because of you.'

'No!' She backed away from him. 'Don't complicate my life, Danny Donovan. Just don't complicate my life!' She turned and fled from the room, throwing open the door of her own room across the passage and disappearing inside.

He pushed against it and his superior strength sent her flying across on to the bed as he burst in.

'Get out of here please . . . !'

He pulled her up off the bed and held her by the shoulders as his eyes burned down into hers. 'What are you running from, Elaine – the truth? Because that's what I'm telling . . . Oh, don't worry, I care about Ireland, maybe not as much as you do, but I care. But I've learned something else since I've been here – I also care about you. And I think you care about me. You do, don't you? Don't you, Elaine?' He was almost shouting at her now.

She looked up at him, the anger in her eyes fading. 'Don't ask me that, Danny, please . . .'

'Why? Why can't I ask you?' His voice was harsh, insistent.

She shook her head wildly, avoiding his eyes.

'Why can't I ask you, Elaine? Because the answer might just be that you feel the same – isn't that it?'

She looked straight at him, her strength evaporating. 'Yes, damn you, yes!'

He was not aware of taking her in his arms, only of the feelings that surged through him as their lips met. His eyes closed as their kiss grew deeper, to open again and look straight at the neat row of petrol bombs that stood, ready and waiting, on her dressing-table top.

Chapter 62

Maeve looked at her elder daughter with obvious pride in her eyes. 'You look lovely, dear.'

'You don't think I'm too dressed up? You don't think Uncle Dermot will think it a bit – well, daring?' Kitty glanced down at the hemline of the off-white minidress that only just skirted her knees. 'I really bought it for Tel Aviv. You don't think it's a bit too up-to-date for Dublin?'

'Now there's a terrible thing to say, and no mistake! The very idea! It strikes me they're every bit as fashionable on O'Connell Street as they are on Fifth Avenue.' She circled Kitty, casting a critical eye on the length of the hem. 'No, I think with your grey jacket on top that's perfectly acceptable in any company. And I reckon Dermot's as keen as the next man on appreciating a good leg!'

'I still can't believe what Danny said on the phone, you know,' Kitty said, changing the subject to the one that was filling her mind, as she picked up her shoulderbag from the chair and slung it over her arm. 'I'm as excited as a five-year-old at the thought of seeing Art again. Can you believe that, at my age?'

Maeve nodded, not trusting herself to speak, as she took her daughter's arm and they headed for the door. She could believe it all right. She could believe it only too well. She could feel her legs begin to quake already at the thought of seeing Dermot again within the hour.

'You don't think we should have phoned?'

'Oh, I'm sure that's not necessary.' She couldn't have borne the idea of talking to that O'Rourke woman on the telephone. 'He's half expecting us anyway.'

Charles Ballantine, Maeve's father, wearing his insignia of the Order of the Garter, gazed down at them from a life-size portrait in oils as they crossed the hall and went out through the front door to where a Rover identical to Charlie's was parked at the foot of the steps. Kitty had hired it that afternoon for the rest of their stay in the city, rather than inconvenience her uncle any longer by constantly borrowing his. 'Will you drive or shall I?' She glanced up at her mother as she searched in her bag for the keys.

'Oh, you do, dear. It's been a long day and I don't feel up to coping with the traffic, although, heaven knows, it's a treat to drive around these streets compared to New York.'

'I do believe you've quite fallen in love with the place again.' Kitty slipped into the driver's seat and leaned across to open the passenger door. 'I can't say that I blame you. If I didn't have so many ties in the States, I might seriously consider staying here myself!'

Maeve was silent as she made herself comfortable in the padded leather seat. The thought had crossed her own mind more than once today. 'It's not as far away as it once was,' she said at last. 'I mean if you want to visit relatives and that type of thing, you can be across the Atlantic in a day. When I left fifty years ago the aviation industry had hardly even got off the ground. At least what aircraft there were looked as if they were tied together by bits of string! We had no choice but go by sea.'

She settled back in her seat, her mind reliving the horrors of that original sea voyage to New York. They still lived with her to this day. It was bad enough coping with morning sickness, being pregnant with Kitty, but to have to put up with the incessant rolling of the ship into the bargain made each passing day more unbearable than the last. The jet in which she had crossed the ocean this time was the last word in comfort compared to her previous journey.

But even the horrors of early sea voyages could not occupy her mind for long and in the few minutes it took for the Rover to turn into the tree-shaded road that had been Dermot's home since the First World War, Maeve could feel nerves begin to get the better of her once again. Kitty had no idea — no idea at all — what this visit meant.

She glanced across at her as the car drew into the kerb. If anything she looked even more like Dermot as she got older. In her fiftieth year, her face had developed a much leaner, more sculptured look, and even from the side like this the resemblance was becoming quite uncanny. She wondered if he would notice. He had asked Katie once, on her wartime visit to New York, to bring back a photograph of Kitty and she had made sure her sister-in-law took back only the best one for him. It was the one taken on Kitty's graduation day, complete with gown and mortar-board. He would have liked that, she was sure of it, although no word of thanks had come from Dublin. In fact, no word of any kind had come from him over these fifty years. Those wasted years tore at her heart as she stepped out of the car into the clear evening air.

They crossed the pavement in silence and entered the wrought-iron gates. 'It looks a big place for one old man,' Kitty remarked, looking up at the serried rows of latticed windows, as they made their way up the drive.

'Oh, it's not just him who lives here,' Maeve said. 'He's got a younger priest who lives with him, a Father Duffy, but I haven't met him yet. He's in the same position as Dermot was in with Father O'Reilly when he first came to live here as a young man.'

'You knew him then, didn't you?'

Maeve tensed and looked down at her feet. 'Yes, I knew him then.'

She let Kitty ring the bell, standing just behind her on the stone step as they waited for the front door to be opened. But to her surprise it was not Cissie O'Rourke who answered it, but a sturdily-built woman of around fifty, with pale-lashed eyes that peered at them curiously from inside the door. 'Yes?'

'Would you care to tell Father Dermot that Mrs Fullerton and her daughter are here to see him?'

The woman's eyes moved from one to the other. They were a bright hazel colour that shone with an amber light in the evening sun. Her hair, Maeve was sure, had once been much lighter, but was now a dull mousy brown, with a faint reddish tint, and hung lankly behind her ears. This was Caitlin, she was certain of it. But, strangely, she felt no jealousy any more, either towards this tired, faded creature, or her mother – only a deep thankfulness that there had been someone here; people who loved him; people who had cared for him through all the years when she herself had been half a world away.

'Would you care to come in?' The woman moved aside to allow them to enter, then closed the door quietly behind them.

Kitty looked around the narrow entrance hall, wrinkling her nose at the unmistakably musty smell that frequent applications of pine-scented wax on the worn linoleum had done little to disguise.

'If you care to wait here, I'll tell him you've arrived.'

'It's hardly the last word in interior décor, is it?' Kitty murmured, as the woman disappeared back down the hall, and she looked around her at the faded wallpaper and varnished woodwork. 'I bet this place hasn't been redecorated as long as he's lived here.'

'You're probably right, for it looks exactly the same as when I was last here – and I don't mean yesterday!' Maeve said, with a rueful smile. 'But I'm sure he hasn't noticed – Dermot never was one for outward shows of any kind.'

'Would you like to step this way?' The voice from the door of Dermot's study cut short their conversation, and Maeve glanced across at Kitty, who had a totally relaxed smile on her face. It contrasted vividly with the strangely fixed expression on her own, as she tried desperately to calm her jangled nerves.

The woman stood holding open the door as they walked side by side down the hall. Maeve clutched at her daughter's hand as they entered the room. There was the welcoming scent of pine in the air from the blazing fire that crackled in the grate, and the last rays of the evening sun were filtering through the net curtains of the tall window on the far wall.

'Thank you, Caitlin. And we'll have that cup of tea now, if you don't mind.' His voice still had the ability to make Maeve's heart turn in her breast. He was sitting in the same armchair by the fire as before, but was no longer in his dressing-gown. He had on his old clerical robes – the only clothes she had ever seen him in. The years seemed to roll back before her very eyes as a smile lit his face and he stretched out a hand in welcome as they crossed the floor towards him. 'At last!'

'You've been waiting for us,' she said softly.

'All day.' His dark eyes glistened as they looked up into hers, and he raised her hand to his lips.

'We'd have come earlier if we'd known.'

554

He shook his head. 'No matter, no matter. You're here now – both of you – and that's what counts . . . So this is Kitty!' His eyes lit up as they fell on the younger woman by Maeve's side.

'Hello, Uncle Dermot.' Kitty came forwards and reached down to kiss him.

The tears that had been lurking beneath the surface sprang to his eyes and ran unashamedly down the paper-thin skin of his cheeks as he clasped her to him. 'I've waited fifty years for this moment,' he whispered, and the words cut into Maeve's heart.

She sat down on the edge of the sofa next to his chair and, fighting to control her own emotions, touched Kitty lightly on the shoulder. The last thing she wanted was to get Dermot upset. 'Sit down here beside me, Kathleen,' she said quietly.

Dermot blew his nose into a large white handkerchief. 'You'll forgive a foolish old man, my dear. I don't usually welcome my guests in quite such a way.'

Kitty gave an understanding smile. The welcome was much warmer than she had expected, but he had been very ill and she felt that must have had its effect upon him.

'Will you be staying in Dublin long?' he asked, directing the question at Kitty, as Caitlin came back in and put a tray with tea and biscuits on a small table in front of them.

Maeve looked across at their daughter, who first smiled her thanks at Caitlin, as she was handed a cup of tea, then answered truthfully, 'It depends. My son Danny's in Belfast at the moment and I'm hoping he'll join us here in a few days.'

'Danny's here in Ireland, too?' Dermot's eyes lit up as he looked from her to her mother.

'Yes, he's here,' Maeve said, feeling a stab of guilt. He had never even seen a picture of his own grandchild. She had denied him so much – so very much. She reached inside her handbag, as Caitlin waited at her elbow with the tea. 'Here . . .' She handed him across the coloured photograph of Danny in his US Marines uniform, then accepted the tea with a murmur of thanks.

He stared down at it, his dark eyes examining the young, open face. So this was Danny . . . Flesh of his flesh, bone of his bone . . . The red hair was completely hidden beneath the army cap, but the fair, freckled skin and the wide, even-toothed smile were all too familiar. The years between faded to nothing as the image of his younger brother filled his mind. 'He's been well-named Danny,' he said quietly, 'for he's the spitting image of his great-uncle.' It was the first slip in fifty years he had ever made on the subject.

'Grandfather,' Kitty corrected him, with an indulgent smile. The slip was understandable. He was getting on in years, after all.

He looked up at her, as if not quite understanding, and, for one heart-stopping moment, Maeve thought he was going to argue with her — to tell her the truth. Then slowly he began to nod, 'Of course, how stupid of me ... He's so like his grandfather.'

A moment's silence fell as they all watched Caitlin refill the teapot from the hot-water jug, then, clutching the empty jug in her hand, she took her leave.

As the door closed behind her, Dermot gazed back down for a long time at the photograph in his hands, then he looked at Kitty. 'Will you bring him to see me, my dear?'

'Of course I will, Uncle Dermot. He's looking forward so much to meeting you.' It was a white lie, but she felt it important to say it.

He smiled. 'Is that so now?' He leaned back in his seat, as if savouring the remark. 'And you're happy? You have a good life and a good man to look after you over there in America?'

A faint flush crept into her cheeks. 'The best. He's flying over here to join me.'

The answer pleased him. 'We can ask for no greater privilege in this life than to spend it in the company of those we love the most ... But God does not always grant us such privileges. Your mother and I know that to our cost. Is that not so, Maeve?'

His eyes found Maeve's, then, as he met the dark-eyed gaze of his daughter, his voice faltered as he said softly, 'This is the happiest moment of my life, but I wish it had never had to take place, that you had never spent a lifetime across the sea. Life is so short, so painfully short, and I wish, with all my heart, things could have been different ...'

As Kitty smiled back at him, oblivious of the pain behind the words, Maeve looked down at the cup in her lap, fighting to retain her composure. Hot tears scalded her eyes, as she said softly, 'I'm glad there's been someone here to look after you — someone who cared.'

'Life has not been easy for any of us in the years that have gone,' he said quietly. 'And Cissie has had as heavy a cross as anyone to bear. She's had very little luck in this life, Maeve. But I like to think that in coming here and tending to my needs, and that of young Duffy and his predecessors, she has found some kind of peace. What I'll do when she goes, only the Lord knows, for Caitlin has her own family to see to.'

Maeve's grip tightened on the handle of the teacup. 'She — she might have to leave?'

'She's got a bad case of osteoporosis. She should have given up this work years ago, but wouldn't trust anyone else to see to my wants, such as they are . . .' he said, with a sigh. 'Oh, I've argued, of course, but she's a stubborn one, there's no doubt about that, although I've been a real burden to her since I got out of hospital. It has really got quite beyond her, but she says she'd have to be sure whoever it is that takes over will care for me as much as she does — and she doesn't believe such a creature exists!'

Maeve took a deep breath as she looked up and found his eyes. Couldn't he see? He no longer needed Cissie O'Rourke and her daughter, she was here now. She was back. A great wave of happiness welled within her, as her resolve hardened. 'But she does, Dermot, she does . . . Such a creature does exist.'

He looked at her and knew exactly what she was thinking. 'No,' he said softly, reaching out to take her hand. 'No, my Maeve, you must go home . . .'

She shook her head. 'No, my love, I'm already home. I've been away, been away for far too long, but I'm back now. I'm back home, Dermot, and here I'll stay.'

A noise from behind made them look round to see Caitlin standing uncertainly at the door. 'Is there anything else you need, Uncle Dermot?'

His fingers closed even tighter on Maeve's, as tears filled his eyes. When he had left hospital two weeks ago, they had given him three months at the most, unless a miracle happened. Three precious months of life. And, after losing his faith the day she walked out of his life, after fifty years of doubt, the miracle *had* happened. She had come back. How could he ever have doubted that there was a God? Who could tell him now that prayers were never answered? The dark eyes glistened as they looked into those of the woman by his side; the woman he had loved for a lifetime. The woman he would continue to love into all eternity. After fifty long years, he could believe in miracles once more.

'I said is there anything else you need, Uncle Dermot?' Caitlin's voice asked.

He shook his head, as his eyes remained locked on those of the woman he loved. 'No, my dear, there's nothing else in this world I could possibly need . . .'

Epilogue

As Maeve and Dermot sat hand in hand in the small, book-lined study of the presbytery in Dublin, their grandson lay on his stomach behind an overgrown hedgerow on the road between Donaghdee and Newtownards. Where the hell was Elaine? She had insisted on going to reconnoitre further up the road and had been gone at least fifteen minutes. She should have been back ages ago. He blamed himself. If they hadn't spent half an hour making love before they left her apartment in Newtownards Road, she would never have started to panic.

An army patrol was due to pass by here in less than ten minutes and they had to have the job done by then. He shaded his eyes and squinted through the evening sunshine at the rooftop of the police station in the distance. Des had chosen it as their target. He had been picked up by the sergeant there a couple of weeks back and had received a good 'going over', as he put it. He was paying the bastards back, Elaine said. Showing them you couldn't treat your own people like dirt. She had got really mad at him when he had suggested that maybe they should wait and let Des get his own back — let him do the job. 'You're not chickening out, Yank, are you?' she had demanded. 'Because if you are, you can get the hell out of it right now.'

'You're only mad because you feel guilty, that's all,' he had told her. 'You feel guilty because you made love with me and not him. You're doing this job to salve your conscience, Elaine, that's all!'

She had stared at him with something akin to real hatred in her eyes. 'Wait here, Yank,' she had said. 'I'm going up there to see if that guy's in there and if he is I'll signal to you from that corner over there and you come and join me with the rest of the bottles.' He glanced down at the remaining petrol bombs packed in old lemonade bottles, lying in the grass beside him. They were still in the same plastic bag in which Des had delivered them earlier that evening. He rolled over on his side and gave them a disgusted shove with the toe of his sneakers. He would throw the darned things all right, but the thing that really stuck in his gut was that he wasn't doing it for Ireland, or any romantic nonsense like that. He wasn't even doing it for Elaine. They were both doing it for that creep Devlin.

He pulled himself up on the grass for a better look. What the hell was going on over there? Why wasn't she signalling for him?

'Jeeeezuz!'

At the moment his head appeared through a gap in the hedge the whole roof of the police station went up in a blaze of flame. 'Jesus God!' The silly bitch must have thrown the whole darned lot for it to go up like that!

Grabbing the plastic bag, he pushed his way through the hedge, leaping the ditch at the other side. 'Elaine! Elaine!' He had to get to her. He had to get to her before they did. The car was parked only yards away; he had to get to her and get the hell out of here.

He had got only ten yards across the road when the army patrol swept round the corner and the bullet got him. Its impact sent him sprawling backwards into the ditch at the other side.

The armoured car screeched to a halt and two soldiers jumped down. They were no older than their victim.

'Got the bastard, sarge, look at this!' The smaller of the two pointed to the bag of petrol-filled bottles that lay a few yards away, its contents broken and seeping out through the white plastic.

'Recognise him?' the taller man with the three stripes asked.

'Not right off.' His companion bent down and pulled at the piece of card that protruded out of the left-hand breast pocket of the victim's denim jacket. It was already soaked in red blood, the bullet having pierced it through the middle; right through the heart of the young man in the picture. The soldier turned it over and saw the words, written faintly in pencil, 'Danny Donovan, Easter Monday, 1916.'

'Fenian scum,' he said, tossing the picture into the ditch beside the dead body of Danny Donovan. 'Another bloody martyr to the cause . . .'